'Leave 'er alone! Leave our mam alone!'

Lizzie, brown eyes afire, small fists clenched, stood daring him to strike. Her thick plait had swung over one shoulder and begun to come loose, brown hair spurting out like strands of wild brown silk.

Tom knocked her sprawling. She could have been a flower on a stem for all the resistance she had to his great strength. Her dad was not so much angry as dumbfounded, for none of the boys had ever tried to defend their mam. This was not cowardice on their part, but knowing it upset their mam even more when he turned on them.

But Lizzie was beside herself with rage – a rage far greater than anything ever felt by Tom.

'I hate yer,' she said in a quiet, expressionless voice, a voice her astonished family had never heard before. 'I hate yer and I wish ye'd been bombed that night. I wish ye'd been here when the soot came down and it choked yer. *I wish yer were dead!*'

There was silence. Kitty felt as if she would faint. Surely Tom would kill them all.

Maureen Lee was born in Bootle and now lives in Colchester, Essex. She has had numerous short stories published and a play staged. *Stepping Stones*, *Liverpool Annie*, *Dancing in the Dark*, *The Girl from Barefoot House*, *Laceys of Liverpool*, *The House by Princes Park*, *Lime Street Blues*, *Queen of the Mersey*, *The Old House on the Corner* and the three novels in the Pearl Street series, *Lights Out Liverpool*, *Put Out the Fires* and *Through the Storm* are all available in Orion paperback. Her novel *Dancing in the Dark* won the Parker Romantic Novel of the Year Award. Her latest novel in paperback is *The September Girls*. Visit her website at www.maureenlee.co.uk

BY MAUREEN LEE

The Pearl Street Series

Lights Out Liverpool
Put Out the Fires
Through the Storm

Stepping Stones
Liverpool Annie
Dancing in the Dark
The Girl from Barefoot House
Laceys of Liverpool
The House by Princes Park
Lime Street Blues
Queen of the Mersey
The Old House on the Corner
The September Girls
Kitty and Her Sisters

Stepping Stones

Maureen Lee

An Orion paperback
First published in Great Britain by Orion in 1994
This paperback edition published in 1994
by Orion Books Ltd,
Orion House, 5 Upper St Martin's Lane,
London WC2H 9EA

11 13 15 17 19 20 18 16 14 12

A CIP catalogue record for this book
is available from the British Library.

ISBN 978-0-7528-1726-2

Printed and bound in Great Britain by
Clays Ltd, St Ives plc

The Orion Publishing Group's policy is to use papers that
are natural, renewable and recyclable products and
made from wood grown in sustainable forests. The logging
and manufacturing processes are expected to conform to
the environmental regulations of the country of origin.

www.orionbooks.co.uk

For Richard

CHAUCER
STREET

Chapter 1

It was still and deathly quiet one April night in the year 1931 in a place called Bootle in Liverpool. Cramped terraced houses, row after regimented row, were bathed in the clear, unearthly glow of a brilliant moon. Windows gleamed dully, front doors were firmly closed.

Not a soul was to be seen.

The cobbled streets, which shone like ribbons of polished lead between each row of houses, had a virginal, untrodden look. There was an air of emptiness, desertion – no sign at all of the overflowing hordes of human beings who dwelt within these two-up, two-down homes. Parents, children, babies, sometimes all crowded into one small bedroom with perhaps a grandparent sharing a room with the older children and unmarried or widowed aunts and uncles, orphaned cousins, often spilling out into the parlour downstairs to sleep on made-up beds or overstuffed sofas.

None of these people knew of the vivid, almost startling moonlight which bathed their homes and their streets, and even if they had, they would not have cared. They were too preoccupied with sleeping off the exhaustion of the previous day and preparing themselves for the next.

The men, the ones who had jobs, put in ten or more gruelling, back-breaking hours on the docks or in blackened, evil-smelling factories where the noise of pounding machinery near split their eardrums, and sparks attacked their eyes and smoke their lungs. Some of the women worked in the same factories, just as hard, but for even less money than their menfolk.

The women had to be up earlier than the men. At the crack of dawn they'd come down to their cold kitchens and put a match to the rolled-up paper and firewood laid on last night's raked-out cinders and then carefully put the coal on, piece by piece, until the fire caught and was hot enough to take the kettle for the first cup of tea of the day and a pan of water for washing.

Just beyond the houses ran the River Mersey, and that night it gleamed a dull and blackish-silver over which the silhouettes of great tall cranes loomed, brooding, waiting like carrion-crows to pounce on any unsuspecting person who might emerge from the neat forest of stiff, silent houses.

Low and fat, tall and thin, the funnels of the ships stood sentinel, bellies half-empty or half-full, waiting for the weary men to come and on-load or off-load their cargoes, and now the hulls could be seen gently moving to and fro in rhythm with the lapping tide.

Suddenly, the air of Chaucer Street was rent by a fearful scream.

In Number 2, Kitty O'Brien was about to give birth to her ninth child. Three of these children were dead, their births occurring at a late and dangerous stage of pregnancy – not because her once-healthy body had difficulty in bearing children but because her husband Tom had beaten her so severely he'd brought on a premature delivery. Kitty was twenty-eight years old.

She'd been trying to hold the scream back, thinking of the children asleep upstairs, feared of waking them, of frightening them. Kitty would have laid down her life for her children.

But the scream couldn't be contained. It burst forth from her throat like water through a broken dam.

'Oh dear God, the pain! Dear God in heaven, make it stop! Make the pain stop!' These words were not spoken aloud, just in Kitty's head. With an effort, she turned her head to see the crucifix hanging over the mantelpiece and the statue of Our Lady which stood underneath.

'Holy Mary, Mother of God, make the pain stop!' She screamed again as an agonizing spasm of hurt engulfed her body.

'That's right, luv. Let it go. Yell all yer like.'

Theresa Garrett, stout and tall, grey hair in steely waves under a thick net, surveyed the torn mess of Kitty O'Brien's female organs. Mrs Garrett was not a trained nurse. She'd never been inside a hospital except as a visitor, but she was the acknowledged midwife for the area that included Chaucer Street. As long as there were no complications, she would come and deliver a baby for anyone who asked, at any time of day or night, as competently as any doctor.

She was not fit to deliver Kitty O'Brien and Mrs Garrett was only too well aware of it. Every time the poor woman gave birth, she ripped herself open again and the tears were never repaired. Mrs Garrett couldn't sew her up. Kitty refused to leave her children to go into hospital and that pig of a husband wouldn't part with a penny to pay for a doctor to come and see to his wife.

Tom was upstairs now, sleeping off his ale. It had been six-year-old Kevin who'd come to Mrs Garrett's Southey Street home to say his mother had begun having the pains.

There was no charge for Mrs Garrett's services, but afterwards, when they were able, people would come round with a small luxury – a home-baked bunloaf, ten good cigarettes or a bag of fruit. She knew Kitty O'Brien would never be able to give something which cost money, but one day she would appear with a crocheted collar, knitted gloves or an embroidered doily made from bits and pieces salvaged from the clothes and bedding given her by the Sisters of the Convent of St Anne. Indeed, in her pocket at that very moment was one of Kitty's handkerchiefs, neatly hemmed and with a rose embroidered in one corner. The material had probably come from an old worn bolster or pillowcase, the silk for the flower carefully unpicked. That was for bringing Rory into the world five years ago. The midwife valued these little gifts more than most others, in her mind's eye imagining Kitty in a rare quiet moment, stitching away, screwing up her eyes to see in the dim gaslight.

Her rather grim features softened as she knelt beside the small heaving body. There was no bed in the house free for Kitty to give birth in. She lay on coarse blankets on the floor in front of the dying kitchen fire.

Mrs Garrett's experienced eye told her it was time for the woman to push. 'Come along, luv. A good shove now and it'll all be over.'

A neighbour, Mary Plunkett, hovered in the back kitchen doorway, waiting for something to do. Pots of steaming water

5

stood on the hearth ready for use.

The baby's head appeared. Dark hair – that was a change. So far, all Kitty's babies had been blond like their father.

Kitty screamed again. 'Dear Jesus, help me,' she whispered.

Upstairs, several childish voices shouted in alarm: 'Mam? Mam?' And twelve-month-old Jimmie began to cry.

Glad to be useful, Mary Plunkett went up to quieten them. 'Nearly done now, luv, just one more shove.'

Mrs Garrett could see the baby's face. Oh yes, a dark one this. Suddenly, the entire body was expelled, taking the midwife by surprise. 'Lord, you're in a hurry,' she said in alarm. There was a slight pause before she added, 'It's a girl, Kitty, a lovely dark lass.'

She shouted upstairs, 'Mary, tell the boys they've got a little sister and then come down and give me a hand.'

Minutes later, Mrs Plunkett put an arm round Kitty's shoulders, lifting her slightly onto a second pillow, so that the mother could glimpse her first-born daughter.

Through a blur of thankfully-receding pain, Kitty saw the long smooth body of her new baby, the sleek hair. She heard the first cry, a sound she'd always found ominous. It seemed to her a signal of suffering to come, rather than an amen for suffering just ended; a heralding of broken nights, teething pains and colic.

She saw Mrs Garrett cut the cord with her large silver scissors and hand the baby to Mary to wash. But what Kitty was expecting to happen, didn't. She thought the colour of the baby's skin would change with the washing. Wasn't it the blood or the afterbirth that made the satiny skin look so dark? But no, the faint fawnish colour remained.

Kitty's heart began to beat so loud and so strong it seemed the very floor took up the sound and made the entire house throb. She felt herself go dizzy. A prayer, even more fervent than the unspoken pleas made during the excruciating birth, pounded through her brain: *Please God, make me die. Holy Mary, make me die this minute.*

'Here, what's the matter with her?' Alarmed, Mary Plunkett placed the baby in the laundry basket which had served as a cot for all the O'Brien children, and came over to mop Kitty's brow with a wet cloth. 'I think she's got a fever or somethin'. She's sweatin' like a pig.'

Mrs Garrett, gently cleaning Kitty with disinfectant, felt her pulse. 'It's racing,' she said worriedly.

'Should we get the doctor?'

'No, he'll expect to be paid.'

'The ambulance, then?'

'Give her ten minutes. Perhaps she'd like a cup of tea .'

A cup of tea! Kitty heard the words from far away. A cup of tea would cure everything. A cup of tea would turn the baby's skin white. Anyway, it seemed she wasn't going to die. Neither God nor Our Lady were going to answer her prayers. She wondered why neither of the other women were shocked by the baby's colour. 'A lovely dark lass,' Theresa Garrett had said calmly, even admiringly.

Almost as if she'd been reading Kitty's thoughts, Mary Plunkett, who was pouring tea into three chipped cups, glanced towards the baby and remarked, 'Isn't she just the colour of Eileen Donaghue's Marian? Wasn't she one o' yours, Mrs Garrett?'

'That's right,' said the midwife, carefully patting Kitty dry with the torn remnants of an old sheet, brought with her. 'Marian must be twelve or more by now. And d'you know Molly Doyle of Byron Street? All her little ones are dark like that. It's the Celtic streak, you know. Like a tribe of little Indians they are.'

'Well, it'll make a change,' mused Mary. 'A small dark sister for five big blond brothers.'

Kitty relaxed. Her body literally sagged with relief. So it was all right. It was quite normal for an Irish baby to be so dark-skinned . . .

The old armchair was brought over – Tom's chair – and Kitty was lifted and tucked up inside it, then Mary handed her a cup of tea. Despite the nagging ache in her gut and her feeling of total exhaustion, the new mother felt warm and comfortable basking in the rarely-afforded attention to her sole comfort.

It was only when a new baby was born that there was a day or two's respite from never-ending housework. Tomorrow, Mary Plunkett would come in again to help and her other neighbours would see the older boys, Kevin and Rory, got to school and they'd look after Tony and Chris and the baby, Jimmie – though he was no longer the baby now she had this new one, this little dark daughter.

The neighbours would also make Tom's tea and his butties for work, but they had their own families to care for and in a few days Kitty would have to look after her ever-increasing family by herself. Jimmie had only just been weaned. Now there was another one to feed and it meant three of her children were under the age of two.

She looked across at the new arrival. Such a pretty baby, sleeping peacefully, long sooty lashes resting on unwrinkled olive cheeks. Celtic streak? Oh, no! Kitty knew, though she would never be able to prove it – not that she would ever, in her whole life, *want* to prove it, it would be her secret forever and ever, amen – but Kitty knew this baby's father was not the beast upstairs. It was not Tom O'Brien, whom she could hear snoring away in the great soft bed where he used and abused her nightly.

No, this baby's father was someone else altogether.

Kitty remembered the night, almost exactly nine months ago. It had been a Thursday and there was no money left, not a penny, and nothing due till the next night when Tom came home with his wages. He was out at the pub, enough in his own pocket for a drink or two, whilst at home his children went hungry and the larder was empty, not even a stale crust left.

'I'm hungry, Mam.'

'What's for tea, Mam?'

Little desperate voices. Her children, asking their mam for food, and the baby whingeing away at her empty, sagging breast. No milk, for she'd had nothing herself that day but water. Four little faces looking up at her accusingly. A crying baby, chewing at her. She was their mam and she couldn't feed them and there was no prospect of feeding them till the next night.

Everything fit to be pawned had long since gone. All the wedding presents. The clock from her family in Ireland, the teaset from Tom's. She'd never had the money to redeem them. The tatty bedding was worthless, the furniture junk. Nothing left to pawn or sell.

8

Of course she could call on her neighbours – throw herself on their mercy. And they would rally round. They always did. Someone would go from house to house till they'd collected enough food to see the family through the night. No matter how short they were themselves, they wouldn't see her starve. She'd given food herself before, raided the contents of her meagre larder when another family was in need. They shared each other's bad fortune and good fortune, though the latter was rare, but when Joey Mahon won money on the football pools, he'd thrown a street party for the children and they'd had jelly with hundreds and thousands on it and real tinned cream.

But it seemed to Kitty – in fact she knew it was the case – that she had to seek her neighbours' help more often than anybody else. She didn't know another woman whose husband kept his family as short of money as Tom did his. Why, she thought with shame, should these other women's men have to work to keep *her* children fed? They had enough troubles of their own.

So, late on that hot moist evening, with her children wanting food and no money in the house and nothing left to sell or pawn, Kitty O'Brien, absolutely desperate for cash or food and leaving her young family behind with strict instructions to behave themselves and take good care of the baby, wrapped her black shawl around her shoulders, slammed the back door behind her and walked along the Dock Road to sell herself.

For there wasn't a thing in the world Kitty O'Brien wouldn't have done for her children.

A fine clinging sea mist had hung over the Dock Road that night nine months ago, making the sky darken sooner than it should have done. There were fewer people about than usual, though the pubs were crowded and the sounds of breaking glass and drunken voices, laughing and shouting, drifted out from time to time. One of those voices belonged to Tom, Kitty thought bitterly, in there drinking whilst his children and his wife starved.

Foghorns sounded, dull and ghostly, and Kitty hurried even faster along the road to the place where the prostitutes plied their trade. She knew this because once, before she was married, not long over from Ireland and on her way into town on the tram, her best friend Lily had pointed out the street where women hung round waiting for paying customers. From then on, every time they passed it, they giggled, fresh-faced, bright-eyed and virtuously shocked.

Could that really have been only ten years ago? It seemed more like a hundred. She hadn't been into town since she'd married Tom and doubted if she ever would again.

The overpowering smell of spices mingled with the mist, tickling Kitty's nose as she came to the street where she had to wait. She didn't know its name but recognized the large brass sailing ship sign above an office on the corner.

Several women were already there, huddled in doorways, and she was worried they might come and shout at her, a stranger, taking away their custom, but in this fog, and they, like her, hidden by black shawls, they all looked the same.

There were no men to be seen, though. Panicking, Kitty wondered how long she'd have to wait, worried for her family, but then a dark figure loomed out of the dimness, approached a woman, and they disappeared together. Kitty strained to hear what was being said. Did you ask for sixpence or a shilling? It might even be half-a-crown. As long as she got enough to buy something for the children to eat, she didn't care. On the other hand, it was silly to ask for less than the going rate. Curiously, she felt no shame, no fear. Yet here she was, a good Catholic woman, intending to sell her body for money.

Kitty had no intention of being choosy. The first man who came along – assuming that he would want a poor worn-out housewife – would do. She had to get home as quickly as possible. Kevin, who was only six himself, was looking after a small baby . . .

But a foreigner! Not exactly dark-skinned but not light-skinned, either, with glowing, intense eyes and hair as black as night and very shiny, so shiny the yellow light was reflected on his thick waves.

By now, two other women had gone off with customers and this man, this foreigner, stood expectantly in front of her. Kitty's heart sank. At the same time she realized it was foolish to expect a tall blond Irishman, a young Tom, to proposition her. This was the docks – most of the men looking for women would be from abroad.

Was she prepared to do it with this man who was gabbling at her in a strange tongue, making exaggerated gestures with his long slender hands? She wondered if he was asking how much. 'Five shillings,' she said faintly, thinking that if it was too much he might go away. He didn't. Instead, he gestured again and Kitty's heart sank still further. He was signalling that they should leave. Together!

She followed him to the end of the street and round the corner. This particular area was notorious – full of criminals or so she'd heard. The man paused and Kitty realized he was waiting for her to lead the way, take him somewhere. Oh, God! Did he expect to go to her house? An hysterical laugh almost choked her, as she imagined turning up at Number 2 Chaucer Street with him, taking him upstairs, the children watching . . .

'This way,' she whispered nervously, turning the corner. There was bound to be a back alley behind the row of shops they'd just passed.

He was surprisingly gentle. No one but Tom had ever touched her there before. She still hurt from having Jimmie, but this dark-haired stranger was not vicious or rough like her husband, and after he had come – a soft, shedding release – he pressed her to him briefly, as though they had shared something remarkable together, and a strange feeling swept over Kitty and she found herself trembling.

She looked up at him, seeing him properly for the first time. His eyes were a lovely golden-brown, a colour she'd never seen before. From a window somewhere in front, a light came on and shone on his face. He was younger than she'd first thought, perhaps only twenty. His expression puzzled her until she realized it was pity, total, all-consuming pity – and she remembered with a shock that Tom had punched her in the jaw last night and it was black and blue and swollen, and she thought how repulsive she must look. If only she could speak his language, she'd tell him it didn't matter about being paid, she probably wasn't worth anything, but then she remembered the children and their hunger . . .

'T'ank you,' the young man whispered. 'T'ank you ver'

much.' He pressed something into her hand and was gone.

Kitty pulled her knickers up, straightened her skirt and shawl and held what she'd been given up to the light.

It was a ten-shilling note!

'What's the baby to be called, luv?'

Kitty smiled, transforming her once-pretty, now caved-in face. Her blue eyes, usually so watery as if loaded with unshed tears, brightened, and for a few seconds at least they looked clear and healthy.

A name for the baby? She'd only been thinking of boys' names. So far, even the dead babies had been boys and all along she'd been expecting another.

'Elizabeth,' she said. She'd wanted to be Elizabeth herself when she was a little girl because it could be shortened to many other names.

Mary Plunkett changed it immediately to the only form she knew. Bending over the still-sleeping baby, she placed her finger in the tiny clutching hand. The baby's brown fingers tightened over hers.

'Jesus, she's strong!' she gasped. She chucked the infant under the chin with her other hand. 'You're going to be a fighter when you grow up, aren't you, Lizzie, me gal?'

'Well, that's what you need to be in this life,' Theresa Garrett said dryly. 'Isn't it, Kitty luv?'

Kitty nodded, smiling no longer. A fighter. Yes, she hoped that's what her Elizabeth, her Lizzie, would become – unlike her mother, who'd become a victim, long ago beaten by life.

Chapter 2

Kitty lost the baby she conceived soon after Lizzie was born and the next a few months later.

Theresa Garrett, summoned to help with these painful miscarriages, demanded that Tom O'Brien call in a doctor to examine the poor, worn-out body of his wife, but he refused, so Theresa decided she'd pay the fee herself.

She asked the doctor to come early one evening when she knew that Tom would be home. Unfortunately, it also meant he would be drunk. Tom always called in at the pub on the way home from work for a few quick ones, and would arrive mildly stewed. After tea, he went out again and usually returned violent and half-mad with drink.

He was in his mild state when Theresa arrived with the doctor, who took Kitty upstairs.

The midwife didn't sit down but stood in the doorway watching the man sprawled in the armchair in front of the kitchen fire. There was no sign of the children. Lizzie, the baby, who was now eight months old, was probably asleep somewhere and the rest of them had made themselves scarce, as they usually did the minute their dad appeared.

Tom O'Brien had lodged opposite Theresa Garrett's house when he'd first come over from Ireland twelve years before. She remembered his buoyant good looks and charm, the spring and the hope in his step as he walked along the street, eventually appearing with pretty fair-haired, blue-eyed Kitty on his arm. For a moment she felt pity, viewing the coarsened, brutal man slouched in the chair. His blond hair, once the colour of sunshine, was now greasy and lank, and had turned to a dirty grey. His mouth and chin had slackened, fallen back out of control and slobber ran down onto his swollen neck and jowls. The oil-stained working shirt was open to the waist exposing a belly swollen by beer, bulging over the rope holding up his trousers.

But the pity didn't last for long. Hundreds, thousands of men came over from Ireland expecting to find the streets of England paved with gold. Had not her own dear husband done so, ending up stoking the engines of trains for twelve or fourteen hours a day till he'd died of emphysema at the age of forty-five? But unlike Tom O'Brien, these men didn't take out their failure, their loss of hope and dreams, on the weak and puny bodies of their wives and children.

The man was a brute and there were no two ways about it.

When Dr Walker, a well-dressed, harassed-looking man who was continually being pressed by his nagging wife to give up this ill-paying practice and move somewhere where the patients could meet their bills, came downstairs after examining Kitty, he said to Tom bluntly, 'Your wife is worn out by all this childbearing. You must let her be, at least for a while. Give her body a rest.'

'Let me wife be?' snarled Tom. Normally impressed by authority, he was too drunk and too angry to care. 'Why d'ya think I married 'er?'

'You'll kill her,' warned the doctor. 'And what will happen to the children if she dies?'

Tom didn't give a damn about the children. If Kitty died, then the Sisters at the Convent could have every last one of them and he would return to County Cork where he would starve in dignity and peace.

'Fuck the children,' he yelled. 'Take yer fuckin' advice and shove it where the monkey shoved its nuts. And fuck yer too, yer interferin' auld hag,' he directed at Theresa Garrett, waiting in the hallway.

When they'd gone he punched Kevin, the first of his children to venture indoors, and then went to the pub, drowning his sorrows by drinking even more than usual. On his return home, he dragged his wife upstairs, taking her so violently that she shrieked in pain and he felt so aggrieved he hit her. Then he feel asleep, half-dressed, his stained, acrid-smelling working trousers twisted round his ankles, so when he got up next morning, he fell over and woke up half the street with his shouting.

During the long night, Kitty tried to turn her head away from the stinking armpit beside her and wondered how on earth she would have the strength to get up in a few hours' time and cope with the drudgery of the day. Her head ached from where Tom had hit her and the pit of her stomach felt as if it had been pierced with a knife. She longed to move to a more comfortable position but if she did, and if she woke Tom, he might have her again and the thought was unbearable. She'd sooner remain cramped and stiff than risk that. Kitty felt her eyes prickle with tears. It wasn't often she felt sorry for herself, mainly because it wasn't often she had the time.

In the single bed jammed in a corner, little Lizzie gave a long shuddering sigh and Kitty held her breath, dreading the child would wake and disturb Jimmie and Chris, asleep at the other end of the bed. She couldn't imagine being able to raise the energy to get up and see to a crying baby just then, apart from which, it might wake Tom, but Lizzie was a good baby, always had been, and she remained fast asleep.

At the age of five, Lizzie started in the Infants at St Anne's Convent School, where she was regarded with mixed feelings by the nuns.

Several of the sisters made pets of Mrs O'Brien's children because they admired their mother's courage. Although all her brood were painfully thin, they didn't smell, their clothes were clean and neatly mended, and their hair was free from nits. The sisters had told Kitty about the clinic where she could get her children injected against illnesses like diphtheria, and be given free orange juice and cod-liver oil, and she'd taken them all, so they were bright-eyed and clear-skinned and all in all, far better turned out and healthier-looking than many of the children from far less poverty-stricken homes.

One or two of the nuns looked down on Kitty, feeling that a woman of whom a man had had so much carnal knowledge must be a bad lot. However, in the main the O'Briens were regarded as individuals, with their separate faults and virtues, but when it came to Lizzie, many of the sisters weren't sure if they approved of what they saw.

For a child so young, she had an almost exotic look; there was a foreignness about her, with her dark creamy skin and bitter-chocolate-coloured hair carefully woven into a great thick plait reaching almost to her waist. And such unusual-

15

coloured eyes – golden-brown with shreds of lighter gold – wise, knowing eyes that belonged to someone years older, not a child of five.

Sister Cecilia had read a book which said a whole tribe of people from India had landed in Wales a long time ago and it was from them this dark alien look had emanated, spreading to Scotland and Ireland too. But there was a different air to Lizzie O'Brien, one that was not apparent with the other dark-haired children. Wrong though it might be to use such a word about a child so young, there was a look of *wantonness* about her.

One who found this more disturbing than most was Sister Augustus, who, when licking her lips, would find moisture on her faint black moustache when she leaned over Lizzie's sums – and she seemed to lean over Lizzie's sums more than anybody else's – and because she took so much pleasure in stroking the little girl's smooth satin arm, a pleasure which she instinctively knew was wrong, she was inclined to blame Lizzie for this, rather than herself, and marked the sums wrong even when they were right as a sort of penance. Why Lizzie should have to pay the penance, Sister Augustus found difficult to explain, even to herself.

None of the other teachers were so prejudiced when it came to marking Lizzie's work, and all agreed she was an exceptionally bright child. All the O'Brien boys were intelligent, but Lizzie outshone her brothers in every subject.

By this time, Lizzie had acquired two younger sisters, Joan and Nellie, the latter almost as dark as Lizzie herself, and another brother, Paddy, who'd been born in between the two girls.

Mrs O'Brien had been forced to make more visits to the Dock Road and carrot-haired Joan, although she would never know it, had a French sailor for a father. Kitty hadn't realized he was a gingerhead until he took his round hat off to say goodbye, and when the flailing red-skinned, red-haired baby was born nine months later, she was past caring. She'd discovered Tom hadn't paid the rent for a fortnight and the landlord was threatening eviction.

The rent arrears required several trips, for the ten shillings she'd earned that first time had turned out to be far above the normal going rate. Apart from being less profitable, none of these subsequent encounters were as pleasant – though Kitty hesitated to let herself even *think* about it in those terms – as her first trip, yet neither were they as unpleasant as what she had to put up with from her husband.

Tom not paying the rent worried her deeply at first, for what he could do once, he could do again. There was no conceivable way she could pay twelve shillings and sixpence a week to Mr Woods, the landlord – her entire housekeeping was less than that. Fortunately, she discovered that Mr Woods waited outside the dock gates to collect rent off his bad payers on the day they emerged triumphant with their wages. Kitty asked for Tom to be included in this arrangement, relying, quite rightly, on him being too proud to refuse with his mates looking on.

This was a relief. The idea of dragging her poor tired body down the Dock Road on a regular basis seemed more than she could bear, though Kitty would have done it – for the children.

So they struggled along, Mrs O'Brien and her children, as did everyone else in Chaucer Street, in Bootle, Liverpool . . . as indeed did the poor throughout the country, hoping, dreaming, yearning for change, for an improvement in their lot.

When change came, in September 1939, in the shape of World War Two, everybody's world, both rich and poor alike, was turned completely upside down.

Chapter 3

Thanks to its proximity to the docks, Bootle became one of the first targets of Hitler's bombs.

Night after night they rained down on the areas alongside the River Mersey, killing its people and destroying their homes.

Along with her brothers and sisters, Lizzie scarcely knew what war meant until it came. The brief amount of history they'd learnt at school had made them think war was something which happened long ago, between men who wore resplendent red uniforms decorated with gold braid, and took place in strange foreign countries. It didn't happen in modern times, and certainly not in England.

But nightly visits to the communal air-raid shelter which stank of sweat and urine and excreta, where babies cried and old men and women spat and coughed and people did the most intimate, private things in front of other people and from which you emerged to find your house demolished or your street flattened or some of your family dead . . . all of these things taught the children that war was something very real that could happen to anybody at any time in any place.

Young men went off to fight, proud in their uniforms, and Kitty O'Brien prayed, oh how she prayed, night and morning, and whenever she had a moment throughout the day, that the war would be over, well over, in four years' time, when Kevin reached eighteen.

War made Tom a little happier, but this had no effect on his relationship with his family. He was deemed an 'essential worker', which made him feel important. He earned more money too and was employed on a regular basis, no longer having to suffer the indignity of waiting at the dock gates to be examined and picked out on a day-to-day basis by some uppity foreman. Tom was needed as much as any soldier in the fight against Hitler.

And how they hated Hitler! Hitler didn't care who he killed with his bombs. His pilots dropped them carelessly, or perhaps even deliberately, any old where, killing women and children, patients in hospitals, demolishing orphanages, old people's homes, even churches, whereas everyone knew that the brave young men in the Royal Air Force only bombed military targets like arms factories or barracks. German civilians were not being killed like British ones.

One night, the air-raid siren went much earlier than usual. A wave of fear gripped Kitty O'Brien's stomach when the awful whining noise sounded. It was only six o'clock and she was frantically gathering the children together to go to the shelter when the bombs began to drop. Normally she had them all prepared. She pushed the smaller ones into the cupboard under the stairs which some people used as a shelter rather than go to the communal one with the common people. There was an explosion close by and the house shook.

Suddenly, the bombardment ceased and at that precise moment, Tom knocked on the front door.

None of the family came in that way. Any other, safer time and Tom would have come in the back as usual. He didn't carry a front-door key.

A second sooner, a second later, they wouldn't have heard his knock.

Tony opened the door to let his dad in and Tom lumbered down the hall into the kitchen. He's been frightened by the raid and, half-drunk, was ready to lash out at his wife if she so much as looked at him in a way he didn't like, when suddenly the bombs began falling all around like confetti. One fell right outside the house and the front door was torn off its hinges and flung down the hall where it smashed to bits on the stairs.

The children looked at the shattered door and tried to imagine it was their dad. He'd escaped death by a miracle.

Tom boasted about it for weeks afterwards. 'Surely the Good Lord looks after His own,' he bragged and went to two masses the following Sunday morning and Benediction in the evening to convey his fervent thanks to Jesus for saving him.

His children, remembering their mother's nightly plea in their joint prayers to keep their dad on a straight and narrow path, wondered if their prayers had therefore been answered and many times in the years to come, wished they'd not prayed so hard or that God hadn't listened and it hadn't just been the front door which had been flung down the hall and smashed to pieces, but their dad as well.

In the mornings, bewildered parents, their crying children clutching at their legs, sat on the smoking wreckage of their homes. Many old people refused to leave the bricks and mortar they felt were just as much a part of them as their flesh and their bones. They rooted through the acrid-smelling dust, unearthing broken mementos of their lives, wedding presents, wrecked furniture and scorched photographs.

Looters hunted through the debris if they thought they could get away with it, though they were chased when spotted. In Birkenhead, a young woman was stoned to death by angry residents, her pockets full of bone-handled Sheffield steel cutlery, somebody's Silver Wedding gift.

Children still went to school, but the O'Briens' school, dangerously close to the docks, was closed down so they went for only half a day, sharing a school with the pupils of another one some miles inland. They whooped and laughed their way to the gate then dawdled outside, hoping the air-raid siren would go because the authorities said that when that happened, they must go to the place which was nearest, school or home. Wherever they happened to be, they went home, whooping and laughing even louder.

Many children had been evacuated to safe areas like Southport or Rochdale, but Kitty O'Brien saw little chance of someone willing to take on nine, soon to be ten – she was pregnant again – and she didn't want the family to be split up. She had visions of being killed herself and her orphaned children left scattered all over Lancashire, never to find each other again.

'If anyone's going to be killed,' she said to herself, 'then let us all be killed together.'

How happy the children were. Not just hers, but all children, in the midst of so much misery. Despite the war and the bombs, the poverty and the hunger, their wornout mothers and drunken fathers, they seemed possessed by an almost unnatural energy which overcame the wretchedness of their lives and their surroundings.

They sang on their way to school and on the way back. *'Oranges and Lemons, said the bells of St Clement's,'* they chanted in the playground. *'One, two, three, four, five, once I caught a fish alive,'* they sang as they ran up and down the street like demons, and *'The big ship sails down the Ally, Ally, O,'* skipping through dark, dank entries or on their way to the grey, soulless air-raid shelters.

Tom O'Brien found a pub where the landlord ignored the legal 'last orders' and looked on the All Clear as his signal to close, no matter how late this was, so Tom never went to the public shelter with his family.

His wife and children were therefore without him when they returned to Number 2 Chaucer Street in the early hours of Christmas Eve, the second Christmas of the war, thankful to find the house still standing and themselves all in one piece. There was a united sigh of relief as Kitty unlocked the door and the family trooped into the back kitchen of their home.

That night a crowd of drunks had descended on the shelter and kept everyone awake with their raucous singing. Had the children been asleep, Kitty would have stayed there till morning, but she was glad to hear the sound of the All Clear so they could leave. There'd been no chance of rest that night, not only because of the drunks, but they'd never known so many bombs to drop. They'd rained down like hailstones and the shelter had rocked and shuddered for hours.

'Shush, now,' Kitty had cuddled this child and that, stroking the older ones' heads, comforting them. She was worried a bomb might drop, a dead hit, and one of her children would not have had the touch of her loving hands before death. Careworn hands they were, the skin wrinkled, silvery and transparent, the prominent veins a dark and vivid blue and they fluttered over her nine beautiful children, soothing, patting, comforting.

The previous week, Kevin had started work as a milkman's assistant. Tom kept back the five shillings Kevin was going to give her, so Kitty would be no better off. She willed her eldest son to sleep for he had to be up at half-past four.

A bomb dropped yards away and the shelter made an odd

grinding noise as if it were about to collapse. Layers of concrete dust fell from the ceiling into their eyes, making them water.

So it was with an even greater sense of relief than usual that people heard the All Clear, and Kitty thankfully shepherded her wide-awake family out of the shelter, stepping over the drunken revellers who'd already begun to celebrate Christmas.

When the family entered the kitchen of their home, Kitty turned up the gaslight and they stopped, aghast at the sight which met their eyes.

Everywhere, absolutely everywhere was black. The dishes which had been left on the table, the furniture, every inch of lino was covered with a blanket of smooth, velvet blackness. Even the coloured paper chains which the children had made at school and which hung from corner to corner of the room were discoloured.

'Jesus, Mary and Joseph!' whispered Kitty O'Brien. 'What's happened to our house? It looks like the divil himself's been here.'

Lizzie bent and rubbed her finger in the blackness. It was powdery and had a sour, pungent smell.

'All the soot's come down the chimney,' she said. 'The bombs shook it down.'

And so they had. Vibration had loosened every particle of soot from every chimney, and investigation of the parlour and bedrooms showed that the same thing had happened there, though the effect was not so drastic as fires were rarely lit in these rooms.

Thankfully, all the children except Kevin were on holiday from school, and after a few hours' sleep, they set to and on Christmas Eve the house was scrubbed from top to bottom. Kitty was grateful for the blackout curtains supplied by the Government, for they didn't need washing, only a good shake to get rid of the soot.

For some inexplicable reason, when Kitty was an old woman she always remembered that day, that Christmas Eve, above all other days, for it seemed to contain all the misery and all the happiness and all the pride which made up her life.

She didn't expect Christmas presents from anyone and as usual had nothing to give her children, yet somehow the day still had a special, excited atmosphere.

At school, the children had been learning carols and as they scrubbed and brushed and dusted, the words of *Silent Night* and *Noël, Noël* filled the sooty, smelly house. The older ones put silly words to some, like 'While shepherds wash their socks at night' and Kitty tut-tutted and said it was sacrilegious, but at the same time hid a smile.

Then there was a knock on the front door and her heart thudded, for more often than not this meant trouble. Immediately, she felt convinced that the horse which pulled Kevin's milk-cart had kicked him to death, but instead it was a lady from a charity who'd been directed to the O'Briens by the sisters of the convent. She'd brought a package of groceries – a Christmas pudding, a cake with icing on, some crackers and a tin of meat.

'And how many children have you here?' she enquired brightly, blinking owlishly behind thick, wire-rimmed glasses.

'Eight,' said Kitty proudly. 'And me eldest Kevin's out at work and I've another on the way.'

'My! What a lovely big happy family,' said the charity lady and handed round presents to them all, only little things – celluloid dolls for Lizzie and Joan, yo-yos and rubber balls for the boys and a rattle, far too young for Nellie but which she loved.

Such a happy day, till Tom came home and said he didn't want charity, and threw the dolls onto the fire where they flared up in sizzling blue flames and melted to nothing and he would have burnt the other toys too if the boys hadn't immediately vanished with them, though he managed to stamp on the rattle.

Joan and Nellie set up such a screaming and yelling at this wanton destruction, that Tom felt bound to express his anger at the row on the person nearest, which happened to be his wife. He slapped her across the face with his open hand. The other side of Kitty's head slammed against the kitchen wall with a thud. Tom had his hand raised, ready to strike again, when suddenly he froze in astonishment. He was being thumped vigorously from behind. The blows had no force, they didn't hurt in the slightest, but their unexpectedness saved Kitty from a further slap. He turned, ready to strike, ready to knock whichever child this was from here to Kingdom Come.

'Leave 'er alone! Leave our mam alone!'

Lizzie, brown eyes afire, small fists clenched, stood daring him to strike. Her thick plait had swung over one shoulder and began to come loose, brown hair spurting out like strands of wild brown silk.

Tom knocked her sprawling. She could have been a flower on a stem for all the resistance she had to his great strength. Her dad was not so much angry as dumbfounded, for none of the boys had ever tried to defend their mam. This was not cowardice on their part, but knowing it upset their mam even more when he turned on them.

But Lizzie was beside herself with rage – a rage far greater than anything ever felt by Tom. A natural rage, not provoked by drink. She felt as if there was a fire inside her head and at any minute, flames would shoot out of her mouth and her eyes and her ears. She saw the breadknife on the kitchen table, a knife mam regularly sharpened on the back step. The blade gleamed dully in the orange gaslight. Picking it up, she approached her dad slowly, the handle in both hands, the point directed at his overhanging belly.

'I hate yer,' she said in a quiet, expressionless voice, a voice her astonished family had never heard before. 'I hate yer and I wish ye'd been bombed that night. I wish ye'd been here when the soot came down and it'd choked yer. *I wish yer were dead!*'

There was silence. Kitty felt as if she would faint. Surely Tom would kill them all.

Tom's drunken brain clicked over, trying to put a name to this hellcat of a child. Then he remembered. This was Lizzie, the eldest girl. The darkest one of the family. He always found it difficult to remember the children's names and sometimes was hard put to recall how many he had. Yes, he was sure this one was Lizzie and she was eight or nine, something like that.

Christ! She was a beauty. He'd never noticed before. Never given her a second glance. And what nerve! She was still approaching him, slowly, fearlessly, the knife pointed at him.

The rest of the family were frozen like statues in a park.

Unexpectedly, quite out of the blue, Tom felt a surge, a throbbing between his legs, but this time it was accompanied by something new, something different. Desire tinged with excitement. There was a flavour, a sensual tingling in this quivering, palpitating need.

But she was his daughter!

Without a word, and to the intense surprise of everyone, Tom turned on his heel and left the house, even forgetting to slam the door.

Chapter 4

By the time Lizzie was twelve, her mother's miscarriages were on the increase. A baby due the first Christmas of the war was born dead, and two more were lost before 1942, when Kitty surprisingly gave birth to twin boys – Sean and Dougal. The following year she had to go into hospital to have a dead baby removed from her womb.

As he operated, the surgeon was horrified by what he saw. The uterus had been stretched in and out like a concertina. Innumerable, repeated tears had never been stitched.

When Kitty came out of the anaesthetic, he was standing by the bed sternly demanding details of her childbearing history. He was horrified to discover she had eleven live children but had lost the same number, born dead or miscarried.

'You can't possibly have any more children,' the doctor told her brutally. The woman was only forty but looked sixty. 'It's too dangerous, both for you and for them.'

'But my husband— ' Kitty stopped, feeling embarrassed.

'He must take precautions, or if you like, I'll sterilize you.' The doctor wished he'd taken that step during the operation. She would never have known.

'What's that?'

'Removal of the ovaries so you can't conceive again,' he explained, thinking to himself how ignorant the poor were. He couldn't wait to finish his training and move to a hospital where he could treat patients of his own class.

'But that's a sin,' replied Kitty, deeply shocked. 'The Pope himself has forbidden birth control and Monsignor Kelly has spoken out against it from the pulpit.'

'Neither the Pope nor Monsignor Kelly have to bear your children or look after them. Nor do they contribute to the running of this hospital which deals with the consequences of such irresponsible behaviour.'

Kitty was even more shocked at this apparent criticism of the Holy Father and Monsignor Kelly.

The surgeon said he would send for Tom, and because when he was sober her husband was impressed and in fear of anybody in authority, whether it be doctors, nurses, policemen or members of the priesthood, when a letter arrived demanding his immediate presence at the hospital, Tom meekly went along.

'Your wife may well die if she has another baby,' the doctor said bluntly and superciliously to the hulking unshaven figure across the desk. Tom had come in his dinner-hour so as not to lose money and was in his working clothes. 'And if she does die, you will be guilty of murder. Do you understand?'

Tom nodded numbly.

'Murder!' the other man emphasized, relishing the sound of the word. 'Not the sort of murder you can be taken to court and tried for, but it would still be regarded as a mortal sin in your religion.'

Not knowing how to answer, Tom stared at his feet. The medical geezer must be right because he wore a white coat – a clear sign of superior knowledge.

'The Pope would consider it a mortal sin, as would your Monsignor Kelly,' the doctor assured him, privately thinking what a lot of hokum pokum this was, though this big oaf of a man seemed to be taking it seriously.

'If you wish,' he went on patronizingly, 'I could give you something to use which would prevent your wife becoming pregnant again.'

'Oh, I couldn't possibly use anything, doctor,' whined Tom. ''Tis a sin, worse p'raps than murder.'

'So your wife implied,' remarked the doctor dryly. 'What strange notions of sin you Catholics have.' He felt as if he was dealing with another race of people altogether. Many of the patients in this hospital, the Catholics in particular, were quite beyond his experience and his understanding.

Tom felt he couldn't tell this educated geezer in the stiff white coat, this God-like being who spoke as if he had a plum in his gob and probably put his prick through a hole so's he wouldn't see himself piss, that sex without knowing a woman took your seed to turn into a baby, was not sex at all. All his life, he and his brothers back in County Cork, and his friends who were Catholic, all of them felt this. That's why whores weren't satisfactory. Everybody knew they took precautions.

Having to pull it out or cover it up or knowing the woman had been messed about with or had something stuffed up her, that wasn't real sex. Basically, it was all about putting buns in ovens, even if you didn't want the damned kids when they arrived. It was a sign of virility to have a big family. Everyone at the docks, everyone in Chaucer Street knew Tom O'Brien was a real man because he made lots of babies.

But it sounded as if this medical ponce knew what he was talking about. It sounded like he'd even discussed it with Monsignor Kelly, and if he got Kitty in the club again and if she died, then the Monsignor would reckon Tom had murdered her. Even worse, God would know and when Tom himself died he would go to hell.

A week later, Kitty came home from hospital and a bed, provided by the sisters, was set up in the little-used front parlour.

'And not before time,' said the nuns, nodding at each other knowingly. 'Let's hope the poor woman gets a rest, for she surely deserves one,' and they made the sign of the Cross to endorse this hope.

Thus did life improve for Kitty O'Brien.

The bombing of Liverpool had virtually ceased and instead the people of London became the target of the Luftwaffe.

Kevin, Rory and Tony were all working and because of the shortage of manpower, their wages were higher than they would have been in peacetime. They bought Kitty several pieces of furniture, only second-hand, but a vast improvement on the battered old stuff she'd had before.

Tom must have felt inhibited by so many teenaged boys in the house growing taller and broader by the day, because he hardly knocked her about at all these days.

And Lizzie was such a good girl, taking a lot of the housekeeping off her mother's hands when she came home from school, and with only the twins to share her downstairs bedroom, Kitty enjoyed the luxury of night after night of undisturbed sleep for the first time since her wedding.

But in the course of time, Kitty's misery was to be transferred onto a pair of shoulders younger and even narrower than her own.

Tom O'Brien felt he was losing his grip on his family. That his power had gone.

He was lost and bewildered. His world of hard work and hard drinking needed an outlet. There had to be someone on whom he could vent his frustrations and his anger at the raw deal he felt he'd had from life. Now, with Kitty forbidden to him by God Himself and the boys growing bigger, becoming men, he began to feel a stranger in his own home, at odds with his entire family. Not that he'd given a fig for his family before, but suddenly they mattered. He wanted their respect.

The other day the older boys, the ones working, had talked about getting some distemper to decorate the parlour. The whole family had joined in the discussion about what colour to have, but no one consulted Tom, their dad, who should have had the last word on the subject. And this furniture which kept appearing – his permission hadn't been sought. He hadn't been asked for money towards it – not that he would have given any. Kevin just kept turning up with the borrowed milk-cart bearing a couple of armchairs or a new sideboard. It frightened Tom to think that his family could exist without his support, that they didn't need him any more.

But the worst thing of all was night after night, month after month, lying alone in the soft creaking bed, one thing on his mind, just one thing. Fucking. He missed it. He was lonely without it, nothing without it and until that bleedin' doctor shoved his oar in, had hardly ever gone without it since the day he'd married Kitty, nineteen years ago. How could a man be expected to make do with nothing when he'd been used to it once, twice, three times almost every night? There was no one to talk to about it. He was too ashamed to tell his mates. He had to suffer alone.

*

Tarts hung out in the pubs Tom used. One night at closing time, aching, burning with need, he asked one how much she charged. He'd given them all a good look over and this was the best of a bad bunch. Her name was Phoebe and she had a vast, bulging chest which strained against a tight hand-knitted red jumper. Her jet-black hair was permed to a frizz and maroon-painted lips gave her a clownish air.

'Five bob,' she answered in a squeaky querulous voice.

Christ! Tom thought of all the ale five bob could buy. Five bob for what he should be having at home for free every night.

'OK.' He had no choice. Otherwise, he'd go mad. 'Where'll it be?'

She'd noticed his face fall and said, 'Yer can have it fer half-a-crown if we just go outside. Five bob's back in me room.'

'Half-a-crown, then.' He arranged for her to go out first as he didn't want his mates to see him leaving with her.

She was waiting for him outside where a light drizzle fell. 'Come on.' She was in a hurry to get it over with so she could return to the pub before closing time and with luck, pick up another customer.

Tom shambled along a few feet behind, trying not to look as if they were together, though few people were about.

''Ere, this'll do.' She pushed open a heavy wooden gate that creaked and went along a short path which led to a deep, dark porch.

'This is a church,' said Tom, shocked.

''S'not Catholic.'

'Yeah, but even so.'

'Oh, come on. Do yer want it or not? And gimme the money first.' Tom fished in his pocket for half-a-crown and handed it over. 'Ta.'

He could dimly see Phoebe struggling to pull her skirt up and felt the full thrust of an erection. He couldn't wait to get inside her. As he began to fumble with the buttons on his trousers, he became conscious that she was holding something out for him.

''Ere, put this on.'

'Eh? What'cha talkin' about? What is it?'

'A French letter. It's a decent one – I got it off a Yank.'

'Fuck off, I'm not wearing that!'

'Well, you fuck off then. I don't want no kids and I don't want no VD neither.'

All desire had gone. He was limp. Empty. This is what happened when you went with a whore. Nothing but money, precautions and disease. It weren't natural.

''Ere, take yer money.' The half-crown was shoved back in his hand. She would have liked to keep it, but Tom was too big and strong to try that on. There wasn't anything to be gained from staying. She'd come across this situation before with the Irish Catholics and despised them for it. They wanted sex, they were desperate for it, 'cos their wives were frigid or dead or overloaded with kids, but show them a French letter and they ran a mile.

Tom was doubled up in agony, alone in the marriage bed. That woman, that bloody Phoebe. Got him all excited, made him feel worse than ever. He felt like going down and giving it to Kitty like she'd never had it before. He half sat up, then remembered. She might get pregnant. She might die. And it would all be Tom's fault. He'd be a murderer. Monsignor Kelly might even denounce him from the pulpit and he'd be damned to the everlasting flames of hell.

He was about to lie down again when his eyes rested on the single bed alongside his where Lizzie, Joan and Nellie slept, the youngest girls at one end, Lizzie at the other.

Tom licked his lips. Sly little bitch. Every time he clapped eyes on her, ever since that night years ago when she'd come at him with the breadknife, he'd been watching her, desiring her. In his drink-sodden mind he put the fault for this on Lizzie herself. He saw her flaunting herself in front of him, brushing against him as she placed his tea on the table. And oh, those sly, tantalizing glances, lowering those great long lashes when she caught his eye and twisting her lips provocatively.

Yes, it was all on her side, not his. Cunning bitch. It was *her* that wanted *him*.

He couldn't contain his pounding, feverish need any longer. He'd been without for nearly a year and if he didn't get it soon, he'd go mad. Reaching over, he lifted the sleeping girl, putting one hand under her neck, the other supporting her knees. Her skin felt slippery beneath the thin nightdress and as he laid her down beside him, his breathing became hoarse and he found himself gasping with desire.

Lizzie opened her eyes and was about to cry out in fear when her dad clapped his great clammy hand over her mouth. She knew what he was going to do. He was going to do what he'd done to her mam every night for as long as she could remember until Kitty had come out of hospital and begun to sleep downstairs. He was going to put his thing inside her and she knew it would hurt because Mam always moaned when he did it to her and cried when it was over and Dad had gone to sleep.

Now he snarled in her ear: 'Don't yer tell anyone about this. Not *anyone*, or I'll kill yer and then I'll kill yer mam too. Understand?'

Lizzie tried to turn her head away from the foul stink of his breath. Her eyes glowed like a cat's in the darkness. Tom was about to hit her for not answering when he realized his hand was covering her mouth. When he removed it, she took a deep, shuddering breath. Christ! He'd nearly suffocated her.

'D'yer understand?' he hissed again. Lizzie nodded. He felt rather than saw the gesture. 'I'll kill yer if yer tell,' he repeated, and, unable to control himself any longer, he forced himself on the unwilling body of his eldest daughter. At first, Lizzie wanted to scream out loud from the pain, but fortunately for her a few seconds later she fainted.

His power over his family restored, in his own mind at least, Tom felt in full control when a letter arrived in a thick white envelope on which his name and address were actually *typed*. It told him that his daughter Elizabeth had passed the scholarship and could go to a good school where she could stay until she was eighteen, and then, according to Kitty, who hovered anxiously in the background, on to university like Mrs Cooper's son from Dryden Street. Tom bellowed an emphatic and confident, 'No!'

Kitty pleaded, the boys pleaded. Even the little ones,

sensing the honour involved, pleaded. Lizzie said nothing, regarding her dad with contempt.

'No,' he repeated. 'This letter's addressed ter me. It's *me* they're asking and I say no. It's me'd have to pay fer the bleedin' expensive uniform and books and things.'

'We'll pay,' said Kevin, Tony and Chris together.

'Yer don't have ter pay fer things anyway, Dad,' said Jimmie, who'd failed the scholarship, as had all the older boys. 'That's what a scholarship means, gettin' things fer free.'

'This sorta fancy education's not fer girls, anyways. Lizzie's the eldest girl and she has to help her mam.'

'I can manage, Tom. Joan and Nellie can always lend a hand. 'Sides which, it doesn't mean she'll go away, does it?'

Kitty was desperate. She wanted him to agree mainly for Lizzie's sake, but also the idea of an O'Brien child leaving the house for school dressed in a velour hat with a badge on and a satchel over her shoulder made her heart swell with pride. She could scarcely believe it. Fancy Lizzie turning out so much cleverer than the boys, particularly with a foreigner . . .

She stopped *that* thought dead in its tracks.

'See, the nearest grammar school's in Waterloo – Seafield Convent.' Kevin picked the letter up. 'She'd only have ter get a bus down the road. It'd take quarter of an hour at most.'

Tom snatched the letter back. 'Look what it sez 'ere,' he snorted. 'What yer need ter buy for this bleedin' convent. A hockey stick! A bleedin' hockey stick!'

Lizzie had crept into the hallway and sat on the stairs listening. Like lots of children, her education had been badly affected by the war, attending school only half a day for several years and missing lots of classes altogether when there were air raids. She should have started senior school a year ago. Now she was twelve and had sat the scholarship late as a special concession. She was too old to sit it again.

It was now or never. With all her heart she wanted to go to a school where she'd learn foreign languages and sciences, subjects not taught in the senior school she was about to go to with Jimmie.

She wasn't keen on having a hockey stick as she hated team games, but she prayed and prayed her dad would give in and let her go. Why had the scholarship people written to him anyway? He'd never been the slightest bit interested in any of them. They should have written to Mam. It was Mam who asked questions about what they'd been doing at school, and even went to the library to get books out on things they didn't understand, like caterpillars or Roundheads or long division, but the library staff always made her leave because the little O'Briens made so much noise and anyway, poor Mam couldn't understand what headings to look under.

Seafield Convent was probably just like *The Fourth Form at St Monica's*, a book Lizzie had borrowed from the school library, or the schools in the *Girls' Crystal*, a magazine which her friend Tessa loaned her every week.

What she would have liked best of all was to go to a boarding school where she could get away from the awful thing her dad did every night. Perhaps all dads did that to their daughters when their mams were ill, though nobody at school ever mentioned it happening to them. Perhaps they'd been sworn to secrecy, like her. Flora Steward's mam had died when she was a baby and she'd been brought up by her dad. Lizzie wondered if she could ask her. She wanted to know if it would always hurt so much, but was scared that if she confided in someone and her dad found out, he would kill her and Mam as he'd threatened to.

Lizzie rarely cried. It was weak to cry, but right now she felt the tears sting her eyes because she wanted to go to the posh school and she wanted her dad to leave her alone at night. She felt so tired.

Suddenly, there was a crash from the kitchen. Tom had pushed the table back and sent the chairs flying.

'Sod the lottya yis,' he screamed. 'She's not goin'. Me mind's made up.'

And with that, he left the house for the pub and although Kitty tried to raise the matter again several times, he flatly refused to discuss it and on one of the occasions, the boys being out, he managed to give her a black eye.

The letter from the Education Department remained unanswered, and one day Kitty put it away in a drawer. In years to come, she would often take it out and re-read it, although she knew the words by heart. She used to wonder . . . if Lizzie *had* gone to the grammar school, how differently would her life have turned out?

Chapter 5

Tom was scared of losing Lizzie. A posh school – even if it was only down the road and she came home each day – could well give his daughter high and mighty airs and put her out of his reach.

Having Lizzie put new meaning into Tom's life, and fire returned to his belly. He looked forward to getting home at night and would even have left the pub early, but of course he had to wait till everyone was fast asleep.

So Lizzie went to the ordinary senior school, where she didn't do nearly as well as expected.

'Well, if this is a scholarship girl,' exclaimed a teacher, 'then all I can say is, it must have been a fluke. She couldn't have coped at grammar school.'

Although Lizzie grew taller and her body began to fill out and her dark creamy skin moulded itself like smooth soft silk over her high, almost Oriental cheekbones, at the same time her brown-gold eyes seemed to be sinking deeper and deeper into their sockets. Purple shadows, so startling they could have been drawn by a crayon, appeared beneath them. She was always tired, always listless. One day, a teacher found her fast asleep in a history lesson and woke her with a sharp slap, which he regretted when the girl came to with a hunted, frantic look on her face.

Perhaps all was not well at home, thought her teacher, but then he shrugged the problem off. After all, it was none of his business.

At home, Kitty was sick with worry.

'When will this awful war end?' she wailed. It was 1944. Kevin had been in the forces a year and now Rory had got his call-up papers.

'Don't worry, Mam,' he laughed. 'It'll soon be over. 'Sides, it'll be fun going ter France and Belgium and foreign places like that.'

'I hope it lasts long enough fer me ter fight,' said Tony wistfully.

'Me, too,' echoed Chris, and at this Kitty shrieked hysterically.

The only consolation she had was that Kevin had been accepted into the Fleet Air Arm. He wore a peaked cap and a uniform like a suit, not a battledress: he looked just like an officer.

Kitty was so proud. She had no favourite child – she loved each and every one as much as any mother could – but on the day Kevin appeared in his uniform, she overflowed with love for her oldest boy.

Except for the fortunate few who obtained supplies on the black market, rationing was a great equalizer. Nowadays, rich and poor ate the same, so the O'Brien children were no longer painfully thin. The older boys' shoulders had broadened and Kitty was sure she was not being prejudiced when she judged her sons to be handsome, outstanding young men.

Kevin's once-flaxen hair had turned dark blond and beneath his cap, his blue eyes twinkled with excitement.

'I'll not be leaving the country, Mam,' he said. 'Least, not for a while,' but shortly after he'd gone, Kitty received a letter to say he was on an aircraft carrier whose whereabouts he couldn't disclose.

Then, before she knew where she was, Rory was getting ready to leave. He'd joined the Royal Air Force.

'It'll be over next year, won't it?' cried his mother, turning to her eldest daughter for comfort, but to Kitty's surprise, Lizzie twisted away and soon afterwards left the house without a word.

'It'll be the periods,' thought Kitty, remembering how a few months ago Lizzie told her she was bleeding between the legs and she'd provided her with a pile of clean rags. It struck her that she hadn't washed any rags for Lizzie for some time, but she supposed that at thirteen, the girl wouldn't be regular for a while.

Lizzie felt sick. She had been vomiting every morning

in the lavatory at the bottom of the yard and the periods which had started four months ago had stopped after two. She knew as much about the symptoms of pregnancy as any grown woman, having slept in the same room as her mam all her life and helped with the births of Dougal and Sean.

She was expecting a baby. She was also desperate and knew no one she could turn to for help. Once or twice she'd walked along Linacre Lane where Dr Walker had his surgery, but she'd never summoned the courage to go in. One drizzly November evening she loitered outside, the rain penetrating her thin coat and shoes. She shivered, knowing if she hung around all night she wouldn't raise the nerve to call on him.

Anyway, Dr Walker charged a fee. Lizzie wasn't sure what it was, but even sixpence would be too much as she didn't possess a penny.

In the past her mam had taken the children to the doctor only as a very last resort and had called him out on one single, solitary occasion when Chris caught scarlet fever. The ambulance was sent for and her brother was carried out in a fluffy red blanket and a crowd gathered to see what was going on.

Right now, Lizzie earnestly wished someone would wrap her up in a blanket and carry her off somewhere safe and warm.

'Hallo, Lizzie.' It was her friend Tessa from school.

Lizzie wanted to be alone. She'd left the house for that reason. 'I'm on a message fer me mam,' she lied. 'She wants it in a hurry.'

'D'yer want me *Girls' Crystal*?' Tessa offered generously. 'I've just finished it. Come to our 'ouse and I'll give it yer now.'

Normally, Lizzie would have been off like a shot to Tessa's. She loved to creep in a corner with her favourite magazine and get lost in the world of boarding schools and mysteries and juvenile romances, but right now all her mind had room for was her horrifying predicament.

'Termorrer,' she told Tessa shortly. 'I'll come termorrer. I've got ter rush now fer me mam.'

She walked away without even saying tarra and Tessa felt hurt and decided to call on Cissy Smythe to see if she wanted the *Girls' Crystal* instead, and Lizzie O'Brien, who'd become proper stuck-up lately, could go without in future.

A third period missed.

Something else Lizzie knew was that the longer you had a baby in your belly, the more dangerous it was to get rid of. Not that her mam had ever even contemplated such a terrible thing, but a few girls at school had mams who'd had abortions even though they were Catholic. There was a woman in Wordsworth Street who did them and she charged a whole five pounds.

It was a sin, a mortal sin to murder a baby, even when it wasn't yet born. It was even more of a sin, though, and much more dreadful, to have a baby when you weren't married.

In fact, it was the worst thing in the world that could happen. The disgrace of having to tell her mam, and the whole street knowing, and having to go to school with a swollen belly. Though maybe she'd be sent away. That would be better, otherwise the baby might arrive in the middle of a lesson or even worse, school prayers, and everyone would stand around gaping, including the boys.

Lizzie lay in bed one icy December morning. Her dad had long ago left for work and she was in the small bed, her feet all tangled up with those of Joan and Nellie. They were both asleep. In the dim light Joan's copper curls were just visible on the pillow she shared with her sister.

Pulling up her nightdress, Lizzie stroked her normally flat belly. There was no doubt about it. It was beginning to swell.

'Dear Jesus. Oh, sweet Jesus,' Lizzie prayed. 'Please help me.'

In actual fact, Lizzie didn't have much faith in prayers. She remembered how hard the family pleaded to God to end the war before Kevin was eighteen, but He hadn't listened and now Rory was gone as well. She'd beseeched Him to make Dad let her go to grammar school, but He hadn't answered that prayer either.

She couldn't go on like this. Someone had to know, though once she'd heard of a girl who lived in a convent home who'd gone the whole way with a baby and the nuns just thought she was getting fat and the girl had given birth to the child in a lavatory and put it in a dustbin where it died. Someone found it and the police were called in.

Lizzie couldn't have done that even if she'd wanted to. When Mam was expecting, she puffed out like a great balloon and probably Lizzie would do the same and there was no way she could keep it secret.

If only she didn't feel so full of sin, so guilty. She hadn't confessed her sin either. If she told Monsignor Kelly or any of the other priests at Our Lady of Lourdes they'd recognize her voice and tell Mam and Father Steele always asked funny questions like, 'Have you been doing naughty things with boys?' or 'Has a boy touched you between the legs?' even when you only went to confess little things like telling a silly lie or saying bad things about the teachers. So if she got Father Steele when she went to confess she was carrying a sinful baby, he was sure to ask who'd done it to her and there was no way she could tell him about the horrible things Dad did every night.

Aching with misery, she dragged herself out of bed, dressed and went downstairs, leaving her sisters sleeping in envied innocence.

'Yer up early, luv.'

Her mam was sitting in front of the kitchen range crocheting. The fire glowed red and Lizzie could smell bread baking.

'I woke up early an' couldn't get ter sleep again,' she said. Could she tell her mam? Looking into those trusting, watery blue eyes in the prematurely-aged face, Lizzie decided she couldn't.

With Kevin and Rory away, her mam was already beside herself with worry and it would be selfish to add to this. Besides which, she felt she'd betrayed Mam by letting Dad do those things to her. Most importantly, Mam would never, never help her get rid of the baby. Mam would insist she had it and if that happened, Lizzie would be a public disgrace like

Norma Tutty from down Chaucer Street who had a little boy everyone said was a bastard and they wouldn't let their children play with him. Lizzie wouldn't want her child to be called names like that.

'D'yer feel all right, Lizzie luv?' asked Kitty anxiously, struck by the haggard, almost desperate look on her daughter's face.

'Yes, Mam. I'm a bit tired, that's all.'

'Yer working too hard at school, that's what it is.'

On reflection, though, Kitty couldn't remember Lizzie doing homework for weeks.

'No I'm not, Mam.'

'Oh well, you'll grow out of it,' said Kitty complacently. The boys had always been as good as gold but she knew several women whose daughters had gone through a sulky, sullen stage around the time their periods started. 'Fetch some water, there's a good girl and I'll make yer a cup of tea. It's time the little 'uns got up. Give 'em a shout, will yer?'

However, her worry returned when she noticed the laborious and awkward fashion in which Lizzie rose to her feet to get the water from the back kitchen. The awful dark suspicion that occasionally flashed through her mind resurfaced, but she immediately pushed it back, unwilling and unable to think the unthinkable.

Jimmie and Lizzie walked to school together. On that same miserable morning, Lizzie told her brother to go ahead, that she'd catch him up.

'Yer not going to scag again, are yer?' His blond hair was flecked with snow. It was freezing.

'Of course not,' she snapped.

'Stop kiddin', Liz. You've been scaggin' lots lately. I know, because Mrs Robinson asked fer yer the other day. I told 'er yer were ill,' Jimmie said.

'Ta, kid.' Lizzie softened towards her brother. She and Jimmie had always been close.

'Better be careful,' he warned. 'Our mam won't half be mad if the Schoolie comes round looking fer yer.'

'I know,' said Lizzie. That was the least of her worries.

'Would yer like me butty, Jim? I don't feel like it terday.'

'Ta, Liz,' said Jimmie, trudging off through the falling snow which was turning to slush as soon as it reached the ground.

Lizzie walked in the direction of North Park. At this time of year the gardens and playing fields were completely deserted, and spiky, half-dead bushes spattered with snowflakes lined the lonely path along which Lizzie wandered.

Exhausted, she sank onto a bench, little caring that the saturated wood soaked through her dress and coat. Her shoes were already wet and leaking and she began to shiver violently. Not only that, her head throbbed as she tried to think of a way out of her predicament. She wondered what would happen if she just turned up at the hospital where they'd taken Chris when he had scarlet fever, but all she could imagine was angry nurses shaking their fists at her and shouting that she was a dirty girl.

She wanted to cry, but was scared, even in this deserted place, of drawing attention to herself. The Parkie might come and want to know why she wasn't at school. If only she could *tell* someone, thought Lizzie – someone sympathetic. As soon as her mam found herself 'in the club' again, as she put it, she'd tell the whole street, half-ashamed, half-proud, and she'd also tell Theresa Garrett, the midwife, to make sure she'd be free about the time the baby was due.

Mrs Garrett! Remembering her kindly manner when dealing with her mam and her gentle handling of all the newly-born children, Lizzie's heart lifted. Of course! She would go and see Mrs Garrett this very minute. She would listen and understand.

Mrs Garrett lived beside a butcher's in Southey Street. The houses opposite had been bombed and the site only roughly cleared. Stained and tattered wallpaper which had once covered people's bedrooms and parlours, blackleaded fireplaces and even a crooked picture of Our Lady were exposed to the world at the end of the row of houses which remained. Jimmie said it looked as if a giant had cut away a portion of the street to eat.

By the time Lizzie reached the house, the snow was falling thick and fast in great wet dollops and had begun to form a slippery carpet.

'Please, oh please be in, Mrs Garrett.'

Lizzie didn't realize she'd spoken aloud until the butcher, who was brushing snow off his step, said, 'You're in luck, luv. She is in, 'cos she's just made me and me mate a cup of tea.'

Lizzie managed a weak smile and hurried to knock on Mrs Garrett's front door.

'Lizzie O'Brien!' exclaimed the midwife in surprise. 'It's not yer mam, is it? I mean, she's not — '

'No, Mrs Garrett,' interrupted Lizzie, agitatedly. 'It's not me mam. Can I speak with yer a minute, please?'

The midwife's house smelled of polish and disinfectant. Had Lizzie not felt so distressed, she might have noticed the bright curtains on the kitchen windows with blackout material on the outside and cushion covers to match, the heavy cream lace cloth on the table and pot plants and ornaments scattered about the room. In pride of place on the mantelpiece stood a photograph of the deceased Mr Garrett.

'What's the matter, luv?'

Mrs Garrett had already decided the girl had come about her periods. Either bleeding had started and she didn't know what it was, or it hadn't and she wanted to know why. Women of all ages consulted her with their female problems, their dropped wombs, their lumps and cysts, tumours and fibroids, and she advised them as best she could.

But when Lizzie began to speak, she couldn't believe her ears. Pregnant! She remembered the night she'd delivered the child quite vividly, the way she'd shot out in such a hurry and how she'd caught her in safe, secure arms.

'I think I've gotta baby in me,' the girl said.

Thirteen years old and been with a boy! Of course it happened. Mrs Garrett wasn't ignorant of the ways of the world, but it didn't mean she had to approve.

'Yer a bad, bad girl to have done that with a boy,' she said severely. 'Yer should be ashamed of yerself.' And so she should be, too. Kitty O'Brien had devoted herself to her

43

children and until now they'd been a credit to her.

'This'll kill yer mam,' she went on, shaking her iron-grey curls disapprovingly. 'And as fer yer dad, what he'll say —' She broke off. Having sampled Tom O'Brien's language in the past, she couldn't very well put into words his likely reaction.

Lizzie became hysterical. 'Yer not to tell me dad,' she screamed and shrank back into the chair, eyes wide, mouth gaping.

'Quiet, girl. Don't yer dare take on so in my house.'

The more Teresa Garrett thought about it, the more shocked she became. Lizzie O'Brien had always been such a pretty thing, quiet and demure – hadn't she passed the scholarship too, though Tom wouldn't let her go to the grammar school, but it meant she ought to have more sense.

Children today! They had no morals. Well, if this was the way Lizzie behaved, despite being brought up in a decent home, then she could put up with the consequences. She spoke her mind, there and then.

'I can't help yer. Yer got yerself into this mess, so get yerself out of it!'

Lizzie fled out into the snow. The friendly butcher had gone back inside his shop. She paused outside, frantically wondering which way to go.

Before the war, the bloody torsos of animals had hung in rows on great metal hooks outside here, but only a few pathetic joints of meat now lay on the white marble slab inside the window for people to buy their allotted amount with ration coupons. Each joint had a skewer driven through it. In her misery, half-taking in the scene, Lizzie remembered how her brothers had found a skewer like that once, a rusty old thing which they kept amongst their few treasures, using it to make holes through the conkers they collected in North Park.

Lizzie gave a deep and desperate sigh. The butcher saw her gazing through the window, winked at her and smiled. This time Lizzie didn't smile back. He wouldn't be so friendly if he knew the truth about her.

Her brain felt as if it had frozen, not just with the cold

and the snow and the ice, but with numb bewilderment. She wished with all her heart she could stand in the sleet outside this shop, her feet so cold she could scarcely feel them, her clothes soaking, staring at the bloody scraps of animals in the window. She would be happy to just stay until she froze to death. To die on this very spot would solve everything.

But it was not to be.

The good-natured butcher came to the door. 'Are yer all right, luv?'

Lizzie gaped at him and for a moment the man wondered if she was right in the head, for the look she gave him was quite wild. Then, without a word, she turned and fled.

When she reached home, Lizzie was grateful to find her mam had taken Dougal and Sean out shopping.

The house was empty.

At last she was able to release the awful, wracking sobs that had been building up all morning. She lay on the stairs in her wet clothes, her body heaving with pent up misery.

Suddenly she thought of something. A solution!

There was no need to ask for anybody's help with the baby. She would deal with it herself.

Theresa Garrett felt irritated when there was another knock on her door only minutes after Lizzie O'Brien had left. If it was that girl again, she'd give her a piece of her mind.

Instead it was her neighbour returning the empty cups. Mrs Garrett and the butcher, Mr Shaw, had an agreement. He let her have a pound of his best pork sausages each week and she made him and his assistant a cup of strong tea with sugar every morning and afternoon.

'That was nice,' he remarked. 'A really nice cuppa.'

He always said that. Mrs Garrett took the cups and noticed he'd forgotten to get his assistant to wash them, which was most unusual.

'Did a girl just call on yer?' he asked. 'Thin, dark kid?'

'Yes, she did,' answered Mrs Garrett indignantly. 'And I sent her packing.' Of course, she didn't reveal the reason why. Never, never would she betray a confidence, whatever the circumstances. She'd no intention of telling Kitty and Tom O'Brien about Lizzie's visit, despite her threat.

'Oh!' Mr Shaw appeared a bit dismayed by her attitude. 'It's just that she seemed a nice girl and she looked a bit . . . well, a bit lost, yer might say, when she went off.'

'Did she now!'

'Isn't she one of the O'Briens? That's right!' He slapped his forehead triumphantly. 'I've been tryin' ter place 'er. I always think, whenever I sees them kids, how well they've turned out, considerin' what they've got fer a dad. An ignorant lout of a man is Tom O'Brien, in my humble opinion.'

Mr Shaw said goodbye and as she closed her door, an awful, sinking feeling came over Theresa Garrett and she began to tremble.

'Oh, dear God in heaven, what have I done?' she whispered aloud to her empty house. 'It's Tom, I know it is. It's Tom who's been at the girl.'

Kitty O'Brien hadn't been pregnant for over a year. She still slept in the parlour. That left Tom in the bedroom with his three daughters, of whom Lizzie was the eldest. She wouldn't trust Tom O'Brien as far as she could throw him and she couldn't throw him an inch.

Grabbing her coat, she half-walked, half-ran to Chaucer Street.

Kitty had just come in and put the kettle on for a cup of tea. With Tony and Chris at work and Kevin and Rory regularly sending money home, care of a neighbour – an arrangement which Tom knew nothing about – she had more money to spend than she'd had in her life before. She'd secretly been buying Christmas presents for the children for weeks – nothing extravagant, else Tom might get suspicious.

She picked up the breadknife, sharpened only that morning on the icy back step, and began to make butties for the little 'uns, at the same time wondering if she dare buy coats for the girls through the club man, as the ones they had were awfully thin for this weather, when Theresa Garrett appeared in the yard and came through the back door and into the kitchen without so much as knocking.

'Why, Mrs Garrett — ' Kitty began indignantly. No matter

how much respect she had for the midwife, she should always knock before coming into someone else's home.

'Where's Lizzie?' the woman demanded abruptly.

'Why, at school, o'course.'

'No, she isn't. Has she come back here?'

'Back here? No. I mean . . . I don't know. Why should she? I've just this minute come in meself,' said Kitty, totally confused.

Douglas and Sean sucked their sweets contentedly and regarded the distraught visitor with wide, solemn eyes.

'Can I look upstairs?'

'Yes. Yes, o'course, but why?' Kitty was frightened by the midwife's behaviour. What on earth was going on?

Mrs Garrett climbed the stairs as fast as her heavy frame would allow. She had no idea what was urging her on, why she had such a sense of foreboding.

Lizzie lay on the bed. Her eyes were closed and the sockets had sunk so far back that her face was almost skeletal. She was so still, so silent, that at first Theresa thought she was dead and her own heart almost stopped beating at the thought, but as she approached, the girl's eyes opened.

Luminous pools of dark golden light stared up at the midwife and Lizzie whispered. 'I'm sorry I've been such a naughty girl. I'm praying to Baby Jesus right now ter fergive me. D'yer think He will?'

Mrs Garrett felt tears running down her cheeks and she laid her large gentle hand on the girl's stomach. To her astonishment, Lizzie screamed in agony.

The premonition that something was wrong, even more wrong than the evil perpetrated by Tom O'Brien against his eldest daughter, the premonition that had prompted her to rush through the snow-filled streets to this house, caused Mrs Garrett to draw the rough blankets away from Lizzie and what she saw made her stomach churn.

From the waist down, the girl's clothes and the bed were soaked in dark red blood and Kitty O'Brien, who was standing bewildered in the doorway, gave a scream of horror.

But all that Kitty could see was the bloodsoaked bed. She

was not close enough to see what Mrs Garrett could.

The circular fingerhold of a rusty skewer which Lizzie had thrust inside to rid herself of the sinful baby.

Chapter 6

A new doctor was on duty in the Casualty Department the morning they brought Lizzie in. He was not only very young, but idealistic, with a wish to heal and mend and care for the poor. He wanted nothing to do with the rich. In the Norfolk village where he was born and his father was a lord, he was known as Sir Rodney Hewitt-Grandby, but to the hospital staff and patients in Liverpool he was just Dr Grandby.

There'd been no cosy wrapping up in a red blanket for Lizzie. She couldn't bend her body an inch. The horrified ambulancemen had the greatest difficulty getting her onto a stretcher and the moment she'd reached hospital, she'd been rushed into the emergency operating theatre where she was swiftly anaesthetized.

So Lizzie didn't know her feet were placed in cold stirrups whilst the metal skewer was removed followed by the dead foetus, a boy, whom the surgeon reckoned was a good three months old. Then Lizzie was disinfected, sewn and mended.

'You're her mother, I take it?' Dr Grandby came into the corridor where Theresa Garrett waited impatiently. Kitty had been persuaded to stay at home with the twins.

'No, Doctor, I've no children of me own. I'm a friend of the family. Will she be all right?'

'Well, her internal injuries are terrible,' replied the doctor gravely. He'd been horribly shaken by Lizzie's self-inflicted wound. 'There's always the chance she'll never have another baby.'

'Oh, my God!' Mrs Garrett knew she'd have this on her conscience for the rest of her life.

'The injuries are not just from the skewer, either . . .' The young man paused, not sure how much he could divulge to someone who was not a relative.

'I'm a close friend, Doctor, and I delivered her and all her brothers and sisters.'

'Well, Nurse, someone's been abusing her for a long time.'

Mrs Garrett didn't choose to correct the doctor's assumption of her profession. She put her hand on his arm in an unconscious, fervent gesture of assurance.

'I know who it was, Doctor. God help me, but I didn't realize it was going on. Perhaps I should've done, but I swear on the Almighty it won't happen again.'

She'd never meant anything so much in her entire life. If need be, she'd stand over Lizzie and her sisters day and night to protect them from that monster Tom O'Brien. He'd have to throw her out of the house, physically pick her up and throw her out, if he wanted her to leave, and if he did, she'd shout the truth to the whole of Chaucer Street.

Dr Grandby looked doubtful. 'This is really a matter for the police.'

Theresa Garrett shook her head fiercely. 'No, Doctor. Yer don't bring the police into private family matters like this, not round here. Would yer like me to ask Monsignor Kelly to come and see yer?' That would be the ideal solution – let him tell the priest what had happened.

'I'll think about it,' he said, unconvinced. 'She won't be going home for a while and I'll have a chat with the girl herself, see what she thinks.'

They had been talking directly outside the double swing doors which led to the ward where Lizzie lay, and through the windows, Mrs Garrett could see her lying, still and pale, her olive-skinned arms limp on the covers. A nurse had swept her great swathe of brown hair to one side and it hung like a silk curtain over the edge of the bed.

Dr Grandby's gaze followed hers and he commented, 'Unusual-looking girl, isn't she? Which side of the family is the foreign blood on?'

'Oh, no, Doctor! Why, she's as Irish as the pigs of Trogheady. It's the Celtic streak that comes out now'n again and makes them dark like that.'

'Oh, I see,' said the doctor noncommittally.

Dr Grandby was engaged to be married. His fiancée Suzanne was a clerk in the Admiralty in London.

The day after Lizzie's admission to hospital, the doctor was due for two days' well-earned leave and he drove down south in the small Ford car which he'd changed to at the beginning of the war as his big Rover used up too many precious petrol coupons. He was longing to meet Suzanne again. They hadn't seen each other for over two months.

That was the day a tramcar overturned in Stanley Road, and although no one was killed, several passengers and pedestrians were injured and a fleet of ambulances carried them to the hospital.

There was already a shortage of beds. An entire wing of the building had been demolished by a landmine the previous year. The senior doctor in charge did a tour of the wards to decide which patients were fit to return home and make room for the new arrivals.

'What's wrong with her?' he asked from the foot of Lizzie's bed.

The Matron who was deferentially accompanying him leapt forward to grab Lizzie's chart.

'An abortion, Doctor,' she said disapprovingly.

'Send her home,' he ordered. 'There's people here with injuries which are no fault of their own who need these beds.'

So, that afternoon, an ambulance took Lizzie back to Chaucer Street.

Kitty was flustered when the official vehicle drew up. Despite the cold, half a dozen neighbours turned out again to see what was going on. She helped her daughter in and hugged her, though she was still unsure what had happened. Mrs Garrett had muttered something about a haemorrhage, and had promised to come and see Kitty 'before Lizzie gets home', expecting her to be in hospital a good week, which she should have been, for the poor girl could hardly walk and was clearly in great pain.

The terrible thought which had been trying to wriggle its way into Kitty's brain tried to break through again, but she pushed it away. She couldn't think that. *She couldn't.* She couldn't even bring herself to ask what had happened. Theresa Garrett would tell her later.

What she needed to concentrate on now was making

Lizzie comfortable. She was so pale and weak, unable to sit down and right now was holding on to the banisters for dear life.

'I can't manage the stairs, Mam. Me legs won't lift up.' She was staring at the floor, unwilling to meet Kitty's eyes.

'Sleep with me ternight, Lizzie luv. Till yer better, eh?'

'Yes, Mam.'

'D'yer want ter lie down now, girl?'

'All right, Mam.'

Dear God! The girl could scarcely move. She shuffled into the parlour, where Kitty helped lower her onto the bed, lifted her legs and placed them gently on the covers, and all the time, Lizzie winced in agony, though she never cried out, not once.

Tom O'Brien lumbered into the house, his clothes soaked with the sweat of a day's toil. He carried with him a strong aroma of olive oil which he'd been unloading all afternoon.

As the years passed, Tom's gut had become even more bloated. Now it bulged out so far that the top of his trousers had disappeared behind a shelf of fat. His features had coarsened to the extent that sometimes Kitty thought he bore no resemblance at all to the mischievous charmer from County Cork who'd asked for her hand in marriage twenty years before – although it seemed more like a hundred and twenty.

As soon as he entered, the usual air of gloom fell over the house and everyone in it; it would not lighten till he left for the pub after tea. Not one of his children spoke to him. They never did. They faded away to sit on their beds or see their friends. Tony and Chris went to the pictures.

After he'd eaten his scouse, Kitty placed a mug of tea before him and said, 'Lizzie's home.'

Tom started. 'Where is she then?'

He'd missed Lizzie badly the night before and couldn't get out of his stupid wife what was wrong and why she'd had to go to the hospital.

'She's in the parlour. They sent her home early. There was a tram accident in Stanley Road and they needed the beds emptying.'

Kitty didn't mention Theresa Garrett was coming to see her about Lizzie because Tom couldn't stand the woman and it would only set him in a rage. She'd cross that bridge when she came to it.

Lizzie! Downstairs! All night long the thought haunted Tom as he sat in the pub drinking pint after pint of foaming beer. Was she going to stay down there forever, like Kitty? The twin boys, Tom couldn't remember their names, had been upstairs in the back bedroom ever since the eldest two had been called up. Kitty had been sleeping alone for months now, so there was plenty of room for Lizzie.

His brain, already half-rotten from the thousands of pints of beer consumed over the years, simmered in crazy confusion. His little Lizzie was being taken from him, moved out of his reach – the only one of his children whom he loved. Then the unimaginable happened. He actually felt tears prick his eyes and all night long remained so morose and silent that his mates wondered what on earth was wrong with Tom O'Brien. He was usually the life and soul of the party, with an endless fund of dirty jokes and patriotic Irish songs.

At closing time he staggered home alone. The streets were covered in black slush which had started to freeze, and swaying round a corner he slipped and fell full-length. He cursed loudly and fiercely. But although his body was cold and his clothes wet, inside he burnt with a feverish rage.

What a situation to come home to after a hard day's work and a hard night's drinking! All the other men had wives to poke. Why not him? He was a man, a real, vital man and he needed a woman. All men needed a woman, but he more than most. It was his right.

But now there was no Kitty, no Lizzie.

The house was silent when he entered. He made no attempt to keep quiet, but the family were used to his noise and usually slept right through it.

Tom threw himself half-dressed onto the bed. That familiar ache crept over him, as if the mere act of lying down, the feel of the mattress, the creak of the springs, meant that there should be a woman there, legs apart, waiting to satisfy his needs.

But there was no one.

*

That night, one member of the family was awake to hear Tom come in. Lizzie lay in the parlour, the pain in her lower abdomen so sharp and violent, there was no chance of sleep. After Dad settled down, she'd wake Mam and ask for more aspirin, which dulled the ache a little.

She heard Dad throw himself into bed, then the springs squeaked rustily, the headboard banged against the wall, and the floorboards creaked. It sounded so loud downstairs in the parlour, directly below.

An awful suspicion entered her mind.

She lay there for several minutes, trying to stop the suspicion from expanding and developing, when from up-stairs there came a stifled cry, a frightened, fearful moan.

Lizzie sat up in bed so suddenly, that the pain inside her enveloped her entire body like fire.

'Lizzie! What is it?'

'It's Joan, Mam. Me dad's got our Joan. And I can hear it, Mam. I can hear it clear as anything so yer must've known, all this time. Yer must've known what he was doing ter me, 'cos I know, the very first night sleeping here, that me dad's got our Joan.'

Lizzie struggled to get up, gritting her teeth, willing the pain not to explode as she staggered to the door. About to go up the stairs, she remembered the breadknife. That had stopped Dad years ago when he was going to hit Mam.

It lay gleaming on the kitchen table ready to cut butties next morning.

Kitty appeared in the parlour doorway. In the dim gaslight left burning at the top of the stairs, her pale eyes looked desperate in her thin haggard face.

'Lizzie, girl, I didn't know,' she wailed. 'Gracious Christ, I didn't. Yer dad, he's always so restless, tossing this way and that, making the bed creak all night long.'

'Yer must've known, Mam,' said Lizzie coldly.

It was agony climbing the stairs. It was as if her legs were scissors, cutting away at her insides every time she took a step.

In the bedroom she could just about see the great half-naked figure of her dad kneeling over a struggling, snuffling Joan. He had his hand over her face, just as he'd done with

Lizzie.

'*Gerroff!*' she screamed. '*Gerroff 'er!*' And she pointed the razor-sharp knife in the direction of the drunken man.

'Come fer a bit too, have yer?' snarled Tom. He'd have the two of them, he would – Lizzie first, then the red-haired bint. He tried to reach across the bed, difficult on the soft mattress and in his wild drunken state. Joan gasped aloud, retching for air when he moved his hand away and she began to push him off, bewildered, not quite sure what was going on.

Scrambling across the bed on his knees, Tom lost his balance and fell full-length, kicking Joan in the mouth when his feet jerked backwards. Intent on reaching Lizzie, he raised himself and lunged foward, unaware that a knife was pointing right at him, threatening him.

He fell off the side of the bed right onto it.

Right through his chest it went, and even though his body was covered with a thick layer of muscle and fat, the long sharp knife plunged in, right up to its handle, piercing his heart virtually right through. He breathed his last choking breath at Lizzie's feet.

Poor Joan, thinking she was waking up from one nightmare to another, crawled to the foot of the bed to see what had happened. Nellie woke and then the boys, all six of them, came into the room, rubbing their eyes. Jimmie carried a nightlight and this illuminated only too clearly the dead and bleeding body of their dad.

But before they saw anything, Kitty had crept into the room and was kneeling by the body, her hand on the knife, trying to remove it.

So only Lizzie knew it was she, not Mam, who'd plunged the knife into the hated heart.

Or so she and Kitty thought. It was many, many years before Lizzie was to discover that one other person had witnessed the true version of events.

Chapter 7

'Going down Central Station ternight, Lizzie?' Marie Gordon shouted from the doorway of the newsagent's where she worked and which Lizzie passed on her way to school.

'You bet!' answered Lizzie, her best American accent emphasized by the fact that she was vigorously chewing gum. 'Got a date with Hank at half-past seven.'

'See yer then. I'll call fer yer about six, okay?'

''Kay,' agreed Lizzie and hands in pockets, hips swinging, she swaggered on her way.

In a few weeks' time she would be fourteen, and she was already taller than everyone in her class except for one boy. Her breasts, which Lizzie regretfully suspected were as big as they would ever be, were small but firm, high and pointed, the nipples prominent through her sparkling white though frayed school blouse. Those swinging hips were as lean as a young boy's, but curved up to an eighteen-inch waist, giving the impression of voluptuousness unusual in someone so slim.

Lizzie tossed her waist-length chocolate-coloured hair as a gesture of rejection at the boys who whistled and catcalled in her direction when she entered the school gates.

The girls mostly ignored her. Tessa was no longer her friend and Lizzie wouldn't have read the *Girls' Crystal* to save her life. *Secrets* and *Miracle* and *Red Star* were now her favourite magazines.

It was said at school that Lizzie O'Brien 'went' with boys, and that was the real reason why they whistled and stared and crowded round her at break-time, vying with each other to walk her home. It wasn't that they found her attractive. They'd pay just as much attention to other girls if they allowed the liberties Lizzie O'Brien did.

No one had any proof of this. Lizzie had never been seen *out* with a boy from school, but surely, the other girls told each other, being so free with her favours could be the only possible reason for her popularity.

It was nothing to do with her erotic looks, they said cattily. Yet those starry golden-brown eyes seemed to issue an invitation to anyone who wished to see an invitation there . . . and there was not another girl in school, nor in the whole of Bootle, with such high, exaggerated cheekbones or with a mouth that, without a touch of lipstick, was such a pretty pink colour. Well, more of a peach colour really. No one had seen a peach since the war began but, thought the boys, if that's what peaches looked like, then they wanted to get their mouths around one.

Lizzie was the cleverest of the O'Brien children by far, the teachers decided as they gossiped in the staffroom, but what a pity she'd waited until her last half-year to prove it. Of course, they'd never met Paddy who'd passed the scholarship and gone to a boy's grammar school in Waterloo, just along the road from the convent where Lizzie would have gone if her dad had let her.

Yes, she'd certainly blossomed since that awful tragedy at home last December when her mother had stabbed her father to death. No more sunken, shadowy eyes and falling asleep in class – but although she turned in more than adequate work without any apparent effort, and appeared to have a quick and lively brain which could grasp facts in a flash, the general consensus was that Lizzie O'Brien was a cheeky little madam with a provocative manner who had an unsettling effect on the boys, not to mention several of the male staff, and all in all, they'd be glad to see the back of her when she left at the end of the summer term.

In class Lizzie yawned. Not through tiredness, but boredom. They'd been doing square roots for nearly a week now and she'd got the hang of it straight away but some stupes kept on asking questions, then more questions, and it was all very tedious.

She stared out of the window and thought about the night ahead.

Marie Gordon, Lizzie's new friend, was a bold and brassy

girl. She worked in the newsagent's on the corner of Chaucer Street and Marsh Lane and a few months earlier, when Lizzie went to buy her favourite magazines, Marie had confided they were her favourites too and saw in Lizzie a spirit equal to her own.

It wasn't long after Christmas and she'd asked Lizzie if she'd like to come with her to Central Station to meet the Yanks who arrived there nightly, entire battalions – or detachments or whatever you called it – of them, searching desperately for girls on whom to shower presents of cigarettes or cookies or gum or, best of all, nylons.

'All yer have ter do,' explained Marie, 'is ter let them take yer out, go to the flicks, or a pub or caff, then afterwards, let them have a little feel – yer know!' She winked at Lizzie knowingly.

'I know,' said Lizzie, who didn't know at all at the time, but since then the two of them had been going to Central Station every night.

With pearl earrings from Woolworths, nylons kept up with garters and high-heeled shoes borrowed off Marie's mother, Lizzie looked three or four years older than her age.

In pubs and dance-hall bars, she sipped gin and It and rum and orange, or funny drinks with slices of lemon and cherries on sticks. She took the cherries home to Sean and Dougal. One Yank, a Captain, had taken her to the Adelphi, the poshest hotel in Liverpool. That was the night Lizzie had inadvertently let slip she was still at school and he demanded her age. When she confessed she was only thirteen, the Captain had given her a stern talking to and told her to go home. Then he almost ran out of the hotel. 'Jailbait,' he'd said she was, which Lizzie didn't quite understand, but to avoid future embarrassment she invented a job. From then on, she said she worked in a florist's.

She gave the cigarettes she got to Mam. Kitty found smoking a great comfort since Tom's death. The rest of the family enjoyed the cookies, sweets and gum. One day Joan was sent home from school for wearing nylons.

'Where do they come from, luv?' Kitty asked querulously. She was a shaky, nervous figure nowadays and scarcely left the house.

'Off some fella,' replied Lizzie casually, not caring what her mam, or anybody, thought. No one was going to stop her from doing anything that took her fancy.

Poor Kitty. Her neighbours felt even more sorry for her than ever. As far as that brute of a husband was concerned, it was good riddance to bad rubbish, but trust Tom to depart the world in such a violent way, leaving his long-suffering wife to cope with the consequences. Kitty felt as if she'd never be able to face Chaucer Street again.

It seemed to Kitty, from the very moment it happened, that it really *was* she who'd plunged the knife into Tom. When she relived the events of that terrible night, she could actually recall the feel of the thick bone handle in her hand and the sensation, the crunching, squashing sensation, of the blade entering her husband's gross, beer-swelled body.

Oh, that awful night!

She'd ordered the boys back to bed, all but Tony who was sent to fetch a bobby. Then she'd helped Lizzie, who seemed to have gone into a trance, down to the parlour and told Joan and Nellie to stay with her.

Once they were all out of the way, she'd struggled to turn Tom's body over. He was lying face down on the bedroom floor. She knew he was dead, yet at the same time she expected an involuntary arm to reach out and hit her as one final gesture of hate.

She knelt over him and tugged at the knife until it came out of the body with an ugly, squelching sound. Then, gritting her teeth and saying a prayer, 'Hail Mary, full of grace,' she turned the weapon on herself, slashing her arms and chest. Her thin nightdress was soon soaked with blood and it wasn't until it ran down her arms and began to mingle with her husband's that she stopped and put the knife back in his heart.

Then Kitty began to weep. For Lizzie, for all of her children, for herself and even for Tom.

She was still weeping when the bobbies arrived.

There were two of them, one as big and gross as Tom had been, the other small and weedy with a narrow, suspicious face. On several occasions in the past when Kevin or Rory had gone to the police station to complain that their mam was being beaten by their dad, the bobbies, including these two, had just laughed and said, 'Good luck ter him. Get on home, lad, it's none of our business.' And now that the victim had fought back, they remained unsympathetic, both towards her and her injuries.

Not so the nurses at the hospital where Kitty was taken, though, nor the Detective Inspector who came to see her early the next day.

A sister whispered, 'Good for you, girl. I bet he deserved it,' and Kitty replied shakily, 'Oh, he did. Believe me, he did.'

It was the least she could do for her Lizzie whom she'd let lie with that beast for all that time.

Of course she'd known!

She, Kitty O'Brien, who thought herself such a wonderful mother, had lain in the parlour, comfortable and alone, whilst at the back of her mind lurked the suspicion, no, the *knowledge* of the awful thing going on upstairs. She'd hidden her head under the clothes when she'd heard the bed creak in that all-too-familiar way, telling herself it was too horrific to be true, that Tom was having a restless night after drinking too much. Never, never would she admit to herself that the unbelievable was really happening, because if she did, then she would have to stop it and because Tom *had* to have a woman, it would be Kitty who'd be upstairs again in the big soft bed subjected to his animal desires.

Yet there'd been only one time, one single time Lizzie had heard him at Joan, her little sister, and she'd been up there like an avenging angel despite the pain of the abortion which Theresa Garrett told her about afterwards.

So, when the Detective Inspector came into the hospital, Kitty was ready to confess, confidently and believably, to the murder of Tom.

'He'd always been violent,' she whispered, 'ever since we was married.'

The Inspector nodded. His men had already told him about the boys coming to the station, pleading for help, and the neighbours confirmed that the dead man had conducted a reign of terror over his family for years. Dr Walker had informed him of Kitty's numerous miscarriages, many caused by kicks and blows.

'Ternight, though,' Kitty said, 'I mean, last night, he came at me with a knife. He'd never used a knife before.'

'Upstairs?' queried the policeman. 'You mean, he brought the knife upstairs?'

'Y . . . yes,' stammered the woman. Her self-inflicted wounds were smarting from the iodine. She was worried sick about Lizzie and to a lesser degree about Joan. As yet, the fact she was a widow hadn't quite registered.

'He . . . he came in drunk, like he allus did,' she went on hesitantly. 'I was already in bed and he woke me slamming the door. He went out ter the lav then came upstairs, swearing and cursing. I thought ter meself, "He's in a worse mood than usual." Alluva sudden, he was in the room, slashing at me with the breadknife. I fell outta bed,' she continued visualizing the scene as if it had really happened. 'And Tom, he tripped over me legs and dropped the knife, so I picked it up, in case he came at me again, like.' She paused, close to tears.

'Go on,' said the Inspector gently. He was a tall, ungainly man who'd interviewed half a dozen women like Kitty since he'd come to Liverpool. Women who'd spent their married lives as punchbags for vicious, brutish husbands. Women who took the beatings, took the violence, year after miserable year, for the sake of their children, of their marriage, or even, God help them, because they actually loved the men who made their lives a nightmare, but suddenly the worm would turn and the men got a taste of their own medicine. It was not until that happened that the Inspector became involved. Ironic, wasn't it, he thought to himself, that a woman can be nearly murdered for a lifetime and no one cared, but let her strike back . . .

Kitty drew a deep breath, forcing the tears back. 'I was lying there holding it, and he did no more than fling himself atop o' me, not knowing I had it like. He probably couldn't see it was pointing up at him, and he landed right on it.'

'I see,' said the Detective Inspector, genuinely believing he did.

'Can I go home now, mister?' pleaded Kitty. 'I've little 'uns there who need their mam. I won't have ter go ter prison, will I?'

The policeman smiled kindly. 'You can go as soon as the doctor says you're fit,' he said. Kitty's lawyer had arranged bail. 'As for going to prison, it's not up to me, but I shouldn't think so.'

There was a trial, though little publicity. The war took up all the headlines in the *Liverpool Echo*, what with Allied landings in Europe and victory in sight, even if only on the distant horizon.

Kitty was accused of manslaughter.

Kevin and Rory, smart in their uniforms, the rough edges of their Liverpool accents already fined down, testified to the continual beatings suffered by their mother at the hands of Tom O'Brien. Lizzie and Joan weren't even mentioned. Kitty was found Not Guilty and only a small paragraph about the case appeared in the *Echo* and this was ringed in pencil and passed round Chaucer Street, where the unanimous judgement was that Tom had only got what he deserved and it was surprising that Kitty hadn't done it long ago.

It was the least Kitty could do for Lizzie, but even so, she sensed her daughter never completely forgave her.

From then on, all Kitty could do was let Lizzie go her own way. Since that awful December night, she'd become a different girl altogether, going out most nights and not coming home till very late. Kitty said nothing. How could she, when it was all her fault?

On Saturday mornings, her eldest daughter lay in bed till midday when the other children were up and about by eight or nine o'clock helping with the housework. What was she doing to get these stockings and sweets and cigarettes and things? Kitty dared not ask.

The two girls waited on Central Station. Marie wore a second-hand green Moygashel frock which she'd bought the Saturday before from Paddy's Market where good quality second-hand clothes could be got without coupons. It was two sizes too big, which meant the shoulders drooped halfway down her elbows. There was nothing she could do about that, but she'd taken up the hem and buckled the stiff-backed belt as tightly as it would go. In fact, she could scarcely breathe.

The Yanks seemed to have so much money that they didn't know what to do with it, and sometimes they'd hand over as much as five pounds at the end of an evening out, so Lizzie went to Paddy's Market as well and she'd also bought a new second-hand frock. That meant she had three frocks and a camel coat. The latest dress was tangerine silk – a wraparound style which seemed in perfect condition until it was ironed, when Lizzie found that the inside seams were flame red, showing that the dress had faded with so much washing, but she didn't mind a bit. It was a hand-made dress and therefore unique, and Lizzie wondered if the previous owner would ever approach her one day and say, 'You're wearing my dress!' It had a wide, separate sash which wound round her waist twice, making it look so tiny that Marie, suffocating in her tight petersham belt, was green with envy.

Lizzie liked the way the tissue-thin material rested on her lean hips. There wasn't a long mirror at home so she had to examine her full reflection in the Ladies Waiting Room on Central Station. The first time Lizzie had done this she got a shock. Of course she'd seen herself full-length before, blurred and distorted, in shop windows, but to see herself properly for the first time was a revelation.

For one thing, behind her in the mirror were scores of other girls painting their faces, combing their hair and generally making themselves as attractive as possible for the Yanks about to arrive from Burtonwood, and Lizzie couldn't help but notice that a lot of the girls had lumpy bodies or stringy hair or faces full of spots. Of course there were *some* pretty ones, but Lizzie, trying not to be conceited, knowing vanity was a sin, couldn't see another pair of legs as slim and smooth as hers or eyes as large or glowing. And without a doubt – and this was not vain – there was definitely no one with such a cascade of silky shining hair flowing right down to their waist, and such a narrow waist at that.

That was the day, the day she saw herself full-length in a

proper mirror for the first time, that Lizzie noticed lots of the girls glancing in her direction, some in admiration, but mainly with expressions of unconcealed jealousy on their faces.

'Hey, shove over!' A fat girl nudged her out of the way. 'Let other people have a go in the mirror,' she said nastily.

'Sorry,' stammered Lizzie, who'd just realized she was beautiful. Uncommonly and strangely beautiful.

Several weeks after that first visit to Central Station, a scraggy scarecrow of a woman, much older than the others, approached Lizzie. 'Does yer mam know yer come here, girl?' she asked.

'O' course,' lied Lizzie.

The woman's face was dead white and powdery as if she'd dipped it in a bag of flour, and her lips were a gash of crimson. Several teeth were missing. Her name was Georgie and she was always the last to leave on a Yank's arm – that is, if she left at all. It was reckoned a Yank would have to be really desperate before he would take on Georgie.

'Yer shouldn't be 'ere,' said the woman. One of her legs was shorter than the other and she would skip along in a fast, lopsided manner. 'Yer mam shouldn't letcha come.'

'She doesn't mind.' Lizzie tossed her head and wished Georgie would go away. For one thing, a train was due any minute and she didn't want to be seen in her company.

But Georgie wasn't to be put off. 'Listen, luv,' she said confidentially, 'in that case, yer should go up ter the Adelphi fer yer trade. Yer'd make a fortune there, a girl with your looks.'

'D'yer think so?' Lizzie answered, wondering what the woman was on about. Then Georgie was forgotten as the train steamed to a halt and Hank came bounding towards her, first through the barrier as usual.

'Hi, y'all,' he drawled in that lovely, lazy Texan accent, and picking Lizzie up he swung her round so high that her skirt swirled into the air and her long legs nearly knocked poor Georgie off her feet.

Like Lizzie and Marie, a few girls waited for definite dates, but in the main, the women were waiting for a Yank, any

Yank, to pick them up, take them out and give them a good time.

Not only had Yanks got money and all sorts of goodies unobtainable in war-starved Britain, but they were incredibly generous and good-humoured. Most were young and handsome, but even the older ones and those who were downright ugly had a smart and glamorous air in their neat, well-cut expensive uniforms, and their film-star accents invested them with a charm the English lads couldn't match.

Hank, Lizzie's date, was a Corporal in the Pay Corps. He could only get to Liverpool three or four times a week and when he did, Lizzie was his girl, or 'gal' as he put it. His hair, bleached by the sun, was almost white-blond and his lifelong golden-tanned skin was just beginning to fade after a cheerless English winter. He was barely as tall as Lizzie when she wore her high heels, which she found strange, used as she was to rubbing shoulders with big brothers all over six feet. Back in the States, Hank's pa was a farmer and right from when he was little, Hank had ridden a horse and herded cattle, just like a real cowboy. He showed Lizzie a photo of himself with a spotted scarf around his neck, wearing a stetson hat and mounted on his favourite horse, Gyp. He looked just like Roy Rogers, only younger.

Lizzie, having only seen broken-down, weary cart-horses dragging coal merchants' or rag and bone men's carts round Bootle, was very impressed – by Gyp, by Hank and by Americans in general.

One night, Hank proposed marriage. Lizzie accepted. She thought it a huge joke. Of course, he said, he'd have to get his Captain's permission. The Captain might want to interview Lizzie and her parents, seeing how young she was and all, not yet seventeen.

Lizzie suggested they wait awhile. 'Let's see how we feel in six months' time,' she said, thinking how very mature and responsible this sounded, and much better than saying there was no question of marriage as she was only thirteen years old!

Lots of girls had received proposals, some as many as four or five. More often than not, they never heard from their prospective husbands again once the men were transferred

65

or had 'got their way', as some girls put it bitterly, knowing their erstwhile suitors were off to Manchester instead to pick up and offer marriage to other innocent young women.

So Lizzie was not so naive as to take Hank's proposal seriously and anyway, she wasn't the least bit faithful to him. The nights he was on duty she still went to Central Station with Marie and joined up with other servicemen. Lizzie was a very popular girl and Marie was glad to be her friend, because it meant that with the boys nearly always in pairs she and Lizzie were always the first to be picked up.

Some nights they went dancing, to the Rialto or Reece's, and Hank or another soldier or airman Lizzie happened to be with would dance very, very close, so close you couldn't have stuck a matchstick between them.

It was so romantic, thought Lizzie, mooning about in class most days, staring out of the window, driving the teachers mad, particularly when they tried to catch her out and sharply asked a question, to discover that although she looked as if her mind was anywhere but in school, she'd understood more than most other pupils.

Hank was really taken with her new tangerine dress. He said she looked 'real cute' and they left Central Station arm in arm, ignoring poor old Georgie waiting awkwardly outside the gents' toilet, winking grotesquely at every man who entered.

Lizzie and Hank, Marie and Clifford – Yanks had such funny names – went to the Trocadero to see *Gone With The Wind* which they'd already seen twice. It made Hank feel homesick, but Lizzie loved every single minute, particularly the ending. It didn't seem possible that the Deep South of America and Chaucer Street actually existed on the same planet.

She made a strict rule and stuck to it: 'No necking during the performance'. She didn't want to miss a part of any picture, and particularly not *Gone With The Wind*.

Hank spoke about the American Civil War as if it had just taken place. It seemed more real to him than the war he was taking part in. He said Lizzie was the spitting image of Vivien

Leigh, except their eyes were a different colour.

'Damn Northerners!' he'd mutter. 'Niggers are scum. Take it from me, they don't get treated like equals on my pa's spread.'

Lizzie had already noticed how the black Yanks stuck together and never mixed with their white comrades. The latter had even been known to beat the black boys up if they saw them in the company of white girls.

After the pictures, they went to Lyon's for a cup of coffee. Despite the blackout, the centre of Liverpool was teeming with people. Nowadays, the air-raid siren rarely sounded.

The café was almost full of Yanks and their girls. The few Englishmen there watched them enviously. A soldier in coarse battledress sitting at an adjoining table, fingered Clifford's smart tailored uniform in admiration.

'You a Captain, mate?' he asked.

'No, pal, I'm a Corporal, just like you,' Clifford told him.

The Yanks all seemed to know each other and they carried on conversations in loud voices across several tables. They were so brash and confident, so wealthy and generous.

After half an hour, Lizzie and Hank got up to leave.

'See yer half-eleven at the tram stop,' hissed Marie as they passed.

'Okay,' said Lizzie.

Hank put his arm around her shoulders as they wandered up Skelhorne Street, turning into a dark cobbled passage where they began to search for an empty doorway. Several they passed already contained couples locked in heaving, panting embraces.

Eventually they came to the back entrance of a laundry – dark, empty and inviting. Hank pushed Lizzie against the double doors and began to kiss her – long, wet, childish kisses. Sometimes Lizzie suspected she was the first girl he'd ever dated.

After a while, he began to breathe heavily and his hands groped her body. He kneaded her breasts with his thumbs, then moved his hands down to her waist, twisting and turning as if he wanted to break her in two.

'Lizzie, oh Lizzie,' he whispered hoarsely. 'I love you.'

'I love you, too,' Lizzie replied dutifully. She liked Hank a lot but didn't love him. The lovemaking she found bewildering. The kissing meant nothing, though she pretended to respond. Sometimes, when he touched her nipples, she felt a slight, pleasant thrill. But it was when he smoothed his hands over her hips, stroking, caressing, pressing his knuckles against the crevice between the top of her legs and her belly, his thumbs creeping closer, closer to the point where the moistness was swelling and throbbing inside that she would pray Hank would go further so that the moistness could be released and she knew, she could tell that when this happened the moment would be joyous. At the same time there was a feeling of disgust, with herself, with her body, with Hank, which she couldn't explain. Anyway, Marie's warning always came to mind in good time: 'Never let them up yer skirt, otherwise they can't control themelves and ye've got a fight on yer hands.'

So, half-sorry, half-relieved, Lizzie pushed Hank away and said, 'I'm going ter miss me tram.'

'Godammit, honey,' Hank gasped, 'I can't even get to first base with you.'

Lizzie didn't answer. She began to walk down the road and Hank ran after her. He put his arm around her, his hand cupping her breast and he kept squeezing it gently as they strolled towards the tram stop.

'When am I going to get to screw you, Lizzie honey? After all, we're practically engaged.'

Lizzie wanted to say 'never', but this might put Hank off and she quite liked having a regular boyfriend. She couldn't very well tell him that good Catholic girls didn't sleep with boys before marriage, even if they wanted to, and she wasn't sure whether she wanted to or not.

'Ye've never gone all the way with Hank, have yer, Liz?' Marie asked on their way home on the tram.

'Oh, no!' Lizzie replied, shocked. 'Not with him. Not with nobody.'

'Me neither,' said Marie. 'I'm still a virgin too, though the way Clifford behaved ternight, it was all I could do ter keep him off me. I'm going ter have to give in or give Clifford up.'

'Then give him up,' advised Lizzie virtuously.

*

That stuff with her dad couldn't have been real. It was just a nightmare she'd had. Those things he'd done, the things she'd dreamt he'd done . . . it wasn't possible, not with Mam downstairs in the parlour. And that day in North Park, so cold, so wet, so desperately unhappy. Mrs Garrett being horrid. Why, Mrs Garrett made such a fuss of her nowadays, coming round to the house specially to see her, taking her hand and asking how she was.

She'd imagined it. It hadn't happened. Lizzie couldn't live with the idea that it was true. Lying on the bed, the rusty old skewer, piercing herself. The pain, the doctor, the hospital.

Lizzie O'Brien, sitting on the tram, so pretty and smart in her tangerine dress and camel coat, could never have inflicted such an horrific injury upon herself.

Joan! Her dad and the bed creaking. The bread-knife always kept so sharp. 'Gerroff 'er.' A scream. Then blackness.

That was where the nightmare ended.

It hadn't happened, Lizzie told herself. It was merely a bad dream that kept returning in the darkness of the night, making her shudder and moan, even when she was awake.

It hadn't happened!

Chapter 8

At the same time as Lizzie was being fondled by her American boyfriend, another US serviceman was coaxing his limping single-seater Mustang down onto the runway of an air base in Suffolk. He'd been as far as Berlin, trying to crack those bloody Germans who wouldn't give in. Jeez, you'd think they'd know they didn't stand a chance, surrounded on every side, with Russians, Americans, English and French, all closing in.

He'd dropped his bombs on a railway terminal. Trucks full of arms exploded like a giant firework, but he'd been hit from the ground. Gone in too low, trying to make sure the bombs were spot on.

Talk about coming back on a wing and a prayer! The engine faltered and spluttered all the way, but here he was, above base, and now the fucking undercarriage was stuck! So they'd got him there too. But he'd land the plane on its belly. It took skill, but he'd done it before.

He pushed the joystick forward delicately, trying to transmit his terror and his wish to live to the aircraft through its instruments. *'Don't explode. Don't crash. Smoothly does it.'*

The plane touched the ground, shrieking like a thousand madmen.

Christ! It veered crazily from side to side and he frantically moved the joystick left, then right, trying to steady course, and as the plane careered towards the side of the runway, one wing demolished a flimsy wooden hut where the mechanics sometimes went for their tea to save the long walk back to the mess.

The collision seemed to help the plane back on its right course. The pilot breathed a sigh of relief and saw an ambulance racing towards him. Report in, a cup of coffee, then bed and forget all about planes till tomorrow night. In fact, by the time he jumped out of the cockpit, he felt quite cheerful.

*

On the tram, Lizzie said to Marie, 'D'yer want ter come to Southport on Easter Monday, the week after next? Hank's taking me.'

'I wouldn't want ter be a gooseberry.' Marie had her pride.

'He's bringing a crowd of mates,' Lizzie told her. 'It's me birthday, yer see. We're having a day out ter celebrate.'

'Gee, Lizzie, I'd love ter come, but the shop'll be open Easter Monday and I've got ter go ter work.'

'Never mind,' said Lizzie, who didn't care if Marie came or not.

In Suffolk, where the young pilot of the damaged plane was having a welcome cup of coffee and comparing notes with his fellow aircrew who'd also survived the night, another young man in overalls was crawling out from beneath the splintered remains of the hut the plane had demolished.

He ran as fast as he could back to base, but every now and then his legs gave way and he fell and every time he fell, he cried like a baby.

Soon he was stammering incoherently at his Sergeant who strained to make sense of him.

'Pull yeself together, man,' commanded the Sergeant roughly. He was a Scot, a regular serviceman who considered all wartime recruits were yellow-bellied cowards. If they weren't, there'd have been no need to call them up; they'd have volunteered. 'Speak up, Rogers. What the bleedin' hell are ye on aboot?'

Rogers starting gabbling again and the Sergeant had to restrain himself from hitting the lad. Then he thought he caught a name. 'O'Brien, did ye say? What about O'Brien?'

'We were in the hut, Sarge, having a cuppa, when we heard this plane coming in. It was in trouble, we could tell, and Rory, I mean O'Brien, he stood up and looked out the window in case we could help, like, and one of the wings went right into us and it knocked O'Brien's head clean off, Sarge.'

There was something wrong.

When Lizzie arrived home, she just knew there was something wrong. The house looked exactly the same. Not a thing had changed. Everywhere was silent, but it was an electric, quivering silence, as if there were voices gabbling away in some far-off place, wanting to break through with an unwelcome message. The nape of Lizzie's neck prickled.

She crept upstairs. Her mam, Joan and Nellie were fast asleep in the front bedroom, whilst in the back the boys snored contentedly. She counted them. Tony, Chris, Jimmie, Paddy, Sean and Dougal. Three apiece in two double beds. All alive and breathing.

Yet the feeling of unease persisted.

Downstairs again, she put the kettle on for a cup of tea. Mam had a proper gas-stove in the back kitchen now.

Lizzie sank into one of the new armchairs. The fire was almost out, though the grey embers still gave off considerable heat. She often sat here by herself when she came home from town and thought about Hank and what it would be like to live in Texas. Then she'd imagine having enough money to buy lots of frocks and shoes and handbags from proper shops, not Paddy's Market. Sometimes she would even design the clothes in her mind, but tonight she couldn't concentrate. No matter how hard she tried to dismiss it, the feeling of foreboding persisted, so she drank her tea quickly and went to bed, deciding she'd be better off asleep.

The war was about to end – in a week, a month, two months . . . Everybody had a different opinion.

Each day, Kitty O'Brien listened avidly to the wireless. It was Kevin she worried about, stuck on an aircraft carrier on some far-off ocean. Rory was all right, safe in England. After the war they'd be able to get good jobs. They had trades now, both of them. When Rory had last been home, he'd said, 'We could move away from Bootle, if you liked, Mam. Get a house in the country – Formby or Ormskirk, like.'

But Kitty wasn't sure if she'd ever want to leave Chaucer Street.

After the older children had gone and she was left with just Sean and Dougal quietly drawing at the kitchen table, Kitty turned on the nine o'clock news. Nothing new, Hitler hadn't surrendered. He was still hanging on in his bunker somewhere in Berlin, refusing to accept the possibility of defeat even though it stared him in the face.

She turned the wireless off and went upstairs to make the beds, picking up clothes to wash, dusting. She'd be glad when these awful blackout curtains could come down. Tony had promised to buy new ones for the parlour so she was saving the coupons and had her eye on some green brocade in a shop in Strand Road.

Kitty sighed. Strange, but when she'd had a crowd of little 'uns, she'd longed for peace and quiet, yet now she had it, perversely, she yearned for a baby to nurse or a tiny hand to drag at her skirt. Sean and Dougal were such self-contained children, absorbed in each other, playing quietly all day long. They were no trouble, didn't need their mam like the others had.

She carried the washing downstairs and put it in a bucket to steep, and decided to have a cup of tea before starting on the baking. As she filled the kettle, she recalled with disquiet the funny question Lizzie had asked that morning before she went to school.

'Did anything happen last night, Mam?'

Kitty assured her that nothing out of the way had occurred and pressed Lizzie to explain why she'd asked, but her daughter just shrugged and wouldn't say any more.

She was just about to ask the little 'uns if they'd like a cup of tea when there was a knock on the front door and Kitty began to shake because she knew, she just knew, it was bad news.

'Oh, no!' she wailed, running down the hall to open the door. 'Oh, dear God, no!'

Sean and Dougal looked up from the table, alarmed by her cries, and they both began to sob as well.

Outside was a boy with a telegram informing her that Rory was dead.

Some people said, 'But you've ten more lovely children, Kitty. Imagine if he'd been the only one,' but Kitty felt as much sorrow for the loss of Rory as a mother who'd had just one child. After all, she reasoned defiantly, if you had a finger cut off, you wouldn't comfort yourself by saying, 'Never mind, I've got nine left.'

Unlike many mothers with large families, Kitty never got her children confused as they grew older. She remembered Rory's birth as clearly as if it were yesterday.

He'd been one of the few to arrive in the daylight hours. Theresa Garrett had been there, of course, and Rory was an easy birth, being only her second baby, and he turned out to be quicker at walking than Kevin but slower with his teeth which had given a lot of trouble. But apart from those restless, painful months, he'd been a sunny child, always good-humoured.

Of course his teething hadn't been nearly so bad as Nellie's. She'd screamed blue murder night after night, so much so that Tom had threatened to throw her out of the window. Rory had insisted on chewing the ring of his dummy instead of the teat and that helped to keep him quiet. Indeed, his first word was 'dum dum', though he hadn't managed that till he was eighteen months old.

Lizzie had been best for talking, though Jimmie hadn't been far behind and he hadn't stopped talking since. Paddy was the cleverest of the boys so far and was at grammar school, going off every day looking ever so smart in a white shirt and tie and blazer, though he kept his cap hidden in his pocket till he got on the bus.

Such lovely, lovely children, all of them.

You gave birth to your children, thought Kitty bitterly, went through hell to deliver them into the world, guarded them, cared for them. You shielded them from violent fathers, took the blows on your own back. Kept them warm in winter, knitted gloves, scarves, patched the soles of their shoes with bits of lino to keep their feet dry, then you scrabbled in the road for vegetable scraps after the outdoor market closed and begged the baker for yesterday's bread to feed them.

You even sold your body to stem their hunger.

Then you walked with them to school on their first day, even if it meant trailing three or four little 'uns along with you and you bathed their bruises, bandaged their cuts, wiped their noses and their tears.

Oh, how you cherished your children. You raised them to be fine young men and women and then in a freak accident, a moment of carelessness, or because a lunatic invades

Poland or some country you've never even heard of before, despite all your love, all your care, your child, your lovely son, is taken from you.

For the first time in her life, Kitty found it hard to get comfort from the church. She wanted Rory here. She wanted to see him, laughing, straight and tall. She wanted to touch and hear him.

Monsignor Kelly said Kitty should be grateful that Rory was in heaven now, but instead of being grateful, she was angry. She couldn't understand how his death was part of God's great plan.

She was so upset at Monsignor Kelly's complacency, his insistence that she should be happy instead of sad, that in a gesture of defiance, she told the Air Force Captain who came to see her a few days later, that she wanted her son buried in Suffolk, near the base. She couldn't stomach the idea of a priest who didn't care, presiding over the Requiem Mass, chanting prayers he didn't mean.

Poor Kitty was nothing without her children. No one ever knew, but she often mourned her lost babies. The ones born dead or murdered in her womb by Tom. The little 'uns who hadn't got as far as this great cruel world. She'd given them all names and never forgot them. There were Peter and Brendan who'd be well into their teens by now, Clare and Kathleen . . . Kitty's heart often bled for her eleven dead babies, just as it bled now for her tall and handsome Rory.

The only good thing to come out of his death, not that Kitty noticed it, was that with so many people calling to express their condolences, and with them being so sincere and sympathetic, promising to remember Rory in their prayers or have special masses said, Kitty began to go out and mix with her neighbours once again.

Lizzie felt numb about Rory's death. Her brothers and sisters and her mam and even people like Mrs Garrett and Mary Plunkett cried openly. Lizzie couldn't cry, couldn't feel sad, and it worried her, watching her family weep as they knelt round Rory's photo at night, saying the rosary out loud, yet she felt nothing.

*

The Air Force people sent train tickets and Kitty and Jimmie went down to Suffolk for the funeral. Rory was to be buried in a tiny cemetery in a country churchyard a long way from the base.

'The nearest Catholic church, I'm afraid,' explained the priest, Father Watts, the first non-Irish priest Kitty had met. 'This isn't Roman Catholic territory, you see, Mrs O'Brien – not like Liverpool.'

Kitty asked to see the body but the Captain explained to the grieving woman that it was too late. The casket had been sealed. They'd made sure it would be, knowing the condition of O'Brien's head.

Really, Kitty thought unhappily, it should be Lizzie with her. It was a daughter's place to be by her mother's side in such circumstances. But Lizzie had refused, made some lame excuse about important work at school. As if anything could be more important that your own brother's funeral. And Lizzie hadn't seemed upset either, not like the other children. Perhaps she had used all her emotions up after that terrible time with Tom and the hospital and the stabbing.

Kitty and Jimmie were driven through fairytale Suffolk lanes, where the trees drooped and met overhead to form leafy tunnels, and they passed by thatched cottages with daffodils dancing on the lawns and long narrow paths which led to great mansion houses, past where sheep and cows grazed on rolling green fields . . .

But neither of them noticed the spectacular countryside. All they could think of was Rory.

Chapter 9

On Easter Monday 1945, Lizzie's fourteenth birthday, Kitty was making a pathetic attempt to organize a special tea. Just back from Suffolk, she was finding it difficult to pull herself together, but she'd managed to buy a present for Lizzie, a nice leather purse, and Tony and Chris had clubbed together and got a real silver locket on a chain. Kevin sent a manicure set from abroad, very smart in a crocodile-leather case.

'Ta, Mam.' Lizzie accepted the purse ungraciously. She knew she was about to hurt Kitty's feelings and felt uncomfortable.

'We'll have a really nice tea, luv. Josie O'Connor's icing a bit of bunloaf fer us and I managed ter get a tin of salmon in the grocer's the other day and some tomatoes and I'll make a jelly later on.'

'Don't bother, Mam,' Lizzie said offhandedly. 'I'm going out.'

'Where to, luv?' Kitty's face fell.

'Ter Southport with Marie.'

So off she went in her tangerine dress and her high-heeled shoes, feeling very grown up because she was fourteen and soon to start work in the dye factory, the biggest employer in Bootle, though her mam didn't know that; she thought Lizzie was staying on at school till summer.

The other children persuaded Kitty to make the special tea anyway, if only because it was Easter Monday, but Kitty was miserable all day long thinking Lizzie would soon be as lost to her as Rory, but in her daughter's case, it was Kitty herself who was to blame. She felt particularly bad when Paddy came home and said he'd seen Marie Gordon serving behind the counter in the paper shop.

Anticipating an entire day out on the arm of a generous American led to an ever greater crowd of women than usual waiting at Central Station that Easter Monday morning.

Georgie, limping and white-faced, waited with them, though she knew it was unlikely she'd be picked up so early. It wouldn't be until a late, late hour she'd get a man, and even then it wasn't certain.

As ever, it was Hank who was first through the ticket barrier and with his usual enthusiasm, he picked Lizzie up and swung her round and round until a shoe flew off.

A crowd of GIs gathered round. One of them picked the shoe up and, bending on one knee, replaced it on Lizzie's foot with a flourish.

'It fits! It fits!' he shouted. '*This* is Cinderella and now she must marry her prince.'

'Honey,' said Hank, 'this is my greatest pal, Tex, who, as you might guess, comes from Texas same as yours truly.' He turned to the rest of the group. 'And this here is my greatest pal, Junior T. And another greatest pal, Duke.'

Tex was thin, lean and blond and could have been Hank's twin they were so alike. Both were dwarfed by Duke, broad-shouldered, flat-nosed and the squad's boxing champion, and also by Junior T, a leathery beanpole of a boy with strange silvery-coloured hair.

One by one Lizzie was introduced to Hank's greatest pals. Fred, dapper and neat, whose real name no one knew. They called him Fred because he danced all the time, just like Fred Astaire. Nero was dark-skinned, dark-eyed and Nero was his surname not his Christian name, and he was Italian and therefore a bit inferior to a real, red-blooded American like himself, Hank explained later, but because he was very, very rich and his paternal uncle was a 'godfather' in the New York mafia, he was considered acceptable as one of the greatest pals. Then came Buzz, with his horn-rimmed glasses and grave expression, who only looked about sixteen.

'He's going to be a great writer some day,' said Hank. 'Always scribbling. And last, but not least, my greatest pal, Beefy. And you can see where he gets the name from.'

'Shut yo mouth, yo Southern trash,' kidded Beefy, who was almost as wide as he was tall. He shook hands in a real gentlemanly fashion. They all did, and Lizzie felt like a queen amidst her adoring courtiers as they crowded round, looking at her appreciatively.

'You sho' was right, Hank boy. You picked a little beauty here,' drawled Junior T, breathing on Buzz's glasses so he couldn't see.

'Hank said you was as pretty as Scarlett O'Hara in that film,' whispered Duke from behind, right in her ear. 'But I reckon he was wrong. You're a whole lot prettier than that there actress.'

What wholesome, healthy and well-mannered boys they were. Not one of them over twenty. Bright-eyed, excited, not making any attempt to pick up other girls, but all set to spend the day with Lizzie to celebrate her birthday.

Most of the still-waiting girls cast covetous eyes as she left with her eight young men, all that is except Georgie, who shouted, 'Good luck, Lizzie, luv.'

To get to Southport meant walking through the centre of Liverpool to Exchange Station. As it was a Bank Holiday, all the shops and offices were closed. Not yet midday, a still-watery sun gave promise of a fine afternoon.

Hank draped his arm possessively round Lizzie's shoulders and as they walked through the deserted streets, the other boys danced around them, paying Lizzie extravagant compliments, walking backwards in front of her and blowing kisses, bowing, laughing, joking. Fred tap-danced on the kerb and invented a special step in her honour.

'C'mon, fellas, she's mine,' Hank protested, kissing her left ear.

'No, she isn't, she's ours. She belongs to all of us,' someone shouted and Lizzie wanted to cry with happiness.

The train was crowded with day-trippers going to Southport or the beaches on the way – Formby, Ainsdale or Birkdale. Despite the general resentment many English people felt towards the Americans on their soil, the unabashed exuberance of the eight young men soon charmed the long carriage full of people.

Beefy produced a mouth organ and in no time, fifty or sixty people were joined together in singing *Run Rabbit Run*, *The White Cliffs Of Dover* and *Yankee Doodle Dandy*.

There was a chorus of goodbyes when they parted at

Southport Station.

This was the furthest Lizzie had been away from Bootle. She was overwhelmed by the beauty of Lord Street with its central, tree-lined reservation, gracious and expensive shops and ornate Victorian arcades. She had never realized that such an elegant and lovely town existed so close to home. Perhaps Mam would like to come here one day.

'Gee, this sure is a stylish place,' said Hank admiringly.

By now the sun shone, bright and warm for an April day.

'How's about some chow?' suggested Junior T.

They went into the first café they came to, not bothering as Lizzie and everyone else she knew would have done, to check the prices on the menu outside. What did they care about money?

A sour-faced elderly waitress joined two tables together and Lizzie was placed at the head, Hank at the foot. She ordered turkey and stuffing, roast potatoes and peas.

Turkey! What with rationing and poverty, a turkey had never made an appearance on the table in Number 2 Chaucer Street, but now here were two thick white slices, which were tough and took a lot of chewing, but Lizzie convinced herself it tasted delectable.

For pudding there was fruit salad and ice cream, and in the salad there was a grape, a genuine grape! So, that was what a grape looked like. Purplish-red, the skin thick and difficult to cut and the inside juicy and green. It tasted tart and sweet at the same time and there were pips which she didn't like to spit out, not with eight pairs of eyes on her, so she ate them as well.

Even the bad-tempered waitress in her rusty black dress and lace cap and apron soon succumbed to the young soldiers' charm, particularly when Nero said she was the spitting image of his mother. She ended up smiling and nodding, and even brought extra milk and sugar for their tea without them having to ask. Then they toasted Lizzie's birthday, holding up their cups, and Hank reminded them they might be getting hitched pretty soon. Lizzie didn't disillusion them. If they learnt she was only fourteen they might disappear, like the Captain in the Adelphi.

'Hey, how many brothers and sisters you got, Liz?' Duke

asked. He was sitting on her left and kept pressing his knee against hers.

'Eight brothers and two sisters,' she replied, entirely forgetting Rory was dead, but when she remembered, she didn't mention he'd just died for fear it would cast a gloom over the occasion and anyway, just thinking of home reminded her of the stuff Mam had bought for the special tea and made her feel real bad.

She didn't feel bad for long because Nero, who was on her right, leaned over – she felt his warm sweet breath on her cheek – and said, 'Y'know, Lizzie honey, you got the sweetest mouth and the cutest nose and the most beautiful eyes I ever seen on a gal. As for your hair — '

'Hey, you two, cut that out!' yelled Hank from the end of the table. 'That's *my* gal you've got there.'

'No, it isn't,' replied Nero, and along with the others, chorused, 'She's *ours!*'

Flushed, eyes like stars, Lizzie basked in their united regard.

Lizzie shrieked. She'd never been so frightened in all her life. Every ounce of breath had drained from her body and she was convinced she was going to suffocate and die.

'Gee, honey,' said Hank, on whom the roller coaster was having no apparent effect, 'calm down now.'

But Lizzie couldn't calm down and she didn't stop screaming until the ride stopped, when she adamantly refused to have another go, much to the regret of the other boys who'd been looking forward to riding with her.

'I'll never go on anything like that again as long as I live,' she vowed.

She did agree to ride the Bobby horses, though, and found the gentle up and down motion enjoyable, especially with a pair of strong arms around her. She lost count of the turns she had, at least one with each of the boys, two turns with some.

Buzz, looking so young and wise in his horn-rimmed glasses, was the only one who didn't kid her along or keep touching her. Lizzie wondered if he didn't like her, but found him watching her intently with a solemn, gentle expression on his face and decided he was just shy.

As the day wore on, she became more and more exhilarated. There'd never been a day like this in all her life and there might never be another, not with so many young men hanging onto her every word and rushing to do her bidding.

'Lizzie, honey, look at this!'

'C'mon, Lizzie, let's go on these dodgem cars.'

They were all so anxious to please. If this was what being pretty meant, then she was glad she'd been so blessed. Perhaps all the rest of her life would be like this; men forever on hand wanting to look after her, asking her opinion, needing her approval for everything they did.

'For you, sweetheart.' Fred bounded up with a furry rabbit and thrust it into her arms.

'Another prize!' she exclaimed delightedly. She'd already got a teddy bear and a golliwog, a comb in a leather case, a doll and a gold glass sugar basin which her mam would love.

Junior T, Tex and Hank were at the shooting gallery driving the stallholder wild. Such good shots, they won every time. He was considering refusing them any more turns, but a crowd had gathered to watch and applaud and he didn't dare turn them away, particularly when they began to give the prizes away.

Every now and again, groups of children would besiege them with cries of 'Got'ny gum, chum?' and the boys would hand out strips of chewing gum to eager, grasping little hands. Nero swopped a pack of cigarettes for an old shopping bag to put the prizes in.

Beefy tried to teach Lizzie how to use a rifle, putting his hefty arms around her from behind, pressing himself close against her. She felt his hand momentarily, accidentally, caress her breast.

'Hold it this way, cutie. That's it. I think you've got it now.'

But Lizzie couldn't stop giggling and missed every time, much to the stallholder's relief.

The fairground eventually lost its interest and together they began to wander towards the Southport sands and the far-off strip of silvery sea.

Beefy began to play a sad lament on his mouth organ whilst Fred did what he called a soft-shoe-shuffle on the sand.

'C'mon, old buddy,' yelled Duke to Buzz who was lagging behind, his hands stuffed morosely in his pockets.

Her boys! Lizzie almost felt like a mother to them all. Hank linked one of her arms and Tex the other. Duke, Nero and Junior T began to play football with an old can.

The late afternoon sun began to dip into the sea, turning the thin line of water into a strip of vivid orange, and the beach shone gold. Behind them were the dunes which the sea never reached, the sand pale and powdery and dotted with clumps of blackened reed, broken and bent by the wind.

The few people about appeared to be making their way back to the town for it was starting to get chilly. The sun was visibly sinking further into the sea and it began to get dark.

Lizzie shivered in her thin silk dress. In her hurry to leave that morning, she'd come out without a coat. Earlier she'd taken off her shoes as the high heels kept sinking into the sand and by now her feet were wet. She turned and began to walk in the direction of the dunes where the sand was dry.

'Let's go back,' she said. The boys stopped dead at the sound of her voice. 'I'm starving and I'm cold.'

'We'll warm y'up, honey chile,' said Tex, and there was something in the tone of his voice that Lizzie didn't like.

She looked from one to the other of her boys and what she saw made her heart begin to pound so loudly and so fiercely that she was sure her body must be shaking too.

They'd become different people, different boys altogether, with hard faces and narrowed eyes and they'd lost their smiles and their gaiety and their good humour. Suddenly they were menacing and didn't look as if they liked Lizzie one bit.

A sixth sense made Lizzie look up and down the beach for signs of life but the only people visible were tiny figures, way out of earshot.

Hank was the nearest to her. He was her boyfriend and would protect her. She moved over to him and took his arm. 'Hank?' She wanted him to explain what was happening and was thankful when he put his arms around her.

'Oh, Hank!' Everything was all right. Hank loved her. Hadn't he told her so dozens and dozens of times?

But she soon realized that Hank's arms weren't protective at all. His fingers dug into her shoulders with such force she yelped in pain. 'C'mon now, honey,' he said in a strange, harsh voice. 'You've bin asking for this all day.'

Asking for what? What was he talking about?

Hank dragged her towards the sandhills out of sight of the beach. She could hear the others following, their footsteps muffled on the sand, and she stumbled on a stunted, brittle bush, dropping her shoes.

She fell forward, full-length, and felt Hank straddle her and push at her dress. With her face buried in the soft, suffocating sand, she couldn't shout, could scarcely breathe. She coughed and choked as Hank tore away her clothes and shouted, 'Just look at that ass, fellas,' and there was a jeering laugh from his friends.

'Turn her over,' one of them said, so Hank did, and as she hoarsely gulped in air, she saw him looking down at her, eyes blazing and a wild cruel smile on his face. His trousers were undone and he held his bulging pink penis in one hand and was trying to force her legs apart with the other. When he couldn't manage it, Junior T and Beefy came over and each took one of her legs and held them apart whilst Hank entered her. Then he yelled to his pals, 'She sho' done this before, I can tell,' and when he'd reached a climax he moved away for Junior T, then Beefy, Nero . . .

Lizzie lost track. Her marvellous boys who'd made this the most wonderful day of her life now took their fill of her and instead of paying her compliments, they called her a 'little whore' and 'fucking English bitch'.

Duke thrust his tongue down her throat so hard it made her retch and he hit her. 'Slut!' he rasped. 'Don't make that noise when I kiss you.' He raised his hand to strike her again but someone stopped him.

When they'd finished and left her lying there, exposed, lifeless, numb, she began to cry. She could hear them on the beach, giggling like naughty schoolboys, sounding almost their old happy selves again. They were discussing what to do with her.

'Leave her,' someone said contemptuously. It sounded like Nero. 'We've shown her a good time.'

'Well . . .' that was Hank's voice. He sounded embarrassed. 'Don't you think we should take her back? I mean, we can't just leave her.'

'I was last,' that was Fred speaking, 'an' she seemed okay to me.'

'C'mon, fellas,' someone called from a distance, as if they were already walking away. 'Won't the English bars be open by now?'

'Duke's right. Come on, don't know 'bout you, but I could really do with a drink.'

And so they went.

The sky had darkened, turned to grey. Lizzie began to tremble uncontrollably. She wondered if she should stay, embedded in the sand until someone found and rescued her. But no, she had to get home, back to Mam, to her family and Chaucer Street.

But how? She had no money. The small amount she'd brought had been spent on postcards and a lavender bag for Mam which had *Welcome To Southport* embroidered on it. Hank had her return ticket.

A voice said hesitantly, 'Lizzie!'

Inside, Lizzie screamed. She thought they'd all gone. Not again. Please, God! Not again.

Buzz was crouched on top of a dune looking down at her, blinking through his glasses. He looked as if he'd been crying.

'Are you okay, Lizzie?'

She nodded dully and attempted to stand. Buzz leapt to his feet and came down and helped her up. He fetched her clothes and turned away as she put them back on and he collected her things together. The postcards were bent and the lavender bag covered with sand. Soft toys were scattered everywhere. Buzz stuffed them in the bag Nero had so charmingly exchanged for cigarettes an hour or so before. Could it really be only an hour? How could the world change so much in such a short time?

'I think you'd be better off without your shoes,' said Buzz, and he carried them as well as all the other things.

Lizzie feld cold and her thighs throbbed with pain. Buzz must have noticed her shivering, because he removed his jacket and wrapped it round her shoulders.

'I never . . . you know, Lizzie,' he said.

Lizzie nodded, though she hadn't realized at the time.

'I'm sorry, Lizzie,' Buzz was saying. 'I could just tell the way things were going.'

Her voice was locked in her throat. She wanted to ask, 'Why didn't you warn me?' but nothing would come. Even so, Buzz answered as if she'd spoken aloud.

'If I'd told you, you wouldn't have taken any notice. You wouldn't have believed me.'

Of course he was right. She would never in a million years have believed dear Tex and good old Junior T and courteous Nero and Duke and Beefy and Fred, felt so badly about her, considered her a whore and a bitch.

Hank was different. He was her fella and it was only to be expected that he'd want to make love to her. But not like that! It should never have been like that, thought Lizzie, stifling a sob.

Buzz coughed awkwardly. When they reached hard ground he returned her shoes and walked with her to the station where he bought her a ticket. Once on the train they sat opposite each other in complete silence till it reached Marsh Lane and Lizzie got off, too miserable to even say goodbye.

'You forgot this.'

She was on the platform and Buzz was standing by the open doors of the carriage holding out the bag of prizes. Lizzie didn't want them, but he looked so pathetic and young and had helped her, trying to make up for what his friends had done, that despite her wretchedness, she couldn't bring herself to refuse.

She took the proffered bag and whispered, 'Thank you. Goodbye, Buzz.'

His face lit up when she spoke to him.

'Goodbye, Lizzie,' he said as the door closed in his face.

Lots of people got off at the same time. Some small children were crying, tired after the long day out, but in the main, everyone was cheerful and happy and they jostled Lizzie as she sluggishly made her way to the exit carrying the bag full of mementos of her day out in Southport.

QUEEN'S
GATE

Chapter 10

'Good luck, Lisa,' sobbed Jackie, who'd had too much to drink as usual. She emptied the remainder of the confetti over Lisa's head. 'Good luck.'

Lisa laughed, crossed her eyes and blew upwards at the bits that had attached themselves to the veil of her hat. Everybody applauded, even the landlord of the pub who'd have to clear up the mess. Brian's hand tightened on her elbow involuntarily, as if warning her not to be silly, to behave. At the same time, he glanced in the direction of his mother to see if she was watching.

She was.

Mrs Smith was the only person from their group sitting down. She didn't drink, disapproved of a reception in a public house, and had tried to insist on a church wedding, but her new daughter-in-law had a mind of her own and refused. She eyed her balefully over her glass of orange squash.

Of course she'd always wanted Brian, her only child, to marry someone pretty. After all, he deserved to. Such a handsome boy with his pale, almost translucent skin, flushed now with the excitement of the day. Baby blue eyes – the same blue he'd been born with – and silky fawn-coloured hair flopping on his forehead. She'd nagged him to get it cut, but for once he'd refused to do her bidding. Apparently Lisa preferred it long.

Lisa!

The girl was lovely, there was no doubt about that. Tall and slim to the point of skinniness, her height accentuated by her pink leather shoes with heels at least three inches high. Her suit was pink too – grosgrain, a tight-fitting calf-length skirt showing off every curve, and a short shaped jacket accentuating her small breasts. Today, her chocolate-brown hair was drawn back into a bun, the severity of the style countered by a pink pillbox hat with matching veil reaching over the eyes then gathered into a big flaring bow at the back. Not too much make-up, Mrs Smith conceded that much – just a touch of eye-shadow and shell-pink lipstick. Yet despite that she looked like a film star, a strange, exotic film star – Hedy Lamarr or Gene Tierney. Not quite English, with those huge brown-gold eyes and high cheekbones.

Mrs Smith had marriage planned for Brian at twenty-six, when he would wed a nice ordinarily-pretty girl – one perhaps not quite so intelligent as himself. A girl she could train to be a real wife, teach how to darn and cook, look after the house and take care of her boy Brian in the way he was accustomed, but most importantly, to provide her with a grandson. Another Brian. Another child to devote her life to. She sighed, impatiently waving away the cigarette smoke when it floated in her direction.

She'd designed her outfit for her son's wedding years ago, had imagined inviting all the old aunts and uncles, her brother and sister-in-law and their children, one or two friends. But Miss Lisa O'Brien had refused to be married in church and didn't want a proper reception, not even in her mother-in-law's home; Mrs Smith had had the menu worked out too. Instead, they were in this rowdy pub with someone playing a piano in one corner and crowds of strangers toasting Lisa and Brian in Guinness and pints of shandy.

In the end, the only guests invited were her brother George and his wife Margery, and there was George, enjoying himself no end, joining in the singing, unable to take his eyes off the bride. But then who could? She was radiant, the cynosure of all eyes, the recipient of dozens of congratulatory kisses.

When Brian told her about Lisa who worked in the bookshop on the ground floor of his office building, she'd built up a picture in her mind of a studious-looking girl and hoped she wasn't too mousy for her son. But when she'd met her – why, the girl didn't look as if she could read a comic, let alone a book! Then there was talk of marriage, and with Brian only twenty-two. She'd tried to make him see sense but he was besotted, so she'd shrugged, started to make arrangements and found just the right wedding dress in Dickins & Jones, but when she told Lisa, the girl just laughed.

'I don't want that sort of wedding,' she said dismissively.

Then Mrs Smith went to see the vicar and had a long talk with him, and despite the fact he hadn't even met the girl, he agreed to conduct the wedding in his church. She'd informed Brian and a few days later he told her Lisa wanted the wedding in a registry office.

As a wedding present, for their honeymoon, Mrs Smith had booked the bed and breakfast hotel in Hastings where she and Brian had spent all their holidays since he was a baby. She had photographs. Such a picture he made, toddling along the beach with his bucket and spade, then older and playing cricket on the sand, but Lisa was indignant when she discovered this. She'd decided on Paris. Paris! Well, she'd fit in there better than Hastings, Mrs Smith told herself spitefully.

She sipped her orange squash and thought with satisfaction, 'Once she's back and living in my house, I'll soon sort out Miss Lisa O'Brien. Or I should say, Mrs Lisa Smith.'

Eyes brimming with tears, Jackie said, 'I'll miss you heaps.'

'No, you won't,' Lisa laughed. 'I'll still be working for dear Mr Greenbaum and I can see you every single day, except Sundays.'

'Sunday is the day I'll miss you most of all,' sniffed her friend, getting ready to cry again. 'I never see Gordon on Sundays, either.'

Gordon put his arm around her shoulders and gave her a clumsy hug. 'Come on, old girl. Stiff upper lip, eh?'

Lisa felt like pouring her glass of wine over him. She hated Gordon with his ridiculous moustache. Forty, married with children, he'd been stringing Jackie along for years. Ex-RAF officer – or so he said. There was something phoney about his wartime slang, as phoney as his love for Jackie. She'd thought that even before he'd made a pass at her that day he'd called when Jackie was away . . . Yet Jackie was so much in love with him and believed everything he told her, about his wife not understanding him and how he'd leave like a shot if it wasn't for the children.

'I won't sell a single book for two whole weeks till she gets back from Paris,' groaned Mr Greenbaum, his eighty-year-old face exaggeratedly mournful. 'The books I've shifted since she came to work for me! I've sold books on mathematics to people who can't add up, novels by Proust to customers who came in for an Ethel M. Dell, and do you know, she once sold an entire set of Dickens to a man who only entered my shop to ask the way to the nearest tube!'

'He'll be bereft without you, Lisa dear,' said Miriam, his wife, looking elegant in her best mauve silk dress and astrakhan coat.

'We all will,' said Ralph. 'Saturday nights will never be the same again, will they, Piers?'

Piers shook his head and gave an impish smile.

Beside her Lisa felt Brian stiffen. He had always resented her friendship with these two men.

'Lisa.' She felt a hand on her arm and turned to see Brian's Aunt Margery. Her heart sank, expecting some sort of lecture. The woman was probably in her late forties, quite smartly dressed. Her face was plain, but her expression friendly.

'Dorothy says you're going to live with her in Chiswick.'

'Only for a while,' said Lisa. 'Till we've saved enough for a place of our own.'

'Well, save quickly, dear. I know this is out of order and I couldn't have brought myself to say it if I hadn't had three gin and tonics, but get Brian out of his mother's clutches as soon as you can.'

'Where is his father?' asked Lisa, out of interest. 'Brian won't speak about him and I don't like to ask Mrs Smith.'

'Did a bunk, dear, when Brian was one. She, Dorothy that is,' Margery lowered her voice and spoke in a stage whisper, 'didn't like *It*. You know – sex. Once Brian was born he was the only male she wanted, so Peter either had to go without forever or find someone else.' She shrugged. 'Poor Brian has had a God-awful picture of his father painted for him all his life.'

'I see,' Lisa nodded sagely. 'Well, thanks for the advice.'

Aunt Margery squeezed her hand. 'All the luck in the world, dear. I wish we lived nearer than Bristol so I could be on hand if ever you need a friendly face.'

'Lisa! Another hour and the train leaves,' yelled Brian. Across the room, Mrs Smith winced.

'Time for one last drink,' announced Mr Greenbaum. 'Champagne, I think.'

Mrs Smith grudgingly accepted a glass and actually came and joined the small circle as they drank a toast to the young married couple.

'To Lisa and Brian,' said Mr Greenbaum, holding his glass high, his wrinkled face wreathed in smiles.

'Lisa and Brian,' everybody chorused.

The ferry swayed and seemed to perch at an acute angle for a long, long time, though it was probably no more than a few seconds before it righted itself. Then it swung the other way, like a giant shuddering seesaw.

Brian, along with at least half the other passengers in the lounge, was sick again. Lisa would have felt fine if it hadn't been for the pools of vomit which turned her stomach. The ship's motion didn't affect her at all. She decided to go up on deck. Brian was oblivious to her presence, too ill to notice her attempts to soothe him.

There were a few hardy souls on top holding firmly to the handrail.

'You'd best not walk on deck in those heels, miss,' said an elderly man clad in a waterproof cape and hat. 'A sudden dip and you'll lose your balance and be over the side. There's an observation lounge up front, you'll be safe in there.'

The small glass lounge was empty. Lisa sat in the front seat. Spray showered against the windows, obscuring the angry, foam-tipped sea outside. She took her hat off – the wind had nearly blown it away and the pins were hurting. Then she leaned back against the hard wooden bench and thought about the last long journey she'd made, from Liverpool to London.

They say – Kitty was always saying it – that time heals everything, but it didn't heal Lizzie. No matter how many months passed since that day in Southport, the horror remained as fresh as if it had happened yesterday.

Nightmarish memories haunted her. If it wasn't Hank and his greatest pals, then Tom entered her dreams. A night rarely passed that she didn't wake up in a suffocating sweat, arms thrashing, tossing and turning and disturbing Mam who shared the bed with her.

Poor Mam! Lizzie knew she was the only one of the children who worried her. The older ones were working, all in good jobs. Kevin had got married the year before and Tony and Chris were courting. All the little 'uns got good reports from school. It was only Lizzie who went around with a long face, some days scarcely bothering to comb her hair, throwing on the first clothes that came to hand before she went to work in the dye factory, a job she loathed. She'd started soon after her fourteenth birthday, but scarcely ever spoke to anyone there and after a while, no one spoke to her.

One day, she slashed the tangerine dress to ribbons and threw it in the bin.

Secretly, or so they thought, Nellie and Joan referred to her as 'old Sourpuss' and Jimmie kept saying, 'You're a real wet blanket nowadays, our Liz,' and he would hug her, try to cheer her up, then become hurt when Lizzie flinched. She couldn't stand anyone touching her, particularly a man, even if it was her favourite brother.

There was such warmth in the house, such love and demonstrative affection, but Lizzie was excluded – not from the getting but from the giving. She felt like a stranger, an alien who didn't belong in Chaucer Street amidst all these happy, outgoing people.

When Lizzie entered the house, people became quiet, just like they'd done when Tom came in, scared to laugh or joke in case they upset her.

On her sixteenth birthday, two years to the day she'd gone to Southport so full of anticipation of a nice day out, Lizzie left home.

She was always the first to wake. Mam was snoring beside her. Lizzie glanced across at her sisters, still sharing the same single bed, one at each end. Their faces were peaceful. Neither had a care in the world. She envied their innocence, their uncomplicated lives.

Mam had a party planned for tonight when Lizzie got home. It was supposed to be a surprise, but Lizzie had seen the birthday cake on the pantry shelf and noticed the jellies left to set on the back kitchen doorstep before she came to bed. Tonight, everyone would kiss her and wish her Happy Birthday and expect her to look cheerful and she couldn't, she just couldn't. Once again, she'd let them down and leave them wondering what had happened to their Lizzie, whom they loved so much, but who couldn't love them back in return. In fact, it was even difficult to raise a smile most of the time, particularly if it was expected of her.

She'd become a blight on her family, like Dad had been. They'd be better off without her.

Stealthily she climbed out of bed and took her clothes downstairs to get dressed. Then she put her Post Office savings book in her bag and was about to leave when she remembered she'd need her ration book too. She took it off the mantelpiece where Kitty kept them stacked in a neat row. The act of removing the book from all the others pierced through her like a knife, as if by this single action she was severing herself from the O'Brien family forever. Yet despite the pain, she felt a stir of excitement as she closed the door of Number 2 Chaucer Street behind her, and as she ran towards the tram stop, actually found herself smiling.

Where did you go when you ran away from home? London seemed the obvious place, the only place really.

Lizzie had to wait outside the Post Office by Lime Street Station for nearly an hour until it opened so she could draw the money out for her fare, which only left her with five pounds.

Buying a single ticket to London was almost as bad as taking her ration book – such a final, separating act. She sat on the train, oblivious to the varying countryside, the towns where the train stopped to pick up more passengers, scarcely aware it was a bright, warm April day, that people were dressed in their summer clothes. All she was conscious of was the noisy rhythm of the train's wheels as it ate up the miles on its way to London, and the enormity of what she had done. She'd left home.

97

She was embarking on The Unknown, all alone.

So this was London. A big, dirty station, little different from Lime Street. Lizzie didn't even know what it was called. She stood outside the ticket barrier, unsure which way to go and feeling slightly panic-stricken. A lot of people were making their way down some stairs marked 'Underground', so she followed and to her surprise found herself in another station. Beneath her feet she felt the rumble of trains. She bought the cheapest ticket, went down an escalator and got on the first train that came storming out of the narrow tunnel. Inside, she studied a map on the wall opposite. The names of the stations meant nothing. Where had she got on? She'd never even met anybody who'd been to London, and she experienced a further bout of panic. Where on earth was she going?

The carriage was only half-full. Opposite her, a young negro sat reading a newspaper, a student's scarf thrown casually round his neck. He had a friendly approachable face and Lizzie tried to pluck up the courage to ask his advice.

The train stopped at several stations and she kept glancing at him nervously when suddenly, he closed his paper and her heart sank. He was going to get off. But no, he was merely turning to another page.

She took a deep breath. 'Excuse me.'

'Hello.' He lowered his paper and gave her a friendly grin.

'I'm looking for somewhere to live.'

'Well, you could move in with me, but my wife might complain.' His grin widened further.

'I mean, I've never been to London before. Where's the best place to look?'

'You want a hostel or a flat?' He noted her shabby clothes and untidy hair.

Lizzie thought a moment. Not a hostel. She wanted to be by herself, not with a crowd of other girls. Surely she had enough money for a place of her own.

'A flat,' she said.

'Try Earl's Court. *Everybody* lives in Earl's Court.'

'How do I get there?'

'Well, you're on the Circle line . . .'

'Am I?'

He looked amused and pointed to the map above his head. 'See the yellow line? That's the Circle. When you get to Gloucester Road, get off and it's just one stop on the District line to Earl's Court.'

'Thank you.'

'Any time,' he said, grinning.

She didn't say anything for a few minutes, then, 'Excuse me.'

'Hello again.'

'I'm sorry to appear so stupid, but when I get to Earl's Court, what do I do? Just knock on doors?'

'Christ, you're a greenhorn. No, you'll find dozens of little shops with cards outside advertising accommodation to let. Want me to come with you? Of course, my wife might divorce me if she finds out, and we've only been married a month . . .'

'No, no,' said Lizzie hastily. 'But thanks for offering.'

'You're very welcome.' He returned to his paper and got off a few stations later. 'Good luck,' he said.

After he'd gone and the space opposite became empty, she caught sight of her blurred reflection in the dark window and was horrified. Wild strands of hair had escaped from the bun into which it had been hastily scraped that morning and the black coat she'd bought from Paddy's Market nearly two years before was about three sizes too big for her. She'd bought it big deliberately, wanting to hide her body from the world and look as unattractive as possible, but now, glancing round the compartment, she saw that most of the women, the young ones particularly, were smartly dressed. She felt like a tramp and searched through her bag for a comb, but there was none so she redid the bun as best she could with her hands.

Earl's Court bustled with people, mainly young, mainly foreign. Even those speaking English had strange accents. It was an exciting, cosmopolitan atmosphere. The afternoon sun beamed down on the crowded pavements.

Right outside the station, a sweet and tobacconist's shop had a window full of postcards, mainly rooms to let. Her heart lifted. This was going to be easier than she'd thought, though rents were higher than she'd expected. Some were as much as five pounds a week, though others were ten shillings or a pound less. There was one for only two pounds ten shillings: 'A girl to share two-roomed flat', but Lizzie dismissed that one, determined to live alone. She made a list of numbers then went into the shop and bought a bar of chocolate, asking for the change in coppers for the phone box.

Lizzie had never used a telephone before and with her first call, she pressed the wrong button and her money came back. Some rooms were already gone. She made appointments to see two within the next hour and set off immediately.

The roads were like caverns with tall, four-storeyed houses looming up each side. She found the first street she wanted almost straight away. A grim-faced woman dressed in a flowered overall answered her knock.

'Yes?'

'I rang about the room.'

The woman looked her up and down contemptuously and said, 'Sorry, it's gone,' and slammed the door.

What little confidence Lizzie had completely ebbed away. For an hour she wandered the streets forlornly before plucking up the courage to keep the second appointment.

This time it was a man who opened the door. His trousers were sagging at the waist exposing a belly swelled by beer, and his shirt-sleeves were rolled up revealing hairy arms covered in tattoos.

'I've come about the room.'

'C'min.' He gestured with his cigarette and ash fell on the lino-covered floor.

The room was on the third floor. It was filthy, the corners covered in mould. Of course she could clean it herself. Wash the bedding. Scrub those walls.

'You share a kitchen and bathroom. They're along here.'

The bathroom contained a toilet and the room stank of urine. Food droppings littered the kitchen floor and the cooker was encrusted with dirt.

Four pounds a week for this!

'I'd like to think about it,' Lizzie said. 'I've got other rooms to look at.'

'Suit yourself,' the man said, shrugging carelessly.

She fled. Round the corner was a square, the centre a delicate garden of pink-flowered trees and bulging shrubs. She sat down on one of the wooden benches and wondered what to do next.

Chapter 11

It was peaceful in the square. The sun glinted on the windows of the tall gracious houses. She wondered what time it was. It must be four or five o'clock by now and she had to find somewhere to live by tonight or waste money on a hotel. But you were supposed to have luggage for a hotel – she read that somewhere, and she had nothing except her handbag.

Pangs of hunger assailed her and she realized she'd had nothing to eat since last night's tea. Then she remembered the bar of chocolate in her pocket and took it out and unwrapped it. As soon as she'd finished eating it, she'd go back to the shop by the station and take down some more numbers.

Two women were approaching, leading a strange-looking dog. The back half of its body was shaven and the front was as fluffy as a powder puff. When they reached her, one of the women said in a hostile voice, 'Do you live in this square?'

'No,' said Lizzie.

'Well, this is private property. You're trespassing. This square is for residents only. They took the iron railings away for the war effort, otherwise it would be locked.'

Lizzie stared at her. What harm was she doing? Perhaps her bewilderment showed, for the woman looked a little ashamed.

'Finish your chocolate. There's no hurry,' she added, but Lizzie was already on her feet. As she walked away, the woman shouted, 'It *is* private property.'

Back at the shop, she peered at the cards again. A lot of them were no good – they wanted someone for an 'all-male household', or 'middle-aged lady to act as companion', or the rents were too high. She made a note of the only suitable numbers which remained and again noticed the card asking for '*A girl to share two-roomed flat*'. It was a pink card, neatly typed. Only two pounds, ten shillings! This time, Lizzie wrote the number at the bottom of her list and went into the telephone box for the second time.

The first number was answered by a foreigner whose accent was so thick, Lizzie couldn't understand a word. When she'd asked for the directions to be repeated a third time, the receiver at the other end was slammed down angrily. The second room had gone. The third had someone coming to view tomorrow. Would she ring back then and see if it was still available? Lizzie promised she would and then dialled the next-to-last number. A frosty voice asked if she had references.

'References for what?' she asked.

'Your character, from a previous landlady or an employer.' Lizzie confessed she hadn't.

'Sorry, but I only take people with references.'

The only number left was the 'Girl to share'. Lizzie hesitated. She could go around looking for another shop with a noticeboard, but it was getting late. Hundreds of people were pouring out of the Underground, coming home from work, the shops were closing and the sun beginning to dip behind the houses opposite. If this flat were still available, she could stay there for a few weeks until she found her feet – that's if the girl was prepared to share with someone who looked like a tramp . . .

Someone rapped sharply on the window of the telephone box. Lizzie had been ages just staring at the telephone, trying to make up her mind. She took a deep breath, picked up the instrument and dialled. The dialling tone sounded just once before the receiver was lifted and a cheerful, breathless voice said, 'Hallo!' and half-sang the number.

Lizzie swallowed. The girl sounded very confident. 'Hallo,' she whispered. 'It's about the flat. You want a girl to share.'

Of course it might have gone. It *was* awfully cheap.

'Ooh, of course I do. Can you come round now? That would be frightfully convenient, because I'm out at work all day. In fact, you're lucky catching me. I don't usually get home till eight.'

Lizzie assured her she could come immediately.

'Do you know Queen's Gate? It's in South Kensington. Where are you ringing from? I put cards in several shops.'

'Earl's Court,' Lizzie told her.

'That's not too far to walk. Of course, you could get the tube but it means changing.'

Lizzie assured her she'd prefer to walk, and took down the instructions carefully. Once there, she was to give three long rings and three short ones on the doorbell. Each flat had its code, the girl explained.

The houses in Queen's Gate were really grand, with tall white pillars and wrought-iron balconies. In one, the first-floor French windows were open and people were standing on the balcony wearing evening clothes. She could hear laughter and the clink of glass. Perhaps this was a cocktail party. Just like a novel, thought Lizzie, hugely impressed. Some of the houses were embassies. She couldn't imagine that anyone living in a road like this would want her, looking like she did, as a flatmate.

She reached Number 5 which was on the corner, rang the bell and waited so long for it to be answered that she began to wonder if the girl had seen her from the window and decided not to let her in.

At last the big stained-glass door opened and Lizzie's mouth dropped. The girl was actually wearing *pyjamas!* Pink satin pyjamas. Her milky blonde hair fell in soft waves and curls around her pretty, over-made-up face. She gave Lizzie a welcoming smile which lit up her wide, smoky-grey eyes and deepened the dimples in her creamy cheeks. She was as tall as Lizzie, but two or three stones heavier, the extra weight laid seductively on wide curved hips and a large firm bust. The backs of her plump hands were as dimpled as her face.

'Christ Almighty, don't you look a mess! Come in. It's a long trek upstairs, I'm afraid. I'm on the fourth floor so take a deep breath. You're frightfully thin, aren't you? That's not a criticism, I'm green with envy.'

Lizzie was taken aback by the garrulous welcome. Although the girl's words could be construed as insulting, they were made in such a friendly way, she didn't take offence. The hallway was impressive, very big with a mosaic floor and a wide marble staircase. The girl began to run up the stairs, her fluffy pink slippers flopping on each step.

'It's two pounds ten shillings a week, by the way. Is that okay?'

'Fine,' said Lizzie, panting to keep up. With each floor, the stairs got narrower and steeper. By the time they reached the fourth, they were concrete and carpetless. The girl bounded ahead, her blonde curls bouncing. Lizzie's heart began to pound.

'Of course, I could afford all the rent, but then I think to myself – fifty-two lots of two pounds ten shillings! All the clothes I could buy with that. Does that sound horribly greedy?'

'No,' gasped Lizzie.

'Oh, you poor thing. You'll soon get used to the stairs. The exercise is good for you.' They'd reached the top landing. She turned towards the back of the house and opened a door. 'This is it.'

The slope-ceilinged room was painted white and the walls were covered with travel posters advertising holidays in foreign countries – Italy, Greece, France. There were two armchairs and a sofa scattered with brightly coloured cushions; a vivid silk shawl was draped over the sideboard which was littered with the petals from a bunch of fading flowers crammed into a glass vase. Beside the flowers, a cream-shaded lamp gave off a cosy, homely look. There was another, smaller lamp on a low table which also held a gramophone. A heap of records was stuffed underneath.

But the mess! The carpet was almost completely hidden by a layer of magazines, newspapers, books and clothes, even dishes.

Following Lizzie's gaze, the girl looked down. 'Gosh! It's in a God-awful state, isn't it? The bedroom's even worse. I'll tidy up tomorrow, though I say that every day. I'm Jackie, by the way, Jackie Rawlinson. Who are you?'

Lizzie was about to answer, 'Lizzie O'Brien', when something prevented her. Lizzie O'Brien belonged to the past. Lizzie O'Brien was not the person about to move, or so she hoped, into this exciting flat with a girl called Jackie who opened the door wearing pink satin pyjamas.

'Lisa,' she said. 'Lisa O'Brien.' She'd always wanted to be Lisa instead of Lizzie, it sounded more sophisticated.

'What a pretty name. Well, Lisa, I must tell you here and now, that I'm murder to live with. Flatmates come and go by the minute. Most girls take one look, make some excuse and run. Two came yesterday and did just that. I drive the ones that stay quite mad. I never put anything away. My mother says I'm a pig who'd be better off in a sty than a flat. Would you like a cup of tea or coffee?'

'I'd love either.'

'There's a kitchen along the corridor, but I only use it to get water. That's another thing – I never wash dishes. It's not that I mean to leave them on the floor, but somehow I always do. I keep an electric kettle here. I boiled it a few minutes ago. Usually I eat out. My boyfriend takes me to dinner after work. Tonight he had to stay late else I wouldn't have been in when you phoned.'

She knelt down, switched on the kettle and picked up two mugs. 'These are *almost* clean. Do you take milk and sugar?'

'Just milk, please.'

After a short search, Jackie found the milk bottle on the mantelpiece.

'Sit down, you poor soul, you look worn out. Where's your things?'

'Things?'

'Clothes, luggage.'

'I haven't got any,' confessed Lisa, adding quickly in case the lack of 'things' deterred Jackie from taking her as a roommate: 'I ran away.' Since she'd arrived, the doubts she'd had about sharing with someone else had completely gone and she desperately wanted to move in. She accepted the proffered cup of coffee, holding the handle in her left hand so as to avoid the bright pink lipstick smear on the other side. Despite the milk being faintly sour, the drink tasted good and at that moment she didn't particularly mind a dirty cup.

'How incredibly exciting. I always wanted to run away, but my parents were so glad to see the back of me there wasn't any need.'

Lisa leaned back in the chair, suddenly exhausted. It had been a long, tiring day.

Jackie looked at her with concern. 'Have you eaten today, Lisa?'

'Well, no, apart from a bar of chocolate.'

'Then let's go out for a meal,' she cried enthusiastically. 'I'm bored out of my mind without Gordon – that's my boyfriend.' A fleeting shadow passed over her lively face. 'We can go to that new restaurant in Gloucester Road.'

Lisa said uncomfortably. 'I'd love to, but will it be expensive? I haven't got much money and by the time I've paid you . . .'

'Oh, blow that. You can pay me next week. As to dinner, it's my treat.' She paused. 'That is, if you want to stay? Do you want to live with a pig, Lisa? You haven't seen the bedroom yet, have you?'

'I'd love to stay,' said Lisa, not caring a fig about the bedroom.

'Goody. I'm sure we'll get along – you look the patient type. But we can't go out like this. You look as if you've been sleeping in a ditch. Is that coat Army surplus? They'll chuck you out of the restaurant. What size are you?'

'I'm not sure. I'm a thirty-two-inch hip.'

'You horrible thing, sometimes my waist's that big! Everything of mine will swim on you. Wait a minute, I've got a dirndl skirt with an elastic waist – and my peasant blouse. Now, I wonder where they are?'

She disappeared into the bedroom and emerged with a flowered skirt and a white embroidered top.

'Shoes! Those lace-up flats look hideous. I suppose you take a three or something?'

'No, a seven.' The shoes had been bought in Paddy's Market at the same time as the unfashionable coat.

'Really! I'm a six. You can have my open-toed sandals – if I can find them. I'll get dressed again.' As she left the room she began to remove her pyjama top, revealing full white breasts. Through the open bedroom door, she shouted, 'I suppose you'll be looking for a job?'

'Yes.' Lisa pulled her jumper off and tried on the blouse. It had a gathered neck and full puffed sleeves.

Jackie appeared fastening her stockings onto a thin black lace suspender belt. She wore matching pants and brassière.

'Do you have shorthand?'

Lisa looked down at her hands in wonder.

Jackie gave a hearty laugh. 'Bloody hell, Lisa. *Shorthand*, can you write it? You know, little squiggly signs for words.'

'No.' Lisa had never heard of shorthand.

'Can you type?'

'No.'

'What can you do?'

'Nothing,' said Lisa.

'Then you'll have to get a job in a shop.'

'I'd quite like that.'

'If you worked in a fashion shop we could get clothes cheap. I love clothes. I've got two old aunts who send me all their coupons. I'll give you some if you like. Sometimes I buy things I don't really want, just to use the coupons up.' She disappeared into the bedroom again.

'Thank you,' Lisa called, though she couldn't imagine ever having enough money to use all her own coupons.

Jackie appeared brushing her corn-coloured hair and dressed in a white linen skirt with black buttons down the front and a short-sleeved black sweater.

Whilst she'd been gone, Lisa had hastily removed her skirt and stepped into the flowered dirndl, ashamed to let Jackie see her petticoat which was grey and shrivelled with so much washing.

'I say, that skirt looks lovely on you. It always made me look fat. You're beginning to look human, though I bet you haven't got any make-up.'

'I'm afraid not. All I've got is what I stand up in.'

'Well, help yourself to mine. There's a ghastly maroon-coloured lipstick somewhere that I've never used. I must have bought it when I was drunk – but it should suit your colouring. Come and sit by the mirror.'

Lisa followed her into the bedroom.

She saw twin beds with white candlewick bedspreads striped with blue, more posters and a pretty pink lamp on the table between the beds. The wardrobe door was open and bulged with clothes. Yet more clothes, dirty sheets and newspapers, covered the floor. The dressing table was loaded with bottles, creams, lotions, perfume, two half-empty cups of coffee and several dirty glasses. In the midst of the chaos stood a dusty black telephone.

Lisa's fingers itched with the urge to tidy up. She would enjoy achieving order out of this chaos.

Jackie pushed her down onto the stool in front of the dressing-table mirror. Despite the mess, she knew exactly where to find everything, and immediately handed Lisa a jar of foundation cream. As she rubbed it into her skin, Lisa was shocked to notice how much weight she'd lost over the last few years. She scarcely ever looked in the mirror at home. No wonder Kitty was forever urging her to eat more. And those purple shadows under her eyes made her face look drawn and skull-like. Her hair had not lost its shine, though. When she undid the tight bun on her neck, it flowed down to her waist, a shimmering, silken curtain, and Jackie gasped: 'Oh, you must borrow my velvet Alice band. It was made for someone with hair like yours.'

Lisa applied the maroon lipstick carefully. Jackie was right – she *was* beginning to look human. The gathered, fine cotton blouse suited her, accentuating her long neck and slim brown arms, and the full skirt flared out from her slender waist. Suddenly, she began to enjoy the feeling of being feminine again.

Behind her, Jackie was applying her own lipstick, her mouth contorted grotesquely 'I can't be bothered washing my face,' she said. 'I'll just apply another layer.' She spat on her mascara and began to brush her eyelashes. 'Want some?' She offered the case to Lisa.

'No thanks,' said Lisa quickly. Dirty cups she could stand, but not mascara covered with Jackie's spit.

'God!' Jackie said admiringly. 'I'd kill for those cheekbones. I've no bones in my face, it's just fat.'

Lisa laughed. With a sudden rush of confidence, she said, 'You're very, very pretty.'

Jackie stepped back, a look of surprise on her face. Lisa watched through the mirror, wondering if what she'd said had been presumptuous.

'Why, Lisa, when you laughed and your eyes lit up, you looked – well, quite beautiful! Isn't this great? I'm pretty and you're beautiful. We're going to get on fine. I'm so glad you saw my card. Gordon will love you and you're sure to love him, he's a pussycat. Come on, let's go and eat, else we won't get a table. It's nearly half-past seven.'

Chapter 12

A pink bath. Pink! And the bathroom walls were tiled, right up to the ceiling, in the same colour.

Lisa lay immersed in rose-scented bubbles, feeling like a Hollywood film star. This was the first real bath she'd ever had. At home they'd bathed in a tin tub in front of the kitchen fire, the girls on a Tuesday, all using the same water.

This room, like the kitchen, was shared by the residents of the other flats on the top floor. Jackie told her that the caretaker who lived in the basement took care of the maintenance of the house, whilst his wife did the cleaning, so everywhere was spotless.

They'd got back from the restaurant an hour ago. Lisa had eaten something called spaghetti bolognese which was delicious and very filling, and Jackie had ordered a whole bottle of red wine, drinking most of it herself. Lisa still felt pleasantly fuzzy after two small glasses.

Back in the flat, Jackie had said, 'I'm just off to have my bath,' as if she had one every single day, so Lisa, not to be outdone, asked: 'Can I go after you?'

So, here she was lying in luxury with Jackie's bubble bath, soap and shampoo at her disposal as well as her thick, fluffy but rather grubby towel and crimson silk dressing gown. It seemed unreal, like a dream. In less than twenty-four hours she had left one life and entered another, so totally different that the enormity of the change was difficult to grasp.

Tomorrow they were going to Knightsbridge where Jackie worked as a secretary in an office right opposite Harrods. She'd paused after saying this, as if waiting for some comment from her companion.

'Harrods?' Lisa said dutifully.

'Haven't you heard of Harrods? Gosh, you're an ignoramus. Harrods is the most famous shop in the world. It's where the very richest people go. I can see the front entrance from my window and almost every day famous people go in and out. Why, on Friday, I saw Herbert Lom outside waiting for a taxi.'

'Really!' said Lisa, impressed. She'd heard of Herbert Lom.

'There's an employment agency on the ground floor of my building. You must go there and see about a job.'

Lisa felt nervous at the idea of looking for work. The interview she attended at the dye factory had been in the company of half a dozen other girls, some from the same school as herself, and had not been in any way intimidating. Still, she had to get a job. There were clothes to buy, make-up, jewellery, and things like her own towel, soap, tooth-brush and of course food. Unlike Jackie, she would make her meals in the kitchen.

She soaped her body, noting how her ribs and hip-bones felt sharp and were covered only with the thinnest layer of flesh. 'I'll soon put weight back on again,' she thought contentedly. After she'd dried herself, she dressed in Jackie's dressing gown. The material felt cool and slippery against her body.

Jackie was back in pyjamas, boiling the kettle for cocoa. 'I'll have a head in the morning,' she groaned. 'All that wine!'

The clothes she'd worn were thrown over the back of a chair. Lisa picked them up, folded them neatly and put them on the sofa alongside the clothes she'd worn herself, then she sat on the chair and leaned back. Immediately her head began to swim and she felt an overwhelming desire to sleep.

'I'm so tired, I don't think I want a drink.'

Jackie, unsteady on her feet and searching for the cocoa tin, said, 'I'll find you a nightdress then. There'll be a clean one somewhere.'

Lisa protested. 'I'll sleep in my underclothes.'

'You'll do no such thing. You'll sleep like a civilized human being in a pretty nightdress.' She disappeared into the bedroom and emerged a few minutes later with a red cotton Victorian-style nightgown trimmed with white lace.

'I told a lie. It's not pretty, but grotesque, but at least I know it's clean because I've never worn it. My mother gave it me for Christmas.'

'It's very nice,' said Lisa, who would have gone to bed in a sack, she was so weary.

A few minutes later she climbed into bed. Jackie was sitting in front of the dressing table removing her make-up with cream. Lisa muttered, half-asleep. 'You've been awfully kind. I don't know why.'

'Because I like you. You're different from all the other girls I've shared with. And anyway . . .'

Lisa didn't catch the rest. She was fast asleep.

They walked to Knightsbridge under a pale sun in a pale sky. Tiny wisps of clouds were moving swiftly to nowhere. It was like being in a foreign country, Lisa mused, and you'd never think a war had not long ended. There were no bomb sites, no derelict buildings with every window smashed, no craters. Not like Liverpool, where signs of war were every-where. And the women they passed, even the older ones, were exquisitely dressed. Their make-up and hair were so perfect, they looked as if they'd just stepped out of a beauty parlour. Even Jackie, considering the chaos at home, looked surprisingly smart in a cream Moygashel suit, frilly white blouse and black patent-leather court shoes with a matching bag tucked underneath her arm. Lisa wore the same dirndl skirt and and blouse as yesterday and a borrowed cardigan.

She'd never seen such traffic: non stop cars, tooting impa-tiently, big red buses stopping and starting as they crawled along the busy roads. The aroma of coffee, rich and strong, came from tiny restaurants, already open. Outside one, people were sitting at pavement tables drinking out of thick brown cups and eating crescent-shaped rolls. A delicious smell of baking bread came from a small corner shop called a 'pâtisserie', and the women who emerged, some carrying long thin loaves, were not dressed like the others she'd seen so far. They wore print overalls and one had a scarf wrapped round her head, turban-style, the way her mam used to. From one large, magnificent house a woman came out wearing a green gaberdine coat and a velour hat, just like a school uniform. She carefully levered a massive pram down the wide steps. As she passed, Lisa looked inside and saw a tiny baby clad in a lace-trimmed bonnet, fast asleep under a rich silk eiderdown.

'Come on, Lisa,' urged Jackie. 'Else I'll be late and I'm *never* late.'

Hard though it was to believe, Jackie was not an ordinary secretary, but Personal Assistant to the Managing Director of a travel company.

'You see,' she explained to Lisa in the restaurant the night before, 'I know how inefficient and scatterbrained I am, so I make a supreme effort at work. I write everything down; when I send letters, when I get them, when somebody rings up. I do the things I have to do straight away so I won't forget. If I'm asked to book plane tickets, I do it there and then, else I know it will slip my mind. You wouldn't believe my filing system, Lisa. I never lose a piece of paper. I'm the perfect secretary. Does that surprise you?'

Lisa conceded it did and Jackie looked pleased, as if she'd been paid a compliment.

'And because of this,' she went on, 'I've got promoted and promoted, till now I'm Mr Ireton's Personal Assistant and I earn twelve pounds a week. That's much more than an ordinary secretary.'

Jackie was a lot older than Lisa had thought – twenty-three.

'That's my office.' She pointed across the road. Lisa only half-heard. She was gaping at the fur coats in a shop window which had price tickets of over a thousand pounds.

'There's the agency. It won't be open for a few minutes yet. Good luck with the job, and see you back at home tonight. Got your key safe?'

Lisa nodded and Jackie dodged through the almost stationary traffic to the other side of the road.

The employment agency had a wide, floor-length window, just like a shop. As she watched, a woman unlocked the door and went in. Her hair was black and carefully waved, and she wore a severe tweed suit. She looked very unapproachable. What if she also asked for references like one of the landladies had? The last thing Lisa wanted was the dye factory being approached for a character reference. It would be all round the building within an hour and someone would be bound to tell her mam. Anyway, the woman over the road didn't look the sort who was used to dealing with people from factories.

She wondered if there was a Labour Exchange in Knightsbridge. That's where people in Bootle went when they were looking for work. Or she could look under *Situations Vacant* in a newspaper. Perhaps if she walked round for a bit, she might gain enough courage to enter the agency, though she doubted it.

If that was Jackie's building, then this shop with the fur coats for over a thousand pounds must be Harrods. She wandered along the pavement marvelling at the window displays. One in particular appealed to her: a wedding scene with six bridesmaids and two pageboys, all in dark-blue satin and velvet. The bride's dress was cream watermarked taffeta, an Edwardian style with a bustle extending to a long, fan-shaped train. The mannequin, gazing expressionlessly at her new husband, carried a bouquet of what looked like orchids, the leaves trailing to the floor. Lisa smiled, imagining Sean and Dougal in those pageboy outfits!

As she passed the main entrance, a man in uniform was opening the doors and almost immediately a woman in a sleek fur jacket swept past him regally without even a glance in his direction. The man caught Lisa's eye and winked. She winked back.

At the end of Harrods, she turned into a side street. By now the sun was shining brightly and she could feel its warmth on her back. Here there were smaller shops; lingerie, then shoes, one with nothing but leather luggage, a sweet-shop – though the elaborate displays of confectionery were unlike anything she'd ever seen before – and a tobacconist's exhibiting rows of strange-looking pipes. There was an art gallery on the corner and Lisa stopped and stared at the paintings hung on the white walls. After a while, she decided they must be a joke. They were nothing but smears and blobs of paint and made no sense at all. Nellie, who was top in art at school, could do better than that.

She came to a row of private houses and peeped through the windows. Such furniture! Brocade chairs and tall antique sideboards which almost reached the ornate, moulded ceilings. Displays of flowers that must have taken hours to arrange. In some of the basements, women in white overalls were preparing food, cutting vegetables or kneading pastry. In one, four small children were sitting around a large scrubbed table, whilst a woman in a grey cotton dress bustled about pouring milk into beakers. Lizzie smiled at the box of cornflakes on the table – it was just like Chaucer Street! As she passed one house, a postman knocked on the glossy red door which was opened by a maid, a real-life maid in a black dress and a small white cap and apron.

She glanced at her watch – well, Jackie's watch. This morning, when Jackie was telling her about the agency, she'd stressed the importance of keeping any appointments made for her on time.

'I bet you haven't got a watch, you poor impoverished thing.'

Lisa shook her head. 'I've never had one.'

'Well, I got three for my twenty-first. I'll lend you one,' and she'd fished in a drawer and brought out an expensive gold model with an expanding bracelet.

It was already nearly ten o'clock and she felt guilty, wandering about, nosily peering into people's houses when she hadn't been near the agency and doubted if she ever would.

She turned into another street – more shops, though not nearly so posh as the ones she'd already passed. There was a grocer's and a florist's, then a bookshop. She looked through the rather grimy window. Books were crammed onto the shelves, which extended from floor to ceiling all around the walls. They seemed to be second-hand books, many very old and bound in leather. Three more high, double-sided shelves took up almost all the floorspace. Behind a desk squeezed in a corner, an elderly man with a long grey wispy beard and wearing a small embroidered skullcap, sat reading.

Lisa stood entranced. The scene was like something out of the nineteenth century. She'd seen *David Copperfield* with Freddie Bartholomew, she'd read *Pickwick Papers*, and this could be a set for a Dickens' film. It was a warm and welcoming oasis in the midst of smart and wealthy Knightsbridge.

She sighed and was about to move on when she noticed a dusty card in the window, '*Shop Assistant Required*' it said in sloping, old-fashioned script. Her spirits rose, but only momentarily. Someone well-educated would be wanted – someone who knew a lot about books. Well, she loved reading, always had, but apart from *Pickwick Papers* and *Treasure Island*, she'd read nothing they'd sell here. Nevertheless, it wouldn't hurt to try. The man could only say no and she'd be no worse off than she was now.

She took a deep breath and opened the door.

The old man looked up. She liked the friendly smile he gave her. At least he wouldn't be rude, she thought.

'Is is something specific you need, or do you just want to browse?' he asked in a deep voice with a faintly guttural accent.

Lisa swallowed. 'I've come about the job.'

For a moment, the man looked puzzled. 'The job? My goodness, I'd forgotten about the card. Is it still there?'

'Yes.' That probably meant the job had gone ages ago.

'You are the first person to apply. Come, sit down. Let's talk.'

The shop smelt of a mixture of dust and leather. Lisa sat down in front of the desk.

'What do you know of books?' The man's face was like a book itself, parchment-coloured and etched with wrinkles as fine as an old manuscript. His thick wiry eyebrows were like grey butterfly's wings above his brown eyes. He wore a flannel shirt and knitted cardigan, worn thin at the elbows.

'I only know I like reading them,' said Lisa.

'What have you read?'

She stood up suddenly. This was a waste of time. She had no answers to give him. 'I'm sorry. I shouldn't have come in. It's just that I'm looking for a job. I'm on my way to an agency now. Well, I'm supposed to be, but I'm going the wrong way. I saw your shop, then your card . . . I've only read *Pickwick Papers* and *Treasure Island*. I shouldn't have come in. I'm sorry.' She turned to leave.

'What did you think of them?'

She stopped. 'I liked the first but not the second. I think *Treasure Island* is a boy's book.'

'If you liked *Pickwick Papers* then you are a good girl to have working in a bookshop. Sit down, sit down. I am not conducting an examination here. When I was your age – what is it, sixteen, seventeen? – I had not read even those books. If you want to work here, let's talk about it.' He was standing, bowing and gesturing towards the chair Lisa had vacated. 'What is your name?'

'Lisa O'Brien and I'm sixteen.'

'And you come from Liverpool?'

'Yes.' Lisa had been doing her best to imitate Jackie's well-modulated speech. Obviously she hadn't been very success-ful.

'The Liverpool accent is my favourite. I was a mimic on the music hall, oh, a long, long time ago, but I still practise. I can do Winston Churchill, just listen. "Rise up ye peasants, throw down your chains and sit at the table of thy masters."'

Lisa burst out laughing. He'd got the voice just right, but it was delivered in a broad Liverpool accent. 'Did Churchill really say that?'

'No, but sometimes I amuse myself by imagining he did.' He slapped his forehead dramatically. 'Ach, there I go, showing off again. It is one of my weaknesses. Behave yourself, Harry,' he told himself sharply. 'This is serious. You want a job, Miss Lisa O'Brien, and I have a job to offer. The pay is not so bad – eight pounds a week. You would not get more in Harrods, though the atmosphere may appeal to some more than my old bookshop. Can you add up?'

'Yes, I was good at arithmetic at school.'

'Congratulations, I was not. My books are a mess. My legs are a mess. Rheumatism is my enemy and although I fight, I think the enemy is winning. My heart is not what it was. It goes too fast – or is it too slow? I forget which. One fine day it will stop going altogether. Until then, I need assistance to run my shop. My wife, Miriam, says I should ask for references. She thought people would be queuing up for this job.' He spread his hands, palms upwards, and shrugged. For a moment Lisa's heart sank. 'But you have an honest face. I take for granted you are not on the run from the police, or you didn't abscond from your last job with the petty cash?'

'Of course not!' Lisa said indignantly.

'I joke, I joke. Another weakness. I joke all the time. Tell me, Miss Lisa O'Brien, when can you start?'

'Tomorrow?'

'Fine, fine. My name is Harry Greenbaum, by the way. I am a Jew. Orthodox. You like my hat?'

'It's pretty,' said Lisa, smiling.

'It keeps my head together. Sometimes I get so angry with the world I think it will explode. You like a drink? Some coffee, tea? I ask from selfishness because I long for one myself and the back stairs to the kitchen are like Mount Everest so early in the morning. In other words, Miss Lisa, will you do your new employer a favour and make him a cup of coffee? Very black, very strong.'

Chapter 13

Eight pounds a week! Eight pounds all to herself for working for a dear old man who made jokes all the time, in a shop like a film set.

She almost skipped back to Queen's Gate, stopping only to buy some groceries. As soon as she got in, she went into the kitchen and made herself a sandwich, although she felt a bit uneasy when she came to spread the butter. In Chaucer Street, even now they were better off, they ate margarine during the week and only had butter on Sundays. She eased her conscience by not smearing it as thickly as she would have liked.

After she'd eaten, she began to tidy the flat.

She discovered thirty-eight women's magazines and Sunday papers going back for months, ten blouses, eight skirts, three nightdresses, eighteen pairs of stockings and five odd ones, three pairs of shoes and a blue slipper without a mate. She didn't bother to count the underclothes, just stuffed everything in a bag for Jackie to take to a place called a 'launderette' – apparently there was one just around the corner. Underneath the mess, she found an assortment of mugs, some empty and covered in green mould, and others in which what had once been coffee or tea had turned into a revolting sort of jelly, and three bottles containing varying amounts of whisky. She poured the contents of two of the bottles into the third and fullest one, then put all the letters and pieces of paper together on the sideboard, stacking an assortment of books, nearly all romantic novels, at the back. Her proximity disturbed the drooping flowers and petals scattered onto the carpet, now revealed as plain green wool. She lifted the vase carefully and took it to where she'd spread newspapers to contain the rubbish and threw the flowers away.

She hung the clothes in Jackie's wardrobe, which was so

packed, she wondered where she would put her own things when she bought them, took the dishes along to the kitchen and washed them, then collected the rubbish and carried it downstairs. There was a row of dustbins at the back of the house and she deposited her parcel in one of them with a sense of satisfaction.

Back upstairs she dusted, flicking cobwebs out of corners and off the low, sloping ceiling. She'd noticed a carpet-sweeper in the kitchen and used it to clean the floors in both rooms. Finally, she moved a small table into a corner for the clean cups and the kettle, adding the bottle of milk and packet of tea she'd just bought.

Finished!

From the bedroom doorway, she regarded both rooms with pride. They looked much bigger now with the floorspace cleared. The carpet in the bedroom was blue and matched the pattern on the candlewick bedspreads. Then suddenly, she felt worried in case Jackie would be annoyed. Perhaps she liked untidiness, and might be offended that Lisa had cleared up so ruthlessly . . .

After a few seconds of agonizing over whether to throw some clothes about to make the place look less spick and span, Lisa decided that as she was paying half the rent, she had the right not to live in a pigsty. As long as she was prepared to do the work, that was all that mattered.

She made herself a cup of tea and looked through the *Guide To London*, one of the books she'd found on the floor. If she turned right outside the house, she could walk to a place called Fulham. Perhaps Fulham was not quite so posh as South Kensington and Knightsbridge, and she could do some much-needed shopping. Although Jackie appeared willing to lend her anything she needed, Lisa didn't want to sponge off her flatmate longer than could be avoided.

Fulham, it turned out, was a working-class area. Lisa felt quite homesick mingling with the harassed-looking women laden with shopping baskets, their shabbily-dressed children clutching at their coats as they trailed behind.

She was relieved to see several familiar shops – a big Woolworths opposite a Boots. In the High Street there was a market where things were even cheaper than in Bootle. She bought a pair of black court shoes, almost identical to those Jackie had worn that morning, for nineteen shillings and elevenpence, and a black pleated skirt for the same amount. A white blouse with a lace Peter Pan collar was seventeen and six. After two pairs of stockings and pants, a bar of soap and a cheap hand-towel, she still had a little money left. It would be nice to buy a jacket or a cardigan, but she'd need to get food during the week.

She reached the end of the market. The last stall was piled high with second-hand clothing and several women were rooting through it. Lisa joined them. There were lots of men's collarless shirts, trousers with frayed hems, children's jumpers and shorts without buttons. The women were picking at the clothes with an almost savage energy, turning the piles over, throwing them to one side and clutching at a garment they'd revealed, examining it briefly, then discarding it contemptuously.

''Ere, 'ere,' said the woman behind the stall in an aggrieved tone. 'Be careful with what's not your own.'

The woman beside Lisa ignored the warning and heaved a pile of clothes upside down. Lisa snatched at the corner of something which caught her eye and dragged it out. It was a Chinese jacket made from royal-blue quilted satin with a mandarin collar and elaborate cord fastenings, crumpled but quite whole. 'Not a break in it', as Kitty used to say when she got a second-hand bargain. She put her purchases on the ground and tried it on.

'That looks nice, darlin',' said the woman who had up-turned the clothes and revealed the precious item.

'Are you sure?' asked Lisa, who would have liked to look at herself in a mirror. The jacket was hip-length and felt all right, except for the sleeves being a bit too long, though she could easily take them up.

'Eh, Vera, don't that look nice?' The woman nudged the person beside her.

'Cor! Not much. Looks a treat,' Vera confirmed.

'How much is it, please?' Lisa asked the stallholder.

'One and six.'

'Come off it, Doris,' Vera snorted. 'This ain't 'arrods, it's

Fulham 'igh Street.' She turned to Lisa. 'Offer her ninepence, darlin'.'

'Will you take ninepence?' Lisa wouldn't have dared make such a low offer without the backing of the women alongside her.

Doris pursed her lips and her weatherbeaten face took on a stubborn look. 'I'm not runnin' a charity 'ere. A shillin's the least I'll take.'

The women began to argue again, but Lisa had already taken a shilling out of her purse and handed it over, worried that Doris might refuse to sell the coveted jacket at all if she were pushed too hard.

She left, the women still arguing with Doris, and on her way home bought some stewing steak and vegetables to make scouse for that night's dinner, then called in at Woolworths for needles and cotton to alter the sleeves of the jacket.

Finally, she bought a bunch of flowers to replace the ones that had been thrown away.

Back in the flat, she prepared the scouse and left it on the stove to simmer. Afterwards, she tried on her new clothes.

She looked like a normal young woman again instead of the grim, frumpy person she'd been these last two years. The fine stockings shimmered on legs made slimmer and more shapely by the high-heeled shoes. The wide waistband of the skirt fitted tight around her slim body, the pleats flaring out to just below her knees, whilst the white blouse with its rounded collar and long full sleeves gave her rather a demure look.

It was the jacket she liked best, though. It added an air of chic to the rather ordinary outfit. Of course, she would never have dared wear it in Bootle, everybody would have laughed, but this morning she'd seen a woman dressed just like a Russian Cossack, with a big fur hat and a muff. A muff! And another woman wearing a collar and a man's tie. Down here, you could get away with outrageous outfits. Everyone would think she wore this satin quilted coat because she'd chosen to, picked it out of a dozen others, and not because it only cost a shilling in a market. At least, she hoped so.

She sat in front of the newly-polished dressing table. The telephone gleamed – just think, when she met people she could give them her number! Tomorrow she'd tell Mr Greenbaum in case he wanted to contact her out of shop hours. She sighed happily and began to comb her hair, experimenting with Jackie's wide collection of slides and combs and bows. Thank goodness she hadn't cut her hair short during the time she'd been trying to make herself look as unattractive as possible. She'd nearly done so several times. It was only the thought of upsetting Mam that had prevented her . . .

Mam!

She'd forgotten all about Kitty. Since she'd walked out of Number 2 Chaucer Street yesterday morning she'd scarcely given her family a second thought. Everything that had happened since had been so exciting and absorbing. But Mam would be distraught with grief, once she realized her Lizzie wasn't coming home again.

At first, she'd probably thought Lizzie had got up early to go to mass, then gone straight to work. She wouldn't have known that she'd left for good till she didn't come home that night. The whole family had probably been sent out to look for her.

What a cruel and thoughtless girl she was, walking out like that!

Lisa got up and began to walk restlessly around the two rooms. The traffic outside was never-ending, but up here the sound was muted and the large house was silent. Presumably everyone was at work.

She couldn't go back to Chaucer Street now, not ever. It held too many bad memories. Every time she looked at the mantelpiece she saw the gold sugar basin Hank had won, a prize for his lovely girl. Since she'd arrived in London, she hadn't thought about Southport, not once, and now she no longer had to sleep in that big double bed, there were no reminders of her dad.

In fact, in the space of less than two days, she felt a different person altogether, as if a part of her that had been dead for years had come alive again. And she *was* a different person, because Lizzie O'Brien no longer existed. Now she was Lisa, with a good job and nice clothes, and the world suddenly seemed a wonderful place.

She slipped into her new coat and went out to buy a postcard for Kitty. On it, she wrote she was fine and not to worry, but she didn't include her address, though she wasn't sure why. Perhaps she couldn't stand the thought of Kitty's sad, demanding letters wanting to know why she had deserted them, her loving, laughing family, or that one of the boys might be despatched to persuade her to go back . . .

She hadn't been home for more than five minutes when she heard footsteps on the stairs. A door slammed, dishes rattled in the kitchen and from downstairs came the sound of music. People were arriving back from work and the house was coming alive.

Tomorrow morning Mam would get the card and know she was all right. 'Anyway,' Lisa thought defensively, 'they'll be happier without me. They're probably glad I've gone.'

Jackie wouldn't be home until eight o'clock. She was having an affair with a married man, she'd told Lisa confidentially in the restaurant the night before. He was thirty-five, had been an officer in the Royal Air Force and his wife didn't understand him. As soon as his children were older, he would get a divorce and marry Jackie. In the meantime, they went for dinner together every night after work. They could never meet at weekends.

'Trust me to fall for someone unavailable,' Jackie said mournfully, her round grey eyes for once sad. 'I mean, I get asked out on loads of dates, but young men seem so callow compared to Gordon. Honestly, Lisa, wait till you meet him, he's gorgeous.'

Lisa was reading when Jackie came in. She'd gone through the books in the flat and rejected most of them, deterred by the description of the plots on the inside covers. Girls married men who turned out to be millionaires; men married girls who had a sordid past; two men loved the same girl, or two girls loved the same man. Then she found a book by the strangely-named Richmal Crompton about a boy called

William Brown. It was so funny that from time to time she laughed out loud. She became so absorbed that she lost track of time and was surprised when Jackie came into the room like a whirlwind.

'I've brought Gordon home to meet you!'

Lisa laid down her book and stood up to meet the gorgeous Gordon. She couldn't believe her eyes when he followed Jackie into the room. He looked older than thirty-five, at least ten years older. He was about five feet ten, of portly build, wearing a loud checked sports jacket, camel-coloured trousers and a military tie. His face was smooth, the skin on his cheeks red and mottled, and his lips were full and fleshy – what you could see of them, that is, for his top lip was almost hidden by a wide moustache parted in the middle with the ends twisted into stiff points.

What on earth did Jackie see in this ridiculous-looking man? Perhaps Lisa should have read one of the romances, rather than the William Brown book, she thought, for it might have given her some insight into why people were attracted to each other. Then she told herself to stop being so critical. Perhaps he had a lovely nature. But she soon decided this wasn't the case, for when she was introduced and took Gordon's limp, sweaty hand, he appraised her quite openly, looking her up and down while Jackie bounced around the flat, in and out of the bedroom, marvelling at the transformation that had taken place.

'I *told* you she was the most amazing person, didn't I, Gordon?' she said excitedly. 'I'm so lucky getting Lisa for a flatmate, I just don't deserve someone so perfect.'

Lisa felt embarrassed. 'Would you like some tea?' she muttered.

She felt Gordon's eyes on her legs when she went to pour the tea out and wished she'd changed back into Jackie's old clothes, but she'd wanted to show her new outfit off to her friend.

Jackie sat beside Gordon on the sofa, cuddling close and smiling up at him adoringly. She'd put a record on the gramophone. It was one of the few bands Lisa recognized, Glenn Miller. Smooth, romantic dance-music filled the room.

Lisa felt uncomfortable and wondered how long Gordon would stay. No wonder his wife didn't understand him! She probably didn't understand why he didn't get home from work till nine or ten o'clock each night.

After a while, he whispered something to Jackie and they stood up.

'We're just going into the bedroom for a while,' Jackie said with an embarrassed smile.

They disappeared and Lisa felt the urge to giggle. How long would they be? Collecting the mugs, she took them down to the kitchen and washed them slowly. She was taking even longer to dry them when a young man came in carrying a tray of dirty dishes.

'Ho, ho!' he said. 'Are you Jackie's new flatmate?'

'I am,' confirmed Lisa.

'Given in your notice yet?' he asked with a grin.

'Not yet,' she replied. 'I quite like it here.'

The young man's features were almost startlingly perfect. His face was tanned a rich gold, slightly darker than his long, curly hair.

'I suppose you're the one who used my pan.'

'Did I? I'm sorry. I thought they were for everybody,' she said contritely.

'No, we buy our own utensils and of course Jackie never cooks. What is that revolting mixture you've got in there, anyway?'

Lisa had made enough for two days. 'Scouse,' she said.

'Scouse? I suppose that's what you are, a Scouse. I'm Piers, by the way, Piers de Villiers.'

Piers! She'd never heard that name before. And de Villiers!

'Lisa O'Brien.'

He put his tray down and they shook hands.

'Pleased to meet you, Lisa. Your scouse may look frightful, but it smells delicious. You must show me how to make it some time.'

'It's just stew, really. I won't use your pan again, I promise. Is there something else I can put this in? A basin? I'll buy a pan of my own as soon as I get paid.'

'Don't be an idiot, there's a good girl. I've heaps of pans. It's just that that one's my favourite. Here, take this one as a gift. It's yours – your very own scouse pan.' He rooted through a cupboard and brought out a pan that was slightly bigger than the one Lisa had used.

'Thanks,' she said. 'You're very kind.'

'Any time,' he said cheerfully. 'New here, are you – I mean to London?'

'It's only my second day.'

'Well, Lisa, my friend's an actor. If you ever want theatre tickets, he gets them free.'

'I'd love some! I've never been to the theatre, but I'm sure I'd like it.'

Piers began to pile his dishes in the sink so Lisa said goodbye and returned to the flat, glad to have been detained and hoping that Jackie and Gordon had come out of the bedroom.

They had. Jackie was in her pink pyjamas, tying the belt of her dressing gown and Gordon, a complacent smirk on his face, was straightening his tie when she entered the room. He winked at her.

'I'm ready for take off,' he said.

Lisa hoped they wouldn't embrace in front of her. Thankfully, they left the room together and a minute later Jackie returned.

'Did you like him?' she asked, and without waiting for an answer: 'Did you mind? I mean, us going into the bedroom like that? That's another reason my flatmates leave. They think I'm immoral. Well, I suppose I am. Are you terribly moral, Lisa?'

'No, I don't think so.'

'Thank God for that.'

'I met a nice young man in the kitchen – Piers. He's given me a saucepan and he's going to get me theatre tickets.'

'Oh, Piers!' Jackie wrinkled her nose.

'Don't you like him?' Lisa was surprised. She couldn't imagine Jackie disliking anyone.

'He's okay, though Gordon hates him – and his friend Ralph. He doesn't like me to have anything to do with them. They're queer, you see.'

'Queer?' Piers had seemed excessively normal to Lisa.

'Queer – homosexual. They're lovers, Piers and Ralph.'

Lisa was trying to digest this piece of information when Jackie asked if she'd got a job. She told her about Mr Greenbaum and the bookshop.

'A bookshop! Oh Lisa, couldn't you have got something more interesting? Clothes, perfume . . . is that all the agency had?'

Ignoring the reference to the agency, Lisa said defiantly, 'I think books are interesting. And it's eight pounds a week, and Mr Greenbaum, he's interesting too and very funny.'

'Oh, God! What an interfering body I am. I'm sorry, Lisa, you've done incredibly well. And the flat – you've worked miracles! You've even bought some clothes. That waist! I'd kill for it. You look truly elegant.'

Lisa showed her the quilted jacket. She put it on and twirled round. 'What do you think, Jackie?'

'That must have cost a fortune. I thought you hadn't got much money. How on earth did you manage to buy all this stuff?'

Jackie didn't look the least bit suspicious, just puzzled. She was so naive and innocent. Lisa felt a sudden surge of anger against Gordon, who probably told her all sorts of lies which Jackie believed.

'I went to a place called Fulham and things there were so cheap. The jacket was only a shilling on a second-hand stall.'

Apparently Jackie had only vaguely heard of Fulham and had no idea it was only ten minutes' walk away. Impressed with Lisa's purchases, she resolved to go the very next Saturday.

Lisa was waiting outside the shop when Mr Greenbaum arrived the following morning. When he saw her he began to hurry, shuffling along in his ankle-length black overcoat.

'I'll give you a key,' he panted, 'so in future you can let yourself in. Now I feel guilty because I have a prompt employee.'

Once inside, he lowered himself onto the chair behind his desk. 'Ach, Lisa,' he sighed. 'Why does my body grow old, but inside my head stay young? Tell me.'

'I have no idea,' she confessed. 'Perhaps some people have

old heads and young bodies.'

'You sound like one of them,' he said accusingly. 'Now, when I get my breath back, I'll show you where things are.'

The books were in sections, marked alphabetically, *Aerodynamics*, *Anthropology* in the far corner by the window, followed by *Biography*, *Biology*, right through to *Zoology* on the opposite wall.

'Here is *Fiction* at the back.' His breath was ragged. Just the short walk round his shop had exhausted him. 'I keep a few modern authors, like Graham Greene, Evelyn Waugh and Somerset Maugham. Mainly they are old, pre-nineteen-twenty – Flaubert, Proust, Bennett, Hardy . . . Have you read *The Way Of All Flesh*, Miss Lisa O'Brien?'

'No, I've only read — '

'Of course, *Pickwick Papers* and *Treasure Island*. I forgot. Samuel Butler is my favourite. I will lend you *The Way Of All Flesh*. And *Erewhon*. Do you know what that is?'

'A place?'

'Yes, a place – a mythical country. It is nowhere. "Erehwon" is "nowhere" back to front. A brilliant, brilliant book.'

Beside the desk there was a small section containing office supplies: reams of paper, typewriter ribbons, spiral notebooks, bottles of ink. Mr Greenbaum explained that there were several offices in the area which sometimes ran out of stationery and bought small amounts from him.

At this point, the letterbox suddenly rattled and a heap of envelopes landed on the mat. Lisa went over and picked them up. The old man chuckled: 'You have earned today's wages already. Picking up the post has become an ordeal lately. Perhaps you could help me open some but first, Miss Lisa, a cup of coffee would be more than welcome. If you want it white, there is a dairy just around the corner.' He laughed again, this time a trifle ruefully. 'Oh, what bliss this is, to be waited on. I'm ashamed of myself, a good socialist like me, sitting back and letting a fellow comrade labour on my behalf.'

'What's a socialist?' asked Lisa.

The old man's jaw dropped. He stared at her with shocked, rheumy eyes. She felt as if he might sack her on the spot.

'I'm sorry,' she stammered. 'I've never . . .'

'Oh, Miss Lisa! Make that coffee and I'll tell you.'

Five minutes later, when she came out of the kitchen with the drinks, he was opening the post, slitting the envelopes with a silver letter-opener. He stopped when she put the coffee in front of him.

'Who is the Prime Minister?' he demanded sternly.

'Mr Attlee,' she replied promptly.

'Thank God, you know that much.'

'Of course I do.' She remembered how just after the war, Kitty had proudly gone to vote and when she'd come back the little ones had been aghast to learn she hadn't put her cross by Mr Churchill's party, though the older boys seemed to understand why she had voted Labour.

'Do you know what Clause Four is?'

She wriggled uncomfortably. 'I left school at fourteen. We never did politics, at least not after Charles the First. I mean, I know they executed him for doing something against Parliament.'

'Forget about Charles the First. Clause Four of the Labour Party Constitution says that we must secure for the workers by hand or by brain the full fruits of their industry. Does that sound right to you?'

Lisa thought for a while. 'It sounds fair. Yes, I agree.'

'There, then! You are a socialist too.'

'Am I?'

'Of course you are. Very soon, Lisa O'Brien, dear Mr Aneurin Bevan will bring in the National Health Service. Free healthcare for all – free spectacles, medicine, deaf-aids. No more people will die because they can't afford a doctor. Britain will become the envy of the world. Oh, it is a good thing to be a socialist.'

'Is it?' Lisa felt bewildered.

'Of course it is. You'll realize that some day. Come, now we've sorted that out, let's finish opening these letters.'

There were at least twenty, several containing cheques.

'These people have already written or telephoned and I have the book they want put away,' Mr Greenbaum explained. 'Others are writing to ask if I have a certain book in stock.' He laid a letter in front of her. 'Now, this person wants Halsey's *Butterflies*. That is extremely rare. I will ring some friends, booksellers, to see if they have it, but it isn't likely.'

'Gosh! This one's from Australia!' gasped Lisa, carefully slitting open an envelope with an airmail stamp. 'He wants *The Road To Wigan Pier* by George Orwell, published by the Left Wing Book Club. Have we got that?'

'We most certainly have. Is that from a Peter Prynne?'

Lisa looked at the scrawled signature. 'Yes.'

'Then I'll send it off this afternoon with an invoice. I know he will pay.'

Just then the door opened and Lisa sprang to her feet. A middle-aged woman entered the shop. Remembering Mr Greenbaum's words when she'd come in herself the day before, she asked, 'Is it something specific you need, or do you just want to browse?'

The woman wanted a Latin dictionary for her son. 'I know I can get a new one, but he said if I do, everyone at school will know he's lost it. Something battered-looking, please.'

Lisa was about to take her to the *Languages* shelf when she recalled that on her quick tour round the shop, she'd noticed a section headed *Reference*. Sure enough, the dictionaries were there, including several Latin ones. A maroon leather-covered one was considered the most shabby.

'How much is it?'

The price was scrawled in pencil on the flyleaf. 'Five shillings,' Lisa said faintly, thinking the woman would make an excuse, leave and buy a new, cheap edition for half the price from somewhere else. Instead, she handed over two half-crowns.

She felt Mr Greenbaum's eyes on her as she faced the till and pressed the *Sale* and 5/- buttons. The drawer sprang open and she put the coins in the correct tray, took a medium-sized paper bag from the shelf under the desk and handed the book over.

'My first customer!' she exclaimed excitedly after the door had closed. 'Did I do it right?'

'Perfectly. If you go on like this, you will make me feel

redundant.'

'Oh, I don't want to do that,' she said, alarmed.

'I joke, I joke. Take no notice of me ninety per cent of the time. I will make a signal when I'm serious. See, I'm wiggling my eyebrows. That means I'm serious.'

Lisa laughed. 'You'd better think of something else.' It looked as if a butterfly was frantically flapping its wings just above his eyes.

'Then I shall speak in a deep, grave voice, just like Mr Churchill. Can you type, Miss Lisa O'Brien?'

She laughed again. His imitation, as before, was perfect. 'I'm sorry, no.'

He sighed. 'Never mind. I can't type either, but I bet your young fingers are better at not typing than mine. Later on, whilst I wrap the parcels, you can reply to these letters.'

The shop door was opened with a quick rush and slammed violently shut. An elderly woman in a black astrakhan coat strode towards the desk. Lisa approached her.

'Is it something — '

'Don't speak to her, Miss Lisa. Ignore her. You horrible woman, go away!'

Lisa stepped back in alarm.

'See, you've frightened her! Coming in looking like Joan Crawford as if you owned the place. Get back to where you came from.'

The woman had once been beautiful. She was still striking. Snow-white hair, thick and shiny, was brushed smoothly back into a coil on the nape of her neck, though the cosmetics she wore accentuated her age rather than reducing it. Bright blue eye-shadow drew attention to the sagging lids, and the residue of rouge in the wrinkles of her cheeks gave them a raddled look. Scarlet lipstick, carefully applied, could not cover the spidery lines in the corners of her mouth and when she spoke, tiny cracks appeared in her lips.

'Shut up, you silly old man.'

Harry Greenbaum sighed deeply. 'Lisa, this is my wife, Miriam. Miriam, Lisa.'

Lisa swallowed in amazement. She'd thought they were

sworn enemies about to attack each other.

Miriam removed her leather gloves and shook hands firmly. 'Is he treating you all right? Oh, he's a slave-driver is that man. I'm surprised you're still here.' She sat down opposite the desk.

'She's only come in to inspect you, Lisa. To warn you off. To confirm I'm spoken for. She thinks every woman is out to seduce me, steal me away. Oh, if only they would.' He raised his eyes to heaven and shook his head longingly. 'If only Minnie Kopek was still around, I should have gone off with her. She pleaded. How she pleaded!'

Miriam hit him over the head with her gloves. 'Stop going on about Minnie Kopek.' She turned to Lisa. 'For fifty years this man taunts me with Minnie Kopek. I never met her. Did she exist, I ask myself?'

Harry gave an enigmatic smile and didn't answer.

'Listen, Greenbaum, I'm going to the dentist which is right by the bank so I thought I'd put the cheques in,' Miriam said.

'That's right, woman, take my money as fast as I earn it. Here! Here's your damn cheques.' He secured them with a paper clip and flung them across the desk in front of her. She reached out for them and as she did so, the old man's hand went out and covered hers. At first Lisa thought he was about to snatch them back, but instead, Miriam turned her own hand upwards and clasped his. For a few seconds they stared into each other's eyes and Lisa saw an exchange of pure, explicit love. They adored each other. This was all a game. She felt a lump in her throat.

She'd brought sandwiches for dinner, though in London everybody had lunch at midday and dinner at night. Mr Greenbaum wandered off at twelve o'clock announcing in his Churchillian voice that he considered her perfectly able to look after the shop alone.

Whilst she munched her sandwiches, she got on with typing replies to the letters which had come that morning. It had been difficult with Mr Greenbaum present, as he chatted away distractingly as he wrapped and addressed the parcels.

She was making a slightly better job of it than he had, judging by the carbon copies of letters she'd been given to show how they should be set out. The old letters were full of overtyping and words joined together. Already she could manage two-finger typing, though the main difficulty was remembering to press the shift key when she wanted a capital.

A customer came in to browse and eventually bought a book on magic by someone called Aleister Crowley. Lisa made a mental note of the name. Magic, Aleister Crowley. Then a girl no older than herself entered the shop and asked if they had the collected works of Byron.

Lisa bit her lip. She had no idea where to look. Who on earth was Byron? 'I'm not sure.'

The girl was chatty. 'It's this ghastly English exam. I've already done Chaucer and quite frankly, that old English script or whatever you call it, may as well be double Dutch for all the sense it makes.'

Chaucer! She'd lived in Chaucer Street and someone at school once told her he was a poet. Close by was Byron Street and Wordsworth, Southey and Dryden Streets. Perhaps they were all poets.

She looked under the *Poetry* section and there was Byron! Relieved, for she would have hated to make a fool of herself, she pointed out several collected editions.

Mr Greenbaum returned just after one. He looked mournful. His beard dripped amber liquid. 'One double brandy, Lisa. Just one and I feel like I drank a bottle. Oh, the trials of old age.'

'Surely that's a good thing,' she said. 'It means you can get drunk cheaper.'

He brightened. 'That's a very postive way of looking at things. I shall present you with all my problems in future and you can make them disappear with your words of wisdom.'

'Have you had anything to eat?' she asked severely.

He put his hands over his ears defensively. 'Quiet! You sound like Miriam. No, I had a liquid lunch. Now, get out of my shop. Have your lunch-hour. Wander around Harrods. If you, a working girl from Liverpool, were not a socialist when you went in, you will surely be one when you come out.'

One Christmas just after the war, Lisa had taken Dougal and Sean along Strand Road to a shop which had a grotto. Inside, it was just like a fairy tale, with frosted glistening walls strung with coloured lights. It was unreal, out of this world. She'd had trouble getting her little brothers out of the magic place.

Harrods reminded her of a grotto. Sparkling chandeliers shed brilliant light over the rich merchandise. Jewellery such as she'd never seen before, necklaces thick with rubies, emeralds and sapphires, twinkled beneath glass counters, next to rings containing stones as big as a shilling piece, and even tiaras.

The scarf counter was like a stall in an Arabian bazaar. Brilliant silks and satins cascaded like streams of coloured rain from their stands. As for the perfume section, it smelt like heaven. In front of one display of expensive scent stood a half-full bottle labelled 'sample'. She dabbed some behind her ears.

'Can I help, modom?' A sleek salesgirl approached.

'How much is it?' Lisa asked.

'Five pounds.' the girl answered.

Trying not to let her astonishment show, Lisa said airily, 'I'll think about it.'

She wandered upstairs. The clothes took her breath away. Voluminous sequinned ballgowns, embroidered cocktail dresses, filmy summer frocks, linen suits exquisitely cut. She looked askance at the price tags. The cost of just one ballgown would have kept the entire O'Brien family for a year!

There were plenty of customers, mainly women, nearly all beautifully dressed in clothes which could have been, and probably were, bought on this very floor. Lisa was struck by how few of them looked happy, though. It seemed to her that to be let loose to look through these lovely clothes with the intent of buying would be paradise itself. Why, then, did they all appear so discontented? They sorted through the racks of garments with no more care and far less enthusiasm than the woman Vera and her friend had done at the stall in Fulham market!

She heard phrases that until then she'd only read in magazine stories.

'I simply *must* get something for Freddy's ghastly preview on Friday.'

'What a frightful bore, darling. As for me, I haven't got a thing to wear for *Aïda*.'

'We're off to Paris on Saturday and if I don't get something today, I'll go in rags.'

All said so petulantly, so loudly, as if they didn't give a damn what other people thought. And they spoke to the assistants rudely, as if they were servants and didn't merit a 'please' or 'thank you'. Lisa felt anger rise in her breast. Did this mean she was a socialist?

It was such a warm day that she'd left her quilted jacket in the shop. Perhaps in her white blouse and skirt she looked like a shop assistant, because a man approached her – a vision, dressed from head to toe in dove grey: shoes, suit, overcoat. His shadow-striped grey tie was held with a pearl clip, and a soft felt hat was clasped in one white hand, on which the fingernails were polished to perfection. Even the slim rolled umbrella over his arm had been bought to match his outfit. A tall man with an authoritative face and pencil-thin moustache, his aquiline nose quivered as if the shop, the entire world, smelt somewhat unsavoury.

'I say,' he barked at Lisa, 'fetch my wife the blue dress, the one she decided against. She'd like to have another try.'

Lisa stared at him. It was an order, not a request.

'Come on, my girl, come on!' His eyes flashed with impatience.

'I am not your girl,' she said icily. 'And it wouldn't exactly kill you to fetch the dress yourself.' Resisting the urge to flee, for there was nothing he could do as she didn't work here, she stared at him, seeing the impatience turn to amazement. Then, to her astonishment, he began to laugh – a high, hysterical, unnatural shriek.

'Ginger,' called a voice from a cubicle nearby. 'Ginger, where is the girl with the blue dress?'

The laughter stopped abruptly.

Lisa haughtily threw back her head and without another glance at Ginger, who was clearly unhinged, she left the shop.

Chapter 14

The afternoon passed swiftly. There were few customers. Mr Greenbaum said sales over the counter just about paid the rent for the shop. He did most of his business by post.

'But,' he added with his expressive shrug, 'I have to keep my books somewhere, so why not a shop?'

'Why not?' agreed Lisa.

When she got back to the flat that evening, she found an envelope pushed under their door. It contained two tickets to see a play called *Blithe Spirit* a week on Saturday, and a note which read: '*Why don't you come and have a drink with us when you get back?*' It was signed '*Piers*'.

She showed the note to Jackie later, after Gordon had left. 'Will you come with me to the theatre?' she asked eagerly.

'I don't think Gordon would like it,' Jackie said doubtfully. 'Not using tickets off Ralph, and as for going for a drink with them afterwards . . .' She wrinkled her nose.

'What right has Gordon to dictate what you do at weekends?' reasoned Lisa. 'If he can't see you, it's none of his business.'

The girl looked uncomfortable for a moment, then her face lit up. 'It wouldn't hurt, would it? You're right – I mean, he can't expect me to act like a nun. Anyway, it's not as if I'm going with another man.'

They were good seats in the rear stalls. Many of the theatregoers wore evening dress. Out of her wages, Lisa had paid her rent and bought herself a gold-braid Alice band and a black silk blouse. In her blue quilted jacket and new blouse, she didn't feel too out of place among the elegantly dressed audience.

At first Jackie was on edge, worried that Gordon might miraculously turn up with his wife and see her.

'What if he does?' said Lisa, trying not to sound impatient. 'You're not doing anything wrong.'

It was the first play she had ever seen. She sat entranced, glued to her seat, disconsolate when it finished.

'Oh, I wish there'd been more,' she moaned as they waited for a bus near Piccadilly Circus.

Jackie had livened up and seemed to have forgotten all about Gordon. 'It's been a super evening,' she enthused. 'I hope Ralph can get more tickets and we can do this often.'

The main room in Piers' and Ralph's flat stretched across the entire front of the house.

Lisa stopped in the doorway, taken aback by the decoration. The walls were painted dark red, the ceiling black. A tall black lacquered Chinese cabinet decorated with red and gold flowers dominated one wall. Against another wall stood a matching sideboard and a black enamelled bookcase. Above the marble fireplace hung a huge mirror with a thick gold frame. The chairs were upholstered in dark red velvet, and white fur rugs were scattered on the polished floor. Two red-shaded lamps provided the only illumination.

'Gosh!' was all she could say. Despite the forbidding colour scheme, the room looked warm and welcoming, though Lisa couldn't have lived in it. The style was too dominant and overwhelming.

'Like it?' said Piers. He wore black velvet trousers and a loose white silk shirt, and seemed pleased by her surprised reaction.

'It's very exotic,' she said. 'And foreign.'

'That's just the effect I wanted – exotic and foreign. It's my job, you see. I'm an interior decorator. I come back here and forget I'm in London, in England. It's like walking into a room in some strange country with an entirely different culture. Oh, I forgot, you haven't met Ralph. He's only just got in himself.'

Lisa hadn't noticed the person sitting reading at the black table at the opposite end of the room. Statue-still and silent, he hadn't even glanced up when they arrived.

He looked nothing like an actor. About thirty, plainly dressed in brown slacks and a fawn shirt, he was more like a comfortable family doctor or bank clerk. At Piers' words he got to his feet and came over to shake hands. He was almost excessively ordinary – neither good- nor bad-looking, of average height, with mouse-coloured hair cut very short. He was polite, but Lisa sensed he resented their presence.

'You already know Jackie,' Piers said and Ralph nodded.

They sat in armchairs around a black octagonal coffee table whilst Piers poured the wine. 'Did you like the play?'

'I could have stayed there all night,' said Lisa enthusiastically, 'I wish there'd been ten acts.'

'Are you a regular theatregoer?' Ralph asked in his subdued, rather colourless voice.

'It's the first play I've ever been to and I want to see every one in London. I didn't just like it, I *loved* it.'

'What did you think of Noël?' asked Piers.

'Who's Noël?' she enquired innocently.

'Christ Almighty, Lisa.' Piers exploded into laughter. 'I'm talking about Noël Coward. He wrote the play and starred in it. Didn't you realize that? Didn't you buy a programme?'

'Are they the leaflets they were selling when we went in?' She turned to Jackie. 'Why didn't you tell me? I didn't know you were supposed to buy a programme.'

Jackie had already demolished her wine. 'Sorry, I was so worried about Gordon I just didn't think.'

Piers refilled her glass. 'More wine, Lisa?'

'Not yet, thanks.' She felt uncomfortable, displaying her ignorance so shamefully. But the person she least expected to, boosted her self-confidence.

'I think Lisa has the makings of a genuine theatre-lover,' said Ralph quietly. Piers had not returned to his seat after pouring Jackie's wine. Instead, he sat on the floor, leaning against Ralph's chair companionably. Lisa wondered if Ralph had been so unwelcoming because he was jealous that Piers had asked her and Jackie in for a drink, and whether this gesture on his friend's part, this move towards him, had shown that his fears were unwarranted.

'Can you get tickets for the play you're in?' she asked. 'I'd love to see you on stage.'

'Would you really?' He looked surprised and flattered.

'Ralph's rehearsing *Pygmalion*,' Piers said proudly. 'He's got a leading part, Alfred Doolittle. It opens next week.'

'Who wrote *Pygmalion*?' asked Lisa.

'George Bernard Shaw,' said Ralph, adding with a smile, 'and he isn't in it.'

Jackie finished her second glass of wine. Lisa had already noticed in the short while they had lived together that she drank a lot. As soon as she came home from work she poured herself a glass of whisky, and the glass was regularly refilled until she went to bed. Lisa decided it was all Gordon's fault. He made her unhappy, deserting her at weekends, stringing her along with lies about his wife – at least Lisa was convinced they were lies and there was no way he would ever get divorced. He was just having a good time at Jackie's expense and didn't give a damn about the consequences. Right now the girl looked uncomfortable, simply because dear Gordon didn't like homosexuals. He'd gone on about them only the other night because he'd met Ralph coming out of the lavatory as he was about to go in.

'Had a narrow escape there,' he'd crowed when he came back. 'Scared the bugger was about to proposition me on the spot.' As if Ralph would fancy horrible, ugly Gordon when he had Piers!

Halfway into her third glass, Jackie suddenly came to life. Spurred on by the wine, her real, sunny nature surfaced. She began to talk about *Blithe Spirit* and the parts which had amused her most.

Piers opened another bottle. Lisa, on her second glass, began to feel faintly tipsy. The conversation turned to the cinema, something she could talk about without making a fool of herself. Going to the pictures by herself had been her only source of entertainment over the past two years, and she had a good memory for everything she'd seen.

Piers rested his head against Ralph's knee. It looked so gentle, so normal. Once Marie Gordon had told her about men who fancied other men, and there were even women who went with each other, apparently. At first she hadn't believed it, but Marie convinced her it was true, and she'd thought, 'Anyone who behaves like that must be a monster and if I ever meet one, I'll know straight away.' But watching

Piers and Ralph together was not the slightest bit disgusting. It was just two people in love.

They stayed until three in the morning and only left after Jackie fell asleep in her chair.

When Lisa awoke, it was midday. She lay there, relaxed and happy, before realizing it was Sunday and she'd missed mass – again! She'd forgotten all about it last Sunday until it was too late.

She jumped out of bed and grabbed some clothes. Jackie slept on, dead to the world. Perhaps she could find a one o'clock service somewhere, though she had no idea where the nearest Catholic church was. Then she remembered about Westminster Cathedral. Perhaps the underground train went there.

She was almost dressed when she stopped in the act of buttoning up her blouse. Going to mass seemed part of her past life, the life she'd abandoned, and would only bring back memories she was trying to forget. Some day she'd have to go to Confession and tell some unfamiliar priest that she'd run away from home – and what would she answer if he asked why?

Best not to go then, she decided, and put the kettle on instead.

She was amazed at how little it seemed to matter. After making herself a cup of tea and some toast, she sat on the sofa reading and the fact she hadn't been to church slipped to the back of her mind and it was almost as if she'd never been at all, ever.

The book she was reading was *Pride And Prejudice* by Jane Austen. When she'd finished *The Way Of All Flesh*, Mr Greenbaum had eagerly asked for her reaction. She said she was amazed and delighted to find it so enjoyable. *Pride And Prejudice* was even better. It was just like the stories in the *Red Star* and *Miracle* – full of unspoken sex and frustration. Passions seethed beneath the sedate surface of the writing. Mr Greenbaum said Jane Austen had written a lot of books, and if Lisa liked them she should read Charlotte and Emily Brontë too.

'*Jane Eyre, Wuthering Heights* . . . Ach, Miss Lisa, you will adore them. Such love stories. And let's not forget *Madame*

Bovary and *Anna Karenina*. My friend, you have a lot of reading to do.'

Lisa looked forward to it. In fact, she looked forward to everything these days. Sitting on the sofa, she glanced up when she heard Jackie stir. In a minute, she'd take her friend in a cup of tea.

She looked forward to going to the theatre every week, particularly to seeing Ralph in that play *Pygmalion* by – she wracked her brains – George Bernard Shaw. She loved her job. When she'd worked in the dye factory, Sundays were spoilt by the thought of tedious, smelly work next morning, whereas the prospect of Mr Greenbaum's bookshop tomorrow held only pleasure. Once there she would contemplate the evening ahead with quiet satisfaction; a period spent reading whilst she ate her meal and listened to the radio until Jackie came home. It was only when she brought Gordon with her that things were not perfect.

It was nice making friends with Piers and Ralph. In fact, life was nicer than it had ever been!

The time spent in London, living with Jackie and working for Mr Greenbaum, was perhaps the most carefree period of Lisa's life. 'The years of innocence', she called them, whenever she looked back . . .

On stage, Ralph was a revelation. At first Lisa didn't recognize him, but hadn't Piers said he played Alfred Doolittle, and wasn't that Alfred Doolittle on stage now? That meant it must be Ralph. This coarse, loud-mouthed, unshaven man, his sagging trousers held up by braces, the sleeves of his collarless shirt rolled up to reveal hairy, muscular arms, this really was the quietly-spoken refined man she'd met last week. The voice, the stance, the manner, were those of a Cockney born in the gutter. It was as if the spirit of some totally different person had taken over Ralph's body.

In the first act, the hilarious speech claiming he was one of the undeserving poor almost brought the house down. Some people even stood up to applaud.

Lisa enjoyed the play more than *Blithe Spirit* – at least, she thought she did. It was difficult to decide.

This Saturday night, Ralph and Piers were coming to the girls' flat for a drink after the performance. Lisa had bought fresh flowers and, allowing for the fact that Jackie would probably drink twice or even three times as much as everybody else, three bottles of wine.

When the two friends arrived, Lisa found she couldn't take her eyes off Ralph. She handed him a glass of wine and when he thanked her, found it incredible to believe that this quietly-modulated voice had so recently filled an entire theatre with its grating power.

Jackie had lost all her inhibitions and was chatting away to Piers about restaurants they both frequented.

'You're quiet, Lisa,' Ralph remarked eventually. 'Didn't you like the play? Were you disappointed by my performance?'

'Oh no!' she said passionately. 'I'm struck dumb with admiration. You were wonderful. I couldn't believe it was really you at first.'

'It's a good part,' he said modestly.

'I think I'd like to be an actor. It must be wonderful to lose yourself like that. I mean, you *were* Alfred Doolittle.'

'You could go to drama classes,' Ralph said

'How could I do that?' she asked eagerly.

'Well, full-time schools like RADA are difficult to get into and the fees are horrendous – and you have to keep yourself.'

Lisa shook her head ruefully. 'Out of the question, I'm afraid.'

'Then you could go to night-school. I know someone who runs a course in Hackney. He charges half-a-crown a lesson.'

Lisa brightened. 'I could afford that much.'

'I'll find out for you,' he promised.

Lisa's life fell into a comfortable pattern. Work, a visit to the theatre every Saturday, then back for drinks with Piers and Ralph, and on Wednesdays her drama class run by a wild-eyed elderly actor, Godfrey Perrick, and his wife, Rosa. She felt like Eliza Doolittle, her Liverpool accent gradually fading as Rosa taught her to speak properly and throw her voice, how to walk and sit gracefully.

Godfrey concentrated on acting itself. They sat in a circle reading from a play and the words came alive when he spoke them. He never criticized, never praised, as they read their lines, just patiently pointed out how a particular phrase could be expressed, to bring out a meaning that they hadn't noticed.

Summer came. The London pavements were hot beneath her feet as Lisa walked to and from Mr Greenbaum's, though once inside the shop it was cool. On Sundays she dragged a sleepy, reluctant Jackie out of bed and they walked to Kensington Gardens at the end of Queen's Gate where they would have coffee in the outdoor restaurant, watch the model boats on the lake and the uniformed nannies wheeling giant prams, with small children in their stiff Sunday clothes following miserably behind.

Autumn. The leaves in the park turned gold and fell from the trees, crunching beneath their feet as they strolled down the narrow concrete paths. It was too cold to sit outside and Jackie suggested they go to a pub for a drink instead.

Lisa bought a winter coat – a real film star's coat in heavy tweed with a wide belt she pulled tight around her narrow waist. Many admiring looks were cast in their direction; at tall voluptuous Jackie with her creamy hair and skin and Lisa, the same height but slim as a model, her dark hair cut shoulder length – she'd had to keep her eyes shut tight whilst Jackie cut whole sheaths off – and arranged in her favourite style – combed low over one eye, like Veronica Lake.

She'd been asked out on lots of dates since she'd come to London. Customers in the shop had approached her, two of the boys in the acting class kept pleading for her to go out with them, and a young man in the flat below had asked her to dinner twice.

Lisa turned them all down. She wanted nothing to do with boyfriends, not yet anyway. Maybe some day she'd feel differently, but in the meantime the men already in her life were quite enough. Harry Greenbaum, Piers and Ralph: they were all she wanted.

Chapter 15

Jackie was going home to Bournemouth for Christmas and she invited Lisa to come with her.

The invitation was tactfully refused. Jackie constantly complained about her parents, particularly her mother.

'You wouldn't believe it, Lisa,' she grumbled. 'My mother's maxim is "a place for everything and everything in its place". The house looks unlived-in, like a museum. You can't put a thing down before it's whisked away and put in a drawer where no one can find it. It drives my father wild. He sits in his surgery, even at night – I've told you he's a dentist, haven't I? It's the only way he can get some peace. The reason why I'm such a slob is probably a reaction against my upbringing.'

Staying with Jackie's parents for two days – the elderly aunts who supplied the clothing coupons would be there too – didn't seem to Lisa the ideal way of spending Christmas. Anyway, as she pointed out, Mr Greenbaum and Miriam had asked her for dinner on Christmas Day.

'I thought Orthodox Jews didn't celebrate Christmas,' said Jackie primly. She usually adopted a rather disapproving manner whenever the Greenbaums were mentioned. Lisa suspected Gordon was an anti-Semite.

'They don't, but they still have to eat,' she answered. 'It'll just be an ordinary Jewish meal. Kosher,' she finished knowledgeably.

She got enormous pleasure buying presents for her family: wooden toys for the little ones, scarves and gloves for her other brothers, brooches for Nellie and Joan and a three-strand pearl necklace with a diamanté clasp for Mam. She wrapped each present individually in holly-patterned paper, tied it with red ribbon and attached little labels to each and imagined the large package arriving in Chaucer Street and the youngsters pouncing, tearing it open and handing the presents round, or perhaps it might come whilst Mam was there alone and she'd put the things on the tree.

She sent a card separately, *'From your own Lizzie with lots and lots of love'* she wrote, but still didn't give her address.

There were heaps of parties to go to. The drama class had a special end-of-term celebration and some students were holding parties of their own. Ralph and Piers had asked her and Jackie in for drinks on the Sunday before Christmas. Piers was also going home for Christmas and Lisa sensed tension between the pair when this was mentioned.

Mr Greenbaum kept his shop open all day Christmas Eve. Lisa said goodbye to Jackie in the morning as she was finishing work at lunch-time and going straight to the station.

'I hope you have a nice Christmas,' Jackie said mournfully when they parted outside Harrods. 'I know I won't.'

'You do not mind, Miss Lisa O'Brien, working on this special day?' Mr Greenbaum asked. 'But you see, all the shops stay open and I might do lots of business this afternoon. Last-minute presents, you know.'

'I mind terribly,' she told him severely. 'But you're such a slave-driver you might sack me if I refused.'

'That's right, taunt an old man, an old man who can't hit back.'

'Whilst you've still got a tongue in your head you'll be able to hit back,' said Lisa. She enjoyed their day-long banter. When they were not talking about books, they traded good-humoured insults.

He sighed. 'Ah, Minnie Kopek! Why did I not listen? You pleaded and pleaded. If only I'd given in, I'd be with you in some heaven and not subjected to the slings and arrows of a wicked wife and a slip of a girl who has no respect for me.'

'Don't give me Minnie Kopek. Who on earth was she anyway?'

'A fat lady. She did a striptease – it was obscene. But I could have rested my head in her ample, ample bosom and had some peace, instead of this . . .' He spread his arms, looked around the shop, at Lisa, and shrugged.

She burst out laughing. 'Come off it, Greenbaum. You love your life, you love Miriam and you love your books.'

'Stop being so clever and so damn right. A Jew enjoys

148

being miserable from time to time. You're spoiling my fun.'

The shop door opened and a boy entered.

'Brian – I haven't seen you in ages. What have you run out of this time? Ink – a typewriter ribbon?' Mr Greenbaum turned to his stationery shelf.

'A ream of foolscap copy paper, please.'

The boy approached the counter, caught sight of Lisa and stopped dead. He stared at her for several seconds, then dropped his eyes in confusion and his baby-smooth cheeks flushed pink. He was good-looking in a rather insipid way, with blond, silky hair and light-blue eyes framed with stubby, almost-white lashes which gave him a short-sighted, frightened look. He looked like a cherubic choirboy. She was amused by the way he kept glancing so furtively in her direction.

Mr Greenbaum also noticed. He said jovially, 'Brian, have you met Lisa? I don't think you've been in since she started. Brian works upstairs,' he explained. 'What sort of office is it? I forget, my old brain . . .'

'Imports and exports,' Brian said. His voice, masculine and deep, belied his youthful looks.

'You've made a conquest,' Mr Greenbaum laughed when he'd gone.

Lisa screwed her face into what Mr Greenbaum called her 'Harrods' expression, a mixture of disgust and disdain. 'A mere child,' she said dismissively.

'He is no child,' said Mr Greenbaum seriously. 'Twenty at least – much older than you. His mother calls for him sometimes and waits outside. She is a dragon. Once she came in and bought a cookery book.'

Someone else entered the shop and Lisa forgot all about Brian.

That evening she walked home along Old Brompton Road. Harrods was closed, though inside, it was still brightly lit, and exhausted assistants were emptying tills and tidying counters. She stopped entranced before each window, as she'd been doing for weeks. After Christmas, these exquisite displays would be dismantled ready for the Sales.

In the first window was a bridal scene, all white and red

velvet, in another a larger-than-life dummy Santa Claus, with elves and fairies clustered at his feet amidst a carpet of real leaves – gold, red, rust. Then the toy window! Even now, at sixteen, Lisa coveted the beautifully dressed dolls with their uncannily-lifelike faces, and wished she could have bought the twins the train-set which chuffed around the floor, in and out of green-painted tunnels, stopping at miniature stations and moving off when the signal fell.

The centrepiece took her breath away. It was a three-storeyed Victorian doll's house, each room furnished with perfect replicas. The chandelier and wall-lights actually worked! A tiny woman stood in the kitchen, hands forever motionless on top of a half-kneaded loaf no bigger than a farthing. In front of the drawing-room fireplace a man in black stood puffing on a pipe whilst his wife sat in a blue brocade armchair sewing, her arm poised in mid-air. Lisa could even seen the glint of a minuscule needle. Children played in the nursery, and in the attic a white-clad woman leaned over a cradle containing a baby.

Lisa sighed. Tomorrow morning some children would be waking up to presents like this, whilst others, through no fault of their own, would get nothing.

The night was balmy, the sky clouded, with a reluctant moon peeping out from time to time to float away almost immediately behind a mass of black. Stars twinkled brightly in the few clear patches of dark blue. It was so different from Liverpool where, right now, icy winds were probably blowing in from the Irish Sea and whipping down the streets.

Shops were emptying, doors were locked, assistants poured out onto the pavements, chattering excitedly, the fatigue of the busy Christmas season falling away as they began their journey home to commence their two-day holiday. Last-minute shoppers, laden with parcels, stood on the kerb, vainly yelling for a taxi.

Outside Brompton Oratory a circle of carol singers stood, their silvery voices scarcely audible against the roar of traffic. As Lisa passed, the faint strains of *The Holly And The Ivy* could just be heard above the noise.

Houses, their doors hung with holly wreaths, had trees

glittering in front windows, rooms laden with decorations.

The atmosphere was almost heady, filled with a sense of delicious anticipation. Lisa felt an excited thrill run through her. Tonight, she was going to yet another party. Tomorrow, to the Greenbaums for dinner, though on Boxing Day she would be alone. Not that she minded. In fact, she was looking forward to a quiet day spent reading.

Tonight's party was in Lambeth, where Barbara from the drama class lived. Someone was calling for her at eight o'clock. She'd wear her green taffeta dress with the heart-shaped neckline and three-quarter-length sleeves. The skirt was an entire circle of material and she loved the feel of it swirling against her legs when she moved. The only problem would be fighting off John and Barry, who'd both been pestering her to go out with them for months. At every party one of them attempted to capture her for a 'snogging session' as they called it, where couples sat for hours and hours in darkened rooms, clutched in what seemed like an endless, suffocating and rather boring embrace.

'Never mind,' thought Lisa serenely. 'I'll get rid of them somehow. I always do.'

The Greenbaums lived on the ground floor of a rather gloomy block of flats in Chelsea. Lisa had already been there several times. The inside of the flat matched the façade of the building and was filled with dark, heavy furniture lavishly decorated with carvings and scrolls. Miriam had covered every surface with ornaments and photographs of long-dead relatives from Austria.

She'd gone to great trouble with the meal.

To start with there was barley soup, followed, to Lisa's surprise, by chicken in wine sauce served with giblet stuffing, fried potatoes and mixed vegetables.

'I don't usually cook in wine, but seeing as it's Christmas . . .' Miriam winked.

Lisa declared the food delicious but said she'd expected something entirely different. 'I thought kosher food would be more . . . well, foreign. Things I'd never eaten before.'

Miriam and her husband exchanged amused glances.

'Kosher food is the same as your food, but prepared in a

different way, that's all. The animals are killed — '

'Don't tell her, not while she's eating!' choked Mr Greenbaum. 'Have some tact, woman. You'll be describing your operations next.'

Pudding was an unusual apple tart. Miriam said it was called 'strudel'.

'That's the nicest meal I've ever eaten,' Lisa said when they'd finished.

Miriam looked gratified. 'It's pleasant to have some appreciation for a change,' she said sarcastically. 'This man here! Never a word of thanks he gives me, even though I slave over a hot stove all day to fill his guts with decent food.'

Mr Greenbaum winked at Lisa.

Over the afternoon and evening, a good-natured argument raged. It appeared Miriam wanted her husband to work part-time in the shop.

'You're a stubborn old goat, Greenbaum, staggering off every day, putting in eight hours. For what? We have enough money. Lis. can look after the place on her own. You're lucky to have her.'

'My shop is my life,' the old man said simply.

'Are you saying I'm not?' Miriam countered furiously.

'Of course you're not! You're a boil on my bum. You think I'd stay at home with you when I can spend my time with a lovely young woman like this?' He gestured towards Lisa.

'I could compete with Lisa once.' Miriam nodded with satisfaction. 'Some day, she will be old too.'

'When Lisa's old, I'll give up the shop.'

'Tch! What do you think, Lisa?'

'I'm not taking sides,' said Lisa with alacrity. She sat contentedly sipping blackberry wine and nibbling frosted coffee biscuits. Privately she thought Mr Greenbaum should work as long as he wanted.

The argument continued and Minnie Kopek was not mentioned once.

On Boxing Day, Lisa had intended to sleep in but she woke at seven and found it impossible to drift off again. After a while, she got up. She dressed in slacks and a white blouse, made a pot of tea and picked up her latest book, *Vanity Fair*.

She loved the character of Becky Sharpe – such a scheming minx and terribly hard-hearted.

Later on, she walked to Kensington Gardens, which to her surprise was crowded. Several little girls were pushing their new dolls' prams and looking very self-important, and a little boy careered wildly along the path, his small feet straining on the pedals of a bright red racing car. By the pond, fathers hovered anxiously as their sons sailed their new model yachts, advising them how to adjust the rigging, some watching in despair as the boats fell sideways and the sails filled with water.

A young couple came towards her, the man in soldier's uniform, his arm round the waist of a girl not much older than herself. With one hand each, they pushed a well-used pram and as they passed she saw a baby girl inside about nine months old playing happily with a rattle.

A sudden feeling of homesickness overcame her. Last January, Kevin had proudly announced that his wife Colette was expecting a baby. Kitty had been thrilled to bits – her first grandchild! In Liverpool, there was a niece or nephew Lisa had never seen and was never likely to see.

Her family! Would they be thinking about her too?

Blinking furiously to keep back the tears, she rushed home.

Not a sound came from behind the closed doors of the flats in Number 5 Queen's Gate as Lisa ran upstairs, not a single voice or note of music. Nearly everyone had gone away, though Ralph had stayed behind. Perhaps he had no family to go to. Later on, she heard dishes rattling in the kitchen and contemplated taking her own along to wash, pretending to meet him by accident, but although Ralph was friendly, it was a reserved sort of friendliness, as though he was just being nice to please Piers and would far sooner have nothing to do with her or Jackie.

It was impossible to get back into her novel. No matter how hard she tried, she couldn't stop thinking about home. She mended some stockings and tidied the flat. As she dusted the dressing table she noticed Jackie's bottle of whisky and stared at it thoughtfully. It seemed to help Jackie cope with her problems. She fetched a glass and poured out an inch, sipping it cautiously. Almost immediately her body was flooded with warmth. She sipped more and her head began to swim. It was a pleasant sensation and coupled with it came the feeling that things were not so bad after all. She drank some more. In fact, life was rather good. As if the sun had risen inside her head, everything turned rosy and she sat on the sofa, contented and sleepy.

There was a knock on the door. It must be Ralph. Too lazy to get up, she shouted, 'Come in.'

To her utter astonishment, Gordon entered the room. Jackie must have given him a front-door key.

'What on earth do you want?' It sounded rude, but she didn't care. 'Jackie's away. Didn't she tell you?'

'It's not Jackie I've come to see,' he said with an unpleasant leer.

'Well, I don't want to see you,' she said firmly.

She might just as well have not spoken. He sat down beside her and she glared at him, wishing now she didn't feel so dizzy and could get to her feet, open the door and order him out. What on earth did the man want? She was dumbfounded by his next words.

'C'mon, Lisa – I've seen you looking at me. You're really turned on, aren't you?'

She regarded him contemptuously. 'Turned on – by *you*!'

The scorn in her voice seemed to reach him. He looked angry. His blotchy cheeks flushed blood-red and his eyes narrowed. The ends of his silly, oversized moustache literally quivered with fury.

'You're a sexy little bitch. Don't think I haven't noticed the way you flaunt yourself around when I'm here.'

'When you're here, all I want to do is be sick.' The whisky seemed to have banished all her inhibitions. She said the first thing that came into her head. 'The thought of you and Jackie together turns my stomach. She's a million times too good for you.'

'Jackie likes a good poke and that's what I give her. Don't you want a good poke, Lisa? Lisa the sexy bitch.'

'If you don't get out immediately, I'll tell Jackie,' she spat.

'Fuck Jackie. I'd sooner have something going with you.'

He clumsily dragged her towards him and she felt his unsavoury breath on her cheek. Then he began to kiss her, his hands fumbling with her breasts. She struggled and screamed, 'Get off me, you bastard.'

'C'mon, Lisa, you're driving me mad. You want it, I know you do.'

She screamed again, but his arms were strong and although she fought, she could not escape his embrace. He tore at her blouse and bent his head to her throat.

Suddenly, she felt him being lifted off her.

Ralph! Ralph had him by the scruff of the neck and threw him onto the floor where he crouched on all fours like an animal, saliva dripping from his mouth.

'Get out,' said Ralph quietly. 'Get out, before I kick you down the stairs, all four flights of them.'

'Bloody pansy,' croaked Gordon, crawling out of reach.

Ralph took a step towards him. '*Out*, I said.'

He crawled along the floor until he reached a chair and pulled himself to his feet. One half of his moustache drooped down over his mouth like an untidy tassle.

At the door, he turned and his expression was obsequious.

'You won't tell Jackie?' he asked in a fawning voice.

Lisa didn't answer.

'*OUT*,' said Ralph.

Chapter 16

They listened to his descending footsteps until they faded and soon afterwards came a faint thud as the front door was slammed shut. Lisa glanced at Ralph and they both burst out laughing.

'What a slimy character!' said Ralph eventually. 'What on earth does Jackie see in him?'

Lisa shook her head in perplexity. 'I don't know. She's in love and love's blind, so they say.' She attempted to stand, but her head swam and she fell back onto the sofa.

'Are you all right? Do you want something?'

'I'm drunk, Ralph. I've never been drunk before. I've been drinking Jackie's whisky. I felt so depressed. I think I'd better make some tea to sober myself up.'

'You should have come to see me – I feel depressed too. In fact, I've been contemplating knocking on your door all day but thought you might prefer to be alone.' He got up, a sturdy, comfortable figure, his usually withdrawn features animated by the recent excitement. 'I'll put the kettle on.'

'There's water already in it,' she said, adding quickly, 'I forgot to thank you. You saved my life, you're not half tough.'

'Not half tough!' He smiled. 'I doubt if it was your life I saved, just your virtue.'

'Oh, that's long gone,' she answered dismissively and could have bitten off her tongue, though he didn't seem to notice.

'What's making you so miserable, Lisa?'

'Just missing my family, that's all. I went to Kensington Gardens and there was a baby. I remembered I have a niece or nephew I've never seen. And you?'

He echoed her words. 'Just missing my family, that's all.'

'Couldn't you go home and visit them?'

'My wife and children, you mean?'

She gaped. 'You're married.'

'She's divorcing me – quite rightly. My parents have disowned me. Piers has gone, temporarily. I realized I was completely alone. It was getting to me more and more. Fortunately for me, *un*fortunately for you, you screamed and broke the spell, the bad spell.'

He poured two mugs of tea and brought them over. 'Can you hold this?'

'I'm not that bad. It's my legs and head mainly, they're all swimmy.' She began to sip the tea eagerly. 'I'll never drink so much so quickly again,' she swore.

'An excellent idea. I'll drink to that.' He held up his mug.

'I just wanted to blot things out, stop thoughts coming.'

'Ah, if only we could!' he said sadly. 'I've been thinking about my kids all day. Imagining how Christmas could be, how it used to be, you know, the few years we were together.'

'What happened? I don't want to seem nosy. Don't answer if I am, but why did you get married?' She glanced at him and wondered how she could ever have thought he looked anonymous. There was anguish in his eyes and his mouth was twisted bitterly.

'I got married because it was the thing to do. All men – well, most men – did it. And I thought I was in love. I can't have been, but I genuinely thought I was. How are you supposed to know what love is? My marriage wasn't perfect, sex was nothing like it was cracked up to be, but maybe it wasn't for anybody.'

He sighed. Lisa watched but said nothing.

'Then I was called up,' he went on. 'I'd never lived with men before. Suddenly it all seemed more natural. I felt more at ease, more myself, my real self. Then I was captured, went in a prisoner-of-war camp and . . . well, you can guess the rest.' He shrugged. 'Once home, I wrote to my wife and told her everything. I knew she'd be shocked, but the letter I got back! Full of filthy insults. The children have been told I'm dead.'

'That's awful.' Lisa laid her hand on his arm. He turned and made an effort to smile.

'Sorry. I'm heaping all my problems on you and making you even more depressed. I've been drinking too, you know. Wine, one bottle, two . . . I can't remember.'

'Don't be sorry, go on,' she urged. 'A trouble shared is a trouble halved.' That was one of Kitty's favourite sayings.

'In the camp I got involved in dramatics. To my amazement, I found I was good at acting. It seemed the logical thing to do when I got home.' He was holding the mug tightly in both hands and she saw the knuckles turn white.

'You know what I want more than anything, Lisa?'

'What?' she murmured.

'To become a famous star. For Ralph Layton to become a household name, like Charles Laughton or Laurence Olivier, then one day my wife might tell the kids who I am, that I'm not dead after all. Maybe things will have changed by then. They won't care that I'm a pansy, a faggot, a queer or any other insulting word you can think of which describes what God made me. Do you think I'll become a star, Lisa?'

'I hope so,' she whispered. 'I sincerely hope so. Anyway, Piers will be back tomorrow and — '

He interrupted harshly. 'Not tomorrow – next week. It's not just a two-day break at the old de Villiers ancestral home, you know. Piers will be having a whale of a time. Of course, he can't take me, as they don't know about . . . He'll be flirting with some girl, softening her up for tonight.'

'You mean Piers — ?'

'Oh, yes. He likes women, though not so much as men. That's why, when he brought you along, I thought . . .' He stopped and shook his head. 'Enough!' he cried in a deep stentorian voice which made Lisa jump. 'You know, you're right – I *do* feel better. Now I've bared my soul, it's your turn. Where's that bloody whisky?'

He half-filled a glass and gestured towards Lisa. 'C'mon, have some more. Help get things off your chest.'

'Do you think I should? Drink, I mean.'

'On second thoughts, no, though you're quite safe with me.'

'I've told you what's wrong. I'm missing my family, that's all.'

'No it isn't, you're holding something back. I could tell when we first met. You're a very deep and mysterious woman for only sixteen. You've lived life far more than Jackie. I can see it in your eyes.'

There was something inherently appealing about confiding in someone, someone as warm and understanding as Ralph, the things she had told no one. Not a single person in the world knew about that day in Southport.

So she told him. Everything, including Tom and his bloody death.

The day grew dark. Neither bothered to switch on the light and by the time she'd finished, the room was illuminated only by the dim, shadowy moon.

He didn't speak for a long, long time. Eventually he sighed and said softly, 'My dear girl, I admire you more than words can say. What a fight you've had. Let's hope you'll always be on the winning side.'

She began to cry softly and he took her hand. They sat together, silently, companionably, until she feel asleep. When she woke, his head had fallen on her shoulder and he was snoring and she quickly dozed off again, grateful for the proximity of his warm, comforting body.

It was daylight when an astonished Jackie came home and found them.

'Sorry, I can't. I have a drama class tonight.'

'Well, what about tomorrow?'

'I wash my hair on Thursdays.'

Brian blinked, obviously considering whether to suggest another day.

Lisa prayed he wouldn't. She didn't want to go out with him and wished he'd take the hint and stop asking. Ever since Christmas Eve, he'd been coming into the shop once or twice a week. Mr Greenbaum had rubbed his hands and ordered more stationery because, as he said with a grin, Brian was rapidly emptying the shelves.

'I wonder if it gets used in the office or does he take it home?' he mused one day. 'Have pity on the boy, Lisa, persuade him to buy books instead. At least he can read them. He must have a dozen bottles of red ink and there is a limit to what a man can do with red ink, other than pretend he is Dracula and drink it!'

Today he'd come for a box of HB pencils. Lisa put them in a paper bag and gave them to him, smiling kindly.

He left the shop looking disconsolate, his head bent to guard against the torrential rain.

The weather this April was actually colder than it had been in December. Rain had fallen relentlessly for days. Jackie and Lisa had been forced to catch a bus to work and Mr Greenbaum had been coming and going in a taxi. Now, Lisa went into the kitchen to check that the hem of her fawn trenchcoat had dried. It had got soaked in the scurry from the bus stop to the shop. The hem was dry but crumpled. She'd iron it when she got home. Lisa was proud of her trenchcoat and wore it with the collar up and her hands stuffed in the pockets, just like Barbara Stanwyck. She was folding the umbrella which had been left standing in the sink to drip, when the shop door opened.

She hurried back. A middle-aged man had entered and was shaking himself on the mat. She blinked at his attire: a loud black chalk-striped suit, patent-leather shoes, topped by a massive sheepskin coat with a fur collar. He removed his hat, a soft suede fedora sporting a bright feather, and began to blow the raindrops off with loud puffs. Lisa wanted to laugh.

'Morry Sopel,' said Mr Greenbaum disapprovingly. This customer, she sensed, was not welcome. 'What can I do for you?'

'Exchange a few words, Harry, that's all. I was in the area on business, I saw your shop and thought to myself, "I've not seen Harry Greenbaum in a long, long time."' He pulled off his suede gloves to reveal dark, hairy hands.

'I have shed no tears over that,' the old man said frostily.

'Harry, boy, don't hurt my feelings.' The man waved his hands. His fingers were covered in rings and a wide gold bracelet gleamed on his thick wrist. He had dark, good-natured eyes and had once been very handsome, though now his chin was slack and deep lines ran down from his nose to the corner of his wide mouth.

He looked up and saw Lisa standing at the top of the stairs.

'Well!' he said, whistling appreciatively. 'I didn't know you had help, Harry. And what help!'

Lisa wore a pale blue polo-necked jumper and a cream skirt with matching high-heeled court shoes. Her hair was parted in the middle and smoothed back behind her pearl-studded ears. She wore little make-up, just shell-pink lipstick and a touch of brown shadow above the eyes. Each morning, she smeared a little vaseline on her long black lashes to give them a silky look.

For some reason she couldn't fathom, Lisa found it difficult to take offence at the newcomer's open admiration. To please Mr Greenbaum, she didn't smile, but came down the stairs into the shop without a word.

'This is Miss Lisa O'Brien.' The old man introduced her reluctantly. 'Morry Sopel is an old . . . acquaintance.'

'How do you do, Miss Lisa O'Brien.' He shook hands, his grip warm and friendly. Mr Greenbaum glowered in their direction. 'Tell me,' said Morry. 'Is it nearly time for this lovely young lady to take lunch? If so, will she do me the honour — '

Mr Greenbaum interrupted, his voice gritty with anger. 'No, she will not.'

'Can't Lisa answer for herself?' said the visitor, his eyes crinkling with amusement.

'I am answering for her. She works for me. She is my responsibility and what's more, she is almost engaged to be married.'

Lisa glanced at him in astonishment.

The visitor was persistent. 'But lunch won't hurt, surely?'

'He works upstairs, her boyfriend, the almost-fiancé. He will be angry if he sees Lisa leave with another man. Won't he, my dear?'

'Why, er . . . yes,' she stammered.

Morry Sopel shrugged philosophically. 'Never mind. It isn't often I come across such a vision. I would have enjoyed treating Lisa to a slap-up lunch in Harrods.'

Lisa would have quite enjoyed it too. She rather liked this garishly dressed visitor and felt slightly irritated by her employer's proprietorial attitude, though she said nothing.

After the man had gone, she was quiet. Mr Greenbaum kept glancing in her direction and eventually he said, 'You're angry with me.'

'No, no,' she protested.

'Yes, you are, I can tell. But Lisa, he is a bad man, that

Morry Sopel. A bad, bad man.'

'He seemed all right to me.'

'Oh, he has charm, I grant you that. Women fall for him. His poor wife left him many years ago, broken-hearted. So many other women she had to put up with.'

'But as he said, lunch wouldn't hurt,' she muttered defensively.

'Ach, Lisa! Forgive me. I was wrong to interfere, but believe me, Morry Sopel is not a man to eat with. Not lunch. Not anything. He mixes with evil people.'

She smiled, convinced the old man was exaggerating. He saw her smile and when he spoke again, his voice trembled with emotion. 'I cannot put it too strongly, my child. Now he has seen you, he may come back. Promise me you will have nothing to do with that gangster.'

'Gangster!' she gasped.

'Yes. That's what Morry Sopel is – a gangster, involved with thieves and murderers. How he has escaped prison, I do not know. Now, promise me, Lisa.'

'I promise,' she said, and shuddered.

The following week, Brian bought her flowers – deep red roses wrapped in silver foil. Mr Greenbaum was just about to leave for lunch as he came in.

'A visitor for you, Lisa,' he said with a mischievous grin.

She was embarrassed and angry. Why on earth wouldn't this boy leave her alone? It wasn't fair to keep pressurizing her.

'I wondered what you were doing on Saturday,' he asked boldly after she had thanked him, trying to keep the irritation out of her voice.

'I'm going to the theatre,' she said. 'With a friend.'

'Sunday, then?'

'I'm sorry.' She tried to make it sound final, to deter him from asking again.

A woman customer entered and Lisa left Brian to attend to her. She was wrapping up the purchase when Morry Sopel came in. He wore the same clothes as before, though this time, his expensive coat hung open to reveal a diamond flashing on his bright blue and green tie. Over the head of the customer, he gave her a massive wink. She regarded him coolly and when the woman left, he came over.

'I waited till I saw old Harry go. Thought I'd ask you out to lunch without the presence of a chaperone who wouldn't even let you speak.'

She felt her insides quiver. This man was a gangster – a real live gangster like Humphrey Bogart or Edward G. Robinson.

'The answer's the same – no,' she said shortly.

He looked unabashed. 'Dinner, then? The Savoy, Claridges? Ever been there?'

'No,' she said. 'And I've no wish to.'

'Come off it,' he said. 'Every girl likes dinner in a top hotel. Five courses, the best wine.'

Privately, Lisa agreed. She would have loved to go to Claridges or the Savoy. 'This girl doesn't,' she lied. 'Anyway, as Harry said, I've got a boyfriend.'

'Don't believe it!' he said flatly and his dark eyes flashed with fun. 'He was lying, was old Harry. He's too honest a man to lie. It doesn't work.'

'He wasn't lying.'

Brian! Lisa had forgotten he was there. He emerged from behind a row of shelves looking and sounding remarkably self-assured. 'I'm Lisa's boyfriend and tonight we're going out to dinner.'

Morry looked disappointed. 'Ah, well. No harm in trying. Goodbye, Lisa. And goodbye to you, young man. You are a lucky fellow. Tell me when you get engaged and I'll send a present.'

That Sunday, Brian took her out to tea then to the pictures.

It had been impossible to refuse his invitation after he had rescued her from Morry. In fact, he turned out to be surprisingly good company. Clearly infatuated, he was attentive, opening doors, pulling back her chair in the restaurant, paying for the best seats in the cinema where they saw *Anchors Away*. It was such a happy film and Gene Kelly's dancing was sheer magic.

Brian didn't say much himself, but he was a good, almost avid listener. She told him about going to see plays every

163

week and getting the tickets off a real-life actor who lived in a flat on the same floor as her own and who was in *Pygmalion* at a theatre not far from where they were now, about her acting classes and Jackie and her awful boyfriend.

'And Piers, he also lives on our floor, is an interior decorator and presently is working for some duchess, I forget her name.'

'Really!'

When they came out of the cinema he spoiled things a bit by saying, 'It would be nice to go for coffee, but I promised Mother I'd be home before ten.'

At the door of Number 5 Queen's Gate, she said, 'I won't ask you in, else you might be late for your mother.'

He was aware of the touch of sarcasm in her voice and muttered something about his mother wanting help with filling in a form.

'Then you'd better hurry,' said Lisa in a chilly voice, thus firing the first shots in the battle which would one day commence between herself and Mrs Dorothy Smith.

When Lisa got in, Jackie was already bathed and ready for bed, clad in lemon silk pyjamas and a short matching dressing gown. She was lounging on the sofa drinking whisky.

'What was he like?' she asked in a blurred voice which told that this drink was not her first.

Lisa wrinkled her nose and said, 'A bit impressionable.'

Jackie giggled. 'You make it sound like he's a little boy.'

'In some ways he is.' Then she recalled the uncompromising manner in which he had dealt with Morry Sopel. 'And in other ways he's very manly and grown up. All in all, I quite enjoyed myself.'

'I suppose you'll be going out with him again?' said Jackie.

'Next Sunday.' He'd pleaded to see her earlier, but she'd been firm, not wanting the relationship to become serious.

'Oh dear, I hate you going out on Sundays. I've got used to you being here.'

'I'll make it another day,' Lisa said quickly. 'Brian won't mind.'

'I wouldn't hear of it.' Jackie was vehement. 'I shouldn't

have complained. After all, I leave you alone most nights till gone eight.'

'We could make up a foursome,' suggested Lisa tentatively. Jackie looked so pretty with her damp curls sticking to her fresh peachy skin and it seemed a waste for her to sit alone in the flat saving herself for that awful man she loved. 'What about this chap in the office who keeps asking you out?'

Predictably, her friend answered: 'Oh, I couldn't possibly do that! I would be betraying Gordon.'

'But he's with his wife all weekend. Isn't that betraying you?'

'Oh no, Lisa. That's a different thing altogether.'

Although Lisa wished they could continue the conversation, she said no more. She hadn't told Jackie about Gordon's visit on Boxing Day, though she agonized over whether this was the right decision. Her main worry was that even if her friend knew, she wouldn't love the man any less, but just be more miserable with the knowledge – and she would make excuses for him, like he'd had too much to drink or he'd thought Jackie would be home sooner. She'd feel guilty about Lisa, too.

So she said nothing, but noticed that ever since Christmas, Gordon's manner with Jackie had been increasingly offhand, almost cruel. At times the poor girl was thoroughly wretched.

Lisa sighed. 'I'll make us a cup of tea,' she said.

Chapter 17

The following Saturday, Lisa woke Jackie before she went to work. 'We're having a party tonight,' she said.

Jackie struggled to sit up, blinking. 'A party! Why?'

'It was my birthday the other day – I'm seventeen.'

'Lisa! You should have told me – I haven't bought you a present. Who's coming to this party?'

'You don't mind, do you? After all, it's your flat.'

'Of course I don't mind. I love parties.'

Lisa had deliberately not told Jackie before, in case she invited Gordon. Although he was supposed to be unavailable at weekends, on odd occasions he had appeared on the scene. Now it was too late for him to be contacted.

'Piers is coming, of course, and Ralph, though he'll be late. I invited the drama class, too, though not all of them can come. And poor Mr Greenbaum can't manage the stairs, I'm afraid.'

'What about food?'

'Sandwiches and biscuits, that's all, And of course, wine. I'll buy it on my way home from the shop.' Lisa finished at one o'clock on Saturdays.

'Oh, Lisa! I'm glad you came into my life. You've made it so much more interesting – something always seems to be happening.'

For her birthday present, Mr Greenbaum gave her a set of Jane Austen novels bound in dark green, gold-tooled leather inside their own special case.

She was so delighted that she spontaneously kissed his yellow wrinkled cheek.

'Thank you, thank you,' she breathed. 'I loved the books so much, I know I shall want to read them over and over again.'

'There's two there you haven't read,' he said. 'And I shan't tell Miriam about the kiss for fear she'll come in here and kill you.'

'Give her a kiss from me.'

'What, kiss that awful woman? Never!' Suddenly, his old face crumpled into an expression she couldn't at first identify. Was it fear? He leaned on the desk to steady himself then sank into his chair.

'What is it?' she asked, alarmed.

'Nothing, nothing. An old man being stupid.'

'Tell me,' she insisted. 'You look as if you're frightened.'

'I am frightened. A thought crossed my mind that when next you read *Pride And Prejudice*, I will be dead.'

'Don't be silly! Of course you won't.'

'Lisa, Lisa, don't patronize. I'm nearly eighty. Inside my head I feel eighteen. How I would have liked to go to your party with my lovely Miriam.'

She began to wish she'd held the party somewhere else, so that he could have come without difficulty.

He saw her concern and gave a disgusted grunt. 'Ach! What a neurotic old man I am, behaving like this on your birthday. Harry Greenbaum, pull yourself together.' He began to sing *Look For The Silver Lining* in guttural bass tones that made her giggle.

'There,' he said after a few lines, 'That's as much as I know and in cheering you up I've cheered myself.'

'Are you sure?'

'Sure I'm sure. Tonight at eight o'clock, when your party starts, Miriam and I shall drink your health. I hope you have as full and as happy a life as I've had, Lisa.'

'So do I,' she said fervently.

She remembered Kitty when the crowd sang 'Happy Birthday'. Jackie put out the lights and came in with a large cake she'd bought that afternoon: seventeen flickering candles, each set in a white rose and LISA written in pink on the smooth white icing surface. As Lisa laughingly blew out the candles, the guests began to sing and she immediately thought of her mam. Even when they were little and there was no money for presents or special food, they still sang 'Happy Birthday' when they sat down to their scouse or bread and jam or whatever Kitty could afford.

She was crying when the lights came on but everyone

thought it was just the emotion of the moment. Except Ralph. As Jackie began to cut the cake he came and sat by Lisa.

'Sad?'

'A bit.'

'I thought you might be.' He squeezed her hand and Piers glanced at them curiously. Since Boxing Day a bond had been forged between Lisa and Ralph. Jackie had noticed it too.

'You are my greatest friend,' she whispered.

'I'm honoured.' He smiled.

'We'll always be friends, even if we don't see much of each other in the future.'

'Always. You can count on me if you're ever in trouble.'

Decades were to pass before Ralph had to keep this promise.

Brian was annoyed to learn that she'd had a party and not invited him.

'It went on till two o'clock this morning,' said Lisa mischievously. 'And I thought your mother might not like you being out so late.' In truth, it hadn't crossed her mind to ask him.

'Do you like my watch?' She pulled back her sleeve and revealed a tiny gold watch on an expanding bracelet. 'It's from Jackie.'

The one Jackie had lent her originally had been returned a long time ago, and Lisa had bought herself a cheap chrome model, which her friend declared looked like a boy's, which indeed it was.

'And I got lots of perfume and jewellery, a set of Jane Austen's novels from Mr Greenbaum and a lovely doll off Ralph.'

'A doll?'

On Boxing Day she must have told Ralph about looking at the dolls in Harrods' window, for he'd bought her a two-foot high Victorian doll with real hair set in ringlets. Only that morning she and Jackie had sat on the floor staring in admiration at the doll, carefully placed on the sofa. It stared back at them with wide blue expressionless eyes.

'What will you call her?' Jackie had asked.

'Victoria – or does that lack imagination?'

'No, Victoria's just right. Just look at those buttons! I mean – they're real, you can undo them.'

'I know,' gloated Lisa. 'I undressed her earlier on. You should see her pantaloons. They're trimmed with lace – and so are her petticoats.'

'Really? Can I play with her this afternoon when you're out?'

'As long as you're careful.'

Then they had both collapsed on the floor in giggles.

'Yes, a doll,' said Lisa to Brian. 'She's lovely. I've called her Victoria.'

Brian looked mystified. Later on, he bought the largest box of chocolates in the cinema kiosk.

'Happy birthday,' he said stiffly. Lisa felt guilty. His feelings were obviously hurt so she was especially nice.

They saw a film called *Rope* with James Stewart. Brian said it was based on a true murder which had happened in America in the nineteen-thirties. It was so gripping that for two hours Lisa forgot where she was.

'That was marvellous,' she whispered when they stood up for the National Anthem.

'Alfred Hitchcock's films always are.'

'Alfred Hitchcock? What part did he play?'

'He was the director. Mother and I see all his films.'

Although he mentioned his mother several times during the evening, Brian didn't say he had to be home early, and suggested they go for coffee. When Lisa invited him back to Queen's Gate instead, he jumped at the idea.

At the flat, Jackie was wafting round clad only in pyjamas and clutching the inevitable glass of whisky. Brian looked embarrassed and Lisa smiled. He was such a baby sometimes.

After she'd seen him out, Jackie said, 'He couldn't take his eyes off you. He's definitely smitten.'

'Is he? I hadn't really noticed,' Lisa said dismissively.

'He's very good-looking, too.'

Lisa grinned. 'I hadn't noticed that, either.'

'I reckon Alan Ladd might have looked a little bit like Brian when he was very young.'

Lisa's opinion of Brian suddenly improved by leaps and bounds, and for the first time she felt flattered to be going out with him. After all, not many girls could claim a youthful Alan Ladd as a boyfriend.

This year, summer was not so fine as last year. The days were misty and damp with just occasional periods of fine hot weather, though autumn was as lovely as ever.

'This is my favourite season,' Lisa said to Jackie as they tramped through Kensington Gardens one bracing October day. A shower of leaves fell from a tree in front and Lisa ran forward, hands outstretched. 'Come on,' she shouted. 'Catch a leaf and make a wish, it's sure to come true.'

'My wishes never come true,' Jackie said bitterly.

'Oh dear!' Lisa came back and took her friend's hand. 'What are we going to do with you?'

Jackie gave a wistful smile. 'Make Gordon love me as much as Brian loves you,' she said. 'Catch a leaf, Lisa, and wish that for me.'

Lisa was seeing Brian twice a week, on Sundays and Thursdays. They nearly always went to the cinema. He searched through the newspapers to find where Hitchcock films were showing and sometimes they travelled out into the suburbs where they saw *Notorious* with Cary Grant and Ingrid Bergman, who was too lovely for words and also starred in the next film they saw, *Spellbound*, with Gregory Peck. Lisa fell in love instantly.

She enthused when they got outside, 'If I was younger, I'd send for his photograph.'

Brian looked annoyed. 'I didn't think he was all *that* handsome,' he said disparagingly.

'Oh Brian, he's *gorgeous*.'

Spurred on perhaps by jealousy, that was the night Brian proposed for the first time. Flattered, Lisa turned him down gently. He was a nice boy, but too immature. Most of the time she felt years older than him, though one day he would make a fine man.

Undaunted, he invited her to tea next Sunday to meet his

mother.

Lisa remembered Mr Greenbaum's description of Mrs Smith. She was a dragon, he'd said. She told him about the anticipated visit next day, knowing he would have some awful tale to tell about Miriam's mother. True to form, he shuddered and said, 'Ach! Mothers-in-law.'

Lisa laughed. 'Was Miriam's mother a dragon?'

'Worse than a dragon, a Brontosaurus Rex. My own mother, she was a reasonable woman, a lovely mother, but as a mother-in-law she was a different person. A monster. Mothers become schizophrenic when their children get married. They show an entirely different face to the poor new son- or daughter-in-law.' He wagged his finger cautiously. 'Put your armour on this Sunday, Lisa. Be prepared for war.'

Lisa wore her new tweed suit — Jackie had advised her to buy one. 'They're useful whenever you're stuck for something to wear, and a suit always looks smart.'

The two-piece was fawn tweed, with a brown velvet collar. Lisa wore it with a frilly cream blouse and brown court shoes.

Brian's mother lived in Chiswick in a road of identical semi-detached houses, each front door containing a panel of stained glass.

'Mother loves her house, it's her pride and joy,' Brian said once.

Lisa couldn't understand why. Once inside, she thought the house unremarkable. There were few ornaments and no pictures, the carpets were faded and the curtains didn't match the wallpaper. It was scrupulously clean, but that was all. It entirely lacked imagination or originality. Although it was Christmas next week, there were no decorations up.

Mrs Smith was a reflection of her house. A tall bulky woman, she used no make-up and her dull, mouse-coloured hair was cut short and permed almost to a frizz. She wore a beige rayon dress with a V-shaped neck and long, ill-fitting sleeves which did absolutely nothing for her. Around the place where her waist had once been, a matching belt strained in the final hole. Lisa noticed the seams were rucked and badly pressed, and realized the woman had made the dress herself. Her only jewellery was a wedding ring which

bit into the flesh of her finger. Brian had once said that his
mother had had him when she was twenty-one. That meant
this woman was only forty-two. She looked well into her
fifties! It was as if she was determined on middle age and
made no attempt to halt it – indeed, encouraged it.

Mrs Smith was looking Lisa up and down quite openly as if
her son had brought home a piece of meat that needed to be
examined, then accepted or rejected if found wanting. It
seemed that at any minute, she might squeeze her wrists to
check her bones. Lisa felt annoyed.

'How do you do?' she said boldly, and stuck out her hand.

Almost grudgingly Mrs Smith shook it. She smelled
strongly of mothballs. 'Sit down,' she said gruffly.

Lisa sat on the rust-coloured armchair, dislodging one of
the lace-trimmed linen arm-covers. Mrs Smith sprang over
and straightened it. There was silence. Lisa glanced around
for a photograph of Mr Smith, for surely that must be who
Brian took after. Delicately-boned and fine-featured, he was
nothing like his mother. There was none.

Brian sat on the edge of the settee and coughed nervously.
'Lisa works in a bookshop, Mother. On the ground floor of
our company.'

'You told me,' said Mrs Smith. 'What does your father do,
Lisa?'

Lisa was taken aback. It was the last question she'd
expected. 'He's dead,' she answered.

'I'm sorry to hear that. What did he die of?'

I murdered him. She felt an almost hysterical desire to tell
the truth, just to see Mrs Smith and Brian's reactions.

'He had an accident at work,' she lied. 'He was on the
docks, you see.'

'A docker?' said Mrs Smith, making no attempt to disguise
her contempt. Lisa felt annoyed again and rather to her
dismay, found herself disliking the woman intensely.
Despite Harry Greenbaum's warnings, she'd come with an
open mind, hoping to become friends with Brian's mother.

'He was a foreman. A ton of rice fell on him one day when
he was supervising the unloading.'

'Ah, a foreman.' Mrs Smith nodded her head less critically
and Lisa wanted to shout, '*It's me that matters, not what my*

father did. I'm the one Brian's going out with.'

'And your mother?'

'She's dead too. I'm an orphan.' Lisa felt her heart twist as she told the lie, but it seemed the best way to stop Mrs Smith from prying.

The woman's next words dumbfounded her. Turning to her son, she said, 'You didn't tell me she was an orphan,' as if Lisa wasn't there.

'I didn't know,' mumbled Brian.

'Have you been submitting a report on me?' She smiled at him, unconsciously separating him from the disagreeable relationship established with his mother.

He blushed and hung his head. Another silence. Then he looked up and said apologetically. 'We mainly talk about films, Mother, and all the interesting people in the house where Lisa lives.'

'Do you now?' She sniffed and added petulantly, 'We haven't been to the pictures together in weeks.'

Brian looked uncomfortable. 'Perhaps we could go on Monday night?'

'Oh, don't mind me.' The air was heavy with resentment.

Brian coughed again. 'Is tea ready?'

'It's been ready since two o'clock,' his mother said unpleasantly, as though they'd arrived late.

Tea comprised watercress sandwiches, a sponge cake and plain biscuits. Lisa, who'd been looking forward to something seasonal like mince pies or shortbread, hated the bitter taste of the vegetable and remembered the teas Kitty made when the boys brought their girlfriends to Chaucer Street. Despite rationing, she always prepared a feast – cold ham and tomatoes, trifle and at least three different sorts of cake.

'Mother does all her own baking,' said Brian proudly. 'She made the cake and biscuits herself.'

'I don't believe in shop-bought confectionery,' said Mrs Smith as grimly as if she was making a statement about religion.

'That's a pity,' thought Lisa, sipping the pale weak tea, 'for the sponge is crisp and the biscuits are soggy.'

'Do you cook?' Mrs Smith smiled as if the question was a silly one and the answer bound to be no.

'Oh yes,' Lisa replied brightly. 'I do all my own cooking. I make cakes all the time.' Another lie. She hadn't made a cake since she'd left home, though if she came again she would bake and bring a sponge, just so Mrs Smith could discover what they *should* taste like.

After tea, she offered to help with the dishes, but the offer was churlishly refused. Lisa sighed and returned to Brian sitting stiffly in the lounge.

'She likes you,' he whispered.

Lisa tried not to let her astonishment show. 'Does she?' she answered noncommittally, then with an effort she added, 'I like her, too.'

Chapter 18

'How did you get on with the dragon?' Mr Greenbaum asked on Monday.

Lisa wrinkled her nose. 'Not very well. I got the third degree and a lecture on home-cooking. I can't imagine us becoming friends, though I'd far prefer it that way.' Kitty treated Colette, Kevin's wife, like another daughter.

He grimaced. 'You didn't get off to a very good start then?'

'No. In fact, she really got my back up. I feel like marrying Brian, just out of spite.'

He proposed nearly every week. He was besotted, so Jackie and Mr Greenbaum said.

'He adores you,' Jackie told her wistfully. 'It must be nice to have a man so much in love with you.'

Nowadays she looked miserable most of the time and drank non-stop when she came home from work, waking every morning with a hangover.

'You'll lose your job,' warned Lisa as they walked to work and Jackie stumbled along beside her complaining of a splitting headache.

'I'm all right once I get there.'

Then, at Easter, something happened that made Lisa review her life and accept Brian's offer of marriage.

There was a note stuck to the stove. *'Hope the sponge had the desired effect. Piers.'*

Lisa grinned. She'd borrowed two baking tins from him on the Saturday to make a cake for Mrs Smith. It had risen well, the surface golden and smooth. Piers said to use his icing sugar to sprinkle on top.

'Mother, this is delicious!' Brian had enthused. 'You must ask Lisa what her secret is.'

That morning, Mr Greenbaum nearly had convulsions

when she imitated Mrs Smith's reaction. 'Do it again, Lisa,' he pleaded over and over again, so she pursed her lips and made her nose quiver, then sniffed, took three deep breaths, flashed her eyes angrily and drew up her shoulders till they nearly touched her ears.

'What's so funny,' she laughed, 'is that Brian thinks his mother is taken with me. "She likes you so much," he keeps saying, but I'm sure she loathes me. She'd loathe anyone who tried to take Brian away.'

She finished reading *Madame Bovary* that night. By the time she reached the last page, she felt close to tears. Poor Emma Bovary, her life was so sad. Glancing at her watch, she was amazed to find it was half-past eight and she'd been reading solidly for nearly three hours. Jackie was late. With any luck, this meant Gordon wouldn't be with her when she eventually arrived.

Her hope was in vain. Not long afterwards, the door opened and a red-faced, angry Jackie marched in, followed by an equally angry Gordon.

'We've been to the pictures,' Jackie said immediately in a loud voice. 'They had an advertisement for people to emigrate to Australia and I've decided to apply. Gordon can't make up his mind whether to come with me.'

'That's not true,' Gordon blustered. 'I've no intention of emigrating, at least not until the children are much older.'

'Then you'll just have to get yourself another mistress, won't you?' Jackie poured a glass of whisky and swallowed it in one gulp.

'It looks as if I might,' Gordon sneered.

They'd forgotten Lisa was there. She slipped out of the room and went down to the kitchen.

Australia! Suddenly, alarmingly, she felt as if the world she loved so much was gradually falling apart. Ralph was leaving soon to make a film in Rome. Only last week, Mr Greenbaum, whose legs were now so bad he could scarcely move from his chair, announced he would only be coming into the shop a few days a week, so the rest of the time she would be alone. The shop wouldn't be the same without him, and the flat would be lonely without Ralph just along the corridor. There'd be no theatre tickets for ages. Now

Jackie was leaving, going to the other side of the earth. Everything was changing. Changing for the worse.

And what was to become of her, Lisa? Where did she fit in this changing world?

'Nothing lasts forever.' Mam used to say that.

It was silly to expect this lovely life just to continue on and on. People were bound to move away, die, get married. So, where did she go from here? For one thing, she doubted if she would ever become an actress. Whenever the group performed a play, she was given the smallest part or no part at all. She was prompt or a stage-hand. Godfrey Perrick never criticized but she knew, just knew, that he thought her hopeless, though Ralph said she must keep on, keep trying.

Some day, Mr Greenbaum would stop coming to the shop altogether. Some day, he would die and it would be sold. She'd have to look for another job. In another shop? She couldn't go back to Chaucer Street, not after all this time. She'd never go home again.

Then, in a flash, she saw her place: it was at Brian's side. She would become a wife – a wife and mother. Hadn't she nursed her little brothers and sisters, cradled them in her arms and loved them as if they were her own? They would buy a house, she and Brian. He had enough money saved – he'd told her, nearly five hundred pounds. She'd have her own kitchen. She'd paint it . . . yellow! Yes, yellow, so the room would always look as if the sun was shining outside. Brian had prospects, too. By the time he was thirty, he assured her, he would be head of his section. Yes, next time he proposed, she would accept.

'You don't love him,' said a little warning voice in her head.

'It doesn't matter,' Lisa argued with herself. 'I respect and like him. I enjoy his company and he loves me. I'll grow to love him in time, I know I will. Anyway, being in love isn't so special. I never want to be like Jackie.' She remembered Kitty telling the girls how much she'd once loved Tom and look how *that* had turned out!

'What about his mother?' came the same cautionary voice. Lisa frowned. 'It's time Brian broke away and asserted himself. She's much too protective and selfish. She'll probably come round once we're married.'

There was the sound of shouting in the corridor and a door banged shut. Lisa peeped outside. Gordon was leaving in a temper, his broad face more purple than ever, his silly moustache quivering.

Back in the flat, Jackie was lying on the sofa in tears. Lisa knelt on the floor and stroked her soft, blonde hair. 'Is it all over?' she asked gently.

Jackie didn't answer and began to cry more violently.

'I think Australia is a good idea,' Lisa said. Presumably Gordon had refused to go and Jackie could start afresh without him.

'Oh Lisa, I've no intention of emigrating! I only said it on the spur of the moment to make him jealous. Instead, he didn't appear to give a damn. That's when I got angry and demanded he come too – either that or we get married.' She sniffed, sat up and added incredibly, 'Poor thing, I've never been angry with him before. I bet he's terribly upset.'

It was Lisa's turn not to answer. She went over and plugged the kettle in, feeling confused.

Jackie wiped the tears off her cheeks with the sleeve of her blouse. Suddenly she smiled. 'So you won't be rid of me after all, Lisa. I'll still be around for a long time yet.'

'As if I'd want to be rid of you!' Lisa said hotly. She paused. It would be wrong to change her mind over her recent decision. 'You'll be rid of *me*, though, but not for a while. I'm going to marry Brian.'

The boat lurched violently and Lisa slid along the wooden seat. She clutched her hat and bag to stop them falling on the wet floor. Although she longed for a cup of tea, she didn't fancy making her unsteady way back along the deck to look for a restaurant, possibly having to pass through the lounge where Brian and lots of passengers were being sick. She'd stick it out here in the observation room till the boat docked. Clutching the back of the bench to steady herself, she stood and peered through the spray-soaked window. Thank goodness land was in sight – a dark line on the horizon. She'd be glad when this journey was over, though not half as glad as Brian would be.

Just married! She fingered her new wedding ring through

the pink suede gloves. A gold engraved band, just the sort, said Jackie sadly when she saw it, she'd always wanted herself. Next to it, her engagement ring. Lisa remembered the day she and Brian had chosen the diamond solitaire. It was a Saturday afternoon and he'd met her from work. She'd only agreed to marry him a few days before, but as soon as she'd said yes, he couldn't wait to get a ring and put it on her finger, as if this proclaimed to the world that she belonged to him. They were going to get married in twelve months' time when Lisa would be nearly nineteen. He'd wanted them to be married sooner, but she'd insisted on waiting a year.

After buying the ring, they'd gone straight to Mrs Smith's house to tell her the news.

'We're engaged,' Brian cried on entering, and his mother looked at them and said in an icy voice, 'You didn't tell me.'

Brian looked deflated. 'We only decided the other day, Mother.'

'You might have discussed it with me first.'

'Sorry, I just didn't think.'

She came to accept the engagement eventually, though with obvious reluctance, and started to make plans for the wedding. One day she called in at the shop. Mr Greenbaum buried his head in a book and pretended he wasn't there.

'I've seen a wedding dress in Dickins and Jones. It's your size, I should imagine, just slightly shop-soiled and reduced to half-price.'

'I don't want that sort of wedding,' Lisa said gently, trying to smile, knowing the woman would be disappointed.

White was for purity. She hadn't been pure for a long time, but she wasn't going to tell her future mother-in-law that. Mrs Smith had just glared at her and left without a word.

One day, Brian brought up the subject of the church.

'Mother knows the vicar of our parish church very well. She asked him and he'd be pleased to marry us.'

'No thanks,' she said. 'I'm a Catholic, though I don't go to mass.'

'A Catholic!' His pale eyes popped and he said in a complaining voice, 'You should have told me before.'

'Why?' she asked. 'What difference does it make?'

'Well, none, I suppose. But if you don't go to church, why

179

does it matter where we get married?'

She wrinkled her nose. 'I don't know. It just wouldn't seem right, getting married by a vicar in a Protestant church. You know the saying, "Once a Catholic, always a Catholic". Sorry, Brian. It'll have to be a registry office.'

Of course, she wouldn't be married in the eyes of God, but neither would she in a Protestant church. A registry office seemed less sacrilegious.

He gave in, as usual. He would have got married in the middle of the street to please her, though he said awkwardly, 'Don't tell Mother you're a Catholic, will you? She's funny about religion.'

One day when they were at Mrs Smith's house, she threw an envelope on the table, saying, 'That's your wedding present from me.'

Brian opened it. 'Mother's booked us two weeks' bed and breakfast in Hastings for our honeymoon, Lisa. We've stayed in this hotel every year since I was a baby. It's very clean and the breakfasts are so big you don't need to eat again till tea-time.'

'Seeing as it's not far away, I might come down by coach the middle Saturday, just for the day,' his mother said.

'I thought we'd decided on Paris,' said Lisa, trying to keep the irritation out of her voice.

'Had we?' Brian glanced at his mother worriedly.

'Yes.' This was a slight exaggeration. They'd only discussed it so far. Ralph said it was an ideal place for a honeymoon and Lisa had some brochures in her bag to show Brian later, along with two passport application forms.

'I forgot.' Brian looked uncomfortable. 'I'm sorry, Mother, I'd forgotten about Paris.' Much as he wanted to please his mother, he wanted to please Lisa more. If Lisa wanted to go to Paris, then she would go.

'Can you get the money back?' he asked contritely.

'Well, does it matter whether I can or I can't?'

Lisa sighed inwardly. She doubted if she would ever be on amicable terms with this woman. 'Perhaps,' she thought hopefully, 'when Brian and I have children, she'll be nicer. She goes on enough about how much she wants a grandson.'

*

Lisa jumped as the boat juddered and made an odd grinding noise as it slowed to a halt. Chains clanked and she could hear voices shouting in a foreign language. They were in France! She jumped to her feet and went to find Brian.

They were going to live with Mrs Smith until they'd saved enough to buy a house of their own. Brian said there was a thing called a mortgage you could get, but it meant borrowing a lot of money on which a high rate of interest had to be paid.

'We only need to save about another two hundred pounds. Mother will let us stay with her rent-free, so we can save up quickly with both of us working,' he said.

'I thought you told me you had enough to buy a little house?'

He definitely had. He'd used it as a ploy to persuade her to marry him, and only revealed this latest news a few weeks before the wedding.

Brian frowned. 'I talked it over with Mother and she said a cheap house wouldn't have a garden, perhaps not even a bathroom. It's best to start off with a decent house, Lisa, one like Mother's.'

Lisa hated the idea of living with her mother-in-law but she couldn't very well tell Brian that. She said crossly, 'It's me you should be talking it over with, not your mother.'

It was the only time she had doubts, but soon dismissed them. After all, his argument made sense. A flat would cost five or six pounds a week in rent and although she wouldn't have minded a cheap house, perhaps something big and modern would be better, particularly if they had children soon. Somewhat reluctantly she agreed. She didn't tell him, but she had more than fifty pounds saved in a Post Office account. She was keeping it as a surprise to buy furniture when the time came.

They arrived back from Paris late on a Saturday night. Fortunately, the weather on the return journey had been fine and the motion of the boat steady. No one was sick.

'Did you have a nice time?' asked Mrs Smith rather grudgingly. She was ready for bed in a thick plaid dressing gown over a washed-out nightdress. Her hair was screwed tight in metal curlers.

'Marvellous,' enthused Lisa. 'Paris is enchanting. I want to go there again and again. We've bought you a present. Brian, where's your mother's present?'

'In this bag, I think.' He rooted through the leather holdall, part of the set of luggage Jackie had given them for a wedding present. 'Here you are, Mother.' He handed her the velvet box which contained a tiny gold locket.

'It's real gold,' said Lisa excitedly. 'And the little stone is a real ruby.'

Mrs Smith stared down at the locket for several seconds. 'Oh God,' thought Lisa, 'she's going to say something rude like "I never wear jewellery", and poor Brian will feel mortified.'

To her relief, the woman said politely, 'It's very nice. Thank you.' Tucking the box inside her pocket, she added, 'I'm going to bed now.'

After she'd gone, Lisa said, 'Let's make some tea. I'm dying of thirst.' She thought Mrs Smith might have offered them a cup.

'You mean make one ourselves – in Mother's kitchen?'

'Where else?'

Brian looked worried. 'I'm not sure she'd like that.'

'Come off it, Brian, we live here now. It's our kitchen too, even if we're not paying rent.'

'I'm not sure.'

'Darling.' She sat on his knee and kissed his cheek. To her surprise, he stiffened and said quickly, 'Don't! Mother might come down for something.'

'Well, we're married, aren't we? Don't married people kiss?'

He wriggled uncomfortably. 'Make some tea then, but put everything back where you found it.'

They were using Mrs Smith's bedroom and she was sleeping in Brian's, which only had a single bed. Her room was large and crammed with heavy furniture: two tall wardrobes, each with several cardboard boxes on top, two matching chests of drawers and a dressing table in the bay window. All were polished to glassy perfection, as was the wooden headboard on the bed. A low-wattage bulb in a parchment shade hung low over the high bed with its chocolate-coloured eiderdown and matching coverlet, folded back. The wallpaper, a shade of putty, had a pattern of fawn trailing leaves. Curtains the same as in the parlour – navy-blue velvet with the reverse of the material turned inwards so only neighbours and passers-by saw the best side, hung at the windows.

'When we have a house, I'm going to have the curtains the other way round,' Lisa said, 'so we see — '

'Shush,' said Brian hoarsely. 'Mother might hear.'

He was already in his pyjamas, the striped jacket buttoned tightly up to the neck. Lisa slipped out of her clothes. She'd been allocated one of the wardrobes, but when she opened the door to hang her honeymoon suit up, the smell of mothballs nearly choked her. There were dozens of them. 'I'll throw them away tomorrow,' she decided, 'and splash some perfume around.' For tonight, she hung the suit outside. Naked, she slipped into bed beside Brian.

She urgently wanted to make love. On their honeymoon, they'd made love every night and morning and sometimes even in the afternoon. Lisa had been almost dreading this side of marriage. During their courtship, Brian had done no more than kiss her, sometimes passionately, but she'd been fearful to respond in case it encouraged him to go further and she wasn't sure if she wanted him to or not. Her experience of sex had been so unpleasant, so violent. But once in Paris, after some initial nervousness, even embarrassment, on both their parts, Brian soon took command of her body and to her utter relief, Lisa found making love was wonderful, more wonderful than she'd ever thought possible. Brian became a different person altogether, a real man, yet supremely tender, forever gentle and he would enter her, deep and satisfyingly, sighing in ecstasy when his climax came.

But tonight he bitterly disappointed her.

'Lisa!' he said when she cuddled close. 'Put your night-dress on.'

'Why?' she demanded. 'Has your mother got X-ray eyes? Can she see through the wall, through the bedclothes?'

'She might come in.'

'Now?' Lisa giggled.

'Of course not, but in the morning maybe.'

She slid her hand down his body and untied the cord of his pyjama trousers.

'Oh, Lisa,' he said in a faint voice. 'Lisa.' He turned to face her, his hands on her body, then raised himself to mount her.

The bed creaked.

'Shush,' he said.

'It can't hear you.'

Cautiously he moved on top of her. The bed creaked again. He stopped. She pulled him down, but he was tense, too scared to make another move lest the bed creaked again.

He lay back beside her. 'I'm sorry,' he said.

'Is it always going to be like this?' she whispered angrily. 'After all, your mother must have done it, else she wouldn't have had you.'

'Don't talk like that. My father — ' He stopped.

'What about your father?'

'Nothing.'

Sulkily, she slipped out of bed and put a nightdress on and they went to sleep, for the first time with their backs to each other.

Chapter 19

Sunlight filtered through the dark-blue curtains when Lisa woke, casting an unnatural ghostly light over the room. She held up her hand to see the time. Only seven o'clock. She'd hoped she might sleep in after the long, tiring journey yesterday. Beside her Brian was dead to the world. The clink of dishes came from downstairs. Her mother-in-law was up. She considered going down herself, but decided against it. On the few occasions she'd been alone with her mother-in-law, conversation had been forced and difficult. For a moment, Lisa desperately wished she was back in the flat and could wander round in her nightdress making endless cups of tea and later on she and Jackie would stroll along to Kensington Gardens, but she sternly told herself to stop thinking like that. She was married and Brian was fun to be with. He'd make a good husband and she would be a good wife, though his behaviour last night was alarming. Did this mean they wouldn't make love again till they left his mother's house in a year's time? In which case, how were they to have the grandchild Mrs Smith kept on about?

She smiled to herself, then sighed. Perhaps coming here wasn't such a good idea. If things hadn't altered in a few weeks' time, she'd suggest they bought a place of their own. The meanest little house would be better than this.

Feeling bored, she closed her eyes and designed some dresses. A few months ago she'd started making her own clothes. A woollen suit would be useful – she'd get coupons for the material off Jackie. Royal blue, with a long fitted jacket . . .

Suddenly, there was a knock on the door and without waiting for an answer, Mrs Smith came in.

Lisa felt a surge of irritation. All right, so it was her house, but what right had she to just barge in? She sat up, half-expecting, half-hoping, a cup of tea was being brought, in which case she'd forgive the infringement of their privacy.

But no, Mrs Smith was standing in the doorway, a bitter, disapproving expression on her face, as if seeing her son in bed with his wife was like coming face to face with the citizens of Sodom and Gomorrah.

'It's nearly half-past seven. You'll both be late for church.'

Brian groaned. He sat up, blinking and rubbing his eyes. Lisa saw him redden with embarrassment.

'Sorry, Mother.'

'I'm not going to church,' said Lisa.

Her hair, so thick and straight, became only slightly ruffled when she slept. From its natural centre parting, it hung down, almost covering her wide, gold-flecked eyes. The strap of her black nightdress had fallen off one shoulder. Brian glanced at her. She saw desire flash in his eyes. Now was her opportunity. She reached beneath the bedclothes for the gap in his pyjama trousers and felt him quiver.

'Brian?' said Mrs Smith. There was a challenge in her voice. She was in her beige rayon dress. Fat bulged above and below the tight belt. Her thick legs were encased in flesh-coloured lisle stockings, wrinkled at the ankles. Brian looked from her to his new wife, sitting so innocently beside him, playing havoc with his body.

He gulped and said in a cracked voice, 'I think I'll give church a miss today, Mother.'

She glared at him. Lisa felt a surge of pity for the woman, but it soon died.

After she'd gone, they lay in silence, touching each other, until half an hour later, the door slammed and he fell upon her.

But it was the last time they were to make love.

Mr Greenbaum was thankful to see her back. Miriam had been helping out and driving him wild.

'She has been moving books round. Every day, she finds one, two, three books which she declares are in the wrong category. "This is a biography," she tells me, as if I did not know, "so what is it doing under *Art*?". "It's under *Art*," I say, "because it's a biography of Vincent Van Gogh and that's where my customers will look for it."' He sighed. 'Still, she's a good woman.'

'And you love her,' grinned Lisa. Behind the grin, she was worried. Her employer looked ill. His shoulders were more stooped than ever and his face was gaunt. Seeing him after a gap of two weeks brought home how rapidly he was deteriorating. When it was time for lunch, she had to help him to his feet, and she felt tears prick her eyes.

Lisa was meeting Jackie at one. They'd decided to lunch together every day, though Brian was annoyed by this. He thought Lisa should have lunch with him. His mother would make sandwiches for her too, he said, and they could eat them in the park. She had refused.

'Jackie is my best friend,' she said. 'Lunch is the only time we can see each other.'

'How is the dragon lady?' Jackie asked after Lisa had described Paris in all its glory and given her a present of expensive perfume which would have cost a small fortune in London.

Lisa laughed. 'Being a dragon. Honestly, even St George would have had his work cut out with her. Yesterday, Sunday, was so tedious. I've never known the hours drag so much. We just sat there, Brian and I, like guests, whilst she had the radio on – non-stop hymns. I wasn't allowed to help with the meals, though I offered.'

She recalled the Sunday dinner. Knotty lamb, the cheapest cut, with boiled potatoes, cabbage and lumpy gravy. Nothing for dessert.

'It's horrible not being able to make a cup of tea whenever you like,' she complained.

'Never mind,' soothed Jackie. 'It won't be for long.'

'Not if I can help it,' vowed Lisa stoutly.

They had the same meal that night, except this time the lamb was cold. Lumps of white congealed fat stared up from the plate and Lisa felt her stomach churn. What real meat there was, was tough and no amount of chewing made it edible. She forced herself to swallow the stringy mess in her mouth. Another 363 days to go, she thought and giggled.

'Lisa!' said Brian reprovingly.

'Sorry, I'm not hungry.' She jumped to her feet. 'Excuse me.'

In the bedroom, she found that Mrs Smith had remade their bed. Although Lisa had made it carefully that morning, folding the sheets back to below the pillows the way Kitty liked it done, now the sheets and blankets were drawn right up to the headboard. Victoria, who'd been left on a pillow, had disappeared and was found stuffed in a suitcase. Lisa picked her up and smoothed her ruffled dress. 'I'll sit you in the wardrobe,' she whispered, 'So every time I open it I'll think of Ralph.'

That morning, she'd moved the mothballs to the other wardrobe which still contained some of Mrs Smith's clothes. When she went to put Victoria away, she found the mothballs had been replaced. Angrily, she put them in a paper bag to throw away. There was a key in her wardrobe door, so she locked it and put the tiny key in her purse.

'What stage is the battle at now?' asked Mr Greenbaum. Lisa and Brian had been married six weeks.

'Well, the goodies – that's my side,' she said, 'are in an advantageous position. The baddies haven't taken any ground at all.' Then she thought about the nights and Brian lying stiffly beside her, too scared to move no matter how hard she tried to seduce him. Under his mother's roof, his desire for Lisa had fled. Of course she couldn't tell Mr Greenbaum that. In actual fact, the baddies, slowly, stealthily, under cover of darkness, were making considerable progress.

'We'd be much happier, Brian, in a place of our own,' Lisa said one night on their way home from work. The tube was packed and they hung onto straps, buffeted to and fro as people pushed their way on and off. It wasn't the ideal place for a conversation, but they were so seldom alone together. Even in bed, he was reluctant to have a discussion.

'Oh, don't start that again, Lisa,' he complained petulantly. She stared at him, surprised by his tone of voice.

'I've only brought it up once before.'

He looked disinterested. Sometimes she thought she was

losing him: now she felt convinced. She *had* to get him away from his mother's influence, or their marriage would die. She said, 'Brian, I don't feel as if we're married. I don't feel a bit like a wife.'

'Shush,' he said, looking round. 'People might hear.'

'Where can we talk when people can't hear?' she demanded. 'We can't talk in your mother's house, not even in bed.'

'We could talk at lunch-time,' he said, spitefully, 'but apparently you have to have lunch with Jackie. Mother thinks that's disloyal.'

Lisa's eyes flashed in annoyance. 'It's even more disloyal to discuss me with your mother,' she snapped. He looked shifty. 'Oh, Brian,' she went on in a rush. 'Your mother doesn't recognize that you've *got* a wife. She acts like I'm an intruder. I mean, in nearly three months I've never cooked a meal. She still darns your socks and mends your clothes.'

'Most girls would be grateful for that,' he sniffed.

'But I'm not a girl, I'm a *wife*,' she insisted. 'We have no privacy, no place to call our own. Whatever way I make the bed, she unmakes it and does it some other way. When I leave the dressing table tidy, she moves everything round. She takes the dirty clothes which I'm keeping to do at the weekend, even if I've put them in a drawer – she goes through our drawers, Brian.'

'But it's her house, her furniture,' he protested.

A seat became vacant and Lisa sat down, too weary to argue any longer. A few weeks ago, she'd suggested they go to the pictures and when Brian mentioned this to his mother, Mrs Smith had declared she'd like to come too, so now, each Wednesday, all three went together and somehow, Mrs Smith always managed to sit between them. Instead of enjoying the film, Lisa sat burning with resentment. On the last occasion, she'd declined to go, declaring she had a headache, so Brian had gone with his mother. 'Just like old times,' Mrs Smith had chuckled.

Lisa remembered when one of her brothers, Jimmie it was, had desperately wanted a bow and arrow. He'd saved his pennies for weeks until he had enough and returned from Woolworths, eyes shining with the pride of possession. After playing with the toy for a few hours, it had been left in the back yard until Kitty had found one of the little ones using it and had hidden it away. Jimmie never even noticed. That's how she felt with Brian – as if she was a toy he'd first seen, appropriately enough, on Christmas Eve, a toy he desperately wanted, had pursued with diligence, but which, once possessed, held no further interest.

The passengers on the train began to thin out and Brian sat beside her. 'I realize it's difficult for you,' he said awkwardly. 'But I promised Mother we'd stay a year. She'd be hurt if we left before. Just nine more months and we'll have enough for a house of our own.'

Lisa didn't answer but inwardly vowed that, whenever it was bought, the house wouldn't be within easy reach of her mother-in-law. Just before they reached their station, she ventured, 'Perhaps we could go away on a little holiday, just for the weekend?'

He frowned. 'Can we afford it?'

'Two nights' bed and breakfast wouldn't cost much. We could go to Brighton, that's not far away.' Mr Greenbaum said Brighton was the most cosmopolitan town in England with all sorts of exciting things to do. Years ago, he and Miriam used to go there every Sunday till the journey got too much for him.

'That's not such a bad idea,' Brian mused. 'A break would do us good.'

She felt so elated, she kissed his cheek and he blinked and looked at her, slightly surprised. 'He doesn't realize what he's missing,' she thought excitedly. 'He's entirely forgotten what it was like on our honeymoon.' She'd pack her black lace nightie and buy some sexy underwear and show him that making love was the most marvellous thing in the world so when they came back he wouldn't care if the bedsprings creaked all night. Either that, or he'd insist on them living in their own house.

Mr Greenbaum had a friend who owned a small hotel right on the Esplanade in Brighton.

'Give him a ring,' he said the next morning. 'Tell him old Harry Greenbaum recommended you and he might give you a discount.'

Lisa telephoned immediately and booked a double room for the weekend after next. They would travel straight after she finished work on Saturday and return Monday morning.

She told Brian on their way home.

'Our room's got a little balcony and looks right over the pier. Oh Brian, I'm really looking forward to it!' It was going to be a turning point in their marriage.

'What sort of room did you book for Mother?' he asked. 'I hope it isn't some little boxroom at the back.'

Mr Greenbaum wasn't in the shop when Lisa telephoned the hotel to cancel the booking. When he brought the subject up a few days later, she said brightly, 'We decided we couldn't afford it, after all.'

He looked at her, a sad, knowing expression on his dear, wise face, but said nothing.

Lisa hadn't bothered to argue with her husband, reckoning it was a waste of time. She'd just said later that perhaps Brighton wasn't such a good idea, adding pointedly, 'We'd be better saving the money for our house.'

On the Saturday morning when Lisa would have gone to Brighton, she was in the shop alone, burning with resentment, wondering what on earth she had to do to save her marriage.

'Perhaps I could move out,' she mused. 'Then Brian would *have* to leave.' But would he? She had the alarming thought he might not, that his mother's grip on him was too strong. She was grateful when the telephone rang to interrupt this depressing chain of thought. It was Jackie.

'Can you come round?' she asked in a despairing voice. 'I'm in awful trouble, Lisa.'

'I'll come as soon as I've closed the shop,' Lisa promised. Brian didn't work on Saturdays which meant she couldn't tell him she'd be late and there wasn't a telephone in Mrs Smith's house. Lisa didn't care. Her friend needed her and that was all that mattered.

She still had her key to Number 5 Queen's Gate and, puffed from climbing the unaccustomed four flights of stairs, arrived in the flat to find Jackie lying on the bed. Lisa had been declared irreplaceable, so no new roommate had appeared to tidy up, and both rooms were littered with clothes and other paraphernalia.

'I'm pregnant,' Jackie cried, bursting into tears. Her face was puffed and red, her eyes raw from weeping. She'd put on a lot of weight since Lisa left. The dimples in her cheeks had disappeared into a morass of fat.

'I suspected as much,' said Lisa. 'What did Gordon say?'

'He's ditched me! I thought to myself, he loves children – that's why he wouldn't leave his wife, because of the children. But they're growing up and if I had a baby, his baby, he'd leave and come to me, but when I told him . . . Oh, Lisa! He said I was a whore, tried to make out I'd slept with other men. As if I would, I love him so much.'

'There, there.' Lisa stroked her friend's head gently. 'You're better off without him.'

'No, no! I can't live without Gordon.'

It seemed to Lisa she had no choice, but now was not the time to say so. 'What about the baby?' she asked. 'Are you going to have it?'

'I've done the most stupid thing. I let myself go four months. I had, well, a suspicion that if I told him straight away he might insist on an abortion, so I left it until it was too late. I've *got* to have the baby, Lisa.'

Oh, God! What a mess. Lisa did the thing she did in every emergency. 'I'll make us a cup of tea,' she said.

As the afternoon wore on, Jackie became even more distraught. She would have to give up her job soon – some of the women at work already suspected she was pregnant. 'I can't go home,' she wailed. 'Mother wouldn't have me. How will I live with a baby I don't want? I got pregnant for Gordon, that's all. I'll never be able to work again.'

'Don't you get money from the State or something?' asked Lisa. 'They won't let you starve.'

'I've no idea,' cried Jackie frantically. 'I don't want money off the State. I want to work, not sit in this flat all day looking after a baby. And the stairs, Lisa, I can't carry a baby and a pram up and down those stairs. I'd have to find another place to live.'

Lisa shuddered, remembering her first day in London looking for a flat. Imagine doing that with a baby. Then suddenly she had an idea that was so audacious that it almost took her breath away.

'I'll have your baby,' she said, then put her hand over her mouth. Had she really said it?

'What d'you mean?' Jackie was so taken aback her hysteria disappeared instantly.

Lisa gulped. 'I'll have the baby. I'll pretend I'm pregnant. Mrs Smith's longing for a grandchild. You stay here for five months and when the baby's born, I'll say it's mine.'

'That's a mad idea, Lisa,' but Jackie's protest was half-hearted. 'D'you think it would work?'

'Of course it would.' She and Brian never made love. He never even saw her undressed. This was the solution she'd been wracking her brains for that morning. Once they had a family, he would *have* to buy a house, and as soon as they were alone together everything would be fine. 'It just fits in with our honeymoon. I'll say I'm three months' gone, not four, in case you're late. I'll pad myself out a bit. Oh, Jackie, it'll be fun. A real joke, fooling everyone.' She giggled and after a while her friend perked up and began to laugh too.

'But what about Brian?' Jackie looked puzzled. 'You can't expect to get away with something like that, not with your husband!'

Lisa laughed ruefully. 'I can with mine,' she said and Jackie looked at her curiously.

Later on, she asked, 'What about the actual birth, Lisa? Brian will expect to come with you to the hospital.'

'Oh, we'll cross that bridge when we come to it,' said Lisa airily. 'We'll think of something.' She got to her feet and danced around the room. 'I'm pregnant, I'm pregnant,' she sang.

'I'm pregnant,' she said.

Brian had come to the door to let her in – she'd never been given a key. He looked more cross than worried. Behind him, Mrs Smith stood with a sly grin on her face. There was an air of togetherness about them. They were the family, she the outsider.

'Where on earth have you been?' her husband demanded. 'It's nearly midnight. We've been worried sick.'

'Well, I've been properly sick. If you were on the phone, I'd have let you know.' Lisa decided the best method of defence was attack. 'I nearly fainted in the shop, so I went to Jackie's and she called the doctor. I didn't feel fit to come home till now.'

'What's wrong with you?' her mother-in-law asked.

So she told them she was pregnant.

Brian was overjoyed. He rushed forward to hug her, but she pushed him away.

'I'm tired,' she said. 'I'm going straight to bed.'

As she climbed the stairs, Mrs Smith said, 'Would you like a cup of tea?' Her eyes were bright and joyful. Lisa had never seen her look happy before.

'No, thank you,' she replied churlishly.

In bed, Brian said, 'Mother's absolutely thrilled. You know she's always wanted a grandchild.'

'Shush,' snapped Lisa. 'She might hear.'

They couldn't do enough for her, Brian and his mother. The following day they fussed around, fetching her endless cups of tea.

'Lisa loves her tea, Mother,' joked Brian, and she wondered why he'd never said so before.

'Of course, you'll have to leave work,' said Mrs Smith. 'You can't spend the day on your feet, not in your condition.'

With a jolt, Lisa realized she would indeed have to leave. If she really had been pregnant, she would have ignored the advice and stayed at the shop for as long as possible, but she couldn't fool Mr Greenbaum, not for six whole months. He was too canny, too wise, to be taken in, besides which, she liked him too much to deceive him. She didn't want to let him in on the lie, either, it might distress him.

This meant that without her salary, she and Brian would be longer saving up for a house of their own.

She was woken from her reverie by Brian.

'What do you think, Lisa?'

'About what?'

'Whether the baby will be a boy or a girl?'

'How on earth should I know?' she said crossly.

Chapter 20

Suddenly, she could do no wrong. At last she was part of the family, though she realized it wasn't *her* they cared about but the baby they thought she carried – Brian's son and his mother's longed-for grandchild.

Mr Greenbaum was stunned when she gave in her notice, and she found it difficult to meet his eyes. 'I'm expecting a baby,' she told him, regretting for the moment at least that she'd become involved in such deception.

'Why, this is marvellous news,' he said when he recovered from the shock. 'Forgive me, Lisa, I am a selfish old man. My first thought was for myself and for my shop. You must be so happy, you and Brian.'

'Well, Brian is,' she thought, 'and so is Mrs Smith. I'm glad to be helping Jackie and the atmosphere's better at home, that's all.'

The months passed slowly. Mrs Smith bought yards of white winceyette and pounds of wool to make baby clothes, and announced she was going to teach her daughter-in-law to knit and sew, though Lisa needed no tuition. Kitty had been an expert needlewoman and taught her daughter all she knew. Her would-be teacher watched in wonder as Lisa sewed the seams of baby gowns with tiny, symmetrical stitches and knitted cardigans, six of each size to cover the baby's first year, and had no difficulty with the lacy panels or crocheted trim, whilst Mrs Smith struggled to make sense of the patterns, clearly chagrined at Lisa's expertise.

Twice a week, Lisa went into town for the day. She was having lunch with Jackie, she lied unblushingly to her husband, then she liked to wander around the shops, sometimes visiting her doctor. In fact, she spent the whole day in the flat.

'You should be resting,' Brian protested. 'And I wish you'd

sign on with our local doctor, then Mother could go with you.'

Lisa didn't bother to argue with him. She went her own way. By now she was theoretically six months pregnant, so she stuffed a folded towel in her pants, jutting her stomach out to heighten the effect. The maternity gowns she made for herself contained a yard more material than the pattern called for, in order to add to her bulk.

Jackie was in the throes of deep depression. She'd left work and spent her days in bed drinking whisky and eating chocolates.

'You should get more exercise,' Lisa told her every time she came. 'You're not doing the baby any good, lying around like this.'

She said it again when she came one day in late September. Autumn, her favourite season. A faint mist hung in the air and the leaves were damp beneath her feet.

'Who cares about the baby?' her friend said sulkily. 'I can't manage those stairs, not in my condition.'

Lisa looked down at her. Jackie was scarcely recognizable nowadays. She must have weighed thirteen stone, if not more. Her fresh complexion had turned grey and her uncombed hair was a mass of knots. Through the creamy curls, Lisa saw her scalp was dirty. Worst of all, she smelt! Jackie, so vivacious, so scrupulous about her appearance, had been reduced to this by Gordon.

'You're still not eating properly, are you?' Lisa said sternly. The only food she could see was the stale remains of a loaf and some cheese she herself had brought on her last visit. 'Where's your ration book and I'll get you something.'

'I don't know,' sniffed Jackie. 'It's wherever you left it on Tuesday.'

'While I'm shopping you can have a bath. I'll go and run it. Come on, out of bed!' Lisa clapped her hands and to her relief saw her friend grin.

'You're a worse dragon than your mother-in-law,' she complained.

An hour later, a freshly bathed and fed Jackie sat on the chair whilst Lisa tried to comb the tangles out of her wet hair.

'Ouch!'

'Well, if you combed it every day, it wouldn't get in this state.'

'Sorry, ma'am.' Jackie saluted and they both laughed.

'Why don't you go to the hairdresser's every week? Have you got enough money?'

'Stacks. My aunts send me cash from time to time and my boss gave me three months' wages. He felt sorry for me. He knew about Gordon.'

'In that case, I'll make an appointment for a shampoo and set next Tuesday – I'll get you down those stairs if I have to carry you myself. Don't forget, the week after next you're due at the ante-natal clinic.'

'I don't know why you put up with me.'

'Because you're my best friend, that's why. There, that's finished. You're completely unknotted.' Lisa sat opposite and asked. 'What will you do after the baby's born?'

'God knows.' Jackie shrugged. 'I thought I might emigrate to Australia – I mean it this time.' She burst into tears. 'Oh, Lisa, isn't life hell? I can't stop thinking about Gordon.'

'Try not to cry,' said Lisa softly. 'He's not worth it.'

'So I keep telling myself.' She wiped her nose on the sleeve of her dressing gown. 'You look lovely,' she said suddenly.

Lisa's maternity gown was red and white gingham with a high neck and long gathered sleeves. A wide frill went from a V between her breasts to the shoulders and the hem was similarly trimmed. Her hair was smoothed back and tied at the nape of her neck with a red ribbon.

'I feel as if I'm wearing a tent,' she said. Glancing at her watch she saw it was time to leave. 'Don't forget your orange juice and vitamin tablets,' she commanded.

'No, Lisa.'

'And I've brought you some fruit – you must eat some every day.'

'Yes, Lisa.'

They smiled at each other. 'See you Tuesday,' said Lisa.

Before leaving, she slipped a note under Ralph's door, hoping and praying that no one would hear and open it. *'Look after Jackie for me,'* the note said. She had deliberately kept away from Ralph these last months. When this was all over, she would tell him the truth, but not yet.

Brian was home before her. She unlocked the front door – her pregnancy had qualified her for a key – and could hear him upstairs with his mother. They were talking in animated voices.

'Lisa, is that you?'

'Who else could it be,' she thought. 'No one else has been in this house since I came to live here.' She found them in the small spare room standing each side of a chipped wooden cot.

'Look! Mother got this from a second-hand shop.'

'It was only five shillings,' Mrs Smith said proudly.

'I'll rub it down and re-paint it, and Mother'll make a new cover for the mattress.'

'Do we really need to buy second-hand things for our baby?'

Brian and his mother glanced at each other and for a second both looked shamefaced. 'Well no, but it's silly wasting money. Once finished, it'll be as good as new. But Lisa,' Brian went on enthusiastically, 'see, the cot fits in this alcove nicely and if we put these odds and ends in the attic, it'll make a fine nursery.'

'Nursery!' said Lisa. 'I thought we planned to move into a place of our own?'

His mother made no attempt to leave the room and let them have their argument in private. In fact, she edged closer to support her son.

'Lisa, you haven't worked for months. We haven't saved nearly enough for a decent house.' Brian spoke slowly and patiently as if addressing a child. 'You wouldn't want to bring our baby up in a flat, would you? Or a scruffy little house? Besides which, if we stay here, Mother can help out. Why, you can even go back to work if you want.'

She stared at him accusingly, her great brown eyes filled with sorrow. After a while, he dropped his gaze and she turned and silently left the room. He didn't follow.

Time dragged interminably by. She rose with Brian and sat with him whilst he ate his breakfast – a boiled egg in his

199

Humpty Dumpty egg cup with bread soldiers to dip in the yolk. Mrs Smith assured her there was no need to get up, but Lisa couldn't stay in bed once she'd woken. If she wasn't going to see Jackie, an empty day stretched ahead. All the baby clothes had long since been made: dozens of gowns, cardigans and vests, bonnets and bootees. Lisa had crocheted two shawls. There was nothing else needed. Mrs Smith spent most of her time in the kitchen, though what she did there mystified Lisa, as the meals she produced were barely edible. The woman considered herself a perfect housewife, yet could neither cook nor sew.

'If I were in my own house,' thought Lisa, 'I would be really busy instead of sitting here with absolutely nothing to do – at least, nothing I'm allowed to do. I'd go shopping, there'd be housework and I'd make curtains and cushion covers and arrange my books and buy flowers.' Once she'd left her Jane Austen set on the sideboard but when she came home it had disappeared. She searched everywhere until eventually she had to ask her mother-in-law where the books were. 'Under your bed,' she'd been told. 'Out of the way.'

'There's nothing of me here,' she thought sadly as she sat in the dull, colourless room. 'Even poor Victoria is shut in the wardrobe. I'm not part of this family and I don't belong in this house. Brian and his mother don't really want me. We should never have come here to live.'

'Now, don't forget,' said Lisa sternly. 'As soon as the baby's born, get someone in the hospital to send a telegram addressed to Mrs *Lisa* Smith, else the dragon will open it. Just say something like "*Eureka*" and I'll know what it means. I'll be with you in an hour. Understand?'

'I understand,' said Jackie. Strangely, as her time approached, Jackie's physical and mental condition improved. She'd begun to eat better and drink less, and she'd lost some of the flabby flesh on her body as if she was already preparing to face the world after the baby's birth.

'Have you got the wedding ring I bought from Woolworths?'

'Of course. I'll not forget to say my husband's abroad, either.'

'Good. Ring for the ambulance the minute you get contractions and they'll help you downstairs.'

'Stop fussing! I may be pregnant, but I'm not an idiot.'

'Of course you are, that's why I like you so much,' said Lisa affectionately.

The baby was due on 14 December. Lisa prayed it wouldn't be late. If it arrived over Christmas it would make things awkward. By now, she'd begun to feel she really *was* pregnant. She'd taken a cushion from the flat and tied it round her middle and when at home, she made a great show of lumbering clumsily around, straining to get up from the chair. 'If Godfrey Perrick saw me now,' she thought dryly, 'he wouldn't think me a rotten actress any more. I'm doing this part perfectly!'

Two days before expected, on a dark wet afternoon, the telegram arrived. The bell rang and she heard her mother-in-law's heavy tread down the hall.

'Any answer?' a man's voice asked.

Lisa leapt to her feet and ran across the room, slowing when she reached the hallway, just in time to see Mrs Smith about to open the envelope. She blushed when she saw Lisa.

'It's for you,' she said.

'*Eureka*' was the message. 'No answer,' she told the delivery man. After he'd gone, she said to her mother-in-law, 'I have to go to Liverpool. My sister's very ill.'

She hadn't expected the woman to be pleased, but even so she was taken aback by Mrs Smith's violent reaction.

'Sister! You've never mentioned a sister. Why didn't she come to the wedding? I thought you said you were an orphan.' The woman's voice was hoarse with pent-up anger.

'She couldn't afford to come and orphans do have brothers and sisters. I'll go and pack a case.'

As Lisa was going up the stairs, her mother-in-law shouted, 'You can't travel to Liverpool in your condition. What will I tell Brian?'

'The truth, that my sister's ill. And I feel perfectly well. The baby's not due for a month.'

Lisa swiftly packed a small case of clothes – she couldn't

wait to get back into her old things again. When she went back downstairs, Mrs Smith was still standing in the hall.

'I don't think I should let you go,' she said aggressively.

Lisa looked amused. 'Are you going to keep me prisoner?'

The woman's eyes were filled with hatred as she stepped to one side.

'I'll be back as soon as I can,' said Lisa. On the step, she turned, trying to think of something kind to say, not wanting to leave with such ill-feeling between them, but even as she opened her mouth to speak, the door was slammed in her face.

Chapter 21

Jackie was sitting up in bed clutching the baby in her arms and looking surprisingly pleased with herself. She was in a small room at the end of the ward. The sister, a cheerful middle-aged woman with rosy, weatherbeaten cheeks rarely seen in the city, said, 'It's not visiting time till half-past six, but as her hubby's abroad and you're her only relative, I'll make an exception. We've put her by herself, so she won't get upset when the other hubbies appear. If you hear Matron, duck under the bed, there's a love, else I'll be for it.'

'How was it?' asked Lisa, sitting beside the bed.

'Easier than I thought,' Jackie said complacently. 'The nurses said I'm made for having children. You know, broad hips and I've got stacks of milk too, so won't have any trouble breastfeeding. Some women do.'

'Is it a boy or a girl?'

'A boy. I've called him Noël, because it's nearly Christmas. He's so beautiful, I just can't believe it.' She looked down at the baby in starry-eyed wonder.

Lisa felt worried. The last thing she had expected was to find Jackie overcome with maternal feeling.

'Let's see him.'

'You can hold him for a while if you like – isn't he lovely?' She handed the tiny bundle to Lisa.

The baby's beetroot-red face was crumpled like that of an old, old man and down the centre of his scalp a tuft of reddish-blond hair stuck up like a cockscomb. The rest of him was hidden, tightly wrapped in a white hospital shawl. Lisa watched with fascination as his tiny mouth opened and closed repeatedly.

'He looks like a goldfish,' she said, noting with increasing alarm Jackie's air of proprietorial pride. 'I've brought some baby clothes with me,' she added.

'You're an angel,' said Jackie gratefully. 'What would I have done without you these last five months?'

'You would have managed.'

'No, I wouldn't. I'd have gone to pieces without you.' She was silent for a moment, then looking faintly embarrassed, she said, 'Lisa, I've done more thinking in the few hours since Noël was born than I've done for months. You wouldn't be doing this if you loved Brian. You wouldn't fool someone you really cared about, no matter how much you wanted to help me.'

Lisa opened her mouth to reply but Jackie shook her head. 'No, for once I'm giving you an order. Shut up a minute. I've been so selfish and wrapped up in myself, that I've hardly thought about you and Brian. You don't love him, do you, Lisa, not like I loved Gordon?'

Burying her head in the baby's shawl, Lisa felt an unexpected flush of tears. 'No,' she whispered.

'Did you ever?'

'Not really. He seemed so immature, but I thought that once he had a wife and family, a house of our own, he'd grow up. There were glimpses, now and then, of what he could be, what he was struggling inside to be. Like on our honeymoon, for instance. I expected I'd grow to love him, but at home he's stuck firmly under his mother's thumb.' She sniffed. 'Oh dear, this is no way to talk. I should be comforting you.'

'No, no,' urged Jackie. 'Go on.' There was an unexpected tinge of sternness in her voice that Lisa had never heard before.

'Well, there's nothing much to go on about,' she said sadly. 'Mrs Smith resents me. In fact, I think she hates me.' She recalled the way the woman had acted less than an hour ago. 'Brian is so used to doing her bidding, so used to them being a couple and doing things together, that he doesn't realize it's *us* that's the couple now and I just get pushed to one side.'

'Will Mrs Smith hate the baby?'

'Oh no,' Lisa said emphatically. 'She can't wait for a grandchild, a grandson, "Little Brian", she wants to call him. It's all she's talked about for months. Brian thinks I should go back to work and she can look after him during the day.

They've made the spare bedroom into a nursery. Why, only the other day, she was talking about putting the cot in her bedroom for the first few weeks so she can see to him during the night.' She smiled grimly. 'There's going to be some battles when — '

'Lisa,' Jackie interrupted harshly. 'That's no place for a baby, for Noël.'

'What?' Lisa's jaw dropped, the suspicions that had arisen since she entered the room confirmed.

Now Jackie looked close to tears herself. 'Oh, gosh! This is an awful thing to do. I can't let you take Noël back to a house with so much hate — you used that word yourself.'

Lisa didn't answer. The baby smacked his lips and wriggled gently. She felt his arms pushing, as if he was attempting to struggle free from his tight wrapping, and her insides began to churn as she realized the implication of her friend's words.

'When I was expecting him,' Jackie said quietly, 'I never imagined I carried a tiny human being. I know that sounds stupid. Even when he began to kick, he never seemed real. But when he was born and they handed him to me, it seemed like a miracle.' She shook her head in wonder and involuntarily stretched out her arms. Lisa placed the baby in them and Jackie bent her head and stroked his face with the back of her finger. 'I can't describe the feeling. It was so unexpected and I began to think, "How on earth can I give him away, even to Lisa, who I'd trust him with more than anyone in the world?"' She smiled at Lisa warmly. 'At first, I felt really terrible. I desperately wanted to keep him but knew I couldn't possibly let you down. Then I began to think about you and Brian and realized how unhappy you were – you are, aren't you?'

Lisa nodded numbly.

'You're a wonderful friend, Lisa, but when you said those things about Mrs Smith! It wouldn't be right for her to get her hands on *any* baby, let alone mine. She'd suffocate him, like she's suffocated Brian. You know that's true, don't you?'

'Yes,' whispered Lisa. 'And I've just realized something else. If he really *was* my baby, I'd feel the same as you.'

'There!' Jackie relaxed back in the pillow, smiling. 'You

don't think badly of me then?'

Lisa didn't answer. She was appalled to discover what a second-class mother she would have been to Noël. If she really *had* been pregnant, she would have insisted on their own place, would have known instinctively that the unhealthy atmosphere in that house was unfit for a baby. And if Brian had refused to leave? Why, she would have left all by herself.

She sighed. Jackie was watching her with concern.

'I've really landed you in trouble, haven't I?'

'At least I don't need to go to Liverpool, that's something,' said Lisa resignedly.

'What do you mean?'

'That's where they think I've gone, and as telegrams show the post office they're sent from, I was going to send one from Liverpool in a few days' time saying I'd had the baby early – I could have got there and back the same day. Then I would have gone to our flat and next week, I'd have just turned up at the house with Noël in a taxi and — ' she paused. 'Oh, my God!'

'What's the matter?' asked Jackie in alarm.

'I didn't know how much I dreaded going back with the baby. I suddenly feel an enormous sense of relief, but more than that, I realize *I needn't go back at all!*' She stared at her friend, eyes shining with excitement, her body tingling. She was free!

'But that means I've broken up your marriage,' said Jackie tragically. 'This is all my fault.'

Lisa shook her head vigorously. 'No, it's Brian's fault and his mother's – and mine for not being firm enough. Anyway, it's not a proper marriage, not a proper marriage at all.'

Her heart lifted as she unlocked the door to the flat and switched on the lamp. She breathed a sigh of relief. It all looked so warm and cheerful compared to where she'd been living. There was a letter addressed to her propped up on the sideboard. It was from Ralph.

'*Reckon you'll read this just as quickly if I leave it here rather than post it,*' he'd written. '*I'm off to Hollywood. Hollywood! Just a smallish part, someone's dropped out, so I'm wanted straight away.*

206

Catching the plane tonight. Wish me luck!'

'Good luck, Ralph,' she murmured aloud.

'Jackie seems much better lately,' he continued. *'I've been popping in every day. What have you two been up to? There's something funny going on!*

'Hope you're happy, my good friend, Lisa. God bless, Ralph.'

Lisa folded the letter and put it away in her bag. She was glad for Ralph, but sorry he wouldn't be there for Christmas. It reminded her that Victoria was locked in the wardrobe at home – no, not home now – in Mrs Smith's house in Chiswick. Somehow she'd have to get Victoria and her Jane Austen books and her clothes. In a few days, she'd write to Brian and tell him the truth, the whole truth – that it had been Jackie's baby all the time. Much as she despised him – and she hadn't realized until she'd spoken to her friend in the hospital just how much she did – she couldn't just disappear into thin air and let him go on thinking for the rest of his life that he had a child he'd never seen. 'If he had been a real man,' she thought contemptuously, 'there's no way I could have fooled him into thinking I was pregnant all those months. In all that time, he didn't touch me, didn't see me without my clothes on, not once.'

After unpacking her bag, she went out and did some shopping, made a meal and returned to the hospital to see Jackie, who by now was almost bubbling over with happiness.

'I want lots more children,' she said the minute Lisa walked into the room. 'Three more, at least. Another boy and two girls.'

Lisa laughed. 'Who is to father this ideal family?' she asked.

'Lord knows – I'll advertise! It won't be Gordon, though, I can tell you that. I've finished with him.'

'That's a relief,' said Lisa thankfully.

'And I've decided what to do. I'll have to leave the flat – it's too small for a baby and the stairs are dangerous. I'll go and live with my aunts. They're not the slightest bit stuffy. Both of them were suffragettes and they'll think having a baby outside marriage is very avant-garde. My mother will come round eventually.'

'I'm so happy you're happy,' said Lisa, and meant it with all her heart.

That Saturday morning, Lisa went to see Mr Greenbaum. She would have gone earlier, but was worried that she might encounter Brian. Every week since she'd left the shop, she'd written the old man a letter, making a variety of excuses for not coming to see him, and he had replied within a few days, often with a long message from Miriam at the end. He hadn't answered her last two letters and she was worried.

She made the familiar journey along Old Brompton Road, past Harrods, its windows ablaze with Christmas lights and decorations, and began to hurry as she neared the shop, longing to see her old employer again.

There it was, the windows thick with dust. She saw the Closed sign written in Mr Greenbaum's old-fashioned script as she approached the door and she thought fondly, 'He's forgotten to turn it round. He's always doing that.' To her surprise the door was locked, but still she peered inside, expecting to see his stooped form bent over a pile of books on his desk; the shop was empty, however. He'd only been coming in half a day since she'd left, but Saturday mornings were one of his busiest times. He must be ill, she thought with alarm, to miss a Saturday, right before Christmas too. She'd go round to his flat straight away.

She turned and bumped into a man who was vaguely familiar, a middle-aged man in a loud tweed suit and a grey overcoat with a velvet collar. His soft felt hat was pulled rakishly down over one eye.

'I've been following you,' he said. 'I came out of Harrods just as you were passing. Lisa, isn't it?'

'That's right. And who . . . oh, I remember, Morry Sopel!'

'Himself,' he said with a grin.

She also remembered he was a criminal and tried to look offhand, but it was difficult with his warm brown eyes smiling into hers.

'Where are you off to?' he asked.

'I came to see Mr Greenbaum,' she said. 'I left months ago to . . . well, I got married.'

'To the little boy I met?' he asked mischievously.

'Yes,' she said stiffly. 'Anyway, the shop's closed. I was just going round to the flat to make sure everything's all right. Goodbye.' She turned to leave but to her dismay he began to walk along beside her.

'Think a lot of old Harry, do you?'

'Of course I do.'

'And he thought a lot of you. I could tell by the way he hovered over you like a guardian angel when I asked you out to lunch.'

'I love him,' she said simply. 'He's been like a father to me.'

Suddenly, he put his hand on her arm. She was about to shrug him away indignantly, when he said in a gentle voice, 'I'm afraid there's bad news, my dear. Old Harry's dead.'

'What!'

'He'd been ill for ages, though you probably knew that. Two weeks ago, he had a heart attack and died a few days later.'

'Oh, no!' She felt an ache in her throat.

'Come on, let's get you a drink.' She numbly allowed herself to be led into the pub on the corner of the street, the one where Mr Greenbaum used to have his liquid lunch.

'What about Miriam?' she asked when they'd sat down.

'Miriam took it very badly. She's gone into a home.'

Lisa began to cry softly.

'He was an old man, Lisa. He'd had more than his share of time.'

'That doesn't make it any easier,' she sobbed.

On Christmas Eve Lisa stood by the window watching the traffic as it crawled along Brompton Road. Cars were bumper to bumper and drivers sounded their horns in frustration. The shops had just closed and people were making their way home along the crowded pavements.

Inside, the house was silent as the grave. Two days ago Jackie had come home from hospital with a thriving Noël. They'd spent one night in the flat before leaving for Bournemouth. Jackie had pleaded with Lisa to come back with her for Christmas.

'You can't stay here on your own,' she said impatiently.

'Ralph's in America and Piers is going home. And with the Greenbaums gone . . .'

'I'll be all right,' Lisa insisted stubbornly. 'I've got to learn to live by myself some time.'

Jackie shook her head in resignation. 'There's no arguing with you, Lisa. I'll telephone on Christmas Day.' She chucked the baby under the chin. His wide blue eyes seemed to stare right into hers. 'Say goodbye to Auntie Lisa, there's a darling,' then she was gone in a flurry of suitcases and carrier bags, Noël clutched to her breast as if she never intended letting him go. Lisa stood on the pavement waving until the taxi disappeared.

She sighed. As soon as Christmas was over she'd have to look for a job and decide whether to keep the flat on. The five pounds rent was more than half her anticipated wages, yet she couldn't bear the idea of advertising for a flatmate and sharing with a total stranger.

The telephone rang. Before picking up the receiver, she took a deep breath. Jackie wasn't expected to ring until tomorrow, so this could be Brian. She'd written to him a week ago and half-expected he might call.

It was Morry Sopel. 'What are you doing tonight?' he demanded.

'There's a good play on the radio,' she replied.

'Beautiful girls like you don't stay in listening to the radio on Christmas Eve,' he said in a shocked voice. 'How about dinner, the Savoy. Come on,' he coaxed.

Despite all she knew about Morry, she was tempted but remembered old Harry Greenbaum. He'd turn in his recently-dug grave if he knew.

'I'm sorry, no,' she said, trying to keep the regret out of her voice.

He rang off, sounding slightly annoyed, and Lisa hoped she'd never hear from him again.

As expected, Jackie telephoned on Christmas Day. Her aunts adored Noël who, in the space of a few days, had learnt to smile.

'Has Brian called?' she asked eventually.

'No,' said Lisa.

'He must be crazy to prefer his mother to you.'

That was the conclusion Lisa herself had reached. She imagined them sitting together in that cold cheerless room and felt enormously relieved that she wasn't there with them.

'How are you getting on? I keep thinking of you, all by yourself.'

'I'm fine,' Lisa said cheerfully. 'I went to Kensington Gardens this morning and I was just about to put some of your records on.'

Later on, she said to herself, 'I *am* fine, I really am. It's only natural to be upset over Mr Greenbaum and the fact my marriage turned out so badly, and it would be lovely if Ralph was here to talk to . . . But apart from all those things, I'm fine.'

A few days later, early on a dismal, grey Sunday morning, she took a taxi to Chiswick and asked the driver to park some distance down the road from Mrs Smith's house. She sat in the back of the cab, chatting to the driver, a gregarious Cockney, waiting for her mother-in-law to leave for church.

'I hope you're not intending to make away with the family silver, darlin',' the cabbie joked. 'Don't want no stolen goods in my vehicle.'

'No, it's just my personal possessions.' Somehow, she'd found herself spilling out the story of her marriage to this total stranger.

As she spoke, the front door opened and Mrs Smith emerged in her brown Sunday coat with Brian behind her. He sprang forward to open the gate and they walked down the road in the opposite direction, as Lisa knew they would. Mrs Smith linked her son's arm and Lisa thought there was something terribly pathetic about the pair, locked in their arid affection. They disappeared into the half-darkness.

'That's them.' She opened the door to alight.

The driver must have thought the same as she did. 'Poor sods,' he muttered.

The house smelled of stale cabbage. She went upstairs and unlocked the wardrobe. Victoria could just be seen, sitting comfortably on top of the set of Jane Austen novels, staring at Lisa in pained surprise.

'You poor thing, have you been lonely?' Lisa gave her a quick hug before laying her on the bed and dragging the suitcases out from beneath it. She quickly packed her clothes, leaving the coats to carry over her arm, and was about to remove her wedding and engagement rings and leave them on the dressing table when she changed her mind and, carrying her burdens downstairs, went into the kitchen. On the draining board stood Brian's Humpty Dumpty mug beside the matching egg cup. She dropped her rings in it and put the front-door key on the table.

When she went outside, the taxi was in front of the house and the driver got out and helped with the luggage.

'That the lot?' he asked, when everything was stowed away.

She nodded wordlessly.

'Goodbye, Brian,' she whispered, blinking back unexpected tears as they drove away. 'I would have made a good wife,' she thought sadly, 'if only you'd let me.'

Chapter 22

On New Year's Day Lisa went to see Miriam. The home was in a small village on the edge of Epping Forest, a large pleasant house in its own spacious, tree-filled grounds.

'She's much better than she was,' the Matron said, 'but every now and then her mind completely goes and she's living in the past.' She took Lisa upstairs to Miriam's room. 'She won't sit in the lounge with the other residents, though she might come round to that in time.'

Without her garish make-up, Miriam looked terrible. At last she was the old woman she'd fought against becoming. She sat crouched and wizened in her chair, her silver hair combed loose.

She recognized her visitor immediately. 'Lisa! Oh Lisa, what am I to do without my Harry?' she cried.

Lisa took her liver-spotted hand. She had no idea what to reply. Eventually she said, 'I don't know, dear, but you're lucky to have such wonderful memories. Not many women are so fortunate.'

Miriam seemed anxious to know what he'd said about her in the shop. 'Was he miserable, Lisa? I used to nag him terribly. Did he complain about me much?'

'Never,' Lisa lied stoutly. 'He was one of the happiest men I've ever known.'

'Really?' Her eyes became moist. 'I loved him dearly, you know.'

'He knew that and he worshipped you.'

Miriam suddenly frowned. 'Are you looking after the shop properly?' She seemed to have forgotten Lisa was supposed to have a baby.

'The shop is closed,' Lisa said gently. Presumably, with Harry gone, it would be sold.

'Closed?' The woman's eyes flashed fire and for a few seconds the years fell away. 'Harry's shop closed! That's very presumptuous of you, Lisa. You must re-open it immediately.'

'But . . .'

'There are no buts about it,' said Miriam angrily. 'There's no way that shop will close while I'm alive. Harry lived for his shop. In fact,' she added bitterly, 'sometimes I think he thought more about it than he did me.'

Lisa was about to argue but the fire in Miriam's eyes suddenly faded and she turned away and began to rock to and fro and speak of things long past. 'Sarah has borrowed my blue satin shoes, Mama,' she said in a little girlish voice. 'And she didn't ask. Sometimes I hate her.'

'Oh, Miriam!' Lisa leaned over, kissed her raddled cheek and left.

She still had her key to the shop. Next morning, she opened it up for business again. The place smelt mustier than usual and there was dust everywhere. She cleaned up quickly and began to attend to the pile of letters that had arrived. A few customers came in and the familiar ones expressed surprise and pleasure to see her again. Most of them knew Harry was dead and offered their condolences.

The atmosphere was strange, uncanny without the old man. Although she'd worked alone before on numerous occasions, it was different now, knowing there was no chance the door would open and Mr Greenbaum would come shuffling in, mumbling something philosophic through his beard. 'At least,' she thought sadly, 'it solves the problem of me getting a job.'

All morning long, every time someone came in, Lisa looked up quickly, half-expecting Brian to walk in wanting stationery. But perhaps someone had told him she was back, because in the three years she remained in the shop they never once came face to face. Occasionally she saw him at lunch-time, clutching his sandwiches on his way to the park, or in the evening, a stooped young-old man going home to his mother.

At times, it seemed to Lisa as if nothing had changed. Then, just as quickly, she'd think everything had changed irrevocably. She re-adopted the old familiar routine, leaving Queen's Gate at half-past eight and walking the same route to work. Yet Harry wasn't there and she returned home to an empty flat which felt as lonely as the shop without Jackie.

'I'm only leading half the life I used to,' she thought sometimes, 'and it's the best half that's gone.'

After she'd worked in the shop for six weeks, Lisa began to get worried. Her salary hadn't been paid and the money in her savings account was almost gone. She didn't like to help herself to the takings and anyway, most of it was in cheques. Much as she loved Miriam, she couldn't work for nothing – the rent had to be paid and she had to eat. She was mulling over the problem one morning, wondering how to approach Miriam and sort out the matter of her wages, when the door opened and a young man came in. He wore a bowler hat and a dark formal suit and carried a briefcase and a rolled umbrella.

'Is it something specific you want or would you just like to browse?'

'Is this Mrs Lisa Smith I am addressing?' He removed his hat.

She couldn't help but grin; his stilted speech was quite funny. 'It is and you are,' she said.

He handed her a white card. 'I represent Harwich Cooper, the solicitors handling the late Mr Harold Greenbaum's affairs. I have a letter for you which he requested be handed to you personally.'

Her heart twisted as she took the crisp white envelope addressed to her in old Harry's lovely curved script. 'Should I open it now?' she asked, preferring to read it later when the visitor had gone.

'Read it whenever you wish,' said the young man stiffly. Lisa wondered if this was the first time he'd been sent on such a mission. 'I have another letter from my principal, explaining a detail of our client's will.' He coughed nervously. 'I understand from Mrs Greenbaum, wife of the deceased, that you have undertaken to look after this shop.'

'Your understanding is correct,' said Lisa, trying not to

laugh. 'I hope that means you're going to pay me some wages.'

'A cheque will be sent monthly,' he confirmed.

'Thank goodness, I can eat tonight.'

'I shall instruct the bank to set up an account in your name so you can deposit the takings and draw cheques. I take it you know how to obtain new stock?'

'Harry mainly got it off people bringing books in, though sometimes he went to book-sales in an hotel near Victoria Station. I'll carry on doing the same.' She felt thrilled at the idea of so much responsibility.

'Good. Well, I think that's all.' His body sagged with relief. 'It's been nice meeting you, Mrs Smith.' He went over to the door. 'I say, I don't suppose you fancy coming for a drink?'

Lisa looked up in surprise. Now the formal business was over, he looked quite cheerful.

'Or lunch?' he added hopefully.

'Not likely,' she said indignantly. 'You seem to forget I'm a married woman.'

'My dear Miss Lisa,

'I asked for this to be hand-delivered in case the dragon opened it. I am leaving you a little something in my Will. It is to buy a house, dear Lisa. It is important that you escape soon, otherwise you will remain in the dragon's lair forever and eventually she will consume you with her fire and you will become ash, like Brian. You can call the house after me, "Harry's Haven", or "Greenbaum's Folly". My hand trembles because I know I will be dead when you get this. Still, death might bring some consolation. Who knows, as you read my letter, I might be having uproarious fun with Minnie Kopek!

'Your dear, good friend, Harry.'

'You silly old man,' whispered Lisa, smiling through her tears. Even in death, he was capable of making her laugh.

The solicitors' letter stated that their client, Mr Harold Greenbaum, had left her a thousand pounds in his Will. When the money came, Lisa put it in her Post Office account. She didn't need a house, but one day she'd spend it on something old Harry would have approved of.

*

Nowadays, Lisa saw little of Piers. He had a new partner, a surly middle-aged man called William who could scarcely bring himself to say hallo when Lisa met him on the stairs. Ralph had never returned from Hollywood, where he was acquiring a reputation as a solid, reliable supporting actor, though his parts were gradually getting bigger and more important. He wrote frequently.

'You MUST start your acting classes again. Godfrey Perrick was an old ham, completely over the top. If he didn't think much of your acting ability, it probably means you're good! Anyway, hardly anyone in Hollywood can act, so why worry? You have no ties in England, why not come and live here? Your life sounds very dull, in the shop alone all day and no one to keep you company at home. Lisa, you're only twenty and too young and lovely to hide yourself away.

'And what about boyfriends – you never mention any? I have another "companion" by the way, Michael . . .'

'I never mention boyfriends because there aren't any,' she replied. 'I'm still too numb over the breakdown of my marriage to start a new relationship. My life seemed to change course completely in the matter of a few days; I left Brian, old Harry died and Jackie went away. For the moment, I'm quite content with this quiet, rather boring life. I have to work SOMEWHERE, and the shop is where I most want to be – anyway, they've increased my wages by fifty per cent which means I can afford to keep the flat on. I couldn't do that working anywhere else

'Your latest film sounds a joke – I can't see you as John the Baptist and hope they don't cut your head off for real!

'Jackie sends her love, Noël is thriving – I go down to Bournemouth to see them every month on a Sunday.

'Your dear, dear friend, Lisa.

P.S. I kept thinking of Harry when Mr Attlee lost power and Churchill became Prime Minister again – that would have killed him if his poor old heart hadn't.'

She'd been back in the shop for over a year and was struggling with the typewriter one morning when a striking-looking middle-aged man came in. He was tall, well over six feet, with a shock of prematurely-grey hair and the face of a Greek god. His clothes were casual, though well-cut and clearly expensive. Lisa felt as if she'd seen him before, very recently.

'Is it something specific you've — '

'My God! What on earth are you doing here?'

His look of amazement was so disconcerting she began to stammer, 'I'm sorry, we must have met before, but I'm afraid I can't . . .'

He interrupted her again. 'Last time I came in here, there was an old man serving.'

'That was Harry Greenbaum, the owner. I'm afraid he died last year.'

'But why are you here? You're the last sort of person I expected to meet in a bookshop.'

Lisa wore a yellow jersey dress with a high neck and long gathered sleeves. The tan leather belt which encircled her narrow waist was the same colour as her high-heeled boots. She'd combed her hair into a pony tail and tied it with a yellow ribbon.

She felt too embarrassed to answer. She also felt slightly annoyed by the man's intense stare, his wide-eyed look of surprise.

'I don't know what you mean,' she muttered eventually.

'You should be on a catwalk modelling clothes or posing for a fashion photographer. You should be a society hostess or an actress.'

Her annoyance grew. 'Well, I'm not,' she snapped. 'I manage a bookshop.' She felt like sticking out her tongue and adding, 'So there!'

He burst out laughing. 'Sorry,' he said abjectly. 'I'm a writer and I continually see drama in the most innocuous situations. You look so out of place in this little drab bookshop. My immediate reaction was to wonder what you're doing here. I suppose I expected someone quite different. Sorry,' he repeated.

'You're forgiven – for the most part,' she said. 'I would describe this shop as interesting, not drab.'

She remembered now where she'd seen him before –

though not in person. His photograph was in the window of a bookshop in Old Brompton Road, along with a display of his latest novel. She recalled thinking how attractive he looked. His name was Clive Randolph and she'd tried to read one of his books once, but took it back to the library in disgust. It was full of self-conscious preening, a selfish intellectual exercise unintelligible to the ordinary man or woman in the street.

Because she hadn't liked his book, she began to get irritated again. 'How can I help you?' she asked coldly.

'I'm looking for something on cannibalism for the background of my next novel.'

He stayed for over an hour and purchased three books. After promising to bring her a copy of his latest novel, he left.

'What did you think of him, Harry?' Lisa asked aloud.

'Good-looking but too clever by half, in my opinion. Needs taking down a peg or two, as my mam used to say.'

She rather hoped he'd forget to bring his novel. Apart from not wishing to read it, she wasn't sure if she wanted to see him again, but in less than two weeks' time, Lisa was sleeping with Clive Randolph.

He telephoned the shop the following day. 'Why don't I give you my novel over dinner?'

She said promptly, 'I'm busy this week.'

'Next week then.'

Lisa was about to turn him down again, when she hesitated. Lately, she'd begun to dread going home to an empty flat.

'All right,' she said grudgingly. 'How about Saturday?'

Saturdays seemed even more lonely than other nights. She was conscious that all over London people were out having a good time.

'Saturday it is,' he said cheerfully.

He spent most of the evening lecturing her on various aspects of modern literature, using his own work as an example of how things should be done. Lisa found him interesting but would have liked to get a word in edgewise now and then.

Outside the restaurant, he hailed a taxi. 'I really enjoyed myself tonight,' he said on the way home. 'We must do this again soon.'

When they reached Queen's Gate, he alighted from the taxi with her. 'There's no need,' she protested. 'You keep it to go home in.'

'I only live a short walk from here,' he said.

She had no intention of asking him in and was trying to think how he could be put off when Piers appeared looking gloomily tipsy.

'I'm in for a wigging off the horrible William,' he groaned. 'I promised to be back hours ago. Shelter me Lisa, please. I'm not in the mood to be told off. I need another stiff drink before I face him.'

'All I've got is wine,' she said.

'I suppose that'll do. What a pity you're not Jackie, then we could have got plastered together.' He sighed mournfully. 'I suppose I should get rid of the awful beast, but I don't know how to tell him his presence is no longer welcome.'

He unlocked the front door and it seemed only natural for Clive to come in too, up to Lisa's flat, where Piers tearfully told them of the ordeal of living with the horrible William. An hour later, fortified by an entire bottle of wine, he left to face the beast.

After he'd gone, Lisa smiled sadly. 'He's missing Ralph,' she said. 'Ralph is — '

Without a word, Clive Randolph fell upon her, crushing her in his arms and pressing his lips against hers. For a second, she was outraged but before she could raise her arms to push him away, her body responded to his kiss and she felt herself sinking, sinking . . .

He half-carried, half-dragged her towards the bedroom and once inside began to tear off his clothes. With equal enthusiasm, she removed her own and they sank on the bed together in a wild, naked embrace.

His hands were all over her, touching, caressing, driving her wild with desire. 'Please, please,' she whispered urgently. 'I can't wait any longer.'

Making love with Brian had been pale compared to this.

She'd never dreamed it could be so glorious.

'Christ Almighty!' he groaned when it was over and they lay glued together by perspiration on the single bed. 'You were made for this. How much will you take to lie there for the rest of your life, waiting just for me?'

She ran her finger down his chest and he shivered. 'Nothing,' she said. 'In fact, I'm going to get up in a minute and make a cup of tea.'

He was married but lived apart from his wife, he told her a few weeks later. Divorce was pending – though, he added quickly, he couldn't make any promises.

'Then don't make them,' Lisa said, just as quickly. She'd grown to like him, but all she wanted was his presence in her bed once or twice a week. He made her feel like a schoolgirl as he continued to lecture her on modern literature and other esoteric subjects.

'You seem to think I'm a complete ignoramus,' she complained one night when they were in bed together.

'I'm not interested in your brain, only your body.' He began to caress her breasts and her insides turned to liquid. Nevertheless, she persisted.

'Wouldn't you like to know what I think about Jane Austen or George Eliot?'

'Shut up.' He began to touch her nipples with his tongue, little soft flickers that made her want to shout with pleasure and she didn't wait for an answer, just let herself be carried away by the passion of the moment.

Gradually he began to bore her. He was too taken up with the sound of his own voice, never asking for her opinion on anything. Nevertheless, she continued to see him.

'I'm not interested in his brain, only his body,' she thought with a grin. 'He'd have a fit if he knew.'

Just before Christmas, Jackie came to London to do some shopping and stayed with Lisa overnight. Noël, who was two, was quite happy to be left with his grandparents, who adored him. Jackie's mother had 'come round', as she put it, a long time ago.

'This is just like old times,' she said, 'except I'm drinking milk instead of whisky.' They were sitting in the flat and the floor was already strewn with paper bags and parcels.

'Not really,' Lisa thought sadly, and it wasn't just the milk. She vividly recalled the fresh-faced sparkling girl in pink satin pyjamas who'd let her into this very flat nearly six years ago. Jackie had aged considerably since she'd left London and had begun to acquire a matronly look. She wore a paisley-patterned, long-sleeved shirtdress, buttoned severely to the neck – the sort of dress that once upon a time she wouldn't have been seen dead in! Her blonde curls were brushed smooth, her only make-up a touch of pale pink lipstick. For some reason she couldn't fathom, Lisa felt a lump in her throat, remembering the spiky black lashes of the old Jackie.

Noël had sent a portrait of his Auntie Lisa – a wild, crayonned scribble. 'It's better than some of the stuff in that art gallery by the shop,' Lisa said dryly. 'The child is undoubtedly a genius. It's hard to imagine he was nearly mine.'

'I wonder if we would have got away with it,' mused Jackie. 'It seems a mad idea now.'

They were both silent for a while, then Lisa said ruefully, 'We've made a rare old mess of our lives, haven't we, Jackie? A few years ago, I was married and you were madly in love and now look at us!'

'Oh, I don't know,' said Jackie in a strange voice and Lisa looked at her quickly. Her friend was blushing.

'You've met someone,' Lisa said gleefully. 'Tell me all about him.'

'You must promise not to laugh.'

'As if I would!'

'It's the vicar. His name is Laurence Murray and he's a widower. His wife couldn't have children and he's longing for a family – he thinks the world of Noël.'

'Do you love him?' Lisa asked cautiously.

'I'm not sure, but I think so.'

'I hope you'll be very happy.' Lisa reached out and clasped Jackie's plump white hand.

'Oh, I will,' she replied serenely. 'I've discovered my

vocation, you see. I want to be the mother of lots of children.'

Lisa went down to Bournemouth for Jackie's wedding in March.

Laurence was a tall, lanky man with a gentle face and eyes only for his new bride. Jackie, in a rather severe blue tweed suit and a white taffeta blouse, was starry-eyed.

'You only *thought* you loved him a few months ago,' Lisa said with a smile. 'It looks as if you're quite sure now.'

'I am, I am.' Jackie kissed her on the cheek. 'And it's so much better than with Gordon. In fact, it's magic!'

After the church ceremony they went back to the old shabby vicarage for refreshments. Lisa felt strangely alone, despite the friendliness of the other guests. 'I've got no one,' she thought bitterly. 'This thing with Clive won't last, I don't want it to. In a few weeks' time I'll be twenty-two. What on earth's to become of me?'

Chapter 23

In the autumn of 1954, Miriam died. The Matron rang Lisa who'd been her only visitor. 'It was very peaceful,' she said. 'She was dead when we went to wake her this morning.'

Despite her sorrow, Lisa felt a sense of relief. Over the last twelve months, the shop had become a burden. She'd longed to leave and start afresh but knew Miriam's time on earth was limited, so waited. Now the shop would be closed and she could get on with her life.

She knew exactly what she wanted to do.

Ralph had sent a list of drama schools in London. The most prestigious ones she crossed off – she hadn't the nerve to approach a place like RADA – and wrote to the remainder for their brochure. In the end she settled on The Bryn Ayres Acting Academy in Sloane Square, mainly because they didn't demand an audition. The fees were horrendous and took half of Harry Greenbaum's legacy, though the remainder would be more than enough to live on during the year's course.

Most of the students at Bryn Ayres came from wealthy families. As long as they could afford to pay, they were taken on. Lisa's expectations were low when she started, so she wasn't disappointed.

The Principal was an American, Harvey Roots, a failed actor. Lisa could remember him in bit parts in old Hollywood films. He took himself very seriously, continually talked about his 'art' and was more interested in name-dropping than in teaching his students how to act.

'As I said to Clark during *It Happened One Night*,' he would drawl, or, 'When Greta and I were making *Ninotchka*.' Sometimes, it was all Lisa could do not to giggle out loud.

Still, it was an acting school, albeit not a very good one, and she was bound to learn *something* there – and it had one advantage over all the others. Every summer, Harvey Roots arranged for his students to spend a season acting in a holiday camp he part-owned in Wales.

'You'll be paid a pittance,' Ralph wrote, when she let him know what she'd done, *'and the plays are abominable, usually farces, though they amuse the campers no end. The good news is you'll get your Equity card, which means you'll be a professional actress!'*

Clive Randolph was impressed by Lisa's decision to become an actress, convinced that his influence had steered her towards a more artistic career. Lisa couldn't be bothered to disillusion him. One night as he was leaving, he said casually, 'I won't be around for a week or so. I'm going away.'

A few days later, she saw his photograph in the paper. He'd got married. The bride was another writer – a grim-looking woman wearing heavy horn-rimmed glasses. Lisa felt annoyed and hurt that he'd just walked out of her life without an explanation. After all, they'd shared some high emotion together. To her surprise, the following week he rang up. 'Same time as usual tonight?' he said breezily.

'But you're just married!' Lisa gasped.

'Oh, you saw that. I rather hoped you wouldn't. It doesn't mean we have to break up, Lisa.'

'Yes, it does,' she replied indignantly. 'I'll not be a party to you two-timing your new wife.'

'I married Patricia for her intellectual ability. She's not terribly interested in sex.'

'In other words, you want a woman for your head and another for your bed,' said Lisa. 'Well, too bad, Clive. Find someone else.'

She slammed the receiver down. Clive's services were no longer required, anyway. At Bryn Ayres there were half a dozen young men clamouring to take her out.

In the little holiday-camp theatre, Lisa was the despair of the producer. As Ralph had prophesied, the plays were mainly farces, requiring the actors to leap about the stage, shrieking their lines at the tops of their voices. Lisa could neither leap nor shriek. She had an almost deadpan delivery and an innate stillness on stage, quite unsuited to the parts she was

225

given. She was almost in despair herself, when a young stagehand approached one night after the performance. He wasn't part of Harvey Roots' group, but was gaining backstage experience and hoped to become a producer himself one day.

'Have you been to a method-acting school?' he asked.

'Why, no,' she replied, somewhat surprised. 'Why do you ask?'

'Because of the way you act, so still and understated. You should be in serious drama, not shit like this.'

Lisa was so pleased, she kissed him. 'Thanks, I really needed that,' she said. After the way she'd been yelled at during rehearsals she was beginning to think the year at Bryn Ayres had been a waste of time and money.

When she got back from Wales, Lisa found a letter from a firm of solicitors to say that their client, Brian Smith, was suing for divorce on the grounds of desertion. She'd almost forgotten they'd been married. She wrote back and said she had no objections. When the Final Decree came through a few months later she felt sad and wondered if she'd still be married to Brian if they'd got their own place right after the wedding. Why, they might even have had several children by now and she and Jackie could compare notes. Her friend had already had another son, Robert, and was pregnant again. If it was a girl this time, she was going to call her Elizabeth. 'Though in fact she'll be Lisa, like you,' Jackie said, the last time Lisa went to stay in the big noisy vicarage.

Over the next year, Lisa, her Equity card tucked in her purse, got three non-speaking parts in films and a walk-on rôle in a West End play which ran for three months. She felt her career had got off to a healthy start and earned what seemed a lot of money for relatively little work.

However, her most important part was played in Bournemouth when she became Godmother to Lisa, a little creamy baby girl, the spitting image of her mother.

'One more and I've finished,' Jackie said as they walked down the path towards the church. Noël, his face unnaturally clean, trotted dutifully behind, holding Robert's hand.

Lisa glanced at the pretty baby in her arms, marvelling at how fast her eyes were turning from blue to Jackie's smokey grey. 'You should have an extra one for me,' she laughed. 'After all, you owe me a baby.'

Jackie squeezed her arm. 'You'll have your own some day,' she said. 'Don't forget, I was twenty-eight before I had Noël.'

'I suppose so.'

'You're happy, aren't you, Lisa? I mean, everything's turned out well for us both, hasn't it?'

'Of course it has,' Lisa said confidently. 'I love being an actress. After all, it's what I've always wanted.'

Afterwards, she wondered if she'd said that to convince herself, rather than Jackie.

She was sitting learning lines one night – next morning she was going for an audition – when the doorbell went, three long rings, three short, which meant it was for her. Glancing at her watch, she saw it was half-past ten and wondered who on earth it could be. She prayed it wasn't Clive Randolph, for every now and then he called or telephoned, pleading to renew their relationship. She always refused.

The man on the step was a stranger – or so she thought at first. 'Hi, Lisa,' he said with a grin.

'Ralph!' She flung herself at him and dragged him inside into the light. 'You look years younger and your hair's different! I didn't recognize you.'

'They made me grow it for my latest movie,' he said shamefacedly. 'Then they dyed it blond.'

'And permed it!' She collapsed giggling on the stairs. 'You don't half look funny.'

'Thanks!' he said dryly. 'The studio would have a fit if they could hear you. They think it makes me look outrageously attractive.'

In fact he did look attractive, though not a bit like the Ralph she used to know. He wore a leather jacket over a black shirt and tight jeans.

'You look gorgeous,' she soothed, linking his arm as they climbed the stairs together. 'So gorgeous, I might not be able to restrain myself once I get you in my flat – so beware!'

*

Ralph Layton was not yet as famous as Laurence Olivier or Charles Laughton, as he'd once hoped, but in his latest film, a thriller called *Raging Fury*, he had the starring role.

'The studio insisted I come over for the British première,' he told Lisa after he'd sat down. 'And I want you to come with me. Would you mind? It's next Tuesday.'

'Mind? Try keeping me away,' she said, eyes shining.

'You'll need an evening dress. I'll buy one for you.'

She bustled around him solicitously. He'd professed himself tired after the long flight from California.

'Would you like some wine or food?' she asked.

'No, but I'd love a cup of tea.' He settled himself comfortably in the chair. 'You know, it's an odd compliment to offer such a lovely young woman, but you make the best cup of tea in the world, Lisa. I've really missed it in Hollywood.'

On Tuesday afternoon, Lisa went to a beauty parlour for the first time in her life. Then she took her new dress and shoes with heels as fine as a pencil, together with a hired mink stole, along to Ralph's suite in Claridges to get dressed. A limousine would pick them up at half-past seven to take them to the cinema in Leicester Square.

When she emerged from the bedroom ready to go, Ralph gasped. 'My God, you're beautiful!'

Lisa already knew. The radiant woman who'd stared back at her from the mirror in Ralph's bedroom had startled her. She literally glowed, seemed almost unreal. Was that really Lizzie O'Brien from Chaucer Street? Her eyes looked huge, bigger than ever now they were emphasized by black liner, the lids touched with gold shadow which brought out the golden shreds in the brown pupils. And what on earth had they done to her hair, to make it ripple and shimmer whenever she moved her head the slightest fraction?

The dress was vivid red chiffon, strapless, exposing her breasts to a degree she found embarrassing and clinging to her body down to the hips, where it flared out in a multitude of frothy layers of material. She was sure she looked indecent, but to her surprise, found she didn't mind a bit. In fact, she rather enjoyed the feeling.

'You're a tart, Lizzie O'Brien,' she told herself with a grin.

'If Mam could see you now, she'd have a fit!'

Ralph came over and touched her arm. 'Oh Lisa, when I look at you, how I wish, I wish . . .' He frowned and shook his head.

Lisa stroked his cheek. 'I wish too, Ralph, I really do.'

There was a crowd outside the cinema, mainly consisting of women. They screamed hysterically at Ralph when he and Lisa alighted from the car onto the red-carpeted pavement. Before entering the foyer, he turned and waved and they screamed again.

'That was frightening,' Lisa said when they were inside. 'They'd have torn you to bits if they'd got their hands on you.'

'You get used to it,' Ralph said easily.

She nudged him, almost beside herself with excitement. 'Ralph! Jill Ireland's over there with David McCallum and there's Diana Dors. Jesus, Mary and Joseph, Dirk Bogarde's actually *looking* at me!'

Ralph squeezed her shoulders. '*Everyone's* looking at you,' he said proudly. 'It's as if you're the star, not me.'

Raging Fury wasn't a very good film. Remembering Ralph's outstanding performance in *Pygmalion*, Lisa felt he was wasted in the part. It required only a mere fraction of his talent, though she began to wonder if there was something about the film which had escaped her, because when it was over, he was showered with congratulations.

'Marvellous!' people said. 'First class, Ralph. Best thriller I've ever seen.'

'Liars!' said Ralph in a quiet moment. 'They all hate it.'

'How can you tell?' she asked, amazed.

'Because even *I* know it's a lousy film,' he said with a grin. 'The only good thing about it was the money I got paid.'

It was gone midnight before the cinema began to empty. 'There's a crowd going back to Donnelly's place,' Ralph told her. 'Want to come?'

'Of course I do! I never want tonight to end.'

Donnelly Westover had written the novel from which

229

Raging Fury was adapted. He was a slight, cheerful-looking man nearing sixty. Ralph and Lisa shared a taxi with him and his wife back to their top-floor West Kensington apartment. The long, low-ceilinged room was already full of people when they arrived.

'This lot weren't invited to the première,' Donnelly explained. 'They've been at it for hours.'

'It' appeared to be drinking. The twenty or thirty guests were in a state of advanced merriment and the shout of welcome which greeted Ralph and Donnelly as they entered almost lifted the roof off its black-painted rafters.

Lisa was besieged by people asking what films she'd been in, and had to confess that her appearances so far had been brief. 'If you blink, you'll miss them,' she said. 'I'm only here as a friend of Ralph's.'

She got separated from Ralph almost immediately, but was accepted without question by Donnelly's friends, men and women alike. Most of them seemed to be writers of one sort or another. One man had written a play with a part in it that was apparently perfect for Lisa. 'You must let me know where you live,' he said, 'and if I ever get it on, I'll contact you.'

The woman beside him laughed. 'Don't take any notice of him, Lisa. It's a lousy play. This is my husband's sneaky way of getting your address.' They began a good-natured argument about the merits of the play.

The rest of the group were involved in a heated debate over the Suez crisis.

'Churchill would never have got us into this mess,' someone said. 'Anthony Eden needs his behind kicking.'

'What! Churchill would have atom-bombed the lot of them,' a young woman cried. 'If a Labour government was in, we would have minded our own business. After all, the Suez Canal doesn't belong to us.'

Lisa hastily moved on, worried she might be asked for her opinion. She was only vaguely aware of the Suez crisis and wasn't even sure if it was over yet.

She joined another group where space flight was the topic of conversation. Donnelly Westover was waving his arms about excitedly.

'Come on, who'll take me on? A hundred quid that the Russians'll have a man in space by the end of the year.'

'I'd give a thousand,' a young man beside Lisa said fervently, 'to be at the launch with my camera.'

She turned to look at him at precisely the same time he became aware of her. He was well-built and tall, over six feet, with a mop of blond hair curling onto his neck. Bright, clear blue eyes, full of laughter, were set wide in his handsome, sensitive face. He wore jeans and a loose brown sweater over an open-necked check shirt, and he looked vaguely familiar.

He was staring at her, frowning. 'Have we met before?'

'I was just wondering the same thing,' she said, though she felt sure she would have remembered if they had.

'We can't have,' he said seriously, 'else I'd have remembered.'

'I was thinking that too.'

They were staring at each other with a mixture of curiosity and wonder when someone pushed between them to join their circle. Then Ralph touched her arm. 'There's a man I'd like you to meet,' he said. Hiding her reluctance, Lisa followed him to the corner of the room where he introduced her to a producer who was planning to stage a musical version of *Pride And Prejudice* in the New Year.

'I'm not auditioning yet, but ring my office in a few months' time and we'll arrange something.' He gave her his card and after tucking it inside her evening bag, Lisa glanced across the room, searching for the young blond man. She caught his eye immediately and wondered if he had been watching since Ralph had taken her away. The young man smiled across the crowded room. Lisa caught her breath as she smiled back.

'Eric was impressed with you,' Ralph whispered. 'I think you stand a good chance there.'

'Eric?' she replied vaguely.

'The producer who just gave you his card,' said Ralph patiently. He followed her gaze. The young man was still watching. 'Ah, I see you have more important things on your mind.' He squeezed her hand. 'Good luck.'

She smiled at him brilliantly. 'Oh, Ralph! I feel very strange. I don't even know his name, we only exchanged a few words, but I feel as if I've known him all my life.'

'That's a good omen.'

'Is it? Do people *really* fall in love at first sight?'

'They do in books and songs. I expect they do it in real life too.' He kissed her cheek affectionately. 'You make a remarkably handsome couple.'

A woman came and dragged Ralph away and Lisa suddenly found herself involved in an argument over foreign food.

'Believe me, one day pizzas will take over the world. What do you think?' a man demanded.

Conscious only of a blond head which seemed to be getting closer, Lisa confessed, 'It's not something I've given much thought to.'

'Pizza, pizza, pizza. Everywhere I go nowadays, I get pizza,' the man complained.

'Personally, I find ravioli a curse. You get given it as an hors d'oeuvre – and then there's no room for anything else. You're full before — '

'Hi, I'm Patrick.'

She turned, her eyes like stars. He'd come for her as she knew he would. His face held an expression of sheer joy mixed with something else – perhaps it was incredulity, she wasn't sure.

'I'm Lisa.'

He took her hand; it was a completely natural gesture. 'I know this sounds foolish, you can call me an idiot if you like, but I think I've fallen in love with you, Lisa.'

'Then I must be an idiot, too,' she said softly.

She felt him shiver. 'This is really weird,' he said. 'Do you feel weird?'

'Weird and wonderful.'

Perhaps they'd been made for each other. Perhaps this was the man she'd been waiting for all her life, just as he'd been waiting for her. That's why he seemed familiar. He'd always existed in a remote corner of her mind, and she in his, so that when they met they'd be bound to recognize each other instantly.

'Let's find a seat.' He put his arm around her and the touch of his large warm hand on her naked shoulder sent a delicious thrill through her body.

They would make love later on. Of that she was sure. They would make love every night for the rest of their lives. She was sure of that too. She had met Patrick. She had come home.

He lived in a flat below Donnelly Westover. 'Though it's less than half the size,' he explained. 'In fact, it's a bit of a hovel.' He was a freelance photographer and until recently only earned money sporadically when he sold a picture. 'Though lately, I've had a couple of commissions. I'm beginning to get known.'

Lisa felt a surge of pride. His career was already important to her.

'What about you?' he asked. They managed to find a space on the edge of the settee and sat close together. Lisa's body moulded into his, the skirt of her dress spilling onto his knee. 'What do you do?'

'I'm an actress, though please don't ask what I've been in because it hasn't been much – yet.'

'Okay, I won't.'

They said no more until the party broke up, both silently marvelling at the fact they'd found each other.

After she had said goodbye to Ralph and collected her coat, she took his hand and they went down to his flat, her whole being tense with anticipation of what was to come and conscious of Patrick trembling beside her.

It was even better than she could have imagined in all her wildest dreams. He didn't switch on the light. The open curtains allowed the bright moon to flood the room with a heavenly golden glow and as he removed her dress, his hands sliding down her slippery, satin shoulders, he gasped when her small pointed breasts were fully revealed to him and groaning, he buried his head between them. When his mouth touched her nipples, Lisa could scarcely stop herself from screaming aloud as an inexpressible sensation of sheer ecstasy tore through her. She pulled the dress away, throwing it to the floor where it lay like a pool of spilt blood. When Patrick removed his own clothes, Lisa reached up and with both hands began to touch him with featherlight fingers. As she travelled down his body, he began to groan again and she felt him, rock hard against her.

Now it was time for their union and as he entered her, Lisa felt as if she had left her body altogether and was somewhere on a higher plane where ordinary feelings were left behind and she was experiencing a joy which was beyond life itself.

When she woke, daylight was just beginning to struggle through the small window. Patrick's hand was flat on her abdomen. She watched him sleeping. He looked young and vulnerable and she had to resist kissing him awake. There was so much she wanted to ask him. About his family, for instance, and where did he come from?

Lisa glanced around the gradually lightening room. The furniture was shabby, nothing matched. The walls were a patchy cream and needed painting. He could come and live in Queen's Gate, she decided, and they'd push the twin beds together to make a double. They'd spend a lot of time in bed. Her swift intake of breath at the thought of them together for the rest of their lives was audible. She glanced at Patrick, half-hoping it had woken him. As she watched, a shaft of pale lemony sun lit up a small section of the room, enveloping him in its soft beam. Lisa marvelled at the way it caught strands of his blond hair and his long thick lashes and turned them gold. A sensation of déjà vu overcame her. How familiar it seemed, watching a fair-haired young man lost in sleep.

The warm touch of the sun must have disturbed him. He blinked and looked at her. 'So, it wasn't a dream.'

She shook her head. 'No,' she said softly.

He began to move the flat of his hand up and down her body and she felt her insides turn to liquid.

'Jesus,' he whispered hoarsely. 'I feel as if I should wait a few minutes, out of decency or something.'

'Don't wait, don't wait,' she pleaded. 'Now!'

'What are we going to do today?' he asked later.

Lisa looked at him coyly. 'What do you want to do most?'

He laughed. 'Okay, we'll stay in bed.'

She sat up and looked around the sun-filled room. 'I spy a kettle. I'm longing for a cup of tea.' She got out of bed. The linoleum under her bare feet was freezing so she slipped her feet into her red high-heeled shoes.

'Christ, you're beautiful.'

Patrick was staring at her nakedness, adoration on his face. She laughed and briefly posed for him before slipping into his check shirt. 'Where's the water?'

'In the kitchen down the hall, but you can't go like that, I'll have a riot on my hands. Anyway, I've only got one mug.'

'I can't hear a soul about and we'll share the tea, though bags I have the first half.'

When the tea was made and she was sitting up in bed drinking out of the large cracked mug, she said, 'Don't think I'm setting a precedent. In future, we'll take turns making the first cup of the day.'

'Yes, ma'am. Any other rules you'd like to set for the next fifty years?' She could sense deep emotion behind his joking words.

'Oh, Patrick!' She touched his shoulder. 'Isn't this wonderful?' He didn't answer but began to caress her underneath the sheets until she was forced to say, 'I'll spill my tea, please stop.' He took no notice and moved his head until it was against the hollow of her waist and began to kiss her. She groaned, put down her tea and slid down the bed into his arms.

She fell asleep. When she woke Patrick was fully dressed and sitting at a small plastic table, writing. The atmosphere inside the small room was so intense, so highly charged, that she had a strong feeling that she and Patrick were the only two people left in the world. 'If I look outside the window,' she thought, 'it will be a wasteland. Everything and everyone will have disappeared except him and me.' She felt a surge of pure love that took her breath away as she watched him, his brow puckered in concentration as he wrote swiftly, the pen clutched in his hand in an awkward, schoolboyish way.

'How old are you?'

He jumped. 'You're awake! You've been spying on me. I was going to wake you soon. I've made more tea – I borrowed a mug off Donnelly.'

'You didn't answer my question. I don't usually sleep with strange men. I hardly know anything about you.'

'I'm twenty-two.'

'Is that all?' Lisa was dismayed. 'I'm years older than you, twenty-five and a half, to be precise.'

'I like older women,' he said contentedly.

'What are you writing? A report on me? What do I get out of ten?'

He laughed. 'No, I write to my mother regularly. She gets worried if she doesn't hear. If I gave you marks, you'd get eleven out of ten.' He tore two pages out of the pad, folded them and stuck them in an envelope. 'I must go out and post this later,' he said, propping the letter up against the wall. 'Now, about that tea . . .'

'Are you an only child?' asked Lisa as he handed her a mug, a pretty china one this time.

'No, I come from a large family, with lots of brothers and sisters. That's a strange thing to ask.'

'I just wondered why you wrote home regularly.' She'd immediately thought of Mrs Smith and Brian, though Patrick didn't give the impression of being a mother's boy. He put his left hand on her neck and began to stroke her cheek with his thumb. She closed her eyes briefly, dipping her head against his palm, little realizing that the next words were to be the most devastating she would hear in all her life.

'Because my mother frets – it seems odd calling her "Mother". At home we call her Mam.' He smiled ruefully. 'You see, one of my sisters ran away from home when she was sixteen – just walked out without a word and never came back. She wrote to us from London, but never gave her address. It broke Mam's – my mother's – heart.'

Lisa felt herself grow cold. 'What was your sister called?'

'Elizabeth, but we called her Lizzie. Hey, don't get up! I was going to join you in a minute.'

'I've just remembered something – I have to go.' She began to struggle into her dress. *'Don't panic,'* she told herself. *'Stay calm or he'll guess something's wrong and he might even guess what it is.'* She tried to smile. 'I have an audition this afternoon, Patrick. I'd forgotten all about it.'

'I'll come with you.'

'No!' She spoke too sharply. He looked at her, surprised and hurt. *Paddy, my dear little brother.* Ah! She felt her eyes fill with tears.

'What's wrong, darling?' He hadn't called her that before.

'Why, nothing,' she said lightly. 'What a fool I am to have forgotten. It's something quite important.'

'Will you come back afterwards?'

'Yes, I promise. About five o'clock.' That was an awful thing to do, make a promise. He'd be waiting and waiting, but how else could she get out of here?

She couldn't manage the zip on her dress. He came to help, burying his head in her shoulder. 'There *is* something wrong,' he said, his voice muffled.

She turned to face him, clasped his dear, handsome face in her hands. 'I love you, Patrick,' she said softly, and kissed him full on the lips. Then, picking up her stole, she glanced briefly at the letter on the table just to make sure, to make absolutely sure.

Mrs K. O'Brien, 2 Chaucer Street, Bootle, Liverpool.

Poor Kitty, what a curse your Lizzie has turned out to be!

Then she left.

Chapter 24

Somehow, she must have hailed a taxi, though she could never recall the journey home. It wasn't until she entered the flat in Queen's Gate that she realized where she was and found herself trembling. She ran a bath and lay in the steaming, scented water for an hour trying to make sense of things.

No wonder Patrick had seemed so familiar. No wonder she'd felt as if she'd known him all her life . . . In her mind, she went back to the party, re-living, re-writing the night's events, meeting him. What had he said: 'Have we met before?'

'No,' she'd answered. 'Else I'd have remembered.' She'd responded with her heart instead of her head. She should have been more curious. Instead, she'd thought it an aspect of love, that a man you'd been waiting to meet all your life would be *bound* to have a certain familiarity about him. She imagined herself answering his first question differently. 'I can't remember for the moment, but let's try and think where we *could* have met,' and one by one they would have crossed off Bryn Ayres, the film sets, the theatres, until it came down to, 'Where do you come from?' and the inevitable discovery that they were related. The attraction would almost certainly have died immediately – and if it hadn't, they would have pretended it didn't exist and would never, never . . . not when they knew they were brother and sister! She cursed herself for her lack of caution. Why, they hadn't even asked each other's surname!

Then she began to think about him, about Patrick. At five o'clock he would be waiting for her to return, but his wait would be in vain. Oh my God, he might even come looking for her! In fact, the more Lisa thought about it, the more certain it seemed. She would search for him, under the same circumstances. He'd ask Donnelly Westover where she lived, and she remembered telling Donnelly in the taxi from the cinema,

'On the corner of Queen's Gate and Old Brompton Road,' she'd said.

There was nothing else for it. She had to get away.

The water in the bath began to cool and she shivered, then shivered again as the memory of the glorious night she'd spent with her brother returned and for a brief, mad moment she considered going back and saying nothing. She could invent a new past, a new name, say she came from somewhere else. He could still come and live here, just as she'd planned. But the thought fled as swiftly as it had come. It could never be the same again, not for her. Not only that, he couldn't keep her hidden from his family forever and Kitty would know who she was straight away, even from a photograph.

'Oh, God!' she groaned aloud. She would remember their hours together for her entire life. There would never be another night like it, but it could never happen again. She must expunge it from her mind, try not to think about it, forget it happened. If she could.

'My brother, my lover, but for one night only,' she whispered softly

Later on, when she was dressed, she made some tea and sat wondering what to do. In a few hours, it would be five o'clock. Despite everything, she had a strong feeling that if Patrick came through the door some time tonight, she would allow herself to be swept up in his arms and . . .

Yes, she had to get away this very afternoon.

But where?

'I'm doing it again,' she thought sadly. 'Jumping out of one life into another totally alien one.' One minute she had a family, then suddenly she had none. She'd come to London a stranger completely alone in the world. Now she was about to depart, equally alone, an empty broken marriage behind her. No ties, no possessions worth speaking of. Not even anyone close to wish her goodbye.

Most people's lives seemed to run smoothly. They stayed on the same path throughout, just changing course slightly from time to time. 'Mine is more like a series of stepping stones,' she thought ruefully, 'and I hop from one stone to another whenever things go wrong . . .

'Where do I go from here?' she asked herself again.

Suddenly, she knew exactly what she would do. She'd go to California, to Hollywood. Ralph had suggested it dozens of times.

But she wouldn't tell Ralph. She didn't want him getting parts for her. She knew the contempt other actors reserved for those who'd got a part, not through merit, but through connections. She'd make it on her own!

Lisa packed her bags swiftly, collecting her favourite clothes, the Jane Austen set, and Victoria, then she wrote a letter to the landlord enclosing a fortnight's rent and apologizing for leaving so many possessions behind. 'Perhaps they could go to charity,' she suggested. On her way out, she'd push the note under Piers' door.

When she'd finished, she stood back and looked at the two rooms for the very last time. She'd left once before, but it hadn't seemed so final then and she'd been looking forward to getting married.

This time it was for good.

What wonderful times they'd had here, she and Jackie. So much laughter, so many bright-eyed, confident hopes expressed for the future, though there'd been sadness too. She remembered all the tears shed for Gordon.

Thunder rumbled in the distance and rain began to splatter against the windows, swiftly turning into a deluge. Lisa looked outside. People were running for shelter and the cars already had their windscreen wipers on.

'Where are they going, what are they thinking?' she whispered. 'How strange life is. No one knows I'm behind this window making one of the biggest decisions of my life.' What was going on behind all those other windows opposite? In some of those rooms, people might be dying or sunk in indescribable misery or having a furious row. On the other hand, they could be making love or happily reading a book. People's emotions were hidden away, behind their windows and their closed doors. In a minute she'd leave this house, walk round to Gloucester Road Air Terminal and ask for a ticket to California – and no one in a million years would be able to tell that last night she'd slept with her brother, and now she was running away to another continent.

The ringing of the telephone made her jump. It sounded extra loud, as if the rooms were stripped bare of everything. She went aross to the bedroom door and stared at it, as if just by looking she'd be able to tell who was at the other end.

She didn't pick it up. It might be the last person in the world she wanted to talk to right now – or was he the person she wanted to talk to most?

'God help me,' she said aloud as she picked up her bag and left the flat. When she opened the big front door, she could still hear the phone ringing four floors above her.

SOUTH OF
SUNSET
BOULEVARD

Chapter 25

Another sunny day. Ever since Lisa had come to California seven months ago, the sun had never seemed to stop shining. Day after day after day, from early morning until dusk, the world was blessed with glorious golden sunlight. She sat up in bed, nudged the white curtain aside and looked out onto the wide road of Spanish-style stucco houses painted in delicate pastel colours – shell-pink, cream, pale green, lilac . . .

Though it must have rained some time; how else could the long lawns be such an unnatural bright green, or the luscious, bulging flowers that filled every garden, grow and bloom so extravagantly? Lally had told her the names. The purple bell-shaped ones were jacaranda and already, a mere two or three weeks since bursting so ostentatiously into bloom, their petals were beginning to fall like confetti. And there were bougainvillaeas, azaleas, gardenias outrageous, brilliantly-coloured flowers, the likes of which she'd never seen before.

The telephone rang in the hall and Roma shouted, 'I'll get it.' Lisa slipped out of bed and went to the door to listen. Roma called, 'Gloria, it's for you,' and Lisa relaxed. She didn't trust Roma, not since the day Dick Broadbent had called Lisa to say Paramount were testing for slave girls for *Desert Princess* and she should get to the studios immediately. In her excitement, Lisa had told her flatmates, Gloria, Lally and Roma, as she ran to get ready. When she arrived at Paramount, however, she was told, 'Sorry, doll, we got all we need.' Two days later, she discovered Roma had taken a taxi before her and been hired.

Now she was out of bed, she might as well stay up. In just over an hour's time she had a singing lesson, and her shift at the coffee shop commenced at midday. After a quick shower, Lisa pulled on a pair of jeans and a yellow sleeveless tee shirt. She twisted and turned in front of the mirror, trying to decide if the tee shirt looked best loose, or tucked inside her jeans. She left it tucked in, inserted a tan leather belt through the loops of the waistband and slipped her feet into a pair of yellow canvas loafers. Sorting through her earrings, she selected a pair of gypsy hoops.

It was important to look her best for work. You never knew who might drop in for a coffee; a producer or director, even a famous star on the lookout for a new face for his or her latest film.

Dick, her agent, advised her not to wear make-up. 'You don't need it,' he said. 'A nice, fresh complexion makes you stand out.' Dick also said to take a few years off her age. '*I* know you're just starting out, but others don't. When you say you're twenty-five, folks'll think you've been hanging round for years.' In April, when her birthday came around, she told her flatmates she was twenty-two and was astounded when Gloria said, 'I didn't think you were *that* old.'

When she first arrived in Hollywood, Lisa stayed in Rollo's, a cheap hotel off Franklin Avenue. The taxi driver who'd brought her from the airport recommended it. 'It's pretty basic,' he warned, 'but you said you wanted somewhere cheap. Well, it's that all right, but clean. An' you'll be safe there. Rollo's particular who he takes in – no dopers, no prostitutes.' Rollo was his wife's cousin.

On her first day, after a dark-haired silent woman had brought her breakfast, she ventured out, but only for a short distance before returning to the safety of the mean, sparsely furnished room, where she lay on her bed and thought about the enormity of what she had done. She was alone in a strange country and not quite sure which way to turn.

On the second morning, she sat up in bed listening for the chink of dishes which heralded breakfast, anxious for her first cup of coffee. To her surprise, it wasn't the dark-haired woman, but a curly-haired, impish-looking young man who came in holding the tray.

'It's Adriana's day off,' he said, 'so I get the honour of bringing the breakfast.' He put the tray down on the cheap plastic table. 'I'm Brett Charwood, scriptwriter extraordinaire and you're Lisa O'Brien – I looked it up in the register. Hi.'

'Hi,' said Lisa. His relaxed, friendly manner made her feel at ease. 'What is an extraordinary scriptwriter doing working in a cheap hotel?' she asked.

The young man grinned. He wore shabby jeans and a tee shirt with a Mickey Mouse face on the front. 'Earning a crust,' he answered. 'Gotta eat, need a roof. Unfortunately, I don't get either from writing – yet. I'm the nightclerk here. Gives me plenty of time to scribble.' He looked at her, his head on one side. 'Understand you're English. Gee, Hollywood must seem strange. Took me a while to get used to it and I'm only from the next state!'

'Well, I haven't plucked up the courage to go far yet,' Lisa confessed. 'I've only been here a couple of days.'

'Expect you've come to take the place by storm?' he said cheerfully. 'What are you – an actress, dancer, singer?'

'Actress.'

'Tell you what, Lisa, I finish in half an hour. Wanna walk with me? I'm going to see my agent about a script idea I got.'

'I'd love to,' she replied.

'Brett!' a voice yelled. 'There's breakfasts down here waiting.'

'A man's work is never done!' He rolled his eyes. 'I'll give you a call when I'm leaving.'

Sunset Boulevard!

She was actually on Sunset Boulevard! It was so incredible that she wanted to shout, loud enough for it to reach Number 2 Chaucer Street: *Look, Mam, your Lizzie is on Sunset Boulevard!*

The atmosphere was exhilarating, vibrant, and the air spun with vitality and optimism. Everyone looked busy, their faces full of hope, their eyes almost manically bright as they pushed and shoved their way through the crowded pavements.

'Feel it?' asked Brett.

She'd forgotten he was there. 'Feel what?'

'The greed, the ambition, the will to succeed. Listen, Lisa, these people'd kill for fame. The actors'd sell their own mother for a bit-part in a B movie.'

'Would you?'

He looked at her, a half-smile on his face. 'Well, I kinda like my mom, but I'd seriously consider trading Grandma for a screen credit on a low budget no-hoper.'

Lisa laughed. 'I don't believe you.'

Brett shrugged. 'Don't bet on it.' He glanced around. 'It's all getting to look rather tawdry, isn't it? Gee, I would have loved to have been here ten, twenty years ago when Hollywood was in its heyday.'

'Isn't it now?'

'Nope – movies are on the way out, for sure.' He laughed at her crestfallen face. 'Don't worry, honey, television's taking over. That means there'll be even more work for us. After all, why should folks pay to see a movie, when they've got a screen of their own, right in their living room?'

She felt relieved. 'I was beginning to think I'd come too late!'

'Nah, don't worry,' he said dismissively. 'My agent's on the next block. Do you wanna hang around or can you find your own way back?'

'I'll look around a bit, thanks, and I can remember the way back.'

'While you're here, why not fix yourself up with an agent? Guess you'll want to start work pretty soon.'

'Can I use yours?'

'No, idiot, mine's literary, though I think there's an actors' agent in the same building. Take a look at the board outside.'

Shortly afterwards, Brett said goodbye and darted into a narrow doorway between a little cinema and a dress shop. After he'd gone, Lisa looked at the list of names beside the door. Quite a lot of agents worked in the building – insurance, literary, employment. On the fourth floor she saw what she was hoping for: *Dick Broadbent, Actors' Agent.*

Lisa took a deep breath, threw her shoulders back and marched up the stairs. 'Dick Broadbent, here I come,' she said out loud.

Later on, when Lally found Lisa was represented by Dick Broadbent, she urged her to change. 'He's eighty if he's a day, and likely to drop dead any minute.'

'I like him,' Lisa said stubbornly. 'He's nice.'

In fact, Dick wasn't quite that old, more like seventy. He worked entirely alone, without even a secretary. A tiny hunchback, no more than four and a half feet tall, much to his regret and chagrin he'd never had a star on his books. When Lisa walked in, nervous and prepared for rejection, he'd welcomed her with open arms. 'Star material!' he crowed. 'I recognize it straight away.'

Lally cautioned that he said this to everyone. 'The little creep has got a jinx on him. Sign with him and you're guaranteed to fail.'

Lisa said she was willing to take a chance, if only to prove Lally wrong.

Not only had Dick taken years off her age, but he'd changed her surname, too.

'Sure you ain't got some Latin blood?' he asked first time they met, staring at her with his rather crooked eyes.

'Positive,' she said firmly. 'I'm pure Irish-Liverpudlian. It's the Celtic streak makes me so dark.' Kitty had told her that.

'Well, you look Latin. Lisa O'Brien gives the wrong impression. You need something more romantic. You can keep the Lisa . . .'

'Thanks,' said Lisa dryly.

He didn't notice the interruption. 'How about Rosa? Lisa Rosa.'

'There's already a singer almost called that, Lita Roza. She comes from Liverpool, too.'

'Hmm.' He put his gnomelike head on one side and stared at her intently. 'Lisa Gomez?'

Lisa shook her head firmly. 'I don't like that much.'

'Lisa La Plante?'

'No.' It had to be something she felt comfortable with. After all, she'd be living with it for a long time, perhaps all her life.

There was silence for a while in the dusty, over-furnished office. Both of them were deep in thought.

'How about Angelis?' Lisa suggested. 'No, Angelis, with the emphasis on the second syllable. Lisa Angelis.' She couldn't remember where she'd heard the name before but it sounded pretty.

249

'Perfect,' said Dick.

A week later she got her first movie work in Hollywood.

The film was a big-budget thriller and Lisa spent a whole day on set as one of the throng of passengers on a mocked-up station. The director, an hysterical, overbearing man, demanded the big chase by the two male stars through the crowds to be shot again and again; daylight was beginning to fail before he pronounced himself satisfied, to the relief of everyone including Lisa, who had a headache.

The clash of several overweening temperaments was nerve-wracking, and there'd almost been a real fight at one point. The hatred of the two male stars for each other was exceeded only by their joint hatred for the director – and he appeared to loathe everyone, extras included.

As for the language! Lisa heard more four-letter words that day than she'd heard in her entire life. Filming in England had been mild compared to this. She'd be glad to get back to Rollo's for some peace and quiet.

She was about to leave the set when a young man came up. 'Can you come back tomorrow, Miss er . . .?'

'O'Bri . . . Angelis, Lisa Angelis. Yes, I can come back.'

'Right, see you at seven o'clock then.'

Her headache disappeared as if by magic.

She spent half the next day with three other extras, two men and a woman about her own age, in the tiny, claustrophobic setting of a lift. Lisa was dressed as a nun, feeling suffocated in the heavy costume. The four extras were instructed to remain impassive and disinterested throughout.

The thirty-second scene, in which the female star entered the lift, examined her face in a compact, and got out again, took all morning to shoot. According to the director, she wasn't casual enough.

'How can I be fuckin' casual, when you're screaming at me like a fuckin' maniac?' the actress demanded furiously. The woman extra beside Lisa whispered, 'And how are we supposed to keep a straight face with all this shit going on?'

Lisa didn't answer – her face felt as if it would never move again, and if she had to wear these clothes much longer she'd melt to nothing.

In the end, the director grudgingly conceded, 'That'll do,' and someone yelled, 'Break for lunch.'

Lisa made her way to the dressing room to rid herself of the nun's habit. Apart from feeling uncomfortably hot, wearing the heavy crucifix around her neck made her feel uneasy and vaguely sinful.

To her surprise, when she came out, the other woman extra was waiting for her. She was the first actress Lisa had come across since she'd arrived in Hollywood who wasn't beautiful. Indeed, she bordered on plain, but there was something appealing about her round, chubby face with its wide mobile mouth, snub nose and sparkling blue eyes. Lisa took to her straight away.

'Hi, I'm Lally Cooper. You're British, aren't you?'

'That's right. My name's Lisa Angelis.'

'I just love your accent.'

'Everyone says that, it's rather flattering.'

'Been here long?' They began to walk towards the canteen.

'Just over a week,' Lisa answered. 'This is my first job, though I did theatre and film work in England.'

'You're lucky getting a part with so much exposure straight away,' Lally said enviously.

'Am I?' Lisa wasn't quite sure what she meant.

'Yeh. I expect you were in the big station scene yesterday.'

'That's right. The director asked me to come back again today.'

'That's a really good sign. It means you've got a noticeable face.' Lally took Lisa's arm and steered her into a self-service restaurant, a tall, bright room with cream plastic tables and chairs. It was already crowded and there was a long queue of people waiting to be served.

While they stood in line, Lally showered Lisa with questions. What had she been in? Where was she living? Who was her agent?

Lisa didn't mind the third degree. It was nice having someone interested. Lally delivered her blunt opinion on Dick Broadbent. 'If you ever decide to ditch him, I'll recommend you to Elmer. He's a Grade-A swine, but a really good agent.'

They carried their food over to a table with two vacant seats.

'You ain't planning on staying in that hotel, are you?' Lally asked.

'Oh no,' said Lisa. 'I want a place of my own. Although it's cheap at Rollo's, I have to eat out except for breakfast, and my money's fast disappearing.'

'Hey, ain't that a coincidence? We'll have a room vacant in a week's time. Why don't you move in with us, Lisa? It'll be real nice, having a Britisher staying.' Lally's blue eyes lit up.

'Who's "we"?' Lisa asked.

'Gloria Grenville, Roma Novatora and me. Pam Redman, that's the fourth, is moving in with some guy. Come round tonight and take a look.'

Lally's apartment comprised the top floor of a pink stone house in a little road off La Brea Avenue, south of Sunset Boulevard. The entrance was up a black iron staircase at the back. Lally ushered Lisa into a narrow hallway which led to a big pleasant room with white, roughcast walls decorated with film posters. Two sofas and several armchairs were covered in coarse red linen and colourful woven rugs were scattered over the black tiled floor. In front of a large wide window was a pine table, a bowl of yellow flowers in its centre.

'It's really pretty,' she said.

Lally smiled. 'No one's ever called it that before. Come and see the room that's gonna be empty. Pam's out somewhere.'

The room was small, about ten feet square. One entire wall was taken up with a built-in wardrobe. Opposite was a single bed and on another wall, a small dressing table with a long mirror. The walls here were white too, as were the thin muslin curtains, and the bed was covered with a multi-coloured patterned blanket.

Lisa said she'd definitely like to move in when Pam left. 'It's five hundred dollars a month,' Lally said. 'We pay a quarter each, plus twenty dollars for extras. Okay?'

'Fine,' agreed Lisa.

'Would you like a coffee?' Lally asked. 'Or do you Britishers only drink tea?'

'Coffee's fine.'

Back in the big lounge, Lisa sat down as Lally disappeared into the kitchen. 'You gotta job yet?' she shouted.

That seemed a strange question. 'Why do I need a job, when I'm going to work in films like you?' Lisa shouted back.

Lally appeared in the doorway, a kettle in one hand, a jar of coffee in the other. She looked astounded.

'You gotta get a job, kid, if you wanna pay your rent and eat. Today was my first movie work in weeks. I've been in Hollywood four years now and I ain't ever made enough from movies to live on. Some day I will. Some day.' She nodded fiercely, as if to convince herself more than Lisa. She disappeared again and emerged shortly with two cups of coffee. 'I work nights as an usherette at the Plaza that's a movie house, case you didn't know. Roma's in an office, though she'd going to get dumped any minute, the way she just disappears at a moment's notice for an audition or takes whole days off if she gets a part.'

'What about Gloria, what does she do?'

Lally's blue eyes twinkled. 'Well, you look the innocent sort, Lisa. I won't say what Gloria does to earn a buck or two, just that she lies down a lot.'

It had come as a shock to Lisa to discover that she was no longer an outstanding beauty. It wasn't that she'd changed, just that Hollywood was filled with women every bit as lovely as herself. Every time she went out, she saw dozens of women as pretty, if not prettier than she was. Tall girls, petite girls, all gliding gracefully along like models, their golden limbs gleaming, their blonde, brunette or red hair floating proudly behind.

She began to feel very ordinary, and understood Dick's advice not to wear make-up. At least this made her different from the others, who all looked as if they'd spent hours in front of the mirror.

When she met Roma Novatora, she understood what it must feel like to be plain.

The day Lisa moved into the apartment, Lally gave her a key before rushing off to work, so Lisa was left alone and had just finished unpacking when she heard the door slam and went out to say hello. She hadn't met Gloria or Roma yet.

A tall, statuesque girl had come in and was standing disconsolately in the centre of the room. Lisa gasped. She had never seen anyone so incredibly lovely. At least six feet tall, her figure was remarkable: large, high breasts, the nipples prominent through her fluffy white angora sweater, above an unbelievably narrow waist. Smooth, long hips arched outwards under a short red pleated skirt and her long bare legs were as smooth and glossy as marble. She jumped when she saw the newcomer. Lisa approached smiling, extending her hand.

'Hello, I'm Lisa Angelis. It's nice to meet you.'

'Hi, Roma Novatura.' The handshake was surprisingly limp and she didn't return Lisa's smile. Her face was as perfect as her figure, with wide, deep violet eyes surrounded by a thick tangle of lashes and a fine straight nose. Her glossy black hair was cut short and lay on the nape of her long white neck like feathers. Lisa felt overshadowed, small and insignificant beside this extravagant and glorious-looking woman. She also felt depressed. What chance had she of making good in films beside someone like Roma Novatura?

'You settled in yet?' She had a surprisingly dull, low-pitched voice.

'Just about. Would you like some coffee? I just put the kettle on.'

'No, thanks. I'd prefer something stronger. I just got dumped, lost my job.' She took a bottle of spirits and a glass from out of a pine cupboard and poured herself a drink.

'I'm sorry to hear that.'

'It happens!' Roma shrugged her perfect shoulders. 'It's not the first time. Tomorrow, I'll find something else.'

'I hope so,' said Lisa sympathetically. Roma threw herself into a chair and stared into space, her lovely violet eyes strangely expressionless. She didn't speak and after a while, Lisa said, 'Where are you going to find another job? I need one myself.'

'What sort?'

Now it was Lisa's turn to shrug. 'Any sort,' she said.

'Waitressing's best if you need time off. You can always get someone to cover. That's what I'm going to look for next.

Office work's a drag, even though the pay's better. Too much hassle.' She returned to staring into space for a full five minutes. Suddenly she looked up and said, 'I've got an idea. If we could get a job in the same place, we could cover for each other.'

'That'd be great,' Lisa said enthusiastically.

'Right. First thing tomorrow, we'll go job-hunting.'

Finding a job was surprisingly easy. Roma, with an air of ruthless determination which Lisa found embarrassing, just went into half a dozen places, from greasy burger bars to expensive-looking restaurants, and asked if they wanted a couple of waitresses. They struck lucky with the sixth – a big, dimly-lit basement coffee shop situated on Hollywood Boulevard and called Dominic's, after the proprietor.

'I don't really need two waitresses,' Dominic said, 'but I've been going through a real bad patch with girls leaving every other week. If I take you both, I'll be overstaffed, but with my luck, someone's bound to take off soon, which means I'll be back to normal.'

A portly, dark-skinned man with a black moustache, he couldn't take his eyes off Roma. Before they left, he introduced them to his mother who was working in the kitchen.

'This is Momma,' he said proudly. 'The best pastry cook in all Hollywood.' Momma looked up from the table where her arms were buried deep in a bowl of flour and smiled at them broadly. 'She don't speak English much,' he went on. 'Here, have one of her chocolate éclairs. But be careful, you could get addicted.'

'It's sheer heaven,' said Lisa through a mouthful of featherlight pastry and fresh cream. Roma had rather churlishly refused, muttering something about them being fattening.

Momma had understood the word 'heaven' and beamed at Lisa.

'I'd appreciate one of you starting tonight,' said Dominic. 'Don't care who it is.'

'I'd like the evening shift,' said Roma with alacrity.

'I don't mind when I work,' Lisa said easily.

She soon regretted being so easygoing. Whilst Roma frequently asked her to take over the evening shift, she never seemed free to help Lisa out in the afternoons. Twice she missed work as an extra because she had to be at Dominic's and Roma couldn't fill in. One day, Lally said, 'Why weren't you there this afternoon?'

'Where?' asked Lisa.

'Warner Brothers. I thought Dick Broadbent called you this morning. They were taking people on for an eight-hour TV epic about the *Titanic*. I got a few days' work, Roma too.'

'I had to be at Dominic's,' said Lisa abjectly.

'You *what*?'

'I had to be at Dominic's,' she repeated. 'My shift's twelve till eight.'

Lally took a deep breath and said in a voice like setting concrete, 'Listen, kid, you don't ever, *ever* miss out on a job in the movies.'

'But I couldn't let Dominic down. He'd have been short-staffed if I hadn't turned up,' Lisa protested.

'Look, kid,' Lally was angry. 'Roma shoulda told you this. Dick, too. If something comes up again, you *go*. Don't mind who you let down. If it means getting dumped, then okay, you get dumped and you look for another job. Shit, Lisa, you're too soft-hearted by a mile. In this town you look after numero uno. Number one. You gotta be hard, real hard – understand?'

'I suppose so,' Lisa said reluctantly.

The thin-faced, sharply-dressed man had been staring at Lisa for nearly an hour, ever since she'd served him with coffee. From the corner of her eye, she saw his head turn every time she passed. It was three o'clock and customers were thin on the ground.

The trouble with Hollywood was that you couldn't get annoyed when people stared. He might be a famous producer wanting someone for his next film.

When the man gestured for the bill, she took it over to his table.

'Bet you're an actress,' he said, fishing in his pocket for change.

'Every woman here's an actress,' she replied pleasantly.

'Except for Momma in the kitchen.'

'Yeah, but you're special. You got star quality, I can tell. You walk good and you got class.' He looked her up and down openly. 'And a real good body, too.'

Lisa smiled nervously, undecided whether to be flattered or to tell him to go to hell.

'My name's Charlie Gruber. I got my own production company. Art movies is what I do. Like to try out for my next project? It's gonna be a real big number. See, here's my card – *Gruber Productions*.'

As she examined the card, a flicker of excitement ran through her. She'd been discovered!

'How about coming along tomorrow for a screen test?' he asked. 'What's your name, by the way?'

'Lisa Angelis.' She told herself to calm down; he might be testing dozens of girls. 'And I can come tomorrow morning.'

'Fine. Ten o'clock, then. The address is on the card. It ain't far from Paramount. Know where that is?'

'Sure.'

'See ya tomorrow then, Lisa. Ten o'clock.'

When Lisa finished work, she walked slowly back down Hollywood Boulevard to Grauman's Chinese Theatre, the ostentatious pagoda-like building where the stars left their hand- and footprints in the cement-covered courtyard. The brightly lit streets were as busy as if it were midday; the bars and restaurants were crowded, and several shops were still open and full of customers. Lisa stared down at the hollowed-out prints. Tomorrow she was going for her first real screen test! Some day her name might be as famous as those immortalized here . . .

'I'm going to be a star too,' she vowed. 'I'm already on the first rung of the ladder.'

To her surprise, Gruber Productions was a small, rickety wooden house in a rundown road on the edge of Hollywood, nowhere near Paramount. Her excitement began to ebb as she stared at the blacked-out windows and the shabby door with its peeling paint. Charlie Gruber must have been watching for her, because the door opened and he greeted her jovially. He still wore the same suit, but in the daylight it looked worn and the collar of his shirt was frayed.

'Come in, Lisa. We're all set.'

Who 'we' were, she never discovered, because Charlie seemed to be alone in the house.

He led her into a large room at the front where a camera was set up in one corner, focused on a threadbare brocade-covered Regency sofa opposite. A dusty, unshaded lightbulb hung from the cracked ceiling. Charlie said, 'There's a rack of clothes over there. If you'd like to get changed, we'll begin.'

A row of flimsy, diaphanous garments, mainly black and red and full of pulled threads and ladders, hung off a crooked wooden rail. Lisa didn't know whether to laugh or cry. She stood in the doorway and made no move towards the clothes. 'What's your new film to be called?' she asked.

Charlie Gruber was fiddling with the camera. He looked up innocently and said, 'I haven't decided on a title yet.'

'Can I see the script?'

'I'm still working on it.'

'Where's my dialogue then?'

'I ain't testing for sound.' They stared at each other for several seconds without speaking. Charlie said, 'You getting changed or not?'

'Not.'

'I'll give you a hundred bucks. It'll only take fifteen minutes.'

'Get stuffed.'

Lisa walked down the dusty corridor and out the front door. She didn't bother saying goodbye.

'Do girls ever fall for it?' Lisa asked Lally in a whisper.

They were sitting on two little pull-down seats at the back of the cinema where Lally worked. The house had just filled up for the eight o'clock show and Lally only had to get up and show the occasional latecomers to their seats. Lisa had come straight from Dominic's, anxious to talk about her 'screen test'.

'Yeh,' said Lally. 'Some do – I suppose about one in ten. I wish I'd known, Lisa, I would've told you not to go. Charlie Gruber's famous as a con-artist.'

Lally had still been in bed when Lisa left that morning so there hadn't been any opportunity to tell her.

'Oh well,' sighed Lisa. 'I really thought he was genuine. But then, you only learn from experience, as my mother used to say.'

'My mom used to say something like that too,' grinned Lally.

Lisa looked in the mirror a final time. As she pulled her belt a notch tighter, her heart lifted, as it did every morning. After all, today might be the day when fate would smile. She picked up Victoria and kissed her, before laying her carefully back on the pillow. 'I've been here seven months,' she told the doll. 'And the longer I'm here, the closer that day comes.'

Chapter 26

Roma's long lovely body was draped disconsolately over an armchair. From time to time she took a deep, shuddering sigh which everyone affected to ignore.

On the floor, Gloria lay with her face covered in a mudpack, a towel wrapped round her head, turbanwise, and her legs resting on a chair. 'The blood rushes to the head,' she declared. 'It's good for the brain.'

'What brain?' demanded Lally, looking up from the Sunday paper. She watched as Gloria gingerly placed a slice of cucumber on each eye. 'My God – if your customers could see you now, they'd pay you to go away.'

'Zip it, Cooper,' Gloria replied good-naturedly.

Despite living in the same house, Lisa never saw much of Gloria. In her early thirties, she was a tiny, fragile woman with a frail, waif-like beauty. Her enormous pale-blue eyes and pearly skin were in startling contrast to her autumn-leaf red hair which she wore in a bouffant style, cut just below the ears. However, the slight and delicate figure which Gloria presented hid a tough, fighting spirit and a wisecracking, cheerful personality which took people by surprise when they first met her.

Gloria made no secret of the fact she was a call girl. 'I make more in a day than you three make together in a whole week,' she boasted to Lisa on one of the few occasions they were alone together.

'Yes, but — ' Lisa didn't go on, not wishing to be offensive.

'Yes, but what?' Gloria had laughed. 'You sell your labour, I sell my body and in this wicked world my body's worth more.'

'Yes, but — ' Lisa began again.

'Wasn't it some famous Englishwoman who said, "I just lie back and think of England"? Well, I do the same but think of money. And if you say "Yes, but" again, I'll scream.'

'Yes, but — ' said Lisa.

Gloria screamed.

'I'm sorry, Gloria. It's just that – oh, I don't know. It seems sort of, well . . .'

'Debauched?' offered Gloria.

Lisa laughed. 'I give up, Anyway, it's none of my business.'

'Y'know, Lisa, I've been in Hollywood ten whole years. Came here all bright-eyed and bushy-tailed and did well my first coupla years.' Gloria gave a rueful smile. 'Musicals – I started out a dancer and got a whole heapa parts, each one bigger and better. I was making fairly good money when – wham, bang! Suddenly, no one wants musicals no more. No one wants *me* no more, along with Howard Keel, Kathryn Grayson, Betty Grable – folks like that.' She stopped and lit a cigarette from the one she'd nearly finished.

Lisa murmured, 'Gee, I'm sorry.'

Gloria waved the cigarette furiously. 'Don't be. I can't stand people being sorry for me. After all, I was in good company. Anyway, I contemplated going home, back to Pittsburgh, but only for about sixty seconds. I thought, "Hell, no. I came here to make my fortune, and by Jeez, I'll make it." By then, I'd got used to the dough and didn't fancy going back to being a waitress or working in some crummy shop with the proprietor breathing down my neck. I had a friend, married, who told me about this agency, an escort agency, really high-class. She only worked one afternoon a week – Wednesdays – to pad the housekeeping out. Her husband never seemed to notice they were eating best steak all of a sudden.' Gloria smiled sardonically. 'Or perhaps he did and kept mum. After all, they say the way to a man's heart's through his stomach. When she told me, I kept saying "yes, but", just like you . . .'

'But you gave in,' said Lisa.

'Saw sense, more like. It was easier than I'd thought. The agency only sends us girls along to clients in first-class hotels, never to private addresses, like some do.' Gloria looked at Lisa, a half-smile on her face. 'If you're interested, I'll introduce you.'

Lisa shuddered. 'No thanks,' she said quickly. 'I'll stick to waitressing.' Afterwards, she felt ashamed of the shudder.

She would never have admitted it to anyone, but sometimes, when she thought about what Gloria did, she found her imagination running away with her in a manner that was not altogether unpleasant.

Lally said, 'Are you gonna eat that cucumber when you've finished?'

'Yeah,' said Gloria. 'It's good for the bowels.'

'Oh, shut up you two,' Roma said petulantly.

'Why?' demanded Lally. 'You don't need to listen.'

'I can't help but listen.'

'What d'you wanna talk about then?' asked Lally.

Roma shrugged. 'Nothing.'

'You expect us to just sit here all quiet and talk about nothing – on a Sunday morning, too?'

Roma glowered at Lally and didn't answer. Her lovely pink mouth was sulky. Whatever mechanism in the brain caused people to laugh or smile was deficient in Roma. Her magnificent good looks brought no happiness. She was eternally sour, as if a crabby, twisted old woman existed inside the body of an angel.

'Any of you got movie work on tomorrow?' she asked suddenly.

'No,' the three other women chorused quickly. Lisa wouldn't have told her if she had, not after that time she'd pre-empted her with Paramount. She guessed Gloria and Lally felt the same. Roma had no shame when it came to pushing for work.

'I haven't had movie work in weeks,' she complained. 'And my last two jobs were as a corpse.'

'You'd be good at that,' said Lally. 'You'd make a perfect corpse.'

Roma stared at her, frowning slightly. Devoid of humour herself, she was never sure when people were joking. Suddenly, she unfolded herself out of the chair and left the room.

'Has she gone?' Gloria lifted the cucumber off her right eye.

'Lally really hurt her feelings,' said Lisa.

'She ain't got any feelings, 'cept nasty ones,' said Lally

indignantly. 'I don't mind hurting nasty feelings. If she had nice feelings, I wouldn't dream of hurting them. What Roma needs is a live firework stuffing up her ass, then she might find she's got feelings.'

'Yeah, but they'd be even nastier,' said Gloria. 'Hey, someone, light me a smoke quick. I'm gasping down here.'

'Lally!' Lisa remonstrated. 'That's an awful thing to say.'

'Awful but true,' Lally answered. She poked a cigarette in Gloria's mouth and lit it.

'If you drop that match on me, I'll sue,' warned Gloria. 'This mud could be highly flammable.'

'Actually, I feel sorry for Roma,' Lally said. 'I mean, she's got that fantastic face and figure, yet she'll never get anywhere in the movies.'

'Why not?' Lisa asked curiously.

'She ain't got no screen presence, that's why,' Lally answered crossly, as though poor Roma had done something terribly wrong. She went on, 'Look at Judy Garland, f'r instance, or Shelley Winters, or Marilyn Monroe – shit, I could reel off a hundred names. All o' them got screen presence in abundance. They glow, radiate, though they're nowhere near as good-looking as Roma. She's got nothing inside, nothing to give. I wasn't joking when I said she'd make a perfect corpse, 'cos on screen, she looks dead.'

'It's come to the pitch,' said Gloria from the floor, 'that she's even finding it hard to get work as an extra. In a crowd, she stands out as looking downright glum.'

'Gee, that's really awful,' Lisa said.

'I mean, there's a limit to the times you can be a corpse,' said Lally with a wicked grin. 'Folks'd start laughing in the most serious movies if every time some woman got murdered it turned out to be Roma.'

Gloria began to giggle. 'Don't make me laugh. I'll crack my mask.'

'Why are you lying down there, anyway?' demanded Lally. 'You lie down so much in your job, I'd've thought you'd prefer sitting when you had the opportunity.'

Apart from Gloria, the women led a remarkably chaste existence, considering they lived in what was probably the most explicitly sensual town in the world. Lally had a serious boyfriend back home in New Jersey and once a month, he flew over to spend the weekend with her and sometimes she went back to see him and her parents.

'Frank's really worried I'll two-time him,' she told Lisa. 'He thinks Hollywood's a den of iniquity. I said not to worry. I told him I didn't have the energy to get laid. Lots of guys come onto me in the Plaza, but by 2 a.m. all I want to do is sleep. Alone.'

'I'm sure that put Frank's mind at rest,' said Lisa dryly, though she understood what Lally meant. Her own days were full, from morning until night. Each morning she took some sort of class in a studio along with anything from ten to a hundred other men and women. A dollar an hour learning how to dance – both ballet and tap – or how to develop her singing voice. Wednesdays she went to a gymnasium to work out. After her shift finished, some nights she went straight to a writing and acting group Brett Charwood had introduced her to, where aspiring writers brought scripts for aspiring actors to read, and other nights she went to the cinema. It was important to keep abreast of the current movie scene.

Every few weeks there was movie or television work. Clad in a skimpy tunic and wearing a silver wig, she'd spent two days frolicking over plastic grass hills as an inhabitant of Utopia, and half a day as a squaw fleeing from a burning wigwam. Her voice was hoarse after a day screaming, 'Off with their heads!' in a film about the French Revolution. So far, it had all been crowd work, though on two other occasions she'd been asked to stay behind, along with some other extras, because a few faces were needed in the background of the next shot.

Lally called this being a first-class extra as opposed to being second-class. 'There's a whole heapa difference between being one in a thousand and one in ten,' she claimed. 'Like that day we were in the lift. It's how you get noticed.' On filming days, the classes and the coffee shop were forgotten and Lisa was up at the crack of dawn and at the studio for seven o'clock when the cameras would, hopefully, roll.

*

One morning in June, Dick Broadbent telephoned, his voice squeaky with excitement. 'I got two lots of good news. Y'know that movie, *Black Corner*?'

'Never heard of it,' said Lisa.

'Christ, Lisa, you were in it! The one with the lift.'

'I remember, but it wasn't called that. It was called — '

'Don't matter,' he interrupted impatiently. 'They must've changed the name. Anyway, it ain't been released yet, but someone must have seen the rushes and Disney want you for their next production. It ain't a speaking part, but you'll get billing.'

'*Disney!* Gee, Dick, that's incredible. *Disney!*' Lisa sat down in the nearest chair, her legs weak. 'What sort of part is it?'

'A fairy o' some sort. The woman from their casting office said you suited your name, 'cos you looked like an angel. Lisa Angelis, the angel,' Dick said with a giggle. 'Anyway, they're gonna fix up a meeting pretty soon.'

'Oh, Dick! I could die with happiness.'

'I ain't finished yet,' Dick said. 'You heard of a writer, Cahil O'Daly? He's Irish,' he added, somewhat unnecessarily.

She remembered that Harry Greenbaum had stocked some of his books, though she'd never read any. 'Didn't he get the Nobel Prize for Literature a long time ago?' she asked.

'The very one! He's about a hundred and fifty now and in town 'cos they're making a movie from one of his books, *The Opportunist*. Thing is, angel, guess where the beginning part of this book is set?'

'I've no idea,' confessed Lisa.

'Liverpool, England!' cried Dick triumphantly. 'And there's a really plum part for an actress, only short, but lot'o of women'll be after it. You've got a headstart, coming from Liverpool. In fact, I got you priority. Tomorrow afternoon, the Cascade Hotel in the Hollywood Hills, we're seeing this O'Daly guy. He got casting approval and wants to look everybody over.'

'What should I wear, Dick?' Lisa suddenly felt nervous.

'Something plain and simple. This woman was a servant, dead poor, so there's no use going all jazzed up in diamonds and stuff. You got anything black?'

'If I haven't, I'll buy something,' promised Lisa.

'Pick you up at one o'clock. Best to have your agent on hand, in case they want to sign you up on the spot.'

Gloria loaned her a simple black dress with a cowl neck and a soft flared skirt.

'I look like a waif and stray,' she decided when she was ready. Lally had woven her hair into a long loose plait. Even Roma proved cooperative for once and let her borrow a pair of flat black shoes. All she carried was a small purse and her portrait folio.

Dick called for her in his car. He'd had the pedals built up so his short legs could reach them, beneath a specially-adapted high seat.

'Do I look all right?' she asked when she climbed in beside him.

'Fine. You don't look poor, but then he can't expect you to turn up in rags.' He looked excited. 'There's a copy of the book in the glove compartment – I bought it yesterday. Seems a bit boring to me. In fact, I only read the beginning, but then I don't expect anyone ever got the Nobel Prize for writing something really interesting.'

'I've already read it,' said Lisa. 'I went to the library straight after you phoned. I quite liked it, though it got a bit wordy towards the end. I think he philosophized too much.'

'You prob'ly gotta do that,' Dick mused. 'To getta prize.'

As he drove out of Hollywood, they discussed the novel. It was clearly autobiographical. Cahil O'Daly had been a seaman as a young man, rising to become ship's captain. The book was a saga of his travels and the women he'd loved, the first being Mary, a poor worn-out woman, older than himself, who'd worked in the seamen's hostel where he'd stayed in Liverpool at the turn of the century. The writer had spread his favours far and wide, but his first love affair was the most tragic and moving. As Dick said, although small, it was a plum part.

Last night Lisa had felt homesick, reading about her home town. 'I used to play on the Dock Road when I was a child,' she told Dick. 'It was strange to think he'd been down the same streets as I have.'

She'd gone asleep thinking about Kitty and Chaucer Street. Dick squeezed her hand. 'Keep that sad look, kiddo, and he'll hire you on the spot.'

True to its name, the Cascade Hotel had bright blue water cascading down the steep, rocky gardens that fronted it. In a corner of the plush reception area a tinkling fountain was surrounded by several palm trees.

'He's in the penthouse,' said Dick. 'There's a special elevator at the end of the row.'

'Which studio is doing the movie?' Lisa asked as they rode up in the spacious lift.

'It's a small independent company,' explained Dick, 'set up a few years back by Busby Van Dolen, the writer, to produce and direct his own movies. He's only made three so far and they didn't earn much dough – they ain't commercial enough – though they got a really great reception from the critics. They call him another Orson Welles.'

The lift stopped and the door opened on a small square lobby with a peach-coloured carpet and half a dozen chairs. There was a six-foot display of imitation grasses in one corner.

Dick pressed the buzzer on the white-painted door twice. He was clearly enjoying himself. On the way he'd told Lisa it was a long time since he'd accompanied one of his clients to an appointment.

An elderly man opened the door. Dick coughed importantly. 'Hi, Mr O'Daly. I'm Dick Broadbent and this is — '

'Mr O'Daly is not feeling very well at the moment. I'm afraid you'll have to wait.'

They were still waiting an hour later and Dick began to get angry. 'He shouldn't ask for casting approval if he's not up to it,' he complained.

Lisa patted his tiny, gnarled hand. 'Calm down,' she soothed, though she was getting worried herself. She'd told Dominic she'd only be a couple of hours late. At this rate, the tea-time rush would be on by the time she got there.

At two o'clock, the lift doors opened and two girls came in. They knocked on the door and Dick stiffened, ready to leap off his chair if they were admitted. 'You'll have to wait,' the girls were told.

Half an hour later, the old man reappeared and motioned to Dick and Lisa to enter.

'Mr O'Daly is in the bedroom.'

They were led through a sitting room crammed with flowers and into a large bedroom. The Venetian blinds on the windows were closed and the room was in semi-darkness. Lisa could just about see an elderly man sitting in a wheelchair beside one of the windows, his eyes shut. He seemed unaware of the visitors. The room smelt like a hospital and she noticed the table beside the bed was full of medicine bottles.

Dick nudged her forward. Lisa took a deep breath and went over and stood in front of the old man, looking down at him. She'd never seen anyone so old. His face was criss-crossed with deep, jagged wrinkles.

She turned and cast a questioning look at Dick. What was she supposed to do? Dick loudly cleared his throat and to her relief the old man opened his eyes. It was clearly an effort; the lids were creased and heavy. He looked her up and down briefly, then the lids sank down again, as if it had all been too much. He mumbled something in a voice that seemed to come from a long way away.

'I'm sorry?' she stammered. His words made no sense.

'He said you're the wrong physical type,' declared a voice.

She turned, startled, unaware that there was anyone else in the room. A tall, bearded man wearing thick horn-rimmed glasses rose from a chair in the far corner.

'Busby Van Dolen.' He strolled over and shook Lisa's hand firmly.

'Gee, Mr Van Dolen, I didn't realize you were there,' said Dick. 'I'm really pleased to meet you.'

'And I'm pleased to meet you, too. Dick Broadbent, isn't it? I've heard your name mentioned a lot round Holly-wood.'

Dick flushed with pleasure as the two shook hands. Cahil O'Daly began to speak again. Busby Van Dolen listened, then said to Lisa, 'He says the part calls for a small, fair woman and you are a tall, dark woman. You're too young, as well.'

'She could always wear a wig,' said Dick eagerly. 'And she's older than she looks.'

The writer shook his head firmly. 'Sorry, she looks far too exotic, I can see that for myself.' He began to usher them out of the room. Lisa turned to say goodbye, but Cahil O'Daly seemed fast asleep.

In the sitting room, Busby Van Dolen shouted, 'Rudy, are there any more girls waiting?'

'Half a dozen.' Rudy appeared out of the kitchen. Seeing him again, Lisa thought he looked almost youthful compared to his employer.

'Show them in, two at a time. Stay there, will you? Make sure he keeps awake.'

'Sure thing, Mr Van Dolen.' The man opened the main door and ushered two girls into the bedroom.

'Why's he doin' this?' demanded Dick. 'I mean, wanting to approve the cast when he can hardly see.'

'It's very important to him. The people in the book were real; he wants them to look right.' Busby Van Dolen gestured towards a group of armchairs. 'Sit down, I'd like a word with you both.' Dick took a sidelong look at Lisa and winked excitedly.

'So, you're Lisa Angelis.' The director regarded her keenly. 'May I have a look at your portfolio?'

'Of course.' She handed over the brown envelope. As he glanced through the large, glossy photographs, she watched him. He was probably in his early to mid-thirties and anything but handsome. His nose was too long for one thing and his black eyebrows were almost as bushy as Mr Greenbaum's, yet he had an agreeable, lazy charm she found immensely attractive.

'Hmm, very nice,' he said, pushing the photos back in the envelope. 'You done much work in Hollywood?'

'She just got a big part in the next Disney production,' Dick butted in eagerly.

The writer's eyes danced with humour. 'Does that mean when I've got the backing together for *The Opportunist*, Lisa won't be free?'

'Well, it's not all *that* big a part,' Dick said hurriedly.

'Good, because I'm seriously considering her. Have you

read the book?' He turned to Lisa. She nodded. 'Good. There's two or three parts I can see you in.' He stood up. 'I better go back to Cahil.' He shook hands with them both again. 'I'll definitely be in touch.'

'Lisa, we've made it! You're gonna be a star, I feel it in my bones.' Dick virtually danced back to the car. Despite his age and his infirmity, he was as sprightly as a teenager. 'I knew it the minute you came into my office. You've got a sort of aura. Jesus! A Busby Van Dolen movie! Y'know, the biggest stars fall over themselves to act for him, even though it means a big drop in pay.'

He chatted all the way home, pointing out the homes of the stars, great colonnaded mansions with vast lawns and shining limousines standing outside. Lisa hardly listened. She was mentally going through *The Opportunist*, trying to think which parts Busby Van Dolen could see her in. It wasn't until Dick said, 'And that's where Ralph Layton lives,' that she looked up and saw a small grey turreted castle. The edge of a tennis court was just visible round the back and someone in white ran over and picked up a ball. The person disappeared before she could make out if it was Ralph.

There was no one in when Dick dropped Lisa off at her apartment. She pirouetted across the living room and fell giggling onto a chair. 'I'm so happy, I could *cry!*' If only there was someone in to share her news with. The coffee shop would be a real anti-climax. She felt more like going to a dance class or a workout where she could put all this bubbling happiness into sheer, physical hard work.

She went into her room and changed into a white silk blouse, a short denim skirt and tennis shoes. A few months ago, she'd stopped wearing a bra and, turning sideways, felt a pleasant thrill, seeing her nipples stand out through the thin material. It was like walking round half-naked. Unplaiting her hair, she combed it loose, parting it in the middle so that it hung in thick brown swathes framing her face.

'Cripes, Lisa mate,' she said in a broad Cockney accent.

'You don't 'arf look a treat, darlin'.' She cocked her head sideways. 'You've definitely got that glow Lally talked about.' Her mirrored reflection glowed back. It was as if a candle were lit inside her head, illuminating the brown-gold eyes, the skin, the whole being of the woman who stared back at her.

Reluctantly, she picked up her bag. She'd better go into work or Dominic would think she wasn't coming.

Suddenly she heard a noise. There was water running in the bathroom. Someone was home, after all. She knocked on the bathroom door. 'Hi, it's Lisa. Who goes there?'

There was a pause before Gloria answered in a scarcely audible voice, 'It's me.'

It wasn't like Gloria to sound so subdued. 'You okay?' asked Lisa.

The door of the bathroom opened and Gloria came out, clasping the collar of a towelling robe to her throat, her head bound in a towel. She had an angry purple bruise on her chin.

'What happened?' Lisa gasped.

'I don't want to talk about it,' said Gloria abruptly. She walked into the sitting room and lit a cigarette. 'No I've changed my mind – I do.'

'What happened?' Lisa asked again, gently.

'Pour me a drink, will you? Something strong and neat.'

Lisa poured out two brandies and handed one to the older woman, who swallowed hers in one go.

'Gee, that feels good!' She sank back in the chair. Without make-up, her face looked drawn and haggard, her white skin waxen. 'I had a client last night. He seemed a nice guy – at first. We had dinner in the hotel restaurant and went up to his room, only to find his friend was there too. I told them, I never do two guys. Never! Some girls don't mind, but I do.' She held out her glass. 'Fill me up, kid.'

As Lisa went to get the bottle, Gloria went on, 'By then, the door was locked and I didn't have much say in the matter.'

'You mean – they both . . .?'

'Yeah.' Gloria managed a weak smile. 'I got this bruise – and a couple of others – somewhere in the middle of the

271

argument.' She let the collar of her robe fall back to reveal purple marks on her neck. 'Reckon they both would have been at it all night if I hadn't gone into the bathroom and locked myself in. They kept hammering on the door, but I stayed there till the maid came this morning.'

'Gee, Gloria, what an awful thing to happen.'

'Isn't it just?' She grinned suddenly. 'Still, it's one of the hazards of the job. Serves me right, don't it, Goody Two-Shoes?'

Lisa didn't answer. She was staring at Gloria, frowning. She'd suddenly had the most amazing idea.

'You know the part I went for this morning? The one I borrowed your black dress for?'

'Gee, Lisa, I forgot to ask how you got on. How *did* you get on?'

'I didn't get it, but it'd be perfect for you.'

'Y'think so?' Gloria's eyes widened.

'Are you up to an interview?'

'I'd get up from my deathbed for a part. Who wouldn't?'

'It calls for a little drab woman in her late twenties, early thirties.'

'Gee thanks, Lisa, you've made my day.'

'Shut up. Don't put any make-up on, not even on the bruises, and wear the black dress you lent me.' Lisa bit her lip. 'The only problem is your hair, It looks too bright and glamorous.'

'No problem,' said Gloria. She pulled the towel off her head to reveal short mouse-coloured curls.

Lisa watched the taxi draw away. Gloria, looking even more fragile without her red wig, glanced out of the rear window and gave the thumbs up sign. There was no doubt about it, thought Lisa. In Hollywood, every cloud really *did* have a silver lining!

The telephone rang and for a moment, she considered not answering in case in was Dominic wanting to know where she was. It would be easier to make excuses once she got there. On the other hand, it might be Dick with another part. Who knows who else might have seen the rushes for *Black Corner*? Billy Wilder or John Huston.

The caller was a woman whose voice was familiar. She often rang and always asked for Gloria. Lisa said she'd be gone at least two hours.

'Would you mind leaving her a message? Tell her Mr Baptiste is in town. He's staying at the Belltower.' The woman phrased her words carefully. 'They've been the greatest friends for a long time and he'd like very much to see her again.'

'I'll leave the message by the phone,' Lisa promised. 'I'm going out myself right now.'

After she'd replaced the receiver, she stared down at the paper in her hand. Mr Baptiste, the Belltower. He sounded more in tune with her present mood than the coffee shop. Her mouth curved into a smile as she crumpled the paper up and pushed it in her bag.

She knocked on the door and a deep voice said, 'Come in.'

A slim, silver-haired man was sitting at a desk writing. He looked up as she entered and gave a start. 'I wasn't expecting anyone just yet. The agency said Gloria — '

'She's not well,' Lisa said softly.

He stood up, slowly, gracefully. Lisa closed the door behind her and leaned against it. The man was watching her intently. His face flushed and she saw desire leap into his eyes. His long thin hands tightened at his side. He took a step forward.

'Stay,' she ordered and he stopped as she threw her bag onto the floor and began to undo the buttons of her white blouse, slowly, tantalizingly, until her small, perfect breasts were revealed in full.

'Jesus!' he moaned, though he still didn't move. Lisa's eyes never left his as she unzipped her skirt, easing it gradually, lazily over her narrow hips. The man began to shake as she languorously reached for her panties and pulled them off. She stood before him naked and dizzy with desire.

She walked over to the bed and lay down, her body stretched out, ready, eager, waiting for him.

'Now,' she said.

Next morning, she found an envelope pushed under her

bedroom door containing two one-hundred dollar bills. The scribbled note with it read:

'I got your part. You got mine. I reckon we're quits. Love, Gloria.'

Chapter 27

'Hi Dick, it's Lisa. Any news yet?'

'You know I would've called if there was,' he said.

'It's months since we saw him,' Lisa complained. 'He promised he'd get in touch – perhaps he told all the girls the same thing.'

'It's only four weeks, angel, and you've called every day since. He said he had to raise the dough. Busby Van Dolen's not the sort to say things he don't mean. Anyone else and I'd take what they said with a whole shovelful of salt, but not Busby. He's a really decent guy.'

'I suppose so,' she said reluctantly.

'You still practising your accents?'

'Sure thing.' There were several parts in *The Opportunist* she might be asked to play and she was being taught how to speak with various foreign accents; French, Italian, Arabic.

'Can I ring off now, angel, and get on with some work?' said Dick, 'You ain't my only client, y'know. I got hundreds on my books.'

'Liar!' she retorted good-naturedly. Nevertheless, she said goodbye and put the receiver down, resolving to stop giving Dick a hard time over Busby Van Dolen. If he was going to call, he'd call, and there was nothing Dick could do about it.

On the wide screen, the dust-covered Cadillac screeched to a halt in front of an isolated roadside café. The two bank robbers got out and looked furtively around. One of them slipped over on the muddy forecourt and the audience burst out laughing. Once inside, the men sat in a corner and began whispering to each other.

Lally approached them, looking pert and pretty, a white apron over her gingham dress and a cap perched precariously on her long blonde wig.

'You wanna order?' she enquired.

The two men looked up, startled.

'What?' one of them demanded.

'You're in a restaurant. We serve food here. You wanna order some?' The audience tittered.

The two men looked at each other. 'I guess so,' one said.

'Huh! Don' do me no favours,' Lally replied sarcastically. 'It's just that it sez FOOD outside, and generally that's why folks come in here. To eat!'

'I'll have a coffee. Black.'

'Me, too.'

Lally made a face. 'Huh! Jack'll be able to sell his truck and buy a bicycle if we get more customers like you.'

'That's it,' hissed Lally as the audience laughed again.

'You were fantastic,' whispered Lisa.

'Y'really think so?' said Lally modestly.

'Shush!' A woman in the row in front turned on them irritably.

'Let's go outside and celebrate,' said Gloria. 'We can always see the rest of the movie some other time.'

It was Lally's first-ever speaking part. The film had been made last year and only just released. She'd already been offered two other parts on the strength of this movie, but was disappointed that they were almost identical to the character she'd just played.

'They've sent me scripts for both,' she complained a few minutes later when they were sitting in a bar, 'and I wear almost the same clothes and speak almost the same dialogue. I wish I had enough courage to turn 'em down.'

'Why?' asked Lisa incredulously.

'Because she'll get typecast, that's why,' said Gloria. 'And after a while, nobody will be able to see her in a different part. She'll be a tough, wisecracking waitress for the rest of her movie life.'

Lally shrugged. 'Oh well, if that happens I suppose I can always go home, get married and have a heap o' kids instead.'

It was a Saturday night and as usual the coffee house was packed. Every table was full and Momma's pastries were being eaten faster than she could make them. Lisa felt as if her feet had swollen to twice their size. She hadn't sat down for a minute since midday. Fortunately, it was nearly eight o'clock and almost time for her shift to end. Tonight, she'd be more glad than usual to get away. There was a man on one of her tables who'd been ordering coffee for nearly two hours now, and every time she took his order, he stroked her hand and insisted he take her to dinner when she finished. Why couldn't some men take no for an answer? she thought irritably. Roma had come in to work a couple of hours ago and looked unusually animated – for Roma.

'I got this really good job,' she said to Lisa as they walked back to the coffee station together. 'On a TV games show.'

It was nearly half an hour before they had an opportunity to speak again. 'What sort of job?' Lisa asked.

'I have to present the prizes. The programme's called *Beautiful Dreams*. There's a new series starting in a couple of months' time.'

'I don't think I've seen it.' Lisa rushed off to take more orders.

Later, Roma said, 'If I go down well, they're going to sign me up for a year. The pay's really good. It means I can quit this job. Jesus, I won't be sorry. My feet are killing me.'

'Best of luck,' said Lisa. 'I wish I could quit, too. *My* feet are already dead.'

Five more minutes to go. She signalled to another waitress that it was time to take over her tables. The girl made an agonized face. Lisa served her final order, putting the coffees down with visible relief. The man who'd been pestering her caught her skirt as she walked past. 'Another coffee, miss.'

'I'm off-duty,' she snapped. 'You'll have to ask someone else.'

'In that case, how about dinner?'

She ignored him and dodged back through the crowded tables.

'Excuse me.' A man stood up to bar her way.

'I'm sorry . . . ' she began. 'Why, Mr Van Dolen!'

He stood looking down at her, smiling through his thick horn-rimmed spectacles. He wore a shabby corduroy suit and a check shirt. 'I've been waiting for you to serve me for nearly half an hour,' he groaned.

'That's not my table.' It was Roma's and she was notoriously slow.

'What time do you finish?'

'I already have. As of this minute, I'm gone.'

To her surprise, he followed her back to the counter and waited whilst she collected her bag.

'Fancy something to eat?' he asked.

Even more surprised, she said, 'I wouldn't mind a hamburger, but somewhere close, please, else you'll have to carry me.'

Smiling, he said, 'I wouldn't mind that.'

Lisa felt a pleasant warmth run through her body.

He was holding the door open for her to leave, when a middle-aged couple entered. 'Why, BD!' the woman cried. 'How are you, darling?' She kissed him on the cheek. The man patted him on the shoulder and said jovially, 'How's things, BD?'

'Stella! Mike! Things are coming along fine.'

'Why BD?' Lisa asked when they were outside.

'My initials, minus the V,' he said. 'You can call me that or Busby. No more Mr Van Dolen, if you please. After all, we're going to be working together pretty soon.'

'Are we?' That must mean he'd raised the money and was ready to start on *The Opportunist*. Suddenly, she didn't feel tired any more.

He ushered her into a nearby hamburger bar. 'Two burgers,' he told the waitress who came up for their order. 'Do you want a coffee?' He turned to Lisa.

She shuddered. 'I never want to see a cup of coffee again,' she said. 'I'll have a beer, please.'

'I like women who drink beer,' he said approvingly after the waitress had left.

'How did you know where I worked?' she asked, adding hastily, 'Assuming you weren't there by accident.'

'Dick Broadbent told me. Unfortunately, he didn't tell me where to sit.' His crooked, easygoing features relaxed into a smile. Smiling came easily to him. Behind the thick glasses, his brown eyes shone with an amused twinkle, as if he found the world and everything in it a never ending source of enjoyment. Even if he hadn't been BD, the famous writer and producer-director of highly regarded movies, Lisa would still have felt thrilled to be with him. He probably charmed everyone like this. As if to prove her point and emphasize his popularity, the door opened and a man shouted, 'Hi, BD. I was just passing and thought it was you. How's things?'

'Coming along fine, Doug,' Busby shouted back.

After the waitress had brought their food, Lisa asked, 'How soon are we going to be working together?'

'Keen, are you?' he asked, grinning.

'You bet!' she said enthusiastically.

'In about a month, I reckon. I booked the studio for two months' time, the outdoor shooting's first. How about your Disney job?'

'That'll only take a couple of days,' she replied. 'Next week I'm a nurse in a Civil War movie. I'll be on screen about half a second.'

'Seems like I got hold of you just in time,' he smiled. 'Another few months and you'd have been snapped up by some big studio.'

She didn't answer, but wondered if he was seeing everyone in *The Opportunist*, or just her. She desperately hoped it was just her. Gloria, who had a far more important part, hadn't mentioned him. Which reminded her, she didn't know what part she was going to play. As if reading her thoughts, he said, 'I've got a script roughed out. I think you'd be perfect for the Italian girl, Catarina. Perhaps we could meet tomorrow and I'll give you a copy?'

She looked at him directly. He stared back, a challenging expression on his face. She could meet the challenge or back away. He wasn't the sort to withdraw the part if she turned him down. It was up to her. She felt her heart quicken with excitement as she said, 'What time?'

To her surprise, he closed his eyes briefly and she thought she heard him give a soft sigh of relief. 'Midday,' he answered, 'I'll pick you up and we'll make a day of it. Go to the beach, have lunch.'

She gave him her address and said, 'I'm looking forward to it.'

'So am I.'

*

He was the best company she'd ever known. They went to Little Venice and ate lunch in a ramshackle wooden restaurant overlooking the crowded beach. They watched a group of well-muscled, suntanned men working out and pretending to ignore the onlookers, mainly women who surrounded them and cheered and whistled their every move. Teenagers sat clustered around radios listening to pop music and there was a serious-looking football match going on over to the left. In the midst of all this noise and activity, dozens of people lay prone on the sand sunbathing, oblivious to everything except the need to get a tan. Far beyond, where the pale blue cloudless sky touched the sea, tiny, white-masted yachts were dotted, apparently stranded on the still turquoise water, and the faint drone of motor boats could be heard as they ploughed through the water, dragging water-skiers in their cream foamy wake.

Lisa stared at the sun-worshippers enviously. 'I'd love a tan,' she said, 'but I can't get into sunbathing. I get bored in five minutes.'

'So do I,' said Busby.

That was about the tenth thing they'd agreed on. In fact, they hadn't disagreed on anything yet. They liked the same authors, the same actors and the same movies. Lisa went along with Busby that *The Maltese Falcon* was the best thriller ever made and they'd both seen *Casablanca* half a dozen times.

They left the restaurant and strolled along the sea front. Busby took her hand companionably. It seemed the natural thing to do.

'Gee, I'd like muscles like that,' he said, pointing to a couple of weightlifters on the beach, their wide powerful shoulders gleaming with oil, strained and knotted, as they hoisted the heavy weights.

Lisa shook her head. 'You wouldn't suit them,' she said. He wore a short-sleeved white tee shirt, revealing arms that were well proportioned though decidedly unmuscled.

A voice yelled, 'Hi, BD. How'ya doin'?'

In the middle of the crowded beach, a man was waving his arms furiously in their direction.

Busby waved back. 'Hi, Joe. I'm doing fine.'

'You know a lot of people,' Lisa remarked. That was the third time today someone had greeted him.

'He was in a movie I wrote a couple of years back,' Busby said. 'Hollywood's a great place for getting to know folk.' Lisa reckoned it was his warm, outgoing personality that made people speak to him. They knew they'd get a friendly response and always looked gratified when he remembered their names.

'Fancy a beer?' He stopped by an open-fronted bar with wooden trestle tables in the forecourt.

'I wouldn't say no. I never drank beer at home,' she said as she sipped the ice-cold drink. 'It was always warm.'

He shuddered. 'Warm beer! I remember that only too well.'

'You've been to England?' she asked, surprised.

'Just for a couple of months during the war.'

As if a cloud had suddenly appeared covering the sun, Lisa felt cold. Dark memories flooded in and she shivered. 'Where were you stationed?' she asked.

'Some little village near London, I can't remember the name.' He looked at her with concern. 'Are you okay? You've gone quite pale.'

'I'm fine. A goose walked over my grave, as my mother used to say.'

'Hey, look at that guy on roller skates!' She knew he said it to distract her and he succeeded. An elderly man with a flowing white beard skated past, his wispy, shoulder-length hair streaming out behind like a sail. He wore nothing but a pair of cutdown jeans and carried a basket full of shopping. Lisa couldn't help but laugh.

They finished their beer and carried on along the pro menade. Loud music could be heard some way ahead and suddenly they came upon its source, a little funfair on the corner of the next street.

To be reminded twice in the space of a few minutes of that Easter Monday in Southport was devastating. Lisa had never been near a funfair since. She'd thought the memory of that day was deeply buried in her mind, though not forgotten. It just showed how close to the surface it was, that Busby's casual words and the sound of a funfair could bring it back with such a sense of shock.

Inhuman screams were coming from across the road and she saw a girl on the roller coaster, her face terrified, clasped in the arms of a young man and she winced, remembering.

'You'll never guess what I can see,' said Busby.

'What?' She tried to sound casual.

He was pointing down the street towards a tiny cinema. 'See what's on – *Casablanca*!'

He bought a tub of popcorn and two cans of drink, and they sat in the back row of the virtually empty cinema, his arm round her shoulders. She rested her head against him, feeling comfortable and safe. At the end of the film, she began to cry. 'It's so sad,' she sobbed. 'I keep hoping that one day they'll have changed the ending.'

When they came out, to her surprise, it had gone dark. The day seemed to be passing unnaturally fast. She remarked as much to Busby.

'It's the company you're keeping,' he said, grinning. 'It shows you're not bored.'

Later, as they drove back towards Hollywood, he asked, 'Are you interested in politics?'

'Not much,' she replied and tried to remember the name of the current American president, without success.

'I wanted to go into politics when I was a kid,' Busby said. 'In a background role, speech-writing, public relations, that sort of stuff.'

'You'd have been good at that,' she said.

'Somehow I got sidetracked into movies, though I never regretted it.' He explained that in America, the Democrats were the left-wing party and the Republicans the right. 'Just like Labour and Conservative in your country,' he said. He was a Democrat, an activist, deeply involved in the local party machine. 'When President Eisenhower – he's a Republican – bows out in 1960, there's a good chance we'll get in. You ever heard of Jack Kennedy?'

'I'm afraid not.'

'You will do soon. He's the Senator for Massachusetts. There's a group of us in California rooting for him to get nominated as our presidential candidate. I met him once.

He's the most decent guy I've ever known. If Jack gets elected . . . ' He didn't finish. She saw his hands tighten on the wheel of the car. Turning towards her, he grinned. 'Sorry. Have I managed to bore you after all?'

Lisa assured him she hadn't been bored at all. 'I should know something about the country I'm living in.'

'Let's stop here for dinner.'

He drove into the forecourt of a roadhouse and as he got out of the car, he took a briefcase off the back seat. After they'd eaten, he handed her a manuscript. 'The screenplay for *The Opportunist*,' he said.

'I'd forgotten all about it,' Lisa confessed guiltily. After all, this was supposed to be the reason for their day out together.

'So had I until we were on our way home. Your part starts on page forty-three.'

'Who's taking the main role?' she asked. 'The Cahil O'Daly character?'

'I got really lucky,' Busby answered, looking pleased. 'Ralph Layton asked if I'd consider him. I took him like a shot.'

'Ralph?' she remarked in delight. 'He'd be perfect!'

'You sound as if you know him.'

'I do. Gee, it'll be really great to see him again.'

Busby stopped the car outside her apartment and said, 'I'd like to see you again, Lisa, but I've got to tell you something first.'

She turned to gaze at him. He looked grave for once. Behind the thick glasses, his eyes were solemn. 'What is it?' she asked curiously.

'I'm married.' Before she could say anything, he went on quickly, 'My wife has left me for another guy and she's suing for divorce, so I suppose you could say I'm married going on single.'

Lisa couldn't imagine any woman in her right mind leaving Busby for someone else. She was stuck for a reply and remained silent for so long that eventually he asked anxiously, 'It's all right, isn't it?'

'Of course.' She put her hand over his and said, 'It's been a lovely day. I'd like to do it again some time.'

283

He leaned over and took her in his arms. His lips were moist and soft against hers. Immediately she began to kiss him back passionately, praying he'd suggest going back to his place so they could make love properly. Instead, he suddenly broke away and began to stroke her cheek. 'My God! You're beautiful!' he said hoarsely.

She felt let down, almost rejected. Perhaps he sensed this because he whispered, 'Let's leave the first time until it's just right.'

'Okay,' she said, smiling, though still disappointed.

As she stood on the pavement watching him drive away, she thought it had been an almost perfect day, marred only by those painful reminders of the past.

Later on, when she was in bed, she thought about Busby. He was so easygoing and laid-back, she couldn't visualize him having the authority or the downright bloody-minded imperiousness needed to direct a film.

'Lisa, Lisa, *Lisa*!' Busby screamed. Then, '*Cut*.'

He sprang nimbly over the rocky beach and grasped her by the shoulders. She shrank back. His hands hurt; the fingers dug into the flesh of her upper arms, though he didn't seem to notice.

'Christ, woman,' he yelled. 'Your lover has gone. GONE! Geddit? You're watching his boat sail away, knowing you'll never see him again. You're heartbroken. You think your life has finished.' He let go of her contemptuously. 'You look more like you've dropped a blob of ice cream down your dress.'

There was a titter from one of the crew. Lisa wished the sand would open up and swallow her. Perhaps she could have managed the look of heartbreak required if the scenes were being shot in sequence, but although this was her first day of shooting, it was her final scene in the film. She had to grieve over the loss of a man with whom she'd just had a passionate affair, yet that part wasn't due to be shot for another two weeks, when they moved into the studio for the indoor work. The isolated beach twenty miles from Hollywood where they were shooting today was supposed to be the coast of Italy; it was the farthest Busby could afford to go on location. He'd planned on finishing the scene by midday, when the company would move on somewhere else. The morning had mostly gone, wasted on Lisa, who by now felt convinced that if she stayed here forever, she would never get the expression Busby wanted. Perhaps, she thought vainly, if the boat she was supposed to be staring at was really sailing past, she could fix her feelings on that. But the ocean was an empty expanse of blue. The boat would be added later.

She stood there, miserable and close to tears, but Busby showed no mercy. 'Let's do it again,' he ordered. 'Take twenty-two, *roll it*.'

The wind machine started up again and Lisa pushed the hair out of her eyes. She felt the skirt of her long black dress wrap itself around her legs and the tears that had been threatening began to well and she swallowed hard, trying to hold them back. The cameraman moved in for a close-up. The tears refused to be held and she felt them coursing down her cheeks. 'I wish I was anywhere in the world but here,' she thought tragically. She wiped the tears away with the back of her hand, ashamed of crying in front of so many people. 'Any minute now, Busby will yell at me again and people will laugh.' Her bottom lip trembled as more tears began to fall and it was all she could do not to bury her face in her hands and weep quite openly.

'Cut!' Busby shouted. 'That'll do. Thanks, Lisa.'

Open-mouthed, she watched him come back over the rocks towards her. He passed without a second glance. She could have been invisible.

It was nearly midnight when he turned up in the bar where cast and crew had gathered hours ago. He slipped into the seat beside her and said, 'Sorry I'm late, I've been watching the rushes. You were great.'

'You know what you are?' she said accusingly.

'What?' He raised his eyebrows.

'A bloody Jekyll and Hyde, that's what.'

He looked genuinely astonished. 'Why, what have I done?'

'If you don't know, it only goes to prove my point.'

*

Lisa sat in a dark corner of the studio watching Busby as he examined the set of her next scene. His tall thin body stooped and intense, he prowled around the old-fashioned drawing room. Suddenly, he paused in front of a sideboard crammed with ornaments and framed photographs, frowning and scratching his beard. Then his face went black as he reached out and grabbed something from the back.

'Who put this photograph here?' he asked in a voice like thunder. 'The clothes are all wrong. Women weren't wearing hats like that in the nineteen-twenties!'

Chas, his assistant, snapped his fingers and a girl in jeans and a man's shirt scurried onto the set, took the photograph, and scurried off again. Busby was a perfectionist. The chances of someone noticing that photo in the few short seconds the sideboard was on screen, were millions to one, but his concentration would have been spoiled by knowing it was there. He opened the door of the set, closed it, came back in, sat down at the table and began to talk to himself. Several people had stopped work and were observing him, fascinated. Busby knew the script by heart and he was acting out the parts, matching movement with dialogue, so he would know exactly what directions to give when shooting began. As far as Busby was concerned, once in the studio, the world outside ceased to exist. Nothing mattered except the film he was making. A bomb could drop yards away and he wouldn't notice, and if someone told him, he wouldn't care.

High up above, somebody started hammering loudly and the sound echoed through the vast building. Everybody jumped, except Busby, who went on talking to himself, saying the lines under his breath.

Lisa opened her script and began to read. She knew her part backwards but was worried that she would forget everything once the cameras began to roll, particularly if Busby was horrible again, though from now on, Ralph would be there to support her.

Ralph! She remembered that first day in the studio. She'd gone in and there he was, sitting in a canvas chair next to Busby. His name was printed on the reverse. He had his back to her and so she crept up and put her hands over his eyes.

'Guess who?' she whispered.

He sat stock-still for several seconds, then 'Lisa!' he shouted in astonishment. He sprang to his feet and clasped her in his arms. 'My dear, dear girl, how on earth did you get here?' He turned to Busby. 'Last time I saw my lovely friend she was in hot pursuit of a handsome young blond gentleman – or was he in hot pursuit of you? What happened?' he demanded.

'We caught each other – but it didn't work out,' she said swiftly.

Busby was glowering at them jealously.

'Where have you been all this time?' Ralph asked. 'I rang the flat and wrote to you, but Piers said you had just disappeared into thin air.'

'I came to Hollywood,' said Lisa. 'After all, you invited me enough times.'

'But you didn't get in touch!' He looked dumbfounded and slightly hurt.

She took his hands and pressed them against her cheeks. 'I knew we'd meet up eventually. In the meantime, I wanted to make it on my own.'

'Well, that's Lisa O'Brien in a nutshell,' he said, laughing. 'The most independent-minded young woman I've ever known.'

'It's Lisa Angelis now,' she said. 'My agent thought O'Brien was too ordinary.'

Later on, when they broke for coffee, he asked, 'What do you think of our magic town?'

'It's like you said, magic,' she replied simply.

And it was. As she watched Busby discussing costumes with Maggie Nestor from the wardrobe department, she thought, 'If I stayed here too long, I'd get confused between real life and celluloid life.' So much more effort was put into the creation of a fictional, ninety-minute or so movie than into ordinary living, that eventually the imagery and myth became more important than reality.

Even more magically, in a few weeks' time Busby the wizard would take the thousands of feet of film shot so haphazardly, a few seconds here, a few seconds there, away to the editor in the cutting room. One day he would emerge, the patchwork complete, the beginning in its proper place, the ending duly at the end. To the eyes of the innocent audience, Lisa would be weeping at the sight of a real ship sailing away from the coast of Naples. In the dark cinema, a miracle would occur. The audience, reality suspended and their imaginations set free, would travel the world. Yet every foot of film had been shot within a few square miles of California.

Hollywood! The dream-maker. The story-teller par excellence.

Lisa tried not to be envious of Gloria, but she couldn't help it. Gloria seemed to get right inside the part of the little Liverpool servant woman, Mary, and Busby never had to raise his voice when she was on set. She understood what he wanted instantly.

'A touch more emotion there,' Busby would say, or 'Make that expression a little harder,' and in the next shot Gloria would do it just the way he wanted.

'Perfect!' he'd crow. 'Absolutely perfect.'

How had she done it? Lisa was lost in admiration. Busby had never said 'perfect' to her once. 'That'll do,' was the most she got.

On the second day of shooting Gloria's part, Busby declared her 'better than perfect', and Lisa decided she couldn't stand it any longer. In between takes, she left the studio, depressed at watching Gloria turn in such an impeccable performance, when she had to be bullied into expressing the most basic emotion.

She emerged at the back of the lot amongst a ramshackle collection of buildings which housed the wardrobe and make-up departments, and came face to face with Ralph, who was just emerging from make-up, his hair back to its original brown, curling onto the collar of his navy pea-jacket.

'What's wrong?' he asked. 'You look upset.'

Lisa said, 'I am. I've just been watching Gloria and according to Busby, she's better than perfect. I'll never be able to act like that.'

'Don't be silly,' said Ralph. 'Those scenes we did together

were really good. Anyway, Gloria's had years more experience than you.' He looked down at her sternly. 'Busby Van Dolen's one of the best directors in Hollywood. He wouldn't have picked you if he thought you'd spoil his movie.'

She made a face and for the first time she could remember, Ralph looked annoyed. 'I don't think you realize what a great movie we're making here, Lisa. It's a real work of art and the best part I've ever had. You should be in there watching and learning from Gloria – and me, come to that, instead of sulking out here.'

'In that case, I'll go back,' she said contritely. She linked his arm and they strolled towards the main entrance. 'How's Michael?' she asked. There hadn't been much time to talk since they'd met again.

Ralph grinned and said, 'Apart from being a two-timing son of a bitch, he's fine.'

Lisa glanced at him. 'You don't mind?'

'Not as long as he comes back to me each night,' he answered. 'You must come and have a drink with us some time. Give *him* something to get jealous about for a change.'

'Cut,' shouted Busby. 'that's it – finito! All wrapped up. Thanks, everybody. Good night and goodbye.'

The crew and cast cheered and began hugging each other. Some of the crew began packing up their equipment.

'You got real Oscar material there, Busby,' someone shouted and there was a chorus of 'Hear, hear.'

Lisa felt a lump in her throat. What was she to do with herself now *The Opportunist* was finished? What were all of them going to do? These last eight weeks, the film had completely dominated her life, all their lives. To her surprise, she heard someone say, 'Thank God that's over. I'm having a few days' holiday, then I'm off to Spain for eight weeks to do a thriller.' 'I've got a couple of weeks in a soap,' someone else said. To them, the movie was already part of their past. They would never forget it, but what mattered was the future and getting on with the rest of their lives.

Busby touched her on her shoulder. 'How about foregoing the wrap party and coming and taking a look at my etchings?' he whispered.

'How dare you, sir,' she answered primly. 'What sort of a girl do you think I am?'

'My sort.' He put his arm around her shoulders and they began to walk towards the exit. A couple of people watched them curiously. This was the first time he'd treated her differently from the other actresses and it made her feel very special.

They'd driven in companionable silence for ten minutes before Lisa asked, 'Where are we going?'

'Beverly Hills,' he replied. 'My place.'

She caught her breath. At last Busby had decided the 'right' time had come. For nearly three months she had been aching for this moment. His brusque, apparently uncaring attitude had hurt and she found herself longing for a kind word, yet the more he ignored her, the more she fell in love. Tonight, he seemed like the old Busby again, the man who had sought her out in the coffee bar and swept her along to Little Venice and other places, content with a kiss when he took her home. Tonight, a kiss wouldn't be enough. Tonight, they would make love.

He lay beside her, fast asleep. Without his glasses, he looked younger. She'd never noticed how long his lashes were before. As he breathed, they quivered gently. He looked contented and satisfied.

Lisa slipped naked out of the giant, oval-shaped bed. There was a dressing gown thrown over a chair and she put it on and padded towards the kitchen where she searched around until she found a box of teabags.

Why didn't she share Busby's contentment? Instead, she felt edgy and unfulfilled. He had brought her to the very brink of passion, but left her there, dissatisfied and frustrated. It had all been over so quickly. There had been no doubt of his love, his longing to possess her, his urgent need, yet . . .

'Perhaps it's my fault,' thought Lisa, 'I expect too much, particularly after Patrick— ' She stopped *that* thought before it could get any further. It had been better with Clive Randolph, even Brian. Yet in every other way she and Busby were perfect together. She thought about the man she'd met in the Belltower – Carl Baptiste – and shivered, remembering the unbridled, savage passion of that afternoon.

'So there you are!'

She jumped. Busby had come into the kitchen. He wore a pair of pyjama trousers. 'I wondered where my robe had gone,' he added.

'Would you like a cup of tea?'

He came up behind her, pulled the robe away and began to fondle her breasts. 'No, I want you.' He buried his head in her neck and whispered, 'That was wonderful before. Was it good for you too?'

'Yes,' Lisa lied. 'The best ever.'

Chapter 28

They'd made love three times and Lisa's body was slippy with perspiration. Then he began to caress her once more, his fingers exploring her most intimate parts. She groaned in delight as he entered her yet again and brought her to the very peak of rapture, keeping her there, poised in a state of almost unbearable, quivering anticipation. Lisa cried aloud. Suddenly, inevitably, her body erupted in a gush of sheer ecstasy. They lay in each other's arms for several minutes, neither speaking. Then he lay back with a deep sigh and said reluctantly, 'I have to go soon.'

'So have I,' said Lisa. With a determined movement, she pushed the clammy sheets away and got out of bed. As she stooped to pick up her underclothes, he reached out and began to stroke her buttocks, first with one hand, then two. 'Your flesh is like silk,' he murmured and pressed his lips in the hollow of her waist. She began to moan softly and he pulled her back onto the bed.

'If I miss my plane, there'll be hell to pay,' he complained a quarter of an hour later.

'I refuse to get out of bed again until you're dressed,' said Lisa. 'It's a waste of time.'

'I refuse to get dressed until you're out of bed,' said Carl Baptiste.

Lisa lay still and after a while, he gave an exaggerated sigh and threw back the clothes. She watched under lowered lids as he pulled on his fine silk clothes, tightening a lizard-skin belt around his narrow, almost feminine waist with thin, brown hands and marvelled at the incredible things those hands had done to her over the last three years.

As he brushed his silver hair, he noticed her watching him and smiled. 'I'll be back in six weeks,' he said. 'Shall I give you a call?'

'If you feel so inclined,' said Lisa.

'I always feel so inclined, you know that.'

'And you know I always want you to call.'

'Asking is all part of the game,' he said. His voice was deep, with the merest trace of an accent. 'You know, I nearly bought you a present this time.'

'Why?' asked Lisa in surprise.

'Our third anniversary. I changed my mind. I thought it might spoil things.' He was having trouble inserting a cuff link into his right-hand sleeve. 'My wife always . . . ' He stopped suddenly. 'Sorry, I forgot our pact. No personal details.'

'And no presents,' said Lisa.

He picked up his cashmere jacket and she noticed the designer label inside. After he'd put it on, he took a wallet out of the inside pocket, and pulled out a note and put it on the desk.

'A dollar, as usual,' he said. He stared down at her curiously. 'Why just one?'

'It makes it more exciting to be paid.' She sat up, pushed the clothes back and stretched extravagantly. He looked down at her hungrily, his eyes narrowing.

'You're doing that on purpose,' he said in a cracked voice.

'What?' she asked innocently, adding, 'You'd better hurry, or you'll miss your plane.'

'I can always get a later one.' He began to drag at his tie.

'No.' She shook her head vigorously. 'That's against the rules.'

He said angrily, 'There should be a rule against your flaunting your body at me once I am dressed.'

'I'm sorry,' she said mischievously, and pulled the sheet up to her neck. 'Is that better?'

He didn't answer and began to throw his belongings into a soft suede bag. When he had finished, he looked at her coldly and said, 'Goodbye.'

'Goodbye, Carl.'

The door closed behind him. She didn't care that he had gone in a bad temper. He'd done it before, riled at her shameless attempts to seduce him when she knew he had to go. She sank back onto the bed. It hadn't been a lie, saying she had to leave soon. In an hour she was due at the studio for a costume-fitting with Maggie Nestor, but she felt too limp and languorous to move. Carl always left her feeling like this, drained and satiated after two or three hours of lovemaking.

It was a perfect arrangement. She hadn't been married to Busby for long before she realized that he could never satisfy her needs – yet she loved him so much! There hadn't been a moment's hesitation in accepting his proposal. He'd asked her soon after *The Opportunist* had been completed and she'd said yes straight away.

'My divorce comes through in the New Year. What say we get married, Lisa?'

It was Christmas Day and they were sitting by his pool. There must have been a hundred people there who'd just turned up to wish him well, all happening to have a bottle of Scotch or wine with them and all free to spend the day at his place.

Busby didn't mind. He loved company. It was rare that at least half a dozen people weren't gathered in his big modern single-storey home for some reason or another. If it wasn't movies, then it was politics. This was why his wife, Sharon, had left. A quiet, timid girl he'd met at college, she couldn't get used to sharing her house with his numerous friends. Worst of all, she hated the film industry. Sharon had gone off with a bank manager, a man as quiet and unsociable as herself.

Lisa was lying on a lounger, her thoughts miles away. It was hard to get used to the idea of wearing a bikini on Christmas Day. Over and over again as she stretched out in the hot sun, she found her thoughts turning to Chaucer Street. It would be evening there, the family would have got together and be gathered round the kitchen fire – or would they? she thought lazily. She tended to think of her brothers and sisters as they were when she left, but that was eleven long years ago; she hadn't recognized Patrick. Most of them would be married and have homes of their own. Wherever they were, the biting Mersey wind would be whipping across the city.

'What did you say?' She opened her eyes, aware that someone had spoken and found Busby, clad only in a pair of baggy khaki shorts, kneeling beside her.

'I said my divorce comes through in the New Year. What say we get married?'

Close by, someone dived into the pool and water splashed them both. Lisa shrieked and Busby took his glasses off and wiped them dry.

'Yes.'

'Yes?' He looked surprised, as if there was a chance she'd refuse! They got on so well, it would be madness to say no. There was that one thing, but as Kitty always used to say, 'practice makes perfect'. After a while, making love would be sure to turn out well.

But it didn't!

They got married by the pool late in January 1958. Lisa hadn't bothered to count the guests who turned up. Two hundred had been invited, and at least as many again gate-crashed.

Married life turned out to be a hectic round of socializing. Except for breakfast, they rarely ate at home, driving into Hollywood for lunch and dinner to eat Chinese or Greek or Italian food, two or three carloads of them, as folk began to drop in from early on. Wherever they ate, Busby was greeted with delight, and even more people were squeezed onto their crowded table and came back to the house. Often when Lisa got up, she found someone already in the kitchen making coffee or folks asleep on the couch or by the pool. She didn't mind. In fact, she loved the friendly, club-like atmosphere and helped Jacob, Busby's black helper, keep the giant-sized refrigerator stocked with beer and the cupboards full of snacks and cigarettes. Several times, they flew to New York to spend a week theatregoing, looking up yet more of Busby's old friends. Somehow, in the midst of this chaos, he managed to tuck himself away in his study to write the scripts by which he earned his regular money. After an exhausting day, they'd go to bed and always made love – but practice did not make perfect. Each time, Lisa was left feeling let down and disappointed, though Busby was more than satisfied. She came to the inevitable conclusion that for all his magnetism and charisma, his warmth and charm, Busby Van Dolen was a lousy lover.

*

One morning, after they'd been married three months, she woke up feeling irritated and on edge. Busby was still asleep. Last night, she'd tried to pour herself into him, stir him into the extra effort which would bring her to the state of joy for which she yearned, but it had been useless. As always, she pretended enjoyment she hadn't had.

She got out of bed, pulled on a bikini and went outside.

The pool was warm, despite the early hour. She swam a few lengths, forging through the water as if she were in a race, trying to rid herself of the feeling of frustration. After a while she climbed out, wrapped herself in a towelling robe and went into the kitchen to make a drink. She still felt as if live wires were rubbing against each other in the pit of her stomach.

As she plugged the kettle in, she noticed the wall phone had a message under it from Gloria. She wanted Lisa to ring back. Gloria! Seeing her name gave Lisa an idea – an utterly audacious idea that sent the live wires into a state of high-speed agitation. She flipped through the telephone directory until she found the number she wanted, then dialled it, her fingers, her entire body trembling with excitement.

'Good morning, Belltower,' a man's voice answered.

'I have a package for Mr Baptiste. Is he staying with you now?'

'Hold on, ma'am, and I'll check.' The man was gone less than a minute. 'No, ma'am, Mr Baptiste isn't due till next week, Thursday.'

'Thank you,' said Lisa.

She'd just turned up, knocked on his door and gone in as she'd done that first time. She'd been going every six or eight weeks since. They knew nothing about each other. He was not an American. He had a passport, but for which country she had no idea. Baptiste wasn't his real name, she knew that much. They rarely talked. There wasn't time. Each satisfied a need in the other. Outside that Belltower bedroom, she might not like him. It didn't matter. All he knew of Lisa was her telephone number and when he arrived in Los Angeles he'd call.

'Your dry cleaning is ready,' was the code. Sometimes it

was Busby who took the call and Lisa was ashamed that she never felt guilty when he passed the message on. Indeed, it seemed to add an extra frisson to the whole thing.

She was going to be late for the fitting. Reluctantly, she got out of bed and went into the shower to wash all trace of Carl Baptiste off her body.

As she stood under the cool water, she seemed to wash the memory of him away too. These enchanting few hours were always difficult to emerge from. As he faded from her mind, she began to think about the new movie and her first starring role.

The last three and a half years, she'd turned down dozens of parts, preferring to stick to Busby's own movies.

'Your heart ain't in acting,' Dick Broadbent said accusingly when he rang to tell her about a part she'd been offered and which she refused, as usual. 'The minute you get married you give up.'

'I do Busby's movies,' she said defensively.

'Huh! Once a year and if Busby wasn't the director, you wouldn't even do them.'

'I quite like being just a wife,' she said meekly. She didn't add that she was desperately hoping to become a mother, too. 'I'm sorry, Dick. Come round to dinner on Friday. It's my thirtieth birthday and Busby'd love to see you.'

He grudgingly agreed. 'I still think you're star material,' he said quickly before he rang off.

That phone call had been nearly a year ago. Lisa stepped out of the shower and began to dry herself with unnecessary roughness.

Her thirtieth birthday!

She remembered that occasion with horror. She remembered staring at herself in the mirror, looking for age lines, seeing none, thinking 'What have I achieved?' The mirror held no answers, so Lisa answered herself.

'You've achieved a lot. You've had parts in three of the most highly regarded films made in America in the last few years.' *The Opportunist* had been greeted with critical acclaim and won prizes in several foreign film festivals. Ralph only just lost out on an Academy Award to Burt Lancaster's *Elmer Gantry* and Gloria Grenville was now a major star, though as usual Busby's film had gone out on limited release. It wasn't commercial enough to appeal to a wider audience, the distributors said, so it was only screened in small 'art' cinemas throughout America.

The same thing happened to Busby's next two projects: *The Lilac Tree* and *Beneath Contempt*. The critics had showered both films with plaudits and Lisa had been picked out for special praise. '*A sparkling, sensitive performance,*' one reviewer wrote. '*Lisa Angelis is a real find.*' As usual, only the same small art cinemas showed them.

'You've done well for a girl coming from Chaucer Street.' She was rich beyond her wildest dreams. Although Busby didn't earn nearly as much as other successful producers, Lisa had more than enough money.

Why then, did she stare at herself, anxiously demanding answers? 'Because compared to other girls coming from Chaucer Street, Lisa, you've never done anything *really* worthwhile!' There was nothing to show for thirty years of existence except a few feet of celluloid film.

'That's not my fault. You know how much I want a baby.' She'd been married to Busby for nearly three years and it wasn't his fault she hadn't conceived. He already had two daughters from his first marriage – pretty, outgoing little girls who came to see him once a month. Lately, Lisa found herself watching and wishing they were hers.

Staring numbly in the mirror on her birthday, she'd decided it was time to see a gynaecologist. Perhaps she had some blocked tubes, or whatever it was that prevented women from conceiving. She was totally ignorant on medical matters.

She had a feeling, a suspicion at the back of her mind of what the result of the tests would be, and her suspicions were confirmed. A long time ago, the doctor said, she'd had a badly injured womb, followed by serious inflammation. Unfortunately, the damage was irreparable.

'You can't expect to get away with having this sort of thing done to your body,' he said angrily. 'Isn't this the result of what you call in England a back-street abortion?'

Despite her premonition, Lisa felt herself go faint. 'So there's no chance, no chance at all of conceiving?' she whispered.

'It would be a miracle if you did,' he said, his face cold and unsympathetic. 'Which is a pity, because otherwise you're an exceptionally healthy woman.'

The shock of that day never paled. Lisa finished drying herself and began to get dressed. Once again, she felt a surge of cold anger at her father for what he had done to her. She'd told no one of her visit to the doctor, not even Busby.

After she'd slipped into her cream silk shift, she sat down at the dressing table and began to draw a thin line above and below her eyes with a black kohl pencil, smearing the lids with gold shadow and brushing her long lashes, curling them upwards. She still didn't use powder or pancake, but finished off by painting her lips scarlet, building the shape outwards with a stiff lipbrush. Pulling a cream band over her hair, she combed forward the recently-cut fringe, then stood up to examine herself full-length.

There was no doubt about it: despite the absence of lines, she had acquired an air of maturity which added an extra dimension to her beauty. There was a sadness in her eyes which she was sure had only been there since she'd learned she could never have a child. Only the other day, Busby had said to her, 'You're like a rose, in its most perfect moment of blooming.'

She'd replied indignantly, 'I don't want to be like a rose, thank you very much. It means at any minute my petals will fall off and I'll just be a nasty twig with thorns on. I'd sooner be a sturdy old nettle which never dies. Least, I don't think it does.'

'I was just trying to be nice,' Busby said in a little-boy voice.

'Well, don't.' Lisa threw a cushion at him and he threw it back, then came over and dragged her onto his knee.

'I'll never be nice to you again,' he threatened.

'Yes, you will.' She snuggled into his arms. 'You can't help but be nice to everybody. Except when you're making a movie,' she added as an afterthought. 'Then Genghis Khan could take lessons in being mean.'

After a few minutes, he said seriously, 'You know, I've never been so happy. I've got you, I've got the finance together for *Easy Dreams* and I've got Jack Kennedy in the White House. The world is perfect.' Busby acted as if President Kennedy had been elected entirely due to his own efforts.

'Let's pause and remember this moment all our lives,' said Lisa. 'The moment when the world was perfect for Busby Van Dolen.'

He looked down at her quickly. 'Isn't it perfect for Lisa Angelis?'

She kissed him. 'Almost,' she said softly. 'Almost perfect.'

Before quitting the hotel room, Lisa checked that nothing had been left behind. Carl had departed in such a hurry. The room was clear. If she caught a taxi, she would just get to the studio in time.

Easy Dreams was set in the 1930s. Maggie Nestor had got hold of top fashion magazines for the period and Lisa's wardrobe consisted of slinky, tight-fitting suits and evening dresses that showed off her slender, curved figure to perfection.

'I've put a zip in this when it should be hooks and eyes. D'you think he'll notice?' Maggie asked. Lisa was struggling into a black lace spangled gown lined with fine, flesh-coloured silk.

Maggie was a homely, plump woman who bought her own ill-fitting clothes through a chain-store catalogue.

'He' was Busby, the monster. 'I wouldn't like to say,' said Lisa cautiously, remembering the way he'd exploded with rage on the set of *The Lilac Tree* when he found a newspaper with an out-of-date headline. 'I'll try and keep my left side away from him, just in case.' She walked to the mirror with difficulty. 'I'll have to learn to walk again in these narrow skirts.'

'You need to mince, not walk,' said Maggie, adding thankfully, 'I'm glad it's not me wearing them.'

'Wow!' said Lisa. 'I look as if I've got nothing on underneath this.'

'That's the whole point,' Maggie said. 'She wears that for the Mayor's ball. Causes a consternation – I read the script. At home, she wears even less. Have you seen these night-dresses and stuff?'

'Wow!' said Lisa again as Maggie pointed to half a dozen sheer garments hanging from the wall. 'They look like nylon. Did they have nylon then?'

'They're all crêpe or silk. I had a helluva job tracking the stuff down. Look at this one.' Maggie unhooked a black diaphanous negligée. 'I managed to buy this from an antiques market. Most of the trimming had gone, so I replaced it with feathers. If it tickles, blame me.'

'I might as well be wearing a sheet of glass,' said Lisa.

'You certainly won't be hiding any of your charms,' agreed Maggie. 'This movie's gonna give the censors a big head-ache. I've certainly never seen one yet with so much nudity. Busby's taking a real big chance.'

'He always takes chances with his movies,' said Lisa, holding the negligée in front of her.

Maggie was staring at her, looking puzzled. 'How you actresses can wear stuff like that in front of an all-male crew beats me,' she said. Then she grinned and added, 'But then, if I had a figure like yours, perhaps I'd be willing to flaunt it round a bit.'

Shooting of *Easy Dreams* went, appropriately, like a dream. Busby said it was the smoothest, least troublesome movie he'd ever made.

Lisa played a beautiful, shallow woman who causes havoc in the lives of four powerful men who are her lovers. Her lines were few.

'You don't need to say anything, you speak with your body,' Busby told her.

For the first time, Lisa seemed to sense what Busby wanted of her without him asking. The part had been written with her in mind and the entire movie centred around Cassie Royale.

'You are everything a man wants in a woman,' Busby said, 'and everything a woman wants to be.' So, oblivious to everyone else in the studio, Cassie Royale enticed her lovers into her bed, standing in the doorway, naked under the sheer black robe, hands resting provocatively on her lean hips.

'Perfect,' said Busby, peering through the viewfinder. 'Perfect . . . Just look at him and lick your lips, slowly. Your eyes hold a promise – you can fulfil his wildest, most impossible dreams. If he gives you money, you'll give him heaven in return.'

The film was a paean to his wife, to Lisa, into which he poured his very soul. On set, he was like a madman, pushing himself beyond exhaustion, expecting miracles from the cast and crew, driving them mad with his impossible demands. Yet no one complained. No one refused to stay late. Everybody seemed to understand they were working with a genius who deserved, was entitled to, their total cooperation and commitment.

The movie was an allegory of the American Dream. It showed that what people were being encouraged to strive for was ultimately rotten and corrupt. Lisa said she didn't think anyone would notice. Busby pointed out Cassie Royale's address – 49 Republic Avenue. 'Americans will notice,' he said.

Unfortunately, they didn't have an opportunity. In the spring of 1963 when *Easy Dreams* was previewed, it was almost universally slammed by the critics.

'A pornographic nightmare.'

'Too avant-garde for its own good.'

'Busby Van Dolen should never be allowed inside a studio again. The film is trashy, boring and wastes the talents of its excellent actors.'

'An abstract mish-mash of images which drives its message home with a sledgehammer.'

'How can it be abstract *and* drive its message home?' groaned Busby. 'That's a contradiction in terms.' He was sitting up in bed reading the reviews. A couple of friends had already arrived to commiserate and were on the floor drinking beer. 'They like you, though, Lisa. Listen to this: "*The dazzlingly lovely Lisa Angelis is enchanting as Cassie Royale.*

Perhaps it is only because she is married to the wretched director that she agreed to take the part."' He threw the paper down. 'I expect the Sundays will be just as bad.'

They were. There was just one favourable review. The critic in a little Greenwich Village magazine wrote, *'Some will call* Easy Dreams *pornographic. Some will say it is unpatriotic. It is neither. It is a movie made before its time. The day will come when every movie will not have to be a glorification of the American way of life. When that glad day comes,* Easy Dreams *will be regarded as a classic.'*

Easy Dreams won prizes at the Berlin and Cannes film festivals, though it was never released in America. Busby said he didn't know whether to laugh or cry when he learnt that a copy had been acquired by a pornographic film club and was now included in their library.

It was not in Busby's nature to stay downhearted for long. Anyway, his beloved President Kennedy was involved in confrontation with right-wing whites as he tried to enforce civil liberties for black people in the southern states. Busby went to Birmingham, Alabama, to march with those fighting for desegregation of schools. Lisa asked to go too.

'No, it's too dangerous. You could get hurt and I just don't want you to see how much Americans can hate each other.'

He was gone a week and Lisa was sick with worry. When Carl Baptiste called, she made an excuse. She couldn't have been unfaithful to Busby then. Night after night, she watched the violence of the marches on the television screen. The vicious hatred, the anger and prejudice were unbelievable. The demonstrators were showered with rocks, spat at, hit with sticks and iron bars. Where did they get their courage from?

Busby came home safe but appalled. 'Some day I'm going to make a movie about it,' he said. 'But not just yet. With my present reputation, it'd be sure to bomb.'

He had, however, made up his mind what to do next. 'I'm going to rehabilitate myself with a nice-as-apple-pie movie with Mom and Pop and a coupla kids and a scruffy dog and scatty neighbours.'

'It's not like you to fall in line so easily,' said Lisa. 'I thought you'd go in for something even more daring than *Easy Dreams*.

He shrugged. 'No point,' he said. 'It'd just be like a red rag to a bull. I'll stick to something safe.'

Inevitably, he threw himself heart and soul into the making of *Mr & Mrs Jones*, but there wasn't the usual excitement on the set. Cast and crew knew they were making just another humdrum movie, not, as they usualy did with Busby, sharing in a passionate adventure to produce a work of art. Lisa was cast as a vampish neighbour, a small, unimportant part. She'd hoped for the main female role, but Busby said she didn't look right and she accepted his judgement without a murmur. Once, when raising finance for a film, a businessman had offered half a million dollars provided his daughter was given a starring part. Busby turned him down. He wouldn't cast someone unless they were perfect for the part, not even Lisa.

Shooting reached its closing stages in November. Busby had never worked with children before and found them difficult to direct. The fact that the pair – a boy of twelve and a girl aged ten – disliked each other and squabbled incessantly off the set didn't help. Even the dog was proving difficult. 'W. C. Fields was right,' Busby groaned to Lisa one night. 'Never work with children or animals. I'm taking his advice in future.'

Today, on the set, the family Christmas dinner was turning out to be a nightmare. The children were tetchy and Grandfather was drunk. They were into the twenty-first take when suddenly, it all began to fall into place. At long last, everything was going perfectly, until a door opened and someone rushed into the studio and right onto the set.

'*Cut!*' screamed Busby. 'What the hell— ?'

It was Maggie Nestor. Tears were streaming down her face. 'The President's been shot! I was watching TV. I think he's dead.'

A pall descended over America. Even Lisa felt heartbroken. Jack Kennedy had seemed so young and offered so much hope. The country had become a better place to live in since he had arrived at the White House.

With cool professionalism, Busby returned to the studio next day and finished filming. At home he was distraught. 'Such a fuckin' *waste*,' he railed. 'He made us feel good about ourselves. He shared our dreams. Ah, shit!' He poured himself a tumbler of Jack Daniel's.

Lisa could think of nothing to say that would soothe him.

One night she went to bed at midnight leaving him with his friends. They were sitting moodily, drinking, not saying much, each preoccupied with his grief. When eventually Busby came to bed, she could smell the liquor on his breath. His voice was slurred. 'Come here, I need you.' He reached out and took her savagely and she felt ashamed. It was the first time he'd ever left her satisfied. 'Oh, my dear, darling Lizzie,' he murmured softly before he went to sleep.

Lisa froze. She lay there for what must have been an hour, her head swimming. Eventually, she eased herself from his grasp, threw on a robe and made her way to his study. Voices came from the kitchen – music, the radio was on. There were still people in the house.

Busby's study was lined on all four walls with books: paperbacks packed tightly together on the narrow top shelves, larger hardbacks below. Beside his desk was a shelf of encyclopaedias and reference books. Lisa bit her lip. She was looking for a photograph album. Busby's parents were dead and he'd been an only child. If there'd been albums, they would have come to him and he'd have kept them. No one threw old photos away. Eventually she found what she was looking for – three blue, leather-bound albums tucked in a corner along with a College Yearbook and school reports.

She knelt on the floor and began to leaf through the books, trying to keep back her sense of rising panic.

The first contained pictures of his parents as children, growing up, getting married, then with Busby as a baby. The second was mainly Busby at school; grade school, high school, college. Towards the end, she found what she was looking for – Busby in his army uniform: a grave and serious-looking Busby, bespectacled, clean-shaven and horribly familiar.

No, it wasn't what she was looking for! Of course not. It was what she'd hoped she wouldn't find. *Busby. Buzz.* The two names chased each other round her brain. Buzz, the only soldier who hadn't raped her that day in Southport. Busby, her husband, who must have known who she was when she came into the Cascade Hotel bedroom years ago. He knew she was from Liverpool. Why had he married her? *Why?*

'So you noticed?' He was standing at the door, looking down. Without his glasses, he always looked so much younger.

'You've never called me Lizzie before,' she said.

'I tried not to.'

'Why didn't you tell me right from the start?' she asked in an agonized voice.

He sighed deeply, came into the room and helped himself to a glass of Scotch. Then he sat down, reached out and touched Lisa's hair. She flinched and his face twisted with grief. He looked close to tears.

'I didn't think you'd want to be reminded of that day,' he said eventually. 'I knew it for certain when we went to Little Venice. I saw how you reacted when I said I'd been in England during the war. That's why I lied and said I'd been stationed near London.'

She remembered the occasion perfectly. 'Why did you marry me? You went out of your way to get to know me.'

'Because I love you,' he said simply. 'I always have, I always will.'

They were silent. Lisa said, 'Can I have a drink?'

He handed her a half-full tumbler. She sat back on her haunches and leaned against the shelves. He watched her. The love in his eyes made her want to weep. She wanted to take him in her arms but she couldn't bear to touch him.

He said softly, 'The day you came into that hotel room I knew my wildest dream had come true. You'd been my first love, my only real love, but I never imagined we would meet again. Oh, that day! If only you knew how innocent you were. How lovely. And so trusting! I could have killed those others.' The knuckles on his hands tightened around his glass, so tight that Lisa feared it would break. 'I could have killed them,' he repeated.

'What happened to them? Do you know?' she asked curiously.

He shook his head. 'All I know is that Hank and Tex were killed in a plane crash just before we were demobbed. I never heard from any of the others – not that I expected to.'

They were silent again. Busby said, 'What are we going to do now?'

'I don't know,' said Lisa. 'Try and carry on, I suppose.'

She slept in the guestroom for several weeks. Eventually, she returned to his bed, but it was no use. Each time he touched her, memories flooded back and she relived that brutal day all over again.

'I'm sorry,' she told him tearfully. 'But I keep thinking that now, nearly twenty years later, you're having your turn.'

'Lisa!' He was shocked. 'Oh, Lisa!'

Although he denied it vehemently, to himself most of all, Lisa felt that she was almost certainly right.

She waited until Christmas had passed before telling him she was leaving. 'Do you love me?' he asked, his voice hoarse with emotion.

'More than I can say,' she answered truthfully.

'And I love you. If two people who love each other so much can't stay together, what hope is there for the world?'

'I don't know.' She began to cry and longed to bury her head against him, feel the warm comfort of his arms around her. 'We'll stay friends, won't we?' she sobbed. 'I'll always want to know you're there.'

'I'll always be there for you, Lisa,' he vowed. 'Always.'

Chapter 29

Despite her protests, Busby insisted she keep his house. 'I've got a heap of friends who can put me up until I buy another place,' he said.

The house was strange and silent without him, without Jacob and the endless, noisy guests. It dawned on her that in all the years she'd lived here, she'd never really looked at it properly before. It seemed half-furnished with rather ugly, featureless modern pieces she didn't like. The white painted walls were bare and discoloured. Perhaps Sharon, Busby's ex-wife, had taken all the pictures and the ornaments and Lisa had never noticed before. She smiled wanly. If she *had* noticed, she probably wouldn't have cared.

As the days dragged by, a few of Busby's friends dropped in to see him, unaware he'd gone. They stayed a while out of politeness, making awkward conversation before leaving. She never saw them again. She hadn't realized how much she had relied on Busby for company, for work, for everything. Suddenly the world seemed bleak and empty. She was alone again and she had no one.

Lally had left Hollywood to marry Frank a long time ago after a string of identical parts. The last Lisa had heard, she was expecting her second baby.

The Opportunist had turned Gloria into a star and nowadays Lisa saw little of her. She was making up for those long years out of work and was always busy, always working, often abroad.

As for Roma, well she'd never been friendly with her, but Roma had just disappeared, no one knew where. Lisa had watched the programme *Beautiful Dreams*, for which Roma had been going to audition, but she wasn't in it.

Ralph only lived a few miles away, but she had gone to dinner there once and it had turned out disastrously. Perhaps foolishly, Ralph had been over-attentive, deliberately trying to stir his consistently unfaithful lover into jealousy. He'd done it too successfully. Michael, an excitable, brown-skinned Adonis, had reacted violently, seizing a knife and shutting himself in his room, threatening to hurt himself.

'I didn't realize he loved me so much,' Ralph had said. 'I'm sorry, Lisa. Let me call you a taxi.'

She had left sad and worried, and hesitated to contact him now, much though she wanted to.

Busby had been gone a week when Jacob came in a van to take his books away.

'How is he?' Lisa asked.

'Bearing up,' said Jacob, shrugging. 'He's got plenty of company, though he's drinking too much.'

After he'd left, Lisa picked up the telephone and dialled Busby's new number. He'd come back like a shot if she asked, but when the receiver was picked up at the other end and she heard his voice, she immediately rang off. Although it broke her heart to acknowledge it, their marriage was irrevocably over.

It was, however, time she got back to work. She picked up the phone again and called Dick Broadbent. It was months since she'd heard from him.

To her surprise – she had expected an enthusiastic greeting – Dick sounded subdued. His normally chirpy voice was flat and tired.

'Got anything for me?' she asked.

'Nothing,' he said. 'Folks got fed up offering parts and you turning them down. Nobody's enquired about you for ages. Of course, it didn't help, *Easy Dreams* having bombed. I know *you* got good notices, but even so, in folks' minds, you're connected with a failure. You know what they say – an actor is only as good as their last movie.'

'So there's nothing,' she said disappointedly.

'All I got is a bit-part in some crummy TV movie.'

'That'll do,' said Lisa. 'Give me the details.'

Dick reacted impatiently. 'Don't be stupid, Lisa. You can't do stuff like that! You gotta reputation to consider.'

'Sorry, Dick.' He didn't answer. 'Are you all right?' she asked tentatively. 'You don't sound yourself.'

'I keep getting these pains in my chest and they make me feel nauseous. Also, I got a splitting headache.' He laughed and added, 'Otherwise, I feel fine.'

Lisa told him firmly to see a doctor and he promised he would. Before ringing off, he assured her he would ask around and call back immediately he found her some work.

He didn't call. A few days later, she rang his office and there was no reply. Such a thing had never happened before. Dick seemed to be at the end of his telephone day and night. There was no reply the next day either, so she went to see him. His office door was locked and there was no sign to say where he was. She had no idea where he lived – sometimes, she used to wonder if he lived and slept in the office. A few days later, she saw in *Variety* that Dick had died at his desk from a massive heart attack. He was seventy-nine. By the time she read the news, he'd already been buried.

Lisa put the paper down and began to cry for Dick. He'd been such a kind, naive little man, full of life and enthusiasm. She smiled through the tears, remembering what Kitty used to say when someone elderly died: 'Oh well, he had a good innings.' Her mam had been so wise, so knowing with an inner strength that brought her through the most dire adversity. Lisa did what Kitty would have done on hearing bad news. She went into the kitchen and made a cup of tea.

She put Cole Porter on the record player and carried the tea out to the pool, together with a pack of cigarettes. Not long after Busby left, she'd starting smoking. Every time she opened a cupboard or a drawer, there was a packet of Marlboros and in the end she couldn't resist trying one in an effort to lessen her loneliness; by now, she was already smoking ten a day.

It was a beautiful evening, but then, evenings were always beautiful in California. Dusk was just beginning to settle and between the tall trees bordering the garden, the last of that day's sun was sinking, leaving a strip of shimmering gold on the horizon. The sky, a lurid mish-mash of deep orange and purple, was zebra-striped with black. Coloured poolside lights, festooned from tree to tree, were reflected, wobbling gently in the pale, almost still water, and the faint scent of flowers hung on the warm air.

Lisa sat in one of the padded chairs outside the open french windows and watched the sun as it sank further, the gold strip narrowing until it became no more than a pencilled line separating land and sky. Then it disappeared altogether and darkness took over. Lisa shivered, overwhelmed by the beauty of the night. She wished someone was here to share that beauty with her. If she stayed in this house for the rest of her life, Lisa knew she would never get used to it being empty. It was Busby's house. His spirit, the spirit of his multitude of friends was everywhere. One day, she'd move, let him have his house back. But not yet. She had to get her life sorted out, get used to living without him. She had to make it on her own, yet again.

The telephone beside her rang and she picked up the white receiver.

'Your dry cleaning is ready,' said a familiar voice.

Carl! She made an instant decision which she hoped she wouldn't regret. 'I'm sorry, I won't be needing dry cleaning any more,' she said.

Dick's list of clients was transferred to a big reputable agency on Vine Street. Lisa received a letter saying a Karen Zorro would be looking after her from now on and to call if she had any queries.

She rang the firm immediately. It was a month since Busby had gone and she was becoming desperate for work, though her pride wouldn't let her tell this Karen Zorro how anxious she was.

The extension number rang just once before a brusque, efficient voice said, 'Zorro here.'

Lisa had scarcely managed to introduce herself before the woman interrupted. 'I was just about to call you, Lisa. There's a real emergency cropped up on *The Matchstick Man*.'

'Another one?' said Lisa. She'd read all about this movie, a comedy thriller which had been plagued with difficulties.

Both male and female stars had withdrawn before shooting had even begun, and so far there'd been three directors, a score of writers and reports of endless trouble on the set.

'I'm afraid so,' said Karen Zorro with a touch of impatience. 'Now the second female lead has walked out in high dudgeon and they're desperate. I know it's asking a lot at such short notice, but could you possibly fill in?'

'I'd be willing to help out,' said Lisa. The calmness in her voice belied her inner excitement.

'Good. I'll call the studio immediately. They might even want you there this afternoon, if that's all right.'

'I had a few things planned for later today, but I'll cancel them,' lied Lisa.

The studio called and wanted her straight away. Lisa said midday would be fine and they promised to send a car.

She showered, scrubbing her body with a loofah until it tingled, then made up her face with extra care. Sorting through her wardrobe, she decided on a clinging cinnamon jersey dress with a deep V neck – one of Busby's favourites. She held her breath as she pulled the zip up at the back. It passed her waist smoothly and she sighed in relief. She'd been worried that the past month of inactivity, lazing round the house, drinking too much tea and Jack Daniel's and not doing any exercises, had made her put on weight. But she was as slim as ever. She pulled on a pair of black lace tights and slipped her feet into a pair of stiletto-heeled black court shoes. Brushing her fringe forward, she combed the rest back and coiled it into a bun on her neck. Finally, she clipped on a pair of gold drop earrings and stood back several feet to examine her full-length reflection in the mirror.

She felt her stomach turn. She had lost her glow, her radiance. Her eyes were lustreless and dull, her face flaccid. Busby going had affected her even more than she had realized.

But she was an actress! No matter how bad she felt inside, it was important not to let it show. She closed her eyes and took several deep breaths. The car would be arriving soon. She was at a crossroads in her career. The movie she was about to make could decide her entire future in films. It was vital to look right. She *would* look right! Straightening her shoulders, she stepped back and opened her eyes. They sparkled back at her. Her pink lips curved into an enticing smile. She was herself again!

A car horn sounded and she picked up her bag and ran outside, dazzling the driver with her beauty.

It would have been easy to lose her short-lived confidence not long after arriving on the almost empty set during the lunch-break. As soon as she went in, the assistant director rushed over to introduce himself.

'Hi, I'm Ben Shadley. I can't thank you enough for stepping in at such short notice. You've really got us out of a hole. We're close on reaching our budget and not a quarter of a way through the movie yet.' He was a plump, anxious-looking man. Lisa soon discovered he had good reason to look anxious. 'Come and meet our new director, Mr Dent. I hope you're thick skinned. Please don't take any notice of his rudeness,' he said pathetically. 'It's never personal – he's rude to everyone.'

Joseph Dent was famous for his histrionics. Over the years, every film he'd made had been cursed with trouble because of his wild, uncontrolled temperament. He could reduce grown men and women to tears and once ended up in hospital when an actor, driven to the end of his tether by his insults, had thrown a table at him. Dent, who specialized in thrillers, hadn't worked for some time. With the contract system ended and actors no longer tied to a particular studio and forced to take parts whether they wanted them or not, big names refused to work with him, despite the fact that his movies were highly regarded and one or two were often included in critics' lists of the ten best thrillers ever made. The company behind *The Matchstick Man* must have been really desperate to put him in charge of a project already in deep trouble.

Lisa had never met the man, but he was a Hollywood legend and everyone had heard of him. Ben Shadley took her arm and ushered her cautiously towards a small figure stooped over a script, one arm draped over the camera.

'Mr Dent,' he said obsequiously. 'This is Lisa Angelis,

who's agreed to take over the part of Honey.'

If ever the devil was needed for a movie, Joseph Dent could have done the part without make-up. Although he must have been nearing sixty, he had the demeanour and build of a man half his age. Thin and wiry, his heart-shaped face was brought to an exact point by a small goatee beard. His black-as-night hair was combed forward into little pikelets on his broad, flat forehead, and black eyebrows turned sharply upwards like the tails of two dark birds. Coal-black eyes flashed fire as he looked Lisa up and down with sharp intelligence.

'She's too old,' he said flatly.

'She's twenty-seven,' said Ben Shadley. 'The script calls for Honey to be twenty-two, but it's not important. Another five years— ' He held his arms out, palms upward, and shrugged.

Joseph Dent looked Lisa straight in the eyes. 'Another *five* years?' he said disparagingly. 'Looks more like ten to me.'

Ben became flustered. 'But she looks the part, Mr Dent. She's the right type – classy, yet innocent-looking.'

'She's too tall for that idiot Gary whatever-his-name-is.'

'He can wear platforms,' Ben said desperately.

Lisa began to feel annoyed. Joseph Dent acted as if she were invisible.

'Does he always do this?' She ignored the director and spoke directly to Ben Shadley.

'What . . . what?' the man stammered.

'Talk about people so insultingly and pretend they're not there?'

'Well, um . . . I don't know.'

'It's frightfully juvenile,' said Lisa in her best upper-class English accent. 'I faintly remember doing it at school. Most people grow out of it. Oh, well.' She turned to go. 'Nice meeting you, Ben.'

'Don't!' Ben caught her arm. Lisa glanced at Joseph Dent and saw he was grinning. The charade she was performing was only hurting poor Ben Shadley.

'But I'm too old and too tall,' she protested.

'I suppose you'll do,' Dent said nastily. 'Beggars can't be choosers.'

'I expect that's what they said when they took *you* on,' said Lisa.

Making *The Matchstick Man* was one of the worst experiences of her life. Busby van Dolen was regarded as a bit of a tyrant on set, but compared to Joseph Dent he was mildness personified. She had never encountered so much unpleasantness and venomous, unnecessary criticism.

The male star, Gary Maddox, was the latest juvenile heart-throb. With his suntanned muscular body and bleached hair falling into his blue eyes with a casualness that was anything but genuine, he was used to teeny-boppers screaming in adoration at the mere raising of a well-plucked eyebrow. Expecting to charm everybody and be charmed in return, instead he found his inadequate acting ability cruelly exposed. Joseph Dent tore him apart, taunted him. 'Mr Beefcake', he called him.

'If Mr Beefcake could bring himself to look intelligent for ten minutes, we might get this scene in the can.' The actor, driven beyond endurance, began to show the dark side of his nature. His arrogant, though easygoing manner turned into ugly aggression. Lisa found it difficult to act naturally, particularly in romantic scenes, with a man who'd just cursed the director, using the foulest language imaginable.

Ruth George, the female lead, coped by becoming mildly drunk as soon as she arrived on set and staying that way all day; the bit players, men and women alike, were constantly in tears, stripped of all pride and faith in themselves by Dent's caustic tongue.

He tried it with Lisa too. 'Christ Almighty, woman,' he screamed. 'You're opening and closing your mouth like a fuckin' fish.' He aped a fish, puckering his lips, pushing them forward, making smacking sounds.

Lisa put her hands on her hips and looked at him intently. 'Very good, Joseph,' she said admiringly – she called him Joseph deliberately to annoy him, knowing he preferred Mr Dent. 'If ever they make *Moby Dick* again, I'll nominate you for the title role.'

Some of the crew laughed and Ben Shadley looked as if he might have a fit, but Lisa had decided that the best way to deal with Joseph Dent was to make fun of him. Strange as it might seem, he was never annoyed and indeed often the first to smile. 'He just needs taking down a peg or two,' she'd thought to herself right from the beginning.

A day rarely passed without there being a row, perhaps two or three. One day, the set had to be rebuilt when Gary Maddox, driven to the end of his tether by the director's ridicule, kicked down a wall.

Despite these traumas, Joseph Dent worked a minor miracle. The movie was brought to its miserable end within the time limit, and only slightly over budget. There was no wrap party when it was finished. No one felt like celebrating. As the last scene was shot, there wasn't a single cheer. Instead, everyone gave a loud sigh of relief.

To the astonishment of everyone, when *The Matchstick Man* was released six months later, it was greeted with universal acclaim. During the course of shooting, it had lost all trace of comedy and ended up a genuine *film noir*. Lisa cut out her favourite review and pinned it to the kitchen wall.

'Joseph Dent, back in top form, has teased top-rate performances out of the cast of this dark, psychological thriller. In particular, Gary Maddox, who so far has shown only a lightweight ability, gives his role a power and strength of which this critic had not thought him capable. Unshaven and unkempt, he attacks his part with raw, cynical savagery that shows great promise for the future. As the tragic, unbalanced heroine, Ruth George is also unexpectedly superb, wafting gently in and out of her scenes with an almost dreamlike quality. Making a welcome return to the screen as the downstairs neighbour is the lovely Lisa Angelis, who brings an air of appealing vulnerability to her part . . . '

Over the next few years, Lisa took every part she was offered and acquired a reputation as someone reliable and entirely lacking in temperament. The 'Un-primadonna', one gossip columnist called her.

Budgets began to expand and movies took longer to shoot. Stars were paid phenomenal salaries – Elizabeth Taylor received over a million dollars for *Cleopatra*, which went way over time and budget. Lisa's latest statement from her bank showed a balance of nearly half a million dollars. Several times she went abroad on location as the film industry in Hollywood began to shrink, television took over, and Europe became the movie capital of the world. She always hated leaving Busby's house and was glad to return to the comfort and shelter of its four walls.

Between filming, she had the house completely redecorated, buying paintings, new carpets and curtains, never forgetting that one day it would be Busby's again, so choosing things she knew he would like. Inevitably, she began to make friends. The Beatles were all the rage and she acquired celebrity status just because she came from Liverpool. Several times she was asked to parties on that account alone, though she always refused. 'The Cavern opened long after I left Liverpool,' she told people honestly. 'I've never met The Beatles and I'm not accepting invitations just because we come from the same city!'

Busby telephoned often and sometimes they talked for hours. Two years after their divorce, he remarried, a young dark-haired actress caled Lulu, but it failed after only a few months.

'She was a substitute for you,' he said, the last time he called. It was midnight and Lisa was asleep. As soon as she heard the telephone she knew it would be him. 'Though I should have known it wouldn't work out. Poor kid! I expected too much of her. I expected her to act all day like Lisa Angelis and she just wasn't up to it.'

'Poor Busby,' Lisa said.

'Poor Busby,' he echoed. 'I've given up on my own company, you know. Now I just make movies, full stop.'

'I know,' she said. 'You told me last time.' Who could blame him? He'd put his heart and soul into his eight films and hardly anybody in America had seen them.

'Now the men in suits have control. They cut my work to shreds, leave out the bits I thought were my best work.'

'I know,' she said again, adding tenderly, 'but one day you'll make your own movies again, I feel it in my bones.'

'Do you? Do you, Lisa?' His voice became hoarse. 'Christ, I miss you. Why do we have to be apart?' Without waiting for an answer, he went on, 'The other day, I was wondering, if we hadn't met, you know, all those years ago in Liverpool, would I still have fallen in love when you walked into that damned hotel?'

'I don't know, darling,' said Lisa truthfully. She dragged a pillow up and propped it behind her back. Busby sounded as if he was in for one of his marathon chats.

'Is there anyone else?' he demanded suddenly.

'No,' she said truthfully. 'There's been no one since you.' She hadn't felt the slightest desire to become romantically involved since he went. In a recent magazine, it said she led a 'hermit-like' existence in Beverly Hills.

'I thought you had something going with Gary Maddox? I keep seeing pictures of you together at premières and stuff.'

This wasn't the time to remind him that it was none of his business, that they were no longer man and wife. 'Gary and I have the same agent,' she explained gently. 'And it suits us to be seen together. In fact, I don't like him much.'

'I see,' said Busby, sounding mollified. He stayed on for another hour telling her about the anti-Vietnam War movement he was involved in. 'Kennedy would never have let us get in this deep,' he said moodily. Now he was campaigning for Robert Kennedy to be elected as Democratic candidate for the presidential elections later in the year.

Compared to his, her own news was prosaic. She'd bought more pictures for the house – Impressionist reproductions. 'Very conventional,' she said. 'Monet, Cézanne, Renoir – and I've learnt to drive. I've got a Chevrolet estate.'

'A Chevy,' corrected Busby. 'No one says Chevrolet.'

He rang off later, still sounding depressed. Lisa got up, made herself a cup of tea and lit a cigarette. His call had disturbed her. She felt guilty for making Busby, of all people, so unhappy.

'Oh, my dear,' she whispered. 'If only we could be together.' But it could never happen. Only a few weeks ago she had seen him across a restaurant where she was lunching with Karen Zorro and immediately his stance, the movement of his shoulders, the glint of light falling on his thick glasses, had brought back the horror of that distant day in a rush of nausea. She stubbed her cigarette out and immediately lit another.

'You're a bloody hypocrite, Lizzie O'Brien,' she said angrily. 'Mooning over a man you two-timed right from the start. *You* might be the right woman for Busby, but *he* certainly isn't the right man for you, and it's about time you realized it.'

A few days later, one Sunday morning, she had an unexpected caller. The record player was on loud, and Lisa was humming along to Charlie Parker's *Laura* when the doorbell chimed. The windows were open to the pale blue March sky. During the night it had rained and the shrubs and trees were moist, glistening under the weak, lemony sun.

She jumped in alarm at the figure standing on her doorstep. A short man, wearing an enormous leather flying-jacket and helmet, with thick goggles pulled up over his forehead. It took several seconds for her to realize that it was Joseph Dent, which made her feel even more alarmed. Lisa stared at him, too taken aback to speak. Eventually she said, 'Where did you land the plane?'

'I came on Dessie.' She looked past him expecting to see a horse tethered outside. Instead, an old motor bike was propped up in the drive.

'Aren't you going to ask me in?' He had the gall to sound hurt.

'When I've got over the shock,' said Lisa. She took a deep breath. 'You can come in now.'

'Thanks.' He came in quickly and looked around with interest. 'Nice place you've got here.'

'Your small talk's not very original,' she said.

'I'm working on it,' he replied. He began to undo the strap of his helmet. 'Is that Renoir real?'

'Well, I can see it too, so it must be.' He was struggling out of the leather jacket with swift, jerky movements, then he put it on the floor where it stood as if the top half of him was still in it. His devilish appearance was emphasized by his clothes, all black, a polo-necked sweater under an old shiny suit.

'You know what I mean,' he said tetchily. 'Is it genuine or fake?'

'It's a copy.' Feeling she'd got the better of the exchange, she took him out to the pool and sat him down. 'Drink?' she asked. 'Coffee, tea or something stronger?'

'Something stronger,' he said. 'Anything'll do.'

She poured two Jack Daniel's. She needed one herself to get over the shock of having Joseph Dent in the house. When she took them outside, he'd got out of his chair and was walking up and down the edge of the pool, snapping his fingers. The sounds were so sharp and explosive that Lisa wouldn't have been surprised to see sparks fly.

'I'll come straight to the point,' he said when she sat down. 'I want you for my next movie.'

Lisa's mouth dropped. 'You must be joking. I wouldn't be in one of your movies again if I was dead broke and starving.'

He grinned. His teeth were surprisingly white and even. 'You always spoke your mind.'

'Didn't you?' she asked pointedly. 'Rather, didn't you always yell or scream your mind?'

'Point well taken,' he said. 'However, I didn't come to exchange insults.' He fished in his pocket and took out a pile of newspaper cuttings secured with a rusty paperclip. 'These are your reviews,' he said. 'All of them. You got good notices for the work you did with Busby Van Dolen, but since then, the only good review you got was for *Matchstick Man*. These last three years, you've made a load of junk. That movie you did in Rome, I can't remember the title . . . '

'*April Flowers*,' she said.

' . . . was one of the worst I have ever seen in my life. What did it cost? One million, two? Whatever it was, they wasted their dough.'

'It wasn't very good,' she conceded.

'It was abominable.' Suddenly, he came over and leaned on the table, his black eyes alight with enthusiasm. He looked like a giant blackbird which had just alighted on a worm. 'This book I got the rights to, *Attrition*, it's a futuristic thriller with a really neat twist ending.' He took a well-worn paperback novel out of another pocket. Lisa fully expected a camera next and he'd start shooting. 'I've brought you a copy. Read it and let me know what you think.'

'Even if it's the best thriller ever written, I don't want to make another movie with you, Joseph,' Lisa said emphatically. 'To be blunt, doing *Matchstick Man* was a truly horrible experience which I never want to repeat.'

She knew she was being rude, but didn't care. He'd never given a damn about other people's feelings, so why should she give a damn about his? 'Any minute now,' she thought, 'he'll fly into a rage and if he does, I'll push him in the pool.' However, instead of looking mad, he grinned again. She'd never been alone with him before and was surprised to find him so calm and so, well, almost *charming*!

'Before you say no— '

'I've already said no,' she said quickly.

He ignored her '— read your cuttings and think about why you're in Hollywood – to turn out bland junk, or good movies? If it's the first, then you're not the woman I thought you were. If it's good movies, then do this with me. Okay, so we'll have a hard time . . . '

'*You* don't have a hard time,' Lisa said sarcastically. 'It's everybody else who has the hard time.'

'But it's the end result that matters, don't you see?' To her surprise, he sat down beside her and grasped her arm. She looked down at the taut, wiry hand and could feel the throbbing of his fingers through her thin blouse. It was almost like getting an electric shock. 'Two of my movies are part of the Film Studies course at several universities. One day, they might include *Matchstick Man*.'

The warmth, the throbbing of his hand spread upwards, to her shoulders, her chest, her entire body. Of course he was right. Not only that, his enthusiasm was catching. She looked up. His ugly little face was close to hers. His broad forehead was moist with perspiration and strips of black hair clung to his skin. Their eyes caught and they shared a moment of understanding. Lisa dropped her lashes, feeling shaken. She moved back in her chair, dislodging his hand.

'Who'll be putting up the cash?' she asked eventually. This might be a ploy to get her financial backing.

'Gary Maddox has got someone to back us.'

'Gary!' She laughed out loud, glad to have the opportunity of being offensive again. That moment their eyes had met she'd found strangely disturbing. 'You mean you've met Gary Maddox and he didn't kill you?'

'*He* approached *me*. Gary's on the skids. His last two movies bombed, not surprisingly, they were brainless fluff. But he really liked the notices he got from *Matchstick Man*. He knows he's got it in him to act – with the right director. In other words, me.' He smirked. God, he was a nauseating little man.

'Fancy yourself, don't you?' she said disparagingly.

'With good reason,' he said, standing up. 'I've got to leave now.'

Lisa felt strangely disappointed and wondered why. He was so unpleasant and obnoxious – why should she care if he stayed or went?

Six weeks later, Busby telephoned. 'Lisa, I just heard the most fantastic rumour.' He laughed nervously. 'You'll die when I tell you what it is.'

'Tell me,' said Lisa.

'Someone said you were going to marry Joseph Dent. I told them not to be ridiculous. It couldn't possibly be true.'

'It is,' said Lisa.

'What?' his voice squeaked.

'I *am* going to marry Joseph Dent,' she giggled. 'It's true.'

Chapter 30

Soon after Joseph Dent's visit, he invited Lisa and Gary Maddox to his home on the edge of the Hollywood Hills for the weekend. The house, which had once belonged to the silent star Vita Reese, was a three-storeyed, oak-beamed, genuine Tudor mansion which had been dismantled, brought over from Suffolk, England, piece by piece, and then put together again with careful precision.

Lisa got out of her car on the Saturday and looked up in admiration. At first-floor level, a stone was set into the white plaster and on it was engraved *Tymperleys* and underneath, 1551. The writing, lashed by centuries of wind and rain, was scarcely readable. She thought wryly how odd it was that the first time she should set eyes on an olde English building like this was thousands of miles away in Hollywood. The white-painted, black-studded front door was wide open.

'Come in,' shouted Joseph Dent. She stepped down into the large, low-ceilinged hallway-cum-lounge with whitewashed walls, furnished with big, comfortable-looking chairs covered in subdued chintz. The wooden floors and the wide stairs, worn away to a curve, were uncarpeted. Four gnarled oak columns riddled with woodworm went from floor to ceiling and the broad brick fireplace was stuffed with bright yellow daisies. Gary was already there. Both men had a drink and Joseph was rocking restlessly from foot to foot.

'I love your house, Joseph,' she said. 'It's full of atmosphere.'

'And woodworm,' he replied, 'though it's static. In spring, you can hear the deathwatch beetles courting. They rub their legs together with a loud grating sound.'

Gary came over and kissed Lisa on the cheek. He'd changed a lot since their first meeting, three years ago. Gone was the bleached hair and carefully casual style. Back to his natural brown, he was already thinning on top. He had a slightly haggard look and needed a shave. Lisa perversely thought he looked immensely more attractive now, more rugged and manly. His stardom had been brief and he'd fallen fast. Last time they'd met, he told her he'd been offered a small though regular part in a TV soap. 'If I sign the contract, it's like signing my death warrant as a screen actor,' he said bitterly.

Dent rubbed his hands. 'Lunch is ready,' he said. 'I got caterers in for the weekend. My cook's speciality is soggy meatloaf so I gave her a couple of days off.'

Lisa shuddered – imagine working for Joseph Dent and being under the same roof all day long!

He led them into a long charming room where a French window opened onto an Elizabethan garden criss-crossed with hedges. Wide stone steps led down to a water-lily-covered lake. A smiling waiter was standing by the table ready to serve them.

The meal was delicious, but halfway through it Dent flew into a rage. 'This meat is tough,' he snarled at the waiter who stepped back, eyes filled with alarm.

'No it's not, Joseph,' Lisa demurred. 'It's just right.'

The director stood up and hurled his plate at the wall. 'Such a simple fucking thing to ask someone to do – to *pay* someone to do.' The waiter rushed across and began to wipe the food off the white-painted wall with a napkin. Lisa put down her knife and fork and went to help pick up the pieces of the smashed plate.

'Don't take any notice,' she said to the man. 'The meat was fine.'

She wasn't surprised to see that Joseph Dent was grinning. 'I get mad when people don't do their job properly,' he said.

'Do anything like that again, Joseph, and I'm going home,' she said.

After lunch they went down into the basement viewing room. 'Vita Reese had this put in first, then the house built on top,' said Joseph.

It was a perfect miniature reproduction of a 1920s cinema with gold and brown painted walls, five narrow rows of velvet-covered tip-up seats, and, covering the screen, matching velvet curtains which drew back at the touch of a button.

'I thought I'd show the movies in reverse order. Shall we begin with *Matchstick Man*?' asked Dent from the doorway of the projection room. Row after row of film was stacked on the shelves behind him.

'Yes, please,' Gary said quickly. He sat down, shoulders hunched, at the end of a row. Lisa sat a couple of rows behind just as the lights went out and the titles came onto the screen.

This was the reason for the weekend – to see all of Joseph Dent's movies and decide if she wanted to appear in his next one. Her first inclination had been to turn the invitation down, but Gary had telephoned the night of the producer's visit to ask what she thought of his proposition.

'I don't quite know what to think, Gary,' she'd replied. 'I suppose he talked a lot of sense, but working with him again . . . ' She didn't finish. Gary would know what she meant.

'Have you read the book yet, *Attrition*?'

'Yes, I started it after he left and I just this minute finished. I couldn't put it down.'

'I can just see it as a movie. I can see myself in that part. Just the two of us on screen for most of the time. Shit, Lisa, it could turn out really sensational.' Gary's voice was raw, pleading. She lit a cigarette and wondered why.

Between puffs, she asked, 'Why does it matter if *I* say yes or no? He can always get someone else. Okay, so no big name will work with him, but there's scores of actresses who've probably never heard— '

Gary interrupted, his voice harsh. 'Because he refuses to do it with anyone else but you,' he said.

'Does he?' She was astonished.

'He's a real bastard, Lisa. As soon as he saw how desperate I was, as soon as he knew he had the power, he started laying down conditions, even though I told him I got the backing . . . '

So, when Joseph Dent called the following day and asked if she'd spend the weekend at his house, she had reluctantly agreed for Gary's sake, even though she'd never cared for him much. Anyway, she thought grudgingly, it was a good book and as Gary said, would make a really sensational movie.

On screen, Gary's face was twisted in an awful rage as the camera moved slowly in for a close-up. Then his expression began to change, to melt into despair. There was no sound, no music. Without a single word he conveyed the suffering in his soul. It was brilliant acting.

Lisa glanced across the tiny cinema. The real Gary was staring at himself as if entranced. Incredibly she saw a tear run down his cheek, and thought how strange ambition was.

Gary's family were wealthy. She knew he could go home tomorrow and never need to work again, but this third-rate actor, by a freak of chance, had got the lead in *Matchstick Man*, a movie written off almost before it had begun. Joseph Dent had tormented him into giving a great performance and now Gary was desperate to give another. Those good notices had acted like a drug and he was willing to abase himself before the man he hated in order to read again that he was a good actor.

Suddenly the lights went on; the film had reached its end. As the curtains swung together, a gaudily-painted organ rose out of the tiny orchestra pit and raucous music blasted from the speakers each side of the screen. Joseph Dent appeared, grinning, went across to the organ and lifted the lid to reveal a fully-stocked bar.

'What's it to be?' he asked.

They watched two more movies that afternoon. Lisa's head began to ache, though she had to concede that Dent was a great director. His work had a dark undercurrent of fear, gripping the audience, right from the very first startling shot. She'd already made up her mind to agree to his proposition. A real actor should consider that the ends justified the means. She wouldn't let Dent know yet, let him hang on tenterhooks for a while longer; it would do him good – though she still wondered why he was so insistent on having her.

Dinner was served on the terrace. The waiter, no longer smiling, hovered over them anxiously. Lisa felt angry with the director for reducing the man to such a state. As the light began to fail Dent said, 'Watch this.' He went inside the French windows and suddenly the hedges and trees were lit by a thousand candle-shaped lights. 'Some sight, eh?'

The spangled garden seemed to stretch for miles. An old-fashioned street lamp shed its soft glow over the lake right into the faces of the creamy-white water lilies, so perfect and so still. Rustling, scrabbling sounds came from the nearby hedges and bushes as though small animals had been disturbed by the sudden intrusion of light on their slumber, and startled birds rose, squawking angrily as they flew haphazardly for a few seconds before settling back into their nests.

'It's breathtaking,' said Lisa.

Before going to bed they watched another movie – an eerie, haunted piece of work with an unexpectedly savage twist at the end that turned Lisa's stomach. She went to bed, having drunk too much whisky and seen too many frightening films. As she lay in the large four-poster, she felt strangely on edge. It had been an unusually weird day. Her feeling of unease was not helped when she half-woke during the night, convinced she could hear a child sobbing. She pulled the covers over her head, wondering if the sound had been made hundreds of years ago and she was only hearing it now.

Next morning, everything was back to normal. The sun was shining through the mullioned windows, dancing on the pink flowered carpet. Lisa was about to get up and have a shower when she froze in fright as the sound of wild, tumultuous music suddenly filled the room – she later learnt it was Wagner. Terrified, she leapt out of bed and could feel the floor throbbing beneath her. She searched for a radio and identified that the sound was coming from a speaker above the bed. There was a switch underneath. She clicked it down and the music ceased, but only in her room. The sound could still be heard outside.

Still shaking, she showered in the modern adjoining bathroom and dressed in white jeans and a bluebell-coloured blouse with wide gathered sleeves, pulling a white band over her long gleaming hair. She didn't bother with make-up. She

327

still looked good without it, and doubted whether Gary or Joseph would notice if she wore it or not.

Downstairs, Joseph Dent said gleefully, 'Wagner woke you up, then?'

'I was already awake, thanks,' she said sarcastically. He explained that he'd fitted up a loud-speaker system throughout the house.

'Like to keep everyone on their toes,' he said. Lisa gave him a filthy look. The music had been changed to New Orleans jazz, which was more relaxing though still too loud.

The caterers had already arrived to prepare breakfast. Lisa said all she wanted was coffee. Gary, looking even more haggard this morning, said just coffee would do him fine, too. 'I'd like to get back to watching movies straight away,' he said. 'I learnt a lot yesterday.'

'Suits me.' Joseph Dent told the waiter to take the food away. 'You and the cook eat it,' he said curtly. Today he wore jeans and an open-necked black shirt. Lisa wondered if he was aware of his similarity to Old Nick and emphasized it by always wearing black.

'Do you mind if I give the first one a miss?' she said. 'I've still got a bit of a headache.'

'In that case,' said Dent, 'I'll set Gary up in the basement and show you around the house.'

When he came back a quarter of an hour later, he said, 'Maddox has turned out different from what I thought he would. He's not so empty-headed after all.' His black eyes glittered and he seemed to be gripped by an energy that threatened to explode.

'This way.' He darted over to the door and was about to forge through, then remembered his manners and held it open for Lisa to go first. As he walked alongside her, he snapped his fingers impatiently in time to the music. 'This is, was, a sewing room.'

'It's lovely!' A tapestry-covered window seat in front of a tiny bow window, a silk-cushioned rocking chair, a carved sewing-box.

'Vita had the original furniture brought over too.'

After a while she ran out of adjectives, though Joseph Dent didn't seem to notice. He didn't linger, just opened a door, let her look, then closed it abruptly. She felt as if he was leading up to something and had to go through the motions of showing her round beforehand.

'And this,' he said eventually, pausing before a door at the end of a corridor, 'is my studio.'

'And this is what you *really* wanted me to see,' thought Lisa, 'though I can't think why.' For some reason, Dent seemed set on impressing her.

The large room looked as if it might once have been a chapel or a schoolroom. Two storeys high, the walls were white and heavily beamed – what you could see of them, because they were hidden by hundreds of unframed paintings. At first Lisa thought he was a collector until she noticed an easel holding a half-done painting at the end of the room.

'Did you do all these?'

'Yes,' he said proudly, pulling at his beard. 'What do you think?'

Lisa walked slowly around the room. Some were paintings of the garden and the house, barely recognizable, just suggestions here and there of a window, a door, a lake, the water lilies. There were numerous portraits of women and children with names scrawled on their foreheads in black. The oil paint was laid on thick in smears as much as an inch deep.

'I like the colours,' she said cautiously – lots of deep mustardy yellow, purple, dark reds, bottle green.

'You fucking moron,' said Joseph Dent, behind her.

She spun round, almost choking with anger. 'You arrogant, insufferable pig of a man,' she spat.

To her utter astonishment, he was smiling. 'I was interested in seeing your reaction.'

She said nothing for several seconds. Then she returned his smile. 'Do you have a favourite?'

'This one.' He pointed to a large painting of what looked like a church at night, yellow light shining out of the half-open door.

Lisa picked the canvas off the wall, threw it on the floor and stamped on it. The stiff cloth split several ways and the interior framework splintered.

'I was interested in seeing your reaction,' she said, edging towards the door so she could escape if Dent decided to attack her.

Instead he looked quite indifferent. 'Actually,' he said, 'I hated that one most. Seriously though,' he went on calmly as if nothing had happened, 'what *do* you think?'

Lisa was outwardly as calm as he was. Inwardly she felt exhilarated by a sense of almost perverted satisfaction. She stepped over the broken painting and stared at the walls. 'I could grow to like them,' she said slowly. 'Who are the portraits of?'

'My wives and children. To save you counting, I had five of the first and sixteen of the second.'

'Where are they?'

'Who knows?' he shrugged. 'Who cares?'

Lisa drove home that night feeling exhausted. It was as if she'd switched off her own life for twenty-four hours and become immersed in a totally different world. When she went in, Busby's house seemed curiously bare and lifeless, and much too quiet. She immediately made a pot of tea – she hadn't been offered one all weekend and felt deprived. As she drank it, she thought about Joseph Dent. He was the most unusual man she'd ever met. There was something fascinatingly awful about him; he was a charming monster, mercurial and unpredictable. Yet so interesting. You never knew what he was going to do or say next. When she told him she would do his movie, his reaction was the opposite of what she'd expected. Instead of being pleased and grateful, he said in an offhand manner, 'You'd be crazy not to.'

'When will we start?' asked Gary. He'd said little over the weekend and his eyes were red-rimmed and weary. Instead of having lunch, he'd watched *Matchstick Man* again, as if he was trying to cram as much as possible into his stay.

'In a couple of months,' said Dent. 'Soon as I'm back from Cannes. I'm on the jury at the film festival there. Like to come with me?'

'You bet!' said Gary with alacrity.

'I didn't mean you, I meant her,' Dent said rudely, nodding at Lisa.

Gary blushed and Lisa felt angry at the director's lack of tact. Sometimes he was barely civilized.

'I'll go if Gary goes,' she said quickly, and Joseph Dent, confounding her as usual, actually laughed and said, 'Good, I'll book the hotel and tickets.'

But before Cannes, in a weak moment – or so she told herself – she'd promised to spend another weekend at his house, this time to see the movies Busby had made before they met. She'd long wanted to see them.

'But this time, no caterers,' she said firmly. 'Soggy meatloaf suits me fine.'

Joseph Dent's cook and maid-of-all-work, a plump black woman called Millie, treated him with utter contempt. With insults flying thick and fast, Dent was at his most charming. It was as if he could only be nice to people who didn't treat him with respect. Anyone who fawned, who was sycophantic, even good-mannered, was at the mercy of his cruel, lashing tongue. Inefficiency drove him crazy. Lack of intelligence goaded him into wild, uncontrollable anger, though Millie soon put him in his place if he shouted at her for not grasping what he meant instantly.

Just before dinner Lisa heard screaming and the sound of breaking crockery coming from the kitchen. Alarmed, she ran down the corridor and found Dent and Millie throwing plates at each other with gusto. With Wagner thundering in the background, it was like a scene from an operatic farce.

'That was one of Vita's,' hissed Dent as a plate narrowly missed him and shattered on the wall behind. 'It came from England and was a hundred years old.'

'I don't care if it came from the table of the Lord Jesus Christ,' snarled Millie. She stood beside the stove, her dark eyes sparking hate. 'You call me a stupid black bitch again and I'll throw *you* the length of my kitchen. Oh, hallo Lisa.' The change in tone was so abrupt that Lisa had to smile.

'We were just having a little argument,' explained Joseph. 'She put the Burgundy in the fridge.'

'What's wrong with that?' asked Lisa.

'See!' said Millie triumphantly. '*She* don't know it's

supposed to be warm, either. I'll put it in some hot water, thaw it out.'

And as if it had never been any other way, the pair were suddenly on perfectly amicable terms again and later Joseph even praised Millie for her meatloaf.

Busby Van Dolen was one of the few people for whom Joseph seemed to have any respect. 'He never compromised,' he said after they'd watched the first movie. 'Never gave into commercial pressure.'

'He has now,' said Lisa sadly. 'Though I can't say I blame him.'

Surprisingly enough, neither did Joseph. 'You can't keep banging your head against a brick wall forever.' Afterwards, Lisa thought it was probably the kindest remark she'd ever heard him make.

She'd been given the same room as before and began to wonder why she needed an entire weekend to watch three films. A single afternoon would have sufficed.

In the middle of the night she woke to find the moon shining through the small windows, sharply illuminating the heavy oak wardrobe. There'd been a noise, a creaking of a hinge, the sound of a door closing. Nervously she peeped from under the bedclothes and shrieked.

Joseph Dent was standing beside her bed holding a tray on which stood a bottle of wine and two glasses. He was totally naked.

She struggled to sit up. He looked so ridiculous that she burst out laughing. 'What do you want?' she managed to say between the laughter.

'What do you think?'

She looked him up and down. 'Well, I suppose it's obvious.'

He came over and put the tray down beside the bed. 'Move over.'

Still giggling, she shuffled along and he climbed in beside her. By now tears were streaming down her cheeks. 'You,' she said with difficulty, 'are the most outrageous man I've ever met in my life.'

'I know,' he said complacently. 'Want a drink?'

'Has it been warmed?'

'It's champagne.'

The bubbly wine combined with the giggles gave her hiccups. 'Drink from the opposite side of the glass,' advised Joseph.

'You do that with water, not champagne, silly.'

'I'll come straight to the point,' he said. 'I want to marry you.'

Lisa hiccuped.

'Is that a yes?'

She hiccuped again and slid down the bed, convulsed with uncontrollable laughter.

Joseph slid down and reached for her. His arms were hard and he took her fiercely and swiftly and silently. No gentle words, no compliments, no avowals of love. Not even a kiss. Despite this, his lovemaking was surprisingly satisfying. When they'd finished he lay with his head propped on one hand, looking down at her. 'Wanna know something?'

'What?'

'When you walked onto the set of *Matchstick Man*, I made up my mind to marry you some day.'

'You could have fooled me. If you said you'd made up your mind to murder me I wouldn't be surprised. What took you so long to ask?'

'I was already married at the time.'

'A genuine enough reason,' said Lisa dryly.

'Then I was casting around for an excuse to call on you, like a movie, for instance.'

'I wouldn't have thought *you'd* need an excuse, Joseph.'

'Call me Joe, all my wives do.'

'In that case, I'll call you Dent. I'd like to keep our relationship formal.'

'I take it you've accepted my proposal. Was that hiccup a yes?'

'Yes,' she said, wondering if she'd taken leave of her senses.

'Tell me what you want most in the world and I'll give it you as a wedding present.'

'An ocean liner.'

'Which one, the *Elizabeth* or the *Mary*?'

'A desert.'

'Will the Sahara do?'

She laughed and then thought of what she wanted most in the world and felt sad. In the bright light of the moon Joseph must have noticed her expression change. 'What is it?'

'Nothing.' She turned away.

'You've thought of something I can't give you. What?'

'A baby,' she said softly.

'I can give you a baby.'

She shook her head impatiently. 'No one can.'

'*I* can give you a baby,' he repeated. He got out of bed and went over to the door.

'Dent,' she called. 'You've got nothing on. Millie might see you.'

'Wouldn't be the first time,' he said airily. Nevertheless, he came back and picked up her white cotton dressing gown. 'How does this look?' He twirled around in the frilly garment.

'Ridiculous,' she said, feeling laughter begin to well up again.

He was gone for ten minutes. She wondered what he'd bring her. A doll? A puppy or a kitten? To her utter astonishment he came back with a small child fast asleep in his arms.

He laid the sleeping child on the bed beside her. 'This is Sabina,' he said. 'She's yours.'

The girl was no more than a toddler. Snuggling into the pillow, she put her thumb in her mouth and began to suck audibly.

'She's beautiful,' gasped Lisa. The child was dressed in cotton pyjamas which were too small, exposing her plump legs to the knees. There was a red mark around her waist where the elastic was too tight. Long black lashes quivered gently on her chubby, butter-smooth cheeks.

'Who put her to bed like this?' she hissed angrily. 'You?'

'The nanny did. Why, what's wrong?'

'Her hair hasn't been unplaited; it must be awfully uncomfortable.' The child's thick, waist-length hair was woven tight, drawn hard back at the base of her skull.

'How old is she?'

'Two, three, four – I can't remember.'

'Dent, you monster! Is she yours?'

He grinned. 'I already said, she's *yours*.'

'She's not an article to be handed out as a gift, she's a living child. Let's put it another way, did you father her?'

'I did. Her mother was a full-blooded Cherokee called Koko.'

'And where is Koko?'

'Gone!' he said dramatically, throwing out his hands wide. 'Left directly her papoose was born. The divorce came through a year ago.'

Lisa was gently undoing the tight plait. When she'd finished, Sabina, still asleep, seemed to breathe a sigh of relief and nestled deeper into the pillow.

'You can keep her there all night if you want,' he said generously.

'Don't be silly,' snapped Lisa. 'She'd be terrified, waking up in a strange room with a strange woman. Take her back this minute.'

'If you say so,' he replied obediently.

Busby said, 'You can't marry Joseph Dent. He's a devil.'

'I know,' she said sympathetically, thankful he couldn't see her smile. 'That's what I've thought ever since I met him.'

'And a misogynist. He hates women.'

'Not just women, darling. He hates everyone.'

'Oh Lisa,' said Busby despairingly. 'Then why marry him?'

'I don't know,' she confessed. 'I think it's because he brings out the worst in me.'

'Your little girl is the image of you,' said a woman at the next table. 'I saw you on deck together this morning.'

'Do you really think so?' said Lisa delightedly. She could think of little in her life that had given her so much pleasure as that remark. Sabina's eyes were much darker than hers, but apart from that they could indeed have been mother and daughter with their long, thick chocolate-coloured hair and deep creamy skin. Even Dent had remarked on it that Sunday morning when he took Lisa up to the nursery.

The room, on the top floor of the house, spanned its entire width and could have looked pretty if the white flowered curtains and matching covers on the junior-sized bed had not been tinged with grey, and the floor not littered with so many toys, most of them broken and looking as if they'd been there for weeks, if not months. With the help of a twice-weekly cleaner, Millie kept the rest of the house spotless. Presumably this part was the responsibility of the nanny.

Sabina, still in her pyjamas at ten o'clock, was leaning over a toy crib draped with soiled broderie anglaise, softly talking to a doll. As she leaned forward, her pyjama pants pulled away to reveal the same angry, red serrated mark Lisa had noticed before, and her hair had been replaited.

As they entered, a woman sitting in the corner reading a paperback book jumped to her feet in alarm. She wore a stained maroon dressing gown and her feet were bare.

'Why, Mr Dent,' she stuttered. 'I wasn't expecting . . . ' She didn't finish, obviously petrified of Dent.

Sabina looked up at them gravely without speaking. You'd think she'd come running over to her father, thought Lisa sadly.

'Hallo, Sabina.' She knelt beside the child. 'What's your dolly called, sweetheart?'

The little girl's grave expression did not alter. She thought awhile then frowned. 'Dolly,' she said.

'I've got a dolly at home called Victoria. Do you think she'd like to meet yours?'

Sabina shrugged. 'Don't know.'

Dent, his usual uncivil self, had not thought to introduce the nurse. Lisa forced herself to smile at the woman. 'Hi, I'm Lisa Angelis,' she said. 'Will you get Sabina dressed so she can play outside, please.'

'Outside! What about the lake?' The woman was about fifty, pale, with a thin, unhealthy face. Her mouth was rimmed with cold sores and her hair hadn't been combed that day.

'She'll be quite safe if she's watched. Do I take it she never goes out to play, Mrs— ?'

'Wright. Mrs Wright. Well, I do worry about that lake.' The

woman glanced nervously at Dent who was twiddling his thumbs and staring at the floor, clearly bored with the whole proceedings.

'Do you, Mrs Wright?' said Lisa brightly. 'Well, the reason we've come to see you is to say that Mr Dent and I are getting married and then going abroad for a while, and we're taking Sabina with us, so I'm afraid your services won't be required any longer. Dent will give you a cheque for three months' salary in lieu of notice. So, if you could pack your things, please . . . '

'Now?' said the woman.

'Now,' said Lisa.

'Why did you do that?' asked Dent curiously as they went downstairs ten minutes later, Lisa holding Sabina's hand. She'd dressed the child herself in a pair of yellow overalls and a tee shirt, the only clothes she could find which still fitted. Everything else was too small.

'Because she plaits Sabina's hair too tight and hasn't got the sense to realize how much it hurts, particularly in bed,' Lisa replied angrily. 'God knows what time she dressed her in the mornings. Her doll hasn't got a name which means she probably doesn't talk to her. She doesn't go out to play and none of her clothes fit.'

'She only had to ask for money,' said Dent reasonably.

'Couldn't you see, she was terrified of you!' snapped Lisa. 'She was too scared to ask.'

It wasn't that Dent was cruel. As far as he was concerned, his responsibility ended when he engaged a nanny for his child. Then he had virtually forgotten she existed. It never occurred to him to play with her, or check whether she was being looked after properly, or if she was happy – and Sabina clearly was neither.

Her speech was limited to a handful of words and she had no idea how to play except with her doll. Once they were downstairs she regarded Lisa solemnly, her great brown eyes bright as if she was about to cry, an impression strengthened when her small mouth quivered. Lisa longed to hug the tiny, pathetic body, but felt that too much demonstrative affection from a complete stranger might upset the child even more.

Instead she said, 'I'm Lisa and we're going to be great friends. Do you know what friends are?'

Sabina nodded and said seriously, 'Dolly fwend.'

Lisa took her into the garden and taught her how to throw a ball and catch it. Dent came out and to Lisa's surprise he joined in and it was actually he who brought the first smile to the child's face when he threw himself dramatically onto the grass to catch her throw.

Later, when Lisa went inside to the kitchen to see about the little girl's lunch, Millie said, 'I'm sure glad to see the back of that Mrs Wright. I kept telling his lordship she was a no-good lazy bitch, but he didn't take no notice.'

'I'm going to marry him,' said Lisa.

Millie burst out laughing. 'Sooner you than me,' she snorted.

Suddenly the roar of a motor bike could be heard and Lisa rushed outside. Sabina had disappeared. Half an hour later Dent returned, his daughter clutching his hand, her cheeks pink, her long hair wild.

'Took her for a ride on Bessie,' he said. 'I think she enjoyed it.'

Lisa groaned. The man was impossible.

'Be a funny sort of honeymoon,' said Dent. 'With Sabina and Gary.'

'You don't mind, do you?' asked Lisa.

'Suits me,' he shrugged.

They were in the silver Duesenberg which had belonged to Vita Reese, on the way back from their wedding. It had been a spur-of-the-moment decision to bring the ceremony forward a few weeks and dodge the reporters who seemed to find it newsworthy.

No guests were invited. Two women from an office next door agreed to be witnesses and Dent had given them a hundred dollars each.

Lisa glanced at him. He had on the same shiny black suit he'd worn the day he'd called on her – could it really be a mere five weeks ago? It seemed an age. This small, virile man, bursting with energy – he was a stranger, really. She wasn't even sure she liked him. Yet, somewhat to her astonishment, she'd married him! Perhaps it was because there were no boundaries with Dent. She could be herself. There was never any need to worry about hurting his feelings, saying or doing the wrong thing. True, he might explode into a rage. But then, she could explode right back. She'd really enjoyed stamping on his painting that day.

'What are you thinking about?' he asked.

'You.'

'That's a coincidence – so was I.'

Dent was terrified of flying. He excused this weakness by declaring that anyone willing to trust themselves to a pressed steel tube thousands of feet up in the air was beyond his understanding. 'They must be stark, raving mad,' he said wonderingly. 'When you think of the things that can go wrong!'

'Trouble with you, Dent, is you think too much,' scolded Lisa. Nevertheless, she looked forward to the trip to Cannes by sea.

Sabina loved the water. With Lisa hovering anxiously behind, the child stood for hours at the stern of the ship, fascinated by the sight of the muddy grey ocean being churned into dirty foam. She held up her doll to watch the V-shaped wake, her brow creased in concentration. Lisa knew she wanted to ask questions but hadn't yet the words to form them. When she told Dent, he treated his three-year-old daughter to a lecture on propellers and velocity and water strength, of which neither of them could understand a word.

Meal-times in the luxury-class dining room turned out to be torture. Dent looked upon the rest of the passengers as morons, particularly the Texas oil millionaire and his wife who shared their table, along with another couple – working-class New Yorkers using their lottery winnings for the trip of a lifetime. The Texan was admittedly loudmouthed, voicing his opinions with a certainty that brooked no argument. Dent either ignored him or demolished the man with stinging rudeness.

'Perhaps we should set up concentration camps,' he said

one night when the Texan had been sounding off on the stupidity of paying welfare to the unemployed. 'Feather-bedding the scroungers', he'd called it.

'Eh?' The man stared at Dent. He wore rimless glasses and behind them his small eyes were puzzled.

'Put the unemployed, the blacks, the sick and the old in concentration camps,' said Dent in a friendly voice. Lisa's heart sank. She knew he was leading up to a whopping insult. She also knew he didn't give a damn about the unemployed. If the Texan had declared the sky was blue, Dent would have demolished his premise with equal nasti-ness just because he didn't like the man. 'Put the able-bodied to work building ovens, then gas the lot.'

Even then the Texan wasn't sure if Dent was being serious or not, 'Well, perhaps that's a bit extreme.'

'That's a preposterous idea,' gasped the woman from New York. Dent ignored her.

'Not too extreme for a fascist like you, surely?' he said.

The Texan, aware by now he was being mocked, exploded in anger. On Lisa's right, Gary gave a little snigger and she felt doubly irritated. Gary's feelings about Dent had done a hundred and eighty degree turn. Now he almost worshipped the man and the longer the two were together, the more like Dent he became. His admittedly superficial charm had gone, along with the bleached hair, and day by day he became more caustic and offensive.

'Please excuse me.' She stood up. 'I think I'll skip dessert.'

On deck she lit a cigarette and stood by the rail watching the smoke disappear into the night air. Suddenly she found herself smiling. Serve that Texan right, expecting everyone to agree with his nauseous opinions. Dent had certainly taken him down a peg.

There was a loud crash from the dining room behind. It sounded as if someone was throwing dishes. Gary told her later that in the process of trying to strangle her husband, the Texan had dragged the tablecloth and everything on it onto the floor. It had taken three waiters to pull him away. Throughout the proceedings, said Gary with a giggle, Dent had adopted an air of injured innocence, saying wonderingly, 'The man just flipped, I can't think why.' The New Yorkers, not sure whose side they were on, asked to be seated elsewhere and the Texan remained out of sight for the rest of the trip so the Dent entourage had a table to itself – to Lisa's heartfelt relief.

Chapter 31

It was truly a glittering event. Lisa had never seen so many women wearing so many precious jewels. The occasion was a reception for the judges, officials and stars of the Cannes Film Festival. The three pink-tinted crystal chandeliers which hung down the centre of the room added yet more sparkle to the big hotel ballroom, its walls hung with richly-coloured oil paintings depicting heroic scenes from the French Revolution.

Lisa wasn't sure if she felt underdressed or overdressed. That afternoon, Dent, who usually didn't give a damn what she wore, had bought her a silver lamé trouser suit. The legs were gathered, harem-style, into wide, multi-coloured jewelled bands; the top was full with a halter neck, the strap a delicate silver chain, and finally, a two-inch-wide belt which matched the ankle-trimming.

'Don't you think it's rather vulgar?' she asked Dent when she came out of the changing room in the tiny, exclusive boutique. He was dancing impatiently about, waiting for her to appear.

'Yeah, but everyone should look vulgar once in a while,' he said.

She agreed to bow to his awesome wisdom and let him pay, though once outside, she gasped, 'Christ Almighty, Dent! Wasn't that the equivalent of three thousand dollars?'

'Something like that,' he said flippantly.

'I doubt if I'll think I'll look as gorgeous as when I paid a couple of shillings for a frock in Paddy's Market,' she remarked wryly.

'Lisa! Someone told me you were here,' cried a familiar voice.

Ralph grasped her shoulder and she threw her arms around his neck in delight.

'Ralph! Have you met my husband, Joseph Dent? And this is our friend Gary Maddox.'

'We've met before,' grunted Gary, and moved rudely away.

Dent said accusingly, 'You wasted your talent in Hollywood. You could've been a truly great actor if you'd picked your parts more carefully.'

'No need to rub it in, old man,' Ralph replied courteously. Later, when Dent was out of earshot, he asked 'Is he always so blunt?'

'Always,' said Lisa.

'It doesn't seem to worry you, though. I've never seen you look so contented.'

'I've never been so contented,' she said. Afterwards, she thought with astonishment. 'That's true! Who would have thought I'd find such happiness with a man like Joseph Dent?'

Back in Hollywood, Dent and Gary were working together on the script of *Attrition*. It was a bitter, uncompromising story, virtually a two-hander, with Gary and Lisa's characters locked in a frightening game of cat and mouse. The studio was booked, the crew hired. To Lisa's disgust, she discovered Dent had been stringing the novelist along for years with repeated options on his book.

'You are a bastard, Dent,' she told him when she learnt that the poor man had been waiting to give up his job to write full-time for ages. 'I hope you pay him an extra large fee. And by the way, how did Gary come to raise the finance?' *Attrition* had a budget of over a million dollars. She knew there was animosity between Gary and his father, who didn't approve of his son's Hollywood career, so the money wouldn't have been forthcoming from that quarter.

'Don't know, don't care,' Dent replied brusquely. 'As long as he's got it, that's all that matters.'

Sabina had been registered at a nursery school. At first, Lisa let her go just two days a week, then, when the child showed every sign of enjoying it, she went full-time. Her vocabulary improved enormously and she mixed well. Those first isolated, friendless years didn't appear to have had any long-term detrimental effect. On her fourth birthday, Lisa invited the entire class to a party, a noisy, chaotic affair. None of the games which Lisa had planned so carefully were played. Instead, Dent led the children on an adventure trip around the vast garden. There were ogres under one tree and witches living up another. Fairy fish, invisible to the human eye, inhabited the lily pond and one little boy fell in, determined to catch one. After the guests had been collected and it was all over, Dent said, 'I enjoyed that.'

'That's because you're little more than a child yourself – at times,' said Lisa.

Marriage had not mellowed Joseph Dent. When they began work on *Attrition*, he was as vicious and cruel as ever. Lisa ignored his rages and, to her surprise, so did Gary Maddox. As if he had taken a vow not to lose his temper, the actor listened patiently to every criticism, responding with almost pathetic obedience.

One night, when they were at home, Dent said, 'I'm not getting the full works out of Maddox.'

'What do you mean?' Lisa asked.

'He's too damned submissive. I need to get under his skin to bring out the best in him. He's *acting* angry and frightened and it shows. I want him to *be* angry and frightened. I'll have to rile him more.'

Next day on set, they were on the ninth take of a scene where Gary thinks he has been betrayed by Lisa and the camera rests on his face as the reality of supposed betrayal sinks in and he is possessed with inward, overpowering rage. Gary just wasn't managing it so Dent managed it for him. Flinging his script onto the floor, he screamed. 'You fucking, lily-livered faggot! What's the matter with you? Ain't you got no balls at all? Too ladylike to lose your temper, is that it?'

Lisa heard gasps from the technicians. This was over the top even for Dent. She watched as Gary's face turned red and ugly. He leapt at the director, fists raised ready to strike. She screamed and Gary stopped, only a yard away from Dent. 'Don't you *ever* call me a faggot again,' he grated.

Dent faced him fearlessly. 'Get back on set,' he ordered. 'We're trying to make a movie here.'

Gary returned sullenly. Passing Lisa, he said viciously, 'One of these days, I'll kill that bastard.'

Attrition was more than three-quarters finished. All that remained to be done were the outdoor scenes, for which Dent had rented an empty house. 'It's real spooky,' he'd told Lisa a few weeks before. 'A little grey castle, thoroughly tasteless.'

To her surprise, the house turned out to be Ralph Layton's. It had a *For Sale* board outside.

'You didn't say it was Ralph's,' she said to Dent accusingly.

'I didn't think you'd be interested,' he replied.

That night, she called the operator and got Ralph's new number.

'Why didn't you tell me you'd moved?' she said straight off. 'Are you somewhere bigger and grander?'

'No,' said Ralph with a laugh. 'I'm somewhere smaller and meaner.'

'Why?' she demanded.

'As they say in England, I was short of a few bob. I needed money for something important and in case you haven't noticed, Lisa, I haven't worked much recently.'

Ralph had appeared in too many lousy films. People had forgotten what a good actor he was. Now in his fifties, he'd been relegated to minor supporting parts. 'I'd half-noticed,' she said apologetically. 'I've been so busy. I have Sabina now and Dent is very demanding.'

'For Chrissakes, Lisa, it's not your fault.' He laughed again, this time somewhat bitterly. 'I went to Cannes in the hope of making some foreign contacts, but no luck. I've shot my bolt as far as Hollywood goes. I was thinking of going back to the stage.'

'How's Michael?' she asked tentatively.

'Long gone. As the money shrank, so did his affection. But there's someone else – someone very special.'

On the final day of shooting, something odd happened.

'All I need now,' said Dent, 'Is a shot of the handyman coming out of the garage.'

'We did that last night,' said the actor who played the part.

Dent stared at the man. 'Last night?' he said, his face creased in a frown. Lisa could see he was struggling to remember. 'Last night,' he repeated to himself. He turned to Lisa for confirmation. To her consternation, he looked frightened and for the first time since she'd known him, unsure of himself.

'That's right,' she assured him. 'You were probaby tired. It'll come to mind eventually.'

Beside her, Gary Maddox sniggered at Dent's discomfiture. Relations between the two had hit rock bottom. Dent had kept the actor on the brink of savage, furious rage for weeks. Several times it had exploded into violence and the two men had come to blows. Gary only spoke to the director when he had to and then he was barely civil.

Lisa was thankful it was all over. She took another vow never to appear in one of Joseph Dent's movies again.

Dent had begun a painting – a massive canvas, ten foot by six. He laid it on the floor and began to throw paint on, smearing it with his hands into shapes that meant nothing to Lisa.

'What is it?' she asked.

'Life,' he snapped.

'Whose life? Yours?'

He shrugged. 'Anybody's.'

Gary Maddox turned up one day a few weeks after *Attrition* was finished. To Lisa's astonishment he was completely back to his normal self. After kissing her cheek, he asked, 'Is Dent about?'

'He's in his studio.'

She expected an explosion of anger when Gary went in, and was even considering getting Dent's gun from the kitchen in case they needed separating. Instead, she heard nothing until two hours later when they emerged together, laughing.

'Gary's had this script sent to him,' Dent said. 'It'll make a really sensational movie.'

Lisa groaned.

*

Millie came out into the garden looking angry. It was Saturday and Sabina was home from school. Dent was teaching her to climb trees and like a great black bird of prey, he was perched halfway up an elderly elm, reaching down to pull her up to the next branch. Lisa, wishing he would teach her something more useful and ladylike, watched anxiously.

'Are you staying in for dinner tonight or not?' demanded Millie.

'Going out,' said Lisa. 'Didn't Dent tell you?'

'Sure, he told me,' Millie said crossly. 'Then half an hour later he says you're staying in.'

'He must have forgotten,' soothed Lisa. 'We're going out.' After Millie had gone, she looked at Dent with troubled eyes. It wasn't like him to get confused. On the other hand, he seemed to be forgetting a lot of things lately. Perhaps he had something on his mind, she decided.

Sabina was growing fast. 'My jeans hurt,' she complained one day. 'They dig into my bottom.'

Lisa immediately felt guilty. 'We'll go shopping after school tomorrow,' she promised. It seemed no time since she'd bought the child a whole new wardrobe of clothes.

Dent was having one of his bored days and decided to come with them. As they walked along Sunset Boulevard, Sabina danced between them, holding their hands. 'That's a pretty dress,' she shouted, darting towards a window. Lisa followed and they stood discussing whether to try the dress on. On closer inspection, Sabina decided it was too fancy. 'Too many bows and frills,' she said. When they turned, Dent had disappeared.

Lisa looked up and down and saw him some distance ahead. He had his hands in his pockets and was staring down into the gutter. She caught up with him and said, 'Why didn't you wait for us?'

He looked at her, his black eyes puzzled. 'Oh, it's you,' he said eventually. 'What goes on down there?' He nodded towards a grid in the gutter.

'It's all muddy and dirty down there, Daddy,' Sabina explained patiently. 'It's called . . . ' she paused. 'What's it called, Lisa?'

347

'A sewer.'

'Really?' said Dent in a surprised, almost childish way, as if it was something he hadn't known.

'Come along, Dent,' said Lisa gently. 'Let's go home.'

'But we haven't bought —' began Sabina in an outraged voice. Lisa quickly squeezed her arm and she fell silent.

Aware something was wrong, something she couldn't understand, on the way home in the car, the little girl put her arms around Dent's neck and rested her head on his shoulder.

When Lisa tucked her up in bed that night, she said anxiously. 'Daddy's all right, isn't he, Lisa?'

'Of course he is,' Lisa said comfortingly, but as she closed the bedroom door behind her, she wished there was someone who would say the same comforting words to her.

Dent's painting was turning into an eye. The giant pupil was black and oily, the iris muddy brown. One day, Lisa went in and found him walking around the edge of his canvas in his bare feet. When he saw her, he grinned. 'You get a really good effect doing this.'

'Sabina turns out better stuff than that at nursery school,' she said disparagingly.

'Who's Sabina?' asked Dent.

'Perhaps he's always been like this,' thought Lisa. 'After all, I haven't known him all that long. Perhaps he's always been vague,' but in her heart of hearts she knew it wasn't true.

'What's he up to?' asked Millie.

Lisa had gone into the kitchen for Sabina's bedtime milk. Millie nodded towards the window where Dent could be seen directly outside. He seemed to be digging. Lisa crossed over to the window and looked down and saw he was levering away at the grid into which the sink waste drained. She watched as he loosened, then lifted, the slatted square of metal. Then he stood, both arms outstretched leaning against the windowsill, staring deep into the black, murky depths. For a long time he remained stock-still and in the kitchen the two women stood silently watching. His sudden sigh was audible and made both of them jump. He looked from right to left, as if wondering why he was there and, frowning, replaced the grid.

Lisa looked at Millie and saw two solitary tears running down her black cheeks. She poured a glass of milk for Sabina and left without a word.

Dent and Lisa were driving home one night in the Duesenberg having been to dinner with some of his old friends, an elderly producer and his wife. Dent was trying to raise the backing for Gary's script and was halfway to talking the man into it when they'd had an argument over a movie they'd both been involved in. Dent flew into a towering rage. Lisa had never known him so angry. She sat with bent head as everyone in the restaurant listened to his blistering, raised voice. Eventually, he leapt up, spilling his coffee over the white tablecoth. Lisa, after apologizing on his behalf, followed him out.

For most of the journey back, they didn't speak. Not far from home, Dent said: 'He was right.'

'What are you talking about?' said Lisa stiffly, still angry over the way he'd behaved.

'It *was* Vince Hobart who took over as assistant director when Bert Kent died.'

'Then when we get home, why not call and apologize?' she said coldly. 'For once, consider saying you're sorry.'

Dent chuckled. 'There's a lot hanging on it, so I just might, Maxine. I just might.'

They got in close to midnight. Except for the orange lantern outside, the house was in darkness. As she drew the bolt on the front door, she asked, 'Would you like a drink?'

Dent was standing at the foot of the stairs, his arms clasped behind him, rocking backwards and forwards on the balls of his feet. He jumped at the sound of her voice.

'No thanks,' he muttered. He stared at her thoughtfully. 'You're very beautiful.'

'Why Dent, you say the nicest things.' Her joking tone belied the anxiety she was feeling.

He turned abruptly and leapt up the stairs two at a time. Lisa went into the kitchen and made a cup of tea. To her surprise, the speaker in the corner crackled and Ella Fitzgerald began to sing *Every Time We Say Goodbye*, her favourite. She smiled. Sometimes Dent could be very thoughtful.

She was sitting drinking the tea when he came in dressed in his leather flying jacket, helmet and goggles. 'I'm going for a ride on Bessie,' he said.

'Dent! Not at this time of night, surely?'

'My dear, don't be so conventional. What on earth does it matter what time I go out?' He came over and kissed her full on the lips. 'Goodbye,' he said.

'Good night, Dent. I'll probably be in bed by the time you get back.'

He didn't answer. She hadn't expected him to. The front door slammed and soon after, Bessie roared and she listened whilst the sound faded into the distance. Leaving her tea half-drunk, she went along to his studio and looked at the portraits: Jennifer, Koko, *Maxine*! Maxine was one of his ex-wives.

Dent had propped his new painting up against the wall. In the pupil of the eye was another eye, and inside that another, until the final eye appeared, so tiny it could scarcely be made out. The painting had a reverse three-dimensional effect, the pupils like a tunnel reaching back into infinity. In the top left-hand corner he'd scrawled in red IT'S ALL MY EYE! Life, he'd called it initially. Life is all my eye!

Ella Fitzgerald was still crooning softly in the background. Lisa returned to finish her tea, but the drink had gone cold. She made more, knowing she was delaying going to bed for some reason she couldn't quite define. Or perhaps she just didn't want to define it. Not yet.

She looked through the window, at the hedges smudged black against the electric-blue, star-freckled sky, vaguely aware of the grandfather clock ticking loudly, cranking and grinding as it worked up to striking the quarter hour.

'Lisa.'

She jumped. Sabina was standing in the doorway clutching Dolly.

'Sweetheart! Can't you sleep?'

'Bessie makes an awful loud noise.'

'Come and sit on my knee a while. Would you like a story?'

'Yes, please. Goldilocks.' She padded over and climbed onto Lisa's knee. Lisa hugged the child close and wondered why her eyes felt moist as she pressed the small body to hers.

It was difficult to concentrate on the story whilst her ears were straining to hear the sound of Bessie returning. She'd stumbled halfway through when Sabina fell asleep, her thumb stuck firmly in her mouth.

The clock began to work up to striking a quarter to two. Lisa wondered how many hundreds, if not thousands, of people had listened to it striking away each fifteen minutes of their lives as they waited for sleep, waited to get up or go out, or for a loved one to come home. Waited for good news. Or bad.

Sabina's body was warm and her head nestled in the curve of Lisa's throat. She stroked the smooth soft cheek with her finger. A floorboard creaked and she jumped, disturbing the child, who began to suck furiously on her thumb. After a while Lisa carried the little girl up to her room and tucked her in. It would be best if she was out of the way when the news came.

Downstairs she switched on the television and sat unthinkingly watching the screen for a long time before she realized the presidential results were coming in and it looked as if Richard Nixon had been elected and Hubert Humphrey had lost. Busby would be heartbroken. She remembered his anguish earlier in the year when Robert Kennedy had been assassinated. 'America is a cursed country,' he had wailed. Dear, sweet Busby, so emotional and easily hurt, entirely different from Dent, who was the ultimate cynic. Dent hadn't voted. 'Politicians are scum,' he said flatly. 'All they want is power and none of 'em ever use their power to do any good.'

Lisa turned the set off, made another pot of tea and sat in the dark, waiting.

It was the headlights she saw first, the beam fanning out over the dark trees, turning the leaves into gleaming satin.

She opened the door as the car drew up. It was a police car, the men in uniforms looking grim and uncomfortable.

'What's happened?' she asked, as if she didn't know.

'I'm afraid we have some bad news. Your husband — '

'Is he dead?'

'I'm sorry . . . yes.'

He had driven off the road at speed, straight into a tree. Even then, Dent's iron constitution had held out. He was still alive when a passing motorist noticed the upturned bike and stopped to help. Still alive when the ambulance arrived and took him to hospital. He had finally died on the operating table, less than an hour before, of multiple injuries. Because he had no identification on him, it was the police who had discovered his name and address through Bessie's registration number.

The police had gone. She assured them there were other people in the house who would take care of her – not that she felt like sympathy. She felt cold and shivery, and almost indifferent to Dent's death. She wandered round the downstairs of the house, made more tea, drank several glasses of whisky and smoked endless cigarettes. Suddenly, a glimmer of light appeared above the green hedges outside and at the same time a bird sang, then another until the air was alive with the dawn chorus and Lisa watched as one by one they appeared briefly, appeared to shake themselves, then settled back into the leaves. She found herself smiling at this innocent hive of activity, when a loud hammering sounded on the front door.

'Lisa! Oh, my dear Lisa!' Gary Maddox, tearful and distraught, took her in his arms. 'I heard it on the radio,' he groaned, his voice muffled as he rested his face in her hair.

'Why, Gary!' she exclaimed, pulling away, holding him by the shoulders. 'You really care!'

'I never thought it was possible to love and hate the same person so much. That bastard! Jesus, the times I came close to killing him.'

'Don't get too upset,' she soothed. 'Remember, Dent wouldn't cry for you. Or me, come to that.'

She woke Millie and told her the news. The old woman burst into tears but soon recovered. 'The old devil's probably watching,' she muttered. 'I'll not give him the pleasure of seeing me shed tears.'

Downstairs again, Lisa said to Gary, 'I think I'll try and snatch a few hours' sleep. You're welcome to stay if you want.'

'Do you mind if I go down and see a few of his movies?'

'Well,' said Lisa, 'if he's watching as Millie says, I think that's what he'd like us to do most of all.'

She sat up in bed, lit a final cigarette and reached behind for a pillow to rest against her back. A note fluttered to the floor. As she reached for it, Lisa recognized Dent's wild scrawling handwriting.

'Lisa. My mind is going — rapidly. Early dementia. There's no cure, I've checked. You know, I can see it in your eyes. It can only get worse and I refuse to live with it. I decided if I ever forgot your name it was time to go. I've had a fucking good life and you were the best part of it. Don't show this to anyone. Have a good life, Dent.'

'I knew it,' whispered Lisa as she put her lighter to the corner of the note and laid it in the ashtray to burn. 'I just knew it.'

She watched the paper brown and curl as the flickering flame swiftly consumed it. In no time, all that remained were some scraps of burnt paper and a heap of grey ash.

Chapter 32

Dent was buried early on a hot, fogbound morning in November. Strange to think how much he'd been loathed, yet at least two hundred people turned up for his funeral. So many that the edge of the crowd was shrouded in white mist.

'They've come to mourn the director, not the man,' whispered Gary. Lisa squeezed his arm affectionately. He'd been a tower of strength since Dent died. Not that she needed much comforting. Dent had come into her life like a whirlwind, stayed briefly, then departed violently by his own hand – though no one knew that but her. Occasionally she felt sad, but it soon passed; she knew Dent would have despised her for being maudlin. No one truly mourned the death of Joseph Dent.

Except Sabina. Deprived of a father for most of her young life, she had come to adore him. Since Dent's death, she had been inconsolable and slept in Lisa's bed, crying herself to sleep every night.

'She'll get over it in time,' said Millie. 'Everybody gets over everything in time.'

Sabina would need a lot of love, thought Lisa, and no one was more willing and anxious to give it than she was. Dent's daughter was his greatest legacy. He'd left Lisa his house and his fortune, two million dollars, but it was Sabina she valued most, her longed-for child.

There were no flowers or prayers at Dent's funeral. They played Wagner in the small chapel and Gary and two old friends spoke a few words, but that was all. Lisa was careful nothing should be done her husband would have sneered at.

When it was over, Gary said, 'A few folk would like to come back to the house. We could watch a couple of his movies, if that's all right?'

'Of course. I asked Millie to get some refreshments ready.'

The sun had appeared, brilliant in a pale-blue sky, when a

354

dozen cars drove in procession back to Tymperleys, Lisa and Gary in the first one.

'I'll be glad when today's over,' she said with a sigh as they turned into the drive. 'There's nothing worse than a funeral.'

Later that night, she was to remember those words.

Lisa knew something was wrong the minute she stepped into the hall. Millie was standing there, a tea-towel in her hands, and a look of horror mixed with grief on her plump good-natured face.

'What's the matter?' asked Lisa immediately, then, with mounting panic: 'Where's Sabina?'

'She's gone,' said Millie in a flat, toneless voice.

'Gone!'

Gary went over and took Millie's arm. 'Where?' he demanded.

'Her momma came and took her.'

Outside car doors slammed and footsteps sounded on the gravel path.

'You two go in the kitchen,' Gary said urgently. 'I'll see to the guests.'

'The food's already laid out in the dining room,' said Millie in the same dull voice.

'What happened?' cried Lisa when the two women were alone. Millie started to cry.

'I was laying out the table when I heard voices in the hall,' she sobbed. 'I didn't take too much notice at first. The front door was open and there's been folks in an' out of here like it was Woolworths all week. When eventually I go to see, there's Koko sitting on the sofa with Sabina. "I've come to take her back with me," she ses. There was this big car outside with the motor running.'

'Oh Millie, and you just *let* her!'

Millie stared at her reproachfully. 'What d'you take me for, Lisa? 'Course I argued with her. I told her there was no way she could just walk out with the child like that. I said you'd be home in an hour and to wait, but she sez, "Sabina's my child and I wants her back." She'd read about Dent dying in some paper in Canada.'

'Canada!'

'That's where she's living now. God help me, Lisa, I would have stopped her, I'm bigger than she is, but — ' she paused, the expression of grief on her face turning to embarrassment.

'But what?'

'Well, Sabina, she *wanted* to go. She said, "I want to be with my mummy." She took to Koko straight away, like she'd always known her. I don't like telling you this, Miss Lisa, but she looked really happy.'

According to Dent's lawyer, if Sabina was traced and the case went to court, Lisa didn't stand a chance of keeping her.

'The mother is always given preference,' he said. 'Always.'

'But she just walked out when Sabina was born!'

'She may be able to give a good reason for that. Anyway, the child was left with her father. Now the father's dead . . . ' He shrugged. 'I understand you called the police when the child was removed, but they refused to take action?'

'They said a mother couldn't be accused of kidnapping her own child,' Lisa said tiredly.

'That's right. It isn't as if your husband had been given custody. Sabina wasn't even mentioned in the divorce proceedings.'

Damn Dent! He'd probably forgotten Sabina existed.

The lawyer went on, 'It might have been different if you'd looked after her since she was a baby, but you'd only known her eight months.'

'Yes, but I grew to love her as if she was my own.'

'It must be upsetting for you,' the lawyer said sympathetically.

'It's rather more than that,' she said bitterly.

She never saw Sabina again, though she hired a private detective to find her and make sure she was all right.

Lisa put a tape of Wagner in the loud-speaker system and the sound crashed through the house for an hour, but when it finished the place seemed more like a morgue than ever.

Millie came in almost straight away. 'Want me to put another tape in, honey?'

'Stop treating me like a baby,' said Lisa shortly.

The old woman stood looking down at her with concern. 'Koko's a nice person. She'll take care of Sabina real fine.'

'You've been telling me that every day for two months.'

'Just trying to stop you worrying, Lisa, that's all I'm doin'. She probably wouldn't have left in the first place if Dent hadn't bullied her so much. You know what a shit he could be.'

'Only too well,' said Lisa dryly.

'That dick you hired come up with anything yet?'

'No.'

'Would you like a cup of tea?'

'Yes, please. Anything to get you off my back.'

'I'll bring it in a coupla minutes,' Millie said solicitously.

After she'd gone, Lisa smiled wanly. Millie, everybody, had been really sympathetic. One morning, she'd come down and found every single reminder of the little girl removed from the house.

She leant back and lit a cigarette. Sometimes it felt as if she'd only dreamt about Sabina, that she'd never been real. Now the lovely, long dream was over, she was awake again, and the memory was submerged, only rarely coming to the surface of her mind, as dreams do.

The basement door slammed. That must be Gary coming up for air after watching Dent's movies again. The other day she'd given him his own key. 'Saves me getting up every five minutes to let you in,' she said, though she was glad of his company and it was a good excuse for putting Busby off when he rang – he'd called a lot since Dent died.

'How're ya doing?' He came in and flung himself into a chair.

'As well as can be expected. I fancy throwing myself into work but there's nothing to throw myself into yet.' The movie Dent had been planning next wasn't due to go into production till spring – if it did at all. Matters were still up in the air.

'I've been thinking, Lisa. Y'know, no one will ever get me to act like Dent did. I'm going into direction.'

She looked at him. Lately, Gary had begun to look and act more like her husband. He'd grown a little goatee beard and combed his thinning hair onto his forehead. He wore black a lot. She'd had Bessie repaired and gave it to him as a memento of Dent, and Gary rode everywhere on it. Now he wanted to become a director. Maybe one day he might ask her to marry him, make yet a further gesture to take over Dent's life.

'I think that's wise,' said Lisa. No one would ever drag a great performance out of him as Dent had.

'Y'really think so?' He looked at her anxiously.

'It's a great idea, but who'll take you on, Gary?' Who'd trust someone so inexperienced with a seven-figure-budget movie?

He grinned. '*I'll* take me on. I'm going to start my own production company. *Attrition* is doing really well at the box office. I'm going to put two million bucks into a company of my own.'

Attrition had been released two weeks before on New Year's Day. Lisa had requested the words, '*This film is dedicated to the memory of Joseph Dent*' to appear at the end of the credits. The movie had received even better reviews than *Matchstick Man*. '*Joseph Dent's posthumous work is perhaps the ultimate thriller,*' one critic wrote. '*A nervewracking two hours of nailbiting tension with superb performances from the two stars.*'

'That's a big step, Gary, and I admire you for taking it.' She smiled at him. 'Dent would have been proud of you.'

'I wondered if you'd like to be a partner,' he said shyly.

'Me!' she said, astonished.

'You could go into the production side for a change. You'd be good at that, you're very organized and you hardly ever blow your top.'

'Gee, thanks! I'd like to think about it a while. I'll let you know in a couple of days,' she said.

The more Lisa thought about it, the more she was drawn to the idea of becoming involved in the business side of making films, raising the finance, reading scripts, identifying locations. In other words, she would become a producer. Lots of actors turned to direction or production. John Derek, who'd been a youthful heart-throb like Gary, had recently directed a well-regarded movie called *Childish Things* with another actor, Don Murray, producing and writing the script. Kirk

Douglas had produced *Paths of Glory* and *Spartacus*, which won four Oscars, and Mai Zetterling had started directing her own films.

'I'll do it,' she told Gary the following week. 'I'll put in a million.'

They decided to use Tymperleys as a headquarters until they found an office. The new movie, as yet untitled, would begin shooting in April as Dent had planned.

Suddenly, the house was full of people – set designers, script consultants, actors. Millie was delighted. 'It's nice to see some happy faces around for a change,' she said, looking happy herself for the first time in ages.

Gary was there from early morning till late at night. One day, Lisa asked if he'd like to move in. After all, she reasoned, he had Dent's hairstyle and Dent's beard and was gradually acquiring Dent's crusty manner. He dressed like Dent and was going to make the same sort of movies. It seemed only natural to move into the man's house.

'I'd like that,' he said and paused. 'There's a friend I'd like to bring with me,' he added in a strange, tight voice.

'Well, it's a big house,' Lisa said lightly.

That night in bed she began to feel worried. She shouldn't have been so impulsive. What if she and Gary's girlfriend didn't get along?

The friend was Ralph! She stared at him, stunned, when he arrived with Gary a few days later, their luggage piled in the back of a big station wagon. So that's why he'd sold his house – to finance *Attrition*.

'You don't mind?' he asked shyly. 'I'm a partner in this new company too.' Ralph hadn't aged well. No chance of him playing the role of a hero or a romantic lead nowadays, with his comfortable, portly figure, thinning hair and half-moon spectacles. He looked more like a grandfatherly bank manager than an actor.

'Mind! If there was one person in the world I'd choose to share my house with, it'd be you.' She danced around, showering him with kisses. 'To think, after – what is it, twenty years? – we're both under the same roof again!'

Ralph turned to Gary. 'I told you it would be all right.'

The younger man shuffled his feet and avoided Lisa's eyes. 'Not everyone understands,' he muttered.

'He's still in the closet,' laughed Ralph. 'Except where you and I are concerned.' By now, everyone in Hollywood knew Ralph was gay. The stars didn't bother to keep their sexual preferences from each other. 'Remember the way he pretended to be rude when we met in Cannes?'

That night when she and Gary were alone, he asked, 'What d'you think Dent would have said if he'd known?'

'Dent wouldn't have given a damn,' said Lisa dismissively.

They decided to call themselves O'Brien Productions after a long, heated discussion that went on into the early hours. A hundred names were suggested and rejected as too grand or too pretentious until, the three of them tired and tetchy, Ralph said, 'Why not O'Brien? It's Lisa's maiden name. O'Brien Productions. It's solid and respectable, trustworthy, even. Investors will have confidence in a name like that, rather than Titan, for example.' He glowered at Gary who'd been arguing for Titan all night.

O'Brien Productions! Lisa got a real kick out of seeing that name up on screen at the beginning of their first movie, even more than Lisa Angelis. The critics had been generous, describing the new company's début as *'efficient and entertaining – a good first effort'*.

Six months after Dent's death, Lisa heard from the private detective she'd hired to find Sabina.

'She's living in an apartment block in Ottawa,' he wrote. *'It's not exactly luxurious, but pretty respectable. Koko Lecoustre has two other children, boys aged one and three. She's now married to a building worker; regular income, hard-working, a decent sort of chap. I observed the child going to grade school and she looks happy.'*

He enclosed a snapshot of Sabina looking strange, all wrapped up in a thick coat and boots, with a muffler around her neck and a woollen hat. She was smiling as she carried her lunchbox to school.

Lisa stared at the photograph for a long, long time, wondering if Sabina ever thought about the stepmother she'd had for eight short months. Then Millie came in and Lisa silently handed her the report.

After she'd read it, the old woman said gently, 'She's better off, honey, with two little brothers and a regular mom and pop.'

'I suppose so,' Lisa said dully. 'Though I'll miss her all my life. Do you think I should send some money?'

Millie shook her head firmly. 'Koko knew Dent was a rich bastard, but she never asked him for a penny. I reckon she'd sooner live like the rest of the folks on the block.'

'He gave her to me, you know. He brought her into the bedroom, laid her on my bed and said, "She's yours!"'

'You don't give children away like presents,' Millie squeezed Lisa's hand. 'Come on, honey, cheer up. The Good Lord's blessed you in lots of other ways. Why, this house has really bin jumpin' these last three months!'

Lisa liked having Ralph and Gary living in her house. They were almost like a family. People assumed Gary was *her* partner, not Ralph's, and she made no effort to disabuse them, not even Busby, who called regularly. Folks could think what they liked. She loved her rather unconventional household, though on Christmas Day, there was another, entirely unexpected arrival.

'We're going to have a real old-fashioned Christmas this year,' she declared. 'Our first one together.' Last year it had passed by almost unnoticed, caught up in the trauma of Dent's death and Sabina leaving.

She threw herself into the preparations, spending hours in the shops buying presents, holly, mistletoe and a giant tree. Much to Millie's disgust, she commandeered the kitchen nearly every day to make mince pies or a Christmas cake or puddings.

'How many folk are you baking for?' the old woman demanded. 'The whole of California? There's only three of you gonna be here.'

'There's a heap of people coming round Christmas night,' said Lisa, slapping pastry around with gusto.

Millie snorted.

361

Lisa bought a pile of seasonal tapes for the loud-speaker system, so the house echoed with *White Christmas* or *Sleigh Ride* or choirboys singing carols.

'Isn't this a bit relentless?' Gary complained. 'Dent would never have approved.'

'You're probably right,' agreed Lisa. 'I never got to spend a Christmas with him. He probably didn't even acknowledge its existence, but I'm not leading the rest of my life according to Joseph Dent.'

On Christmas Day, after they'd eaten dinner and Millie had gone off to spend the day with her daughter, the three of them sprawled on the patio, too full and too lazy to move. The table was laden with their dirty dishes and several half-drunk bottles of wine.

'We'll have to wash the dishes,' Lisa yawned. 'We can't leave them for Millie when she gets back.'

'Later,' groaned Gary. 'Much, much later.'

Lisa lit a cigarette and thought how incongruous it all was, the decorations, the tree, the Christmas dinner, yet here they were sitting outdoors in the brilliant afternoon sun. It was an aspect of Californian life to which she would never get used. Over to the left of the garden, a digger was waiting beside a half-excavated pool. *That* was something she *had* got used to – she'd really missed having a pool since she'd left Busby's. The workmen would finish in a couple of weeks' time.

The doorbell chimed and Ralph said weakly, 'I'm immovable. You go, Lisa, you ate the least.'

Lisa cursed them both and staggered inside to open the door.

A tiny old lady was standing on the step rooting through her handbag. She looked up and her pretty violet eyes danced with laughter. 'Shit! I lost my key again.'

Before Lisa could reply, the old lady pushed past, trotted over to an armchair and sat down.

'Get me a drink, Bobby. Rum and orange and go easy on the orange.'

'I think you've got the wrong house!' It was difficult not to laugh. She was such a dear little thing, dressed all in black – a cotton dress with long sleeves, a little straw hat with a veil and cuban-heeled, lace-up shoes.

The old lady didn't seem to have heard. Lisa sat down opposite. 'I think you've got the wrong house,' she repeated. The old lady had certainly been a beauty once, judging from those lovely eyes, long dark lashes and little rosebud mouth. Curly silvery hair fluffed out from under her cloche hat. 'And I'm not Bobby, either,' she added.

'Don't be silly, dear. You're having another one of your turns. Fetch me that drink and make it snappy. I'm as parched as a rhinoceros on heat.'

'This is Tymperleys . . . '

'Of course it's Tymperleys, idiot. Now where's that fuckin' drink?'

'Just a minute.'

Lisa scurried out onto the patio, convulsed with laughter. Ralph and Gary looked up in astonishment. 'What's the matter?'

Scarcely able to speak for laughing, she managed to say, 'There's a little old lady in the hall with the sweetest face and the foulest tongue, who seems to think she lives here!'

The three of them went back to the hall where the old lady sat tapping her foot impatiently. Lisa poured her a Jack Daniel's with ice.

'I'm afraid we're all out of rum,' she apologized, handing over the drink.

'Tut, tut,' said the woman, knocking the drink back in one gulp and holding out her glass for more.

Ralph knelt beside her and said gently, 'You've come to the wrong house '

The old lady interrupted him. 'You think I don't know my own fuckin' house,' she snorted, 'when I had it brought over brick by brick from England!'

'Vita Reese!' they cried in unison.

'Who else? Though I don't usually need to identify myself when I get home.' She turned to Lisa. 'Who are these guys, Bobby?'

'Friends of mine,' gulped Lisa. 'Give her another drink, someone, I'm going to ring Millie.'

'I was just having an after-dinner nap,' Millie complained.

'Whassa matter, can't you live without me or something?'

Lisa ignored the sarcasm. 'Did you ever meet Vita Reese?'

'What a thing to ask a body on Christmas Day! No, I didn't. That old devil Dent was already there when I came.'

'So you don't know what she looks like?'

'No, but she left a heap of her own movies behind – Dent used to watch them sometimes. I expect I thought she was dead.'

'I expect I did, too,' said Lisa. 'Except she's down the hall, claiming she still lives here.'

'What! Well, hold on to her a while, I'm coming over.'

The old lady was already on her fourth glass of whisky when Millie appeared, looking tough and ready to rout the intruder.

'Delilah!' The violet eyes sparkled. 'Am I glad to see you! There's some confusion here. Tell these people who I am.'

Millie's face collapsed into tenderness. She laid her large black hand on the tiny, birdlike shoulder. 'Why, you're Vita Reese,' she said comfortingly. 'Of course you are.'

'I've no idea who she is,' Millie confessed later. After finishing off the whisky, the visitor had fallen asleep in the chair. 'I just felt sorry for her, that's all. What are you going to do with her?' she added sharply.

'I don't know,' said Lisa helplessly. Everyone she'd rung to ask about Vita Reese had replied, 'She's dead,' but no one knew when or how she'd died. Ralph had looked her up in one of Dent's anthologies where it said she was born in 1894; as it was now 1967, this would make the old lady in the hall seventy-three. 'I suppose people just assumed she'd died,' he said.

Gary put one of her silent movies on and they went down to watch it. The woman on the screen looked nothing like the one in the hall, but over forty years had passed, so that wasn't much help.

'She's lovely, though,' said Ralph. There was no doubt about that. They watched Vita Reese kneeling at an altar, sunlight streaming onto her fair curly hair, as she mouthed a prayer, her cupid mouth twisted tragically whilst her enormous dark eyes held an expression of deep despair. The background music soared majestically and violins quivered on their topmost note as Vita threw herself full-length on the altar steps.

'They don't make eyes like that any more,' said Millie. 'I think it's her.'

'What did the police say?' asked Ralph. Gary had forgotten why they were there and become immersed in the movie.

'There are no five-feet-tall, seventy-three-year-old ladies missing from anywhere,' replied Lisa. 'They're going to check on all the old people's homes and ring back. They asked if I wanted her taken away.'

'And what did you say?' demanded Millie.

'I said I'd think about it. I don't suppose it'd do any harm if she stayed on for a couple of days, except we'd soon be out of liquor.'

Three years later, Vita Reese was still at Tymperleys. Nobody ever found out where she'd been in the twenty years since she'd sold the house to Joseph Dent. As far as Vita was concerned, she'd never left. Lisa suspected she wasn't quite as vague as she pretended, that she was *acting* and dressing the part of a sweet old lady. If so, she did it very well and Lisa was the only one to have doubts. The others took Vita Reese at face value and listened avidly whilst she regaled them with tales and gossip from the 1920s. She spent a lot of time in the basement cinema with Gary watching her old movies.

In fact, everybody loved Vita. She was no trouble – unless you counted the drinks bill doubling.

Lisa was worried that things might change. She remembered when she lived in Queen's Gate and life was perfect, then gradually people left or died and she ended up alone. Now life was almost perfect again with her makeshift family all around her.

She tried to take things one year at a time. Christmas, 1971. They'd all be there as usual. Most of the presents were bought and she'd ordered the tree. This year they were going to Busby's after lunch.

As fate would have it, however, it turned out to be Lisa herself who deserted Tymperleys and its disparate residents that Christmas . . .

Chapter 33

The first-class section of the plane was only half-full, and most of the passengers were asleep, though one or two overhead lights were still on.

Lisa looked out of the window. There was nothing to be seen except blackness, not even a glimmer of light. They must be over the Atlantic. The sky was inky, the horizon difficult to make out, just black ocean merging indistinctly with the dark sky.

The engines droned interminably on. Every now and then the aircraft seemed to pause and shudder as if it was stopping to take a breath, and Lisa's heart would miss a beat, convinced they were about to crash, but the engine just changed tone and they forged onwards.

If only she could sleep. She really envied those who'd just tipped back their seats and fallen into a deep slumber. Perhaps a drink would help relax her. She rang the bell and knocked Nellie's letter, read a dozen times since it came that afternoon, off her knee. She was reaching down, trying to locate it, when the stewardess appeared.

'I'll get that.' The girl bent down. 'You must have kicked it back with your heel.'

'Thanks,' smiled Lisa. 'Can I have a whisky, please? With ice.'

'Straight away.' The girl looked no more than eighteen, pretty and slim with white-blonde hair drawn back in a French pleat. What a responsible job for someone so young.

'You're Lisa Angelis, aren't you?' The girl was already back, the drink on a tray.

'That's right.'

'I hope you don't mind me saying this, but I saw *Attrition* a few weeks ago in Hong Kong. You were really wonderful.'

'Why should I mind you saying that?' smiled Lisa. 'I'm flattered, though I think Gary Maddox stole the acting honours.'

'You were every bit as good. Well, enjoy your drink.'

So *Attrition* was still being shown four years after its release. Not surprising, really. Like *Psycho*, it would go down in cinema history. None of O'Brien Productions' movies had come close to getting the same ecstatic reviews. Lately, she'd come to think that thrillers weren't Gary's forte and tried to suggest they try something else, but he was determined on becoming another Joseph Dent. Still, the company showed a healthy profit.

She put the whisky down – she was drinking it too quickly – and Nellie's letter nearly fell again. She folded it up and put it in her bag. She knew the contents almost off by heart. What a bombshell, though, to hear from her family after all these years!

Lisa rarely read her fan letters. Usually the studio or her agent took care of them, though occasionally, a particularly sensitive or sweet letter was directed on to her and she would write a short note and send a signed photograph.

When Nellie's letter arrived at the O'Brien Productions offices in Beverly Hills, the blue air-mail envelope was passed on to Lisa opened but with a little slip attached, saying *'This looks personal.'* She'd found it on her desk when she went in the next morning.

The sender's name on the reverse was: *Mrs Helen Clarke, 30 South Park Road, Crosby, nr Liverpool, England*.

'Oh, no!' she said aloud.

The writing was neat and clear. She unfolded the letter and looked at the signature. It finished, *'Your loving sister, Nellie.'*

Lisa groaned and began to read.

'Are you OUR Lizzie?' the letter began. *'If not, throw this away immediately. I'm sorry to have bothered you. If you ARE our Lizzie, read on, please.*

'How did I find you? (If I have!) Well, five years ago on Mam's birthday, Joan and I took her into town to the pictures and we saw a film called April Flowers. *As soon as you appeared Mam said, "That's our Lizzie!" As you can imagine everyone turned round and either laughed or told her to shut up, including Joan and I. Nevertheless, she insisted throughout it was you. In fact, she ruined*

*the whole evening! Next night, she badgered Joan into taking her
again and on Saturday she tagged along with Jimmie and his
girlfriend after persuading them to go and confirm the discovery of
her long-lost Lizzie.'*

Lisa groaned again. It was rare nowadays she thought
about her family, and she wasn't sure if she wanted to be
reminded of them now. She briefly considered tearing the
letter up before she read another word, but that would be
irresponsible. She sighed and continued reading.

'Ever since, the family have scoured the Liverpool Echo *every
night to see if a Lisa Angelis film is on, and have taken Mam far and
wide to see it. We even went over to the Continentale in Seacombe
once to see a beautiful film called* The Opportunist. *Mam was even
more convinced by that because you were younger, though none of
us recognized you. You seemed far too elegant and lovely to be our
sister! I think she even wrote a couple of letters, though Joan never
posted them.*

*'Anyway, no one took much notice of Mam, though we tried to
humour her and she fretted, not getting any reply to her letters.
(Would they have reached you, I wonder? Would you have answered
if they had? If you* ARE *our Lizzie, that is.)*

*'Why am I writing now? Well, last week Stan (my husband) took
me to the pictures. I can't remember what we saw because I got just
as excited as Mam did all those years before. I didn't think twice at
"O'Brien Productions", but when "Producer, Lisa Angelis" came
up a minute later, I thought, "That's too much of a coincidence!"
and I decided to write myself.*

*'I'll come to the reason for my letter — you must be getting
impatient. It's a sad, sad reason. Our mam is dying. Lung cancer.
All those cigarettes! Sixty a day by the end. She's in Walton
Hospital and has a week left, possibly two. If you really* ARE *our
Lizzie, please come. Please. It would make Mam's end so happy. She
mourned as much over losing you as she did Rory, you know. It
broke her heart when you left. Mam loved you so much, Lizzie —
Lisa. She loved us all so much.*

*'I'm getting emotional. Before finishing, in case you can't come or
won't come, I'll just say we're all fine. I've been married fourteen
years and Stan is a great husband. I'm assistant headmistress at a
primary school in Waterloo and have two lovely children, Natalie,
12, and Luke, 8. (Mam had a fit at the names. Natalie isn't a saint*

and Luke is a PROTESTANT *saint!) Kevin's oldest Sarah is 24 and married, so our Kevin is a grandfather twice over. (He has two more daughters.) Tony and Chris are both married, both happy, two kids each. Jimmie got divorced (much shock horror from Mam, as you can imagine) and went to live back home for a while, but his new marriage is working out fine.*

'Where are we? Paddy . . . ' Lisa's heart missed a beat *' . . . has done really well. He's a press photographer and gets sent all over the world. We hardly ever see him. Mam worries because it can be dangerous. At the moment, he's in Vietnam, so I suppose she's right to worry. Next Joan. I'm afraid Joan has turned out – well, I won't use Natalie's description – let's say, she's a not very happy spinster. Somehow she felt obliged to stay at home with Mam, though there was no need, and now feels she has sacrificed her life. Stan calls her a "self-made martyr". Last but not least, Sean and Dougal, our baby brothers. They both went to the same university, where Sean took Physics and Dougal Chemistry. Now they work together in a research establishment just outside Chester. They got married on the same day – my, what a do we had! The whole of Chaucer Street went to the church to watch. (Mam still lives in the same house, by the way.)*

'I'll finish, my dear Lizzie, I hope this letter doesn't upset you.

'Your loving sister, Nellie.'

'Fasten your safety belts, please.'

Lisa woke up with a start. Trust her to fall asleep just as the plane was about to land. Outside, grey clouds were massed above and below; the plane seemed to stall briefly and the engine coughed as it began to descend out of the skies. They passed through a bank of cloud and she saw houses, rows and rows of them, and green fields and the silver glint of a river. Then cars became visible and tiny people, no bigger than the head of a pin.

England! Home – or was it? Where exactly *was* home?

As soon as she'd read the letter she rang the airline and booked a seat. There were none available until the ten o'clock flight that night. On the way over, she would gain eight hours and arrive in London the next afternoon. She drove home to Tymperleys to pack.

Ralph came out to see who'd arrived. 'I'm going home,' she cried.

'What's the matter?' Dear Ralph, his face was full of concern.

'My mother is dying. I must go back.' She couldn't live with herself if she didn't try to reach Kitty before she died.

'Of course you must, I'll drive you to the airport.'

That evening, when they were on their way, he asked, 'Will you be back for Christmas? It won't be the same without you.'

'I'll do my best. The letter took a week to come, so poor Mam might already be dead by now,' though she was praying Mam would stay alive to see her Lizzie.

'Mam! I've never heard you say that before.'

'Make sure Vita eats, won't you?' And give Millie a surreptitious hand. Everything's getting a bit too much for her lately.'

'You don't have to worry about anything here,' promised Ralph.

It was freezing at the airport, which meant it was bound to be even colder in Liverpool. She'd decided against packing her sable, her only warm coat. She would have felt a fool turning up at Walton Hospital in a three thousand-dollar fur A swank, that's what they used to call people who wore too-posh clothes. Lizzie O'Brien, the swank, coming all done up in expensive fur to see her mam die. The next warmest coat she had was a fine, biscuit-coloured jersey. As she waited for a taxi at Heathrow, she felt the wind whipping through the thin material. The temperature here must be forty or fifty degrees down on California. She sat shivering on the back seat of the cab and when they reached London, wondered if she could spare a couple of hours and ask the driver to take her to Oxford Street where she could buy something heavier, but decided against it. In those few hours, Kitty might die and the journey would have been in vain. She'd get something in Liverpool tomorrow.

The sky was steely grey and sleet slashed against the taxi windows. The change in time, together with the cold, made her feel disorientated as she stared out at the shops, heavy with Christmas decorations.

At Euston Station, she just had time for a cup of tea before the next train to Liverpool. Inside the restaurant, loud with carols, everyone was wrapped up warmly; even a tattered tramp, sitting in a corner seat surrounded by his life's belongings in torn carrier bags, wore a thick tweed overcoat. A few people stared at her and she felt conspicuously underdressed. It was ridiculous, she thought wryly. She had millions of dollars in the bank, yet at this moment in time, an old tramp was more appropriately dressed than she was!

The journey to Liverpool seemed to take forever. The train kept stopping in the middle of nowhere or it slowed down to a snail's pace for mile after mile. At least the heating system was efficient. Too efficient, in fact; the air blowing out from under the seat burnt the back of her legs.

It was after midnight when they finally drew into Lime Street Station. The sudden change in temperature when she stepped off the overheated train was breathtaking. The drivers of the waiting taxis stood in a circle, stamping their feet, their breath white clouds in the dark, cold air.

A middle-aged man came over and took her bag. 'Where to, luv?' His adenoidal Liverpool accent came as a shock.

'Walton Hospital.' She could hardly speak, she felt so cold.

The man looked at her with concern as he took her suitcase. ''Ere, luv, get in quick,' he said. 'I've gorra rug in the front. Wrap this round yer. Jesus Christ, yer teeth are rattling so loud people'll think I've gorra rumba band in the back.'

He was leaning over, tucking a tartan rug around her legs. Lisa felt tears sting her eyes. Liverpool people, they were truly the salt of the earth.

'C'mon, luv, have a sup'a this.' He handed her a bottle of whisky. 'That'll warm the cockles of yer heart.' Lisa took the bottle. Her mouth felt numb and whisky dribbled down her chin as she took a gulp. The driver got in his cab and steered the car out of the station.

He chatted all the way to the hospital. Where had she come from? California! Jesus Christ, had she forgotten the world had different temperatures? Didn't she know

Liverpool got cold in the winter?

'I should do, I was born here,' she said.

'Yer've lost yer accent then?'

'I've been away a long time.'

Why had she come back then, he enquired. Oh, her mam was dying. How sad. But what a lovely girl she was then, coming all the way from California for her mam. 'She won't half be pleased to see yer. What ward is she in?'

'I've no idea,' confessed Lisa. 'No one's expecting me.'

'When we get ter the hospital in a minute, you stay in the back and I'll find out for yer, then I can take yer right ter the door. Save yer wanderin' round, like. What's her name, luv?'

'O'Brien. Kitty O'Brien. And thanks, you're an angel.'

He laughed. 'Wait till I tell the missus I had a lady from California in my cab tonight and she called me an angel.'

When they reached the hospital, he leapt out and was gone for several minutes. He came back and said, 'She's in F2,' and drove right to the door.

After she had paid him, he said, 'Look, luv, I'm on duty till eight o'clock this morning. Here's the company telephone number. If yer want ter leave before then, ring and ask for Sam and if I'm there I'll come and get yer. Okay?'

She could hear the lights buzzing on the Christmas tree in the foyer. Apart from that, the hospital was eerily quiet and her footsteps echoed sharply on the tiled floor as she walked down the deserted corridors following the signs for F2. She passed a lighted office where a nurse was sitting at a desk writing and the woman looked up, startled. Feeling guilty, Lisa began to tread on tiptoe until she came to her mother's ward.

She put her hand up to push the swing doors open when her courage failed. After coming thousands of miles, the last few yards were beyond her. What would Mam look like now? It was almost a quarter of a century since she'd seen her.

The door opened and a young nurse jumped back with a startled cry. 'Sorry, you gave me a fright. Who are you looking for?'

'My mother, Mrs O'Brien.'

'She's in the first bed.' The nurse looked bright and

cheerful, considering the hour. 'Her other daughter's been here every night for weeks. I just persuaded her to go and have a sleep.'

'Which daughter – Nellie?'

'Sorry, I don't know her name. She's got red hair.'

'That'll be Joan.'

'Mrs O'Brien must have been a lovely mother. She has more visitors than all the other patients put together.'

'She was,' said Lisa.

The ward was long, at least ten beds to a side, each one filled with a sleeping, silent woman. Decorations were strung along the putty-coloured walls and a dim red central light gave the room a sinister look. 'Hell might look like this,' thought Lisa.

Kitty was beside a dimly-lit, glass-walled office where another, older nurse could be seen looking through a filing cabinet. The curtains round her bed were the only ones drawn.

'She's asleep.' The nurse drew the curtain back a few inches and motioned her to enter. Lisa took a deep breath and stepped inside and heard the swish of the curtain being closed behind her.

They'd propped Mam up against three pillows so she was almost sitting up in her sleep. She wore a pink brushed-nylon nightdress, the bones on her neck showing sharp through the thin material. Her arms rested on the white sheet, which was drawn tight across and tucked under the mattress. There was so little of Kitty left that the sheet scarcely seemed to curve over the wasted body.

Lisa stood staring down at her and felt the years fall away. *Mam, oh, Mam.*

She sat down beside the bed and took Mam's thin hand. The waxen skin looked and felt like soft silk and the veins stood up as if the hand had been threaded with bright blue string.

'Mam,' breathed Lisa. She bent down and pressed her cheek against the shrunken, caved-in face. They'd taken her teeth out and Mam's jaw had fallen back so far she looked as if she had no chin. Her pale eyelids fluttered, though her eyes didn't open. Mam said, 'Lizzie?'

How did she know?

'Yes, Mam?'

'You're really there?' Her slurred voice was barely discernible.

'Yes I am, Mam. I'm holding your hand.'

Mam's eyes blinked as if the effort of opening them was too great. Eventually, her effort was rewarded and her eyes opened. She was staring at the empty chair on the opposite side of the bed.

'Where are you, Lizzie, luv?'

'I'm here, love.' Lisa reached out and turned Mam's face towards her. The blue eyes were covered with a milky glaze.

'I knew you'd come.' She dragged her other hand over and put it on top of Lisa's. 'There's something I want ter tell you.'

'No, Mam, there's no need to tell me anything.'

'There is, luv.' Lisa bent her head. She could scarcely hear what Mam was saying. 'I'm sorry about what happened, luv. Yer were right, I did know. I'm sorry, Lizzie, luv.'

'It doesn't matter, Mam. It never did me any harm.' The lies you tell at a deathbed, thought Lisa.

Kitty shook her head and began to cry. The tears were huge and they wobbled slowly down her wizened, lined face. Lisa fished in her pocket for a handkerchief but there was none so she wiped the tears away with the back of her hand.

'Please don't cry, Mam. I'm fine. You can't imagine how fine I am.'

'Terrible thing . . . '

'Mam, don't exert yourself. Let's sit together quiet now.'

' . . . fer a mam ter do . . . ' Her voice faded and her eyes fell closed. It had clearly been an effort to get those words out. ''Nother thing.' It came out like a soft sigh. 'Tom, he wasn't yer dad, luv. Someone else, a foreigner . . . '

Christ! What had she just said? She must be rambling, out of her mind. Lisa clutched the thin hands in her own and could feel the pulse throbbing faintly against her palms. She laid her head briefly on the breast that had succoured her, then sat staring at the ravaged face. Somewhere in the ward, a woman cried out and the nurse's brisk footsteps sounded as she went to attend to her.

Lisa had no idea how long she sat there. One hour, two. At one point she glanced at the big white clock at the end of the ward and it had just passed midnight. Memories chased each other through her mind, memories of her mam during the war when they were in the shelter, the way she kept touching them all, hands fluttering from one to the other, her lovely children. Her mam covered in bruises after a beating from Tom, or sick with worry when Kevin, then Rory, had gone off to war. That party she'd got ready for Lizzie's fourteenth birthday . . . the jelly, the purse she'd bought for a present – and Lizzie had just walked out. Lizzie had better things planned for her birthday – a day out in Southport with her Yank boyfriend.

'I won't cry,' vowed Lisa. 'I won't. It might wake her up, she'd be upset and I don't want to upset her, I've done that enough.'

She looked down at the frail form which made so little impression on the bed and thought how remarkable it was that this tiny body had produced eleven children, eight big healthy boys and three daughters.

Suddenly, Kitty's breathing began to get hoarse, became louder. Lisa felt the pulse begin to race. She stood up in alarm and knocked on the window of the office. The older nurse came out immediately. She took hold of Mam's wrist almost roughly, her fingers pressing, moving, pressing again.

'I'm sorry, love. I'm afraid she's gone.'

Lisa sat down on the chair and began to cry softly.

'You bloody hypocrite!'

She looked up. A raw-boned, red-haired woman was looking at her, eyes burning with hatred. Joan! This couldn't be Joan, two years younger than her yet looking fifty, sallow skin, thin mouth tight and drawn back like a cat in anger.

'Joan, it's Lizzie.' Joan hadn't realized who she was. Lisa darted towards her eagerly.

'I know bloody well who it is. Turning up now and crying like the bloody hypocrite you are. Being with our mam when she died, when I've sat here, day after day, night after night . . . '

Lisa reached for Joan's hand, but she snatched it away.

'Don't *touch* me!'

'I'm sorry, I'm sorry.' She felt like an intruder, a stranger who'd forced her presence on a poor dying woman.

'It's too late to be sorry. Why don't you get out – go away from here. Get back to your posh house in America and leave our mam alone.' Joan began to sob, great wracking sobs that shook her blade-thin shoulders, and threw herself on top of Mam's dead body. As the nurse began gently to pull her away, Lisa looked at them both helplessly, then, picking up her suitcase, she ran out of the ward, conscious of the terrible clatter of her heels in the empty corridors. There was a telephone in the foyer. She fumbled in her bag for Sam's number. 'I'm sorry, Sam's gone to Speke Airport,' said the woman who answered. 'Shall we send someone else?'

'Please, straight away.'

She went outside into the black hospital grounds, oblivious to the icy wind which penetrated her thin coat. Joan was right, she was a hypocrite. For all Lisa knew, Kitty could have been dead for years and she'd rarely given her a second thought. Now here she was, pretending to be upset – no, not pretending, she *was* upset, yet . . . it didn't make sense.

Up and down the concrete path she walked, arguing with herself, struggling with her emotions, whilst the wind whistled through the tall, bare trees. She stumbled against a bush and felt thorns tear at her leg just as there was a screech of brakes and a car turned into the drive.

Her taxi! She ran back towards the entrance, but the car turned out to be an ordinary saloon. Two men got out – tall, fair-haired men. They slammed the doors and half ran into the building. Her brothers, though she wasn't sure which.

She longed to call out to them, identify herself, 'I'm Lizzie,' but hadn't the courage. It was as if she was no longer Lisa Angelis, the Hollywood star who had more money in the bank than her family would earn together in their lifetime. Suddenly, she was little Lizzie O'Brien again, nervous and scared. Her brothers might turn on her the way Joan had done and she couldn't have borne it.

Shrinking back into the dark shadows, she waited for her taxi.

*

She had to sit in the waiting room for hours until the first train left at six o'clock, and she felt as if life had turned full circle. Throughout the long wait, and later on, during the journey from Lime Street to Euston, she was oblivious to everything except her own emotional upheaval and the realization that, yet again, she was running away from her family.

Chapter 34

The return journey was fast and there were no hold-ups, though Lisa scarcely noticed. The night's events churned over and over in her mind. Mam dying, Joan's hatred. Her sister's reaction was understandable, though Lisa should have stood her ground, insisted Nellie had asked her to come. At least *she* would have been pleased to see her.

She got Nellie's letter out and read it again. Guilt rose up in her throat, choking her, and she remembered Mam saying, oh, lots of times, 'It's no good being sorry after the event.' If only Lisa had written from time to time to say how she was. She remembered when Kevin joined the Fleet Air Arm and Paddy went to grammar school and how proud Mam had been. Imagine her knowing Lizzie was a film star! Lisa couldn't help but smile. Mam would have been unbearable.

And that incredible thing she'd said about Tom! The idea of her weary, broken mother having an affair was too ridiculous for words.

When she reached London, she wandered down a road beside Euston Station looking for a hotel and found a small, four-star establishment a few hundred yards away. She could have gone straight to Heathrow, but felt too weary to face the long flight home just yet. There'd only been that snatched half-hour of sleep on the plane the night before last. She'd fly back tomorrow after a good night's rest.

The hotel foyer was welcoming with a log fire burning in the wide, old-fashioned fireplace and red-shaded brass lamps on the oak-panel-lined walls. A tall Christmas tree stood in one corner, its jewel-coloured lights snapping on and off.

'I'd like a room, please,' said Lisa.

The receptionist, a sour-faced, middle-aged woman, asked churlishly, 'For how long?'

'Just one night, and I'd like to go to bed immediately.'

The woman sniffed and looked Lisa up and down almost contemptuously. 'That's ten pounds, in advance.'

Lisa didn't bother to argue though the woman's request was insulting. The sudden warmth inside the hotel made her feel faint and she swayed on her feet. She paid and was directed to her room on the first floor. In the corridor a young girl was wheeling a trolley full of sheets and towels. She smiled and said in a broad Irish accent, 'I've just done that room.'

With an effort, Lisa smiled back. The thought of bed and sleep had brought on a feeling of total exhaustion. Once inside the room, she was about to throw herself on the bed fully dressed when she caught sight of herself in the mirror. No wonder the receptionist had been suspicious. She looked an absolute fright! Her coat was crumpled, the lapels stained with whisky, and the right leg of her tights was torn and bloodstained where she'd caught it outside the hospital. The make-up she had put on nearly two days ago had worn away, except for the mascara, reduced to black smudges underneath her eyes making her look faintly ghoulish. Her hair had escaped its bun and hung wildly about her face.

'I don't care,' she muttered as she threw herself on the bed. Within seconds, she was fast asleep.

When she woke, it was daylight. At first she thought she'd slept through the night and it was morning, but the clock beside the bed showed half-past three.

It was the dream that had woken her. She was at Mam's funeral wearing her sable coat and hiding behind a tree whilst her family stood shoulder to shoulder around the grave. Paddy was there, so incredibly handsome, a camera strung around his neck. Then a voice yelled, 'She's here, she's here,' and Joan was up the tree, laughing and pointing down. Her brothers and sisters had picked up soil to throw onto the coffin. At Joan's words they looked up and began to march towards Lisa, their faces twisted with hatred, hands full of clumps of earth, ready to throw it at her. Paddy, Patrick, had recognized her and his eyes were filled with sick horror. Somehow, Joan had got down from the tree and was at their head. 'You bloody hypocrite,' they all screamed.

Her body was soaked with perspiration, yet she was freezing cold. For a while, she lay there shivering, almost lightheaded, trying to remember where she was.

When she got out of bed her legs felt like jelly. She gritted her teeth and forced herself to walk. Perhaps a hot bath might help. As she lay in the water, she realized she'd eaten nothing since she'd landed in England, though right now the idea of food seemed repugnant.

Later she dressed in one of the two outfits she'd brought with her, a lilac-ribbed jersey suit. She was beginning to feel human again – or was she? Out of the mirror, a stranger stared back – a hollow-eyed, gaunt-looking woman with a pinched mouth. This wasn't Lisa Angelis! This wasn't her! Who was she, this unpleasant, mean-faced person looking grimly into her eyes?

'I don't feel real. I don't exist. Who am I?'

The questions hammered at her brain, so hard, so loud, she put her hands up to her head to try and stop them. 'Who am I?' The woman in the mirror merely asked the same question.

Lisa turned away and a wave of dizziness hit her. She willed herself to stay upright, and picked up her coat. There was something wrong with the coat but she couldn't remember what it was. She left the bedroom and walked along the corridor and down the stairs to the hotel foyer, gaining confidence as she went. Why, she could walk fine!

As she went by reception, a woman shouted, 'Miss O'Brien!'

Lisa ignored her – she didn't know a Miss O'Brien. Outside, a taxi was passing and she hailed it. 'Where to?' the cabbie asked.

'Queen's Gate and Brompton Road corner.'

'Right you are, darlin'.'

The window of the flat was dark. Jackie must be having dinner with Gordon. Lisa felt angry. She'd been relying on Jackie to tell her who she was.

'We're 'ere, darlin'.'

The cabbie had turned around and was looking at her impatiently. Lisa shrank into the seat. 'I don't want to get out.'

'Whatcha wanna do then, ducks, stay there all night?'

'No, take me to Kneale Street, down the side of Harrods.'

There was no sign of Mr Greenbaum's shop. Lisa couldn't understand it. The shop had been there only yesterday, surely? There was a chemist's, a sandwich bar, a dry cleaner's, but no bookshop.

The taxi edged down the street. 'I don't suppose you're gonna get out here, either?' the cabbie said resignedly when she made no move.

'Just drive slowly, I'm looking for something.'

'No chance of going fast, darlin', not in this traffic.'

She couldn't remember where the shop should be. Two men came out of a door beside the sandwich bar. 'Goodnight, Brian,' called one. The other man, the one called Brian, muttered something and shuffled off down the road, his shoulders stooped and weary as if he carried the cares of the world. Lisa frowned, wondering why the man looked so familiar. Then she remembered. This man was her husband, yet he looked so old, so hunched. She was about to open the door when the taxi suddenly shot forward and somehow it didn't seem to matter that she'd not spoken to Brian.

'Where next?' asked the driver.

'Back to the hotel,' she said, hoping he remembered where it was because she couldn't.

That night in bed, between fits of shivering, she remembered Harry Greenbaum was dead. What a fool she'd been, riding around London looking for a dead person. And what a fool Brian would have thought her, if she'd leapt out of the taxi and confronted him as if she'd only seen him yesterday. In fact, it was really very funny and she began to laugh hysterically, imagining his astounded reaction. She laughed long and hard and the bed began to shake and after a while someone knocked on her door and called, 'Are you all right?'

'Yes,' she shouted and pulled the clothes over her head and began to cry instead. Then she remembered Jackie. It had been silly looking in Queen's Gate. Jackie had got married and moved to Bournemouth.

'I'll go and see her,' she thought triumphantly. 'I'll go to Bournemouth tomorrow and maybe Jackie will tell me who I am.'

In the mirror next morning she decided she looked much better. Her eyes were star-bright, her cheeks flushed deep red. She got dressed and went downstairs where the disagreeable receptionist was already on duty. Lisa asked her which station the trains to Bournemouth went from.

'Waterloo,' the woman answered. Lisa turned to leave when the woman asked surprisingly, 'Are you all right?'

'I'm fine,' cried Lisa. 'I've never felt so well.' She had a lovely, slightly tipsy feeling.

'Have you had breakfast?'

Lisa frowned, wondering why this strange woman should care. She couldn't remember whether she'd eaten or not. 'Probably,' she replied.

Outside, a light snow had begun to fall and as soon as the white flakes touched the ground they were transformed into grey slush by the heavy traffic. Lisa drew in a sharp breath. Breathing in was like swallowing ice, and another wave of dizziness swept over her. She grabbed the metal railings to prevent herself from falling. The dizziness soon passed and she hailed a taxi to take her to Waterloo.

By the time she reached Bournemouth, the snow was falling thick and fast and the ground was covered with a lethal carpet of slippery ice. The grey leaden clouds seemed low enough to touch and the day was dark, more like dusk than mid-morning. In the taxi, she prayed Jackie would still be living in the same house. It was years since she'd last had a letter and vicars got moved to other parishes. Jackie might be living somewhere else by now. She should have checked before she left London, but these last few days she hadn't been thinking straight.

When they drew up outside the old rambling house she asked the driver to wait a while. 'Let me make sure my friend still lives here.'

The vicarage was exactly as she remembered it: mellow,

russet-coloured bricks, the curtains shabby, the windows and doors in need of painting. A car was parked in the drive, an old Morris Minor, full of rust and minus a wheel. A stack of bricks was propped where the wheel should have been. Despite the weather, someone lay underneath the car and she could see a teenaged boy standing in the open garage. The person beneath the car yelled, 'Hand me that spanner, Rob.'

The boy in the garage ran out and crawled under the car. Lisa smiled and put her hand on the gate to enter. There was a light on in every room of the house. It *must* be Jackie's, she thought. Jackie never turned a light off, ever. The gate creaked and a cat ran across the frozen grass and began to scratch at the front door. A Christmas tree stood in the corner of the room where the wedding reception had been held and two young girls were dancing a minuet, their faces grim with concentration, yet at the same time you could tell they were on the verge of giggling. Lisa felt strangely reluctant to enter. She looked down at her hand poised on top of the gate, watching the snow fall, and soon her hand was covered in white. What was holding her back? The house looked warm and inviting, yet she remained outside. In the stillness, she could hear music, a jazzed-up version of *Silent Night*.

A woman appeared in an upstairs window and glanced down at the car, an anxious expression on her face. Jackie! A plump, matronly Jackie with a cloud of almost-white hair. Raising the window a few inches, she shouted, 'Noël! Robert! Get indoors this minute. You'll catch your death of cold out there!' She slammed the window shut and almost immediately opened it again, calling, 'There's coffee made.' The watcher at the gate went unnoticed; covered in snow, she had become part of the wintry landscape. Seconds later, Jackie came into the room where the two girls were still dancing and all three of them began to laugh. She put an arm around each girl's shoulder and they left the room just as the two boys crawled from underneath the car and ran down the side of the house. They were probably all in the kitchen at the back sitting round that big chipped wooden table drinking their coffee, joking together, chaffing each other, a loving caring family.

Lisa felt rooted to the spot, unable to move, as the knowledge, the sure and certain knowledge swept over her that she would give up everything she owned, every cent she had, for a husband like Laurence and children of her own. It was all she had ever wanted from life, all she cared about. She felt a rush of raw, naked envy for Jackie who had everything, whilst she, Lisa, had nothing except a house full of misfits, a pretend family who meant nothing to her or to each other. Even Sabina, her only chance of a child, had been taken from her.

She had never felt so alone in all her life. Part of her wanted to escape the searing cold, knock on the door and be welcomed, kissed, fussed over, but the other part knew that this would only make her feel worse, more isolated than ever.

Turning to the taxi driver, she said, 'Take me to the station, please. It was the wrong house, after all.'

The journey on the virtually empty train back to London was a nightmare. Her body was so chilled she felt as if her blood had turned to ice yet when she touched her cheeks they were burning. The ticket inspector looked at her with alarm, 'Are you all right, miss?'

'I'm fine,' she insisted through chattering teeth.

After he'd gone, she felt tears slipping down her cheeks though she had no idea why she should cry. The sky had turned so black it could be night and by now a blizzard blew and large clumps of snow were being hurled at the train windows. Suddenly, Mam appeared outside the window in her pink nightdress. She flew alongside the train, holding out her arms beseechingly. Lisa cried out and tried to open the window so she could bring Mam in from the cold, but it was jammed shut.

A wave of nausea swept over her and she fell back on the seat. Everything was too much effort. Even sitting up was hard. She struggled to keep her body upright on the seat, but it was impossible. Slowly, unable to help herself, she crumpled sideways.

*

Later, she learnt that it was the ticket inspector who found her, unconscious and rambling, when the train stopped in London.

Chapter 35

'Where am I?'

The room was empty. She was in bed and outside the open door she could hear loud, cheerful voices and the sound of laughter. She looked around; tall green-painted walls, white flowered curtains, an easy chair, a small table holding a bunch of pink carnations in a chipped vase and lots more flowers on the windowsill. Her handbag stood on a cabinet beside the bed, along with an unlit metal lamp. It was definitely not the hotel. She couldn't remember much about it, but she was sure it had been more luxurious than this.

'Ah, awake at last!' A young man wearing a white coat came in.

'Where am I?'

'You're in St Brigid's Hospital.' He came over and sat on the corner of her bed with a sigh of relief. Despite his reassuring smile, his eyes were blinking with tiredness. 'How do you feel?'

'I don't know.' Her body felt like cotton wool. 'I feel as if somebody's turned on a tap and drained off all my energy. What's wrong with me?' She could vaguely remember passing out on a train.

'You've had pneumonia, a pretty severe case. If you hadn't got the constitution of an ox you might have died.' He reached for her pulse. 'Yes, you're definitely alive.'

'Are you sure?'

He grinned. 'Pretty sure. Ah, here's Sister Rolands.'

A tall bulky woman bristling with authority entered the room, her nurse's uniform starched and ironed to perfection.

'Our star patient is back in the land of the living, Sister.'

'And about time too,' boomed the nurse. 'Well, Doctor, you can get on with your rounds now, I'll see to this patient.'

The doctor went obediently to the door. 'I'll see you again in the morning,' he said to Lisa.

'Why am I your star patient?' she asked when the doctor had gone.

Sister Rolands chuckled as she smoothed the bed where the doctor had sat. 'I hope that isn't a sign you've lost your memory, Lisa Angelis, the famous film star, in a National Health Service ward along with all the common people! I hasten to add I'd never heard of you, but my nurses tell me you're quite famous.'

'How did you know who I was?'

'We went through your bag, of course – how else could we locate your relatives? We found a bill for the Columbine Hotel. They said you'd been staying there but under a false name – O'Brien, I think it was.'

'That's my real name. Angelis is false,' protested Lisa. 'I felt so lousy when I registered that I must have used it by mistake.'

Sister Rolands gave a royally dismissive gesture. 'Doesn't matter. We also found an airmail letter with a Liverpool name and address on the back, which turned out to be your sister. Mrs Clarke has rung every day and said to tell you that as soon as the funeral's over she'll be down to see you. In other words, she'll be here tomorrow. You woke up just in time.'

'Oh dear!'

'I don't allow "Oh dears" on my ward,' the nurse said sternly. 'Just be grateful you've got a family who cares – look at all the flowers they've sent!' She pointed to the windowsill. 'Oh, and we despatched a telegram to the Los Angeles address, by the way. We would have telephoned there too, but according to the American operator your number wasn't listed.'

'It's under my married name, Dent.'

'Three names!' The Sister's shoulders heaved with laughter and her stiff uniform crackled. 'One real, one false, one married. Anyway, a gentleman called Ralph also calls every day. He said everyone sends their love and he'll be over after Christmas to take you home.'

'I won't be staying in England for Christmas,' Lisa said quickly.

Sister Rolands gave a grim smile. 'I'm afraid you will,' she said in a voice that brooked no argument. 'It's Christmas in four days' time and you won't even be fit to get out of bed by then.'

'Four days! How long have I been here?'

'Let's see.' She unhooked the chart off the end of the bed. 'You came in last Saturday and now it's Wednesday.'

'Shit!'

'Tut, tut. Language!' Sister Rolands frowned and wagged a broad finger, though her mouth twitched. 'Wait till I tell my girls our star patient uttered a four-letter word. They're all after your autograph, by the way, but I said to wait until you leave.'

'Why am I in a room by myself?'

'Because you kept us all awake with your shouting, that's why. I think you were re-enacting all your pictures. It was all highly dramatic. You can go in the general ward if you like, but let's wait a while till you've got some strength back.'

Lisa sighed. 'I'm starving. I could eat a horse!'

'The NHS is so hard up you may well have to. Tea will be ready in half an hour. I'll tell them to bring yours first.' She marched out, her uniform crackling.

Lamb chops with mint sauce, mashed potatoes and peas, followed by trifle, all delicious but not nearly enough, were duly served. Lisa ate ravenously, scraping the gravy up with a piece of bread and butter. Afterwards, she still felt famished. The young nurse who had shyly brought her meal came in to collect the tray.

'I'm still hungry,' Lisa said hopefully.

'Sister said you might be, but we're not to give you any more in case it makes you sick.'

'Bitch!'

The nurse giggled. 'Isn't she! But her bark's worse than her bite. Would you like me to sit you up so you can comb your hair for visitors?'

'I'm not expecting anybody, but I'd like to make myself respectable. I can manage on my own.' She struggled to raise herself but after a while fell back exhausted. 'No, I can't. You'll have to help, I'm afraid.'

After lifting her upright, the nurse laid her handbag on her knee. When she'd gone, Lisa took her compact out. With a sense of relief she found that although her face was much thinner, her eyes enormous and surrounded by deep purple shadows, it was once again *her* face. The horrible-looking woman encountered in the hotel had gone. She looked like Lisa Angelis again.

A bell sounded and a stampede of visitors clutching flowers and parcels passed the open door of Lisa's room on their way to the main ward. She lay and watched, feeling unreasonably envious of the other patients. After all, people had been telephoning every day about her, and Nellie would be down soon.

Sister Rolands marched in with a bundle of magazines and newspapers. 'Thought you might like something to keep you occupied,' she barked. 'According to one of my nurses who reads such rubbish, there's an article about one of your pictures in this.'

She threw a paper on Lisa's knee. 'Don't tire yourself now, or there'll be trouble,' she said threateningly as she marched out.

'I wouldn't be so tired if I was fed properly,' Lisa called and heard an answering 'Humph!' from the corridor.

She turned the pages of the paper eagerly. The article was on a centre page, accompanied by a photograph of Gloria Grenville in *The Opportunist*. It was called HOW TO TURN A CLASSIC INTO A FLOP – *Throw Money At It*!

She knew *The Opportunist* was being re-made. Busby had called more than a year ago with the news that Cahil O'Daly's heirs had sold the rights of his novel to another company, this time for a colossal sum. 'They've got a ten-million-dollar budget,' he said gloomily, 'a host of star names, and they're going on location all over the world.'

'It won't be half as good as yours,' she said soothingly, though this made him even more gloomy. Whether good or bad, the new movie would probably be shown throughout America and the world, whereas his, made on a shoestring and acknowledged by critics as a work of genius, had long ago sunk without trace, scarcely shown except in a few small cinemas.

According to the article, the new movie was a flop, a dismal failure. The script was poor, the acting terrible and the direction barely noticeable. Numerous critical comparisons were made between the first version, made fourteen years ago, and the current one – all to the advantage of the original.

'Fourteen years!' said Lisa aloud. 'It seems like only yesterday.'

'*Van Dolen's feeling for the novel was inspired, as was his direction, and his casting was perfect,*' she read, her excitement increasing. She must keep this and send it to Busby! The critic then mounted his very high horse and declared it sinful that such a perfect movie, a gem, a work of art, had been so cruelly neglected. '*Busby Van Dolen must be persuaded to re-release his version instantly,*' the writer thundered, '*so the world can see it isn't cash that makes a good film, but talent.*'

'Persuaded?' laughed Lisa. 'Busby won't need much persuading!'

There was a postscript to the article. in view of the renewed interest in Busby Van Dolen's work, a season of his films would be shown on BBC 2 later in the year.

'Shit!' said Lisa. 'I'm so happy, I could cry.'

Later on, Sister Rolands came in, took one glance at Lisa and clapped her hands disapprovingly. 'Just look at you!' she cried, 'You're over-excited.' She touched Lisa's cheek with the back of her hand. 'Burning!' she announced. 'I bet your pulse is racing.'

'How can anybody get over-excited reading the paper?'

'I don't know, but you seem to have managed it,' Sister barked.

'I feel wonderful. I'd feel even more wonderful if I had something to eat. Do you always starve your patients?'

'Only the famous ones.' She looked at Lisa critically. 'A tablet for you tonight, madam. You don't look in the mood for sleep.'

'Can I telephone my husband?' asked Lisa hopefully. She longed to talk to Busby.

'One of my nurses said you're a widow. One piece of equipment we *don't* have is a paranormal telephone.'

'I'd like to ring another husband, a live one. This one's an ex.'

'Well you can't, so there.' She bustled out, grumbling, 'These temperamental film stars, they'll be the death of me,' and Lisa grinned.

Shortly after Sister left, another young nurse came in with a plate of sandwiches. 'Sister said to say you're a bloody nuisance.' She giggled. 'I've never heard her swear before.'

'Gee, thanks.' Lisa grabbed the plate. Bread and cheese had never tasted so good.

'I'll be back in ten minutes with your tablet.'

She must have gone to sleep the second her head touched the pillow. If she had dreams, she couldn't remember them when she awoke to the rattle of a trolley being pushed down the corridor. Through the drawn curtains she could see it was still pitch-dark outside. The trolley stopped outside her room and a young girl in a green overall came in with a cup of tea.

'Good morning,' the girl sang cheerfully.

Lisa groaned. 'What time is it?'

'Five o'clock.'

'Jesus Christ, why do I have to be awake so early?'

'Don't ask me, darlin', I only work here. Up you come and drink this.' The girl hauled her into a sitting position and put the tea on the bedside table.

'What time's breakfast?'

'Half-past six. Tara for now.'

Another hour and a half before she ate. Lisa doubted if she could live that long. As she sipped her tea she remembered that Nellie was coming today and felt apprehensive. How would they greet each other? Would Nellie be cross with her for running away from the hospital? They might be really awkward with each other after all this time.

'Lizzie! Oh, my dear, dear Lizzie!'

Lisa had been half-asleep and woke to find herself being scooped up in a pair of strong arms and showered with kisses.

'Nellie! I wasn't expecting you for ages.'

'I got the first train out of Lime Street. Let me look at you! Christ, you look thin, thin but lovely.' She hugged her again and began to cry. Unable to help herself, Lisa too felt tears coursing down her cheeks. The two sisters stayed wrapped in each other's arms for several minutes, until, sniffing, they disentangled themselves. And she'd been worried Nellie might be cross, thought Lisa shamefully. Her sister was sitting on the bed, wiping her eyes. 'Oh, dear. I put mascara on specially for you. I don't usually wear it and now it's smudged.'

Nellie had only been twelve when Lisa left. She'd grown into a fine-looking woman with a rosy-cheeked, healthy beauty. Her thick brown hair, only a shade lighter than Lisa's, was cut in short curls in which the occasional silver strand shone and her brown eyes danced with merriment. 'I can't remember you having a nose like that,' said Lisa. It was short and snub.

'Stan punched it that shape,' Nellie giggled, adding hastily, 'That's a joke. He's a super bloke. I'd like you to meet him and the kids some time.' Then her face became serious and she said, 'We were all really angry with Joan for driving you away. You poor dear, coming all that way to see Mam die, then her turning on you. When she told us, so virtuously, as if she expected our approval, we could have killed her! Of course, no one could say much. Poor Joan, she was more upset over Mam dying than anybody.'

'I deserved it,' said Lisa.

'Nonsense,' said Nellie stoutly. 'Next day, we rang the airlines, trying to find out if you'd flown back, then all the posh London hotels. I was almost thankful when the hospital got in touch to say you were ill.' She gasped. 'Christ, Lizzie. I've been here all this time and haven't asked how you feel!'

'Strange as it may seem, I feel marvellous. I'm terribly weak, I can't even sit up by myself, but it's very relaxing just lying here being waited on and everybody's very nice, Sister Rolands especially.'

'Good.' Nellie looked at her fondly then began to tell her about the burial. 'It was a typical Liverpool funeral – a couple of flaming rows, mainly with Joan, lots of tears at the cemetery, then back to Chaucer Street where everybody got drunk and we ended up singing all Mam's favourite Irish songs.'

'I wish I'd been there,' said Lisa sadly. It was strange, but since she'd woken up in the hospital, she'd scarcely thought about Mam. It was as if those terrible, delirious hours between leaving Liverpool and collapsing on the train had expurgated her feelings of guilt.

'So do I.'

They talked all morning. Nellie told her about the wives – her sisters-in-law – and her multitude of nieces and nephews. Kevin was the only one so far with grandchildren, but Tony was about to achieve this status any minute. 'Everyone wants to come and see you,' she said, 'but I told them you mightn't be up to it yet.'

'I'm not,' said Lisa quickly. 'I feel far too emotional at the moment. What with Mam dying, then Joan . . . seeing you is enough for now.' She'd break down, she knew she would, if her brothers came. 'Next time there's a wedding I'll come over, I promise.'

'That's a wonderful idea – providing you mean it.'

'I mean it,' Lisa said sincerely, adding casually, 'Did Patrick come home for the funeral?'

'Patrick? Oh, you mean Paddy. No. We sent a telegram to his last-known address but there's been no reply. Naturally, we're all worried about him, but then we always are.'

Thank goodness! She had visions of Patrick living in London and dropping in to see her. Hopefully he wouldn't recognize her after all this time, but even so, Lisa preferred to put off the reunion as long as possible.

Sister Roland came in and clapped her hands imperiously. 'Time for the patient to have a little nap.'

'I don't feel the least bit tired,' protested Lisa.

'Do as you're told.' Nellie jumped to her feet. 'I'll do some last-minute Christmas shopping in Oxford Street and come back later.'

On Christmas Eve, Nellie returned to Liverpool. 'Don't let it be another quarter of a century before we meet again,' she whispered as she hugged Lisa close. 'I know I've promised to come again after Christmas but I'm worried you might disappear before I get here.'

'Sister Rolands says I'm going to be here another ten days. I'd be too frightened to disobey.'

'Lisa, my darling,' Ralph cried, 'How are you?'

'I'm fine, completely better. Which phone are you on?'

'The outside one. I'm on the patio, why?'

'I'm trying to visualize the scene.'

'It's a beautiful morning. I can just see Vita, fast asleep and pissed as a lord already. When she's sober, she keeps asking after Bobby.'

It was New Year's Day and Lisa was in Sister Rolands' office having been pronounced fit to take a telephone call. Ralph had arranged to phone in the evening, six o'clock British time.

'We missed you at Christmas,' Ralph added.

'And I missed all of you terribly.'

'When are you coming home?'

'I'm being discharged the day after tomorrow and I'll fly home immediately. I'm longing to see sunshine again.' She glanced out of the window which overlooked the hospital car park. A solitary orange lamp lit up the few vehicles which were parked there, their windscreens covered in thick frost. She shivered.

'I'll come over and bring you back.'

Lisa laughed. 'Darling, I'm as fit as a fiddle, a bit weak, that's all. I can manage perfectly well by myself.'

On the morning she was due to be discharged, Lisa was packing her few possessions in the suitcase which had been brought over from the Columbine Hotel when one of the nurses approached her. 'Are you taking your Get Well cards with you?'

'I hadn't thought about it,' Lisa replied. The top of her bedside cabinet was bulging with cards and there were more stuck to the metal headboard of the bed with sellotape – the latter concession only allowed because of Christmas. 'Why, do you want them?'

'Would you mind?'

'Of course not, help yourself.'

'We're going to share them out,' the nurse said. 'Why, there must be a card from every star in Hollywood here.'

Word must have got around that she was ill. Not only did she hear from friends, but actors she scarcely knew sent messages and flowers. Sister Rolands said disapprovingly, 'This ward is beginning to look like the Chelsea Flower Show,' as yet another extravagant bouquet arrived.

And it hadn't just been the Hollywood set who'd thought of her. She'd even heard from friends of her mam who'd gone to the funeral, where Nellie had told them Lizzie had been coming all the way from America but had fallen ill in London. One particularly poignant messsage, the most touching of all, had been from Mrs Garrett, the midwife who'd delivered her over forty years ago. Now nearly ninety, she sent a little round crocheted doily. *This was given to me by your mam for delivering Chris and it's been on my sideboard ever since. I'd like you to have it now.*

She was packed and ready to leave when a familiar figure came through the swing doors of the ward.

'Ralph, you idiot!' she cried. 'I said there was no need to come.'

He threw his arms around her. 'I *had* to. When I said I wasn't, Gary decided he'd better fly across and I swear to God Millie and Vita were threatening to come together.'

'How come I love you so much?' she whispered.

'Beats me,' he said warmly. 'I'm just glad you do.'

She felt so ashamed now of the awful thoughts she'd had in the snow outside Jackie's house, when she'd felt so lonely and isolated, and had mentally spurned her strange, unconventional family.

'Haven't you left yet?' Sister Rolands marched into the

ward and glared at Lisa. Then she transferred her frown to Ralph. 'My poor nurses are all of a twitter. I understand this is another film star causing chaos on my ward. You look vaguely familiar. I think I might have seen you in my youth.'

'I'm not sure whether I should feel flattered or not,' responded Ralph with a grin.

Turning to Lisa, Sister said, 'Well, I suppose it'll be a long time before we get another such distinguished patient.'

'I hope so for their sakes,' laughed Lisa. 'After a few weeks of being bullied by you they won't feel all that distinguished.'

'The National Health Service treats all patients equally. There's no special treatment for film stars,' the nurse said tartly. 'Even so, despite the fact you reduced my nurses to a flutter – after all, not many people can boast they gave a bedpan to Lisa Angelis – I'm sorry to see you go.'

'And I'm sorry to be going,' said Lisa quietly. 'I never thought I would enjoy a stay in hospital. As for your nurses, they're worth their weight in gold.'

Sister Rolands shook her hand firmly. After she had gone, Lisa turned to wave goodbye to the other patients and saw some eyes reflecting her own unshed tears. Several of these women were dying. Before Christmas as many patients as possible had been allowed home, some permanently, others to return after the holiday, so there had been only six left in the main ward – those too ill to be moved, and Lisa. She had been deeply affected and surprised by the strong emotional bond that had almost miraculously been forged between them, despite their differing ages and backgrounds. They had exchanged the most intimate, the most private confidences and by Boxing Day, she felt as if she had known them all her life. Those who were dying, three of them, spoke openly of their fear of death, yet incredibly, found the courage to laugh away these fears, and it was more often than not the three who still had life to live who cried and needed comfort. In that short time, a time of great joy and great sadness, Lisa learnt more about the real meaning of life than she had done in all the years that had gone before. From now on she would treat each new day as a blessing and feel lucky to be alive and well.

Chapter 36

Gary had been offered what he called a really hot property and was raring to go, subject to Ralph and Lisa's approval.

'Another thriller?' said Lisa after she had read the script. 'I think we should diversify.'

'After we've made this movie,' Gary promised.

'That's what you said last time.'

'There's a really good part in it for you,' he coaxed.

The story involved a mother and daughter living in a New York apartment block, being terrorized by an anonymous phone-caller.

'You'd be perfect as Zoe,' Gary added.

Lisa said idly, 'I'll think about it.' Zoe was the mother. She had initially thought Gary meant the daughter.

Later on she went upstairs and examined herself closely in the mirror. It was a month since she'd got back from England and not only had she regained the weight lost, but long hours lazing by the pool meant she had at last acquired the tan she'd always wanted. Her dark golden limbs, smooth and silky, were shown off to perfection by her white shorts and halter top. She bent forward so her face was only inches away from the glass. Underneath her eyes she could see fine, barely discernible lines, though there were none around her mouth or on her forehead. She blinked. The close inspection had strained her eyes and she remembered the difficulty she'd had in reading Gary's script; she'd blamed it on a worn typewriter ribbon, though the depressing fact was that she probably needed glasses. Sighing, Lisa stepped back in order to see her full reflection. There was no doubt about it – she was still a beautiful woman, but there was equally no doubt that she was a beautiful *forty-year-old* woman.

'I'll look better with some make-up on,' she thought, grabbing a jar of cream. She was smoothing it into her cheeks when she stopped, aware of the slightly frantic expression on her face as she tried to rub away the years. She put the jar down and smiled at herself. Everybody grew old and there was no reason to expect the Almighty to excuse her from the aging process. What did a few wrinkles matter anyway? In hospital she'd exchanged addresses with the other women in her ward, and yesterday had received a letter to say that two of them had died. One, Donna, had been only twenty-five; she hadn't been given the opportunity to grow old and wrinkled.

Lisa marched downstairs and told Gary she'd be happy to play the part of Zoe. 'I've been thinking,' he said. 'You look too young to be the mother. Perhaps we could turn them into sisters.'

'Please yourself,' said Lisa. 'I don't mind.'

She did mind, though. After an inward struggle she decided she was only human after all and couldn't deny that she felt immensely flattered.

Later that year she worked with Busby Van Dolen again. His first eight movies had been re-released and at last reached the audiences they deserved. Even his final independent production, the lighthearted *Mr & Mrs Jones*, was declared to have qualities unnoticed at first – much to his amusement – though it was *Easy Dreams* and *The Opportunist* which received particular acclaim. Lisa suddenly found herself in great demand. After making Gary's thriller, she went straight to Busby's set.

Her ex-husband had lost none of his old enthusiasm. Apart from the fact that his bushy hair and beard had turned grey, it could have been the old Busby again, urging, cajoling and bullying them into giving their finest performances. With finance no longer a problem – nowadays he was *approached* by investors eager to sink money into his films – he could afford the very best sets, or go on location wherever he wanted. Busby being Busby, he sought out all the old technicians, the cameramen, the set-designers with whom he used to work. Even Maggie Nestor, who'd long ago taken reluctant early retirement, was unearthed to provide the costumes for the new production. When they all met again, not a few tears were shed as they recalled old times. Again,

Busby being Busby, he got impatient with them all and told them sternly to pull themselves together and concentrate on what they had to do now.

The leading man was an actor of some repute – a tall, rakish Welshman called Hugo Swann, a notorious womanizer with a penchant for the bottle. Lisa came prepared to dislike him, but like everyone else on set was quickly bowled over by his lazy, irresistible charm.

'I always sleep with my leading ladies,' he drawled when they met.

'I thought you always married them.' He'd just gone through a messy, very public divorce from his fifth wife.

'Is that a proposal?' He smiled down at her, his blue eyes twinkling.

Lisa felt her stomach give a pleasant quiver. 'Definitely not. I'm too old, anyway. You only seem to marry teenagers.'

'Ouch!' He pretended to wince. 'How about mothering me, then? Take me out to dinner tonight, then come back to my hotel and tuck me in.'

Lisa was tempted. Her bed had felt lonely since she'd got back from England, but with Busby around it could prove embarrassing.

'I'm sorry, but no,' she said regretfully.

If only things had been different, thought Lisa later, watching Busby prowl around the studio. If he hadn't called her Lizzie that night, they might still be together, though that would mean she wouldn't have met Dent, wouldn't have been living in Tymperleys.

Perhaps Busby was thinking along the same lines, for on the final day of shooting he said casually, 'Like to come back to my place and talk about old times?' and Lisa, nostalgic for the past, agreed.

But nothing had changed. He made love briefly and inadequately, then fell asleep whilst she lay beside him aching with the passion he had the ability to arouse but which he could never satisfy. Even if he hadn't called her Lizzie, in the long run their marriage would never have worked, she thought sadly.

Stealthily, she crept out of bed and went into the kitchen

where she put on her glasses and looked through the directory for the number of Hugo Swann's hotel.

'Are you alone?' she asked immediately he answered.

'Sad to say, yes,' he replied morosely.

'In that case, would you like me to come round and tuck you in?'

It was well over a year before Lisa returned to Liverpool.

'*I've been nagging someone to get married so you can come,*' wrote Nellie. '*But all of a sudden young people feel it's all right to live in sin. Can you imagine the reaction if one of us had just gone off to live openly with someone of the opposite sex! Remember the endless gossip when a girl had an illegitimate baby? Nowadays no one gives a damn. I'm not sure whether I feel censorious or envious! Anyway, Chris's son Stephen is getting spliced in April . . .*'

Lisa bought a moderately-priced plain grey flannel suit, not wanting to stand out in something outrageously fashionable and expensive.

'What do you think?' she asked Millie when she got home.

Millie looked her up and down and asked what prison she intended working at. 'They'll be disappointed, you turning up like that,' she said flatly. 'They expect you to look like a film star, not like you've come to arrest them. Take it back and get something different.'

Vita came in carrying the inevitable glass of whisky. 'Hi, Bobby. You joined up or something?' She saluted.

'I like folks who speak their mind,' said Lisa. 'Both of you have given my confidence a really big boost.'

'Don't be so damn sarcastic. If you don't want a body to give an honest opinion, you shouldn't come asking for it,' Millie said. 'Now get out of my kitchen before I throw a plate at you.'

'Have these houses always been here?' Lisa asked.

'No, they built them because you were coming, Liz,' Jimmie grinned.

She jammed her elbow into his ribs and remembered doing the same thing when they were children. 'You know what I mean,' she giggled. 'The only part of Liverpool I'm familiar with is Bootle. I never knew houses like this existed.'

The girl Stephen was marrying came from Calderstones. 'Where the really well-off people live,' Nellie said. As they drove to the church, Lisa was surprised to see big detached houses which wouldn't have been out of place in Hollywood.

'Stephen's father-in-law is a solicitor,' explained Jimmie, adding with a wicked grin, 'I never thought the day would come when an O'Brien would marry into a family that votes Conservative.'

'Now don't you start an argument at the reception,' warned Nellie. She was sitting with her husband, Stan, in the pull-down seats opposite. 'Heath isn't such a bad chap. He doesn't get under the skin the way Macmillan did.'

'Who's Heath?' asked Lisa.

'Edward Heath, the Prime Minister.' Jimmie regarded her with mock astonishment. 'Christ, you've grown up ignorant, Liz!'

'Don't take any notice of him,' said Stan mildly. 'If you could make a living getting up people's noses, he'd be a millionaire.' Stan was a bespectacled bookish-looking man who worked for a transport company. On the other side of Jimmie, his new young wife, who had so far remained tongue-tied, murmured heartfelt agreement.

Lisa turned to look out of the window. It was a fresh and sparkling morning, though the brilliant sunshine was deceptive; there'd been a chill in the air when they left Nellie's house. The trees, full of young green leaves, swayed gently and dappled shadows danced on the grass verges. Even from inside the car, she could smell the freshness, the vibrant tang of spring.

'We're here,' someone said and the limousine drew to a smooth stop outside the church.

As they walked up the path, Lisa felt glad she'd taken Millie's advice and bought another outfit – a vivid scarlet linen suit with tan leather inserts on the shoulders, a wide leather belt and a red straw picture hat – when she noticed the bride's parents and relatives were far more expensively and showily dressed than the O'Briens. 'They're rotten with money,' Nellie whispered.

Chris came over and took Lisa's hand. She'd met him, along with all her brothers – except Paddy – the night before at Nellie's. 'C'mon, I'm going to enjoy introducing you to the in-laws. This guy was Lord Mayor of Liverpool once and never stops telling you.'

He took her up to a stout couple, oozing self-importance and wealth. The woman wore an emerald-green brocade coat and dress, and a pillbox hat decorated with billowing green ostrich feathers. She had a five-strand row of pink pearls around her reddening neck.

Tony introduced them. 'Charles and Rita Slattery. This is Stephen's auntie, my sister, Lisa Angelis.'

'Not *the* Lisa Angelis?' The woman blanched as they shook hands and looked Lisa up and down, her eyes narrowing in surprise.

The man plucked at his striped waistcoat uncomfortably. 'Stephen mentioned it once. We didn't . . . well, we thought . . . '

'That he was having you on?' Chris said gleefully. 'Well, he wasn't. This is Lisa – our Lizzie – in the flesh.'

The rest of the occasion passed in a daze. They went from the church to the reception in a large hotel in Woolton. As time went on, Lisa felt the gap of years away from her family dwindle until it seemed as though they'd never been apart. Her older brothers were their normal demonstrative selves – she remembered vividly the amount of hugging and kissing that used to go on in Chaucer Street. Every now and then she noticed one of the twins, Sean and Dougal, who'd grown into quiet, serious-looking young men, staring at her curiously. They'd only been four when she left. To them she was little more than a stranger. Paddy was away again; the best man read a telegram from Syria.

In the middle of the afternoon, Lisa suddenly noticed that most of the men had disappeared. 'Where's Stan?' she asked Nellie. 'And all the boys?'

'Where do you think?' her sister said sarcastically. 'They've gone to the match. Liverpool are playing at home. Even the bride had a job making Stephen stay behind.'

Lisa said quietly, 'I see Joan isn't here.'

Nellie looked uncomfortable. 'I hoped you wouldn't notice.'

'I noticed the minute we got to church.' She'd looked for Joan straight away, hoping to make up with her.

'Once she knew you'd be here she refused to come. Poor Joan,' said Nellie with a sigh. 'She's spent her whole life cutting off her nose to spite her face.' She looked at Lisa anxiously. 'It hasn't spoilt your day though, has it?'

'Of course not,' Lisa assured her. 'It's great seeing my family again – and my new family. All these nieces and nephews and sisters-in-law I never knew I had, not forgetting my sole brother-in-law, Stan. He's a lovely chap, Nellie. You're very lucky.'

'I know I am.' Nellie nodded then looked at her sister keenly. 'But what about you, Liz? Have you got anybody?'

'I have a lover,' Lisa said bluntly. 'Though we don't see each other very often, just between movies.'

'Is it someone we know?'

'Hugo Swann.'

Nellie's jaw dropped. 'Hugo Swann! Jesus, Mary and Joseph, d'you mean to say I've got a sister who's sleeping with Hugo Swann?'

Lisa grinned. 'You have.'

Just then, Nellie's son Luke came rushing over and grabbed Lisa's hand. 'Auntie Lisa, come with me a minute.'

'Not now, love,' said Nellie.

'I'll go,' Lisa said quickly. 'You know I can't resist him.'

She'd fallen in love with Luke the night before. A happy outgoing nine-year-old with wide, innocent eyes and a shock of blond curly hair, he was a typical O'Brien. 'He's exactly the son I would have wanted myself,' thought Lisa wistfully, the minute she set eyes on him.

'Surely you shouldn't be in here,' she said. Luke had dragged her into the bar, full of strangers who were nothing to do with the wedding.

'This man won't believe you're my auntie.'

He stopped in front of a stout man clutching a pint of beer and swaying backwards and forwards, very much the worse for drink.

'Tell him you're my auntie,' demanded Luke.

'I'm his auntie,' Lisa said.

The stout man peered blearily at her. Gradually, recognition dawned in his glazed eyes. He carefully put his glass down on the nearest table and fainted dead away.

'One last toast,' said Kevin, 'and one last song. The toast is "Mam", to our mam, the best mother anyone could ever have, and the song is *When Irish Eyes Are Smiling*, to be sung by our Lizzie, the prodigal returned.'

'I couldn't possibly,' Lisa gasped. 'I'm far too drunk.'

'Sing, sing,' everybody chanted. It was nearly half-past ten and the new in-laws and their assorted relatives had long ago broken up their staid circle and come to join the O'Briens. Charles Slattery was playing a rowdy piano when Lisa found herself being picked up, carried over to the piano and placed on top. Charles stood up and gave her a wet kiss. 'What key do you want?'

'Any key?'

'Good, that's the only one I know.'

She began to sing. All those lessons years ago, yet this was the first time she'd sung in public. Halfway through her début, she thought of Mam and broke down, but by then the song had already been taken up by the crowd. The wedding party ended in tears and laughter. 'As all good weddings should,' said Nellie with a satisfied smile when they were on their way home to Crosby.

Chapter 37

Ralph had been threatening to return to the theatre for years. His film career had long been over, though Lisa and Gary always tried to create a part for him in their current movie. Sometimes this was almost too obvious and Ralph smilingly turned the part down. Lisa wondered if the smile hid a sense of hurt.

In the summer, he gathered together a group of actors – old hands like himself and half a dozen youngsters waiting for their big break. 'I'm not going to tout around for parts any longer,' he announced. 'I'll start with my own little touring company.' His name was still big enough to attract audiences in small-town theatres. 'Would you like to join us?' he asked Lisa hopefully.

She recalled how it was seeing him in *Pygmalion* that had inspired her to become an actress. Nothing she had seen since, either on stage or screen, had impressed her so much as his powerful performance in that play. Nevertheless, she made a face, saying, 'A live audience would frighten me to death. I might forget my lines!' Anyway, she was deeply involved with O'Brien Productions, acting in some movies, producing others, and sometimes even doing both.

She and Gary flew over to Maine for the opening night of Ralph's first stop on his tour of the eastern states. The play was *Uncle Vanya* and Ralph's acting was poor; he kept stumbling over his lines and lacked the power and presence of his younger days. When they went backstage, Lisa was trying to think of a tactful way of criticizing his performance, but to her relief he seemed well aware of his shortcomings.

'I'll grow into the part,' he said confidently.

A rosy-cheeked young actor who had a minor role came up and put his hand on Ralph's shoulder. 'The press would like a word,' he said. There was something familiar about the gesture and beside her Lisa felt Gary stiffen.

Ralph groaned. 'I can just imagine the notices: "*A crowd of old has-beens and would-be hopefuls inflicting their negligible talents on us iggerant out-of-towners.*" Instead, when he posted the reviews to them a few days later they were quite flattering. The reviewer wrote that although there'd been a few hitches on the first night, he'd felt privileged to have seen the great Ralph Layton in the flesh.

Nellie and Stan came over with the children the following Christmas. Natalie, a typical bored teenager, was determined not to be impressed by anything, but Luke was bowled over by everything he saw, particularly the pool.

'Can you teach me to swim, please, Auntie Lisa?' he pleaded.

Lisa promised and took the family on a tour of Tymperleys, Vita trotting behind pointing out things she missed. 'To think of an O'Brien owning a property like this!' said Nellie in amazement. 'And we thought we'd moved up in the world when we bought a semi-detached.'

Lisa showed Gary a script she said she'd been sent by a writer called Mary Smith about six women spending Christmas together in a hospital ward. 'It's both funny and sad,' she said. 'I think we should do it.'

After he'd read it, Gary said he liked the basic idea but the dialogue was appalling, too contrived and unnatural. 'We could get an experienced scriptwriter to work on it, but the main characters should be cut down to four. Six is too many to give much depth to in ninety minutes. The title is a definite no-no, too. *Christmas at St Elspeth's* is too clumsy by a mile. Write to the author and get his opinion.'

'Her opinion,' corrected Lisa. 'I've already spoken to her on the phone and I know she won't mind.'

The script was handed to one of their writers, and when a revised version arrived a few months later with a new title, *Hearts and Flowers*, Gary began to get enthusiastic. 'I suppose you see yourself as the actress?' he said to Lisa.

'I'd feel at home in the part,' she replied. She'd no intention of telling anyone she'd written it. It was too private and intimate.

Work began on *Hearts and Flowers* at the end of the year and Lisa threw herself, as she'd never done before, into the part of the wealthy actress who finds herself in a charity hospital over the Christmas holiday.

With an almost feminine intuition, Gary seemed to recognize how women would feel in this situation, and Lisa was impressed by the sensitivity with which he directed them. Sometimes the four actresses found themselves shedding real tears which did not cease when the cameras stopped rolling, though on the other hand, there were times when they couldn't stop laughing either.

When the film was complete, Gary claimed it was his best work to date. 'Do you think Mary Smith will come to the opening?' he asked.

'No,' Lisa replied. 'She's too shy.'

Gary gave one of his rare smiles. 'Gee, that's a shame,' he said innocently. 'Y'know, I feel as if I know Mary already. Isn't that strange? Maybe she'll write something else one day.'

'I doubt it. Mary Smith only had the one script in her.'

'Well, I'm glad I was the guy who got it.' He rubbed his hands together with a mixture of anxiety and nervousness. 'I've never felt quite *this* uptight before an opening. I didn't realize till now, but I've never put so much of myself into a movie before.'

Remembering how cruel the critics had been to Busby, Lisa found herself equally on edge as the June opening drew close. She too felt she had given her finest performance, the best of which she was capable. 'I'll never act so well again,' she thought. If the critics slammed her, she decided she'd give up acting altogether.

'I didn't know whether to laugh or cry.'

'This heart-warming, heart-rending movie had me leaving the theatre emotionally drained.'

'Plucks at the heart-strings.'

'Oscar-winning performances from all four women.'

'Gary Maddox has proved himself one of our finest directors.'

409

They'd been standing on the corner of Hollywood and Vine for half an hour, waiting for the early-morning editions of the newspapers to arrive. There were a dozen people there – most of the small cast of *Hearts and Flowers* and Hugo Swann, Ralph and Vita – all drunk, more with excitement than alcohol. When the van drew up with a screech of brakes and several bundles of newspapers were thrown at their feet, they pounced and tore the bundles apart with eager, desperate hands. 'If the reaction of the audience is anything to go by, the notices are bound to be good,' someone said hoarsely.

Then they began to read the reviews to each other, all yelling at once. 'Listen to what Maurice Edelman says!' 'Hey, we even got Pauline Kael to cry!'

They stood staring at each other, lightheaded with relief, voices tremulous with excitement.

'What do we do now?' asked Gary. 'We can't go home, I'm on a high.'

'This calls for a slap-up dinner,' drawled Hugo. 'Come on, folks, let's find a restaurant. The meal's on me.'

'*Dinner*?' Vita's face was a mixture of disgust and disdain. 'After *my* premières, we used to have a fuckin' orgy.'

For three years, Ralph had been doggedly touring the country with his small band of actors. When he came home in the summer to rehearse a new programme of plays, a mixture of the classics and comedy, Lisa was thrilled to find *Pygmalion* had been included. She suggested he use Dent's studio as a rehearsal room, and for two months the house was loud with the laughter and noise of actors, young and old, as they rehearsed from early morning, often until midnight.

'You're certainly working me hard my last month,' complained Millie. 'I made more meatloaf these last few weeks than I made in my whole doggone life.' Millie had decided the time had come to retire. At the end of the month she was going to move in permanently with her daughter. 'I'm too old to be on my feet all day long.'

'I don't want to let you go,' whispered Lisa. She stood behind the old black woman and put her arms around her neck. 'The house won't be the same without you. Why don't you stay and I'll hire another cook?'

'For Chrissakes, Lisa! You can't go round filling your house up with everybody you sets your eyes on. You gotta learn to live by yourself someday. Now, out of my kitchen and let me get on with some work.' Millie banged a saucepan down on the stove – a clear indication she was moved.

The rosy-cheeked boy Lisa had seen in Maine was still with the company and she wondered if Gary minded. One day when they'd both been sitting in on a rehearsal, she noticed the youth lean against Ralph affectionately when the play had finished, and she turned to look at Gary curiously. To her surprise he gave a wan smile. 'He's old and easily flattered,' he said gently – Ralph had passed his sixtieth birthday earlier in the year. 'I don't mind as long as he comes home to me.'

'I remember him saying that once about Michael.' Lisa felt bemused. She would have expected Ralph to be the one to remain steadfast and loyal, but instead it was Gary, the one-time blond and handsome heart-throb whom she'd once considered superficial and shallow.

Nellie wrote to say that Patrick had got married in Saudi Arabia. 'He sent a photo of Pita, she's half-Indian, really beautiful – a bit like you in looks. He's forty-one, you know. I wonder why he waited so long? Still, better late than never, as Mam always said.'

She finished, 'Things have been exciting here politically. The Conservatives have elected a woman leader, Margaret Thatcher. She'll be no match for Harold Wilson, but imagine the country led by a woman! If they get in again, it'll feel strange. What do you think?'

Lisa sat staring at the letter for a long time. She didn't know what to think – about anything.

Gary was nominated for an Oscar for Hearts and Flowers along with one of the actresses, Dorothy West, who'd played the part of a woman twice her age. Lisa felt a twinge of jealousy when she first heard the news but brushed it aside. Their good news was equalled by Ralph's when he rang to say the off-Broadway production of Pygmalion had reached the attention of national critics and he'd had an offer to go to England to play King Lear. When he came home a few weeks later she heard him arguing angrily with Gary.

'Doesn't he want you to go?' she asked Ralph later.

'It's not that at all. I'm scared to go and he insists I should.'

'I think you should too,' she said, doing her best to sound convincing. Millie had left a few months ago and if Ralph went he could be gone a whole year. Secretly she hoped he'd stay.

'I'm worried I'm past it.'

'They wouldn't have asked you if they thought that.' She patted his shoulder. 'Dent was right, you know. You wasted your talents in Hollywood. There's still time to be a great actor, though I'd lose some weight if I were you. I'm sure King Lear isn't supposed to be a fatty.'

Gary came back to Tymperleys from seeing Ralph off on the plane to England. Lisa expressed surprise. 'I thought you'd go straight to the set,' she said. 'I only stayed at home to make a heap of telephone calls.' O'Brien Productions had just started on a political thriller loosely based on the Watergate affair. Lisa's part wasn't due to be shot for another two weeks.

'I've been feeling really lousy for a while.' Gary rubbed his forehead. He looked flushed, as if he had a chill. 'I think I'll go and lie down for the rest of the day. I would have done before, but I didn't want Ralph to know I felt bad in case he didn't go.'

He went upstairs. When Lisa looked in on him during the evening he was fast asleep. It must be really serious for Gary to take a day off when he was making a movie. Next morning he said he felt better and went off early to the studio. When Lisa arrived later, Les Norman, the assistant director said, 'Gary had to go home. He kept going dizzy.'

'Perhaps he's run-down or something,' Lisa said worriedly. That night, after finding Gary in bed with a raging temperature, she said, 'I think I'd better call a doctor.'

Dr Myerson had been a friend of Dent's. He came within the hour – a stocky middle-aged man who rarely smiled.

'You should be up and running within a week,' he said to

the patient, though seven days later Gary's condition was unchanged. The doctor came back and pronounced himself mystified. 'I think you'd better come into hospital straight away and have some tests.'

'He can't,' said Lisa, who was hovering in the background.

'Absolutely not,' Gary concurred. 'Tomorrow night's the Oscars and I'll be there if they have to carry me.'

'I wonder if Dent is watching.' Gary looked up as if he half-expected to see Joseph Dent hanging like a big black bat from the roof of the large theatre where the Oscars ceremony was being held.

'I doubt it,' said Lisa. 'If he's in a position to watch anything, it'll be one of his own movies.'

Hearts and Flowers didn't win any awards, but the next best thing happened: Busby Van Dolen won the Oscar for Best Director. The night out seemed to do Gary good and next day he returned to work, apparently recovered.

'I think Gary's driving himself too hard. He looks like death.' Les Norman came over and spoke to Lisa between takes. She glanced across the studio. Even from here, she could see perspiration glistening on Gary's forehead and his face was drawn, his cheeks hollow.

'He's lost a lot of weight, too,' Les added. Gary's clothes were hanging loosely on his suddenly gaunt body. 'I guess he must be really run-down or something.'

'I've only just realized how bad he looks,' said Lisa. Last night she'd joked with Gary, 'You missing Millie's meat-loaf?' when he'd pushed his plate away, the food scarcely touched, yet Chloe, the woman hired to take Millie's place, was a good cook. It dawned on Lisa that he'd done that a lot lately.

'I think you should go into hospital and have those tests the doctor suggested,' she said gently to Gary that night.

He looked up, his eyes drawn and tired. 'I'm too scared,' he confessed in a shaky voice. She began to argue with him, but he just pushed his untouched dinner away, saying mutinously, 'I'm going to bed.' Seconds later there was a crash, and she found that Gary had passed out on the stairs.

When Lisa went to collect him from the hospital a few days later, Gary was still in bed and he looked terrible. 'What's wrong?' She felt frightened.

'I've got PGL,' he said with a weak smile.

'What on earth's that?'

'Persistent generalized enlargement of the lymph nodes. In other words, I got lumps all over me that shouldn't be there. I should have told the doctor before.'

'You mean you've had these lumps a long time?' she asked angrily.

'A few months. I was worried it was cancer.'

A young woman came into the room. 'Hi, I'm Dr Evans. Your friend's pretty sick. We can keep him here longer if you like.'

'What do you mean, if I like?'

'Well, there's nothing we can do for him. Once he gets over his viral infection, the swellings will go and he'll be fine. He just needs looking after in the meantime.'

'Can't I look after him at home?' asked Lisa.

'If you're willing.'

'Of *course* I'm willing! He's family.'

Gary made a half-hearted protest. 'I can't expect you to — '

'Shut up,' she told him. 'You're coming back with me this minute.'

'It'll have to be by ambulance,' said the doctor. 'I doubt if he can make it to the car.'

'I can't understand it,' said Dr Myerson to Lisa. 'No matter what I give him, he gets worse instead of better.' He'd come downstairs from seeing Gary, looking both mystified and worried. 'I keep in touch with Dr Evans from the hospital and quite frankly, we've run out of ideas. It's really peculiar, to put it mildly.'

'The lumps haven't gone?'

'No, and that rash is really bad.'

'He didn't say he had a rash,' said Lisa, pulling a face.

'That's because he doesn't want to worry you. It's all over his body.' The doctor sighed. 'I wonder if you should contact his family.'

'Is it *that* serious?' Lisa was horrified. Was he suggesting that someone as apparently healthy as Gary could die from a chill?

Dr Myerson fiddled with the handle of his black bag. 'He's gay, isn't he?'

'Yes,' she replied bluntly.

Looking uncomfortable, the doctor continued, 'One of my colleagues told me about a patient he'd heard of with the same prognosis as Gary and – well, I'm afraid he died. He was gay too.' He shrugged. 'It's probably just a coincidence.'

'I'll get in touch with his father. His mother died a few years back.'

The doctor's words still ringing in her ears, Lisa went upstairs. Gary was asleep and she looked at him as a stranger would and was shocked at the deterioration. He was like a skeleton, the skin on his face a strange ivory colour and tissue-thin. Vita was sitting beside him, completely sober. She'd taken his illness really hard. 'He's not gonna get better,' she whispered.

'Don't say that!' said Lisa angrily, but Vita ignored her.

'I hate people dying. It's bad enough when old people go, but when young people die, I hate it.' She picked up Gary's hand and stroked it gently. 'He's a really nice kid. I like him and he's a truly great director. He's the only one here who treated me like a fuckin' actress and not an eccentric old woman.'

'You're a fuckin' eccentric old actress.' Gary had opened his eyes and was looking at Vita blearily. 'Y'know what I'd like, Lisa?'

'What, darling?'

'I'd like my bed moved downstairs into the cinema so's I

can watch movies.'

'I'll get someone in to do it in the morning,' she promised.

Les Norman called in to see Gary. 'My God, Lisa,' he said afterwards, 'he looks terrible! What's the matter with him?'

'I don't know,' Lisa answered. 'No one does. They took him back into hospital for more tests last week. All they can think of is his immune system has gone.'

'What does that mean?'

'It means he can't recover from anything he happens to catch. He was going in for radiotherapy for his rash but the side-effects made him feel so bad he refuses to go again. Anyway, that wasn't doing him any good, either.'

Les said casually, 'What's going to happen with O'Brien Productions, Lisa? We're scheduled to start on *Central Park* in two weeks' time.'

The Watergate movie had been completed under Les's direction and was due to be released soon. He'd done a competent job but lacked Gary's flair. 'I've got most of the production side sorted out,' said Lisa, 'though I'll be in each day to check how things are going. Should we hire a guest director, or can you manage?'

'I can manage,' Les said with alacrity.

'Good,' she replied, cynically noting the way his eyes lit up with greedy excitement.

'You haven't told Ralph I'm ill?'

'I promised I wouldn't,' said Lisa.

'And under no circumstances tell my father.'

'I won't.' In fact she had telephoned Gary's father weeks ago and he'd said, 'As far as I'm concerned he's been sick ever since he moved in with that old actor, so don't bother me again,' and slammed the receiver down.

Vita cut down on her drinking and spent all day with Gary in the cinema, where the middle rows of seats had been removed to take the big bed. The pair of them sat hour after hour watching films.

'It's not good for either of you. You're getting no fresh air,' Lisa complained.

'Fresh air ain't half as healthy as the air inside a movie-house,' said Vita. 'Watchin' that screen is a far better tonic for Gary than sitting under a fuckin' tree or something.'

The two of them burst into giggles and Lisa smiled. Sometimes there was almost a party atmosphere in the cinema as the old woman regaled Gary with her fund of dirty jokes and a string of lurid tales from her days in silent movies. The other day Lisa had come in while they were watching one of Vita's old films and found him almost falling out of bed from laughing.

'See this bit?' Vita was saying, pointing to a love-scene with a male star who'd become a household name. 'I'm supposed to be saying I'll love him till death do us part and all that crap. 'Stead, I told him his breath was worse than a goat's fart and if he stuck his tongue down my throat again I'd bite if off and stuff it you know where!'

At other times she found them singing together, Vita's voice surprisingly youthful, Gary's cracked and hoarse. No doubt this was an unconventional way to lend a sick, possibly dying man, but he seemed as happy as anyone could be under the circumstances. In fact she was surprised at the equanimity, the stoicism with which Gary had accepted changing from a healthy, vigorous man into a virtually bed-bound invalid in the course of three or four months. Only occasionally did his remarkable control give way and he would cry, 'What's happening to me? When am I going to get better?'

Vita excused herself. 'I'm just going to the ladies' room.'

After she'd gone, Gary clasped Lisa's hand. 'I'm not gonna make it, am I?'

'Don't be silly,' she began, but he squeezed her fingers with a strength that surprised her.

'Shush,' he whispered. 'Don't lie to me.'

She stroked his face with her other hand and thought how terrible he looked. What was left of his hair grew in little tufts out of his shining skull – she'd shaved his beard off weeks ago – and his sunken eyes seemed to stare out from the back of his head. At the same time there was a strange beauty in the gritty heroism of his expression. His next words surprised her. 'You never liked me much, did you?'

'Not at first,' she said honestly.

'I never liked you much, either.'

She smiled. 'Then what are we doing here like this?'

He looked puzzled. 'I ask myself that sometimes. I suppose people just get thrown together and . . . ' He sighed and didn't finish.

'And what?'

'I dunno.' He began to cough and she could hear the raw grating noise inside his chest. She took a paper handkerchief and wiped his mouth. 'Thanks,' he muttered. Neither spoke for a few minutes, then Gary took a deep breath. 'I gotta tell you this now before it gets too late, but I love you, Lisa, far more than I ever loved Ralph, but it's not sex. It's just . . . ' He licked his dry lips. Finding the right words was an effort. 'Pure love, I guess.'

Lisa felt a rush of tears. 'Oh Gary, I don't want you to die.' She pressed her cheek against his and began to cry. 'You see, I've grown to love you too,' she sobbed.

When Gary could no longer get out of bed, she hired a night nurse to sit with him, but after two nights the woman declared she wasn't coming any more. 'I don't like what's wrong with him. I never seen anything like it before. Whatever it is, I don't wanna catch it.' So Lisa gave up going into the office and took turns with Vita sitting with the patient, though for all the old woman's cheerfulness, she was beginning to look exhausted and sometimes when Lisa went into the cinema she found both of them asleep, Vita's head resting on Gary's sharp jutting knees, a bright blank screen in front of them and the noise of the projector whirring behind.

'This is a perfect way to die,' said Gary. At least, that's what Lisa thought he said. These last few days his words had become slurred and difficult to understand. 'Watching movies.' He blinked. His sunken eyes were red-raw from viewing the vivid, flickering images only twenty feet away. 'Next best thing to makin' them. Thanks, Lisa. Thanks for everything.'

'I think you should rest your eyes,' she said softly. 'How about some music for a change?'

'Music? Dent's music? That'd be nice.'

'I'll put the loud-speaker system on. What would you like?'

'That stuff he played the first morning we were here.'

'Wagner?'

'Yeah, I liked that.'

Lisa went upstairs. Over the past week the weather in Los Angeles had been strange. Through the lattice windows she could see dark threatening clouds drifting across the livid angry sky, and thunder rumbled in the distance. Another storm was on the way. She inserted the tape and vibrant, turbulent music filled the old, dark rooms, together with the equally restless spirit of Joseph Dent. Lisa shivered. The house seemed to be crackling with an almost palpable tension. She decided that before going back to Gary, she'd make a cup of tea and a sandwich.

The kitchen was spotless. There was no sign of Chloe, who went home each evening. Lisa glanced at the clock on the stove. Just before six – though whether that was morning or night, she didn't know. She'd been with Gary for so long she'd lost track of time. Thunder growled, closer now, and she heard rain splatter against the windows. She jumped when Vita came into the kitchen, still in her dressing gown, her eyes blinking with tiredness. Lisa had never seen her look so old.

'I overslept, dammit,' she complained. 'These storms, they seem to sap all my energy.'

'Go back to bed, dear. I'm just making some tea. Would you like to take a cup back with you?'

'No, but I'll go and sit with Gary while you get some rest.' Vita turned and swayed, clutching at the door for support. Lisa leapt over and helped her back upstairs, Vita complaining all the time, 'I want to sit with Gary.'

'After you've had a sleep. The storm might be over by then.'

'I like that music.'

'Is it too loud? Shall I turn it down?'

'No, we used that for one of my movies. I can't remember which.'

Lisa pulled the bedclothes up. 'Goodnight, or perhaps it's good morning!'

Vita managed to smile. 'You're a good sort, y'know that Lisa?'

As Lisa ran down the stairs, she realized it was the first time Vita had called her by her real name.

In the cinema, Gary's eyes were closed. Lisa sat beside him, touching his hand to indicate she was there. He lifted a finger to acknowledge her presence and mumbled, 'Is Dent with you?'

'No, darling.' For some reason she felt the hairs on her neck stiffen.

'He's somewhere about. He's in the music.'

Down here the sound seemed to be crashing against the walls, as if they were within a swiftly-moving ball of music that would never stop.

'There were an awful lot of movies I still had to make.'

'I know.' She'd long ago stopped pretending there was hope. 'Someone will make them.'

He began to cry silently. Lisa held his hand, too full of sadness to speak. After a while, unable to help herself, she began to doze and was woken by a crash of thunder that rocked the room. Terrified, without thinking, she clutched at Gary's hand, more for her own comfort than his and was shocked to find it icy cold. Frantically she began to rub it warm. Then she noticed that Gary's head had fallen to one side, and his mouth hung open. She stood up and straightened his head, closed his mouth and picked up his other hand to tuck under the quilt, but that was frozen too and finally, reluctantly, her tired brain told her Gary was dead.

She telephoned Dr Myerson, who promised to come immediately, then she went upstairs to tell Vita. But perhaps Vita already knew. Something had told her that she'd played her last part. She lay, curled on her side, exactly as Lisa had left her, with the smile still on her face, and she was as cold as Gary.

Chapter 38

The big house had never been so quiet or felt so cold. Lisa was convinced she could hear the whispering of age-old ghosts behind the closed doors of the empty rooms as she wandered around the corridors of Tymperleys.

'Why, oh why do things have to change?' she moaned aloud, as if God would stop people dying to please her! Vita had been over eighty and not long for this world, anyway.

She went out to the pool; outside seemed warmer than in. The recent spate of thunderstorms had ceased about a week ago and there was a tangy freshness to the mid-morning air as if it had been cleansed and renewed, though by midday it would be baking out here. The pool-boy had arrived earlier and was scrubbing the rim of the bright-blue mosaic basin. He wore trunks and his body had been burnt nutmeg brown by the sun.

When he saw her the boy waved. 'Hi, Miss Angelis.'

Lisa tried to remember his name. Daniel, that was it. 'Hello, there,' she shouted. 'Would you like some lemonade and cookies when you've finished, Daniel?'

'Gee, thanks, but no, I've got another two jobs later,' he shouted back.

She sighed and sank down on a lounger to watch the boy. He was no more than thirteen or fourteen. The budding muscles in his young back rippled as he worked and she wondered dispassionately if the baby she'd carried those few short months when she was his age had been a boy. What joy it would have been to have had her own family – children conceived and carried in her womb, though the time would have come when they too would have left to live their own lives. By now, all might have gone and she could still be alone, though there might have been a husband. She backtracked over her life: if this had happened or if that *hadn't* happened, how would things have turned out?

The telephone began to ring and she ignored it. Chloe was out shopping so it would stay unanswered. Busby had called a lot lately. 'Darling, you can't stay in that big house all on your own.' He implored her to move in with him, but she refused. No point in starting *that* all over again, yet she was moved by his reliability, the dogged persistence of his love for her. Hugo Swann had taken flight when Gary first became sick, frightened by the mere mention of illness. A few months ago he'd married a model thirty years his junior.

Lisa knew she was being awkward. Several folk from O'Brien Productions kept demanding to know when she'd be back, though as she pointed out, the still-expanding company was quite capable of functioning without its three founders. Les Norman said there was a part in the next movie which would be perfect for her.

'I don't want to rush out and bury myself in work. I want to sort my mind out in my own time in my own home,' she said to herself.

Ralph tried to persuade her to come back to London with him. He'd arrived, numb with shock, for Gary's funeral. 'Why didn't you tell me he was ill?' he demanded angrily.

'He was adamant I shouldn't,' Lisa replied. 'He said your career was at a point where it shouldn't be interrupted.'

Ralph said nothing for a long time and after a while Lisa asked, 'Would you have interrupted it? I don't mean for a quick visit, I mean for all the months it took him to die?'

'I was wondering that myself,' he said in a tight voice.

'After all, the show must go on,' she said lightly.

He looked uncomfortable and said, '*You* didn't think so.'

'Perhaps we have different priorities. Looking after someone dying seemed more important than making a movie.'

'Gary wouldn't have agreed with that,' he argued.

She managed to laugh. 'I did what was right for me.'

Next morning, when she drove him to the airport, he said, 'Think about coming to London for a while, a holiday.'

'I will,' she promised, and meant it.

At the ticket barrier, he kissed her and she felt him trembling. 'What's the matter?' she asked with concern.

'You know the saying "death goes in threes"? I keep

423

thinking I'm to be the next. It seems only right. Vita, Gary, then me.'

'It might be me.' She remembered this was one of Kitty's more ghoulish sayings – and often she'd been right.

'Don't be silly, Lisa, you'll go on forever.' He turned swiftly and went through the barrier.

Frightened, she shouted, 'Call me as soon as you get back.'

It was midnight and she was in bed when the telephone rang. He had arrived safely. 'Thank God! For a minute there you had me thinking your plane would crash.'

She replaced the receiver and remained sitting up in bed listening to the creaks and groans of the old house. '*Somebody else is going to die*,' said a voice. She jumped and felt herself go cold, but the voice had been inside her head. Even so, she tossed and turned for hours, unable to sleep. At one point she opened her eyes and Dent was standing by the bed. He held a tray of champagne and was entirely naked. Lisa began to laugh and suddenly the room was drenched in sunshine. She'd fallen asleep, after all.

The boy had only one more side to clean. His movements grew slower as his strength began to ebb. Lisa felt admiration for his initiative. Cleaning three pools in one day for a few dollars' return showed great strength of character. She recalled how one of her brothers, she couldn't remember which, had done a paper round, going out early in all weathers for a few pennies a week to give Mam, though he'd had to wait till Dad left for work else the money would have been taken off the housekeeping.

Lately, she'd found herself thinking a lot about Chaucer Street. Perhaps it was because Nellie had told her it was about to be demolished and Joan was being moved into a council flat. Lisa had always imagined that one day she'd go back, but perhaps that would have raked up too many bad memories. Anyway, Nellie said she'd never recognize the place. 'It was all modernized years ago, with a proper kitchen and central heating . . . '

Busby said she shouldn't grieve alone; she should mix with people. 'I'm not grieving,' she protested and she wasn't, though the loss of two good friends was hard to take. It was watching a relatively young man die before her eyes that shocked her. What had Gary done to deserve such a cruel fate when other, lesser men lived? Gary, who had so much to give, so much to do – a good, decent man who harmed no one?

'God moves in a mysterious way,' Millie said at the funeral and Lisa felt annoyed with God. What right had He to be so mysterious? Why couldn't He be a little more forthcoming?

Most nights she went down to the little cinema and watched movies, usually Gary's, marvelling at him, young, blond and good-looking, acting his heart out in *Matchstick Man*, recalling the terrible animosity he'd felt towards Dent and the way they'd ended up the greatest friends. It was their obsessive love of movies that had brought them together. By the end of the night she was always in tears for what had been, for what might have been, and knew she was being maudlin again and over-sentimental.

'But I don't care,' she thought rebelliously. 'That's how I am, that's how I'll always be. I cling to memories, they haunt me. I can't forget the past, and after all, it's the past that shapes the future.'

After the funeral, Lisa received a letter from Gary's lawyers. As she read, she felt her eyes fill with yet more tears. He'd left her the bulk of his considerable fortune, as well as his share in O'Brien Productions. She took off her glasses and lay back in the chair, touched to the heart.

Something would have to be done with this money – she wasn't sure what, but one day it would be put to good use.

'Phew! I'm all done, Miss Angelis.'

The boy was standing beside her. She'd been so lost in her thoughts that she'd forgotten all about him. By now the heat outside was intense. It was far too hot. She'd better go indoors once he'd gone.

She sat up and said, 'Thanks, Daniel, you've done a fine job. Is Daniel right or should I call you Dan?'

'My ma calls me Daniel, everybody else says Dan.' Close up, she noticed his knees were grazed and there was a bright bruise on his shin.

'How much do I owe you?'

'Ten dollars.' Lisa picked up her purse and gave him twenty. 'Gee, thanks!' His eyes lit up.

'What are you going to buy with that, Daniel?'

'My folks are taking me and my brothers on a camping holiday this fall. I'm getting my spending money together.' The telephone began to ring again and he said, 'Your phone's been going all morning.'

'I know,' she smiled. 'I forgot to bring the extension out and I'm too lazy to go indoors. *What's more, I don't want to,*' she added inwardly.

'Want me to answer it for you?'

The telephone stopped and immediately began again. Lisa groaned and started to get up. You never knew, it might be important.

'I'll get it.' The boy darted through the open windows and the ringing stopped. He re-appeared, clutching the receiver to his chest. 'It's all the way from Liverpool, England,' he said in an awed voice. 'And they said it's urgent.'

Lisa felt a terrible premonition. *A third person was going to die!* Jesus Christ, who was it?

She ran into the house and snatched the receiver out of the astonished boy's hands. He mumbled, 'Well, I'll be off now, Miss Angelis,' as she screamed, 'Hallo, hallo!'

'Lisa, it's Stan. I've been trying to phone all night.' He was scarcely audible.

'Stan, what's happened? Is it Nellie?'

'No, Lisa, it's Luke.' He began to cry. 'Our Luke is dead.'

Lisa was aware of the atmosphere of death as soon as she entered the house: a gloom, the soft murmur of sad spirits chanting a requiem.

'Thanks for coming,' Stan said dully when he opened the door. He made a brave attempt to be polite and welcoming. 'Nellie asked specially for you. She's in a bit of a state, I'm afraid. Natalie's shut in her room, she won't answer to anyone.' He led her into the big living room, usually so bright and cheerful.

Nellie was hunched in an armchair, her eyes red-rimmed and bloodshot. When she saw Lisa, she stretched out her arms. 'Oh, Lizzie, Luke's gone.'

'I know, love.' Lisa knelt and embraced her sister. 'How did it happen? Do you want to talk about it?'

'He drowned. He was with some boys in New Brighton and they went swimming. Luke swam too far out – he was probably showing off. When they reached him, it was too late. Oh, my lovely Luke,' she wailed. 'He was only thirteen. I can't believe he's dead.'

Lisa listened for a long time, saying little. When she looked across at Stan, he was sitting in the corner, his head buried in his hands.

'I'll make some tea,' she thought. 'That's what we need, a cup of tea.'

To her surprise, there was already someone in the kitchen – a scraggy, raw-boned woman with faded red hair. She was bent over the sink washing dishes with a furious, intense energy.

Joan!

Lisa said nothing but just watched, noticing the scrawny neck, the freckled, yellowing skin, the wrinkled elbows. Unexpectedly, she felt conscious of her own beauty and wondered how on earth this plain woman could be her sister, could be Nellie's sister? She thought of the boys, all fair, handsome and well-built, nothing like this unpleasant looking scarecrow of a woman. Yet Joan had been pretty as a child. What had made her turn out like this?

Joan suddenly became conscious of her presence. She looked up and her face flushed. 'So *you're* here,' she said in a flat voice.

'I am,' said Lisa lightly.

Her sister shook her wet hands in the sink and began to dry the dishes.

'You'll rub the pattern off,' said Lisa. The muscles in Joan's neck were rigid cords and the plates squeaked from the pressure of the cloth. She didn't answer.

'Joan, why can't we be friends?'

'Huh!'

'What does that mean?'

'It means no. I don't want to be your friend. You've caused nothing but misery for this family.'

427

Lisa thought of Tom. 'Perhaps this family caused nothing but misery for me, at least when I was a child.'

Joan looked at her contemptuously, her green eyes full of hate. 'I don't know what you're on about. All I know is Mam seemed to think the sun shone out of your arse. It was "our Lizzie" this, "our Lizzie" that. "I wonder what our Lizzie is doing now?" she'd say whenever it was your birthday. She never seemed to realize it was me, me who stayed at home and looked after her. Never a thought for our Joan.'

'There was no need to stay,' Lisa said gently.

'How would *you* know?' asked Joan sharply. She began to stack the plates carelessly, angrily, each one landing on top of the other with a sharp crack. 'You were away having a good time. I could have got married, you know. There was this chap — '

'Perhaps you should have. I'm sure Mam would have preferred it.'

Joan turned and looked at her, a strange, bitter expression on her plain features. 'Are you saying I wasted my life?'

'Of course not,' said Lisa hastily. 'I just meant Mam would have liked to see you happy, that's all.'

'You seem to know more about our mam than me, despite the fact you never saw her most of your life.'

Lisa said despairingly, 'You twist everything. I don't know what else to say.'

'Then don't say anything, just go away. If you hadn't taught Luke to swim, he wouldn't be dead. It's all your fault!' The words were spat out with such viciousness that Lisa stepped back, appalled.

'I only came because Nellie asked,' she stammered. 'She wouldn't want me if she thought I was to blame.'

Joan seemed to freeze. 'Oh, God!' thought Lisa. 'Now I've hurt her even more.' Nellie already had a sister close at hand, yet it was Lisa she'd wanted by her side in her misery.

That night, when everybody else was in bed, Lisa went for a walk on the sands close to Nellie's house.

It was a brilliant night, the sky a coverlet of shimmering, blinking stars, the moon a curve of gold. Was that a new moon or old? Lisa stared, but couldn't remember which side was which. Dent had explained it to Sabina on the boat on their way to Cannes.

Sabina! Her nearly-child, her dream. Which was worse, to have longed for a child all your life as she had done, or to lose one, like Nellie? Right now, she decided, it was worse for Nellie, much worse.

The beach was deserted – not surprisingly, as it must be midnight. All that could be heard was the soft sound of the River Mersey lapping against the sands. She went down and stared into the black water. What was it all about? What was it all for? Why had Luke been chosen as a sacrifice by some capricious God?

Questions, questions, always questions, but never any answers. The water began to lick her feet, but she didn't notice until a clump of seaweed wrapped itself around her ankle and she leapt back. Her shoes were soaked.

She thought of Joan, her sister. It hadn't taken much to turn her into a shrew, eaten through with bitterness. Yet far worse things had happened to Lizzie – the abortion, the stabbing, and that awful time in Southport, but Lizzie had come through. Things hadn't gone the way she wanted, but she was Lisa Angelis, successful, admired and, most of the time, happy. Yes, she'd overcome adversity and come through with honours.

True, life was a struggle, but she was forty-five and still on the winning side. Nothing was going to get her down, ever. For the next few weeks, she'd stay with Nellie, then she'd continue with the struggle on her own, as usual.

She shook her fist at the stars, 'I don't care what you've got in store for us, you bastards,' she yelled. 'But you've got a fight on your hands with Lizzie O'Brien, that I can promise.'

FERRIS
HALL

Chapter 39

'Lisa, this is Tony Molyneux. He's been nagging something awful to be introduced,' Barbara Heany pushed a tall, silver-haired man wearing evening dress in the general direction of Lisa.

'How do you do?' She shook hands and someone knocked against her, thrusting her forward into the man's arms.

'Whoops!' he said as he caught her.

'Sorry, I think I've spilt some wine on your tie.' Lisa began to dab at the stain with a paper napkin.

'Don't bother, I never liked it anyway.' He smiled, showing white, even teeth. His eyes were an unusual colour, dark grey with flecks of blue, and he had a delicate, gentle face.

'If you can't get the mark out, I'll buy you another,' she promised.

'In that case I definitely won't get the mark out.'

Lisa looked at him; there was slightly more than a flirtatious tone to his words. He was watching her with a quirky smile on his fine, thin lips, though his dark eyes were grave.

'What's this party for, anyway?' he asked suddenly.

'If you don't know, you must be a gate-crasher,' she said accusingly. 'No wonder it's so crowded.'

'Let's go and pretend we're watching a play.' He took her arm and guided her off the stage and into the fifth row of seats. Quite a few people had already escaped the crowd and were sitting in the front stalls. She could see Ralph with his new friend, Adam.

'You didn't tell me what the party was for.'

'You didn't admit to being a gate-crasher,' she said sternly.

He looked faintly bemused. 'I'm not, at least I don't think so. I came with Carter Stevenson and his wife. They assured me they'd been invited backstage after the show.'

'Carter Stevenson? That name sounds vaguely familiar,'

said Lisa.

'I should hope so, he's the Home Secretary.'

'There's no need to sound so shocked,' she said indignantly. 'Not everyone's interested in politics.'

'Whoops again,' he said. He spoke in the slightly strangulated manner of the English upper classes, with long, exaggerated vowels. 'This party,' he insisted in mock exasperation, 'is the reason for it secret?'

'It's a highly confidential state secret but I'll tell you because you're with the Home Secretary. Tonight was the last performance of *The Curtained Window* starring Ralph Layton and me. Also, it's my birthday.'

'Many happy returns,' he said warmly, raising his glass. 'Is your age a secret too, or shouldn't a gentleman ask?'

'You know what a gentleman should ask better than me,' she answered tartly. 'In Hollywood they took four years off my age but it seems silly to keep pretending. I am what I am – in other words, I'm fifty.'

'Fifty!' He looked astonished. 'I would never have believed it.'

'People have been saying that all day, and it really bugs me that I feel so flattered.'

'You're the most beautiful fifty-year-old woman I've ever met,' he said sincerely. 'Mind you, I'd say that if you were twenty, thirty, forty.' He smiled into her eyes and she found herself smiling back. As if embarrassed, he dropped his gaze and jumped to his feet. 'I'm going for a refill, how about you?'

'I've had enough, thanks.'

She watched him climb the stairs at the side of the stage, a tall, slender, rather aristocratic figure in expensive, well-cut clothes. Within seconds he was lost in the crowd. Idly she began to speculate on what it was that attracted people to each other; was it looks, temperament or just sheer sex appeal?

Why had he been nagging to be introduced? She hoped he hadn't heard about that wild, furious time when she'd left Nellie in Liverpool, pale and sad-eyed, but fit to go back to her teaching job, and arrived in London, with her own grief still bottled up.

434

For nearly a year she'd gone from party to party, sleeping with anyone who took her fancy, and occasionally with someone who didn't. By the time she woke mid-morning in the bed of some stranger, her head thumping from a hangover, it was time to prepare for the night ahead. Another party, another stranger, no time for the aching frustration of wondering why, why, why?

Of course she'd come to her senses eventually, bought herself a little house in Pimlico, not wanting to move too far away from Nellie just yet. There was plenty of time to go back to Hollywood.

'Penny for them,' said a voice.

Lisa looked up, startled. Tony was back, looking down at her with a quizzical smile on his mild, good-humoured face.

'They weren't worth that much,' she said.

'That lovely head can't possible have cheap thoughts.'

'You'd be surprised,' she said. 'I was wondering, why did you ask Barbara Heany to introduce us?'

He looked puzzled. 'I just wanted to shake your hand, that's all. It's not often one has the opportunity to meet a famous actress, particularly one as beautiful as you.'

Lisa suddenly tired of compliments and silly conversation. 'What do you do?' she asked in a matter-of-fact voice.

He seemed to sense her change of mood and answered, equally matter-of-factly, 'I'm an MP.'

'Military Police, or Member of Parliament?'

'The latter.' he sounded slightly hurt and she hid a smile. 'What party?'

'Conservative, of course,' he replied with a pained expression, as if the idea he could be anything else was offensive.

Lisa laughed. 'Oh dear, what would my family say if they knew I was talking to you!'

'Are they Labour?'

'Emphatically so . . . well, most of them.' In the 1979 election two years before, Stan had voted Conservative, according to Nellie. 'In a way, I don't blame him,' Nellie had said. 'When his mother died last winter they had to keep her body in the morgue for weeks, as the gravediggers had gone on strike in Liverpool. How would we have felt, Liz, if we couldn't have buried Mam?' Now, every time an O'Brien lost his job in the recession, they blamed Stan.

'How about you?' He was looking at her with real interest.

'I didn't vote. I'm apolitical.'

He raised his fine, rather startlingly black eyebrows. 'Ah, fruitful ground. I'll have to get to work on you.'

'Tony, do you want a lift to the station?' A small plump man had come to the front of the stage and gestured in their direction with his glass. 'You'll miss the midnight train if you don't leave soon.'

'I'll be right with you, Carter.' Tony turned to Lisa and said, 'I have to be in my Yorkshire constituency tomorrow. May I see you again? How about coming up next weekend? I'm having a few people to stay.'

Lisa wrinkled her nose. 'It's not hunting, shooting and fishing?'

'Absolutely not. It'll just be wining and dining and general chat.' He kissed the back of her hand. 'Say you'll come, please.'

'You've talked me into it,' said Lisa.

After he'd gone, she remained in her seat and watched the revellers on stage. She saw Barbara Heany, their producer, catch the arm of the author of *The Curtained Window*, Matthew Jenks, a middle-aged, strikingly handsome man with a fine head of black wavy hair, and felt her lip curl. He was a good playwright, brilliant even, but she felt nothing but contempt for the way he'd gone about achieving his success.

It wasn't long after she'd moved to Pimlico four years ago that Ralph had called to say he'd come across a play, a two-hander that was perfect for them both. 'I met this guy, Matthew, on the train coming back from the Edinburgh Festival,' Ralph said. 'We got talking and – well, he moved in with me – you know there's been no one since Gary died. It turns out he's a playwright. Why don't you come over one night and we'll read it together?'

Lisa had gone, just to humour him, and had to agree *Dead Wood* was excellent. 'But I'm a screen actor, Ralph,' she protested. 'I'm far too nervous to go on the stage.'

'Matthew thinks you're ideal for Sarah Wood,' insisted

Ralph. 'When I told him we were friends, he suggested I approach you,' and Matthew, hovering behind in his tight jeans and threadbare sweater, concurred.

'I didn't know when I was writing the play, of course, but as soon as Ralph mentioned your name I knew I'd had someone like you in mind.'

'I'd be petrified,' she said weakly. 'Even if I knew my lines backwards, I'd be worried I'd dry up.'

'Just give it a try,' coaxed Ralph. 'To please me, to please Matthew. We'll go into rehearsal, quietly, without publicity, then if you still feel the same, you can drop out and we'll get someone else.'

So Lisa reluctantly agreed and somehow, despite Ralph's promise, there was a great deal of publicity. 'Hollywood Star To Appear On West End Stage', she read in the theatre pages a few weeks later, though Ralph swore he knew nothing about it and she was inclined to believe him.

The rehearsals were murder. She was stiff and self-conscious, and although word-perfect off stage, as she had predicted, once on, nerves took over and she forgot everything. But for the fact everybody knew the play was in production, she would have withdrawn. The producer, Barbara Heany, an untidy ragbag of a woman with a growing reputation, was in despair and Lisa's understudy was visibly licking her lips, hoping to get a few nights' stardom during the preliminary tour of the provinces before another major actress was hired.

But something happened on the first night, Lisa was never sure what. They started off in Norwich and the theatre was packed. Her nerves were completely on edge so she sought Ralph out in his dressing room, hoping for some words of comfort, but found him looking ill, his face as white as chalk.

'Are you all right?' she asked, filled with alarm.

'No, I'm terrified. My stomach's where my mouth should be, but I always feel like this before the show first goes on.'

'Oh God!' she groaned. 'I think I'll kill myself.'

The house-lights dimmed, the curtain went up and Ralph sauntered onto the stage. There was a burst of applause. Lisa stared at him in amazement. He looked calm and perfectly in control.

'You're on, Lisa.' Someone gave her a push and she burst on stage, waving her arms like the half-mad woman she was supposed to be. The applause took her breath away, she hadn't been expecting it. Ralph came towards her and suddenly everything fell into place. She was conscious of the audience hanging onto every word, and felt they were behind her, urging her on. The lines, the movements became effortless and as time passed she sank deeper and deeper into the character she was playing until by the end, she *was* Sarah Wood, the schoolteacher's wife.

'I never in my wildest dreams thought I'd *enjoy* it,' she said to Ralph later. 'I was really sorry when it ended. I have never felt like that making a movie.'

Stage-acting was like a drug, far more potent than the cinema. During the year-long run of *Dead Wood*, Lisa found herself aching for the evening to come when she would go on stage and lose herself in her part. She knew precisely when the audience would laugh or gasp, and the sound would urge her on to please and captivate them more. After she and Ralph had taken their curtain calls she still felt exhilarated, and some nights it took quite a while to return to being Lisa Angelis.

'Why didn't you persuade me to do this before?' she teased Ralph. 'I feel as if it was what I was born for.'

As soon as *Dead Wood* was established as a hit, Matthew Jenks went back to his wife and children.

'I didn't know he was married,' Lisa said in astonishment.

'Neither did I,' said Ralph bitterly.

'You're not gay at all, are you?'

'No,' said Matthew flatly.

'You just used Ralph. I think you're despicable!' He'd come into her dressing room with a new script. 'I'd like you to read it,' he'd said on entering.

He didn't appear the least bit perturbed by her insult. 'It was a means to an end, that's all.' He shrugged.

'Did you really meet him accidentally?' she asked curiously.

'No. I'd been in Edinburgh trying to make contacts, unsuccessfully, I might add. I was on my way home when I saw Ralph getting out of a taxi by the station so I spent the last of my cash on a first-class ticket and sat opposite him. The fact that he's gay is no secret. I made the right noises and he asked me to come home with him.'

'And later you revealed that by strange coincidence you happened to be a playwright,' she said scornfully.

'You got it in one,' he said unashamedly.

'Didn't you have enough faith in your plays to get them on in the normal way?'

He laughed sarcastically. 'What's the normal way?' he demanded. 'Dead Wood had been rejected by eighteen theatres; some directors kept it a year and sent it back unread. I've half a dozen other plays, all as good, at home. Shakespeare would have a job getting Hamlet on in London now – it's all sewn up. I'm just an ordinary guy who'd come to realize talent is worthless without contacts. When I saw my opportunity, I grabbed it with both hands.'

'I still think you're despicable,' she said coldly.

'You're entitled to your opinion. I'd call it ambitious, myself.' He went over to the door. 'If I recall rightly, you married two directors in Hollywood. I wonder how far you'd have got without them.'

'But I loved them both,' she protested.

'Well, I quite like Ralph,' he said. 'That's why I'm giving him first option on my new play.' He nodded towards the script. 'That's the best thing I've ever done. I hope you won't be influenced by what's happened, you'd be cutting off your nose to spite your face. Ralph's keen and this time I did write the part specially for you.'

Matthew had noticed Lisa sitting in the stalls. He gave her a sardonic smile and raised his glass. She ignored him, though she conceded that it was thanks to him the last few years had been so productive and rewarding. She'd never expected to get so much satisfaction out of acting.

Barbara Heany was saying her goodbyes. Lisa went on stage and caught up with her in the wings. 'Let's share a taxi home and you can tell me all about Tony Molyneux,' she suggested.

For a woman who appeared totally incurious about people's lives, Barbara seemed to know everything about everyone important, mainly because she devoured the *Guardian* every day from cover to cover.

'I only know what I read in the paper,' she told Lisa on their way home. 'Did he tell you he was a Baronet? It's *Sir* Anthony Molyneux.'

'A Sir!' Lisa said, impressed.

'The title's been in the family for centuries. Tony inherited it when his father died a few years back and he became MP for Broxley in 1979, but I haven't a clue what he did before. He's divorced, no children, and lives in a run-down stately home, Ferris Hall.' She grinned suddenly. 'He was awfully anxious to meet you. I said it was your fiftieth birthday party, I hope you don't mind.'

'You told him? He acted as if he didn't know,' said Lisa.

'He was probably looking for an excuse to flatter you,' said Barbara. 'Looks as if he was successful, you seem interested enough.'

'Only vaguely,' Lisa said airily.

Chapter 40

On Saturday morning, she and Tony travelled together on the train to Yorkshire. 'I hope you don't mind – I don't like driving long distances,' he said when he called to make arrangements for the journey.

She assured him she felt the same. 'I hate motorways, the lorries frighten me to death.'

He led her to a first-class compartment. He wore a British warm and cavalry twill trousers. 'Thank you for the flowers,' she said when they were seated. 'They were lovely.'

'I spent ages in the florists trying to decide which flower most suited you. In the end I decided it was a tiger lily but they didn't have any so I had to plump for roses, though they don't do you justice.'

He was a charming and attentive companion, though as the train sped through the diverse countryside, she began to tire of the never-ending compliments and sensed he indulged in flattery to cover his rather surprising lack of confidence. He seemed unsure of himself, slightly ill at ease in her company. Gently, she probed him on his work and he launched into a description of life in the House of Commons which was not only a relief, but fascinating too.

When the train drew into York Station in the early afternoon, he said, 'We get off here. There's a branch line to Droxley, but the trains seem to run when they please. Someone will be here to meet us.'

A somewhat ancient Mercedes was waiting outside the station and the driver, a stooped man in his sixties, approached them. 'Good afternoon, Sir Anthony,' he said courteously.

'Afternoon, Mason.' Tony nodded briefly and ushered Lisa into the back of the car, leaving their cases for Mason to stow in the boot. He made no attempt to introduce her and she thought how different the employer-employee relationship was in England compared to America, where the hired help often became friends, part of the family, like Millie.

'It's lovely here,' she said. They'd left the environs of York some time ago and were driving through narrow lanes lined with grey, moss-covered walls. Beyond, the fields rolled gently by, a patchwork of green and brown and yellow. An occasional stone house could be seen, nestling comfortably at the foot of a hill or perched proudly at its top. The area had a craggy, breathtaking beauty.

They turned into an even narrower road edged with hawthorn thick with red and white spring blossom. The hedge finished abruptly, to be replaced by a high, stout wall and shortly afterwards the car turned through a wide entrance bordered by two granite pillars. The word *Ferris* was worked into one of the open wrought-iron gates, and *Hall* in the other. Ahead of them was a solid-looking three-storey mansion of buff-coloured stone. On one side scaffolding had been erected, though there was no sign of workmen.

'This is it,' Tony said proudly. 'Ferris Hall.'

'It's lovely,' she said dutifully. Privately she thought it probably had been once, though now it looked run-down and decrepit. The frames on the tall, arched windows were eaten away with rot and the stonework was pitted and crumbling.

Inside, the house was pretty much the same. The high-ceilinged hall had patches of damp in the corners and she could hear the floorboards creak as they walked. The furniture was old, but unlike that in Tymperleys, had been neglected and was in urgent need of repair.

'Mason will show you to your room,' said Tony. 'Then perhaps you'd like to come down and have a drink.'

When she came downstairs, Tony was in a long, gracious though sparsely-furnished room, talking to a red-cheeked man with a shock of brown curly hair. 'Lisa, my dear.' His eyes lit up with pleasure, as if surprised to find her there. It was these unconscious, boyish actions that attracted her to him. He came over and took her hand, 'This is Christy Costello, my agent.'

'How do you do?' The agent's handshake was firm, almost

painful. He was tall, in his early forties and had an open-air, healthy look.

'Is that an Irish accent I hear?' she asked.

'Most definitely – Belfast through and through. Don't tell me you're Irish too. I refuse to believe it, not with those looks.' There was something slightly familiar about the way he looked at her.

'Then I'm afraid I'm going to confound you: both my parents were Irish, though I've never been there.'

'I'll be damned! You've got the most un-Irish eyes I've ever seen.'

The weekend guests turned up later – two couples in their forties, the husbands full of plans to further their joint construction company for which they sought Tony's help, the wives shy and tongue-tied, not speaking even to each other.

Christy Costello joined them for dinner and during the meal the men would have monopolized the conversation with their business talk if Lisa hadn't decided to draw the wives into the discussion. After all, Tony had sat her at the head of the table, so presumably he expected her to act as hostess.

In fact the women turned out to be far more interesting than their husbands. One was a part time social worker, the other ran her own boutique. With Lisa's gentle encouragement, they began to talk about their jobs, their lives, their children.

'Have you any children, Lisa?' one asked.

'No, I'm afraid I've been too tied up in my career,' she lied.

'And what career is that?'

She smiled. There'd been no sign of recognition when Tony introduced them. 'I'm an actress,' she said.

One of the men burst out with, 'Does that mean you're *the* Lisa Angelis, the film star?'

'Didn't you recognize me?' Lisa laughed.

'Well, I haven't seen you in twenty years or more. Christ, woman, I was madly in love with you once.' He stared at Lisa, eyes wide with admiration. 'You're even better-looking close up than on screen.'

'Bob!' said his wife warningly. 'You'll embarrass her.'

They began to ask the inevitable questions. 'Have you met John Wayne? James Stewart? Did you ever know Marilyn Monroe? What's it like living in Hollywood?' She handled the inquisition easily, fending off some questions, answering others, at the same time signalling to Tony to refill the glasses.

The evening ended on a note of hilarity when Bob went down on one knee and proposed to Lisa. 'I used to dream of doing this,' he said. 'It's the only dream I've ever had that's come true.'

After the two couples had gone to bed Christy said, 'That's the best evening I've had in a long time. You're the perfect hostess, Lisa.' He turned to Tony and said jokingly, 'Snap her up quick if she's free. She's worth her weight in gold to an ambitious politician.'

The two couples left after Sunday lunch, the men looking highly satisfied with themselves. 'I can't promise anything,' she heard Tony say as they shook hands in the hall, 'but rest assured I'll get the motorway idea planted in the mind of the appropriate department head.'

'That's all we ask, Sir Anthony,' one of the men replied.

Afterwards, Tony took her for a walk on the fells surrounding the house. When they reached the top she looked back. Ferris Hall, in its wall-lined enclosure, looked like a doll's house from this distance, and its grey slate roof shone in the bright spring sunshine. The house had a look of permanence about it, an impression of having grown from the rich brown earth as had the massive oak trees surrounding it.

'It's very *Wuthering Heights*,' she said. 'Romantic and wild.'

'I'm pleased you like it so much,' he said almost bashfully. 'I desperately hoped you would.'

That night they went out to dinner in a small public house in Broxley. Lisa wore a plain shirtwaister dress of scarlet cotton topped with a black bolero. She brushed her hair back smoothly, securing it Spanish-style with an ornate red comb.

Tony was waiting at the bottom of the wide staircase and his eyes widened in admiration as she came towards him. 'You look lovely,' he said in an awed voice. He tucked her arm in his and led her outside to where the Mercedes was parked. 'I can't believe my luck, having you here. In fact, I'm scared to close my eyes lest you disappear.'

Lisa laughed. 'I've no intention of disappearing, believe me.'

Tony drove into town. He was a hesitant, nervous driver and she found herself pressing an imaginary accelerator to make the car go faster along the narrow, leafy lanes. They entered Broxley through a sprawling red-brick housing estate where children played on the pavements, though the town centre was old and well-preserved, and there were a lot of stone cottages, which, like Ferris Hall, looked as if they'd been there forever. At the end of the High Street stood a large sooty factory with the name *Spring Engineering* on a board attached to the padlocked iron gates.

'That's a real eyesore,' said Tony as they drove past. 'I'd like to get rid of it.'

'Why?' she asked. 'It's where people earn their living. I don't suppose they care if it's an eyesore.'

He was too busy manoeuvring the Mercedes into the car park of a public house to reply. As they entered the low-beamed building, the landlord came over and shook hands heartily. 'Good to see you, Sir Anthony. It's been a while since you were in town.'

'Pressure of work, Clough. There's a lot to do in West-minster.'

'Fergus seemed to find time for us.' The landlord's friendly expression didn't change, but Lisa sensed criticism in his words. 'Always on hand when you needed him, was Fergus.'

Tony muttered something unintelligible and when they were seated, he said, 'We shouldn't have come here. Clough was a crony of Fergus Lomax. I don't think he likes me.'

'He might do if you called him by his first name or put "Mr" in front of Clough,' Lisa commented. 'It's almost medieval addressing a person by his surname. Do you expect him to touch his forelock?'

Tony looked at her blankly. 'But he's only a publican.'

'Well, you're only an MP.'

He frowned and she could see he was struggling to make sense of her words. 'I think I see what you mean,' he said eventually. 'Come down to their level, in other words.'

'That's not the way I'd put it,' she said crisply. 'Just treat everyone as an equal, that's all.'

He smiled suddenly. 'You're good with people, aren't you? In future, I shall heed your advice.'

'In that case, when we leave, shake Mr Clough's hand, say the meal was delicious and ask if he has any problems you can sort out.' As Tony nodded thoughtfully, she asked, 'Who's Fergus, by the way?'

'Fergus Lomax represented the constituency for over thirty years. When he retired at the last election he took a large personal vote with him, I'm afraid. My majority's less than half his.'

'Then Sir Anthony Molyneux must work hard to get a personal vote for himself,' said Lisa. 'So at the next election your majority increases.'

Before leaving on Monday morning, Lisa sought out Mrs Mason who had prepared the excellent meals over the weekend. She and her husband occupied a small flat over the garage. A small stick of a woman, her forehead was furrowed in what looked like a perpetual frown, and her iron-grey hair was encased in a thick black net. She looked up in surprise when Lisa walked into the old-fashioned kitchen, with its scrubbed wooden worktops, deep white sink and stone tiled floors. Even the fridge and chipped cooker looked as if they were antiques and the room was cold and draughty. Plaster crumbled in all four corners.

'I've just come to thank you for the food. It was lovely! I never realized Yorkshire pudding could be so tasty.' Considering the conditions in here, the woman worked wonders.

'Why, thank you, madam,' Mrs Mason muttered, as if being thanked was not something she was used to.

'Please don't call me madam, I hate it. If we're going to be friends, I'd prefer Lisa – or Miss Angelis, if you can't bring yourself to use my first name.'

'Does that mean you're coming back?' the woman asked curiously.

'So it would seem,' smiled Lisa.

Tony courted her assiduously. Almost every day an exquisite bouquet of flowers arrived at Lisa's Pimlico house, often accompanied by a small gift – perfume, a silk scarf, expensive chocolates. Early one morning he turned up with a Harrods food hamper. 'It's a beautiful morning,' he cried. 'I think breakfast *al fresco* in Hyde Park is in order.' On another occasion a miniature portrait was delivered, oval-shaped in a heavy gold frame. It was of Lisa and she recognized the pose from a photograph outside the theatre where *The Curtained Window* had been staged. '*Even Rembrandt would have found your beauty difficult to transfer onto canvas*' said the accompanying note.

Every few weeks she went to Ferris Hall and began to get fond of the bleak, cold house. She was rehearsing a new play and Tony came so frequently to watch, then take her out to dinner, that she remonstrated with him. 'Surely you should be in the House of Commons? After all, it's what you're paid for.'

He seemed to like her reprimanding him and would smile coyly like a little boy. 'It's boring. I'd sooner be with you.'

He took her to the House on several occasions. She sat in the visitors' gallery and found the proceedings fascinating, particularly the way the elected representatives behaved, like spoilt, fractious children. Margaret Thatcher, the Prime Minister, was in her element at the despatch box, a formidable, commanding figure, though Lisa nursed considerable affection for the leader of the opposition, Michael Foot, a courteous, gentlemanly figure with a gift for heartstopping oratory.

She knew Tony was leading up to a proposal of marriage and sometimes wondered if she should discourage him. It would be cruel to string him along then turn him down, though she found herself unwilling to end the relationship. He made her feel precious and wanted, a very special person. When inevitably he asked her to marry him, she said, 'I'm fond of you, Tony, but I'm not in love with you.'

'But I adore you,' he said passionately. 'I have enough love for both of us. Say yes, please! We get on so well together, everything is right between us.'

'I know it is, but I'd still like to think about it first.'

Marriage was a lottery – she'd realized that a long time ago. Two people could be madly in love and end up hating each other because there was nothing behind the love; no liking, no friendship. Anyway, perhaps it was too much to expect, to fall in love at fifty, though Tony had managed it. Fondness, a need for companionship, were probably a better basis for marriage at their age.

When she was invited to Chester in August for a christening – Dougal's wife had just given birth to twin boys – she thought to herself, 'I always go up north alone. I've never once taken a partner.'

She asked Tony to come with her and he agreed with alacrity. He bought gold watches for the babies and Lisa exclaimed, 'They're only two weeks old!'

He said bashfully, 'I'd no idea what to buy. I suppose they'll grow into them.'

During the short visit, Tony was nervous and on edge.

'They're all sizing me up,' he whispered when they came out of the church. 'Trying to make up their minds if I'm good enough for you.'

'What do you think of him?' she asked Nellie later.

'He seems very nice, rather shy, but incredibly generous. Those watches must have cost a small fortune. Remember what Mam used to say? "Generosity covers a multitude of sins".'

'I remember, but I was never sure if that was a good or a bad thing,' Lisa said dryly.

Nellie squeezed her hand affectionately. 'I think it's good. He's madly in love – the way he looks at you! But if you're wondering whether to marry him, Liz, only your own heart can answer that question. All I'll say is I worry about you all the time, living on your own.'

That evening, she and Tony caught the train back to London.

'Whew!' He sank back in his seat with a heartfelt sigh.

'That was an ordeal. Do you think they liked me?' he added anxiously.

She laughed. Considering his position in life, his lack of confidence and wish to please was quite endearing. 'They loved you,' she said soothingly.

He gave his little boy grin. 'That's something, I suppose. Even if *you* don't love me, your family does! Perhaps I should ask them to marry me.'

Lisa didn't answer. It had been nice having someone of her own at the christening. People were made to go in pairs and she'd had no one for a long time. Even if she never grew to love Tony, it didn't matter. As he said, they got on so well. She looked out of the dark window and could see Tony's reflection, sitting opposite. He was watching her, an eager expression on his gentle face.

'I suppose I'd be an idiot to turn you down,' she said eventually and he leaned across, caught her hands in his and began to shower them with kisses.

They decided on a small registry office wedding. Lisa invited Ralph and Adam, Barbara Heany, Nellie and Stan.

'A Conservative MP! It's a good job you didn't mention that at the christening. Jimmie might have lynched him,' Nellie said after the ceremony. 'As for Mam, she's probably turning in her grave. On the other hand, Chaucer Street would never have heard the last of it, her Lizzie becoming Lady Lisa Molyneux. She was a terrible snob was our mam, in her own quiet way.'

'Lady Lisa! It sounds like a brand of cosmetics. I'll never use the title if I can avoid it, but when I do, it'll be Lady Elizabeth.'

'Married again, eh? This is the third wedding of yours I've been to.' Ralph kissed her. 'Let's hope this one's for keeps.'

They honeymooned in America, at Tymperleys. Lisa had only been back a few times since Luke died. Chloe and her husband Albert had moved into the nursery flat and between them kept the old house in immaculate condition.

When she arrived with Tony, Lisa made a particular point of kissing Chloe and Albert before presenting them both as her good friends. She was pleased when Tony showed no obvious sign of embarrassment at being introduced to servants. She'd yank her new husband up into the late twentieth century by his bootstraps if necessary.

'This furniture must be worth a fortune,' he said as she showed him round, his jaw dropping further with each room they entered. She took him into the studio and felt a sudden twinge of nostalgia, remembering Dent's outrageous behaviour when he'd brought her in here on that memorable weekend. The man beside her was so totally different from Dent – from Busby too, come to that. She had always been drawn to eccentric, exciting men with over-the-top personalities. How could she expect to live the rest of her life with this shy, diffident man who, now she thought about it, had few interests and only limited conversation? Her feeling of nostalgia turned to fear. Had she made a monstrous mistake? She turned to him blindly, close to tears, needing comfort, but Tony was walking around the studio, examining the paintings, and he didn't notice her distress.

'I suppose these could be valuable one day,' he said.

She composed herself. 'I'd never sell Dent's pictures,' she said quietly. 'Though I might take a couple back with me.'

'You know,' he said later, 'you could get quite an income by renting out Tymperleys, or you could sell it. What do you think it would fetch?'

'I've no idea. I've no intention of renting or selling.' She laughed to hide her annoyance. 'I didn't realize you were so interested in money, darling. I feel as if I've married my bank manager.'

He was instantly contrite. 'It's just that I'm so impressed,' he said apologetically. 'Tymperleys is a positive treasure trove.'

'I'm sorry,' Tony muttered. 'Really sorry. This has never happened before. I don't know what's wrong.'

'You're probably nervous,' said Lisa, kissing him softly. Was it her imagination, or did she sense him stiffen at the touch of her lips. 'Shall I help you?' She slid her hand down his body. This time she knew it wasn't her imagination when he jerked abruptly away.

'It'll come right soon,' she said gently. 'Don't worry.' She would have liked to talk about it but he lay there, stiff and unspeaking, so she turned over and tried to sleep. Over the months she'd known him, his only attempt at intimacy had been a kiss on her cheek, but she'd put his reticence down to gentlemanly old-world courtesy rather than lack of desire. There had been enough desire in his eyes and his words to convince her that he was aching to make love. Perhaps that was still the case. Perhaps he hadn't made love to a woman for so long that gentle wooing on her part was needed to restore his confidence.

After a long time he said softly, 'Lisa?' She could tell from the tone of his voice that he wasn't trying to attract her attention, but checking if she was asleep. She didn't answer. Seconds later, she felt the covers move and he slid furtively out of bed and left the room.

After he'd gone, she turned on her back and lay staring at the ceiling. 'Shit!' she said in a loud voice. 'Why do I always have such lousy luck with men?'

Chapter 41

'You mean you've *never* made love?' said Nellie in an astonished voice. 'In eighteen months of marriage?'

'Never!' said Lisa dramatically.

'Gosh, Liz, that's terrible! Why don't you get divorced?'

Lisa was stretched out on the floor with her back against a chair. She looked up at her sister with amusement. 'That's a fine question – coming from a Catholic!'

Nellie blushed and said defensively, 'You've already been divorced twice. I didn't think another one would matter.'

'That's probably why I've never considered it,' said Lisa. 'I didn't want to admit failure again. Anyway, it hasn't failed really – in every other way we get on perfectly. Tony still acts like a devoted lover and sends me heaps of flowers and arranges little treats. He makes me feel very wanted and special.'

It was almost midnight, a Sunday. Nellie was going to a head-teachers' conference in the morning and staying with Lisa overnight. They'd been out to dinner earlier and when they got back to the house in Pimlico Lisa opened a bottle of wine, then another, and by now both sisters were slightly tipsy and in the mood for confidences. Nellie had kicked off her shoes, undone her skirt and half-sat, half-lay on the settee.

The women were silent for a while, deep in their own thoughts. Lisa picked up the wine and refilled the glasses.

'Are you happy, though?' Nellie asked suddenly.

Lisa didn't answer straight away. 'Yes,' she said eventually. 'I'm really enjoying life at the moment. The fact that Tony and I haven't got – what would you call it? – a *proper* relationship, means I don't feel obliged to stay by his side, so I go to America whenever I please. As you know, I made a movie there last year. During the run of my plays I live here, though Tony thinks I should sell this house and move into his Westminster flat when I'm in London. Most weekends I'm up in Yorkshire being an MP's wife and find myself getting more and more interested in politics. In fact, I know more about it than Tony does now. I've never been so busy. There's only ten or fifteen minutes each day I feel lonely.'

'When's that?'

'When I get into bed at night,' said Lisa.

'Oh, Liz!' Nellie reached out and touched Lisa's shoulder briefly. 'Did Tony manage it with his first wife, I wonder?'

'I've no idea.' Lisa shrugged. 'All I know is he didn't have any children. He won't talk about his ex-wife, though I suppose that's understandable.'

Nellie was looking at her with a worried expression. Lisa said quickly, 'I wish I hadn't told you. It's the wine, it always loosens my tongue. Honestly, Nell, I'm very happy, please don't worry about me.' She managed a brilliant smile to reassure her sister all was well, adding, 'Let's change the subject. Earlier on, you said Jimmie had been made redundant again. I wish they'd let me help out financially.' All her older brothers had refused her offer of money to help them through the recession.

'They look upon it as charity, I'm afraid, though I don't know if their wives would agree.' Nellie ran her fingers through her almost white hair leaving it standing up around her head like a wiry halo. 'I know I'd take it, but I bet Stan wouldn't let me.'

Lisa shook her head impatiently. 'I think families should stick together in emergencies. I've got millions in the bank doing nothing.'

'I'll have a word with the wives,' Nellie promised. 'See if they can bang a few heads together.' She reached down for her glass and her wedding ring fell off. 'One of these days I'll lose this.'

'You should get it altered, made smaller,' said Lisa.

'Stan won't let me. He says it's me who's got to get bigger.'

Lisa glanced at her sister. Since Luke died, Nellie had shrunk to a shadow of her former self. Noting the peaked, sad face, Lisa said softly, 'How are you, Nell? Have you gotten over . . .'

Nellie interrupted, her voice bleak: 'I'll *never* get over Luke dying, Liz. Never. Even on my deathbed, I'll be wishing he was there to see me off. I doubt if a day, an hour, goes by without me thinking about him. He would have been twenty now and at university – he wanted to study Economics. In my mind he's still alive and leading the life he would have led. I try to imagine what he would look like, how tall would he have grown, what size shoes would he take, would he have let his hair grow long and become a typical, scruffy student? When I see mothers with their grown-up sons, I feel so angry and so jealous, I want to scream, "It's not fair, it's not fair!"'

Nellie's voice became harsh but she didn't cry. Perhaps there were no tears left, thought Lisa.

'I'm sorry, Nell, I shouldn't have asked.'

Nellie shook her head vigorously. 'I'm glad you did. I feel better for talking about it. Stan and I never do and nobody ever mentions Luke in case they upset me, though I'd far prefer they did. I begin to wonder if Luke existed when his name is never spoken.'

She got off the sofa with a sigh. 'I'd better get to bed, I need to be up early in the morning.' Catching sight of her reflection in the mirror, she grimaced. 'I look like something the cat's dragged in, as Mam used to say.' She glanced down at Lisa curiously. 'I wonder why we're all so different?'

'What do you mean?'

'The O'Briens. The boys are so alike, there's no getting away from the fact they're brothers, but us girls! Joan's pale-skinned and red-haired, and we're both dark.' She frowned. 'Dad had blue eyes, didn't he?'

'I think so.'

'And Mam did too. I'm sure I read once that blue-eyed people couldn't have brown-eyed children, something to do with genes.' She laughed, 'D'you think Mam had a bit on the side?'

Lisa remembered the strange thing Mam said just before she died. She'd scarcely thought about it again, putting it down to the ramblings of a sick old woman. Despite what Nellie had just said, that was what she preferred to go on thinking.

'What – Mam?' she scoffed. '"Pigs might fly", as she was also fond of saying!'

*

After Nellie had gone to bed, Lisa remained sitting on the floor and poured the last of the wine into her glass, 'Waste not, want not,' she said to the empty room. She thought about her conversation with Nellie. 'I *am* happy,' she told herself. 'I lead a deeply fulfilling life and Tony is a charming companion, attentive and caring. In his own way, he thinks the world of me,' though she wondered sadly why he'd never attempted to come into her bed again after that first night. Perhaps he was too ashamed, worried he'd fail again. By now she was used to separate rooms, though it still seemed strange at Ferris Hall to say goodnight to your husband and go through different doors to bed. How could he adore her, as he claimed, yet never want to touch her? Once or twice she'd tried to talk about it, but he changed the subject impatiently, just as he did when she asked about his first wife.

Upstairs the bed creaked as Nellie turned over, the sound as clear as if it had been made in the same room. The small house was part of a row of terraced properties built for artisans at the end of the last century and the partitions were paper-thin.

Lisa glanced around the room affectionately. She'd fallen in love with the place as soon as she stepped off the busy Pimlico pavement into the narrow hall and felt a strange sense of familiarity, as if she'd been there before. The estate agent had been surprised when she offered to buy. 'I thought you'd prefer something grander,' he said, though the price was grand enough to make her jaw drop in surprise.

The previous owners had modernized it tastefully. The downstairs rooms had been knocked into one, a brick arch the only reminder that a wall had ever been there. What had been a wash-house was now a bathroom, covered to the ceiling with magnolia tiles flecked with gold, and by dint of clever planning, the small kitchen had been fitted with every conceivable labour-saving device. Sometimes Lisa wondered what the original tenants would have thought if they could see the luxurious fittings in what had been their working-class home – the lantern-style wall-lights, the plush carpets, the candy-striped covered chairs. She'd put one of Dent's paintings up, a brilliant oil of Tymperleys, though no one ever guessed it was supposed to be a house.

She turned off the lights; the room remained semi-lit, illuminated through the rear window by the night-long floodlit patio – in other words, the old backyard. Suddenly, she realized why the house had seemed so familiar when she first entered it. Its basic geography was identical to Chaucer Street! She walked around the room. This part would have been the parlour with its flowered lino and Mam's bed when she slept downstairs, and over there the big black grate which had Tom's chair at an angle in front.

Perhaps she'd drunk too much wine, because she strongly felt that if she closed her eyes and opened them again, she'd be back in Chaucer Street and everything that had happened since she left would dissolve into nothing and she'd be fifteen again, her whole life yet to live.

No, she'd never get rid of this house, no matter how much Tony persisted. The flat in Westminster was usually full of his cronies playing cards. She'd never be able to learn her lines and there wasn't room to put people up. Why, she thought, did he keep on about selling? Not only here, but Tymperleys, too – even her share in O'Brien Productions.

Because he only married you for your money, that's why.

There, she'd acknowledged it at last! She'd been unwilling to admit it, even to herself, for months.

She sank into a chair, longing for a cigarette. She'd given up when Mam died from lung cancer twelve years ago, but there were still times she ached for one. At the start he'd just dropped gentle hints; the roof of Ferris Hall needed over-hauling, slates were broken and rain poured into the attics. She offered to pay, estimates were called for and she'd written a cheque for over five thousand pounds, yet rain still seeped through the cracked slates and Tony was vague as to when the workmen would arrive.

The same thing had happened with the central heating. 'What a boon it would be,' he kept saying and his grey eyes lit up in delight when she joked, 'I'll buy central heating for your Christmas present!' But although she'd given him a cheque, wrapped in gift paper on the tree, the house remained cold and unheated. 'I'm still not sure which system is the best,' he'd said last time she mentioned it.

When it came to re-wiring – he claimed the existing installation was dangerous – she'd arranged for electricians to do the work herself. Although he accepted this in his genial, good-natured way, she had a feeling that deep down he was annoyed. She tried not to think he was getting money out of her, his wife, under false pretences.

A few months ago he had approached her with, 'Darling, would you mind terribly settling a few bills?' He was so charming about it, looking at her uncertainly, unsure of himself, a boyish smile on his face.

'Of course,' she said unhesitatingly, taking the bunch of invoices. After all, she lived in Ferris Hall and it was only right she should share in the running costs. The bills were for electricity, car tax, half a year's rates and other household expenses. Although she paid them willingly she felt slightly resentful when, the following month, she found another pile on her dressing table, alongside a beautiful bouquet of red roses. 'He might at least ask,' she thought to herself. It was almost as if the flowers were a bribe.

From what she'd gleaned from Mrs Mason, Sir Cameron Molyneux, Tony's father, had left a tidy sum together with a healthy portfolio of Blue Chip stocks and shares. What had Tony done with all this money, so that only five years later he had to ask his wife to pay basic expenses?

Nellie's bed creaked again and Lisa hoped she wasn't finding it difficult to sleep after all the wine. Suddenly, she felt an overwhelming desire to go upstairs and say, 'Nell, I was lying. I'm not happy at all, at least not with certain aspects of my life, in other words, my marriage.'

She didn't though. Tomorrow, in the daylight, everything would be all right again.

The sound of the telephone woke her. She picked up the extension beside the bed and gave the number, her voice husky with sleep.

'Lisa, did you watch the television last night?' It was Ralph and he sounded agitated.

'No, Nellie's here and we—'

'Dear God, Lisa, this is an awful thing . . .' He gave a hoarse sob.

She sat up quickly, wide awake. 'Darling, what's happened?'

'I saw a programme on TV last night about this new illness, AIDS. Have you heard about it?'

'Yes, I read an article in the paper.' Jesus, had Ralph got it?

'It must be what Gary died of, the symptoms are identical.'

'I wondered about that too,' she said, also wondering why Ralph should be so upset after all this time.

'Don't you see, Lisa?' he said despairingly. '*It was me that gave it to him!*'

'Oh Ralph, you can't possibly know that!'

'I do. They referred to it as the gay plague. I was Gary's only lover – I'm the only person he could have caught it off. I killed him, Lisa. If it wasn't for me, he'd be alive now. What am I going to do?' he wailed.

Lisa drew a deep breath and said crisply, 'There's nothing in this world you can do to help Gary. You know in your heart you wouldn't have hurt him deliberately.'

He groaned. 'But if I hadn't been unfaithful!'

'He didn't mind, he told me.'

'Did he really? What did he say?'

'I can't remember, it was a long time ago. Ralph, dear, it's all over now, in the past, but I'll tell you what you *can* do.'

'What?' he demanded eagerly.

'Help people who've got it now. I've still got the money Gary left me. I'm going to send a huge donation towards AIDS research. I think he would have liked that, don't you?'

She managed to calm him and he rang off sounding almost his normal self. Lisa sat staring at the telephone, thinking that if that article was right, Ralph must have AIDS in his blood – what was the condition called? HIV positive – which meant that one day he would die like Gary! She shuddered. Perhaps it was her age, but sometimes she felt that as each day passed, the world became a more frightening place in which to live.

Christy Costello said, 'Tony's very lucky. If he hangs onto his seat next time, it'll be entirely thanks to you.'

'I enjoy helping people,' Lisa said simply.

They were in Tony's 'surgery', a converted shop in the centre of Broxley which was open every Saturday morning for his constituents to bring problems which he might, or might not, be able to solve. Tony hadn't turned up yet. He frequently didn't, always seeming to find something more interesting to do in London. Usually Christy sat in on his behalf and when Lisa was free she took her husband's place.

That morning there'd been a string of people with complaints of one sort or another, some trite, some heartrending, like the old lady being browbeaten out of her lifelong rented cottage by a developer who wanted to modernize and re-sell. Lisa had a list of letters to write and telephone calls to make, though Christy would attend to these.

By one o'clock the surgery was empty and she felt satisfied that she'd done a good job of work.

'He's a lazy sod, our Tony,' Christy said with a grin. 'Wants his arse kicking, if you'll pardon my language.'

'I've heard worse than that in my time,' she replied.

'Fancy a drink?' he said. 'The Red Lion's just across the road.'

Lisa did fancy a drink, but wasn't sure if she should take one with Christy. She found her feelings for him confusing. Sometimes she liked his bluff, hearty manner, but there was a streak of hardness in him that warned her not to get on his wrong side. Occasionally she found him looking at her, a hungry expression on his broad red face, though what disturbed her most was the answering flicker in her own body which she always tried to shrug away. Still, a drink wouldn't hurt.

'Okay, I'll have a beer.'

'Lady Elizabeth Molyneux can't be seen quaffing a pint of best bitter!' He pretended shock. 'It's got to be sherry, dry at that.'

'If I can't have beer, I'm not coming,' she said stubbornly. 'I'm not changing my drinking habits just because I've got a title.'

He brought the beer in a half-pint glass. 'Looks better this way,' he hissed.

After he sat down Lisa said, 'Christy, you know these

businessmen who ask Tony for help to get contracts for roads and stuff, is he allowed to do that?'

Christy's eyes grew blank and he stared down into his drink. 'What do you mean?' he asked.

'I think he's using his influence as an MP to fatten people's wallets and it doesn't seem right.'

He said vaguely, 'It's nothing to worry about,' and changed the subject, which she perversely took to mean there was.

When she got back to Ferris Hall she was surprised to hear raised voices coming from the kitchen. Tony and Mrs Mason were having a row. Lisa crept along the passage, curious to know what it was about.

'You can't expect me and Mason to work for nothing and we haven't been paid in weeks,' Mrs Mason shouted angrily.

'You know it'll be forthcoming eventually,' snarled Tony. 'And don't forget you live here rent-free.' Lisa felt her mouth drop open in surprise. She'd never heard him use that tone of voice before; in fact, she hadn't thought him capable of sounding so fierce. Usually he was so gentle and courteous.

'Eventually's no good, sir,' Mrs Mason said stubbornly. 'We need money to spend, like other people. As for rent-free, the accommodation's part of the job. Another thing – the butcher won't give any more credit till his bill's paid and the off-licence refuses to give credit at all – to anyone, not just you. Now you've used up all Sir Cameron's cellar, you need to start buying wine.'

'If you're going to make trouble,' Tony said coldly, 'I might consider looking round for new staff.'

Mrs Mason laughed sarcastically. 'Not when you find out what you'd have to pay them, you won't.'

'I'll have to see what I can do,' Tony said abruptly.

'You'll make it soon, won't you, sir?' Mrs Mason spoke with a mixture of contempt and pleading.

Lisa hurried back along the hall and when Tony emerged she leaned back against the door as if she had just come in.

'Darling!' His face broke into a warm smile of welcome. 'I didn't realize you'd arrived.' He came over, took her hands and rubbed his cheek against hers. Could this be the same man who'd just threatened Mrs Mason? Lisa began to doubt her hearing. He put his arm around her shoulders, led her into the drawing room and seemed so genuinely pleased to see her that all her misgivings about him faded. No one could be such a good actor as this.

'Sit down, my dear,' he said solicitously. 'I'll fetch you a drink. Where have you been? Mason said you arrived early this morning.'

'Where *you* should have been,' Lisa answered reprovingly. 'Taking care of your surgery.'

'You should let Christy do that, it's what he's paid for.'

'No, Tony, it's what *you're* paid for. Christy's only paid to be your agent.'

'I doubt if people notice who's sitting behind the desk whilst they pour out their silly worries,' he said disparagingly as he brought her a whisky. 'Anyway, last night I went out with some chaps and didn't notice the time. When I did, I'd missed the midnight train.'

She shook her head, smiling. 'Honestly, Tony, you're incorrigible.'

Later on she went to see Mrs Mason and asked how much Tony owed. When the woman told her, Lisa was shocked to discover how little it was, virtually slave wages.

'I'll pay you from now on,' she promised. 'And it's about time you had a raise. I reckon a fair rate would be more than double that.'

That night, when she went to change for dinner, she found a single orchid in a slender cut-glass vase on her dressing table beside a clutch of bills. They included final demands for the telephone and electricity and a long overdue invoice from a local garage for repairs to the Mercedes. The butcher's bill she'd heard all about, so she'd better settle that before she left Broxley if they wanted to eat next week. She felt indignant when she saw one from a Savile Row tailor for over a thousand pounds. Tony could smile and charm her all he liked, but she wasn't going to buy his clothes. Picking up her chequebook and the bills she marched along the corridor to his room, pausing outside, wondering whether to knock or

461

just walk in. After all, he was her husband. In the end she knocked and he shouted, 'Enter.'

He'd changed into a dinner jacket and was sitting on the bed tying his shoelaces.

'I'm not prepared to pay this,' she said bluntly, handing him the tailor's invoice.

He made a horrified face. 'Darling, did I slip that in with the others? I'm so sorry.'

Despite his show of sincerity, she had an uneasy feeling that he was lying, that he'd put the bill there deliberately, hoping she'd settle it without question. 'I'll write cheques for the others now, else the phone and electricity might be cut off – you should have given me those before – and the garage are probably waiting for their money. It's six weeks since they fixed the car.'

'I could do with a new car,' he said hopefully.

'You can always borrow mine,' she said absently. She'd bought a Cavalier to use in Yorkshire. She sat on the bed beside him and opened her chequebook. Suddenly she heard him gasp. What's the matter?' she asked.

'The top stub!' His voice was hoarse. 'It's for half a million pounds!'

'That's right, it was for charity.'

He was trying to read her scribbled record. 'The Challenger Trust, is that it?'

'Yes, it's an AIDS charity. A close friend died a few years ago; this is just a gesture in his memory.'

'A gesture!' His face was working furiously and his breath was raw. 'You mean you can just sit down and write a cheque for half a million?'

There was something almost frightening about his stupefaction. His face was like that of a starving man being taunted with food he couldn't reach. She cursed herself for letting him see the chequebook. 'It was his money,' she said eventually. 'He left it to me.'

'And you gave it all away? When I—' He broke off.

'I felt obliged to,' she said. She went over to the door, anxious to get away. In fact, half a million pounds was only a fraction of Gary's money but she wasn't going to let Tony know that. She'd been waiting for a just cause and now she'd found it. If necessary, the whole lot would go towards AIDS research. There was no way she'd spend the revenue from *Hearts and Flowers* and the other movies Gary made on her husband's tailor's bills.

At dinner, Tony was back to his normal self, as gracious and affectionate as ever, though he seemed to look at her with new respect and Lisa thought ruefully, 'It's only because I'm even richer than he'd first imagined.' Her misgivings returned in force. It was a really miserable situation. After all, at the wedding ceremony they'd promised each other all their worldly goods. If, at the beginning of their marriage, he'd told her he needed money, she would have given it to him. 'What's mine's yours,' she might have said, and even suggested a joint bank account. But Tony seemed incapable of being straightforward and she resented the way he dropped hints, wheedling money out of her so insidiously and telling lies. Anyway, what did he need all this cash for? Their lifestyle was modest and an MP's salary was not exactly a pittance, so what on earth did he spend it all on?

A general election was called in the spring of 1983. Suddenly Tony was alerted to the fact that he might lose his seat. The local newspaper published his poor voting record and his abysmal attendance in the House of Commons – both of which came as a shock to his unsuspecting wife – together with an article claiming he lacked commitment to ordinary voters.

'*Sir Anthony seems far more concerned with management than with workers,*' the reporter wrote. '*He fails to realize that he was elected to represent the entire constituency, not just the élite few. Broxley's large and expanding council estate has been gradually filling up with Labour voters over the last few years and this could well tip the balance against him when Polling Day comes.*'

Lisa had a trip to Hollywood planned but cancelled it so she could remain at Tony's side as he frantically began to canvass support for re-election. Despite the fact that he had neglected them, the people he met on the doorstep were clearly susceptible to his eager, boyish charm.

'This is what you should have been doing all along,' Christy Costello said irritably. 'Not waiting until three weeks before an election.'

Lisa went into the Party office and threw herself into a chair. Kicking off her shoes, she exclaimed, 'Phew, I'm beat.' That morning she had attended a press conference with Tony, visited a hospital and canvassed several streets.

She looked over at Christy, who was on the telephone. She expected a smile of recognition, but he ignored her. She could hear a faint voice on the other end of the line which seemed to be arguing fiercely. When the voice stopped, Christy said, 'I've already told you, freedom of the press can go fuck itself. Sir Anthony's taken out an injunction, so you repeat a word and you're breaking the law and I'll see your rag closed down if it's the last thing I do.' His face was even redder than usual and he practically spat his words into the receiver.

She listened with alarm. He was glaring at a magazine open on the desk in front of him. Lisa reached for it and he suddenly became aware of her presence. His hand slammed down, just missing the paper as she pulled it away. It was the satirical magazine *Private Eye*, and a section had been marked with a red felt pen. She began to read, conscious that Christy had transferred his glare in her direction.

Sir Anthony "Cardsharp" Molyneux, laid-back Tory MP for Broxley in South Yorkshire, has managed to reduce this once-solid Conservative seat to a marginal. Cardsharp, who took over from the well-loved and highly-respected Fergus Lomax at the last election, finds the atmosphere in Grundy's Casino more to his liking than the House of Commons, and only rarely graces the latter with his presence. Those with a suspicious turn of mind might wonder if Cardsharp's spectacular losses at Grundy's, where the minimum bet is four figures, together with the even more spectacular collapse of BrixCo, the offshore investment company in which he had a major share (currently being investigated by the Fraud Squad) is in any way connected with the sudden flurry of planned new roads and buildings in Broxley, where the old library, a fine example of late Victorian architecture, will be demolished to make way for a new modern eyesore, together with the cottage hospital. Locals claim themselves satisfied with the old buildings, and say that the motorway which will cut through the beautiful dales is unwanted and unnecessary. Is it just coincidence that the contractors for the new building works are regular guests at Cardsharp's ancestral home, Ferris Hall?'

Christy slammed the telephone down. 'That was the editor of the *Broxley Gazette*. I frightened the shit out of him. He won't publish.'

'Is this true?' she asked, indicating the article.

He seemed resigned to the fact that she'd read it.'Well, there's no smoke without fire, as they say.'

'So it is then.' She laid the paper on her knee with a sigh. 'I suppose that's where the money for the roof and the central heating went.' She felt numb, though not surprised. In her heart of hearts she'd suspected something was going on. If the magazine was right, Tony was a fanatical and committed gambler. That's where his salary went, his father's money and the thousands he'd tricked out of her.

'Has he really taken out an injunction?'

'He's thinking about it, just to keep the local press off our backs till after the election. Once it's over, the fire will go out in the editor's belly and he'll return to heel. Normally, no one takes much notice of *Private Eye*. You're never sure whether what they print is the God's honest truth or a load of cobblers.' He sighed. 'We never had a whiff of scandal with Fergus, he was as straight as a die.'

'Were you his agent, too?'

'Yes.' His rather hard features softened. 'Elections were fun in those days; even his opponents loved Fergus. Everyone called him by his first name, they still do. It was more like a three-week carnival than a campaign. But with Tony!' He gave a disgusted shrug. 'All these photo opportunities. I mean, Tony visiting schools, Tony walking around hospital wards, shaking people's hands. Makes you want to puke when he only does it every four years. Fergus did it all the time.'

'Why do you stay?' she asked.

He looked at her quizzically. 'I could ask you the same question. As for me, I think I'll review my position when the election's over.'

'After reading this,' said Lisa, 'I might do the same thing myself.'

The atmosphere at the count in Broxley Town Hall was tense with excitement. Lisa walked along the long trestle tables and watched the votes pile up in what looked like equal quantities for the three candidates, for Tony, Liberal and Labour. Christy, who was standing behind her, muttered, 'Broxley has deserted us, but the vote from the villages still looks solidly in our favour. He might just scrape home.'

Despite the qualms she felt over her husband, Lisa hoped the three weeks of hard campaigning she'd done on his behalf wouldn't be in vain. As the night wore on and the thousands of votes were being counted, Tony began to bite his fingernails nervously. 'I'm getting worried,' he said.

'It's a bit late for that,' Lisa said caustically and he looked at her, a hurt expression on his face. She hadn't discussed the *Private Eye* article with him and didn't know if Christy had told him she'd read it.

Suddenly, as if by magic, the tables were empty and there were no voting slips left to count. Instead, they were stacked in the centre of the room, in bundles of one hundred before each candidates' name, and a Town Hall official was slipping through them counting the bundles. Christy and the other agents were hovering anxiously around. From where she stood, Lisa felt sure the row in front of Tony's name stretched slightly further than the other two. There was a whoop of joy followed by loud cheers and suddenly Tony was back at her side. 'We've won,' he cried.

His majority had gone down yet again to less than a thousand votes. Labour and Liberal had virtually tied for second place.

Lisa went on stage with Tony for the official declaration, along with the other candidates and their wives. After it was over, he was swept away by his supporters for a celebration party. 'Come on, Lisa,' she heard him shout before he was almost carried out of the door.

'Won't it be a bit subdued?' she said to Christy as she followed him out. 'Under the circumstances?'

'Winning is all that counts, at least tonight,' he replied. 'If it had been by just one vote they'd be equally happy.'

When they got outside she went over to her car. 'Where are you going?' he said in surprise. 'The party's only across the road.'

'I'm not in the mood to celebrate. I'm going home.'

Back in Ferris Hall she telephoned Heathrow and booked a flight to California for the next day. O'Brien Productions had been making a lot of dud movies over the past few years and she urgently wanted to rap a few knuckles. She'd cancelled the visit arranged for the previous month in order to campaign for Tony. It was early evening in California, so somebody would still be in the office. She got through and arranged a meeting of senior staff for the following Monday.

After she'd removed the jacket of the blue suit she'd bought to campaign in, she poured herself a whisky and turned on the television. According to the election results already received, it looked as though Mrs Thatcher was heading for a landslide. After a while she turned the set off with a sigh. She felt a sense of anti-climax. The last few weeks had been hectic, emotional even. People got so passionate over politics. It was the same when you finished a movie, or a play ended its run. Life seemed to stop and you felt convinced nothing would ever be exciting again. She knew what would lessen this feeling of emptiness, but there was no chance of that with Tony! Not that she would have welcomed it now, it was too late. Maybe she should have gone to the party to pass the time.

Feeling irritated with herself, she went over to the window. There was no moon and the dales were muffled in blackness. In the far distance, the street lights of Broxley glowed orange and the town looked as if it was on fire.

Headlights swept up the drive and her heart sank. She didn't feel like talking to Tony just now. The front door closed quietly, footsteps sounded in the hall and she wished she'd had the forethought to rush up to bed. A man's reflection appeared behind her as she remained staring out of the dark window and she started in alarm. It wasn't Tony, but Christy. There was a soft thudding feeling in her stomach as he came towards her, his large frame swallowing up her own reflection, and she felt his hands on her waist, warm through the thin material of her blouse. A voice told her to move away, to stop him, but the words remained locked in her throat and by now she had hesitated too long. His hands moved up and began to caress her breasts and his lips were on the nape of her neck and the hunger she had suppressed for so long was aching to be satisfied. She gave a groan of supplication as she turned towards him and he picked her up in his broad strong arms and carried her upstairs.

Chapter 42

Could she bring herself to sell Tymperleys, a house with so many rich memories, where she'd lived with Dent and Sabina, where Gary and Vita had died, where once she'd been so happy?

The meeting yesterday had been heated and passions flared. 'The company should go public. We need a massive injection of cash before we can make the sort of movies you're talking about,' she'd been told. 'Nowadays, any movie worth its salt costs thirty, forty million dollars. Our yearly budget is less than half that.'

'But just because our movies are cheap, they don't have to be crap,' she raged. 'And crap is all you've been making these last few years.'

She scarcely knew the people she was addressing, accountants all of them, young men with anonymous faces who cared more about money than quality and knew nothing about making movies. They made her feel old, as if her values were out of date, no longer relevant in today's climate, where making a quick buck was more important than making a good movie. It was her own fault. She'd neglected the company shamefully for years. It had moved on without her and she couldn't expect these people to reverse direction just because she'd suddenly noticed they were on the wrong course – or at least a course of which she disapproved.

Lisa said threateningly, 'Perhaps I should sell my two-thirds share,' and was saddened by the alacrity with which they fell on her suggestion. Ralph had sold out several years ago.

They didn't give her a chance to change her mind, not that she wanted to. Contracts were produced so swiftly she realized they must have had them ready, and she signed, to the tune of five million dollars, although she knew she could have got double if she'd bothered to argue. But there was one thing on which she did insist – that they change the company name.

'O'Brien is *my* name,' she said forcibly. 'Quite frankly, I don't want it associated with the rubbish you're turning out.' She thought this might make them feel ashamed, but it didn't.

'That's an idea we've been toying with ourselves,' one of them said smugly.

Tymperleys was so quiet, so peaceful, so welcoming. In the early evening sunlight the house had a warm, tranquil air. Chloe had been expecting her and there were flowers everywhere and the smell of lavender polish, the sort Millie used to use. Lisa sat on the patio and as dusk fell, she switched the garden lights on and put Wagner on the loud-speaker system. If she closed her eyes, it might be possible to imagine things as they used to be, before everything changed. She closed them, but snapped them open almost immediately. This was not the time for reminiscing, for raking over things past. She was too fond of doing that. This was time to think about the future.

No, of course she couldn't sell Tymperleys! It would be selling memories. After all, Dent's ghost was here and by now Vita and Gary's spirits would be hovering in the rafters. She smiled to herself. No they wouldn't; if Vita and Gary's spirits were anywhere they'd be down in the little cinema and in the middle of the night, when Chloe and Albert were asleep, the two of them would be sitting in front of the flickering screen watching movies. She thought about those movies; some were works of art, others great majestic films that left you choked with emotion and a few were just ordinary, competent works. All had been made without much money, though with much love and with the blood, sweat and tears of everyone involved.

As if she could draw a line under that! There was no way this would be the end of her Hollywood career. One day, she'd start another company with Gary's money and her own. That's what he would have liked most for her to do – make the sort of movies of which he would have been proud.

The old house creaked – perhaps it was giving a sigh of

relief, knowing it wasn't going to be sold and that one day she would be coming back.

She'd only been back in Pimlico half an hour when the doorbell rang. As she went to answer it Lisa prayed that it wasn't Tony, for she hadn't yet worked out what she wanted to say to him. To her relief, it was her neighbour, Florence Dale, an elderly widow who'd lived next door for over fifty years. In her hands she held a square cardboard box filled with holes.

Lisa invited her in. Every time she entered the house the old lady marvelled at the alterations. 'It's difficult to believe this house was once the same as mine,' she said for the umpteenth time. 'I just came to tell you half a dozen bunches of flowers arrived while you were away. I've put them in water so they're still quite fresh.'

'Please keep them,' said Lisa. 'If they're not in the way.'

'Are you sure? They brighten up the parlour no end. This came for you too.' She opened the box and Lisa gasped. A tiny blue-grey Persian kitten stared up at her with round frightened blue eyes.

'Isn't she sweet!' she cried.

'He – it's a boy. I've christened him Omar, though you can change it. We've had some interesting conversations these last few days. He's a good listener.' The old lady smiled. 'I'll be sad to see him go.'

'Would you mind keeping him too? He's adorable, but I'm away so much he'd be cruelly neglected.' She couldn't resist picking the kitten up and pulling him on her shoulder. His little heart was pounding, but as she stroked his fluffy back he started to purr and she felt his soft paw against her neck as he began to play with her earrings.

'You're a handsome young man, Omar, and I'd love you to be mine, but Florence has more time for you.' Reluctantly she handed the kitten back.

'There's a card inside the box. Omar did a little job on it but I washed it off.' Florence produced a stained piece of cardboard as Lisa giggled. *To my wonderful, dedicated wife in gratitude for all your hard work during the election,'* Tony had written.

*

After Florence had gone, taking Omar with her, Lisa rather regretted giving the kitten away so hastily. Perhaps she could have arranged joint ownership and looked after him whilst she was home. Right now she too needed a good listener. She had to rehearse what to say to Tony when she told him she wanted a divorce.

It hadn't been a hard decision. In fact, she thought ironically, it showed how empty and shallow the marriage was that she could so easily rid herself of a husband, yet cling to a house. This weekend she'd go to Ferris Hall and have things out with him. In a few weeks, rehearsals would begin for a new play and it would be nice to make a fresh start, unencumbered by a husband whose behaviour worried her deeply. One day the revelations in *Private Eye* might reach a wider readership and she didn't want her name mixed up with his dubious activities.

Lisa travelled to Ferris Hall on the Saturday. Tony must have seen her drive up in the Cavalier which she'd left at the station, for he came running out to meet her. 'Darling, where on earth have you been?' he cried. 'I've been trying to contact you for the past fortnight.'

'I've been in the States,' she said shortly.

'You didn't come to our post-election party. I missed you terribly – if it hadn't been for you I mightn't have won.' He kissed her cheek and as they walked into the house he threw his arm around her shoulders, squeezing her tenderly. As ever, his welcome was so warm and he seemed so pleased to see her that she began to feel guilty for doubting him.

'I've a few friends here,' he said. 'They're staying the night.'

She groaned inwardly. That ruled out the heart-to-heart talk she'd planned for tonight and by tomorrow, if Tony kept this charm offensive up, she might even have changed her mind about divorce!

The friends were three middle-aged businessmen, new members of the moneyed classes, still with their bluff Yorkshire accents, oozing that noisy bright-eyed confidence that often seems to come with quickly acquired wealth.

There was a certain sameness about them and even after Tony introduced them, she found it difficult to tell them apart.

Christy was there, but Lisa didn't meet his eyes. It was embarrassing to recall the almost animal-like vigour of her responses when they'd made love.

After dinner, one man, perhaps the most voluble, said, 'Right, then, let's get down to brass tacks, shall we?'

Tony raised his eyebrows at Lisa. So, he wanted her to leave! She ignored the signal and the man who had spoken glanced from one to the other. When Lisa remained seated, he said, 'You don't want to bother your pretty head with rather dull business matters, Lady Elizabeth.'

Christy burst out laughing. 'According to the *Financial Times*, that pretty head has just sold her share in a film company for five million dollars.'

There was a gasp from the guests and Tony's cup crashed in his saucer. Christy laughed again and Lisa glared at him. Tony had frequently urged her to sell out from O'Brien Productions and she would have preferred him not to know about the hefty rise in her bank balance.

'Well, I never!' The man who seemed to have appointed himself spokesman shrugged. 'I'll bring you up to date on what we discussed last week. I've done a bit of spadework, at least my solicitor has, and found that the property Spring Engineering occupies is covered by two leases, one for the ground, the other for the buildings themselves. The former is a nominal yearly charge that hasn't been changed since before the war, of two hundred and fifty pounds.'

One of the other men said contemptuously, 'That's chickenfeed in this day and age. Is it up for sale?'

'It could be. The owner is an old chap, a pensioner, who hasn't the faintest idea what it's worth. Offer him a couple of thousand quid and he'd be a knockover.'

'What about the buildings?' Tony asked.

'That's a bit more difficult. The rent is two and a half thousand a year and the owners, a London-based property company, are well aware of its value, but I reckon six figures would see them right.'

'So we could get the entire thing for just over a hundred thou?'

'Is this the factory in Broxley High Street you're talking about?' asked Lisa.

'That's right, Lady Elizabeth.'

'What on earth use is that to you?'

One of the men answered, 'Once we own the leases, we raise the rents.'

'But it would take forever to get your money back,' she said.

'Darling, don't you see?' Tony leaned towards her eagerly. 'That site is ideal for an hotel, right in the heart of town.'

'You mean you'd close the factory down?'

'The factory would have to close itself down when it couldn't meet its new rents,' the self-appointed spokesman said.

'And nearly two thousand men and women would be put on the dole! Why, that's a terrible thing to do,' she said angrily.

'I knew you wouldn't understand, Lisa,' Tony said stiffly. 'Anyway, there'd be loads of jobs available in the hotel.'

'That wouldn't be for years and anyway, skilled engineering workers can't be expected to become bottle-washers and wait on tables.'

There was an awkward silence. Someone said slyly, 'Think what the return would be if you invested some of your own capital.'

Lisa didn't answer. She sat staring down at the table, fuming inwardly at the idea of people's livelihoods being in the hands of such greedy, grasping men. Suddenly she got up, pushing her chair away with such force that a leg caught on the fraying carpet and it flew back, landing on the floor with a thud. Everybody jumped as she left the room without a word.

She wondered if Christy would come to her room tonight. But how could he, with Tony in the house? It was gone midnight when she heard the visitors go to bed, their voices loud and angry as they argued about something in the corridor outside. Then a car drove away, it could only be

Christy's, and Tony's soft footsteps passed her room and the door of his bedroom opened and closed.

Sleep was a long time coming and she tossed and turned, still angry when she thought about the night's conversation. She had almost drifted into sleep when she was abruptly brought awake by someone slipping into bed beside her. Christy!

'I thought I heard you drive away,' she whispered. His hands were all over her body and she shivered in delight.

'I left it on the road and walked back.'

He began to kiss her and she felt herself melt into nothingness. It didn't matter that her husband was just across the corridor. All that mattered was this man thrusting against her, with his hard, demanding lips, his seeking hands. She gave herself up to him and just lay there, supine and willing, whilst he took her again and again.

His body was huge and she felt tiny and vulnerable as he crouched over her. Once again she experienced a dizzy, delicious pressure mounting inside her that ached to be released. She was poised, feverishly anticipating the glorious culmination of their lovemaking, when somewhere beyond, in a corner of her brain that must have remained alert to other things, she heard a noise, a soft clicking sound. Christy, his eyes closed, lost in passion, heard nothing. Lisa turned her head and saw the door to her bedroom was open a crack. Perhaps he'd not closed it properly when he came in. Then the door moved and she could see the white of a hand on the knob outside.

She said urgently, 'Christy! There's someone watching.' The door closed swiftly and silently.

He collapsed beside her, groaning, 'You must have imagined it.'

'I didn't. The door just closed, I saw quite clearly.'

'Shit,' he said.

'Who could it be?' She wasn't sure why she felt so frightened.

'Who do you think?'

'Tony?' She was horrified.

Christy laughed coarsely. 'That's about the limit of his sex-drive I should imagine, a peeping Tom, a voyeur.'

'You can't know that,' she muttered.

'My dear Lisa, you acted with me like a person who'd been stranded in a desert without water. It's obvious you haven't been made love to in years, yet you're a lovely, passionate woman and I feel flattered you drank from me.'

'What are we going to do?' she asked.

'I'm going to continue what I'm already doing, looking for another job.' He propped his elbow on the pillow and looked down at her. 'Will you come with me when I find one?'

She shook her head. 'Now it's my turn to be flattered, Christy, but no. I've finished with men forever.' She was trying to be tactful. A person in a desert dying of thirst would accept a drink from anyone. Almost any man who'd looked at her as Christy had might have ended up as he was now, beside her in bed. In certain ways he wasn't much better than Tony when it came to integrity.

In the dim moonlight she could see that he didn't look the least bit upset. In fact he smiled. 'What were we then – two ships that pass in the night? A tugboat and a luxury liner, both Irish registered.'

'I suppose so,' she said. 'And now we must signal goodbye.'

He began to dress swiftly, stuffing his tie in his pocket. When he'd finished, he sat on the edge of the bed and looked at her, his normally hard features softening.

'I take it you're going to divorce Tony?' he said.

'Yes. I'd intended bringing the subject up last night, but those men . . .'

'Be careful, won't you, Lisa? I don't want you ending up like Rhoda.'

'Who's Rhoda?'

'Tony's first wife. He cleaned her out of every penny and as soon as her money had gone, he divorced her. Afterwards, she killed herself.'

The pale, early morning sun rose like a quickly blossoming flower out of a bank of snow-white clouds, and droplets of dew glistened like jewels on the rough, uneven grass. As Lisa jogged up and down the hills she could see the dew spurting underneath her feet like sparks from a Roman candle and the ankles of her tracksuit were soaking wet.

This was the part of the weekend she enjoyed most, running over the dales in the early morning.

The fresh air had cleared her mind and as usual the problems of the night assumed their true proportion in daylight. Although it was nauseous to think of Tony spying on her, what did it matter now she had decided to divorce him? There was no way she'd end up like his poor first wife. She'd continue paying the household bills, but apart from that Tony wasn't getting another penny out of her.

Her breath was hoarse as she virtually staggered up a hill. This was her first exercise in weeks. When she reached the top, she stared at the magnificent view, the rolling green dales, lost in admiration. This was what she would miss most of all when she no longer came to Ferris Hall.

After she got her breath back, she turned and began to run home, though by the time she arrived the run had become a walk.

Mrs Mason was waiting for her in the hall. 'There's been a phone call for you from Fergus Lomax. I've written the number on the pad. He wants to see you. It's urgent.'

'Thank you for coming so quickly.' Fergus Lomax was sitting in a high-backed chair in front of the open window, his legs wrapped in a woollen blanket. The house was unpretentious – a moderately-sized Victorian villa surrounded by a sweet-smelling garden. The window opened onto a figure-of-eight shaped fishpond and she could see a frog sitting amidst the bordering plants, its gullet throbbing violently.

Fergus's wife had let her in – a tall, commanding woman who looked Lisa up and down disapprovingly. 'Don't tire him now,' she said sternly. 'He's not up to visitors.'

'He invited me,' said Lisa indignantly.

'I know that, but what I say still goes. He's not up to visitors and he shouldn't be tired.' She showed Lisa in and disappeared.

'I apologize for Gertie,' Fergus Lomax said as she entered the room. 'I'd never see a soul if it was up to her. I also apologize for not getting up. I'm afraid my legs have forgotten what they were put there for and no longer support me. Sit down, my dear, here, beside me, and let me look at you. Yes, you're every bit as lovely as people say and even nicer in the flesh than in your photographs.'

'Why, thank you!' He was flirting with her. She could tell he'd been a devil in his day. No wonder his wife was so protective! His bushy hair was still mainly black, gradually turning to silver on his lush, curly beard. He looked like a jovial Long John Silver.

'Why haven't we met before?' he demanded. 'I'd have thought Tony'd be in touch from time to time, but I never hear a word from him.'

'I'm afraid you'll have to ask Tony that.' She didn't say that Tony resented any mention of Fergus Lomax on the assumption it meant criticism of his own performance – which it usually did.

'One thing I'm famous for,' Fergus said, 'is coming straight to the point, so that's what I'll do now. What's your husband doing to my old constituency? Is he intent on bleeding it totally dry?'

The question was so unexpected that she felt her eyes widen in surprise. 'What do you mean?'

'I understand that after the fiasco of the new library and cottage hospital, and the motorway to nowhere which will desecrate our beautiful countryside, he now intends to close down Spring Engineering, Broxley's main employers. I also understand that you disapprove of this, which is why I don't feel it's an impertinence to raise the subject.'

Lisa felt even more surprised. 'How on earth do you know all that?' she demanded. 'They only talked about it in detail last night.'

He winked, looking more like Long John Silver than ever, and tapped his nose. 'I have my informant.'

'In Ferris Hall? It must be Christy.'

'I'm not telling, least not yet, not till I know you better. About Spring Engineering . . .?'

'As you seem to know so much, I don't feel disloyal to Tony by telling you you're right, though he – and his friends – don't so much mean to close it down as raise the rents so high that the firm has no alternative but to close itself down.'

'And build an hotel?'

'That's right,' agreed Lisa. 'I think it's a terrible idea, putting all those people out of work.'

'Do you now!'

She began to feel angry again. 'It seems wrong. Surely people should have some control over their destiny.' A memory came to her of words spoken years, perhaps decades ago. She wracked her brain. 'It was explained to me once, I can't remember how it went, something about common ownership of the means of production. That's how it should be.' Of course, it was Harry Greenbaum who'd said it. Who else? she thought affectionately.

Fergus Lomax was staring at her, his face a mixture of disbelief and astonishment. As he stared his face turned bright red and he laughed. He roared until tears ran down his cheeks and he began to choke and gasp for breath and the laugh became more of a husky wheeze.

The door flew open and his wife came in. 'What have you done to him?' she demanded.

'I've no idea,' said Lisa nervously.

'You'd better take a tablet.' She grabbed her husband by the shoulder and tried to force a white capsule into his mouth.

'Get away, Gertie. No tablet can stop people laughing and I hope one's never invented. Leave me alone, there's a good girl.'

Gertie left reluctantly, throwing a murderous glance at Lisa as she went out of the door.

'What's so funny?' Lisa felt slightly annoyed.

'You know what you just quoted? Clause IV of the Labour Party constitution. Pure Marxism, my dear. Does Anthony know you're a dyed-in-the-wool socialist?'

'If I am it's unintentional. I've never really thought about it.'

'Then perhaps you should. I admire firm convictions, even when they are the opposite of my own. In fact, the best friend I have in the world is a socialist – Eric Heffer, the Liverpool MP.' He made an impatient gesture. 'I'm wasting your time. I asked you here to discuss the dismal future of the main source of employment in our town. What are we to do about it? The firm has been struggling to stay afloat as it is, with short-time working and redundancies, and the shareholders' dividends have been negligible, though I think things will start to pick up in a year or two. Until then, any increase in outgoings, rent for instance, would be a death blow and the company won't be there to be picked up when the time comes.'

'The obvious solution is for someone else to buy the leases first,' said Lisa.

'Yes, but where's the money to come from?' said Fergus glumly. 'It would take a fool to put up over a hundred thousand pounds without a hope in hell of a return on their investment for years, if ever. Mind you, I'm fool enough to do it, but all I could afford is the ground lease.'

'My mother used to say "a fool and his money are soon parted".' Lisa took a swift decision. If Fergus was willing to risk his money, she'd risk hers too. 'I'll buy the other lease, but I'd like to take a look around the place first. In the meantime, I'd appreciate you keeping my name out of things. I'll telephone tomorrow afternoon.'

Instead of going straight home, Lisa called in at the Red Lion and had a ploughman's lunch. If she missed the meal at Ferris Hall, Tony's visitors might have left by the time she got back. When she drove up to the house later, she was thankful to see their cars had gone.

Tony came out into the hall when he heard her come in and she regarded him warily, but there was nothing about him to indicate he'd recently seen his wife make love to another man. In fact he looked unusually happy and his normally pale cheeks glowed pink.

'I'm going back to London soon, darling. Like to come with me?'

'No, I've a few things to do in Broxley tomorrow,' she told him.

There was no one else in the house apart from the Masons. It was an ideal time to discuss divorce, but she found herself hesitating. It was important to be around Ferris Hall over the next few weeks whilst this business with Spring Engineering was so up in the air. The divorce could wait. She smiled at Tony and said, 'I think I'll go and lie down for a while. I hardly slept a wink last night.'

The words were scarcely out of her mouth before she realized how true they were! It was difficult to keep a straight face. Tony said something about being gone by the time she got up and she ran upstairs and collapsed on the bed, laughing. Better to laugh than cry, she thought when she calmed down, though it would be easy to cry when she thought what a mess she'd made of her life.

The smell and the heat in Spring Engineering were suffocating. As the young receptionist led her across the factory floor towards the manager's office, Lisa could scarcely breathe, though possibly the noise was even worse than the smell and the heat, a pounding monotonous hammering sound that seemed to echo off the dirty brick walls. Although she'd only been in the place a few minutes, she could already feel damp patches under her arms, and her neck was moist against the white collar of her blouse, fresh that morning.

It had taken a long time to choose the right outfit. She didn't want to appear to be slumming by wearing something too casual, on the other hand, it would be offensive to turn up in a designer outfit which had cost what these men could only hope to earn in months. In the end she'd decided on a plain black suit over a crisp white blouse, though the blouse no longer felt crisp. She'd left her hair loose for a change, drawing it back from her forehead under a black velvet Alice band.

The girl paused before the door of a glass-partitioned section in the corner of the building. 'This is Mr Oxton's office.'

Mr Oxton was the manager, and even though the receptionist had rung through to say Lisa was here, he jumped up nervously, knocking an empty cup over on the desk. There was no roof to the room so the smell here was as vile as in the factory, though there was an added odour which she couldn't identify.

'How do you do, Lady Elizabth. This is indeed an honour.' But he didn't look honoured, in fact he looked petrified.

'Please don't call me that,' she said pleasantly. 'It makes me feel uncomfortable.'

'Wh . . . what, then?' he stammered.

'What's your first name?'

'Arthur.'

'Well, if I call you Arthur, will you call me Lisa, please?'

They shook hands and she wondered why his palms were so clammy and why he still appeared so nervous and ill-at-ease. An elderly man with a stooped back and weak, flaccid features, he looked long past retirement age. He wore a khaki overall coat over stained, pin-striped trousers.

'What can I do for you, Lady . . . er, Lisa?'

'I've just come to have a look round,' she explained. 'That is, if it's convenient.'

He paused and she wondered if he was going to say it wasn't convenient and to get the hell out of his factory. Instead, he picked up the telephone and dialled two numbers. 'Can you come in here, Jim?'

Whilst they waited, he shuffled nervously from foot to foot without speaking. At one point he licked his lips and glanced longingly towards the top drawer of his desk and Lisa immediately understood the reason for his agitation when she recognized the extra smell in the office. Arthur Oxton had been drinking, even though it was not yet nine o'clock. Not only that, he was aching for another drink which was almost certainly kept in his desk.

There was a quick knock on the door and a man entered without waiting for a reply – a broad-shouldered, straight-backed man of about fifty with grizzled handsome features and steady brown eyes. His dark curly hair was slightly scattered with grey and cut short without any pretentions towards style. He wore a navy-blue overall coat over jeans and an open-necked shirt.

Arthur Oxton said with obvious relief, 'Jim, this is Lady Elizabeth Molyneux – Lisa – and she'd like to look around.' He made a hurried gesture towards the newcomer, muttered to Lisa, 'Jim Harrison, the foreman,' and ushered them out, clearly anxious to be rid of them.

'Have you come to do a valuation, see what we're worth?'

the foreman said sarcastically. He spoke slowly, in a deep husky voice with a soft Yorkshire burr, and made no attempt to shake hands.

'I haven't the faintest notion what you're on about,' Lisa said indignantly, taken aback by the bitter tone in which he spoke and the expression, almost of hate, on his face. 'I've come to do precisely what I said, in other words, look around.'

'This way then.' He walked so quickly – she was sure he did it deliberately – that she had to run to keep up. Every now and again he muttered, 'The tool-room,' or, 'This is the stores.'

'It's very run-down,' she said at one point and he turned on her, eyes blazing. She shrank back.

'Shareholders are good at taking money out of firms, but not so keen on putting it back,' he said angrily. He stopped in front of a big machine, half-eaten away by rust. 'See this?' He pointed to a plaque screwed on the front. Lisa could see the name of the manufacturer and underneath the date 1925 'That's when this lathe was made, nineteen-twenty-five. It's long past its usefulness. A modern machine would do the work required in less than half the time.'

'Why don't you buy some new machinery, then?' she asked innocently.

Even above the pounding noise, the man operating the lathe heard her question and she saw him exchange a grin with the foreman. She flushed, feeling ignorant and stupid, then thought defensively, 'They wouldn't know how to make a movie or act in a play. Why should I be expected to know all about their jobs?'

She wondered if her burning cheeks were obvious. If so, Jim Harrison showed no mercy. He led her to a large partitioned section where half a dozen machines stood empty. 'This is where we used to train apprentices,' he said coldly, 'in the days when the firm could afford it.' He showed her the canteen with row after row of chipped plastic-covered tables, crammed so close together there was little room to move between them, then the old-fashioned kitchen where several women in green overalls were already at work peeling potatoes and making pastry. They looked up and Jim Harrison said in a loud voice, 'This is Lady Elizabeth Molyneux, our MP's wife. She's come to have a look around,' and the women eyed Lisa curiously. She tried to smile but perhaps she didn't manage it because none of the women smiled back and after they left she heard shrieks of laughter.

He pushed through a pair of swing doors and suddenly they were outside. She gulped in the fresh air. 'How do people breathe all day in that atmosphere?' she said, more to herself than her companion.

'In order to earn a living wage,' he said caustically. 'To pay their rents and their mortgages and feed their children, but you wouldn't know about that, would you?'

She stared at him angrily. She had come to help and this man had humiliated her, treated her with total contempt.

'You know nothing about me,' she said coldly. How dare he assume she didn't care if people lost their jobs?

'I know all I want to know,' he snapped.

They glared at each other. His brown eyes were the colour of tobacco and despite the dislike she felt, she had to concede that even in his working clothes, there was a dignity about his bearing that Tony, for all his aristocratic upbringing, didn't possess. In some strange, inexplicable way she found herself longing for his approval. She wanted to say, 'I come from a home as poor as any in Broxley, probably poorer, and I started work in a factory just like this when I was fourteen,' and then tell him the real reason for her visit. But why should she explain herself? He'd allowed her to be laughed at, and treated her so patronizingly, let him stick to his horrid assumptions!

She noticed her heel had speared a piece of thin metal and bent down to remove it, almost losing her balance. His hand came out involuntarily to prevent her falling, and she was conscious of his iron grip on her upper arm. Just as spontaneously, she smiled her thanks and for a second their eyes met and she knew, she could tell that behind the surly manner, the hard voice, he was attracted to her. Then he released her quickly and walked away, as if ashamed she had read the message in his eyes.

'What's it going to be then? Are you going to tell your

husband this is the perfect place for a hotel?'

Another assumption, that she'd come to spy on Tony's behalf, 'Rumours fly round Broxley with amazing rapidity,' she said tartly.

'And so they should when people's livelihoods are at stake.'

If only he knew how much she agreed with him, but she wasn't going to disillusion him by saying so. He thought she'd come to spy and he could go on thinking it. She said bluntly, 'Yes, I am going to tell him that. As you say, it's the perfect place, absolutely perfect.'

Later, she telephoned Fergus Lomax and Gertie grudgingly allowed her to speak to him. 'I'll buy the buildings lease,' she said, 'though I don't know why. Arthur Oxton is a drunkard and the foreman, Jim Harrison, is the rudest man I've ever met.'

Fergus laughed. 'Jim's one of the most honourable men I know,' he said. 'We're the best of friends, though I've never been able to persuade him to vote for me. He's a bit of an amateur poet is Jim, often gets published, so I understand. Once you get to know him, you'll like him very much.'

'A poet? You amaze me,' said Lisa. 'He didn't give the impression of knowing enough words to write a poem, let alone make one rhyme.'

'It shows how much you know about poetry. Anyway, that's no way to talk about a fellow socialist.'

'Sorry, that was awfully patronizing,' she said apologetically. 'About the leases, can I leave matters in your hands? Do you need the money now? I haven't the faintest idea how you go about these things.'

'I'll see to everything,' he promised. 'Once I've got the details, I'll be in touch. You can give me the money later. Everyone knows Fergus Lomax's word is as good as his bond.'

Before she left, Lisa found twice the usual number of bills on her dressing table. Tony must have put them there last night and she hadn't noticed because this time there were no flowers, no 'bribe' as she called it. Angrily she stuffed them in her bag and wondered with a grim smile if there'd be an invoice for Omar amongst them. Florence Dale had told her that Persian kittens cost at least a hundred pounds.

Chapter 43

Lisa was trying to learn the lines of a new play due to go into rehearsal later that week, but it was difficult. The dialogue of *Pacemaker* was trite, the words meant nothing. Matthew Jenks was right, she thought. The play had been written by a long-established playwright famous for his lightweight, entertaining comedies, but his latest offering was a various hodge-podge of innuendo and plain bad taste. She reckoned there were probably thousands of plays lying around, immeasurably superior, yet this was getting a West End showing, just because the author was well-known. Fortunately, her part was small as the play had an all-star cast – eight big names in all – and the last she heard, the theatre was already booked solid for months ahead.

When she turned up for the first rehearsal, the other actors were already word-perfect. They sat in a semi-circle, Lisa the only one with a script on her knee, and she found her thoughts drifting away from the theatre to the world outside. She wondered if Fergus had managed to track down the leases for Spring Engineering. She thought about the workers in the factory, their livelihoods at the mercy of Tony's friends, rich uncaring men, their pockets already full of money yet greedy for more and willing to get it by stamping on their fellow men with no more thought than if they were stamping on an insect.

And that was the sort of man she'd married! Ironically, this stage was the very one where they'd met two and a half years ago. With a blinding flash of intuition she knew that although she'd long suspected Tony had married her for her money, she hadn't realized quite how unscrupulously he'd gone about it.

She remembered Barbara Heany saying, 'He's been nagging to meet you,' then later that she'd already told him it was Lisa's birthday, yet Tony had pretended not to know. Both had thought this an insignificant deception, an excuse to flatter. 'You're the most beautiful fifty-year-old woman I've ever met,' he'd said. And she'd been vulnerable to his flattery right from the start – she still was.

He'd sought her out, had Tony. There'd been a lot of articles about her in the newspapers since she'd come back to England, listing her most successful movies, the fact that she was Joseph Dent's widow, and mentioning her company, O'Brien Productions. He'd deliberately and coldly courted her, showering her with flowers and gifts, arranging those delightful surprises – the picnic in Hyde Park, the cosy little dinners. And he'd kept up the charm to keep her sweet so she would pay the bills whilst he poured away his inheritance and his MP's salary at the gaming tables and into shady investments.

Suddenly, she was conscious that everyone was looking at her.

'I know it's a lousy play, Lisa, but let's do our best with it, eh?' the producer said tiredly. 'Learning your lines would be a start.'

'I'm sorry,' she said in confusion. 'I was miles away.' She picked up her script. 'Where are we?'

When she arrived in Broxley that weekend, Tony was already home. As soon as she entered the house, he came out of the drawing room and looked at her coldly. 'What have you been up to?' he demanded, his voice as icy as his expression.

She cursed herself for being so weak; despite everything, she was so used to his affectionate, exuberant welcomes that his coldness upset her. Was he such a good actor that he'd been *pretending* all this time? Surely he felt *something* for her? Deep in her heart of hearts she felt a certain fondness, albeit reluctant, for him.

'I don't know what you're talking about,' she said coolly, praying that Fergus hadn't broken his promise to keep her name out of things.

'I'm talking about the leases for Spring Engineering. Who did you blab to?'

She looked at him indignantly. 'I didn't "blab", as you call it, to anyone.' She hadn't, either. There was undoubtedly a mole in Ferris Hall, but it wasn't her. 'Has something happened?' she asked, wide-eyed.

'It most certainly has.' He wasn't quite sure whether to believe her or not. 'Sowerby's just been on the phone, he's coming to dinner tonight.' Sowerby, if she remembered rightly, was one of the businessmen who'd been here a few weeks ago, the one with the most to say. 'When he approached the leaseholders, they'd already sold. Someone had got there before us.'

'I'm sorry to hear that,' she said virtuously, 'but I gave nothing away. It might have been one of those other men trying to get all the profit for himself.'

'You could be right,' he said eventually. 'I suppose it could have been Christy. A final gesture just to spite me.'

'Have you asked him, or should I say accused him, too?' she asked pointedly.

He flushed. 'Christy's left, gone to another constituency in Cornwall.' He came over, took her hands and crushed them against his lips. 'I'm sorry, darling. I felt convinced you'd betrayed me but I should have known you'd never do anything like that.'

Lisa didn't answer. Inwardly she felt delighted that Fergus Lomax had been successful. She'd call in over the weekend and give him a cheque.

Tony and Colin Sowerby were subdued throughout dinner and the conversation was forced. Despite Lisa's efforts to be a good hostess, brightly relaying theatre gossip, Tony only managed an occasional smile and Colin Sowerby was almost rude in his indifference. She was glad when the meal was over and Mrs Mason had cleared the dishes. Now they might get down to business. However, after an hour of desultory conversation, she realized they had no intention of discussing anything of importance whilst she was there. In the end she said, 'I think I'll have an early night, it's been a hectic week,' and they both gave such an obvious sigh of relief, she almost laughed.

Outside the door she paused and listened, but all she could hear was the sound of muffled voices, nothing distinct. She went down to the kitchen to get a glass of milk and was

489

surprised to see the dinner dishes still piled in the sink waiting to be washed. Mrs Mason, with her back to the door, had her ear pressed against a rubber tube which hung from an old-fashioned communication system used to converse with the servants when the house was built two hundred years before. Lisa had assumed it no longer worked.

'What on earth are you doing?'

Mrs Mason nearly jumped out of her skin. She dropped the tube and turned to face Lisa, her face crimson with embarrassment. 'I thought you'd gone to bed,' she muttered.

Lisa went over, picked up the tube and put it to her ear. She could hear every word that was being said in the dining room!

'Can they hear us?' she whispered.

Mrs Mason shook her head. 'Only if they listened at the grille by the fireplace.'

'So *you're* the informant Fergus Lomax told me about?'

The woman nodded defiantly. 'My son works at Spring Engineering. I wasn't going to sit back and do nothing while they closed it down. I knew Fergus would help.'

'Do you often listen in?'

'Only when there's people like that man who came tonight,' she mumbled. 'That's how we found out he was taking bribes.'

'Who, Tony?' What a stupid question. Who else could it be?

'That's right,' Mrs Mason added proudly, 'It was my son who sent the information to that magazine.' She pointed to the tube. 'They'd started talking about Spring Engineering as soon as you left the room, something about approaching it from a different angle this time. Buying shares, I think that man said.'

Lisa put her ear to the tube and listened hard.

'I'm quite enjoying this,' she said to Fergus Lomax next morning. 'How do we foil them now?'

He regarded her with twinkling eyes. 'Thank God you're not the typical loyal Conservative wife,' he said.

'If this hadn't come up, I'd be well on my way to a divorce,' she replied ruefully. 'They're going to buy fifty-one per cent of the shares – what does that mean?'

'It means they'll have complete control of the company and can shut it down overnight. Before you can say Jack Robinson there'll be a hotel at the end of Broxley High Street and your husband will be a rich man, though if he runs true to form, it won't be for long.'

'But not if I buy the shares first?'

'Precisely, though it'll have to be done pretty damn quick.' He slapped his knee. 'You know, I'm quite enjoying this myself.'

'I'm just as ignorant about shares as I am about leases. Can you do it for me?'

'I'll get on to my stockbroker first thing tomorrow,' he promised. 'At the moment, the shares are at an all-time low, but even so, you realize this won't be cheap? That is why Tony and his friends didn't do it in the first place.'

'How much will it cost?'

'At least half a million pounds.'

'Oh, that's okay,' Lisa said lightly.

He looked impressed. 'I think I took up the wrong profession. I should have been an actor.'

'Errol Flynn would have had to look to his laurels,' she laughed.

'Do you still want to remain anonymous?'

Lisa nodded. 'Isn't life funny?' she mused. 'Who ever thought the day would come when I owned an engineering company? I don't even know what they make there.'

'Combustion engines,' said Fergus.

She groaned. 'I shouldn't have asked. What on earth are *they* for?'

The critics considered *Pacemaker* to be possibly the worst play ever seen in the West End. One wrote, *'This worm-eaten monster crawled onto the stage already half-dead. By the end of the first act, all life had gone from its mouldy body and we had to spend the second act watching the twitching of the corpse.'*

The actors had signed six-month contracts and as the box office reported healthy bookings on the strength of the eight star names, there was no alternative but to plod on and do their best. Lisa knew her performance was probably the worst of her career, though the play was so wretched nobody seemed to notice. She was never able to get into her role and even after several weeks' peformance, she still forgot her lines. By now it seemed unreasonable to blame it on the play. In fact, she seemed to be forgetting an awful lot of things lately – appointments, telephone numbers and worst of all, names. Even more worryingly, sometimes her head seemed so fuzzy and she felt so vague and detached, that she began to worry for her sanity.

One night, in the middle of the second act, she felt herself go hot and without warning, her body was covered in perspiration. It occurred again a few days later when she was at home and looking in the mirror, she saw she'd turned an ugly dark red.

When it happened a third time she went to see her doctor. As soon as she explained her symptoms, he said abruptly, 'It's the menopause.'

'The menopause?' she repeated foolishly.

'It happens to all women, you know,' he said impatiently. 'It's not going to kill you.'

'Is there something I can take for these hot flushes?'

He shook his head. 'They'll go away eventually,' he said. 'In the meantime, you'll just have to grin and bear it.'

'I wonder if you'd be so flippant if it happened to men,' she said.

At least knowing helped; she wasn't going insane after all. She took herself in hand, determined to adopt a positive attitude, though felt angry when her body disobeyed her firm instructions and a hot flush seized her in the most embarrassing situations – on stage, out shopping, once on the train on her way to Broxley.

Fergus Lomax telephoned to say she was now the proud owner of Spring Engineering, but she found it difficult to get excited. He sent cuttings from the local paper. *'Mysterious Buyer Obtains Majority Shareholding In Local Company.'*

Nellie came to stay and was full of sympathy. 'You poor darling! What about HRT?'

'What's that?'

'Hormone Replacement Therapy. It works wonders for

some women.'

'But my doctor said there was nothing I could take,' Lisa protested. 'He claims I must grin and bear it.'

'Then get another doctor,' Nellie said firmly. 'Preferably a woman.'

HRT didn't exactly work wonders for Lisa, but it helped. Within a few weeks she was almost back to her old self. She telephoned Nellie to thank her. 'I was getting really worried,' she confided. 'If I can't cope with the menopause, how on earth would I cope with a real illness?'

Nellie laughed. 'You're a real stalwart, Liz, you underestimate yourself. Anyway, there's no chance of *you* getting a real illness. You're one of the healthiest people I know.'

That was four days before Lisa discovered the lump in her breast.

She was having a shower and at first thought it was something in the soap and looked down, expecting to see a flaw, a bump, but it was as smooth as cream. She touched her breast again, the left one, on the outside, almost under her arm. The lump was no bigger than a pea, but it was definitely there, no doubt about it, and as hard as a pea too, those dried ones Mam used to buy and leave soaking in a bowl overnight. She felt her entire body tingle with goosepimples as she examined the breast in the mirror. Nothing! It looked as smooth and creamy as the soap. She pulled the flesh taut. Still nothing, yet when she let the flesh go the lump was there.

Cancer!

'Jesus Christ!' she wailed and began to cry. She looked at herself in the mirror again. She was so lovely, even at fifty-three. She felt proud of her lithe curves; although her skin no longer had the satin glow of youth there wasn't an inch of superfluous fat. She imagined the breast sliced off leaving a bloody, gaping hole and wept once more.

Her immediate reaction was to call someone. Nellie was the most obvious, but with her hand poised over the receiver she thought, 'I'll only worry her. There's nothing Nellie can do, there's nothing anyone can do.'

Except a doctor, who'd cut her breast off, deface her body

and the beautiful Lisa Angelis would become an ugly, disfigured freak.

She went out and bought a book on cancer. The lump could possibly be benign or just a harmless cyst, she read. Only a small percentage were malignant. She breathed a sigh of relief and for a while her worries faded but as the day wore on she began to think, 'Somebody's got to have the small percentage of malignant lumps. Why not me?'

When she got to the theatre that night, Lisa tentatively brought up the subject of breast cancer with the actress who shared her dressing room. To her amazement the woman refused to discuss the matter, looking at Lisa with frightened eyes as if sensing the reason for her casual remark. At the end of the performance, she removed her make-up and left the room with almost unseemly haste.

'Perhaps if I changed my diet, ate more healthily, the lump might go,' thought Lisa, so she cut out meat and ate only salads and fruit. She began to go to a gymnasium each day and spent hours on a rowing machine or exercise bike, willing her body to return to perfect health.

Her life became dominated by the tiny, pea-sized lump in her breast. She was surprised when she discovered Christmas was only a few days away and went up to Ferris Hall for the first time in weeks. Tony was as effusive as ever. 'I've been worried about you, darling. Where on earth have you been?'

She looked at him. This man was her husband, yet he seemed like a stranger. Would she ever know what he was really like behind that bland, smiling mask? She'd still done nothing about a divorce but again this didn't seem the right time. As soon as the lump disappeared and life resumed normality, she would see her solicitor and commence proceedings.

Although she didn't tell him so, it wasn't for Tony she'd returned to Broxley. The place had come to feel like home. When she walked down the High Sreet, almost everyone said hallo. She felt as if she belonged. When she divorced Tony, she'd buy a house close to the dales so she could go jogging every morning.

She said coldly, 'You have my London number, Tony, you

know where I live. If you've been worried you could have contacted me.'

He said nothing, but his face darkened as if he realized everything was over between them.

On Christmas morning she jogged over the dales, shivering at first as the icy wind cut through her tracksuit, but after a while she became accustomed to the temperature. She gulped the bracing, unpolluted air and thought it was probably doing a lot of good as it spread down to her lungs, her chest. All that exercise was proving its worth as already she'd run twice her usual limit and didn't feel the least bit tired. She slid her hand inside her tracksuit top to see if the lump was still there. It was.

It was exhilarating flying so effortlessly like this, her feet scarcely touching the wet lumpy grass. She must start coming to Ferris Hall every week again. Jogging in London, breathing in the poisonous fumes and smoke, was probably more dangerous than sitting at home.

She'd nearly reached Broxley. Fergus Lomax's house was on the other side of this hill. Would it be all right, she wondered, to call on Christmas Day? Surely it wouldn't hurt to drop in and wish him Merry Christmas – that's if Gertie would let her!

To her surprise, Gertie actually seemed pleased to see her, to the extent of planting a welcoming kiss on her cheek. 'All this cloak-and-dagger lease and share-buying business has really done Fergus good, made him feel important again. Would you like a drink?'

Lisa had stopped drinking alcohol. 'Just water,' she said.

When Gertie showed her into the room where Fergus sat in front of a roaring fire, she found he already had a visitor. At first she didn't recognize the man who got to his feet politely as she entered – a solid, broad-shouldered man with light brown eyes and a slow, dignified bearing, wearing dark trousers and a subdued-patterned sweater that looked as if it had been a gift that morning. Then Fergus said jovially, 'I think you've already met Jim Harrison.'

That pig of a foreman from Spring Engineering! Fergus had said he was a friend. Lisa managed a smile, though it was an effort. 'Nice to meet you again,' she murmured as he came over and shook hands. Better late than never, she thought. He hadn't condescended to the first time.

'I've just been congratulating Jim,' Fergus said. 'He's been made manager of Spring Engineering.' His eyes twinkled mischievously. 'You remember, don't you, Lisa? You took a look around the place once. Didn't think much of it, if I recall rightly.'

'The staff weren't very friendly,' Lisa replied. She thought Jim Harrison might look embarrassed, but instead he had the gall to smile as if she'd said something funny. 'How's the company doing?' she enquired innocently. 'I understand there were plans to close it down and build an hotel instead. Did nothing come of it?'

'A strange thing happened,' said Fergus with equal innocence. 'Some mysterious benefactor turned up and bought the leases and a majority of the shares right from under the noses of the would-be developers!'

'We can't be sure he's a benefactor yet,' warned Jim. 'We don't know what his plans are. Until he starts investing in new machinery, I'll be worried he hasn't got some trick up his sleeve.'

'Damn!' thought Lisa. 'It looks as though I've got to start buying lathes and stuff.'

After a while she said, 'It's time I went. Mrs Mason will be upset if I'm not back in time for lunch.' Not that Lisa intended eating much, but she'd better keep Tony company at the table.

'I'll be off too, Fergus. Annie's home, preparing her first Christmas dinner. I offered to help but she told me to get lost.' Jim Harrison stood up and came over to the door with Lisa.

When they got outside he asked, 'Where's your car?'

'I ran here,' she said.

'You can't run all the way back!' He looked shocked. 'You'll be lucky to be home for tea, let alone lunch. Let me give you a lift.'

'No, thanks,' she protested. 'I'd sooner run.' In fact, the idea of a lift home suddenly seemed welcome. Whilst she'd been in the house, a stiff, penetrating wind had sprung up.

She shivered and Jim Harrison took her arm and led her to his car. After a half-hearted protest, she let herself be virtually pushed into the passenger seat.

Neither spoke for the first mile or so. Every now and then she glanced at him surreptitiously as he stared ahead, concentrating on his driving. These narrow roads could be tricky, particularly if someone came round a bend too fast on the wrong side. He had a firm, strong chin, already shadowed by a faint suspicion of stubble, as if he needed to shave more than once a day, and a long nose with wide, flaring nostrils. His lashes were long and straight and a darker brown than his eyes. As he drove his brow wrinkled in regular straight lines, like corrugated paper. Somewhat unwillingly, she had to concede he was attractive in a quiet, reassuring way. He was a man you would feel safe with, a man you could trust completely. 'Not like Tony,' a mean voice reminded her. He turned and found her looking at him and she felt herself blushing. If she had a hot flush now, she'd kill herself. Anyway, what was a woman in the middle of the menopause doing sizing up a member of the opposite sex!

'Who's Annie?' she asked suddenly to cover her embarrassment.

'My daughter. She's home from university for Christmas.'

She longed to ask where his wife was and found herself hoping he was widowed or divorced. Drat, she was doing it again! Becoming attracted to a man she didn't particularly like and who probably hated her.

'To save you asking, my wife and I divorced about fifteen years ago,' he said suddenly. 'She's in Canada with her new husband.'

'I had no intention of asking,' she lied, and felt half-glad and half-sorry when she noticed him wince.

'Look,' he said quickly. 'I want to apologize for the way I behaved when you came to the factory. It was inexcusable, and I'm truly ashamed.'

'Why apologize? What makes you think I didn't come for the reason you first thought, to size the place up on behalf of my husband?'

'Because I *know* you didn't – now.' At first she thought

Fergus had confided in him, but then he said, 'Paul told me you were on our side.'

'Paul?'

'Paul Mason. His parents work at Ferris Hall.' He smiled. 'Am I forgiven?'

'I can't very well refuse an apology on Christmas Day,' she said stiffly. 'It would be un-Christian.'

'So I'm forgiven?'

'I suppose so.'

'Good.' He grinned broadly. 'That's made my day!'

'There's no reason why it should,' she snapped. She knew she was being deliberately rude because she found him so attractive. After Christy, she'd sworn to give up men altogether.

Without her realizing it, they'd reached Ferris Hall. As they drove up to the door, she saw her husband outside. He and Mason were standing by the Mercedes having an argument and Tony was waving his arms about like a spoilt child.

Jim Harrison looked at him, then glanced back at Lisa, a puzzled expression on his kind, strong face. 'Why on earth did you marry him?' he seemed to be asking – a question Lisa increasingly asked herself.

Chapter 44

Pacemaker closed at last. The mood of relief was so great that the actors put all they had into the final Saturday-night performance, so much so that the producer exclaimed indignantly, 'If you'd done that right from the start, we might have made something out of it!'

A party had been arranged for afterwards but Lisa took one look at the greasy sausage rolls and vol-au-vents laid out backstage and was sickened by the idea of stuffing herself with such unhealthy food, full of preservatives and chemicals. What she intended doing was catching the midnight train to Broxley and tomorrow she would run over the dales, breathing in the pure, unadulterated air. The fitter she got, the more likely it was that she would get rid of the lump which stubbornly persisted in her left breast despite all her efforts. Although it was no bigger it was still there every time she checked, several times a day.

She was alone in the dressing room and had just finished wiping off her make-up – the actress she shared with was keeping out of the way until Lisa finished, something she'd done ever since the dreaded word 'cancer' had been mentioned – when there was a knock on the door and a voice shouted, 'You've got a visitor, Miss Angelis.'

A woman entered. She was as big as a house, panting with the sheer effort of walking and bringing with her the salty smell of perspiration. Most of her long, pure-white hair had escaped from the bun on her neck and stuck up from her scalp like the bleached snakes of Medusa. She wore a silk dress with an unflattering V neck which hung on her overweight frame like a tent. Although she looked sixty, the skin on her face was as fresh and smooth as a young girl's.

She sank into a chair with a sigh and said, 'You don't recognize me, do you?'

'I'm terribly sorry, but no,' said Lisa, trying not to sound irritated. She wasn't in the mood for visitors.

'It's Jackie.'

'*Jackie!*' Jesus, how could that lovely curvacious girl she'd known all those years ago have turned into this . . . this freak! 'Why, how lovely to see you!' Lisa cried, conscious of how false and unenthusiastic the words sounded. 'How are Laurence and the children?'

'Laurence died four years ago,' said Jackie flatly. 'He was much older than me, you know, seventy when he went.'

Lisa made the appropriate soothing noises. 'I'm terribly sorry to hear it. How awful for you.'

'As for the kids, I had four in the end. Two boys followed by two girls. You knew about Noël, of course.' Jackie giggled. 'That was a rare old palaver, wasn't it? You met the middle two, Robert and Lisa, but by the time Constance arrived, you'd left the flat and my letters were returned marked Gone Away.' She paused for breath, as if the long speech had tired her.

'I'm sorry about that,' said Lisa, irritated again at being made to feel guilty after all this time. 'But I moved suddenly.'

'Anyway,' Jackie continued, 'the children are all married – Noël's in Australia and the others are scattered all over the country and I've already got three grandchildren. Of course, I don't see as much of any of them as I'd like, but I suppose all mothers feel that.'

'I expect so.' There was an awkward silence. 'Are you still living in Bournemouth?'

'I had to move out of the vicarage when Laurence died and there'd never been the money to save for a house of our own.' She giggled again but this time Lisa sensed a touch of desperation in her voice. 'You'll never guess where I am now! Earl's Court, no more than a stone's throw from our old flat. Quite a nice little bedsit, but a bit noisy.'

Oh, Jackie! All that loving and mothering and caring and you end up at sixty all alone in a bedsit in Earl's Court. 'Why on earth didn't you stay in Bournemouth?' Lisa asked curiously.

'I had to get a job, that's why I came to London, but in all this time, I've only had a couple of weeks' temping. The job market is virtually non-existent at the moment.'

That wasn't true, thought Lisa. The job market had long since begun to pick up again. The more likely explanation was that firms wouldn't want to employ someone looking like Jackie. She turned to the mirror and began to apply her ordinary make-up as Jackie chattered away. 'I passed the theatre the other day on my way to another agency and saw your picture outside. I recognized you immediately – you haven't changed a bit in all these years. You're still as lovely as ever,' she said admiringly.

Out of sight she sounded just like the old Jackie, as bright and cheerful as ever. There wasn't a hint of envy in her voice. She was pleased her old friend had remained slim and beautiful, despite her own appearance. Lisa half-expected to turn around and find her sitting there with her bright blue eye-shadow and spiky lashes, her creamy blonde hair cascading around her face. There was nobody in the world she would rather have met now than Jackie. She could tell her about the lump and Jackie would understand her fears and offer the warm, uninhibited sympathy Lisa remembered so vividly. But there was something inherently depressing about this woman with her ugly, obese body, deserted by her children, living in a London bedsit. Lisa gave an involuntary shudder and hoped Jackie wouldn't realize the reason for it.

'Laurence and I could never afford to go to the pictures,' Jackie was saying. 'Else I suppose I would have realized who you were years ago. I suppose it's living in London again, but recently I keep thinking about our old place. Gosh, we had some good times there, didn't we, Lisa?'

'We certainly did.' Wonderful times. Lots of laughter, lots of sadness too, but there'd been a freedom and a gaiety about those years that had never been recaptured. Why couldn't she bring herself to respond to Jackie, to kiss and hug her, welcome her back into her life?

There was another awkward silence. Lisa could think of nothing to say and Jackie seemed to become aware that she'd been doing all the talking, and suddenly dried up.

'Well,' with obvious effort she hoisted herself out of the chair, 'I'd better be getting along.'

With a feeling of relief, Lisa stood up and shook hands. 'Perhaps we could have lunch one day?' she said. 'Let me have your number and I'll be in touch.'

Jackie tore a page out of her diary and scribbled the number down. 'It's a communal telephone, so you'll have to ask for me, Jackie Murray.' Her eyes were sad and faintly accusing. *I know darned well you'll never ring,'* they seemed to be saying.

Lisa had been turning down parts for months. She wanted nothing to do with the theatre, with anything, whilst she concentrated on getting rid of the lump. Surely you should have sufficient control over your body to *will* the bad parts away? She saw a television programme which claimed that fruit and vegetables were sprayed with so much fertilizer that they could actually *cause* cancer, so she changed to organically-grown produce. These and water comprised her daily diet. She ate nothing cooked, drank no tea, no coffee or alcohol.

'The water,' she thought frantically one day. 'It's full of fluoride and all sorts of chemicals. No wonder the lump hasn't gone!' She began to buy bottled water, gallons and gallons of it.

Nellie's daughter Natalie got married at Easter. Lisa travelled up to Liverpool and this time Patrick was there, as tall and handsome as all the O'Brien boys, though his tan and easygoing confident manner gave him a more glamorous air. He brought with him his beautiful Anglo-Indian wife, Pita.

'One of my main recollections is of you doing your homework at the kitchen table and complaining we were disturbing your concentration,' Lisa said, willing him to remember that and nothing more.

'Well, we were a noisy lot,' he said ruefully. 'Remember the argument when you passed the scholarship and Dad wouldn't let you go to secondary school?'

Lisa shuddered. 'Only too well!' She wondered if, at the back of his mind, he treasured the memory of the night he'd spent with Lisa, the girl who'd come into his life then vanished so mysteriously. Looking at him, his blond hair bleached almost white by the sun, his smiling blue eyes and long, sensitive hands, she told herself she felt nothing. How could she, when he was her brother?

At Ferris Hall, Mrs Mason said worriedly, 'Are you all right? I wouldn't have thought you could have got much thinner, but you have.'

'I don't look ill, do I?' asked Lisa, alarmed.

'No, that's the funny thing. You look as if you're brimming over with health, though if you keep on eating this rabbit food you'll fade away to nothing, particularly with all that jogging about you do.'

Tony probably wondered why she still came to his home. If he'd asked her, what would she have replied? 'Because I love it here and Broxley feels like home. Because I own an engineering company, and some day, when this bloody lump goes, I'm going to start investing in new machinery and you'll find out it was *me* who prevented you from making a fortune. Not only that, one day I'm going to buy a house here and settle down and I'm going to divorce you, Tony, before long.'

They scarcely spoke nowadays. In fact, she tried to avoid him, though she still found bills on her dressing table which she dutifully paid.

In the autumn Busby telephoned. She was so pleased to hear his voice that she burst into tears.

'Darling, what on earth's the matter?' He sounded so concerned that she cried even harder.

'Oh Busby, I think I'm going to die.' There, she'd told someone at last! It was a relief to get the words out.

'What's wrong?' he pressed. He sounded close, as if he was in the very next street not thousands of miles away in Los Angeles.

'I've got a lump in my breast,' she sobbed. 'And the damn thing won't go away, no matter what I do.'

'Shall I come over? I can catch the very next plane.'

'No, but I'd like to come to you. Do you mind – are you in the middle of something?' Busby's reputation had grown over the years. Nowadays he made big, stupendous films with fifty-million-dollar budgets. His latest was showing in

London and had got rave reviews.

'No, I'm in between movies, but it wouldn't matter if I wasn't. You know I'd drop everything – for you. Dammit, Lisa, you should have told me about this before. When would you like to come?'

'Soon – in a few days.' She began to feel excited for the first time in months. 'Oh darling, I'm really looking forward to it.'

'Don't you want to know why I called? I'm having a house built and the builders haven't even started yet. I was wondering if I could rent Tymperleys for a while?'

'Of course you can.' She had a vision of him sitting round the pool with his friends. 'But I wouldn't want to go there, not just now.'

'How about New York – the same hotel where we spent our honeymoon? There's an Indian summer at the moment, so it'll be hot but exhilarating. Remember what Doctor Johnson said: "To be tired of New York is to be tired of life".'

'I think you've got your cities wrong, but I'm sure he would have said it anyway.'

'New York it is, then. I'm looking forward to it already.'

'Darling, there's just one thing,' Lisa said cautiously, hoping he wouldn't be offended. 'Could we be – what's the word – platonic? Celibate? I'm just not in the mood for that sort of thing right now.'

He laughed and didn't sound the least bit hurt. 'Can I quote you a little poem I read once? "A man is not old when his hair grows grey. A man is not old when his teeth decay. But a man is nearing his last long sleep, When his mind makes appointments his body can't keep." I think that just about describes Busby Van Dolen at the present time.'

It *was* hot in New York. The sun shone down with relentless, burning intensity on the ravine-like streets and was reflected back off the baking pavements so Lisa felt as if she was walking through an oven. She and Busby strolled round Central Park and ate in dark cool restaurants, where he bullied her into eating proper meals for the first time in months. They spent a small fortune in Macy's on silly, extravagant and useless presents for everyone they could think of, and at night went to the theatre – not the big expensive shows, but off-Broadway productions. 'I'm always on the lookout for new talent,' Busby said.

His hair and beard were completely grey now and the lenses in his glasses much thicker than she remembered, but for all that, he was the same old enthusiastic Busby, still fun to be with. Now he had a new enemy, President Ronald Reagan, to complain about. 'You wouldn't believe what he's doing to our country, Lisa,' he groaned. 'Welfare benefits slashed and families living in their cars or on the streets.'

'Wouldn't I?' she replied witheringly. 'I never thought I'd see kids sleeping on the streets of London, either. Nowadays, it seems everyone's out for himself.'

He put his hand over hers. 'We always agreed on things.'

At night they lay in the same bed, his arms around her, but just that, nothing more, though on the final night he kissed the lump in her breast. 'You know you are the love of my life,' he said softly. 'When your divorce comes through, couldn't we . . .'

Lisa laid her fingers on his lips. 'No, Busby, it's too late.'

'It's never too late,' he protested. 'We can spend the rest of our lives together.'

For a moment she was tempted. He was such a dear, sweet man and he'd been in love with her his entire adult life. It no longer mattered that he was Buzz, the young GI who'd come to Southport with her all that time ago – she scarcely thought about that episode in her life now – but it seemed wrong to go back to him after all this time.

When he came to the airport to see her off, he said, 'As soon as you get back, promise me you'll see a doctor about that lump.'

'I promise.'

She flew home feeling slightly more cheerful. Several times she picked up the telephone to call her doctor – after all, she'd promised Busby – but put it down again almost immediately, too scared to dial. After a few days she was gripped by a deep, dark depression. What if the lump was malignant and it had spread, was still spreading through her body like the dark and dirty roots of a tree? It was simply no use trying to cure herself.

Mrs Mason was right: if she kept on eating like this, she'd fade away to nothing.

There was nothing else for it. She picked up the telephone and dialled her doctor's number.

Margaret Ashleigh was a glamorous redhead who looked more like a model than a member of the medical profession. 'How long have you had this?' she asked after she'd examined Lisa's breast.

'Nearly a year.'

Lisa expected a stern lecture on her foolishness. Instead the woman said sympathetically, 'I suppose you've been too frightened to come?'

'You probably think I'm very silly.'

'Well if you are, you share it with an awful lot of women. All of us want to keep our bodies whole, though nowadays they can do wonders with cosmetic surgery. Anyway, let's hope such drastic measures won't be necessary.'

She arranged for Lisa to have a biopsy the following day.

That night, she thought, 'If it's serious, if I'm going to die, Tony will inherit all my money.'

She immediately wrote six-figure cheques to half a dozen charities and scribbled out a Will leaving everything to her family. Then she asked both her neighbours to witness it.

When Florence Dale was asked for the second signature, she looked at Lisa in alarm. 'What's all this in aid of?'

Lisa attempted to laugh. 'I just thought I'd like to put my affairs in order, that's all.'

'A bit sudden, isn't it? Is something wrong?'

She avoided the old lady's eyes. 'Nothing serious. I'm going for a test tomorrow, that's all.' She picked up Omar and kissed him. Although fully grown, he was still as playful as a kitten and began to jab at her pearl necklace with his paw. 'Omar, you are a very immature cat. It's about time you began to behave like an adult.'

Florence said, 'Tell me how you get on, won't you?'

'I won't know the result for a while, but I'll let you know, I promise.'

*

Benign!

When Margaret Ashleigh told her a few days later, Lisa fainted.

Mrs Mason said, 'I wasn't expecting you this weekend so I haven't got any salad stuff in.'

'I don't care,' Lisa sang. 'Just give me roast beef and potatoes, a double helping of Yorkshire pudding and drown the lot in a shovelful of your thick, lumpy gravy.'

'My gravy's never lumpy!' Mrs Mason replied indignantly. She looked at Lisa shrewdly. 'You're feeling better, aren't you? Not that you ever looked ill, you just acted it. I know something's been wrong.'

'There was,' said Lisa happily. 'But it's all over now.'

She ran across the misty dales and had never felt so happy. Exhilarated by her sense of newfound freedom, she laughed out loud and the sound was swallowed up by the white mist which surrounded her on all sides, ethereal, yet protective as a curtain. It was damp and cold, but Lisa felt as if she were running in heaven.

Suddenly, almost miraculously, when she reached the top of the hill, the mist disappeared and the sun came out and she could see for miles and miles. The view was glorious. As if lifelong blinkers had been stripped from her eyes, she saw the scene with a clarity never known before. The grass had never been such a vivid green or the fields such a rich brown, almost purple. Bare trees were stark, their branches crazy shapes against the now blue-grey sky and the roofs of the half a dozen scattered houses shimmered with a silvery glaze in the unnaturally bright sun. She had never felt so alive.

'When are you going back to London?' she asked Tony over lunch.

'Not till tomorrow morning,' he answered. 'Why?'

'I'd like a few words with you tonight.'

'What's wrong with now?'

Was it just her imagination, or had his face grown mean over the years since they'd met? Perhaps it was because he no longer looked at her in the same way, no longer smiled or

507

showered her with those empty, meaningless compliments that had taken her in so convincingly. This was his *real* face, no longer gentle, but hard and empty of emotion.

'I can't now,' she said. 'It's Fergus Lomax's birthday and I've been invited for drinks at two o'clock.'

'They didn't ask me,' he said petulantly.

She dressed in a new white jersey frock, simply styled with a round neck and long straight sleeves. The fine material clung to her waist, which was slimmer than ever, falling in soft folds over her hips to the tops of her white leather high-heeled boots. After getting the result of the biopsy, she'd joyfully bought half a dozen new outfits – she seemed to have spent most of the previous year in a tracksuit. She brushed her hair thoroughly till it shone, parted it in the middle and left it loose. A final glance in the mirror told her she looked radiant. She'd never known her eyes shine back so brightly, so full of the delight of being alive. 'Anyone would look radiant if they felt as I do,' she thought. 'It's not peculiar to me.'

Fergus, so full of life and impishness, interested in everything that went on in Broxley and the wider world, was rapidly fading away.

'You're looking well,' she lied as she bent to kiss him.

'Don't tell fibs,' he snapped. 'I look awful.' Nevertheless, he managed a leery wink. 'Christ, I wish I'd known you twenty years ago. I would have shown you a good time.'

'Don't be foolish, dear.' Gertie came up behind him and slapped his hand. 'You're embarrassing her.' She smiled at Lisa over the chair but the smile didn't touch her eyes. 'I'm going to lose him soon and I can't bear it,' she seemed to be saying.

The room was crowded, full of his old friends from all the political parties, perhaps realizing that this was the last birthday Fergus would have.

'Hallo, there.' Someone touched her shoulder and Lisa turned to find Jim Harrison standing behind her. He looked strange in a dark suit and tie and a white shirt, and she noticed the collar hadn't been ironed properly. 'It seems ages since I last saw you, so how come you've grown younger?

You look wonderful.' There was a strange reluctance in his voice, as if he found compliments difficult and the words had been forced out against his will. His eyes held a similar expression – a grudging admiration.

Lisa understood how he felt. Despite the dislike they had for each other, underneath there was an undeniable attraction. On this perfect day, however, she had no time for deep psychological theories.

'Why, thank you!' She licked her lips provocatively. 'Perhaps it's because I feel wonderful inside.'

She'd never thought she'd flirt again. It was ridiculous, someone of her age fluttering her eyelashes and looking coy. No doubt she was making an exhibition of herself but she didn't care, not today. He seemed to sense her mood. Although she could tell he wasn't used to it and probably felt awkward, he couldn't resist responding in a like manner, and in no time at all they were acting like a couple of teenagers who'd just met at their first dance – there, that showed her age – nowadays it would be a disco. Glancing around, she saw no one was taking a blind bit of notice – not that it would have mattered anyway.

After a while he said, 'You haven't got a drink.'

'I've got wine somewhere. I think that's it on the mantelpiece.'

Through lowered lids she watched him cross the room to fetch her glass and thought what a solid, reassuring figure he made, though at the same time there was an air of recklessness about him that she'd never noticed before, as if he was capable of great, unexpected passion – well, a poet would be, surely! She felt that old quiver of desire in the pit of her stomach and thought to herself, 'I hope they don't send a handsome priest to give me the Last Sacraments, else I'm quite likely to grab him, even on my deathbed.'

'What are you grinning at?'

He was back with the wine. 'I daren't tell you,' she laughed. 'It was sacrilegious.'

'It sounds as if it might be interesting.'

By five o'clock, Fergus began to look tired and people started to leave. When they were outside, Lisa went over to her car.

'I'm surprised you didn't run over,' said Jim. Perhaps the fresh air had brought him back to earth, as he sounded faintly sarcastic.

'Not in these boots,' she replied. 'Goodbye, perhaps I'll see you in another year.' As she got into her car, she noticed he was walking down the drive and wound down her window to shout, 'Can I offer you a lift this time?'

'But it would mean you going in the opposite direction,' he protested, though coming hastily back. 'My car's in getting a new clutch,' he explained and Lisa wondered why she felt so glad!

As she drove into Broxley, their conversation turned to more mundane topics. 'Have you lived here long?' she asked.

'All my life,' he answered simply.

'That must be strange, to have lived in the same place forever.'

'It means you know where you are in the world,' he laughed. 'I don't mean that literally. It's just I know where I belong. The town is as familiar to me as the back of my hand.'

'I wonder why people say that?' she mused. 'The back of my hand isn't the least bit familiar to me. I'm sure I wouldn't recognize it out of half a dozen others.'

'That's because you've been too busy rushing around the world to stop and look at it.'

They were passing Spring Engineering. 'I wonder if the new owner could be persuaded to give it a lick of paint,' he said, half to himself.

'I reckon so if you asked nicely.'

'I don't know who to ask. I'm sure Fergus does but he's keeping pretty tight-lipped about it.'

'He must have his reasons,' she said casually.

Jim told her to take the next right turn. 'Would you like to come in for a cup of coffee?' he asked when she stopped the car.

He lived down a narrow unmade road. His was the last house on a row of terraced properties with long front gardens. At the end of the road the moors sloped gently upwards.

'No, thanks. I'd better be getting home,' she said, trying to keep the regret out of her voice. There was no way she would agree to being alone with this man today – although it wasn't him she distrusted, but herself. He was holding the passenger door open, looking down at her, a half-smile on his face. 'Some other time, maybe,' she added.

'Some other time, then.'

He slammed the door and as she drove away, she tried to push him out of her mind. Over the next few hours she'd need all her wits about her. It was time for the showdown with Tony.

She'd never thought him capable of such rage. Astonished and afraid, she wondered how she could ever have thought him gentle, and almost hoped Mrs Mason was listening and would come to her rescue if he attacked her. She tried to contain her own anger and remain patient.

'You surely realized it was over between us a long time ago,' she said quietly. She'd tried to be reasonable from the start. 'I want a divorce,' she'd said and he reacted with instant, implacable virulence.

Now he was walking up and down the room, waving his arms like a child deprived of a favourite toy. At one point he even stamped his elegantly-shod foot in temper. 'I thought you liked the life I gave you,' he spat. 'A title, a stately home, a position in the community.'

'You forget I already had Tymperleys, my dear,' she said, trying not to sound sarcastic. 'And I've always been proud of my own status, not just in this community. As for the title, I never use it. I've never been entirely happy being called "Lady".'

'That's because you were born in the gutter,' he sneered. 'It takes a certain amount of breeding to carry a title.'

His insults weren't worth answering. After a while she said, 'I'm sorry you're taking it like this, Tony. Why can't we part friends?'

'Friends!' He stopped and looked down at her contemptuously. 'What sort of friend have you been to me, making me beg and grovel for every penny of your money, just like my father did?'

Lisa looked at him in amazement. 'That's a lie! I've been paying your bills for years at the rate of a couple of thousand pounds a month.' She couldn't be bothered adding that if he hadn't been so sneaky and dishonest right from the beginning, she would have been willing to share everything with him. All she wanted now was to get to her room and sleep in Ferris Hall for the last time, but perhaps if he got all this hate and resentment out of his system, the divorce would go ahead more amicably.

Suddenly his attitude changed. He sat opposite and gave a sly smile. 'I've been half-expecting this,' he said. 'And I've already been in touch with my solicitor. He thinks I should be entitled to a settlement from you, either that or alimony.'

'What!' Now it was her turn to be enraged. 'I'd give every penny away before I'd let you fritter my money away at Grundy's.'

His grey eyes narrowed. 'How did you find that out?'

'It doesn't matter. There's no chance of anything off me, Tony,' she said emphatically. 'No chance at all. Forget it.'

'One of my colleagues in Westminster got a massive amount off his ex-wife,' he said virtuously. 'In fact, she was almost thrown in prison for refusing to pay.'

'He sounds a nice type. I'm sure you're the greatest pals.' She stared down at the table. A cigarette! What she wouldn't have given for a cigarette right now to calm her shattered nerves. 'Tony,' she began with forced patience. 'I had intended the divorce to be on the grounds of marital breakdown . . .'

Before she could continue, he interrupted with, 'I've got a better idea. Why not adultery – with Christy Costello?'

'You saw and you said nothing?' She looked at him open-mouthed.

Her bewilderment must have made him feel uncomfortable. 'It didn't bother me,' he muttered. 'Why should it?'

'Because I'm your wife, that's why. What I was going to say before was, if you in any way attempt to get money off me, I'll forget all about a breakdown, but give non-consummation as my reason. I don't think we'd even need a divorce then – the marriage could be annulled. That would give your macho friends at Grundy's a good laugh.'

This time he said nothing. She stood up. 'I think I'll go to bed. Let's not quarrel any more, Tony. Let's sort this out like civilized human beings.'

'It's too late for that.'

His voice was so raw, so filled with hate, that she shivered. At the door, she turned. 'I don't want any unpleasantness, but if you insist on war then I'll use all the weapons at my command. What about your first wife? You used all her money and she killed herself after the divorce. That won't look good in court, Tony.'

The knuckles tightened on his long thin hands. He looked at her with an expression of utter loathing on his white face. 'I suppose Christy told you that, but you'll have a job proving it.'

She went upstairs feeling incredibly sad. This wasn't the way she'd expected the day which had started so gloriously to end. Halfway up the stairs a voice hissed, 'Lisa!'

Tony was standing in the hall looking up at her with burning eyes.

'What?'

'I'm going to get you for this – you just wait and see. This marriage never turned out the way I wanted it, but I'm going to make damn sure the divorce does.'

'What are you going to do?' she asked listlessly.

'Just wait and see!'

Chapter 45

She ripped Tony's face into little pieces, separating his eyes, his nose, his mouth, and flung the pieces in the waste-paper basket. The portrait he'd had painted was already in the bin. Outside, Omar was sitting on the wall between her yard and Florence Dale's, watching with interest.

'It's a good job I gave you away,' she called out severely. 'Otherwise you'd be in here too.' She wanted no reminders of Tony left. Picking up the box-file which held all her favourite notices and photographs, she tipped the contents onto the floor – she'd been meaning to put them in albums for years – then put them back one by one into the file, removing all mementos of her husband. A leaflet from the last election with Tony smiling charmingly at the camera was screwed into a ball, a photo of their wedding torn to bits.

One by one, she put the cuttings and pictures back and as so often happened when the file was got out for some reason, began to reminisce . . . She re-read the review of *The Matchstick Man* which had taken everyone by surprise, then an article about Dent, cuttings from a Maine newspaper praising Ralph's lousy acting in *Uncle Vanya*, and she smiled at a snapshot of herself and Jackie in Kensington Gardens. A young man had asked if he could take it. They'd given him the Queen's Gate address and he'd sent them the photograph, along with a plea to take Jackie out to dinner. Although they'd laughed over it, Lisa had tried to talk her into going. The young man had seemed nice, a million times nicer than Gordon.

Jackie! The way she'd loved that horrible man! So trusting and childlike, she was too innocent for this scary, cruel world. Lisa remembered standing at the vicarage gate in the snow watching Jackie and her family. She'd known all she had to do was knock and be welcomed with open arms, drawn into that close family circle, made to feel part of it. Jackie would have been there when Lisa needed her, even after all those years. But Lisa had rebuffed her friend when *her* support was needed. God, how could she have been so cold and churlish? Of course there'd been the dreaded lump to worry about, but that was no excuse.

Had she kept Jackie's number, she wondered urgently, and began to search through the bureau – but there was no sign of it. She went upstairs and looked through her handbags, eventually finding it shoved carelessly in a pocket. The crumpled page from Jackie's diary showed a whole week in March, yet nothing, absolutely nothing was written on it except Jackie's number in her familiar untidy scrawl; this meant that during that week, Jackie had had no appointments – no lunch or dinner dates, nothing.

Lisa telephoned the number and a young man answered, his voice scarcely audible above the ear-shattering music in the background. She had to ask for Jackie Murray three times before he understood. 'Hold on a minute while I fetch her,' he said eventually.

It was a good five minutes before he came back. 'She's there all right, but she won't answer. I hope she's okay.'

'Give me your address and I'll come straight over.'

'Jackie, it's Lisa. If you don't open the door I'll fetch the landlord with the key.'

'You'll be lucky,' said the youth behind her, the one who had answered the phone. 'He's in Mexico.'

'What's he doing there?' asked Lisa, hammering on the door again.

'Spending the money he gets off this flea-pit, I guess.'

'*Jackie!*' Lisa thumped with both hands. 'She probably thinks this is part of the music, an extra dimension to the bases.'

'It's not all that loud,' he protested.

'Then I reckon you should get your hearing tested. You'll probably find you're almost deaf.'

Lisa pressed her ear against the door and was sure she could hear a shuffling from inside. 'JACKIE!' she yelled. 'Open this bloody door!'

The door opened a crack and no further. Lisa widened it

gingerly. Jackie was walking away and threw herself face down onto the bed like a great floundering whale.

'She's all right then?' The young man looked relieved.

'Yes, thanks for your help. There's one more thing you can do.'

'What's that?'

He was quite a nice young man really. Lisa gave him a wide grin. '*You can turn that bloody music down!*'

'Turn over and look at me,' commanded Lisa. On the way over she'd decided to take control, just like she'd done when they were young. It would probably do Jackie more good than sympathy.

Jackie sniffed and sat up. She looked at Lisa miserably.

'What's the matter, you silly dollop? Why didn't you answer the door? You had that young man really worried, not to mention me.'

'Oh, Lisa!' She burst into tears. 'I feel so utterly wretched.'

'I'm not surprised, living in a dump like this. Just look at it!' The room was a reasonable size with a large window overlooking a pretty, tree-filled square, but Jackie had reduced it to a tip. Her clothes were everywhere, over the backs of chairs, on the floor amidst old newspapers and magazines, and the small round table was covered in dirty dishes. 'Honestly, Jackie, I feel as if I'm in a time warp. It's just like walking into Queen's Gate half a lifetime ago.'

'I'm sorry.'

'And so you should be! Get out of bed this minute and help tidy up.'

She noticed the difficulty Jackie had in hoisting her huge body upright. Jackie caught her look and said defensively, 'I keep intending to lose weight. I hate being fat like this.'

'It's bad for your heart,' said Lisa severely and Jackie suddenly smiled. Lisa almost gasped, as it took years off her age and she felt an ache, as if the old Jackie had miraculously appeared.

'I feel as if I'm in a time warp, too. It brings it all back, you bossing me about like this.'

Amidst the clothes Lisa found a pile of greasy fish and chip papers and bags from a confectioner's smeared with cream, and she remembered the way Jackie had overeaten when she was depressed and expecting Noël. She had turned to food for comfort, which meant she badly needed comforting right now.

Once the room had been tidied, the clothes put in the wardrobe and the rubbish in several plastic carrier bags, it began to look quite habitable. It was only then that Lisa noticed the music downstairs had been turned down considerably. She washed two mugs in a small corner sink and plugged in the electric kettle.

'I think we deserve a cup of tea after that,' she said with a sigh of satisfaction. 'What brought all this on, anyway? Locking yourself away and refusing to answer the phone?'

Jackie had found a dressing gown, a hideous flowered silk thing that hardly met across her stomach. 'Yesterday I was sent to a firm in Holborn,' she said, 'solicitors, and they gave me this awful electronic typewriter to work on. I'd only just got used to using an electric model. It was manuals when I left to have Noël. I've always been a good typist – I used to do Laurence's sermons and all his correspondence – so I never lost my speed, but this thing! It just ran away with me and my fingers turned into thumbs. At lunch-time they suddenly said they didn't need a temp any more, but it was just an excuse to get rid of me. I don't blame them, I was useless.'

'That was awful, no wonder you feel wretched,' Lisa said softly.

'It was the last straw. Sometimes I feel there's no point going on, what with Laurence dead and the kids so far away. I'm no good at being anything except a wife and mother.' She began to cry again. 'I can't get used to everyone being gone and being by myself after all this time. It was such a busy life at the vicarage, really hectic, but I loved it. There were kids everywhere, not just mine. Now everything's so empty.'

Lisa couldn't think of anything to say. After a while, she ventured, 'You could go to night-school and learn to use one of those new typewriters,' though it was a pretty lame suggestion.

'I've thought about that. Word processing would be even more useful, but who's going to employ me, Lisa? I'm sixty and I look a fright. I'm sure that's why the kids don't ask me up to stay more often,' she said despairingly. 'They're ashamed of me.'

'We're going to have to sort you out,' Lisa said briskly.

'How?' said Jackie hopefully.

'First thing is a diet. Join a club where you'll make friends with other people. Will you do that?'

'Yes, Lisa.' Jackie gave a half-smile.

'And remember when we first met and you gave me your clothes and lent me your gold watch and we shared the clothing coupons off your aunts?' Jackie nodded. 'Well, now it's my turn to do something for you. I'll buy you one of those word processor things – no, I insist.' Jackie had opened her mouth to argue. 'Once you've got the hang of it you could become a freelance temp or start your own agency – I know heaps of writers who need scripts typing.'

Jackie didn't say anything for a long time and Lisa began to wonder if she was offended. After all, what a cheek barging in like this, issuing orders on how Jackie should run her life . . .

'Thank you for the word processor, Lisa. I'm truly grateful and I'll do the things you suggest, but you know, I'll only be half-alive for the rest of my life without Laurence and my children.'

That night, as she returned home in a taxi, Lisa thought, 'I'll buy a proper flat, somewhere central where she can start an agency, and pretend it belongs to a friend who only wants a low rent. I can't leave her in that crummy bedsit.' She'd nearly asked Jackie back to Pimlico to live but the house was so small they might get on each other's nerves after all these years. It had been different when they were young, privacy didn't seem to matter, and anyway, there was a limit to how much charity a person could take. Jackie had her dignity to think about.

The day's events had taken Lisa's mind off her own problems, at least. Tomorrow morning she was going to see a solicitor about the divorce, and she dreaded the unpleasantness ahead.

'Of course you can't *prove* the marriage wasn't consummated,' said Alan Peel. He was a grave, portly man with an old-fashioned manner that made him appear older than his years – she guessed he was about her own age and she felt embarrassed discussing such intimate matters with him.

'He can't prove it was,' she replied.

'The question is, why stay? If you claimed non-consummation a week, a month, after the wedding, it would be more convincing. Four years and it becomes questionable. People will wonder why you didn't leave.'

'Don't *you* believe me?'

'Of course I do,' he said soothingly. 'But we have to look at this from the judge's point of view. Why *did* you stay?' he asked curiously.

She shrugged. 'At first, I thought one day he'd . . . well, manage it, though he never tried again. Then I'd got used to the life we led. I began to enjoy politics and I loved Ferris Hall – that's his home – and Broxley. I was fond of Tony, too, in a way. We got on famously for a long time though I gradually became disillusioned. Now there's nothing left except hate on his side and indifference on mine.'

'I see,' he said blandly. 'Now, about the settlement he mentioned. It's been done before, the man getting alimony or a lump-sum payment when the wife is the wealthier partner.' He gave a dry smile. 'When you think about it, it's only fair. You'd expect something off him if things were the other way round.'

'Fair!' she gasped. 'He only married me for my money.'

'And women never marry men for theirs?'

'If that's how you think, I'll get someone else,' she said angrily.

'My dear lady, I'm only pointing out the realities.' Did all solicitors look and sound so pompous, she wondered. 'I'm on your side in this, of course, that's what you're paying me for, but surely you prefer the facts to blandishments?'

'I suppose so,' she muttered. 'But it seems unfair in my case.'

'Well, I'll get things in motion and be in touch.'

Lisa stood up. As he accompanied her to the door, the solicitor said, 'We were at boarding school together, you know.'

Her doubts returned. 'You and Tony? But should you be acting for me, in that case?'

He raised a reassuring hand. 'Don't worry, I've never met him since. I wouldn't want to, to be perfectly frank. He was never a very popular chap. Had a thing about his father, always complaining he kept him short of cash. I remember he was a bit of a gambler, even then.'

Perhaps she should get involved in something, Lisa thought vaguely. A play, a movie, something to take her mind off the divorce rather than just sitting waiting for things to happen. A few weeks ago she'd been offered a role in a four-part television drama, though it was probably too late to take that up now. Nothing had come in since and there was no doubt about it, the older an actress became, the fewer parts she was offered. It was even worse in films, where the Robert Mitchums and John Waynes went on forever, playing romantic leads well into their sixties, usually opposite women less than half their age.

Maybe Tony had got over his rage by now and had come to see sense, and everything would go through without a hitch. After all, she knew so many awful things about him which could be brought up in court and make him seem unworthy of a settlement. There was little he could say about her – only that business with Christy . . .

Jackie was the first to telephone. 'Have you seen this morning's *Meteor*?' she asked.

'You know I'd never read a rag like that,' said Lisa indignantly. 'I'm surprised you do.'

'I only bought it because of the front-page headline. I think you'd better get a copy straight away, Lisa.'

'Why, what does it say?'

'It's best you read it for yourself.'

'*MP TO DIVORCE EX-PORN QUEEN WIFE.*'

The *Meteor* was stuffed in a wire rack outside the news-agent's shop along with all the other dailies, and when Lisa read the headline she didn't immediately connect it with herself and wondered what on earth Jackie was talking about. Then she looked more closely at the full-length photograph of a young, virtually naked woman beneath it and several seconds later, realized it was a still from *Easy Dreams*. The picture was of Cassie Royale – in other words, herself – wearing that black negligée with the feather border, and standing in front of a window, one arm stretched upwards holding the curtain, the other on her hips and looking the wanton, abandoned woman she was supposed to be.

'Oh bugger!' she said out loud.

'Sir Anthony Molyneux, Conservative MP for Broxley in South Yorkshire, yesterday instituted divorce proceedings against his wife, the aging beauty, Lisa Angelis. Sir Anthony claimed it had been brought to his notice that his wife had once starred in pornographic films.

'"Of course I never knew this when we married," Sir Anthony told our reporter yesterday. "But now I do, it leaves me with no alternative but to ask for a divorce. After all, I owe it to my constituents. A person in my position must have a wife who is above reproach . . ."'

Lisa took off her glasses and folded the paper in disgust. *'Aging!'* she said to herself incredulously. *'AGING!'*

Gertie Lomax telephoned later. 'We've had a couple of reporters round asking questions. Nearly everybody here is on your side, but Fergus said Tony's got a private detective digging into your past, so be prepared for more stuff like this.'

'Are you upset?' asked Nellie, calling from Liverpool.

'Not a bit,' said Lisa. 'I only took my clothes off in one movie. It was daring then, but not now, and *Easy Dreams* is regarded as a classic of its kind. It's even been on television a couple of times – they wouldn't do that if it was pornographic. All that bothers me is being called aging.'

Alan Peel said, 'This kind of publicity won't do any good, I'm afraid. Judges are very conservative and even if this newspaper report is totally exaggerated, it'll look bad if it's produced in court.'

*

Lisa had several more sympathetic calls that day and a few from newspapers asking for her opinion on the *Meteor*'s revelations.

'I wouldn't call them "revelations",' she told them. '*Easy Dreams* has always been available for anybody to see. One thing, though – would you refer to someone only fifty-four as "aging"?'

In fact, the publicity turned out to be advantageous. The following day, Lisa was offered three new parts – two stage plays and a movie – and she accepted the latter, an Edwardian comedy called *Barney's Castle*. It didn't matter that the pay was a tenth of what she would have got in Hollywood. The film was being made in London, which meant she wouldn't have to move away. She needed to be on hand in case Tony had any more tricks up his sleeve.

'*TEN THINGS "LADY PORN" WOULDN'T WANT PEOPLE TO KNOW.*'

It was several weeks later, and although this time the article wasn't on the front page of the *Meteor*, it still took up a lot of space on page eight. As she read it, Lisa felt a sense of real fright. How on earth had Tony's detective discovered some of this?

'*Angelis walked out on her first husband after nine months of marriage. Brian Smith never remarried and his mother Dorothy claims he is a broken man.*

'*Angelis shared her Hollywood home with TWO men.*

'*Angelis' third husband, Joseph Dent, was the most hated man in Hollywood.*

'*Angelis began an affair with fellow actor Hugo Swann during the making of a movie directed by her second husband, Busby Van Dolen.*'

. . . and so on.

Lisa felt sick. The rest of the article was lies, nasty gossip, claiming she'd had affairs with people she'd never met, caused scenes on set, slapped a director's face, but it was horrible to think of people delving into her past and inventing fictional stories to blacken her. Thank goodness Dorothy Smith hadn't told them about the baby Brian thought he'd fathered. that would have sounded really awful. Probably Brian was too ashamed to let people know.

'No comment,' she told other newspapers when they called.

'Aren't you going to fight back?' one reporter asked. 'Surely there's some dirt to be dug up on your husband?'

Alan Peel had advised her to say nothing to reporters. 'If they start printing stuff about him, it'll only make him more anxious to get at you. Keep your distance and your dignity, stay above the fray and people will get tired of a one-sided slanging match. Tony will start to look as if he's hounding you.'

Lisa told the reporter, 'No comment on that, either. However, I'd just refer you to *Private Eye*, the June 1983 edition. You might find something interesting there.'

No one on the set of *Barney's Castle* took any notice of the *Meteor*'s exposure. In their time several had been targets of the gutter press and to Lisa's relief they all regarded it as a bit of a joke.

Where was Ralph? It wasn't until Jackie asked about him that Lisa realized she hadn't seen him for ages – the older you got the faster time seemed to fly by and it was more than a year since they'd last met. She asked around, but nobody knew where he was. Adam, his friend, had disappeared too. Then out of the blue she learnt that Matthew Jenks, the playwright, had died of AIDS a few months before. Ralph had probably known Matthew was dying and she remembered how distraught he'd been, knowing he was the cause of Gary's death.

Lisa felt deeply hurt that he'd just disappeared without letting her know, but despite all her efforts to discover his whereabouts, there was no trace of Ralph anywhere.

The divorce proceedings seemed to take forever. A month would pass between each exchange of letters and when Lisa demanded the reason for the delay, Alan Peel said patiently, 'These matters can't be hurried.'

Tony was still seeking a settlement and she continued to

refuse. 'He's not getting a penny,' she insisted.

'I feel bound to advise that if you agreed to pay him a large sum now, a million pounds say, this harassment in the press would cease,' her solicitor told her. 'He just wants to blacken your name so that when the case comes to court it will go in his favour. He'll demand a settlement and might get *more* than a million if it's left to the judge to decide.'

'If and when the case comes to court, there's a lot of things I can reveal about Tony,' said Lisa, thinking of the bribes and the gambling, and the attempt to close down Spring Engineering – not to mention his first wife's suicide.

'As you wish,' said Alan Peel with a sigh.

'Something's happened here,' said Nellie in a frightened voice. 'We've had a reporter sniffing round asking questions about you, and Joan's told him something.'

'What on earth could Joan have said?' laughed Lisa. 'There's nothing she knows that you and the boys don't.'

'I've no idea,' Nellie answered. 'But whatever it was, she said he'd paid a lot of money for it. She came round last night and I've never seen her so excited – she was really on a high. You know she's always hated you since Mam died.'

Lisa wondered why her stomach felt on edge when she woke up next morning. Then she remembered – *Joan*. Although she'd laughed off Nellie's warning, after she'd put down the phone a nagging sense of worry set in and last night she'd lain in bed thinking about things she hadn't thought of in years. Unpleasant, horrible things she'd deliberately pushed to the back of her mind. Had Joan known about the abortion, for instance? That awful time was suddenly so real again, so clear in her mind that she could remember the pain as acutely as if it had happened yesterday.

All of this was Tony's fault and she cursed out loud, calling him every foul name she could think of until she remembered how thin the walls were and that Florence Dale might be listening.

The telephone rang beside her bed. 'What have you got to say about the article in today's *Meteor*?' a voice demanded.

'No comment!' She slammed the receiver down, got out of

bed and threw on some clothes. It seemed strange later that she actually noticed what a lovely day it was – brisk and sunny, the streets still deserted at this early hour. The newsagent's was open but it was too soon for the papers to be outside. She asked for the *Meteor* and folded it so she wouldn't see the headline until she got home. Perhaps it was just her imagination, but did the Pakistani man who ran the shop, usually so friendly, deliberately avoid her eyes?

'*PORN QUEEN KILLED FATHER*'

'*In a sworn statement to our reporter, Joan O'Brien, sister of Lisa Angelis, the porno actress, revealed that in 1945, her sister stabbed their father to death.*

'*"I saw her," claimed Joan, who lives in a council flat (Angelis is a millionairess several times over!), "and she let my mother take the blame." Joan went on to say that she has never forgotten that terrible night. "I don't know why Lizzie" (as Angelis was once known) "did it, but all I know is, as God is my witness, I saw her and I've never forgiven her for it."*

'*Joan O'Brien went on to say that whilst her father was not exactly the ideal parent, "He was a good, hard-working man who cared for his family in his own way and we were always well-fed and well-clothed."*

'*In a final emotional outburst, Miss O'Brien claimed, "It's a relief to get this out of my system. It's been gnawing away at me for years but I could never bring myself to tell anyone – until the* Meteor *came along!"*'

Jackie came within the hour, though by then there were already two reporters banging on the front door, so she had to enter via Florence Dale's, and sneak in by the back door.

'Oh, you poor, poor thing!' She took Lisa in her arms and pressed her against her still-ample bosom. 'Here, let me make you some tea.' She took over answering the telephone. 'No comment!' she barked several times that morning. Sometimes it was friends calling to offer condolences, as if Lisa were dead, or one of the O'Briens to say they were right behind her. Even Busby had heard the news thousands of miles away in Los Angeles and offered to come over immediately but Jackie, in response to Lisa's mouthed 'no', told him there was no need.

It was midday; the telephone rang for the umpteenth time and Jackie picked it up. 'It's your solicitor,' she whispered. 'Do you want to speak to him?'

'I suppose I'd better.' Lisa got up listlessly.

'I've spoken to my partner who specializes in libel,' Alan Peel said brusquely. 'He thinks you should sue. This time Tony's gone too far.'

'It's no use,' said Lisa dully. 'What the *Meteor* says is true. I *did* kill my father.'

Chapter 46

'My father was an animal who used my mother as a punch-bag for years,' said Kevin. On television he looked dignified, the salt of the earth, a working man, but getting old now. His face was more wrinkled than Lisa remembered. Unafraid of the camera, he spoke with the integrity of one confident that what he said was the complete and utter truth.

The news had actually reached television, had become a *cause célèbre*, far more interesting than politics or foreign affairs – a juicy item on a par with the Jeremy Thorpe case, the Profumo affair, Lord Lucan's disappearance.

'So your sister Joan is lying, then?' said the interviewer.

Kevin was standing outside his house, a modern semi-detached in Litherland. 'She probably doesn't remember much about Dad. He drank his wages and he didn't give a sh . . . a damn about us kids, except to give us a swipe when we went near him. It was our mother who kept the family together.'

'But what about this amazing accusation, that it was your other sister, Lisa Angelis, as she's now called, not your mother, who stabbed your father to death?'

Kevin began to look uneasy for the first time. 'I'm afraid I know nothing about that,' he said. 'It came as a total shock to me.'

'Your sister, Lisa, was invited to come on this programme, but she refused. What do you say to that?'

'I suspect she's in a state of shock. Wouldn't you be if something like this came up out of the blue after forty years?' demanded Kevin.

They'd even dug up a copy of the *Liverpool Echo* which reported that Kitty had been found Not Guilty of manslaughter. The newscaster concluded, 'Miss Angelis is in the middle of a bitter divorce battle with her husband, Sir Anthony Molyneux, MP for Broxley. Today, Sir Anthony said he was upset by the revelations. "Whatever my feelings for my wife, I think the *Meteor* has gone too far this time."'

'Bloody hypocrite,' seethed Jackie. 'What are we going to do?'

'I've no idea,' said Lisa.

'Oh my dear, you must come to. Stop acting like a zombie! We've got to fight this thing.'

'What would *you* do?'

Jackie paused. 'I've no idea,' she said eventually.

Somehow they managed to smile. 'What time is it?' asked Lisa.

'That was the ten o'clock news, love.'

'Mam used to call me love,' said Lisa. 'Poor Mam.' She lit a cigarette from the stub of her last one. Jackie had gone out and bought a hundred pack and there was hardly any whisky left in the bottle.

'Lisa,' Jackie said softly, 'I heard you tell your solicitor the newspaper story was true. Do you want to talk about it?'

So Lisa told her everything. When she'd finished, she told Jackie, 'You know, I'm almost pleased it's in the open. Like Joan said, it's been gnawing away inside me all my life. I've always had this restless, discontented feeling and could never identify the reason for it. Now I know what it was: guilt, a need to confess and make atonement for my sins.'

'Shall I open the post again this morning?' asked Jackie, coming in from the hall with a fat bundle of letters. Yesterday it had been mainly requests for interviews, a few anonymous letters which Jackie said there was no need to read, and messages of support from friends.

'Please,' said Lisa. After two nights of broken sleep she still felt unable to cope with the situation.

'More demands for a personal interview – this one offers five figures for your story. Oh, you'd better read this.' She handed over a letter typed on stiff white paper.

Alan Peel no longer wished to represent her. '*Under the circumstances arising over the past few days, I do not feel I am the right person to act on your behalf in the divorce proceedings instituted against your husband.'*

'Shit!' said Lisa.

'That's good,' said Jackie.

'What's good?'

'You swearing. It means you're starting to feel your old self again.'

'I'll *never* feel my old self again.'

'You will,' Jackie said confidently. 'Hey, this looks interesting. Milo Hanna would like you to be a guest on his chat show.'

'Not likely!' said Lisa. Milo Hanna was a national institution, a puckish Irishman who hosted a chat show which went out at peak viewing time every Wednesday to an audience of millions. 'I wouldn't dream of going on television. I hate those programmes where people are persuaded to tell their all by some ghoulish interviewer – Milo Hanna being one of the worst – and everybody, including the audience, ends up in tears. All that false emotion makes me want to puke.'

'You're definitely getting better,' said Jackie firmly. 'If that's the case, it's time you started putting your side of the story about. If your lousy solicitor hadn't told you not to speak to the press, then your equally lousy husband mightn't have gone as far as he did.'

Lisa lit another cigarette. 'Honestly, Jackie, I haven't a clue which way to turn. I'd love to fight back, but how do you fight the truth? If I revealed that Tony ate newborn babies for lunch, so what? It has no bearing on this.'

'You could say *why* you did it,' Jackie said. 'Why you killed him.'

'Jesus, Jackie, I could never, *never* do that! I feel unclean just thinking about it. No, the best thing to do is hide out somewhere till it blows over. When the ratpack go away, I'll escape.'

'You know it'll never blow over. They'll track you down wherever you are. I think you should come out fighting.' Jackie was opening another letter, a small square envelope containing a sheet of cheap lined paper. 'Here's another you'd better read.'

The writing was barely legible, a shaky childish scrawl.

'Dear God, Lizzie, what have I done? I'm sorry, I'll never forgive myself. That man was so persuasive and he asked so many questions. I keep thinking of Mam and how she would have hated me. I'm truly sorry for everything. Joan.'

'Poor Joan,' said Lisa. 'She probably feels worse than I do.'

Jackie nodded. 'Probably.'

'And Nellie and the boys are really angry with her. Perhaps I should go and see her.'

'Not now, Lisa, wait till things have simmered down. You're probably both too emotional just now.'

'Perhaps you're right.' Lisa grinned. 'You've been right an awful lot lately. I used to think I was the only one who was right and you were always wrong.'

'That's right,' giggled Jackie. 'Sorry, I shouldn't laugh.'

'Please do, it makes me feel better. After all, what's the saying – "Laugh and the world laughs with you . . ."'

'"Cry and you cry alone",' finished Jackie. 'Or what about, "laughter is the best medicine" – though it depends on what's wrong. It wouldn't do a burst appendix much good.'

'Damn it all, Jackie,' Lisa said suddenly, 'let's get thoroughly plastered like we used to. Where's that whisky bottle?'

'It was me that got plastered, you never did. Anyway, it's nearly empty,' Jackie said ruefully. 'I could buy another – sod my diet.'

'There's half a dozen under the sink. Busby sends them by the crate, best American bourbon.'

Milo Hanna himself telephoned that afternoon. By then Jackie was too hung over to answer and it was Lisa who managed a slurred 'Hallo.'

'I'd love to have you on my show next week,' he coaxed in his lilting Irish voice.

'Absolutely not,' said Lisa. To her surprise she couldn't help thinking how nice he sounded and almost felt mean for refusing.

'You know I was born in the same village as your mam?' he said. 'My auld mam remembers her distinctly. A pretty little

Irish colleen, Mam says she was, blonde and blue-eyed with skin as soft as clover.'

He'd done his homework, finding out where Mam was born. Perhaps Kevin had told him. She found herself smiling and said accusingly, 'I know your sort, a silver-tongued Paddy who was born kissing the Blarney stone. I bet you could talk the hind leg off a donkey.'

'Only if he wanted to be three-legged,' laughed Milo Hanna. 'If you came on my show, I wouldn't ask questions you didn't want. We'll talk about your film career, your favourite plays, the people you knew in Hollywood. We'd work out a list of questions beforehand.'

Lisa imagined his impish leprechaun face grinning into the receiver. 'I don't like you much,' she said with a hiccup. 'In fact, I hardly ever watch your show.'

'Ah Lisa, I'll cry myself to sleep tonight. You are a cruel, cruel woman to be sure.'

'You'll get over it.'

'I never will, you've cut me to the quick,' he said sadly. 'Still, I suppose it was too much to ask. It would take a lot of courage to face several million viewers feeling as you must do now.'

'Are you suggesting I'm a coward?'

'Of course not! It's just that I understand your reluctance. Only a very special lady could raise the nerve to come on my show and be interviewed, even though the questions would be as gentle as the breath of a newborn lamb.'

Lisa burst out laughing. 'For Chrissakes, all right, I'll come on your show, but I don't know what good it will do me.'

'What have I done?' she said later in an appalled voice. 'I must have been mad to agree.'

'You weren't mad, you were pissed,' said Jackie. She rose to her feet unsteadily. 'I'm going back to Earl's Court for a bath.'

'But you can have a bath here,' protested Lisa.

'In a few months maybe, but not yet. Your bath's so narrow, last night I got stuck and had visions of the fire brigade hoisting me out. Anyway, I'm in the middle of packing. Don't forget I'm moving into my new flat next week. Will you be all right on your own? I'll be back first thing tomorrow.'

'Of course I will.' Lisa didn't feel nearly as confident as she sounded. 'You've been an absolute rock these last few days, I don't know what I would have done without you.'

'You would have managed,' said Jackie. 'People always manage. Even I did, in my own, muddled way.'

'I won't drink any more,' thought Lisa when Jackie left. 'In fact I'll soak in the bath for an hour and then make a cup of tea.'

She glanced out of the window. The reporters had disappeared. After two days of her refusing their noisy demands for an interview, they'd finally gone home disappointed.

It wasn't until she sank into the warm bath that Lisa realised how exhausted she was. Her body throbbed with tiredness and in no time she fell asleep and woke to find the water had gone cold. She put on a robe and combed her wet hair. The face that stared back from the dressing-table mirror was yellow with fatigue. She certainly looked an 'aging' beauty tonight, she thought dejectedly.

'How come you never change?' she demanded of Victoria, who was sitting on the bed, staring at her wide-eyed. 'You're as pretty now as the day Ralph gave you to me.'

She was putting the kettle on when there was a knock on the door. She glanced at the clock. It was nearly midnight, which meant it could only be Jackie, who'd had second thoughts and decided to come back, or possibly Nellie who'd been threatening to come for days.

It was neither Nellie nor Jackie but Jim Harrison who stood on the doorstep.

She took his coat, sat him down and offered him a cup of tea.

'You're the last person I expected to see,' she said as she sat opposite, conscious what a dismal picture she must make, compared with the last time they'd met, at Fergus's party the previous year.

'Fergus died yesterday,' he said abruptly.

She groaned. 'I'm so sorry, he was a lovely person. I'll write to Gertie tomorrow.'

'He was one of the finest men I've ever known,' Jim said simply. 'Though he always knew I never voted for him.'

'He'll be sadly missed in Broxley.' It was an effort to stop herself from bursting into tears.

'When I told Gertie I was coming to see you she let me into a secret.' He looked at Lisa accusingly. 'Why didn't you tell me you'd bought Spring Engineering?'

'I didn't see the need,' she said defensively. 'Have you come all the way from Yorkshire to be angry with me?'

'Of course not!'

'Then why have you come?'

He didn't answer immediately, then he said awkwardly, 'I'm probably making a fool of myself.'

'You're good at that. You made a fool of yourself when we first met and a fool of me at the same time.'

He managed a grin. 'Ouch! Don't rub it in. I thought you'd come to suss us out on behalf of your charming husband.'

'You shouldn't make such sweeping assumptions.'

'I never have since.'

'How do you intend making a fool of yourself tonight?' She had a feeling about what he was going to say and hoped she was right. He'd occupied her thoughts a lot since they'd met at Fergus's party and she felt safe with him there. Nothing could happen to her whilst he was here, so big and reassuring, looking uncomfortable in that silly little striped chair.

'We have a strange relationship, you and I. We seem to meet once a year, yet—' he paused.

'Yet what?' she pressed him.

He still hesitated. 'Yet I feel there's something between us,' he said eventually, the words coming out in a rush. 'Am I making a fool of myself, Lisa? Is there some other man in the background waiting to marry you when your divorce comes through?'

'There's no one,' she said softly.

'What about us? Is it all a product of my overheated imagination?'

She laughed. 'You're far too steady and conventional to have an overheated imagination.'

He gave her a look that made her insides shiver. 'You'd be amazed at how unconventional my imagination can get at times, Lisa. Now it's you who's making assumptions.'

'I'm sorry.' She took a deep breath. 'You're right – there *is* something between us. Even on the day we met when I hated you, I liked you. Does that make sense?'

'Perfect sense.'

'What happens now?' She suddenly felt relaxed and happy for the first time in days.

'This,' he said and came over and sat beside her on the settee and took her in his arms. He didn't kiss her, just wrapped himself around her and put a big hand on her cheek and pressed her head against his shoulder. She could feel his strong chin against her still-wet hair and after a while she fell asleep. When she woke up it was still dark outside and her left arm was stiff. She moved it gently, so as not to disturb him, but he was still awake.

'I only came down to sort things out between us,' he whispered. 'I thought it might help while you're in this fix to know I'm always there if you need me.'

'It does,' she said happily and snuggled back into his arms.

When she woke up again a glimmer of daylight showed through the curtains. This time he was asleep and she moved her head and watched him. After a while she picked up his hand which lay heavily on her hip and moved it inside her robe onto her breast. He stirred, his eyes opened and she reached up and turned his face towards her own and kissed him softly on the lips.

Oh God, she had never been made love to like this before, so slowly, so passionately, so satisfyingly. She'd spent her entire life waiting for this, the ultimate, perfect giving between two people in love, the mutual respect, the adoration of each other's bodies.

When they had finished and she lay naked in his arms, he said softly, 'I have to get back, I've a factory to run.'

Lisa nodded sleepily. A few minutes later she felt her robe

being tucked gently around her, then the door clicked and he was gone.

When Jackie let herself in, later in the morning, she found Lisa fast asleep on the settee. 'You idiot! Fancy dropping off down here. I bet you'll feel half-dead all day, you can't have slept properly.'

'I had the most perfect night's sleep ever.' Lisa sat up with a yawn. 'But I wouldn't say no to a cup of tea.'

'Where are the other guests?' asked Lisa.

The smartly dressed young woman who showed her into the hospitality room said, 'You're the only one.'

'But he usually has three.'

'Not always. If it's someone special, Milo gives them half an hour.'

'Why am I special? I didn't expect half an hour.'

The woman's eyes glazed over. 'You'd better take that up with Milo, darling. He'll be along in a minute. Help yourself to refreshments while you wait.'

She left and Lisa said to Jackie darkly, 'I'd only expected a ten-minute interview.'

Jackie had leapt on a plate of sandwiches and was rapidly devouring the lot. 'I'll be glad when this is all over, it's played havoc with my diet. Here, have some wine, calm your nerves.'

'It's a good job I don't want a sandwich to calm my nerves, they're nearly all gone.' She lit a cigarette and took some wine. 'Where's that bastard Milo Hanna?'

'Have you got your answers rehearsed?' said Jackie through a mouthful of bread.

'It's rude to speak with your mouth full. No, I haven't. We've agreed on a list of questions, but I haven't prepared the answers in case they sound forced.'

'Ah, my dear Lisa! Begorrah, you look lovely tonight.' Milo Hanna came in dressed in a velvet suit and a flowing black and white bow tie. With his dark wavy hair, he looked like a middle-aged Rupert Brooke.

'Why have I got a whole half hour?' she demanded

immediately. 'You usually have three guests. Why —?'

He held up his hands defensively. 'Because we're showing a few sequences from your movies,' he said quickly. 'My darling girl, don't be so suspicious.'

'I've good reason to be suspicious, Milo. I hadn't agreed to do your show for five minutes before it was advertised on television.'

'That was so you couldn't back off, have second thoughts.'

'I did.'

'So, I did the right thing.' He gave a sly, mischievous grin. 'Have some more wine, my lovely one. We'll be on in ten minutes.'

'Y'know, I reckon that man's a bloody fake,' said Lisa when he'd gone. 'I bet he's been no nearer Ireland than those sandwiches. He was probably born in the Home Counties and talks like Noël Coward at home.'

'I think he's lovely,' said Jackie comfortably. 'How do you feel?'

'Terrified!' Lisa went over to the mirror. 'How do I look?'

'Lovely, brave, terrified.'

Lisa had agonized for hours over what to wear. It took days to settle on a calf-length strapless dress of soft turquoise crêpe and a dark green velvet jacket. Her hair was drawn severely back into a plump bun on the nape of her neck.

'Oh God, Jackie, I've got a grey hair – no two, three. What a time to find out!'

'You're lucky, I went grey before I was forty. And look at me now!'

'Three minutes, Miss Angelis.' The young woman had come back.

'Good luck, Lisa.'

'This is worse than any first night. Is everybody frightened?' She clasped the young woman's hand tightly as she was led to the side of the set. Milo Hanna was waiting, a script in his hand, unsmiling for once. The warm-up comedian was coming to the end of his spiel. Lisa glanced at the audience. Christ, the whole of Broxley was there: Jim and the Masons, Gertie Lomax, half a dozen other people she recognized . . . Nellie and Stan were there too, and all her brothers – some with their wives – though she'd known they were coming.

The familiar introductory music began and as soon as it faded, Milo Hanna ran on stage to a burst of enthusiastic applause. She couldn't quite hear what he was saying and was surprised when she was pushed out and suddenly she was walking towards him, her hand out in greeting and he kissed her fondly as if they were lifelong friends.

He began by asking about her Hollywood career, about Busby and Joseph Dent. He showed clips from several of her movies, beginning with *The Opportunist*, her first speaking part, then *Easy Dreams* – much to her relief she was fully clothed – followed by *The Matchstick Man*, *Attrition* and finally, *Hearts and Flowers*. Every time the short sequences ended the audience clapped.

'You've had a long and distinguished career,' said Milo Hanna. 'Several of those films are regarded as classics.'

'I've been very lucky,' she said modestly.

'Tell us about Joseph Dent. He had the reputation of being a bit of an ogre. What was it like being married to him?'

Lisa's eyes lit up as she described Dent's strange personality. 'I loved him dearly,' she said finally.

'What about Gary Maddox? If I remember rightly, your name was linked with his for a long time. He lived with you, didn't he?'

She shifted uneasily in her seat. Gary was down on the list of questions she'd agreed to answer, but only in the context of a fellow actor and director, co-founder of O'Brien Productions. Milo Hanna had departed from the script.

'Gary was one of my closest friends,' she said eventually. 'That was all we were, friends.'

'And what a good friend you turned out to be, Lisa,' he said warmly. 'I understand Gary was one of the first AIDS victims and you nursed him till he died.'

She looked up at him quickly, her eyes filling with unexpected tears. Who on earth had told him that? His researchers were better than Tony's. 'That's what friends are for,' she muttered.

To her amazement, the audience began to clap and she felt

a surge of anger at such an intimate revelation being regarded as entertainment.

Milo, perfectly attuned to his guest's mood, changed the subject to the theatre. He asked her about Matthew Jenks' plays and how she liked acting with Ralph Layton. Then, 'You got married again, didn't you, and acquired a title, Lady Elizabeth Molyneux?'

'I did,' she said coldly. If he asked her questions about Tony or the divorce, she'd pour the jug of orange juice over him. That was also a subject she'd declared out of bounds.

'Not only a title, but an engineering company. That's a strange thing for an actress to buy. Why did you do that?'

She didn't answer for several seconds and someone in the audience shouted, 'Tell him, Lisa.'

'Someone was planning to build a hotel on the site. I thought it should remain a factory.'

There was another burst of applause and with an autocratic gesture Milo held up his hand and the clapping ceased. 'Was this someone your husband?' He was like a bloody magician the way he manipulated her – and the audience.

'It was my husband, yes,' she answered, wondering if Tony was watching.

Milo began to talk about Liverpool – 'City of the Stars' he called it – and ran through the famous names who had been born there.

'Do you miss it?'

'No,' she said, immediately regretting her honesty. If he asked why, all she could say was that it held too many bad memories and he might want to know what they were. She looked at the studio clock. Another ten minutes to go! Surely they'd reached the end of the agreed questions?

He was looking down at the script in his hand, biting his lip as if the next question was going to be difficult. Lisa could tell it was a deliberately staged gesture on his part.

'Did you kill your dad, Lisa?'

Oh, Jesus! The audience gasped then went silent and Lisa stared down at her hands. What good was there in denying it? she thought despairingly.

'I did,' she said eventually. 'Yes, I did. I killed him.'

There was a hissing sound as three hundred people drew in their breath simultaneously and Lisa felt her head begin to spin.

'And why should a thirteen-year-old girl stab her auld dad to death, now?' asked Milo Hanna gently.

She looked at him accusingly. 'You've betrayed me, you bastard,' her eyes said. He stared back at her unblinkingly, his face full of what looked like genuine concern.

The audience could have disappeared for all the sound they made. She could imagine them, Nellie, her brothers, Jim, all on tenterhooks waiting for her reply.

Milo Hanna reached out and took her hand. 'You'll feel better for the telling,' he whispered. It was another staged move; the whisper would have been perfectly audible to the viewers through his mike.

Suddenly, she began to speak, though she hadn't meant to. Words began to pour from her mouth in a rush she couldn't stop. She felt as if she no longer had control of her vocal chords. It was someone else, a stranger, who was babbling all this stuff.

'Because he had been abusing me for a long time,' the strange voice said. 'Because he made me pregnant when I was thirteen and I didn't know what to do. There was no one to turn to, no one. I was ashamed and terrified. What would Mam think? I tried to abort the baby myself with a metal skewer that belonged to my brothers and —' The voice stopped. Lisa looked at Milo Hanna in surprise. Had she really said all that?

Apparently she had because he asked, 'And what happened then, my love?'

'I can't remember much. They took me to hospital, but it wasn't until years later I found . . .' she paused.

'Found what?' he said encouragingly.

'I could never have any more children. I would have loved my own children.'

There were only the two of them in the entire world, her and Milo, under the bright lights together. He was looking at her protectively and quite out of the blue, her feelings for him changed and she felt an unexpected surge of love.

'About your auld dad,' he said softly. 'How did the

stabbing come about? Did he come after you again, then?'

'He probably would have done, eventually. It was Joan he was after the night I killed him.'

'Joan!' Milo pulled his chair forward until their knees were touching. 'Why don't you tell us about it, Lisa?'

She felt as if she would do anything for him. 'It was the night I came home from hospital,' she said. 'I was in the downstairs bed with Mam. Dad came in. He was drunk – he was always drunk. After a while I heard the springs of the bed go and Joan cried out. I knew what he was going to do, I just knew, so I got the breadknife to warn him off and sure enough, when I got upstairs he was after her. I can't recall how it happened – but I killed him,' she finished simply.

There was another swift intake of breath from the audience and Lisa turned round, startled. She'd forgotten they were there.

Milo Hanna was asking another question in his soft, cajoling way. 'But my love, if *you* could hear your dad so clearly, couldn't your mam have heard him too?'

Lisa burst into tears. 'That's the worst part of all,' she sobbed. 'Realising that Mam knew *and she never did anything about it*. Perhaps that's why I didn't care when she took the blame for killing him.'

She wondered why there was music and why, although Milo was still holding her hand, he was talking to a point beyond her, his voice still thick with sympathy as he said goodnight and announced his guests for next week.

'There, I expect you'll feel a whole lot better now.' He patted her arm and got up. Lisa heard him say to someone, 'The whole country'll be in tears after that,' and she was left sitting alone feeling as if the world had turned upside down.

As the spotlights were turned off, the studio lights came on and there was a buzz of conversation. Lisa saw Nellie and her brothers coming towards her, tears streaming down their cheeks. For a minute she watched them numbly, then jumped to her feet and ran to the hospitality room where Jackie had been watching the programme on a monitor.

'Lisa, love!' she cried, but Lisa took no notice. She snatched up her bag and left the room, running out of the building as fast as her unsteady legs would carry her.

EPILOGUE

Chapter 47

She'd been in the cottage less than a week when the dog appeared out of the wild, overgrown garden. He stood growling at her, a tatty, unkempt-looking animal, incredibly ugly with one eye half-closed and long ears caked with dirt. Bones jutted through his mangy knotted fur. Despite his aggression, he had a pathetic, desperate air, as if he wanted to be friendly but didn't know how.

Lisa had no experience of dogs. 'Here, boy.' She patted her knee but he refused to budge, though when she went in the house through the back door, he followed furtively, shambling awkwardly on his too-short legs, going straight for the gap between the sink and the old cooker. He sniffed and turned dejectedly away. She wondered if he'd belonged to the previous tenants and that's where his food had been left.

She looked through the fridge for something a dog might eat and found some ham.

'Here, boy.' He was standing outside, looking lost and lonely. When he saw the food, he bounded over and gobbled it up whilst his stub of a tail wagged briefly. 'Poor boy, are you hungry?' He growled again. 'You're not very friendly, are you?'

There wasn't much else to give him. She smeared jam on a few slices of bread and filled a dish with water. 'Your manners are atrocious,' she said as he demolished the food and drank the water with loud satisfied gulps.

He refused to come into the house that night, though in the morning he was waiting outside – to Lisa's surprise she found herself hoping he would be – still growling, but looking up expectantly. She put an old cushion in a cardboard box and left it in the kitchen with the back door open. A few days later she went out and found him in it, fast asleep, though when she approached his head came up and he growled. By then she'd bought dog food from the small supermarket in the village and was feeding him daily. He began to sleep regularly in the kitchen and one night when she was watching television, he nudged the door open with his black billiard-ball nose and slunk in, throwing himself in front of the fireplace with a deep, heartrending sigh.

'I've got to call you something,' she said thoughtfully. 'How about Rambo? You seem a very tough dog.' Later, she felt his nose snuggle against her feet. She reached down and gingerly patted him. His only response was to stretch his nose further across her slippers. The following week he allowed her to bath him, emerging from the filthy water like a drowned rat. When she tried to dry him, he ran around the kitchen like a mad thing, snatching at the towel. In the end, she gave up, and was astonished to find that when he had dried naturally, his fur had turned into a mass of dark brown fluff.

'Can I comb you?' she pleaded. She'd already bought a wicked-looking metal-toothed comb. He stood patiently as she pulled at the knots in his fur and by the time she'd finished, he bore little resemblance to the creature who'd emerged out of the long grass a month ago. She picked him up, cradling him in her arms like a baby. 'You're *still* ugly, Rambo, but you've got charm, there's no doubt about it. We're going to be the greatest friends because we need each other.'

For her, the cottage was a halfway house, a place where she could learn to live again. Once its exterior plaster walls had been painted pink, but the pink had faded to a washed-out sickly oatmeal. An old man had lived there until he died ten years ago and relatives were still embroiled in litigation over his Will so the cottage had been rented furnished to a variety of tenants. Only those desperate for a roof over their heads would want to live in such an isolated spot, the only house in a long narrow unmade road, which led from one village to another. The road was hardly ever used: years ago, a proper one had been built two miles away.

The house was full of the old man's furniture. 'Could this ever have been new!' thought Lisa when she first walked into the big living room which led directly off the front door. A leatherette three-piece, a chipped veneered sideboard, a scratched gate-legged table. The stone floor was covered with faded, rotten linoleum, eaten away at the edges.

She only bought a few things: new mattress and bedding, a fridge and television, a couple of table lamps – enough to sustain her, make life comfortable. The cottage had been rented sight unseen through a local estate agent. It bore little resemblance to the description she'd been sent but it didn't matter. She liked its quiet, lonely situation and no one in the village appeared to recognize her, at least if they did they said nothing, respecting her privacy

It was a year now since she had moved in; she had come in the summer when the garden was abuzz with insects and filled with the vivid scent of flowers. In the garden shed, Lisa found a pair of rusty shears and an old-fashioned mower and she attacked the garden with vigour. She could have bought a modern mower and done the work in a fraction of the time, but stubbornly persisted with the old implements until the grass was cut and a relatively smooth lawn was revealed. Then she dug up the borders and pruned the shrubs, repairing the fence with odd pieces of wood.

As she stood at the top of the long garden early in the autumn throwing a ball for Rambo, she'd rarely felt so proud of her handiwork. He came galloping up the garden on his tiny legs and she held out her arms; he leapt right into them and began to lick her face. She rolled over, laughing, trying to escape his excited show of affection and he licked the back of her neck and behind her ears.

She'd never dreamt it was possible to love an animal so much. Perhaps it was because his love for her was so unreserved and spontaneous it was hard not to respond. His previous owners had treated him badly, she'd been told, leaving him to fend for himself whilst they went away, sometimes for weeks on end. Then they'd left for good without him.

Sometimes she put him in the back of the car and drove to Broxley dales where they ran till both were exhausted and his tongue hung out the side of his mouth like a moist pink tassel. Then she'd go home and spend the rest of the day replying to the letters which had arrived after the Milo Hanna programme.

Those letters! Those awful, tragic letters.

She'd rushed out of the studio onto the street without any idea of where she was, for she hadn't noticed the route the car which had collected them from home had taken. What time was it, what day, what year? What did it matter, anyway? The embarrassment and shame she felt left little room for anything else, though after a while she stopped running when she became conscious of the odd looks on the faces of the people she passed, some drawing back in alarm as she came rushing towards them. Her breath was ragged, her feet hurt in the spiky heeled shoes. Eventually, she stopped altogether and saw that she was in the Strand; the sun was dipping behind the buildings on her left, which meant it was late evening.

What was she to do now? Where was she to go? She could never appear in public again. Never! There was a large hotel opposite and she went in and booked a room, registering herself as Mary Smith. 'Could you send a bottle . . . no, a pot of tea up straight away, please.'

At midnight she rang home, hoping Jackie would be there. She was.

'I don't want to talk,' Lisa said in response to the demands to know where she was, how did she feel and to please, please come back straight away. 'I only called to say I'm all right and I'll be in touch again soon.' She replaced the receiver in the middle of Jackie's rush of questions.

The front page of next morning's *Meteor* was stark.

'*WHAT A PERFORMANCE!*'

'*Lisa Angelis, the actress, gave the greatest performance of her life on the Milo Hanna Show last night. In an emotional display that made the blood curdle, the ex-porno queen attempted (unsuccessfully) to present herself as a saviour of the working man, a friend of the dying and an abused child. Surely no one was taken in by this? Even if it were all true, the fact remains that this woman is a confessed murderess . . .*'

548

Lisa screwed up the paper and threw it in a bin in the hotel lobby. It had all been a waste of time. All she'd done was to make things worse – and she cursed Milo Hanna with all her heart.

She remembered Ralph saying a long, long time ago: 'I'll always be there if you need me.'

The television had been on all day and she had her meals served in the room, though she scarcely touched the food. Most of the news bulletins showed an excerpt from the Milo Hanna Show, always the same one, the last few minutes when she'd broken down, and she stared at herself curiously. She hadn't thought herself capable of such an agonized, painful expression. On one subsequent programme, a child psychologist explained how child abuse could affect people over their entire lives and a lawyer was interviewed on the legal position. 'There's no way she would be prosecuted after all this time,' he said. Unlike the *Meteor*, the coverage was entirely sympathetic.

The late-night news had reached a halfway point and was about to break for adverts when the announcer said, 'In the second half we'll deal with the question "Why has this woman been persecuted?" – and there she was on screen again, sitting next to Milo Hanna.

The adverts had never taken so long. She sat, willing them to end and the bulletin to begin again. When it did, the same excerpt was shown, followed by the child psychologist, the lawyer, then, to her surprise, all the damning *Meteor* headlines. Then the announcer said, 'Miss Angelis is in the throes of a bitter divorce battle with her husband, the Member of Parliament for Broxley, Sir Anthony Molyneux. It was revealed today that the industrialist, Colin Sowerby, a close business associate of Sir Anthony, is a member of the *Meteor*'s board of directors. People may well ask the question, "Should the press be used to persecute people on behalf of their friends?"'

'Oh, my God!' said Lisa. 'Now it all makes sense.'

The newscaster hadn't finished. 'In a final, dramatic move, Ralph Layton, the distinguished actor of stage and screen, issued a statement from his remote Scottish home where he is suffering from AIDS. *"In response to the* Meteor's *claim that Lisa Angelis made up the facts about her father, every word she spoke is true,"* he said, *"I know, because she told me those same facts more than thirty years ago."'*

She felt better, but it didn't really make much difference. She still couldn't face people, not with them knowing what had been done to her, what she had done to herself and to her dad, even though he had deserved it and she would do it again under the same circumstances.

After the programme finished, she called Jackie again. 'I'm going away for a while. Will you look after the house?'

'Of course I will. I'll move in here instead of the flat,' Jackie said tearfully. 'But Lisa, love, there's no need to hide. You wouldn't believe the calls we've had, the letters and visitors. Jim Harrison – you kept *him* a tight secret – is going up the wall with worry. He stayed here last night waiting for you and the studio said they've been inundated with mail; they're going to send it over.'

'Then you'll just have to re-direct it,' Lisa said. 'I'll let you know when I've found a place to live.'

Where in the world did she most want to go? The answer came immediately. Broxley! Not the town itself, but one of the nearby villages where she wouldn't be recognized. There she would decide what to do with the rest of her life.

But first of all, she had to find Ralph. She was devastated by the news that he had AIDS, though she'd suspected something was wrong for months. She telephoned the television studio and asked for the location of his home in Scotland.

'Even if we had that information, we wouldn't release it,' a cold voice told her. 'We've already had half a dozen calls from the press, I think he deserves to die in peace, don't you?'

'I'm not the press,' Lisa said quietly. 'I'm Lisa Angelis.'

'Oh!' The voice changed tone, became friendly. 'I was telling the truth before. Someone called Adam phoned the message in. He wouldn't give the address, just said it was up in the wilds of Scotland, though I've got a number. We had to phone back and check, in case the call was just a ruse. You can have that if you like. We promised to keep it confidential, but I guess it's okay to make an exception with you.'

'Please, oh please,' breathed Lisa.

She called immediately, her hands shaking as she pressed the numbers. Adam answered.

'It's Lisa,' she cried. 'Can I speak to Ralph?'

Adam said ruefully, 'We thought you'd track us down.'

'I want to see him, Adam. I want to be with him when —'

'When he dies?' he finished for her.

'Yes,' she sobbed.

'He doesn't want to see you, Lisa. He doesn't want to see anyone.'

'But he can't refuse to see me, not *me*!'

Adam didn't say anything for a while and she could hear a whispered mumbling in the background.

'He has difficulty speaking,' Adam said eventually, his voice wracked with pain. 'He said you did enough for Gary and he wants you to remember him as he used to be.'

Lisa wanted to argue, insist she come, but how could you force yourself on a dying man who didn't want you? She could hardly speak for crying. 'Tell him I'll never forget *Pygmalion*.' Such magnificent acting, such presence and that voice, filling the theatre with its grating power.

She heard the same sound again, that slightly hoarse mumble and Adam came back, close to tears himself. 'He says he thinks about you all the time and you'll pull through your present difficulties, you always do.'

'Put the phone by his ear, let me say goodbye to him,' she demanded.

Adam said gently, 'No, Lisa. You know, sometimes there can be too much emotion.' He paused. 'I'm going to ring off now, he's getting distressed.'

'Goodbye, Ralph,' she shouted. 'Goodbye.'

The receiver at the other end was quietly replaced.

She'd only intended staying in the cottage a few months, but had reckoned without the letters. Letters often full of misery, of hopelessness and despair, mostly from women, though several were from men. They'd watched her tell her story on

551

television and wrote to tell their own. She read them carefully. Not all were sad. Some wrote to say they had survived the terror of their childhood and married good men who understood what they'd gone through. '*You'll feel better for having told,*' they said – hadn't Milo Hanna said something like that too? Nearly all ended, '*Putting these words on paper makes me feel a great weight has been lifted.*'

Jackie opened the letters in London – she didn't read them, the contents were for Lisa alone – and sent a typed acknowledgment promising a personal reply in due course. Lisa rarely managed more than four or five handwritten replies each day and even as she wrote, more letters came from women who'd been waiting to pluck up the courage to write.

Other things were happening in the outside world, but she was disinterested, though some affected her personally. Even the fact that Tony was in serious trouble failed to stir her. The newspapers had followed up *Private Eye*'s revelations and now the police were investigating allegations of bribe-taking; the Fraud Squad were mounting a prosecution against his offshore company.

The divorce, with a new solicitor, went through without a hitch and Lisa didn't even have to appear in court.

The only thing to upset her was an item on the news one night. Ralph was dead. She cried all night at the loss of a true friend.

She had never been so popular as an actress. Play and movie offers poured in, and one in particular caused her to smile: Masthead Movies, once O'Brien Productions, wanted to make a film of her life!

Most of this went over Lisa's head. All that mattered was answering the letters. The long feverish hours daily spent holding a pen caused a painful lump to appear on the middle finger of her right hand where it remained for the rest of her life.

She tried to lift the spirits of the writers and offer hope for the future. Sometimes, with her head aching and her right hand taut with cramp, she thought about asking Jackie to type the replies, but always changed her mind. 'If it takes the rest of my life I shall answer each one personally.'

It took a year. Suddenly, it was July again, and she'd reached the end of her task and began to think about what to do next.

On one matter she'd already made up her mind. Months ago, a charitable organization set up to help victims of abuse had asked her to become their president and she had accepted.

'I can't take up the position immediately,' she replied, 'but I would like to become an active president, not just a name on your letterhead.' By then, she would be ready to face the world to which she had so publicly confessed her secret.

Only Jackie knew where Lisa was. As the months passed and her confidence increased, Lisa began to call her family and friends on the old-fashioned bakelite telephone in the lounge, though she made them promise not to come and see her. She had difficulty in stopping Busby from flying over immediately. 'Damn you, Lisa, I've been worried sick,' he said angrily.

'We'll meet soon,' she promised. 'Are you still in Tymperleys? I'm longing to see it again.'

'Are you all right?' demanded Nellie. 'Swear you're all right.'

'I'm fine,' Lisa assured her. 'I'll come to Liverpool in the New Year.' She'd already made up her mind that she'd stay in the cottage until New Year's Eve, then begin a new life.

Winter began to close in again. Last year had been mild, but suddenly Lisa became conscious of draughts sweeping across the rooms under the ill-fitting doors and through the windows. She had logs delivered for the big black fireplace and Rambo began to sleep on her bed. One morning, she found the dishes frozen to the wooden draining board.

'Bloody hell, Rambo, I wouldn't like to be here if it snowed. We could be stranded down this lane for weeks.'

He looked at her intelligently with his odd eyes – one still stubbornly remained half-closed – and gave a woof of agreement.

Perhaps she should move back to London immediately

before the cold really set in, Lisa thought, but then decided against it. Her mind had been programmed like an alarm clock which would ring on New Year's Day. To leave the cottage now would be like getting up at five o'clock when the alarm had been set for seven and you hung about, feeling a bit lost and wondering what to do with the extra hours. She'd leave on the day originally planned.

She supposed it was inevitable that in time she'd meet someone she knew from Broxley.

It was a Sunday morning in November and she and Rambo had been for a run across the dales, only a short one as the air was damp and penetratingly cold. She shut him in the car and was about to climb in the front, looking forward to getting home where she'd left a roaring fire burning, when a car passed and she heard a screech of brakes.

She looked up and her heart sank. Jim Harrison was striding towards her, an expression of incredulity on his face.

'What on earth are you doing here?' he demanded.

'I've been for a run,' she said awkwardly. Rambo began a furious, possessive barking in the back of the car.

He moved to take her in his arms, but she shrank back, dropping her eyes to avoid his look of hurt. She'd scarcely thought about this man since they last met.

'You're not living at Ferris Hall, surely?'

'Of course not. I've rented a cottage.'

'Where?'

She considered refusing to answer, but it seemed childish. When she told him where it was, he said angrily, 'That place is a dump. All sorts of hoodlums have lived there. They might come back – it's dangerous.'

'I've been there for over a year and had no trouble,' she argued.

'A year! And you never let me know?' He said this in an uncomprehending voice, more to himself than Lisa.

'Hardly anyone knows where I am,' she said defensively.

He was looking at her curiously. 'Did that night mean nothing?'

Lisa blushed and looked down at her feet. She hated treating him like this. He was such a good man through and through, decent and sincere. She should feel flattered, a man like this being in love with her. Instead, she felt nothing, just a desire to escape, to get back home where there was only Rambo to talk to. 'It meant everything – when it happened.' Then she looked him full in the face. 'But not since.'

'I see.' He began to back away and the agonized, bitter look on his face made her feel physically sick.

'You don't understand!' she cried. 'You can't possibly understand.' She opened the car door and Rambo tried to scramble over the back of the seat to welcome her. Jim had almost reached his own car. His broad shoulders were bent and she felt a surge of tenderness mixed with pity. Despite this, she shouted, 'You won't come and see me, will you?'

He turned, looking at her coldly. 'As if I would,' he shouted back.

Rambo lay on his back in front of the roaring fire, his little legs stuck up like flagpoles. Lisa looked up from the child's exercise book she was scribbling in and regarded him affectionately. He'd been the best company she could have had these last eighteen months. She smiled and returned to her writing. It was Masthead Movies' offer to make a film out of her life that had inspired her to begin setting it down on paper. She'd started jotting down trivial things that had stuck in her mind, like that Christmas Day kosher dinner with the Greenbaums, the time Mam sent Jimmie out a with a penny to light a candle to Our Lady to implore her to make the jelly set in time for a party, the day Vita arrived in Tymperleys. She already had two notebooks full of reminiscences. When she got back to London she'd start joining them together with the important events in her life, and Jackie had promised to type the manuscript out when it was finished.

After a while, the lump on her finger began to throb and she sucked it to ease the pain, then took a sip of bourbon. Busby had sent a crate for Christmas. It was already beginning to take effect and she felt pleasantly tipsy. She would have liked a cigarette, but had given up – for the second time – when she came to the cottage.

'Cheers, Busby,' she said aloud and imagined him sitting

by the pool at Tymperleys, surrounded by his friends who'd 'just dropped in'. She closed the exercise book, lay down on the settee and stared into the fire, watching with fascination as vivid blue flames ran up and down the logs and deep orange, ash-framed grottoes appeared in the gaps between them. The fire and the little capiz-shell-shaded lamp were the only illumination in the room and the ugly furniture was lost in dark shadows. In fact, thought Lisa, the room had never looked so lovely as it did now, on her last night.

It was New Year's Eve and her things were packed, ready to leave first thing in the morning. Rambo would hate the Pimlico house with its little backyard. She'd look around Broxley for a place to buy and spend a lot of time here. In last week's local paper, she'd read that Ferris Hall was up for sale. Could she live there, she wondered, after all that had happened with Tony?

Snuggling into a cushion, she decided not to think about it just now. Tomorrow, next week, next month, would do. There were lots of decisions to make, not just about where to live, but how to continue with her career. There was a play script she really liked and the movie company she'd vowed to start, another O'Brien Productions.

She picked up the remote control for the television and began to flick from channel to channel – typical New Year's Eve programmes, a games show with celebrities as panellists, a Victorian Music Hall, but on Channel 4, a movie which looked vaguely familiar. She left it on and suddenly a face from the past appeared on screen. Lally Cooper! Lally, in her blonde wig and waitress's uniform, saying, 'It's just that it sez FOOD outside, and generally that's why folks come in here. To eat!' This was the film that was going to launch her to stardom, though the last she'd heard, Lally had five kids and was probably a grandmother ten times over by now. Lisa raised her glass. 'Cheers, Lally.' When she disappeared from the screen, Lisa turned the sound down.

The logs spat and the sound disturbed Rambo. He began to scramble up and she leaned down and stroked him. 'Go back to sleep,' she ordered and he looked up at her adoringly before closing his eyes.

This was the second year she'd spent Christmas and New

Year entirely alone, but she didn't care. She'd turned down invitations to Liverpool, London, California. It seemed like a test of strength to stay in this lonely, isolated house with only Rambo for company.

She listened; the silence was so complete it could be felt, though a few minutes later the faint drone of a plane could be heard, muted and distant, but when it had gone the silence became even more total.

Rambo got unsteadily to his feet and staggered towards the door. Obviously nature called. Lisa sighed and swung her legs off the settee. She needed to get up anyway to put more logs on the fire.

'You're such a good little dog,' she said lovingly as she opened the door and he shuddered at the icy blast of air which met him before padding reluctantly down the path with his awkward clumsy gait.

Shuddering herself, Lisa closed the door and drew the collar of her velvet dressing gown up to her throat. Away from the fire the room was freezing, but she was well prepared for this in her thick woollen slipper socks and warm nightdress. She threw some logs in the grate, picked up her glass and went to get more ice out of the fridge. The kitchen itself was as cold as the fridge and she hurried back to stand in front of the fire, watching the flames begin to take hold of the fresh wood. A chrome mirror, spotted with age, hung above the fireplace and she looked at her blurred reflection.

'At least I've gone grey glamorously.' Two symmetrical wings of silver had appeared just over her ears. It would be good to start buying some new clothes, wearing make-up again, going to a beauty parlour. She bet she could still turn a few heads, even though she'd be fifty-six in a few months. In the half-dark room, the face that stared back at her from the dim, cloudy glass was unlined and beautiful. This was the Lisa Angelis of *Easy Dreams* and *Matchstick Man*. She moved back and Lizzie O'Brien of Bootle was suddenly in the room with her.

No! She quickly turned away. It was too ghostly, particularly on New Year's Eve.

She sat on the edge of the settee, reluctant to get comfortable again until Rambo came back. He'd probably got used to the cold by now and was chasing a rat or some other poor unsuspecting creature.

Glancing at the television, she saw the programme had changed and a familiar face was mouthing words she couldn't hear. Milo Hanna! 'Cheers, Milo.' She toasted him, hoping there wouldn't be many more faces she recognized, else she'd be paralytic by morning. She still wasn't sure whether he was a fake or not, but he'd helped sort out her life. 'Not completely,' a little voice reminded her. 'What about Jim?'

Jim Harrison! She'd forgotten all about him during the year spent answering those tragic letters, but then she'd forgotten about everybody. Could they get together again? Did she want to? More importantly, did he, after that disastrous meeting? She thought about the night they'd spent together. It had been so good, so perfect, yet the memory meant nothing. Why? she wondered.

It was nearly midnight. She turned the television up; it would be nice to have someone, particularly Milo Hanna, wish her a Happy New Year, though people would begin telephoning soon. She especially wanted to talk to Kevin. When she began her book she wanted his advice on the background. There were things about Chaucer Street he could help with. Maybe he could remember the night she was born . . .

Only a minute to go before the New Year came in. In the distance, above Milo's soft Irish voice, came the roar of a car engine, gradually getting louder as it approached the cottage. It wasn't often anything came this way and it must have been doing a hundred, the noise it made. She winced as it passed, then heard the shriek of brakes and a bumping sound and she screamed, '*RAMBO!*'

The car was just red tail-lights in the distance and Rambo was lying on his side, completely still. Lisa screamed again, scooped him up in her dressing gown and ran into the house. His body was limp, a dead weight, but there was no blood. She sat down, buried her face in his warm fur and began to cry, rocking back and forth and clutching his sturdy little body.

She cried all night, great wracking sobs that grated her ribs, threatening to tear out her insides. After a while, she stopped crying for Rambo and cried instead for her mam, for Ralph, for Nellie and her dead son, for Jackie and Sabina, for everyone she could think of, even, at one point, her dad. Vaguely she heard the telephone ring and it never seemed to stop. Beyond the ringing, the television blared and people laughed and sang and cheered. Then a movie began and she wondered if it was one of hers because the music was familiar: passionate, haunting music that made her weep harder. Finally, she cried for herself. Nothing would ever go right for her. Nothing.

'I'm going to die tonight,' she whispered. It was only right that she should die in this lonely spot with Rambo still warm on her knee. 'I don't want to go on living, anyway.'

Closing her eyes, she leant back in the chair. She was drowning, drowning, and as if a film was being fast-forwarded, Lisa saw her life pass before her eyes, from its raw, uncompromising beginning to now, its bitter end. She was a child again in Chaucer Street where there was so much hate and so much love. A young girl in her best dress going to Southport on her birthday, then Jackie appeared in her pink satin pyjamas, dimpled, creamy skinned and smiling and she saw Harry Greenbaum in his bookshop, a misty figure, so wise and good. Patrick! Oh, Jesus, Patrick, my lovely brother. Hollywood, Busby, there'd been some glorious times making movies together. Then Dent, Dent the monster, carrying Sabina into the bedroom, grinning his wicked grin. Ralph, dear Ralph. Gary dying, a sad time, yet the memory strangely uplifting. Tony Molyneux, you bastard, Tony. Milo Hanna, the letters, the letters . . .

She was eight years old and bombs were falling all over Bootle and Dad was banging on the door demanding to be let in. 'Leave him,' Mam said in a hard voice and the children chorused gleefuly, 'Leave him, leave him.' Then a bomb dropped outside and the front door flew down the hall, followed by Dad. When he reached the stairs, he exploded, and lay there, split open, oozing blood. The children started jumping up and down, shouting, 'He's dead! He's dead!' Their footsteps thumped on the lino-covered floor and Mam began to jump too and the noise was so tremendous it drowned out the sound of the bombs.

Lisa opened her eyes. What a weird dream. Oh God, it was cold in here. She shivered and was about to get up and stir the mountain of grey ash in the fireplace, trying to revive a hopefully hidden flame, when she noticed Rambo on her knee and moaned aloud. The thumping sound in her dream still persisted and she realized the noise was real. Someone was banging on the front door.

She got up, still clutching Rambo, and opened it. It was snowing outside and Jim Harrison was standing with his hand poised, ready to knock again. He wore an old duffel coat and urgently needed a shave. She walked away, leaving the door open, and returned to her seat. He came in and stood looking down at her.

'Are you all right?'

Lisa stared at the floor and didn't answer.

'That was a stupid question,' he said gently. 'You look terrible. Let's do something with this fire then I'll make a drink. Here, have a sip of this first.'

He poured out an inch of bourbon and sat beside her, holding the glass against her lips as if she was an invalid. The drink burned her raw, aching throat. She blinked and found her eyes were sticky with crying.

There were still some logs smouldering underneath the ash and he coaxed them back into life and soon a small fire was burning.

'Why are you here?' she asked.

He looked at her quickly, as if relieved to hear the sound of her voice. 'Jackie telephoned. She was worried. Apparently she'd been calling all night and you didn't answer.'

'I fell asleep,' she lied. 'I didn't hear anything.'

She could tell he didn't believe her. 'New Year's Eve isn't a good time to be alone. I would have come over if —' He didn't finish. 'If I'd thought you wanted me to,' he was probably going to say.

'It wasn't that,' she tried to explain. 'Just thoughts, memories, getting out of hand, that's all.' She wasn't going to tell him about Rambo. He'd think her too emotional and stupid, wanting to die because her dog had been killed. She moved Rambo's still-warm body onto the settee, settling his head carefully on a cushion. He'd grow cold now, away from her. After Jim had gone, she'd bury him in the garden.

'That's exactly what I meant. You've been by yourself too long. It's time to return to the land of the living again,' he said seriously.

'Things are easy for you, aren't they? Everything's black or white. With me, life has been all shades in between.'

'You're making assumptions again.' He smiled. 'I learnt a long time ago to take each day as it comes. I've had my ups and downs too, you know. Some day I might tell you about them.'

'I'm sorry.' She plucked at her dressing gown as the telephone rang.

Jim answered it. 'Yes, she's fine. Fit and well, just drank a bit too much, I reckon, and fell asleep.' Lisa heard Jackie laugh. 'Yes, I'll tell her that, goodbye.'

'She said she's been inundated with calls, people trying to get through and worried when you didn't answer.' He paused. 'You're very lucky, having so many people care about you. Some people'd give anything to be in your shoes.'

He was right, she thought. So right. It had been selfish to cut herself off all this time and refuse to let people who loved her come and visit. She smiled at him wryly. 'I needed that advice, thanks.'

'Are you feeling better? Got over your bad thoughts?'

She glanced down at Rambo. 'Most of them,' she said.

'Do you want me to leave? I don't want to be in your way. Jackie said you were going back to London today.' Lisa looked at him. He would have hated to know how much his eyes were pleading, desperately pleading for her to answer, 'Stay, please stay.'

'I don't know,' she said eventually.

'Lisa, can't we begin again?' he said urgently. 'Let's pretend we met this morning . . .'

She knew she would be happy with this man, this safe, secure man who loved her so passionately, but . . . 'I suppose we could – begin again, that is,' she said slowly. 'But I can't promise anything and I'd hate to let you down again.'

'I'll take that risk,' he said quickly.

'And I have loads of things to do. I'm writing a book and I want to start making movies again and I'm involved in a charity.'

'Well, I have a factory to run,' he laughed.

'I'm even thinking of buying Ferris Hall.'

'I could stand that.'

He made no attempt to touch her, for which she was grateful. There would be time for that in the future – possibly.

'You know, you should get out of here straight away. Would you like me to load your things in the car while you get dressed? In fact,' he added hopefully, 'I could drive you down if you want.'

'Well . . .' She rather liked the idea, but what about Rambo? 'I'd appreciate that, but can you come back for me in an hour?'

He looked puzzled. 'Why?' he demanded. 'I can see you're packed. What's wrong with now?'

She couldn't think of a reason to give, except the true one. She burst into tears. 'Because Rambo's dead and I've got to bury him, that's why. A car came racing down the lane last night and ran him over.'

'Oh Lisa, my love. Why didn't you tell me?'

My God! There were tears in his own eyes. He knelt by Rambo and touched his chest with the flat on his hand. 'He's still warm.'

'That's because I've been holding him all night.'

'There's the barest flicker of a heartbeat. He's still alive, you stupid woman. He's concussed, that's all – look at this bump on his head. The car must have glanced off him.' He stood up and said peremptorily, 'Get dressed and we'll take him to a vet immediately.'

She sat beside Jim in the car with Rambo wrapped in a blanket on her knee. The snow had thickened and was beginning to stick to the bare hedges and the fields were peppered with white. It was a desolate lonely scene, but Lisa thought the world had never looked so beautiful.

She felt as if she was waking up after a long, stifling dream and suddenly her blood began to race and her body tingled with excitement at the thought of the future. 'It's going to be wonderful, I know it is,' she whispered. Of course, there were bound to be more ups and downs, but so what? Everybody had them. After these last eighteen months, she was convinced she'd learnt to cope with life, but it only took Rambo's supposed death for her to completely go to pieces. She'd give up learning to cope, and vowed to do what Jim did and take each day as it came. Well, she'd try! She remembered taking that vow before on more than one occasion.

Jim touched her arm. 'How are you feeling?'

'Fine,' she said. 'Absolutely fine.'

She turned and watched his lovely broad, handsome face, his strong hands firm on the wheel and thought again about the night they'd spent together and suddenly there was that old familiar tingle in her stomach. She laughed.

'What's so funny?'

'Nothing,' she said happily.

A New Year.

A new man.

A new life.

Another stepping stone . . .

If you have enjoyed
Stepping Stones
don't miss

LIME STREET BLUES

Maureen Lee's latest novel
in Orion paperback

Price: £5.99
ISBN: 0 75284 961 1

Chapter 1
1939–1940

'Rose!' Mrs Corbett bellowed. 'Where are you?'

'Up here, madam.' Rose appeared, breathless, at the top of the stairs. 'Making the beds.'

'I'd have thought you'd be finished by now.'

'I've only just started, madam.'

'Huh!' Mrs Corbett said contemptuously. She always seemed to expect her maid to have begun the next job, or even the one after that, leaving Rose with the constant feeling that she was way behind. 'Well, get a move on, girl. I want you in uniform by eleven o'clock. The vicar and his wife are coming for coffee.'

'Yes, madam.' It was exceptionally warm for June and there were beads of perspiration on Rose's brow when she returned to the colonel's room and began to plump up pillows, straighten sheets and tuck them firmly under the mattress. Colonel Max was Mrs Corbett's son, a professional soldier, presently home on leave. He was a much nicer person than his mother, very kind. She was always sorry when he had to return to his regiment.

Mrs Corbett, on the other hand, was never kind. She apparently thought the more Rose was harried, the harder she would work. But Rose already laboured as hard as she could. That morning, she'd been up at six, as she was every morning, to light the Aga. On the dot of seven, Mrs Corbett had been taken up a cup of tea, two slices of bread and butter, and *The Times*. The colonel had been given his tea on the dot of eight, by which time his mother was having a bath, the coal scuttle had been filled, the washing had been hung on the line, the numerous clocks had been wound, and Mrs Denning, the cook who lived in the village, had arrived to make breakfast.

While the Corbetts ate, Rose sat down to her own breakfast, although, more often than not, the bell would ring and she would scurry into the dining room to be met with complaints that the eggs were overdone, the kippers not cooked enough, or there wasn't enough toast, none of which was Rose's fault, but Mrs Corbett behaved as if it was.

Breakfast over, she'd start on the housework; shake mats and brush carpets, dust and polish the furniture, which had to be done every day, apart from Sunday, Rose's day off, but only after ten o'clock, when the Aga had been lit and, if it was winter, fires made in the breakfast and drawing rooms, the morning tea had been served and the beds made.

Today, the housework would be interrupted because the Reverend and Mrs Conway were coming for coffee and she would have to change out of her green overall into her maid's outfit; a black frock with long sleeves, a tiny, white, lace-trimmed apron and white cap. Thus attired, Rose would answer the door and show the visitors into the drawing room where coffee and biscuits were waiting on a silver tray and Mrs Corbett would rise to greet them, her big, over-powdered face twisted in a charming smile.

Rose wasn't required to show the visitors out. She would change back into the overall and get on with other things; cleaning the silver, for instance, or ironing, the job she disliked most. Mrs Corbett examined the finished work with a hawk's eye, looking for creases in her fine, silk underwear and expensive *crêpe de chine* blouses. Even the bedding had to be as smooth as freshly fallen snow. Rose would be bitterly scolded if one of the pure Irish linen pillow slips hadn't been ironed on both sides, something she was apt to overlook.

'You'll make some man a fine wife one day,' Mrs Denning had said more than once.

'I can't imagine getting married,' Rose usually replied. She did so again today. Both women were in the kitchen, where the windows had been flung wide open in the hope a breath of fresh air might penetrate the sweltering heat. A red-faced Mrs Denning was preparing lunch and Rose was sorting out yesterday's washing, putting it into different piles ready to be ironed. Mrs Corbett was still entertaining the Conways in the drawing room.

She picked up the iron off the Aga and spat on it. The spit sizzled to nothing straight away and she reckoned it was just about right. She put another iron in its place.

'You'll get married,' Mrs Denning assured her. 'You'll not be left on the shelf, not with those big blue eyes. How old are you now, Rose?'

'Fifteen,' Rose sighed. She'd been working for Mrs Corbett and keeping The Limes spick and span for over two years, ever since her thirteenth birthday. Holmwood House, the orphanage where she'd been raised, wasn't prepared to keep the children a day longer than necessary and Mrs Corbett had been to examine her and assess her fitness for the job, which for some reason involved looking inside her ears and down her throat.

'I want someone strong and healthy,' she'd said in her loud, sergeant-major voice. She was a widow in her sixties, a large, majestic woman with enormous breasts that hung over the belt of her outsize brown frock. She wore a fox fur and a tiny fur hat with a spotted veil that cast little black shadows on her dour, autocratic face.

'Apart from the usual childhood illnesses, I've never known Rose be sick,' Mr Hillyard, the Governor of Holmwood House, had smoothly assured her.

'But she doesn't look particularly strong. In fact, I'd describe her as delicate.'

'We have another girl that might do. Would you care to see her?'

'Why not.'

Rose was sent to wait outside Mr Hillyard's office and Ann Parker was fetched for Mrs Corbett to examine, but rejected on the spot. 'She's too coarse; at least the other one has a bit of refinement about her.' Every word was audible in the corridor outside. 'What's her name again?'

'Rose Sullivan.'

'She'll just have to do. When can I have her?'

'She'll be thirteen in a fortnight. You can have her then.'

Two weeks later, at the beginning of May, a car had arrived to take Rose away from Holmwood House, a place where she had never been happy and where the word 'love' had never once been mentioned or felt. The driver got out to open the door and take the parcel containing all her worldly possessions. He was a handsome man, old enough to be her father, with broad shoulders and dark wavy hair. His skin was burnt nutmeg brown from the sun. She learnt later that his name was Tom Flowers and he was, rather appropriately, the gardener who doubled as a chauffeur when Mrs Corbett needed to be driven anywhere.

He hardly spoke on the way to The Limes, merely

muttering that if she was good and behaved herself, she'd get on fine with her new employer. 'She's a hard taskmaster, but her bark's worse than her bite.'

Rose was soon to discover the truth of the first part of this remark, but never the second.

The Limes was a square, grey brick building with eight bedrooms set in five acres of well-tended grounds. Inside was comfortably furnished, though on her first day she didn't see the rooms she would soon come to know well, as Tom Flowers took her round to a side entrance, through a long, narrow room with a deep brown sink, a dolly tub, and a mangle. A sturdy clothes rack was suspended from the ceiling.

He opened another door and they entered a vast kitchen with a red tiled floor and white walls, from which hung an assortment of copper bottomed pans, from the very small to the very large. Waves of heat were coming from a giant stove. The shelves of an enormous dresser were filled with pretty blue and white china and there was a bowl of brightly coloured flowers on the pine table that could easily have seated a dozen.

'Mrs Corbett's out for the day,' Tom Flowers informed her, 'and Mrs Denning, the cook, won't be back for a while. I'll show you your room. Once you've unpacked, perhaps you'd like to go for a walk around the village. Ailsham's a nice place, you'll like it. Just turn right when you leave the gates and you'll come to the shops about a mile away.'

'Ta,' Rose whispered.

'Come on then, girl,' he said brusquely. 'You're on the second floor.'

He marched out of the kitchen, up a wide staircase, then a narrower one, Rose having to run to keep up.

The door to her room was already open, her things on the bed. Tom Flowers said something that she presumed was 'goodbye', closed the door, and Rose was left alone.

She sat on the bed. It was quite a pleasant room with a sloping ceiling. The distempered walls, the curtains on the small window, and the cotton coverlet on the bed were white. There was a rag rug on the otherwise bare wooden floor, a little chest of drawers, and a single wardrobe. Later, when she opened the wardrobe to hang her too short winter coat, she found a black frock that was much too long and a green overall that would have fitted someone twice her size.

But Rose felt too miserable to unpack then. Unhappiness rose like a ball in her throat. Tom Flowers' footsteps could be heard, getting further and further away, and with each step, the unhappiness grew until she could hardly breathe. She lay on the bed and began to cry into the soft, white pillow. She wanted her mother. That could never be because her mother was dead, but she wanted her all the same. All she could remember was a blurred face, a soft voice, soft music, arms reaching for her as she toddled across the room, being cuddled by someone who could only have been her mother. Then one day the soft voice stopped and the music was no more. She had never been cuddled again. The voices since had been harsh, even when she was told that her mother had died. The birth certificate she'd been given with her things stated 'Father Unknown'. She had no one. Now she didn't even have the orphanage, where at least she'd felt safe. She was completely alone in the world.

More than two years later, Rose was still not happy, but she had settled into The Limes. Mrs Denning was a cheerful soul and they got on well. She had two sons, one a year older than Rose, the other a year younger, and kept her amused with tales of their escapades. She would never grow used to Mrs Corbett's sharp tongue and being told she was lazy and stupid, but it didn't upset her as much as when she'd first arrived. Her favourite time was evening when she enjoyed the solitude of her room, her head buried in one of the books she'd borrowed from the library van that parked by Ailsham Green for two hours every Wednesday afternoon. She was supposed to have time off when lunch was over and before the afternoon visitors were due to arrive. It was wise to escape from the house, otherwise Mrs Corbett was liable to forget it was her free time and demand she get on with some work. Discovering the library van had been a blessing. She liked romances best, stories about men and women falling in love. Rose wanted someone to love her more than anything in the world.

She had just finished the ironing when Tom Flowers tramped into the kitchen for his midday meal, followed by Colonel Max. Neither man was married and they were the best of friends. The same age, thirty-nine, they had played together as children. Tom's father, grand-father, and great-grandfather before him, had tended the gardens of The Limes since the middle of the last century.

The colonel was delighted to see her. 'I swear this young lady grows prettier by the day,' he exclaimed. 'What do you say, Tom?'

Tom glanced at her briefly. 'Aye,' he muttered. He was a taciturn man, though always polite. Rose found it strange that the gardener, with his tall, strong frame and square shoulders, looked far more the military man than

7

Colonel Max, who was small, almost bald, and rather endearingly ugly.

'One of the pleasures of coming home on leave is having my morning tea brought by the best-looking girl in Ailsham,' the colonel enthused.

'I was just saying, she'll make someone a fine wife one of these days,' Mrs Denning put in.

'If I were twenty years younger, the someone would be me.'

Mrs Denning grinned. She knew, they all knew, including the colonel himself, that Mrs Corbett would sooner be dead than allow her son to marry a servant.

Rose's cheeks were already burning and they burnt even more when she noticed Tom Flowers was looking at her again, not so briefly this time. There was an expression on his face almost of surprise, as if he'd never seen her properly before. She caught his eye and he quickly turned away.

'Lunch will be ready in ten minutes, Colonel,' Mrs Denning sang. 'C'mon, Tom, sit down and take the weight off your feet.' She and Tom were also friends, having gone to the village school together, though Mrs Denning had been in a lower class. In fact, everyone in Ailsham seemed to be connected in one way or another. Rose felt as if she was living in a foreign country and would never belong.

'I suppose I'd better get changed.' The colonel left the room with a sigh, from which she assumed he would much prefer to eat in the kitchen with the servants than with his autocratic mother, but that would have been almost as terrible a crime as wanting to marry one.

Was she really all that pretty? Rose examined her reflection in the mirror behind the wardrobe door before setting out on her afternoon walk. She had brown hair, very thick and wavy, a bit wild, framing her face like a halo. It seemed a very common-or-garden face, she thought, with two eyes, a nose, and a mouth. She smiled at herself to see if it made any difference and several dimples appeared in her cheeks, still pink as a result of the colonel's comments. She shrugged and supposed she wasn't so bad.

The shrug reminded her that her brassiere was too tight and she needed a bigger one, size thirty-six. The black frock that had been too big when she first arrived would soon fit perfectly.

The countryside surrounding Ailsham was too lonely to wander around on her own and a bit dull. Rose had got into the habit of walking as far as the village where she usually treated herself to a bar of toffee or chocolate, or a quarter of dolly mixtures.

Ailsham was pleasantly ordinary, not the sort of village that often featured in the books Rose so avidly read. There wasn't a thatched cottage to be seen, nor an ancient stone church with a steeple. She had yet to find a gurgling stream, a hump-backed bridge, or a pretty copse. There were no gently sloping hills, this part of Lancashire being very flat. There was a brook somewhere off Holly Lane, but to get there meant walking along the edge of two ploughed fields and perhaps getting lost.

The village was served by a tiny station, from which trains ran hourly to Liverpool, fifteen miles away, and Ormskirk, only four. The Ribble bus ran twice a day to the same places, early morning and late afternoon, though not on Sundays.

The shops were still closed for lunch when Rose

arrived on this particular day; the butchers, where one of Mrs Denning's sons, Luke, worked, the bakers, Dorothy's Hairdressers and Beryl's Fashions where Rose bought all her clothes, including the pink and white gingham frock she had on now and the blue silky one she wore on Sundays. Beryl also sold ladies' underwear, wool, and sewing things. The biggest shop was Harker's, which was actually five shops in one; a general store, a greengrocers, newsagents, tobacconists, and post office.

She sat on a bench at the edge of the green and waited for the shops to open. The pub, the Oak Tree, which got its name from the huge tree on the green directly opposite, was busy and customers, all men, were sitting at the tables outside. The pub, the shops, and most of the houses that she'd passed had posters in the windows advertising the Midsummer Fête to be held on the village green a week on Saturday. It was being organised by the Women's Institute of which Mrs Corbett was a founding member and chairman of the committee. For weeks now, groups of women had been meeting in the drawing room of The Limes to make final arrangements for the fête. There was a perfectly good Women's Institute hall between the school and the Oak Tree that would have been far more convenient, but the chairman preferred the committee came to her house. Rose wasn't the only person Mrs Corbett bossed around.

The butchers threw open its doors, followed by the bakers. Soon, all five shops were open, but Rose didn't move from the bench. She was watching two girls of about her own age, both vaguely familiar, walking along the path that encircled the green, arms linked companionably.

'Oh, look,' one remarked as they drew nearer. 'The door's open, which means I'm late. Mrs Harker will have my guts for garters.' She abandoned her companion and began to run. 'See you tonight at quarter to six by the station,' she shouted. 'I'm really looking forward to that Clark Gable picture.'

'Me too.' The other girl sauntered into Beryl's Fashions and Rose recognised her as Heather, Beryl's assistant. Beryl mustn't mind her being late.

Rose would have liked to work in a shop and quite fancied going to the pictures, but what she would have liked most of all was to have a friend, someone to link arms with. She rarely met anyone her own age except in the shops. If, say, she went into Beryl's and bought the brassiere she obviously needed and Heather invited her to the pictures – a most unlikely event – she couldn't possibly go. At quarter to six, she would be setting the table for dinner, which would be served at precisely six o'clock. It would be well past seven when her duties were finished. By then, she would be too weary to walk as far as the station. Anyway, the picture would be half over by the time she got there.

She jumped to her feet, bought a whole half pound of dolly mixtures, and ate them on the way back to The Limes.

Music was coming from the barn that Colonel Max's father had turned into a games room for his sons – the colonel's elder brother had been killed in the Great War. It had a billiard table, a dart board, and a badminton court. The music was jazz, which the colonel only played out of earshot of his mother, who couldn't stand it. Rose loved any sort of music. She danced a few steps on the gravel path, but stopped immediately, embarrassed, when she saw Tom Flowers regarding her with amusement from the rose garden.

'You look happy,' he said.

'Oh, I am,' she said, but only because it seemed churlish to say that she wasn't.

She went through the laundry room into the kitchen, which should have been empty as Mrs Denning went home as soon as lunch was over and didn't return until half four to make dinner. Rose was surprised to find a cross Mrs Corbett waiting for her, demanding to know why she hadn't answered the bell she'd been ringing for ages.

'It was my time off, madam. I've been for a walk,' Rose stammered.

'Oh!' Mrs Corbett looked slightly nonplussed. 'Well, you're late back. I'm having a bridge party this afternoon. I want you in uniform immediately. My guests will be arriving very soon.'

In fact, Rose was five minutes early, but Mrs Corbett would only have got crosser if she'd pointed it out.

A week later, the colonel's leave ended and he left for France. Lots of people telephoned or called personally to wish him luck, which had never happened before.

'Look after yourself, Max, old boy.'

'Take care, Colonel. Keep your head down, if only for your mother's sake.'

War between Great Britain and Germany was imminent. Once it started, the colonel's regiment would be on the front line. Mrs Corbett, who'd lost one son in the 'war to end all wars', retired to her room after Colonel Max had gone, and stayed there all morning, emerging as steely-eyed as ever at lunchtime and complaining bitterly that the lamb was tough.